READER'S DIGEST
CONDENSED BOOKS

With the exception of actual personages identified as such, the characters and incidents in the fictional selections in this volume are entirely the product of the authors' imaginations and have no relation to any person or event in real life.

www.readersdigest.co.uk

The Reader's Digest Association Limited 11 Westferry Circus Canary Wharf London E14 4HE

Printed in France
ISBN 0 276 42737 8

READER'S DIGEST CONDENSED BOOKS

Selected and edited by Reader's Digest

CONDENSED BOOKS DIVISION

THE READER'S DIGEST ASSOCIATION LIMITED, LONDON

CONTENTS

When Charlie and Oliver Caruso stumble across three million dollars in an abandoned account at the bank where they work, they are tempted to steal the money. But even as they breach the bank's security system, things start to spin out of control. The brothers find themselves caught up in a much bigger crime with far higher stakes than they could ever have imagined. A lively and intriguing roller coaster of a novel.

PUBLISHED BY
HODDER & STOUGHTON

Tom and Pippa Drummond live an almost perfect life: they have a delightful home on the Sussex Downs, work they both enjoy, and a sixteen-year-old daughter they adore. Then, on a summer holiday in Tuscany, their idyllic existence is shattered and Tom must learn to make sense of his life once more. Alan Titchmarsh writes from the heart in this best-selling novel that celebrates life's simple pleasures.

PUBLISHED BY SIMON & SCHUSTER

GONE FOR GOOD page 273

Harlan Coben

Years ago Will Klein's brother, Ken, went on the run after being accused of murdering Will's ex-girlfriend. The family assume Ken is dead—until one day Will's mother tells him that Ken is alive. As Will struggles to deal with this news he discovers that his adored girlfriend, Sheila, is missing. Suddenly the nightmare seems to be happening all over again. A stunning thriller, from an award-winning author, to be devoured in one sitting.

PUBLISHED BY ORION

BLACK ICE page 419

Matt Dickinson

At a remote base in the Antarctic, scientist Lauren Burgess and her team are on the brink of an astounding discovery. But when they answer an SOS call and rescue explorer Julian Fitzgerald, he endangers the project and the team's lives by pursuing his own dreams of glory. As winter closes in a desperate struggle for survival begins. An atmospheric adventure story by a writer who has experienced, first hand, the dangers he writes about.

PUBLISHED BY HUTCHINSON

THE MILLIONAIRES

BRAD MELTZER

IMAGINE DISCOVERING THREE MILLION DOLLARS LYING UNCLAIMED IN A LONG-FORGOTTEN BANK ACCOUNT.

IT'S THERE FOR THE TAKING.

NO ONE WOULD KNOW.

NO ONE WOULD CARE.

WHAT WOULD YOU DO?

CHAPTER 1

I know where I'm going. And I know who I want to be. That's why I took this job in the first place . . . and why, four years later, I still put up with the clients. And their demands. And their wads of money. Most of the time, they just want to keep a low profile, which is actually the bank's speciality. Other times, they want a little . . . personal touch. My phone rings and I tee up the charm. 'This is Oliver Caruso,' I answer. 'How can I help you?'

'*Where the hell's your boss?*' a Southern chain saw of a voice explodes in my ear.

'E-Excuse me?'

'Don't piss on this, Caruso! I want my *money*!'

It's not until he says the word 'money' that I recognise the accent. Tanner Drew, the largest developer of skyscrapers in New York City and patriarch of the Drew Family Office. In the world of high-net-worth individuals, a family office is as high as you get. Once hired, the family office supervises all the advisers, lawyers and bankers who manage the family's money. You don't speak to the family any more—you speak to the office. So if the head of the clan is calling me direct . . . I'm about to get some teeth pulled.

'Has the transfer not posted yet, Mr Drew?'

'You're damn right it hasn't posted yet, smartass! Your boss promised me it'd be here by two o'clock! *Two o'clock!*' he screams.

'I'm sorry, sir, but Mr Lapidus is—'

'I don't give a raccoon's ass where he is—the guy at *Forbes* gave me a deadline of today; I gave *your boss* that deadline, and now I'm giving *you* that deadline! What the hell else we need to discuss?'

Every year, the Forbes 400 lists the wealthiest 400 individuals in the United States. Last year, Tanner Drew was number 403. This year, he's determined to bump himself up a notch. Or three. The only thing standing in his way is a $40 million transfer to his personal account that we apparently still haven't released.

'Hold on one second, sir, I . . .'

'Don't you dare put me on h—'

I push the hold button. A quick extension later, I'm waiting to hear the voice of Lapidus's secretary. All I get is voicemail. With the boss at a partners' retreat for the rest of the day, she's got no reason to stick around. I hang up and start again. This time, I go straight to Lapidus's cellphone. No one answers.

I click back to Tanner Drew and grab my own cellphone.

'I'm just waiting for a callback from Mr Lapidus,' I explain.

'Son, if you ever put me on hold again . . .'

I'm not listening. Instead, my fingers snake across my cell, dialling Lapidus's pager. The moment I hear the beep, I enter my extension and add the number 1822. The ultimate emergency: 911 doubled.

'What time does your last transfer go out?' Tanner Drew barks.

'We officially close at three . . .' The clock on my wall says a quarter past three. 'But sometimes we can extend until four. Now what's the account number and bank it's supposed to go to?'

He relays the details, which I scribble on a Post-it. Eventually, he adds, 'Oliver Caruso, right? That's your name?'

'Y-Yes, sir.'

'OK. That's all I need to know.' With that, he hangs up.

I page and dial every partner. No one answers. I find the number for the University Club—home of the partners' retreat. By the time I start dialling, I swear I can hear my own heartbeat.

'You've reached the University Club,' a recorded voice answers. 'All operators are busy—please hold.' Grabbing my cell, I dial frantically, looking for anyone with authority. Baraff . . . Bernstein . . . Mary in Accounting—Gone, Gone and Gone.

I hate Fridays close to Christmas. Where the hell is everyone?

I'm tempted to call Shep, who's in charge of the bank's security, but . . . no, too much of a stickler; without the right signatures he'll never let me get away with it. So if I can't find someone with transfer authority, I need to at least find someone in the back office who can—

I got it. My brother.

With my receiver in one ear and my cell in the other, I shut my eyes and listen as his phone rings. Once . . . twice . . .

'I'm Charlie,' he answers.

'You're still here!'

'Nope—I left an hour ago,' he deadpans.

I ignore the joke. 'Do you know where Mary in Accounting keeps her username and password?'

'I think so . . . why?'

'Don't go anywhere! I'll be right down.'

My fingers dance across my phone's keypad, forwarding my line to my cellphone—just in case the University Club picks up.

Dashing out of my office, I head for the private elevator at the end of the hallway. I don't care if it's just for clients. I enter Lapidus's code at the keypad above the call buttons, and the doors slide open. I step inside and pound the *Door Close* button. Three floors to go.

'WELL, WELL, WELL,' Charlie announces, looking up from a stack of papers with his forever-boyish grin. 'Look who's slumming!'

I ignore the jab. It's something I've had to get used to over the past six months—which is how long it's been since I got him the job at the bank. He needed the money, and Mom and I needed help with the bills. If it were just gas, electric and rent, we'd be fine. But our tab at the hospital—for Charlie, that's always been personal. It's the reason he took the job in the first place. And while I know he just sees it as a way to pitch in while he writes music, it can't be easy for him to see me up in a private office with a walnut desk and a leather chair, while he's down here with the cubicles and Formica.

'Whatsa matter?' he asks as I rub my eyes. 'The fluorescent light making you sick? If you want, I'll go upstairs and get your lamp—'

'Can you please shut up for a second!'

'What happened?' he asks, suddenly concerned. 'Is it Mom?'

That's always his first question when he sees me upset—especially after the debt collectors gave her a scare last month. 'No, it's not Mom. One of our clients . . . Lapidus was supposed to put through a transfer, and I just got my ass handed to me because it hasn't arrived.'

Charlie tips his chair back on its hind legs and grabs a yellow can of Play-Doh from the corner of his desk. Lifting it to his nose, he cracks open the top, steals a sniff of childhood and lets out a laugh.

'How can you think this is funny?' I demand.

'That's what you're worried about? That some guy didn't get his walking-around money? Tell him to wait until Monday.'

'Why don't *you* tell him—his name's Tanner Drew.'

Charlie's chair drops to the floor. 'Are you serious? How much?'

My answer's a whisper. 'Forty million dollars.'

'Forty mil? Are you on the pipe?'

'I could really use your help,' I say.

'Tell me what you need me to do,' my brother says.

SITTING IN CHARLIE'S CHAIR, I enter Lapidus's username and password and wait for the computer to kick in. I may not be at the top of the totem pole, but I'm still an associate. The youngest associate—and the only one assigned directly to Lapidus. In a place with only twelve partners, that gets me further than most. Like me, Lapidus didn't grow up with a money clip in his pocket. But the right job, with the right boss, led him to the right business school, which launched him up through the private elevators. Now he's ready to return the favour.

Tanner Drew's corporate account lights up the computer screen. Charlie sits sidesaddle on the armrest and his eyes go straight to the balance: $126,023,164.27. '*A la peanut butter sandwiches!* My balance is so low I don't order sodas with my meals any more, and this guy thinks he's got a right to complain?'

It's hard to argue—even to a bank like us, that's a lot of change. Of course, saying Greene & Greene is just a bank is like saying Einstein's 'good at math'.

Greene & Greene is what's known as a 'private bank'. That's our main service: privacy—which is why we don't take just anyone's money. In fact, clients don't choose us; we choose them. Like most banks, we require a minimum deposit. Our minimum is $2 million.

'I knew it,' I say, pointing at the screen. 'Lapidus didn't even cue it in the system. He must've completely forgotten the whole thing.' I quickly type in the first part of the request.

Under *Current Activity*, Charlie spots three cheque disbursements, all of them to 'Kelli Turnley'. 'I bet that's his mistress,' he says. 'Jenni, Candi, Brandi—it's like a pass to the Playboy Mansion—show the "i" and you get right in.'

'First, that's the stupidest thing I've ever heard. And second—'

'What was Dad's first girlfriend's name? Was it . . . *Randi*?'

With a quick shove, I push my chair back, knock Charlie off the sidesaddle, and storm out of his cubicle. I head up the hallway, still listening to recorded greetings of the University Club on my cellphone. I stop at an unmarked metal door. 'The Cage', as it's known throughout the bank, is home to our money transfer system.

There's a punch-code lock above the doorknob. Lapidus's code gets me in. Managing Director goes everywhere.

Ten steps behind me, Charlie enters the six-person office. 'Why do you always have to blow up like that?' he asks as he catches up.

'Because I work here!' I shout, spinning round. 'And you work here—and our personal lives should stay at home!' In his hands, he's holding a pen and his notepad. The student of life. 'And don't start writing this down. I don't need this in one of your songs.'

'I'm sorry,' he laughs, jotting a few final words in his notepad.

'What'd you write?' I demand.

He holds up the notepad. '*I don't need this in one of your songs*,' he relays. 'How good an album title is that?'

Without responding, I approach Mary's desk. 'Can you please just show me where she keeps her password?'

Strolling over to the neatest, most organised desk in the room, he reaches for the plastic picture frame that stands next to her computer. There's a photo of three children. Charlie turns it upside-down. Under the base of the frame is her username and password: marydamski—3BUG5E.

I turn on Mary's computer and glance at the clock on the wall: 3.45pm. Fifteen minutes to go. Using her password, I go straight to *Funds Disbursement*. There's Tanner's transfer queued up on Mary's screen—waiting for final approval. I type in the code for Tanner's bank, as well as the account number he gave me.

'*Requested Amount?*' It almost hurts to enter: *$40,000,000.00*. I look at the clock: 3.49pm. I move the cursor to *Send*. Almost done.

'Can I ask you a question?' Charlie calls out. Before I can answer, he adds, 'How cool would it be if this whole thing was a scam?'

'What?'

'The whole thing . . . the phone call, the yelling . . .' He laughs. 'With all the chaos blowing, how do you know that was the real Tanner Drew? D'you even know what his voice sounds like?'

My body stiffens. I let go of the mouse and try to ignore the chill that licks the hairs on the back of my neck. I turn to face my brother. 'What're you saying? You think it's fake?'

'I have no idea—but think how easy that was: some guy calls up, threatens that he wants his forty million bucks, gives you an account number and says "Make it happen". The moment you hit that button, the money could be headed to some bank in the Bahamas.'

I stare at the eleven-digit number on the screen in front of me. 'No,' I insist. 'There's no way it's a set-up. I overheard Lapidus talking about the transfer last week. It's not like Tanner's calling up out of nowhere.'

'Unless, of course, Lapidus is in on it . . .'

'Will you stop already? You're starting to sound like a paranoid lunatic divorced from reality.'

'I'll have you know I'm offended by the word *lunatic*. And the word *from*.'

'Maybe we should just call him to be safe.'

'Not a bad idea,' Charlie agrees.

The clock says I have four minutes. I dial the family office number.

'Drew Family Office,' a woman answers.

'This is Oliver Caruso at Greene and Greene—I need to talk to Mr Drew. It's an emergency.'

'What kind of emergency?' she snips.

'A forty-million-dollar one.'

There's a pause. 'Please hold.'

I look at the clock. Three minutes. I click back to the wire transfer menu and put the cursor on *Send.* Charlie's back on sidesaddle, grabbing the shoulder of my shirt in an anxious fist.

Thirty seconds later, I hear the secretary back on the line. 'I'm sorry, Mr Caruso—he's not answering his work line.'

'Does he have a cellphone?'

'Sir, I'm not sure you understand . . .'

'Actually, I understand just fine. Now what's your name, so I can tell Mr Drew who I was talking to?'

Again, a pause. 'Please hold.'

We're down to a minute and ten seconds.

'What're you gonna do?' Charlie asks.

'We'll make it,' I tell him.

Fifty seconds. My eyes are glued to the *Send* button. I put the phone on *Speaker* to free my hands. On my shoulder, I feel the grip of Charlie's fist tighten. Thirty seconds.

'Where the hell is this woman?' We don't have a chance.

'This is it,' Charlie says. 'Time to make a decision.'

He's right. The problem is . . . I just can't. I look over my shoulder at my brother. He doesn't say a word, but with twenty seconds to go, he nods his head slightly.

I turn back to the monitor. *Push the button*, I tell myself. But as I go to do it, my whole body freezes and the world starts to blur.

'C'mon!' Charlie shouts. '*Oliver, push the damn button!*'

He says something else, but all I feel is the sharp yank on the back of my shirt. Pulling me out of the way, Charlie leans forward. His hand comes thundering down, pounding the mouse. On screen, the *Send* icon blinks into a negative of itself, then back again. A rectangular box appears three seconds later: *Status: Pending*.

'Does that mean we—?'

Status: Paid. That's it. All sent. The forty-million-dollar email.

We both look at the speakerphone, waiting for a response. My mouth hangs open. Charlie finally lets go of my shirt. And then, there's a crackle from the phone. A voice.

'Caruso,' Tanner Drew growls in a Southern accent that's now as unmistakable as a fork in the eye, 'if this isn't a confirmation call, you better start praying to heaven above.'

'I-It is, sir,' I say, fighting back a grin. 'Just a confirmation.'

'Fine. Goodbye.' With a slam, it's over.

I turn round, but my brother's already gone.

Racing out of the Cage, I scan for Charlie—but as always, he's too fast. At his cubicle, I grab on to the top edges of his wall, boost myself up and peek inside. With his feet up on his desk, he's scribbling in a spiral green notebook, pen cap in mouth and lost in thought.

'Listen, I'm sorry for freezing like that,' I tell him.

'Don't worry about it, bro. Happens to everyone.'

'How about coming over tonight and letting me say thank you with some dinner?' I ask him.

Charlie pauses, studying me. 'Only if we don't take a private car.'

'The bank would pay for it after everything we did tonight.'

He shakes his head disapprovingly. 'You've changed, man—I don't even know you any more . . .'

'Fine, fine, forget the car. I'll pay for a cab.'

'A cab it is.'

Ten minutes later, after a quick stop in my office, we're on the seventh floor, waiting for the elevator. 'Think they'll give you a medal?'

'For what?' I ask. 'For doing my job?'

'Face facts, Superman—you just saved this place from a forty-million-dollar nightmare.'

'Yeah, well, we were still stealing other people's passwords to do it. You know how they are with security around here—'

Before I can finish, the elevator pings and the doors slide open. A broad-chested man in his late thirties is leaning against the back wall. Shep Graves—the bank's head of security.

'*Shep!*' Charlie shouts, stepping into the elevator. 'How's my favourite manhandler of misappropriation?'

'You see what they got going at Madison?' Shep asks with a grin.

There's a trace of a Brooklyn accent, but wherever he's been, they trashed it out of him. 'They got a girl who wants to play boys b-ball.'

'Good. When do we see her play?' Charlie asks.

'There's a scrimmage in two weeks . . .'

Charlie grins. 'You drive; I'll pay.'

'Scrimmages are free.'

'Fine, I'll pay for you too.' Noticing my silence, Charlie motions me into the elevator. 'Shep, you ever meet my brother, Oliver?'

We both nod. 'Nice to see you,' we say simultaneously.

'Shep went to Madison,' Charlie says, proudly referring to our old rival high school in Brooklyn.

I nod and hit the *Door Close* button. The doors slide shut.

'So what're you guys doing here with everyone else gone?' Shep asks. 'Anything interesting?'

'No,' I blurt. 'Same as usual.'

'Didja know Shep used to be in the Secret Service?' Charlie asks.

'That's great,' I say, my eyes focused on the call buttons.

The elevator slows at the fifth floor. 'This is me,' Shep announces, heading for the doors. 'Enjoy the weekend.'

'You too,' Charlie calls out. Neither of us says another word until the doors shut. 'What's wrong with you?' Charlie lays into me. 'He's a nice guy—you didn't have to blow him off like that.'

'All the guy ever does is lurk around and act suspicious. Then suddenly, you walk in and he's Mr Sunshine.'

'See, there's where you're wrong. He's always Mr Sunshine—in fact, he's a rainbow of fruit flavours—but you're so busy angling with Lapidus and Tanner Drew and all the other big shots, you forget that the little people know how to talk too.'

The elevator doors open and Charlie races into the lobby and past a grid of antique roll-top desks. I'm right behind him. 'Don't worry, though,' he calls out. 'I still love you . . . even if Shep doesn't.'

Reaching the side exit, we punch in our codes at the keypad just inside the thick metal door. It clicks open and leads us into a short anteroom with revolving doors at the far end. We spin through and get dumped out on the black, snow-lined streets of Park Avenue. Behind us, the bank's subdued brick façade fades inconspicuously into the landscape. The only sign out front is a designed-to-be-missed brass plaque that reads: GREENE & GREENE, EST. 1870.

A hand in the air gets us a cab; a gas pedal sends us downtown.

Eventually, the cab pulls up to a 1920s brownstone just outside Brooklyn Heights. Technically, it's part of the rougher Red Hook district, but the address is still Brooklyn. True, the front stairs have a loose brick or two, and the metal bars on my basement apartment's windows are cracked, but the cheap rent lets me live on my own in a neighbourhood I'm proud to call home. That alone calms me—until I see who's waiting for me on my front steps. Oh God. Not now.

Our eyes lock and I know I'm in trouble.

Reading my expression, Charlie follows my gaze. 'Oh jeez,' he whispers under his breath. 'Nice knowing you.'

'Here! Pay!' I shout, tossing him my wallet and kicking open the cab door. He fishes out a twenty, tells the cabbie to keep the change and bounces his butt out of there. No way he's missing this.

Skidding across the ice, I'm already in apology mode: 'Beth, I'm so sorry—I totally forgot!'

'Forgot what?' she asks, her voice as calm and pleasant as can be.

'Our dinner . . . inviting you out here . . .'

'Don't worry—it's already done. I have my own key, remember?' Beth steps round me, but I'm still confused.

'Where're you going?'

'Soda. You were all out—I'll be right back.' She turns away from me, and it's the first time she sees Charlie.

'What's shakin', bacon?' He opens his arms for a huge hug.

She doesn't take him up on it. 'Hi, Charlie.'

'So how's the world of corporate accounting?' he asks.

'It's good.'

'And your clients?'

'They're good.'

'And your family—how're they?'

'Good.' She smiles, putting up her best defence. Not an annoyed smile; not a jaded smile. Just a nice, calming Beth smile.

'And whattya think of vanilla as an ice-cream flavour?' Charlie asks.

'*Charlie*,' I warn.

'What?' Turning to Beth, he adds, 'So you sure you don't mind if I crash all over your dinner?'

She looks to me, then back at Charlie. 'Maybe it'd be better if I left you two alone.'

'Don't be silly,' I jump in.

'It's OK,' she adds with a wave that tells me not to worry about it. 'You two should have some time together. Oliver, I'll call you later.'

Before either of us can stop her, she walks up the block, her beige camel-hair coat fanning out behind her.

'Like Darth Vader—only boring,' Charlie whispers.

'Why do you always have to make fun of her like that?' I ask.

'I'm sorry—she just makes it so easy.'

I spin round and storm for the door.

'C'mon, Ollie—I'm only teasing,' he says, chasing me down the wobbly-brick stairway.

I stuff my key in the door. 'Why do you hate her so much?'

'I don't hate *her*, I just hate everything she represents. The quiet smile, the inability to express an opinion . . . that's not what I—not what you should want for yourself.'

'Really?'

'I'm serious,' he says as I work on the third deadbolt. 'It's the same thing as this teeny basement apartment. It's like taking the blue pill and waking up in an urban twentysomething sitcom nightmare.'

'You just don't like Brooklyn Heights.'

'You don't live in Brooklyn Heights,' he insists. 'You live in Red Hook. Understand? Red. Hook.'

As I shove open the door, Charlie follows me into the apartment. 'While I appreciate what you're trying to do,' he says, 'the whole thing's a symptom of a deeper problem.' He repeats the last few words. '*Symptom of a deeper problem.*' Stopping in the kitchen, he pulls out his notepad and jots them down. His head bobs as he puts together a quick melody. On his notepad he starts scribbling. As he flips to the next sheet, I spot a tiny sketch of a man bowing in front of a curtain. He's done writing—now he's drawing.

Charlie can be an incredible artist. So incredible, in fact, that the New York School of Visual Arts was willing to give him a full college scholarship. Two years into it, they tried to steer him into commercial work, like advertising and illustration. But the instant Charlie saw career and art converge, he dropped out and finished his last two years at Brooklyn College studying music.

On my bed, I open my briefcase to flip through some paperwork.

'Don't you ever stop?' Charlie asks. 'It's the weekend—relax.'

'I need to finish this,' I shoot back.

He knows that tone. In silence, he curls up on the foot of the bed.

Two minutes later, the lack of noise does the trick. 'Sometimes I hate rich people,' I finally moan.

'No, you don't,' he teases. 'You love 'em.'

'I'm serious,' I say. 'Once they get some cash—bam!—there goes their grasp of reality. Look at this guy . . .' I pull the top sheet from the pile and wing it his way. 'He misplaces three million dollars for five years. Five years he's forgotten about it! But when we tell him we're about to take it away from him—he wakes up and wants it back.'

He reads the letter signed by someone named Marty Duckworth—'*Thank you for your correspondence . . . please be aware that I've opened a new account at the following bank . . . please forward the balance of my funds there*'—but to Charlie, it still looks like just another normal wire request. 'I don't understand.'

I wave the short paper stack in front of him. 'It's an abandoned account. Under New York law, when a customer doesn't use an account for five years, the money gets turned over to the state.'

'Who would ever abandon their own cash?'

'Mostly dead people,' I say. 'It happens in every bank—when someone dies, or gets sick, sometimes they forget to tell their family about their account. The cash just sits there—and if there's no activity on the account, it eventually gets labelled inactive.'

'So after year five, we just ship that money to the government?'

'When it hits year four and a half, we're required to send out a warning letter saying "*Your account's going to be turned over to the state*." At that point, anyone who's still alive usually responds.'

'Like Mr Three-Million-Dollar Duckworth over here.'

'That's our boy. The only bad part is, he wants to transfer the cash.'

Looking down, Charlie rereads the grainy type on the faxed letter. Something catches his eye. I follow his finger. The phone number on the top of the fax. He makes that face like he smells sewage.

'When'd you get this letter?' Charlie asks.

'Some time today, why?'

'And when does the money get turned over to the state?'

'Monday—which is, I assume, why he sent it by fax. What's wrong?'

'Lookie here,' Charlie says, pointing to the return fax number at the top of the letter. 'Does this number look familiar to you?'

I study it. 'Never seen it before in my life. Why? You know it?'

'It's the Kinko's round the corner from the bank.'

I force a nervous laugh. 'What're you talking about?'

'I'm telling you—the bank doesn't let us use the fax for personal business—so when Franklin or Royce need to send me sheet music, it goes straight to Kinko's—and straight to that number.'

I look down at the letter. 'Why would a millionaire send us a fax from a copy shop that's right around the corner?'

Charlie shoots me a way-too-excited grin. 'Maybe we're not dealing with a millionaire.'

'What? You think Duckworth didn't send this letter?'

'You tell me—have you spoken to him lately?'

'We're not required to—' I cut myself off, suddenly seeing what he's driving at. 'All we do is send a letter to his last known address, and one to his family. But if we want to be safe, there's one place open late . . .' I flick on the speakerphone and dial.

The first thing we hear is a recorded voice. 'Welcome to Social Se—' Without even listening, I hit one, then zero, then two on the phone. I've been here before. 'Thank you for calling Social Security,' a female voice picks up. 'How can I help you?'

'Hi, this is Oliver Caruso calling from Greene and Greene Bank in New York. We have a loan application that we're working on, and we just wanted to verify the applicant's Social Security number.'

'Do you have a routing number?' the woman asks.

I give her the bank's nine-digit ID. Once they get that, we get all the private info. That's the law. God bless America.

'And the number you'd like to check?' the woman asks.

Reading from the print-out of abandoned accounts, I give her Duckworth's Social Security number.

A second passes. Then another. 'Did you say this was for a loan application?' the woman asks, confused.

'Yeah,' I say anxiously. 'Why?'

'According to our files here, I have a June 12th date of death.'

'I don't understand.'

'I'm just telling you what it says, sir. If you're looking for Martin Duckworth, he died six months ago.'

CHAPTER 2

I hang up the phone and stare down at the fax. 'I don't believe this.'

'Me either,' Charlie sings. 'How *X-Files* is this moment?'

'It's not a joke,' I insist. 'Whoever sent this—they almost walked away with three million dollars.'

'What're you talking about?'

'It's a perfect crime. Pose as a dead person, ask for his money and once the account's reactivated, you close up shop and disappear.'

'But won't the government notice their money's missing?'

'They have no idea,' I say, waving the master list of abandoned accounts. 'We send them a printout, minus anything that's been reactivated. They're just happy to get some free cash.'

'Who do you think did it?' Charlie asks.

'Got me—but it has to be someone in the bank. Who else would know when we sent out the final notice letters? Not to mention the fact that they're faxing from a Kinko's around the corner . . .'

Charlie nods his head in steady rhythm. 'So what do we do now?'

'We wait until Monday and then we turn this bastard in.'

No more nodding. 'Are you sure?'

'What else are we gonna do? Take it ourselves?'

'I'm not saying that, but . . .' Charlie's face flushes red. 'How cool would it be to have three million dollars?' He jumps to his feet and his voice picks up speed. 'You give me cash like that and I'd . . . I'd get me a white suit and hold up a glass of red wine and say things like, "I'm having an old friend for dinner . . ." '

'Not me,' I say, shaking my head. 'I'd pay off the hospital, take care of the bills, then take every last penny and invest it.'

'Oh, c'mon, Scrooge—what's wrong with you? You have to have some insane wastefulness '

'You're so right, Charles,' I say in my best British accent. 'And the best part is, no one would know the money was gone.'

Charlie stops. 'They wouldn't, would they?'

'What're you talking about?'

'Is it really that crazy, Ollie?' he asks, his voice now serious. 'I mean, who's really gonna miss that cash? The owner's dead, it's about to be stolen by someone else, and if the government gets it . . . oh, they'll really put the funds to good use.'

I sit up straight. 'Charlie, what you're talking about is *illegal*.'

'You said it yourself, Oliver—it's the perfect crime—'

'That doesn't mean it's right!'

'Don't talk to me about right—rich people . . . big companies . . . they steal from the government all day long—but instead of *stealing*, we just call 'em *loopholes* and *corporate welfare*.'

'C'mon, Charlie, you know the world's not perfect . . .'

'I'm not asking for perfect—but you know how many breaks the tax code has for the rich? People like Tanner Drew barely pay a dollar in tax. But Mom—who's barely making twenty-eight grand a year—half of what she owns goes straight to Uncle Sam. Between the mortgage, and the credit cards, and everything else Dad stuck us with when he left—you have any idea how long that'll take to pay off? And that's not even including what we owe the hospital. What's that at now? Eighty thousand?'

'Eighty-one thousand four hundred and fifty dollars,' I clarify. 'But just because you feel guilty about the hospital, doesn't mean we—'

'It's not about guilt—it's about eighty thousand dollars, Ollie! And it's still growing every time we head back to the doctor!'

'I have a plan—'

'Oh, that's right, your great plan! How's it go again? Lapidus and the bank bring you to business school, which'll bring you up the ladder, which'll make all our debt disappear? Does that cover it? Cause I hate to break it to you, Ollie, but you've been there four years and we're barely making a dent. This is our chance to set Mom free. She doesn't have to be second class any more . . .'

'She's not second class.'

'She is, Ollie. And so are we,' Charlie insists. 'Now I'm sorry if that ruins your priceless self-image, but it's time to find a way to get her out. Everyone deserves a fresh start—especially Mom.'

Charlie knows exactly what he's doing. Taking care of Mom has always been top priority. For both of us. Of course, that doesn't mean I have to follow him over the cliff. 'I don't need to be a thief.'

'Thieves steal from *people*,' Charlie challenges. 'This money doesn't belong to anyone. Duckworth's dead—he's got no family. All we'd be taking is some cash that would never be missed.'

'Oh, OK, Lenin, so when we're done redistributing the wealth, then what do we do? Retire on the beach, open a bar and write sappy little songs for the rest of our lives?'

'It's better than wasting another four years kissing corporate ass.'

I hop off the bed. 'You know business school is the best way out, and you know I can't go there directly after college,' I insist, shoving a finger in his face. 'You have to work a couple of years first.'

'Fine. A couple of years—that's two. You're finishing four.'

'Charlie, I'm applying to the top schools in the country. Harvard, Penn, Chicago, Columbia. That's where I want to go—anything else is second best and doesn't help anyone, including Mom.'

'And how many opportunities did you give up because Lapidus put his grand plan about B-school in your head? How many companies have you refused offers from? You should've left the bank years ago. Instead, it's been back-to-back B-school rejection letters. You're one of the most brilliant people I know. Stop being so scared of living.'

'Then stop judging me!' I explode.

'I'm not judging you . . .'

'No, you're just asking me to steal three million dollars—that'll solve all my problems!'

'It's the only way we're ever gonna dig out of this.'

'See, that's where you're wrong!' I shout. 'You may be thrilled, nursing paper cuts in the file room, but I've got my eyes on something bigger. Once I'm done with business school, Mom's never gonna see another bill again. Sure, the path is safe and simple—but it works.'

'Really? So you think that even though you've single-handedly brought in over twelve million dollars' worth of new accounts for Lapidus, and even though every partner in the firm went to one of the four business schools you're applying to, it's still possible you've been rejected two years in a row?'

'That's enough!'

'Uh-oh, sore spot! You've already thought it yourself, haven't you? Do you have any idea what a pain it is for Lapidus to hire someone new and train him to think exactly like he does? You gotta find the right kid . . . preferably a poor one with no connections . . .'

'*Shut up!*' I yell, rushing forward.

Charlie ducks under my grasp and races back towards the eat-in kitchen. On the table, he spots a B-school catalogue from Columbia and a file folder with the word 'Applications' on it. As he picks it up, a letter-sized envelope falls to the floor. There's a signature across the back, right where it's sealed. *Henry Lapidus.* The signature on the envelope is required by all four schools—to make sure I don't open it. The typed pages inside are the most important part of any business school application—the boss's recommendation.

'OK, who wants to play detective?' Charlie sings, waving the envelope over his head so it scrapes the basement's low ceiling.

'Give it back!' I demand.

'Oh, c'mon, Oliver. At least this way you get the truth. If this guy's bashing you in the letter—he's ruined the whole plan. Your way out—how to pay Mom's debts—everything we're counting on.'

'*Let go of it!*' I explode. I plough straight at him, but he hops backwards onto my bed and bounces like a seven-year-old.

'Get off my bed!' I shout. 'You'll pop one of the springs!'

Charlie stops jumping. He steps to the edge of the mattress, bounces off the bed and springboards to his feet. 'Oliver, I don't care about the money.' He slaps the envelope against my chest. 'But if you don't start making some changes soon, you're gonna be that guy who—when he hits his forty-third birthday—hates his life.'

'At least I won't be living with my mother in Brooklyn. Get out.'

Shaking his head, Charlie heads towards the door. It slams behind him and I look through the peephole. He bounds up the stairs. 'Open it and find out!' he shouts from outside. And just like that, he's gone.

TEN MINUTES after Charlie leaves, I'm sitting at my kitchen table, staring down at the envelope. Behind me, the water in the kettle is starting to boil. I tell myself it's because I'm in the mood for some instant coffee, but my subconscious doesn't buy it for a second.

It's not like I'm talking about stealing the money. It's just about my boss. It's important to know what he thinks.

Across the table, I spot the most recent bill from Coney Island Hospital: $81,450. That's what happens when you miss an insurance payment to juggle your other bills. It's another two decades of Mom's life. Two decades of worrying. Unless I can get her out.

My eyes go to the envelope. Whatever's inside, I need to know.

I grab the envelope, shoot out of my seat and stand in front of the kettle, watching the geyser of steam. Holding my breath, I grip the bottom of the envelope, lower the sealed side into the steam and pray to God that this works just like it does in the movies.

Carefully, I slide my thumb into the edge of the envelope and prise open the smallest of spaces. Letting it fill with steam, I work my thumb in deeper and try to inch the flap open. Finally the glue gives way. Tossing aside the envelope, I yank open the two-page letter.

Dear Dean Milligan. *Personalised. Good.* I'm writing on behalf of Oliver Caruso, who is applying for your MBA programme . . . *blah, blah* . . . Oliver's supervisor for the past four years . . . *blah and more blah* . . . sorry to say . . . *Sorry to say?* . . . that I cannot in good conscience recommend Oliver as a candidate to your school . . . much as it pains me . . . lack of professionalism . . . maturity issues . . . for his own sake, would benefit from another year of work experience . . .

My hands clamp tightly round the letter. My eyes flood with tears. Spinning round, I race to the closet and pull out my coat. If Charlie's taking the bus, I can still catch him. I yank open the door and—

'So?' Charlie asks, sitting there on my front steps. 'What's new?'

I screech to a halt and don't say a word. My head's down. The letter's crumpled in my fist.

Charlie studies me in an instant. 'I'm sorry, Ollie.'

I nod, seething. 'Were you serious about before?' I ask him.

'Y'mean with the—'

'Yeah,' I interrupt, thinking about Mom's face when all the bills are paid. 'With that.'

'SO WHATTA WE DO NOW?' Charlie asks as he shuts the door to my office early Monday morning.

'Just what we talked about,' I say, grabbing the fax from Friday night and sliding it in front of my computer. At noon today, the abandoned accounts have to be sent to the state or returned to their owners. That gives us three hours to steal $3 million.

I start copying from the Duckworth fax.

'Now what're you doing?' Charlie asks.

'Same thing our mystery person did—writing a fake letter that claims the money—but this one puts it in an account for us.'

Charlie nods. 'So any new ideas on who the original thief was?'

'Actually, that was going to be my next . . .' Picking up the phone, I read the number from the Duckworth fax and start dialling. Before Charlie asks, I put the phone on speaker so he can hear.

'Directory Assistance,' a mechanised voice says. 'For what city?'

'Manhattan,' I say. I read from the fax: 'Midland National Bank.' Where the thief wanted to transfer the money.

I dial the new number.

'Midland National,' a female voice answers. 'How can I help you?'

'Hi,' I say. 'My name is Martin Duckworth, and I just wanted to confirm the details for an upcoming wire transfer.'

'I'll do my best—what's your account number, sir?'

I once again read it straight from the letter.

We hear a quiet clicking as she types it in. 'I have it right here, sir. The transfer will be coming from Greene & Greene, and then we have your instructions to send it to TPM Limited at the Bank of London, into account number B2178692792.'

Charlie scribbles down the number. Next to *TPM Ltd.*, I take his pen and write, *Fake company. Smart.* 'Wonderful. Thanks . . .'

'Is there anything else I can help you with, Mr Duckworth?'

Charlie moves closer to the speakerphone. Dropping his voice down to his best impersonation of me, he adds, 'Actually, as long as I have you on the line . . . I haven't got my last few statements—can you please check and see if you have my right address?'

Oh, the boy's good.

'Let me take a look,' she says. 'OK, I think I see the problem. Which address do you want us to send it to?'

'You have more than one?' I jump in.

'Well, there's the one in New York: 405 Amsterdam Avenue . . .'

'. . . Apartment 2B,' I agree, reading from the address on the letter.

'And then I have another in Miami . . .'

Charlie flings me a Post-it, and I dive for a pen.

'1004 Tenth Street, Miami Beach, Florida, 33139,' she reads.

Instinctively, Charlie writes down city, state and zip. I write down the street address. It's the way we used to remember phone numbers: I get the first half; he gets the last. 'Story of my life,' he used to say.

There's a loud knock on my office door. I jerk round just in time to see it open. 'Anyone home?' a deep voice asks.

Charlie grabs the letter. I grab the receiver, killing the speaker-phone. 'OK, thanks again for the help.' With a crash, I'm off.

'H-Hey, Shep,' Charlie sings, putting on his happy face.

'Everything OK?' the head of security asks, stepping towards us.

'Yeah,' Charlie says.

'Absolutely,' I add. 'So what can I help you with today, Shep?'

'Actually, I wanted to talk to you about that transfer you made to Tanner Drew.'

'That was a perfectly legal transfer,' I challenge.

'*Listen*,' Shep interrupts. 'Spare me the tone. I already spoke to Lapidus—he's thrilled you had the balls to take charge. Tanner Drew's happy; all is well. But from my side of the desk . . . well, I don't like seeing forty million dollars go zip . . . especially when you're using someone else's password.'

How'd he know we—?

'You think they hired me for my looks?' Shep asks. 'With thirteen billion at risk, we've got the best security money can buy.'

'Well, if you need any back-up, I've got a pretty good bike lock,' Charlie adds, trying to keep things light.

Shep turns towards him. 'Oh, man, would you love it, Charlie—I got this one option—you ever heard of Investigator software?'

Charlie shakes his head. He's out of jokes.

'It lets you do keystroke monitoring,' Shep adds, all his attention now on me. 'Which means when you're sitting at your computer, I can see every word you're typing. Email, letters, passwords . . . as soon as you hit the key, it pops up on my screen.'

Oh jeez. The fake letter . . .

'It's really amazin',' Shep continues. 'You can program it like an alarm—so if someone's using Mary's password, and the security system says she's no longer in the building . . . it'll pop up on your screen and tell you what's going on.'

'Listen, I'm sorry I had to do that . . .'

'Don't worry about it,' Shep says, taking a few steps towards us. 'Like I said, Lapidus didn't give a squat. He doesn't care that I can see when someone types in Mary's name, or his name . . .' Shep glances over my shoulder. 'Or even that I can see when someone's using a company computer to write a fraudulent letter.'

Charlie jumps out of his seat.

'I'll tell ya, they never had that when I was in the Service,' Shep continues. 'These days, you can have computers notify you of anything. Forty-million-dollar transfers to Tanner Drew . . . or three-million-dollar transfers to Marty Duckworth.'

I'm paralysed. I can't move.

'It's over, son. We know what you're up to.'

Charlie laughs. 'Whoa, Shep—you don't think we—'

Shep ploughs past him, a finger pointed straight at my face. 'I knew from the second you sent that first fax.'

'The first fax?' Charlie protests. 'The Kinko's one? You think that was *us*?' He puts a hand on Shep's shoulder. 'I swear to you, buddy, we never sent that . . . In fact, when we got in this morning we . . . we were trying to catch the thief ourselves. Isn't that right, Oliver?'

'Knock, knock—anyone home?' a scratchy voice shouts as the door to my office swings open. Shep spins round and finds the source of the voice—the paunchy middle-aged man who's now approaching my desk—Francis A. Quincy, head financial partner of the firm. Behind him is the boss himself. Henry Lapidus.

'Look who it is—the forty-million-dollar man!' Lapidus sings. He wipes his hand across his mostly bald head—it's part of his constant state of kinetic motion. Despite his six-foot-three frame, Lapidus is like a hummingbird in human form . . . flap, flap, flap, all day long.

'And guess who we brought for you?' Lapidus asks. Stepping aside, he reveals a turtle-faced kid slicked up in a way-too-expensive Italian suit. He's our age and looks familiar, but I . . .

'Kenny?' Charlie blurts.

Kenny Owens. My freshman year roommate at NYU. Obnoxious Long Island rich kid. Haven't seen him in years—but the suit alone tells me nothing's changed. Still a putz.

'Been a long time, huh?' Kenny asks. He's waiting for an answer, but Charlie and I are both eyeing Shep.

'I thought you'd like some time to catch up,' Lapidus says.

'Old friends and all that . . .' Quincy adds.

Something's up. As a rule, Quincy hates everyone. Like most CFOs, all he cares about is the money. But today . . . today, we're all family. And if Lapidus and Quincy are personally taking Kenny around . . . he must be interviewing for a job.

Lapidus follows our gaze to Shep. 'And what're you doing here?' Lapidus asks. 'More lecturing about Tanner Drew?'

'Yeah,' Shep says drily. 'All about Tanner Drew.'

'Well, why don't you save it for later,' Lapidus adds. 'Let these boys have some time alone.'

'Actually, this is more important,' Shep challenges.

'Maybe you didn't understand,' Quincy jumps in. 'We want these boys to have some time alone.' Right there, the fight's over.

'Thanks again for doing this,' Lapidus says to me. Leaning in close, he whispers, 'And take it from me, Oliver—helping us get Kenny—it's a perfect way to round out your B-school applications.'

Charlie and I sit there silently as Shep grudgingly follows Lapidus and Quincy to the door. Just as they leave, Shep turns round and pegs Charlie with a javelin glare. The door slams shut.

'So, do I look good?' Kenny asks as soon as they're gone.

'What're you doing here?' I snap.

'Nice to see you too,' Kenny says. 'You always so warm to guests?'

'Yeah . . . no. . . . Sorry—just one of those days,' I stammer. 'So tell us what's going on. What position are you interviewing for?'

Kenny laughs. 'I'm not here for a job—I'm here as a client.'

THE INSTANT THE DOOR slams behind Kenny, I sink down in my seat. Charlie's pacing, unable to stop. 'Maybe we should call Shep,' he says.

'Just give me a minute . . .'

'We don't have a minute—he's gonna be here any second and if all we do is sit around . . . I mean, what're we still doing here anyway? It's like pulling the pin and waiting with the grenade in our pants.'

I think for a second. 'Yeah. What *are* we still doing here?' I get up from my seat. 'Shep just had us nailed for swiping three million bucks—but does he tell Lapidus? No. He walks away and saves the conversation for later.'

'So?' Charlie says with a shrug.

'So what's the first rule of Law Enforcement? Don't let the bad guys get away. If Shep smells something wrong, he's supposed to go straight to the boss.'

'Maybe he's just giving us a chance to explain.'

'Or maybe he's—' I stop mid-step. Up goes the suspicious eyebrow. 'How well do you know this guy, Charlie?'

'We hang out at work.' He rolls his eyes. 'Oh, c'mon . . . Now you think *Shep's* the thief?'

'How else would he know about the original Duckworth fax?'

'He saw it come in . . .'

'Hundreds of faxes come in here every day. There's no way Shep would find it. So—'

'—he knew it was coming,' he says, completing my thought. His mouth gapes open. 'You really think he . . . ?'

'We should get out of here,' I blurt. 'The longer we sit here, the more likely we'll be tagged as scapegoa—' Tearing the door open, I look up. There's a figure in the doorway.

Shep steps forward, forcing me back. Once he's in the room, he whips the door shut. He studies Charlie and me, taking our measure.

'I'll split it with you,' Shep says. 'Three ways—a million each.'

'So it *was* you who sent the first letter,' I say. 'You were just in here blaming us, and now you expect us to hold hands and be partners?'

'Listen, Oliver, chew my head off all you want, but if you blow the whistle on me I'm gonna blow it right back on you. So you can either be a mule and get nothing, or you can share the profits and—'

'I vote for the profits,' Charlie interrupts.

'Screw this,' I say, storming to the door. 'Even I'm not that stupid.'

Shep reaches out and grabs me by the biceps. Not hard—just enough to stop me. 'It's not stupid, Oliver. If I wanted to turn you in I'd be talking to Lapidus right now. Instead, I'm here.'

Even as I pull away, Shep has my undivided attention. 'So how do we know you won't take the money and run?' I ask.

'What if I let you pick where the transfers go? You can start from scratch . . . put it in whatever fake company you want. I mean . . . with your mom here . . . you're not going on the run for two million dollars—that's the only guarantee I need,' Shep says.

'And you really think it'll work?' I ask.

'Oliver, I've been watching this one for almost a year,' Shep says. 'In life, there're only two crimes where you can't be caught: One is where you're killed, which isn't too great an option. The other is when no one knows that a crime took place.' He motions to the paperwork on my desk. 'That's what's here on a silver platter.'

I stare at the clock on my wall. Two and a half hours to go. After that, the opportunity's gone. The money'll be transferred to the state.

'Think of what we can do for Mom,' Charlie says. 'All the debt . . .'

Back in my seat, I take a deep breath and spread my palms flat on my desk. 'You know we're gonna regret this,' I say.

They both break into smiles. Two kids.

'We have a deal?' Shep asks, extending a hand.

I shake Shep's hand. 'So what do we do now?' I ask.

'Know any good fake companies?' Shep replies.

That's my department. When Arthur Mannheim divorced his wife, Lapidus and I opened a holding company and an Antigua bank account in an hour and a half. It's Lapidus's favourite dirty trick—and one I know all too well. I reach for the phone.

'No, no, no,' Shep scolds, pulling my hand away. 'You can't call these people yourself any more. Everything you do is a link, just like a fingerprint. You need a go-between—a professional, not just some schlub off the street. Someone who you can send a thousand dollars and say, "Make this phone call for me and don't ask questions . . ."'

'Like a mob lawyer,' Charlie says.

'Exactly.' Shep grins. 'Just like a mob lawyer.' He stands up and leaves my office. Thirty seconds later, he returns with a Jersey phonebook. He tosses it on my desk. 'Time to find the stutterers.'

Charlie and I look at each other. We're lost.

'The first alphabetical entries in every category,' Shep explains. 'AAAAAA Flower Shop. AAAAAA Laundromat. And the most likely to do anything for a buck: AAAAAA Attorneys At Law.'

Charlie dives for the phonebook and flips through it. 'I got it!' he shouts. He spins the book round and points to the spot. All it says is 'A'. Under it, the text has one word: *Lawyer*.

This time, Charlie's the one who leaps for the phone. Shep pounds him in the knuckles. 'Not from here,' Shep says. Heading for the door, he adds, 'That's why God invented payphones.'

'Are you crazy?' I ask. 'All three of us hovering over a payphone? Yeah, that's inconspicuous.'

Turning back, Shep says, 'I suppose you have a better idea?'

CHAPTER 3

'Hi,' Charlie coos with a beauty-pageant smile as he glides up to the black granite reception desk. We're on the fourth floor of the Wayne & Portnoy building: it's across the street from the bank and it's home to the largest stuffed-shirt law firm in the city.

Behind the desk, a receptionist is yammering into her headset.

'I'm waiting for Bert Collier to come down,' Charlie says, 'and I was wondering if I could use a phone for a quick private call.' Norbert Collier was just one of the names listed on the directory in the lobby.

'Past the elevators,' the receptionist says without even hesitating.

Hiding round the corner, Shep and I wait for Charlie to pass, then fall in behind him. I point to the wood-panelled door and usher them into a conference room. The words CLIENT SERVICES are on a brass plate outside the door. It's not a huge room. Small mahogany table, a few upholstered chairs, a fax machine against the wall and four separate telephones. Everything we need to do some damage.

Shep slides into a seat, pulls the number from his pocket and grabs the phone. As he dials, Charlie hits the hands-free button on the starfish speakerphone system that's at the centre of the table.

'Law offices,' a male voice answers.

Shep keeps it cool and calm. 'Hello, I'm looking for a lawyer and was wondering what type of law Mr . . . uh . . . Mr . . .'

'Bendini.'

'I was wondering what type of law Mr Bendini specialises in.'

'What type of law are you looking for?'

Shep nods to the two of us. Here's our man. 'Actually, we're looking for someone who specialises in keeping things . . . low-profile . . .'

There's a short pause at the other end. 'Talk to me,' Bendini says.

'I'm gonna put on my associate,' Shep tells Bendini, nodding to me.

'Mr Bendini,' I start. 'I want you to call the following number . . The place is called Purchase Out International, and you want to ask for Arnie. When you get him on the line, tell him you need a same-day four-layer cake, endzone in Antigua. He'll know what it is.'

'Believe me, kid, I know how to stack corporations,' Bendini interrupts in a brickyard Jersey accent. 'What name you want to put it in?'

'Martin Duckworth,' all three of us say simultaneously.

I swear I hear Bendini roll his eyes. 'And for initial ownership?'

He needs another fake name. This one doesn't matter—everything's ultimately owned by Duckworth. 'Ribbie Henson,' I say, using the name of Charlie's imaginary friend from when he was six.

'Fine—Ribbie Henson. Now how do you wanna pay Arnie's bill?'

'Tell him we'll pay when we request the original paperwork—right now all we need is a fax,' I decide. I add, 'It's what he does with the big fish—they don't pay until the money hits. Tell him we're whales.'

'And when do you need it by?' Bendini asks.

'How's a half-hour sound?' I reply.

'I'll do what I can,' Bendini says, unfazed. Clearing his throat for emphasis, he adds, 'Now how'm *I* gonna get paid?'

'I'll give you a thousand if you can do it in a half-hour,' Shep says.

'A *grand*?' Bendini asks. 'Boys, I don't piss for a grand—even when I have to. The minimum is five.'

Shep shoots a panicked look to me. I can't help but nod. There go some B-school funds—and hospital bills.

'OK,' Shep tells Bendini. 'We'll wire it as soon as we hang up.' Reading from the white sticker on the fax machine, Shep relays our phone and fax numbers, thanks the price-gouger and hangs up.

'So you think it'll work?' I ask anxiously.

'As long as your buddy Arnie comes through . . .' Shep says.

'Trust me, Arnie'll have it done in ten minutes. He's this hippie left-over who lives in the Marshall Islands and sticks it to the government by plucking shelf corps off the wall all day long.'

'Shelf corps?' Charlie asks.

'Corps . . . corporations. Arnie registers them all across the world—gives them names, addresses, even boards of directors.'

'And you think he's gonna be able to set up an entire company in the next half-hour?' Charlie asks.

'He's set these up months ago. ABC Corp. DEF Corp. GHI Corp. The paperwork's already done . . . each corporation is just a note-book on a shelf. When we call, he scribbles our fake name into the few blanks that are left and gives it a quick notary stamp.'

The phone rings and Charlie answers it through the speakerphone.

'Congratulations,' Bendini says. 'Ribbie Henson is now the proud owner and sole shareholder of Sunshine Distributors Partnership Limited, in the Virgin Islands, which is owned by CEP Worldwide in Nauru, which is owned by Maritime Holding Services in Vanuatu, which is owned by Martin Duckworth in Antigua.' Four layers—endzone in Antigua. When law enforcement digs, it'll take them months to sort through all the paperwork. 'Sounds like you boys are in business. Just make sure you wire my cash.'

Over the next five minutes, the fax machine vomits up the paper-work—from bylaws to articles of incorporation—everything we need to open a corporate account. I check the clock on the wall: two hours to go. Mary asked for the paperwork by noon. Damn. All three of us know this can't be like Tanner Drew. No stolen pass-words. It's gotta be done by the book.

'Can we make it?' Charlie asks.

'If you want, we can hand the original letter to Mary right now,' Shep offers. 'My Duckworth accounts are already set up—'

'Not a chance,' I interrupt. 'Like you said, we pick where the money goes.'

Shep's tempted to argue, but quickly realises he can't win. 'Fine,' he says. 'But if you're not using the existing Duckworth account, I'd go offshore as soon as possible.'

Nodding, Charlie pulls a thin stack of red paper from my briefcase. The Red Sheet—the partners' master list of favourite foreign banks, including the ones that're open twenty-four hours. It's on red paper so no one can photocopy it.

'You want to send it to foreign banks,' Shep continues, 'because they're the ones who're least likely to cooperate with law enforcement. But if you transfer it too fast, the banks will tag it as suspicious and put the IRS on your tail. So focus on short logical jumps. Now, what's the number one location where we bank abroad?'

'England,' I say.

'England it is,' Shep replies. 'Mary does almost thirty transfers there a day. She won't think twice. Now once you're in London, France is the easiest—nothing suspicious about that. And their regulations are softer, which means the world opens up a little. Personally, I like Latvia—slightly smarmy . . . the government hasn't decided if it likes us yet. And for international investigations, they only help us about half the time, which means it's a perfect place to waste an investigator's day. From there you slam the Marshall Islands, and from there, you bounce it close to home in Antigua. By the time it gets there, what started out as dirty cash is now so untraceable, it's clean.'

I skim through the Red Sheet and pick a bank for each territory.

'Listen, I should go check in with Lapidus,' Shep says. 'How 'bout we meet back in my office at eleven thirty?'

I nod, Charlie says thanks, and Shep hightails it out of the office.

The moment the door shuts, I once again dive for the speakerphone, and punch in the phone number for the Antigua bank.

'Hi, I'd like to speak to Rupa Missakian,' I say, reading from the sheet. Within five minutes, I've relayed the tax ID number and all the other vital stats for Sunshine Distributors' first bank account.

As I shut off the speakerphone, Charlie points to his Wonder Woman watch. Twenty minutes, start to finish. Forty minutes left and four more accounts to open. Not good enough.

'C'mon, coach,' Charlie says. 'Get me in the game.'

Without a word, I rip two pages from the Red Sheet and slide them across the table. One says *France*, the other *Marshall Islands*. Charlie darts to the phone on his far right; I race to the one on mine. Opposite corners. Our fingers flick across the keypads.

'Do you speak English?' I ask a stranger from Latvia. 'Yes . . . I'm looking for Feodor Svantanich or whoever's handling his accounts.'

'Hi, I'm trying to reach Lucinda Llanos,' Charlie says.

There's a short pause. 'Hi,' we both say simultaneously. 'I'd like to open a corporate account.'

'OK, CAN YOU READ me the number one more time?' Charlie asks a Frenchman who he keeps calling Inspector Clouseau. He calls it out to me: 'Tell your English bloke it's HB7272250.'

'Here we go—HB7272250,' I say to the rep from London. 'Once it comes in, we want it transferred there as soon as possible.'

It's the third time we've played this game—relaying the account number of one bank to the bank that precedes it.

'Yeah . . . yeah . . . that'd be great,' Charlie says, switching to his I-really-gotta-run voice. 'Have a croissant on me.'

Charlie hops out of his seat as I lower the receiver. 'Aaaannnd . . . we're done,' he says as the phone hits the cradle.

My eyes go straight to the clock. Eleven thirty-five. 'Damn. We're late.' In a blur, I rake the loose pages of the Red Sheet back into my briefcase. And we're gone.

'WHERE THE HELL were you guys?' Shep asks as we plough into his office. Ten minutes and counting. He leaps out of his seat and jams a sheet of paper in front of my face. 'Transfer request—all you need to do is fill in where it's going.'

Ripping the paperwork from my briefcase, I flip to the Red Sheet marked *England*. I copy the account info as fast as I can.

'So where's it finally going?' Shep asks.

I stop writing. 'I thought you said—'

'—that you could pick where the money goes,' Shep interrupts. 'I did—and you can—but I want to know the final stop.'

'That wasn't part of the deal,' I growl.

Shep leans in. 'The deal was to give the two of you control . . . not to freeze me out altogether. All I'm asking for is some insurance.'

'No, all you're asking for is *our* insurance.'

'Just tell me where the damn bank is!' Shep explodes.

'Why? So you can leave us chewing dirt?'

'Dammit, you two, no one's leaving anyone!' Charlie shouts. He reaches out and grabs my stack of Red Sheets.

'What're you doing?' I yell, pulling them back.

'Let . . . *go!*' Charlie insists with one last yank. The top two pages tear in half and I fly backwards. Spinning towards Shep, Charlie flips to the bottom of the pile, pulls out the Red Sheet marked *Antigua* and folds it back so you can only see one bank on the list.

'*Charlie . . . don't!*'

Too late. He covers the account number with his finger and rams it in Shep's face. 'You got it?'

Shep studies it with a quick look. 'Thank you . . . that's all I ask.'

'What the hell is wrong with you?' I shout.

'If we sit here arguing, no one's getting anything,' Charlie shoots back. 'So finish it and get going. We've got only a few minutes!'

Spinning towards the clock, I check for myself.

'Go, go, go!' Charlie shouts as I jot in the last line. He just gave away our entire insurance policy—but it's still not worth losing everything. Not when we're this close. Stumbling out of the door, I've got a stack of forty abandoned accounts under my arm.

'ABOUT TIME,' Mary says as I enter the Cage. 'You had me worried.'

'Are you kidding?' I ask, smiling anxious hellos to the other four officemates who look up as I cross the industrial carpet. 'I still have a good three minutes . . .'

'And worse comes to worst, you can always do it yourself, right?' Mary asks, wiping a smudge from the glass of her picture frame.

'Listen, about Tanner Drew . . . I shouldn't have . . . I'm sorry.'

'I'm sure you are.' She lowers her head, ready to blow. But out of nowhere, her high-pitched laugh cuts through the room. Then Polly, who sits next to her, joins in. Then Francine. All laughing.

'Y-You're not mad?'

'Honey, you did the best you could with what you had . . . but if I ever find out you use my password again . . .'

I wince slightly, waiting for the rest of the threat.

Once again, Mary smiles wide. 'It's a joke, Oliver . . . it won't kill you to laugh.' She pulls the stack of abandoned accounts from my hand and lightly slaps me across the chest with it. 'You take things too seriously, y'know that?'

I try to answer, but nothing comes out. All I see are the forms as they wave through the air.

Turning to her computer, Mary clips the stack to the vertical clipboard attached to her monitor. She knows the deadline. No time to waste. Luckily, the transfers are already keyed in—all she has to do is enter the destinations. 'I don't see why the state gets this,' she adds as she opens the *Abandoned Accounts* file. 'Personally I'd rather see it go to charity . . .' She says something else, but it's drowned out by the blood rushing through my ears. On the screen, a $20,000 account gets zapped to New York's Unclaimed Funds Division. Then a $300 one. Then a $12,000. One by one, she works her way through the pile earmarked for the state.

Flipping to the next sheet in the pile, Mary finally gets to a

$400,000 transfer to someone named Alexander Reed. I expect her to make some comment about the amount, but at this point, she's dead to it. She sees it every day.

She leafs to the next sheet in the pile and lowers her fingers to the keyboard. There it is: *Duckworth and Sunshine Distributors*.

'So what'd you do this weekend?' I ask, my voice racing.

'Oh—tried to show up all my relatives by buying them better holiday presents than the ones they bought me.'

Onscreen, the name of our London bank clicks into place.

'That sounds great,' I say vacantly.

Digit by digit, the account number follows.

'*Great?*' Mary laughs. 'Oliver, you've really got to get out more.'

The cursor glides to the *Send* button. The *Send* icon blinks to a negative and then back again. *Status: Pending*. *Status: Paid*.

THERE'S SOMEONE watching me. I didn't notice him when I left the bank—it was after six and the December sky was already dark. And I didn't see him trail me down the grimy subway stairs or follow me through the turnstile—there are way too many commuters to notice any one person. But as I reach the subway platform, I swear I hear someone whisper my name.

I spin round but all that's there is the typical Park Avenue post-work crowd. The majority stare down at reading material—and one man abruptly lifts a *Wall Street Journal* to cover his face. In no mood to take chances, I head further up the platform.

The train barrels into the station. I make my way towards the subway car and take one last peek down the platform. The man with the *Journal* is gone.

As the train makes its way downtown, the crowd thins and I see who's waiting for me at the far end of the car—the man hiding behind the *Wall Street Journal*. Without the crowds, it's easy to give him the quick once-over. That's all I need. I plough towards him and rip the paper from his hands. 'What the hell are you doing, Charlie?'

My brother ekes out a playful grin, but it doesn't help.

'You want to tell me what this is about, Charlie, or should I just add it to your ever-growing list of stupid moves?' I scold.

'Ever-growing?' he asks. 'I don't know what you're—?'

'With Shep,' I snarl. 'How could you give him our final location?'

'I didn't give him anything,' Charlie growls in a low whisper. 'When I showed him the Red Sheet . . . I pointed to the wrong bank. Of course you were so busy yelling, he believed every word.'

WE WALK UP the broken sidewalks of Avenue U in Sheepshead Bay, Brooklyn, and make a right on Bedford Avenue. The garage door storefronts give way to a 1950s six-storey apartment building.

'I see handsome men!' a female voice shouts from a window on the third floor. I don't even have to look up to know who it is.

'Thanks, Mom,' I mutter. Keep the routine, I tell myself as I follow Charlie towards the lobby. Monday night is Family Night.

The elevator reaches the third floor and we head to Mom's apartment. 'Who wants a nice baked ziti?' she shouts, opening the door even before we hit the doorbell. As always, her smile's wide and her arms are outstretched, searching for a hug.

'Ziti?' Charlie sings, jumping forward and hugging her back. 'We talking original or extra-crispy?'

'Hi, Ma,' I say, still waiting at the door.

She turns back, the smile never leaving her face. 'Ooooh, my *big* boy,' she says. 'I love seeing you in a suit. So professional . . .'

Weighing in at over 180 pounds, my mom's never been a petite woman . . . or an insecure one. When her hair went grey, she never dyed it. When it started thinning, she cut it short. After my dad left, the physical nonsense didn't matter any more—all she cared about was me and Charlie. She's always had more than enough love to go round. The least we can do is pay her back.

Heading for the kitchen, I reach for the Charlie Brown cookie jar and tug off the ceramic head. I pull a stack of papers from inside.

'Oliver, please . . .' Mom says. 'You don't have to pay my bills.'

'Ma, you don't have to worry. This is a pleasure.'

Besides, if she didn't need the help, the bills wouldn't be where I could find them, and we'd be eating steak instead of ziti. Her lips slightly quiver and she bites nervously at the Band-Aids that cover her fingertips. The life of a seamstress—too many pins and hems. She opens the window in the kitchen and leans out.

At first, I assume she must've spotted Mrs Finkelstein—Mom's best friend and our old baby sitter—whose window is directly across the alley between our buildings. But when I hear the familiar squeaky churn of the clothes line we share with the Fink, I realise Mom's bringing in the rest of today's work.

One by one, I flip through the monthly bills, figuring out which ones to pay. Sometimes I just do the credit cards and the hospital . . . Other times, when the heating gets high, I do utilities. Charlie always does insurance. As I said, for him, it's personal.

Scanning through the credit card bill, my bank instincts kick in.

Check the charges; protect the client; make sure nothing's out of place. Groceries . . . sewing materials . . . Vic Winick Dance Studio?

'What's this Vic Winick place?' I ask.

'Dance lessons,' my mother says.

'Dance lessons? Who do you take dance lessons with?'

'Wif me!' Charlie shouts in his best French accent. He grabs my mother and pulls her close. They bob and weave round the narrow kitchen, my mother flying, her head held high.

'Lookin' good, sweet momma—lookin' good!' Charlie yells, his hand waving in the air. 'You're gonna be sleepin' easy tonight!'

I'VE MADE THIS WALK at least a thousand times. Out of the subway, up the stairs, through the crowd and straight up Park Avenue until I hit the bank. But today . . . I'm done counting the days I've put in. From now on, it's a countdown until we leave.

By my estimate, Charlie should be the first out—maybe a month or two from now. After that, it's a coin toss between me and Shep.

Continuing up Park Avenue, I can practically taste the conversation. 'I just wanted to let you know I think it's time I moved on,' I'll tell Lapidus. No need to bring up the B-school letters—just a mention of 'opportunities elsewhere' and a thank-you for being the best mentor anyone could ask for. The whole thing brings a smile to my face . . . until I see two navy-blue sedans in front of the bank. I've seen enough black limos and privately driven town cars to know they're not clients. And I don't need sirens to tell me the rest. Unmarked cop cars stand out everywhere.

My chest constricts and I step back. No, keep walking. Don't panic. As I edge towards the car, my eyes skate to the US GOVERNMENT placard on the dashboard. These aren't cops. They're feds.

I'm tempted to turn and run, but . . . not yet. Keep it calm and get answers. There's no way anyone knows about the money.

Praying I'm right, I shove my way through the revolving door.

'Excuse me, sir, can I speak with you?' a deep voice asks.

On my left, in front of the reception desk, a tall blond man approaches with a clipboard. 'I just need your name,' he explains.

'W-What for?'

'I'm sorry—I'm from Para-Protect. We're just trying to figure out if we need to increase security in the welcoming area.'

It's a clean answer with a clean explanation, but last I checked, we weren't having security issues.

'And your name?' he reiterates, keeping the tone friendly.

'Oliver Caruso,' I offer.

He looks up—not startled—but just fast enough that I notice. He grins. I grin. Everybody's happy. Too bad I'm ready to pass out.

On the clipboard, he puts a tick next to my name. There's none next to Charlie's. Not here yet. As the man leans against his clipboard, his jacket slides open and I get a peek at his leather shoulder-strap. This guy's carrying a gun. Security company, my ass. We're in trouble.

'Thank you, Mr Caruso—you have a nice day now.'

'You too,' I say, forcing a smile. The only good sign is that he lets me pass. They don't know who they're looking for. But they are looking. They just don't want anyone to know.

My first instinct is to go and see Shep, but it's no time to be stupid. Instead, I take the elevator to the seventh floor. If I want to get to the bottom of this, I need to start at the top.

'I DON'T CARE what they want!' Lapidus screams into his phone. 'Tell them it's a computer problem—until they hear otherwise, it's staying shut down!' He slams the receiver as I shut the door. Following the sound, he jerks his head towards me—but I'm too busy staring at the person sitting in the antique chair on the opposite side of his desk. Shep. He shakes his head ever so slightly.

'Where the hell've you been!?' Lapidus yells.

Before I can answer, there's a knock on the door behind me.

'Come in!' Lapidus barks.

Quincy opens it halfway and sticks his head in. He's got the same look as Lapidus. Gritted teeth. Manic head movements. Pale face. It's not anger. It's fear. 'I have the reports,' he says anxiously.

'So? Let's hear 'em,' Lapidus says.

Standing on the threshold and refusing to enter the room, Quincy tightens his glance. Partners only. With a swift push away from the desk, Lapidus climbs out of his leather wingback and heads for the door. The moment he's gone, I go straight for Shep.

'What the hell is going on?' I ask, fighting to keep it to a whisper.

'They set us up, Oliver. They were watching the entire time . . .'

The door swings wide and Lapidus storms back in the room. 'Shep—your friend Agent Gallo's waiting in the conference room—'

'Yeah,' Shep interrupts, leaping from his seat.

I shoot him a sideways glance. *You called in the Service?*

Don't ask, he motions, shaking his head.

'Oliver, I need you to do me a favour,' Lapidus adds. 'I want to have someone downstairs as people start coming in,' he says. 'No offence to the Service, but they don't know our staff.'

'I don't underst—'

'Stay by the door and watch reactions,' he barks, his patience long gone. 'I know we've got an agent taking attendance, but whoever did this . . . they're too smart to call in sick. That's why I want you to keep an eye on people when they walk in. If they've got a guilty conscience, the agent alone'll freak them out. You know the people, Oliver. Find out who did it for me.' He ushers me to the door.

Downstairs in the lobby, I slide up to a teller booth, grab a deposit slip and pretend to fill it out. It's the best way to watch the door. Follow orders. Anything else is suspicious. But the longer I sit there, the less the whole thing makes sense. For me and Charlie, $3 million is a solid hunk of change, but around here it's not a life-changer.

I glide towards the revolving door—

'Have you signed in?' the agent with blond hair snaps.

'Y-Yeah,' I say. 'Oliver Caruso.'

He checks his list, then looks up. 'Go ahead.'

I push through the door, out onto the street. Ignoring the pain of running in formal shoes, I race up Park Avenue, and make a sharp left on 37th. The moment I hit Madison Avenue, I slam on the brakes and slide up to an outdoor newsstand.

'Do you have phone cards?' I ask the guy behind the counter.

He motions at his world of wares. 'Whattya *you* think?'

'I'll take a twenty-five-dollar one,' I tell him.

He pulls one from the clipboard, and I toss him two twenties.

Waiting for my change, I rip off the plastic wrapper. Then I dart back towards Park Avenue and stop at a payphone diagonally down the block from the bank's entrance. It's the best possible location for spotting Charlie. I take out my wallet and pull a scrap of paper from behind my driver's licence. Using the phone card, I punch in the ten-digit number I'd written on the paper in reverse order.

'Thank you for calling Royal Bank of Antigua,' a digital female voice answers. 'For automated account balance and information, press one. To speak to a personal service representative, press two.'

I press two. If someone stole it from us, I want to know.

'This is Ms Tang. How can I help you today?'

I spot Charlie trailing a pack of people across the street.

'Hi, I just wanted to check the balance of my account.' I wave to get Charlie's attention, but he doesn't see me.

'And your account number?' the woman asks.

'It's 58943563,' I tell her. When I memorised it, I didn't think I'd be using it this soon.

'And who am I speaking with?'

'Martin Duckworth,' I say. 'It's under Sunshine Distributors.'

'Please hold while I check the account.'

When the Muzak starts, I cover the receiver. '*Charlie!*' I scream.

He's already too far past. He doesn't hear. Making his way up the block, Charlie steps off the kerb and gets his first good look at the bank. He spots the unmarked cars and freezes. I expect him to run, but he glances round, instinctively searching for me.

'Mr Duckworth . . . ?' the woman asks on the other line.

'Y-Yeah . . . right here.' I wave, and this time Charlie sees.

'Mr Duckworth, I'm going to need the password on the account.'

'*Fro Yo*,' I say to the woman from the bank.

'Now what can I help you with today?' she says.

'I'd like the balance, and the most recent activity on the account.'

'According to our records, there's only one transaction on the whole account—a wire transfer that was received yesterday at twelve twenty-one pm.'

'So the money's still there?'

'Absolutely,' the woman says. 'I'm looking at it right now. A single transfer—for a total of three hundred and thirteen million dollars.'

CHAPTER 4

'We've got *what?*' Charlie shouts.

'I don't believe this,' I stammer, my twitching hand still resting on the hung-up receiver. 'Do you have any idea what this means?'

'It means we're rich,' he shoots back. 'Obscenely, grotesquely rich.'

'We're dead,' I blurt. 'There's no way to explai—'

'We'll tell 'em we won it in the Super Bowl pool.'

'How can you make jokes, Charlie. They'll kill us for this . . .'

'Only if they find it—and last I checked, this bad boy's foolproof.'

'Foolproof? Are you nuts? The only way it works is if no one knows it's gone. Three million fits in our pockets . . . but three hundred and thirteen . . . do you realise what they'll do to get that back?'

I turn back to the payphone.

'Who're you calling?' Charlie asks.

I don't answer, but he watches my fingers pound the digits. Shep.

'I wouldn't do that,' he warns. 'If they're smart, they're watching incoming calls. Maybe even listening. If you want information, go inside and talk to him face-to-face.'

I stop mid-dial. I can't argue with the logic. I slam down the phone and brush past him.

A stop at the local coffee shop gives me an eight-ounce cup of calm and an excuse for why I left the building in the first place. Still, it doesn't stop the Secret Service agent at the front door from putting another tick mark next to my name—and one next to Charlie's.

'What's with the anal attendance taking?' Charlie asks the agent.

The agent jabs us with a look as if the tick mark alone should bring us to our knees—but we both know if they had a semblance of a clue, we'd be walking out in handcuffs. Instead, we're walking in.

On most days, I go straight for the elevator. Today I let Charlie drag me towards the maze of rolltop desks. As always, it's packed with gossiping employees, but today that's actually the payoff.

'Howya doin'?' Jeff from Jersey calls out, cutting us off and patting Charlie on the chest.

'There it is,' Charlie sings. 'My daily pat on the chest.'

It's clear what my brother's after. Jersey Jeff may violate your personal space, but when it comes to office gossip, he's king bee.

'What's the story with Mr Attendance?' Charlie asks, elbowing towards the blond guy at the front door.

Jeff smiles wide. Finally, a chance to strut. 'They say he's doing some security upgrade, but no one believes it. I'm betting on a pickpocket. Inside job.'

'What?' Charlie whispers, playing up the outrage.

'It's just a theory,' Jeff begins. 'But you know—this place doesn't change the toilet paper without firing off a memo—suddenly, they're redoing all of security without even a heads-up?'

'Maybe they wanted to see our normal routines,' I offer.

'And maybe they didn't want to scream fire in the crowded movie theatre. It's like when they caught that woman embezzling from Accounts Payable—they try to keep everything quiet. If it goes public, the clients'll panic and start taking back their cash.'

'I wouldn't be so sure,' I add, refusing to give in.

'Hey, believe what you want—but there's gotta be some reason all the bigshots have been up on the fourth floor all morning.'

The fourth floor. That's where Charlie's desk is. I look at Charlie and he looks at me. Fourth floor it is.

THE INSTANT THE ELEVATOR doors open, Charlie takes a quick recce. Nothing's out of place. Still, it doesn't take a genius to know where the action is—up here, there's only one place where the bigshots can hide. Weaving towards Charlie's desk as if it's just another day, we both focus on the office at the far end of the room. The Cage.

The door slowly opens and the Cage empties. Quincy's the first to leave, followed by Lapidus. I duck. Charlie stays up. It's his desk.

'Who else is there?' I whisper, my chin kissing his keyboard.

'Behind Lapidus is Mary,' he begins.

'Anyone else?'

'Yeah, but I don't know 'em . . .'

I pick my head up just enough for a peek. Mary is followed by a squat guy in a poorly fitted suit. He walks with a slight limp and keeps scratching at the back of his buzz cut, right above his neck. Even with the limp, he's got the same meaty look as Shep. Secret Service. Behind Mr Squat is another agent, much thinner in both hair and weight, carrying what looks like a black shoebox with a few dangling wires. FBI had the same thing when they prosecuted that woman in Accounts Payable. Hook it up to the computer and you get an instant copy of the person's hard drive.

It takes another second for the clown car to spit out its last passenger—the one person we've been waiting for. As he steps into the hallway, Shep's eyes lock on Charlie. I expect a grin, or maybe even a fiendish Elvis lip-curl. But all we get is wide-eyed anxiety.

'Everything OK, Shep?' Mr Squat calls out as he and the rest of the zoo crew wait for the elevator.

'Y-Yeah,' Shep stammers. 'I'll meet you up there in a second. I forgot something in my office.' Heading to the other end of the hallway, he shoves open the metal door and ducks into the stairwell. Just before the door closes, he shoots us one last look. He's not running up the stairs. He's just standing there, waiting. For us.

As Mr Squat turns our way, I duck back down, staying out of sight until I hear the elevator doors slowly slide shut.

'C'mon . . .' Charlie says. 'Let's go get some more coffee.'

I follow him out to the coffee machine—which just happens to be next to the stairs. We duck into the stairwell, but it's empty. He looks over the banisters, up and down.

'Not exactly what we had in mind, now is it?' a deep voice asks as the door slams. We spin round. Behind us is Shep.

'Not a bad day's work,' Charlie whispers.

Shep is focused on me. 'So it's all in the account?'

'Forget the account. Why'd you call in the Service?' I insist.

'They were here when I got here,' Shep snaps back. 'I'm guessing it was Quincy or Lapidus—but believe me, the Service is better than the FBI. At least we're dealing with friends.' Leaning over the banister he eyes the floors above us. He mouths two words: 'Not here.'

'So where do you want to go for lunch?' Charlie asks. Smart. We need a place to talk. Some place private. 'How about Track 117?'

I smirk. Shep's lost. A quick whisper in his ear fills him in.

'Trust me,' Charlie says. 'No one even knows it exists.' Watching us carefully, Shep doesn't have much of a choice.

'So I'll see you at noon?' Shep asks. The two of us nod our heads, and he takes off up the concrete stairs.

CHARLIE AND I race up Park Avenue, zigzagging in tandem through the lunchtime crowd. We cross 42nd Street and approach the brass and glass doors of Grand Central Station.

'You ready?' Charlie asks, pulling open the door and bowing.

I step inside. According to the station clock, we only have about three minutes. I turn back to Charlie. 'What's the easiest way to—?'

'Follow me,' he interrupts, taking the lead. I may have heard of where we're going, but I've never been there. This place is Charlie's. With me barely a step behind, he weaves through the commuters and tourists, races down a staircase, and takes off through the lower level of the station, eyes glued to a left-pointing arrow at the base of a vintage-tiled sign: TO TRACKS 100–117.

Up the hallway, we've got a food court on our left and turn-of-the-old-century track entrances on our right. At the far end of the hall, I quickly spot the rabbit hole to Tracks 116 and 117.

Darting through a door, we're at the top of a tall staircase, looking down at the platform. There's a train pulled into Track 116 on the right. On the left, though, there's no chance that a train's coming. Not ever. Simply put, Track 117 doesn't exist. The space is there, but it's not an active track. Instead, it's filled with a long row of prefab construction trailers.

'This is where you used to play?' I ask.

'No,' he answers. 'This is where we used to hide.' Reading the confused look on my face, he explains, 'When I was a junior in high school, me and Randy Boxer used to go track-to-track, playing music for Friday-night commuters. His harmonica, my bass. The transit cops chased us at every opportunity, but the lower level had the best places to disappear. Here—behind 117—was where we'd reconvene.'

'Are you sure it's safe?' I ask as he rushes across the catwalk that runs over Track 117. It's not the catwalk that's giving me pause—it's the metal door at the end—and the brown, faded words painted on it: EMPLOYEES ONLY. STOP! LOOK! LISTEN! DANGER. I hit the brakes.

'Don't be such a wuss,' Charlie calls out as he grabs the handle to the door and gives it a yank. As the door swings open, a duststorm tumbles towards us. Charlie steps right into the whirlwind.

I follow him through into a huge underground station, beside an abandoned set of tracks. A good place to hide, no doubt.

'Close the door,' Shep calls out from further up the platform.

I don't hesitate. The door slams with a muffled thud.

'How bad is it?' I ask. I'm not wasting a second.

'Ever heard of the *Titanic*?' Shep asks. 'Lapidus is threatening to unleash the ten plagues on anyone who leaks the info to the public. Across the table, Quincy's screaming through the phone at the insurance company and clicking his calculator to figure out just how much they're personally on the hook for.'

'Have they told the other partners yet?'

'There's an emergency meeting tonight. In the meantime, they're waiting for the Service to dissect the computer system and possibly get a nibble on where the money went after London.'

'Fine,' I say. 'Now how do you think we should turn ourselves in?'

'*What?*' Shep exclaims. 'Oliver, don't be hasty,' he adds. 'Even if it's a tornado now, it'll eventually slow down.'

'Oh, so now you think we can outrun the Secret Service?'

'All I'm saying is it can still work out,' Shep replies. 'It'll take the Service at least a week to figure out if they can find the money. If they do, we turn ourselves in with a full explanation. But if they don't . . . why walk away from three hundred and thirteen million?'

There's a loud thump and we all stop.

'Let's get out of here,' Charlie says.

But just as he turns to the door, there's another noise. Not a thud. More like a creak. It's not coming from the walls. It's lower.

Shep spins round and checks out a section of flat wood planks that are built into the ground like a mini-life-raft.

'What're those?' I ask quietly.

'Vertical passageways. Underneath the planks, they lead down to the tracks below,' Charlie explains. 'That's how they move the big equipment and generators—they just take out the wood and lower them through the holes.'

There's another creak. Then another. Shep looks up and rescouts the entire tunnel. If it is an echo, it has to start somewhere.

Through the planks, the pace of the noise gets even quicker. Like a soft scraping . . . or someone walking . . . no, more like running.

There's a sharp crash in the corner and the door bursts open. '*Secret Service—nobody move!*' a beefy man shouts, rushing into the room with his gun pointed straight at my face. I back up. He slows down, and I spot his limp. Mr Squat. The lead investigator.

'He said *don't move!*' a blond-haired agent yells, racing in right behind him. Like his partner, he aims his gun straight at us.

'Officer . . .' I stutter.

'Agent!' the bull-necked man corrects me. 'You must be Oliver.'

'How'd you—?'

'You really thought you could leave the bank twice without being followed?'

'What the hell're you doing, Gallo?' Shep calls out. 'I was just about to bring them in. All I needed was—'

'Don't bullshit me!' Gallo barks, pushing between me and Charlie to aim his gun at Shep. 'I'm not a moron. I know what you're up to!'

'It's not how it looks,' I cry. 'We were about to come in!'

'Enough,' Gallo interrupts. 'It's over, Oliver. Y'understand? The only thing that's gonna make your day better is if you spare us some headache and tell us where you hid the money.'

It's a simple question. Spill the beans, hand over the money and take the first step to getting our lives back. But the way Gallo asks it . . . the anger in his voice . . . the way he grits his teeth . . . you'd think he had a personal interest. Something's up.

I look to Charlie, who slowly shakes his head. He sees it too.

'Oliver, this isn't the time to play hero,' Gallo warns. 'Now I'm gonna ask you again: Where'd you put the money?'

'Don't tell him!' Shep shouts. 'Once you give it up, we've got nothing left! It's our only bargaining chip!'

'*You want to see a bargaining chip?*' Gallo explodes, his face a deep red rage. He lifts his gun and points it directly at Shep.

'What're you doing?' Charlie asks, stepping forward.

Gallo turns his gun to Charlie's face. My brother backs up, hands in the air. 'DeSanctis!' Gallo shouts to the lanky blond agent.

'I got him,' DeSanctis says, aiming his gun at Charlie's back.

'Last chance, Oliver,' Gallo warns. 'Tell me where the money is, or we start with Shep and work our way to your brother.'

'Don't fall for it,' Shep says. 'They're Secret Service, not hit men. They're not gonna kill anyone. Isn't that right, DeSanctis?'

Without a word, Gallo pulls back the hammer of his gun. There's more riding on this than just some lost cash.

'C'mon, Jim,' Shep laughs. 'The joke's over . . .'

But Gallo isn't laughing. He tightens his grip and his finger slithers across the trigger. 'I'm waiting, Oliver.'

'*Don't say it!*' Shep warns. Turning back to Gallo, he adds, 'Can we stop this? You've already caught us—what else are you hoping to—?'

The two men stand face to face. Gallo lets out the slightest smirk.

Shep's expression falls. 'You want the money for yourself, don't you?'

Gallo doesn't answer. He just steadies his aim.

'Don't do it!' I plead. 'I'll tell you where it is!'

'So the big dollars were yours?' Shep asks. 'Who brought you in? Lapidus? Quincy?'

The answer never comes. Gallo licks his lips. 'Goodbye, Shep.'

'Jimmy, please . . .' Shep's voice cracks. As big as he is, his whole body's shaking. Gallo doesn't flinch. He just pulls the trigger.

The shot hisses like a dart from a blowgun. Then another. And another. All three explode in Shep's chest, sending him crashing back into the concrete wall. He grabs at the wounds, but the blood's already everywhere. His eyes wide with fear, he tries to breathe, but all that comes out is an empty wheeze. Unable to hold his weight, his legs buckle, and the big man falls forward, straight for the creaky wooden slats in the floor.

'*Shep!*' Charlie screams, racing out and sliding knees-first next to Shep. Ignoring the puddle of blood, Charlie shoves his hands under Shep's shoulder and waist, and tries to flip him onto his back.

'*Nobody move!*' Gallo barks.

Charlie lets go, and Shep's body sinks back to the ground. The blood is already seeping between the grooves in the planks. I look away and gag. Gallo steps towards me and shoves the barrel of his gun into my cheek. 'Now I'm going to ask you again, Oliver.'

'Don't tell him squat!' Charlie shouts. 'You give him a dime and he'll leave us lying here with Shep.'

'Shut your mouth!' Gallo snaps. Pointing his gun at Charlie, Gallo pulls back the hammer. 'How much is he worth to you, Oliver?'

Leaving nothing to chance, DeSanctis moves in behind me, his gun digging into the back of my neck. Gallo is watching me.

Kneeling next to Shep's body, Charlie cranes his neck round to get my attention. We both know the outcome. No matter what we give Gallo, he's not letting us leave. Not after everything we've seen. Still, Charlie searches my face, looking for something . . . anything . . . to get us out of here. It doesn't come.

Charlie turns away and stares back at Shep. It's not until I notice Shep's blood seeping down through the wood in the floor that I see our one way out. Charlie has his back to me, but I spot the sudden pitch in his shoulders. He sees it too. Hunched over as if the pressure's too much, Charlie kneels in close to Shep's body, and carefully wedges his fingers round the edges of the loose plank in the floor.

'You know how to save him,' Gallo warns, still focused on me. 'Just tell us where the money is.' From where Gallo's standing behind Charlie, he can't see a thing. Three feet away, I see it all. As quickly as I can, I angle my body so DeSanctis can't get a clear view.

'Please don't hurt him,' I stall. 'The information's all yours—I just need to get it from the bank—I don't have it on me.'

Pretending to brace himself for the gunshot, Charlie curls down even tighter—and wraps his fingers round the sides of the wood. It wobbles slightly, but not enough. There's still a nail holding it in place. Focused on the thin gaps between the planks, Charlie wedges his fingers in as deep as they'll go. Almost there. He pulls as hard as he can without revealing himself. It starts coming loose.

'Oliver, you're too smart not to've memorised it,' Gallo warns as he aims at my brother. 'Three seconds. After that, you sweep up his brains yourself. One . . . Two . . .' His finger slips round the trigger. 'Thr—'

'Please—don't do it! If you want it, it's in an account in An—'

There's a sharp crack as the wood comes loose.

Following the sound, Gallo turns away from me and spins towards my brother. He looks at the ground, but Charlie's already on his feet, swinging the plank like a baseball bat. The flat side catches Gallo square in the jaw, knocking him—and his gun—to the floor.

I feel a sharp tug on the back of my shirt. DeSanctis tosses me backwards. He's trained to go after the threat. He turns to Charlie and aims his pistol for the killshot. Instinctively, my brother holds up the plank as if it's a shield. DeSanctis pulls the trigger.

The plank flies from Charlie's hands, cleaved in half by the gunshot. DeSanctis has already readjusted his aim. Straight at Charlie.

'*Don't!*' I yell, ploughing into DeSanctis from behind. The gun jerks, and a shot goes off—tearing at the wall on my right and sending a cloud of loose concrete crumbling into the corner. The impact keeps DeSanctis off-balance enough for me to jump on his back and grab him in a quick choke-hold. Within seconds, though, training overtakes surprise. DeSanctis whips his head back, cracking me in the nose. The pain is ferocious. I don't let go.

'I'll kill you, you bastard!' DeSanctis shouts as I hold on. Reaching back and clawing over his shoulder, DeSanctis still tries to get at me. That leaves his gut wide open. It's all Charlie needs. Picking up the broken plank, he rushes forward, plants his feet . . . and swings away. As the plank collides with DeSanctis's stomach, he doubles over. I tumble to the concrete—but DeSanctis clearly took the worst of it.

'You OK?' Charlie asks, offering me a hand.

I nod repeatedly, unable to catch my breath.

Behind Charlie, there's a noise. He spins round and spots Gallo crawling to reach his gun. Scrambling next to him, Charlie scoops up Gallo's gun and stuffs it in the back of his trousers.

'You're both dead,' Gallo whispers, coughing up blood.

Charlie lifts the plank over his head like a woodchopper and—

'Don't!' I call out. 'We're way out of our league. C'mon—let's go!'

Charlie drops the wood, and we fly for the metal door in the corner. With a quick shove, I'm through the door and across the catwalk. Charlie follows. I can hear Gallo coughing. We leap out of the rabbit hole, into the food court. Behind us, we hear the metal door crash against the wall. They're faster than we thought.

I make a sharp left and race back the way we originally came.

'Wrong way!' Charlie shouts, heading to the right, old instincts flooding back. At the far end of the hall, he leaps for the escalator and scrambles up the moving steps. 'They still behind us?' he asks.

'Just get us out of here,' I say, refusing to look.

At the top of the escalator, the only clear path veers left, back to the main concourse. Charlie keeps running straight, pushing through a service door into an industrial beige hallway. In front of us, two automatic doors blink open. We glance around at the fifty or so cars parked bumper-to-bumper in the underground garage.

Charlie motions towards the steep ramp that leads up to the snow-lined street. Before I can nod, he takes off and runs straight up it.

Back on the street, we're quickly consumed by the lunchtime crowd, but in the distance I already hear the sirens.

I look at Charlie; he studies me. We're not just thieves any more. By the time Gallo and DeSanctis are done with us, we're murderers.

'Should we call Mom?'

'No way,' I counter. 'That's the first place they'll look.'

The sirens get closer, and we step into the line that's curving out of a nearby pizza place. At the end of the block, two police cars are screeching towards Grand Central's Vanderbilt Avenue entrance. Within seconds, four uniformed officers are racing inside.

'C'mon,' I say, jumping out of line.

'You know where we're going?' he asks as he follows.

I'm already running towards the opposite end of the block. 'Not really,' I say. 'But I have an idea.'

JOEY WAS THE EIGHTH to be called. The first was the underwriter at KRG Insurance who wrote the policy. Lapidus chewed his head off and forced a fast transfer to a claims analyst, who, when he heard the amount, called the head of the claims unit, who called the president of claims, who called the CEO. The CEO made two calls: one to a forensic accounting firm and one to Chuck Sheafe, of Sheafe International, to request their top investigator. Sheafe recommended Joey.

'Fine,' the CEO said. 'When can he be here?'

'You mean *she*.'

'What're you talking about?'

'Don't be a pig, Warren. Jo Ann Lemont,' Sheafe explained. 'Now do you want our best or do you want a boy scout?'

That's all it took. The eighth call went to Joey.

'So do you have any idea who stole it?' Joey asked from the seat opposite Lapidus's desk.

'Of course I don't know who stole it,' Lapidus barked back. 'What the hell kind of stupid question is that?'

Stupid, maybe, Joey thought—but she had to ask it. If only to see his reaction. If he was lying, there'd be some sort of tell. A look-away, an uneasy grin. As she brushed her short auburn hair from her forehead, she knew that was her gift—sharpening focus and finding the tell—she learned it playing poker with her dad, and honed it during law school. Sometimes it was in the body language. Sometimes it was . . . somewhere else.

'Now is there anything else, Ms Le—?'

'It's Joey,' she interrupted, her chocolate eyes looking up from her yellow legal pad. 'Please . . . call me Joey.'

Across the room, the door to Lapidus's office flew open. Quincy stepped in, but didn't say a word. He just held tight to the doorknob.

'Is he in there?' a hoarse voice shouted from the hallway. Before Quincy could answer, Agents Gallo and DeSanctis shoved their way into the room. Joey grinned at the interruption. Baggy suit . . . barrel chest . . . cheap shoes scuffed up from running. These two weren't bankers. Which meant they were security or—

'Secret Service,' Gallo snapped, flashing her the badge on his belt. 'Can you excuse us for a moment?'

Joey couldn't help but stare at the swollen cut on Gallo's cheek. 'Actually, I think we're all on this together,' she said. 'I'm here from Chuck Sheafe's place.' It wasn't often that she dropped her boss's name, but fifteen years ago Chuck Sheafe was third in command of the Secret Service. To fellow agents, that meant he was family.

'So you're working for the insurance company?' Gallo asked.

It wasn't the reaction she was looking for, so Joey just nodded.

'Then that still makes you a civilian,' Gallo shot back. 'Now like I said: please excuse us.'

Joey headed for the door. All four men watched her as she crossed the room, which wasn't something that happened often. With her athletic build, she was attractive, but not gawking attractive.

As the door slammed behind Joey, Lapidus rubbed his palm against his bald head. 'Please tell me you have good news.'

Quincy tried to answer, but nothing came out. He stuffed his hands in his pockets to stop them from shaking.

'Shep's dead,' DeSanctis blurted.

'*What?*' Lapidus asked, his eyes going wide. 'How did he . . . ?'

'Shot in the chest three times. We rushed in when we heard the noise, but it was already too late.'

Lapidus sank in his seat. 'W-Was it for the money?'

'That's what we're still trying to figure out,' Gallo explained. 'We're not sure how they got it, but it looks like they had help from Shep.'

Lapidus looked up. 'What do you mean, *they?*'

'That's the other part . . .' DeSanctis said. 'As near as we can tell, Shep was killed by either Charlie or Oliver.'

'Oliver?' Lapidus asked. '*Our* Oliver? That kid couldn't—'

'He *could*—and he *did*,' Gallo insisted. 'So don't talk to me about some bullshit little-boy innocence. Thanks to these two, I've got a financial investigation that just flipped to a homicide.'

Lapidus just sat there, collapsed in his chair—the consequences settling heavy on his shoulders. Then, out of nowhere, he shot up in his seat. His voice was racing. 'On Friday, Oliver used my password to transfer money to Tanner Drew.'

'See, now that's something we should know,' Gallo said as he took a seat. 'If there's a pattern of misapprop—' Cutting himself off, Gallo felt something on the cushion of the seat. Reaching under his thigh, he pulled out a pen emblazoned with the logo of the University of Michigan.'Where'd you get this?' he barked, jamming the pen towards Lapidus. 'Is it yours?'

'I don't think so,' Lapidus stammered. 'No, I've never seen it.'

Gallo pulled off the cap, furiously unscrewed the barrel of the pen and shook both pieces over the desk. Out popped a pen refill . . . a metal spring . . . and from the back part of the pen: a clear plastic tube filled with wires, a miniature battery and a tiny transmitter. A pinhole in the base held the built-in microphone.

'Son of a bitch!' Gallo exploded. Knocking his chair to the floor, he raged to the door and tugged the doorknob. He looked up the hallway . . . near the bathrooms . . . by the elevator. He was already too late. Joey was long gone.

THE BACK SEAT of the black cab is covered with a stained brown towel that smells like feet. I'd roll down the bubbling tinted windows for some air, but right now—after hearing those sirens—we're better off behind the tint. Ducking down so no one can see us, Charlie and I haven't said a word since I waved down the car.

'Make a right up here,' I call, peeking above the headrest so I can get a better view of Park Avenue. The driver makes a turn on 50th Street and gets about halfway up the block. 'Perfect. Right here.' As the car jerks to a halt, I toss a ten-dollar bill between the armrests, kick open the door, and make sure he never gets a good look.

'Let's go,' I call to Charlie, who's already a few steps behind. I head for the door of the Italian bakery right in front of us. But the moment the driver speeds away, I turn round and walk out.

'C'mon,' I say, rushing into the December wind. As soon as we turn back onto Park Avenue, I bound up some concrete steps. Behind me, Charlie looks up at the ornate pink brick structure and finally understands. Nestled between the investment banks and the law firms, it's the one island of piety in an ocean of the ostentatious. More important, it's the nearest place I could think of that wouldn't kick us out—no matter how late we wanted to stay.

'Welcome to St Bart's Church,' a soft voice whispers as we step inside the arched stone foyer.

I shove two dollars into the donation box and head through the doors of the main sanctuary, where I'm hit with the smell of incense and old wood. A dozen worshippers are scattered throughout the pews. Hoping for something a bit less crowded, I glance round. When a church is this big, there's usually . . . There we go. Three-quarters of the way down the lefthand wall—a single unmarked door.

Trying not to be too noticeable, Charlie and I keep the pace nice and smooth. There's a loud creak as the door opens. I cringe and give it a fast push. We rush forward into the stone room, which is just big enough to hold a few benches and a brass votive stand filled with burning candles. We're the only ones in the private chapel.

The door slams shut and then my phone rings. Reaching into my suit pocket, I quickly shut it off.

'No answer,' Lapidus said, hanging up the receiver. Turning to the photocopied letter that Gallo left on his desk, Lapidus looked down and skimmed it. 'So this is how they did it?' he asked. 'A fake letter?'

'According to the tech boys, that's the last document Oliver typed into his computer,' Gallo explained. 'And from the hard copy we found in Shep's drawer, it looks like Shep was helping them.'

'So the three of them met this morning, and when things went sour, Oliver and Charlie took his head off,' Quincy hypothesised.

'That's the only thing that makes sense,' DeSanctis said.

'And what about the investigation?' Lapidus asked. 'As you know, we have a number of important clients who rely on our promise of privacy. Any chance of keeping it out of the papers?'

'I completely agree,' Gallo replied. 'If we throw this to the press, they'll broadcast our every move straight to Charlie and Oliver.'

'So you think you'll be able to find them?' Lapidus asked as Gallo picked up the phone on the corner of Lapidus's desk.

Gallo glanced at Quincy, then back to Lapidus. 'Why don't you leave that to us.' Quickly dialling a number, Gallo raised the receiver to his ear. 'Hey, it's me,' he said to the person on the other line. 'I got a cellphone loose in the city—you ready to do some tracking?'

I don't turn the phone back on until I'm ten blocks away, and it takes me another block and a half to work up the nerve to dial. As I wait for someone to answer, I try to keep my balance in the back of the bus while it crawls uptown. Sure, the subway is more inconspicuous but, last I checked, my phone didn't get a signal underground. And right now, I need to put distance between me and the church.

'Welcome to Greene and Greene Private Bank. How can I assist you?' a female voice sings through my cellphone. I'm not sure who it belongs to, but it's not any of the phonebankers I know. Good. That means she doesn't know me.

'Hi, this is Marty Duckworth,' I say. 'I had a quick question I was hoping you could answer.'

She checks my account and Social Security number. 'What can I help you with today, Mr Duckworth?'

'I just wanted to check the most recent activity on my account,' I tell her. 'There was a large deposit that came in, and I need to know what day it posted.' Clearly, it's a nonsense question, but if we plan on figuring out what's going on, we need to know how Duckworth's $3 million turned into $313 million.

'I'm sorry, sir, but in the last week . . . I'm not showing any deposits. According to our records, your current balance is zero, and the only activity on record is a three-hundred-and-thirteen-million-dollar withdrawal yesterday afternoon.'

'What about the day before?' I ask, watching the passengers on the bus. No one turns round. 'What was the balance on the day before?'

'It's the same amount, sir—three hundred and thirteen million. And on the day before. I have no record of any recent deposits.'

It can't be. It's not possible. How can we—?

'Mr Duckworth?' the woman interrupts. 'Can you hold on a second?'

'Of course,' I agree. The line goes silent. I can't help but wonder where she went. It's the first rule they teach you—never put rich people on hol . . . hold on. This is a company line. And the longer she keeps me on it, the easier it is for the Secret Service to tra—

I slap the phone shut, hoping I'm fast enough.

The phone vibrates in my hand. I check the number on Caller ID. It's nothing I recognise. Last time, I ignored it. This time . . . if they're tracing it, I need to know. 'Hello?' I answer, keeping it confident.

'Where the hell are you?' Charlie asks. There's no phone in the chapel. If he's risking a call from the street, we've got problems.

'What's wrong? Are you—?'

'You better get back here,' he demands.

'Just tell me what happened.'

'Oliver, get back here. *Now!*'

I pound the bus's *Stop-Request* strip with the base of my fist.

CHAPTER 5

As the bus pulls up on the corner of 81st Street, I dial the number for the Kings Plaza Movie Theater in Brooklyn and hit *Send*. When the prerecorded voice picks up, I grab a newspaper from the seat next to me, wrap my cellphone in it and slide the phone package underneath my seat. If they're tracing it, this should buy us at least an hour—and the infinite loop of movie times should give them a working signal that'll have them goosechasing all the way to Harlem.

The bus bucks to a stop, the doors open and I'm gone.

It takes ten more minutes for the bank teller at Citibank to empty the $3,500 that's left in my account.

Back at the church, I keep my head down and speedwalk through the main sanctuary, straight towards the private chapel.

Shoving the door open, I rush into the candlelit room and find Charlie. 'So what's the emergency?' I ask.

'I can't find Mom.'

'I told you not to call her!'

'Just listen,' Charlie begs. 'I called her from a payphone seven blocks away . . . she never once picked up.'

'So?'

'So, it's Tuesday, Oliver. Tuesday afternoon and she's not there?'

As a seamstress, Mom spends most of her time either in the house or at the fabric store—but Tuesdays and Thursdays are reserved for fittings. Out goes the coffee table; in come the clients. All day long.

'Maybe she was in the middle of measuring,' I suggest.

'Maybe we should go check it out,' he shoots back.

'Charlie, you know that's the first place they'll look. She'll be OK. As soon as we get out of here, we'll figure out a way to get in touch.'

He nods to himself, trying his best to believe it. 'What happened with Duckworth? You find out where he got the money?'

'Not exactly,' I say, carefully relaying my conversation with the woman at the bank. As always, Charlie's reaction is immediate.

'I don't get it. Even though when we checked, it said three million, Duckworth had the three hundred and thirteen all along . . . ?'

'Charlie, you know how many clients have over a hundred million in assets? Seventeen at last count . . . and I can name every one of them. Marty Duckworth isn't on that list.'

Charlie stares at me, completely silent. 'How's that possible?'

'Obviously, someone was doing a primo job of making it look like Duckworth only had three million to his name.'

'You really think someone can just hide all that cash?'

'Why not? That's what the bank's paid to do on a daily basis.'

'So with a speciality like that,' Charlie adds, 'there's gotta be someone here who's figured out how to make an account look like one thing and actually be another. *Yes, Mr Duckworth, your balance is three million dollars—wink, wink, nudge, nudge.*'

'When Mary transferred the balance, we got the whole megillah.'

'It's not bad,' Charlie admits. 'But for an insider to pull that off . . .'

'Not just an insider—whoever it was, they were getting help . . .'

'Gallo and his buddy in the Service?'

'You heard what Shep said—he wasn't the one who called them in. They showed up the moment their money went poof.'

'So they were in on it from the start?' Charlie asks.

'You tell me. What's the likelihood that two Secret Service agents would wander into a case and then kill Shep just to turn a quick buck? I don't care how much money's at stake, Gallo and DeSanctis weren't randomly assigned. They came to protect their investment. Maybe they've been working with the bank all along.'

'You mean like money laundering?' Charlie asks.

'Whatever it was, these guys had their hands in something bad.'

'So who do you think they were scheming with?'

'Hard to say. You can't spell Secret Service without *Secret*.'

'Yeah, well, you can't spell *Asshole* without Lapidus or Quincy.'

'I don't know,' I say doubtfully. 'You saw their reactions—they were even more scared than we were.'

'Yeah . . . because you, me and everyone else were watching. Besides, if it wasn't Lapidus or Quincy, who could it possibly be?'

'It could've been anyone. It still leaves us with the original question: where'd Duckworth get three hundred and thirteen million?'

'Why don't you ask the man himself?' Charlie says.

'Duckworth? He's dead.'

'You sure?' Charlie asks, cocking an eyebrow. 'If everything else is a hall of mirrors, what makes you think this is the only wall?'

It's a good point. 'Do you still have his . . . ?'

Charlie reaches into his back pocket and pulls out a folded-up sheet of paper. 'That's the beauty of rewearing yesterday's slacks,' he says. Unfolding the paper, he reveals the Duckworth address that was on the Midland National Bank account: 405 Amsterdam Avenue. With his fuse lit, he takes off for the door.

'Charlie . . .' I whisper. 'Maybe it's better to go to the police.'

'So they can turn us over to the Service, who'll put bullets in our heads? No offence, Ollie, but the fact we have the money and the way they set us up with Shep—no one's gonna believe a word.'

I close my eyes, trying to paint a different picture. But all I see is Shep's blood . . . all over our hands. It doesn't matter what we say. Even I wouldn't believe us. 'We're dead, aren't we?'

'Don't say that,' Charlie scolds. 'If we find Duckworth, that's our first step to finding answers.' Yanking the door open, he disappears into the sanctuary.

TURNING ONTO OLIVER'S block and bundled up in an ankle-length winter coat, Joey looked like any other pedestrian in Red Hook. Yet while her eyes stayed locked on Oliver's run-down brownstone, her fingers were busy kneading the empty black garbage bags in her left pocket and the red nylon dog leash in her right.

Convinced she was close enough, she pulled out the leash, letting it dangle by her side. Now she wasn't just an investigator; she was a member of the community, searching for her lost dog. Empty leashes took you anywhere: up driveways, across back yards, even into the narrow alleyway that ran along the side of the brownstone and held three plastic garbage cans full of Oliver's and his neighbours' trash.

Slipping into the alley, Joey counted eleven windows that overlooked the garbage area: four in Oliver's brownstone, four in the brownstone next door and three in the one directly across the street. Without a doubt, it'd be better to do this at night, but by then the Service would have already picked through it.

A small microphone was clipped to the top button of her shirt, and a tangle of wires ran down to a belt-attached cellphone. She plugged an earpiece into her right ear, hit *Send* and, as it rang, quickly flipped open the lids of all three garbage cans.

'This is Noreen,' a young female voice answered.

'It's me,' Joey said, snapping on a pair of latex surgical gloves.

'How's the neighbourhood?' Noreen asked.

'Past its prime,' Joey said. 'I assumed young banking preppyville. This is a blue-collar, can't-afford-the-city first apartment.'

'Maybe that's why he took the money—he's sick of being second class.'

'Yeah . . . maybe,' Joey said, happy to hear Noreen participating.

A recent graduate of Georgetown Law's night-school programme, Noreen spent her first month after graduation getting rejected by Washington's largest law firms. The next two months brought rejections from the medium and small firms as well. In month four, her old Evidence professor placed a call to his good friend at Sheafe International. *Top night student . . . first impression's mousy, but hungry as can be . . . just like Joey the day her dad dropped her off.* Those were the magic words. One faxed résumé later, Noreen had a job and Joey had her newest assistant.

Reaching into the first garbage can, Joey ripped open the bag on top. She angled it to get a good peek, searching for anything with . . . there it was. Phone bill. She checked the name on the first page. Frank Tusa. Same address. Apartment 1. The bag below stank of rotted oranges. Envelope addressed to Vivian Leone. Apartment 2.

The middle garbage can was empty. That left the one on the far right, which had a cheap white bag. Joey tore it open, stared inside and held her breath at the old banana smell. 'Uh-oh. He's a recycler.'

'How do you know it's Oliver's?' Noreen asked.

'There're only three apartments. Trust me, it's his.' Joey pulled a black garbage bag from her pocket, lined the empty garbage can and quickly tossed Oliver's brown banana peels into the waiting bin.

Item by item, Joey shovelled through the muck, transferring fistfuls of leftover spaghetti and macaroni. 'Lots of pasta—not a lot of cash,' she whispered to Noreen. 'A plastic deli bag . . .' She pulled the label close to read it. 'A pound of turkey, the cheap stuff . . . Empty bags of potato chips and pretzels . . . He's bringing lunch every day.'

'How's take-out look?'

'No Styrofoam . . . no Chinese delivery containers,' Joey said, continuing to dig around. 'He doesn't spend a dollar ordering out.'

'Packaging materials?'

'Just a wrapper for some Tampax—looks like our boy's got a girlfriend.' At the bottom of the bag, Joey raked through the coffee grinds. 'That's it. A week in the life.'

'I bet it's still in his apartment,' Noreen says.

'Only one way to find out . . .' Shoving the garbage cans back in place, Joey took her leash on a walk towards the front of the house and down Oliver's shaky brick stairs. Next to the door was a single blue-and-white sticker: 'Warning! Protected by Ameritech Alarms.'

'My butt,' Joey muttered. *This kid won't order Domino's; he's certainly not springing for an alarm.*

She reached into her bag and pulled out a zippered black leather case. From there, she removed a thin, wire-tipped instrument and shoved it straight into Oliver's top lock. With a quick flick of the wrist, the lock popped and the door swung open.

'WHY'RE YOU MAKING such a big deal?' Joey asked, flipping through the filing cabinet that served as Oliver's nightstand.

'I just think it's odd,' Noreen said. 'I mean, Oliver's supposed to be the mastermind behind a three-hundred-million-dollar swipe—but according to what you just read me, he's writing monthly cheques to cover Mom's hospital bills and paying half her mortgage.'

'Noreen, welcome to your motive. Oliver spends four years at the bank thinking he's going to be a bigshot, then wakes up one day and realises all he has to show for it is a stack of bills. There's a moment of opportunity and voilà—the dish runs away with the spoon.'

'I guess,' Noreen said, anxious to get back on track. 'What about the girlfriend? See anything with a phone number on it?'

Flipping through the recycling bin, Joey quickly pulled out the magazines. *Business Week* . . . *Forbes* . . . *SmartMoney* . . . 'Here we go,' she said, grabbing a *People* magazine and going straight for the subscription label. 'Beth Manning, 201 East 87th Street, Apartment 23H.' Tossing the magazine back into the bin, Joey ran towards the bathroom and jerked open the medicine cabinet. Toothpaste . . . razor . . . shaving cream . . . deodorant . . . nothing special. In the trash was a crumpled-up bag with the words BARNEY'S PHARMACY in black letters. 'Noreen, the place is called Barney's Pharmacy—we want a list of outstanding prescriptions for Oliver and his girlfriend.'

'Fine. Are you done?' Noreen pleaded.

'Done?' Joey asked. 'I'm just getting started.'

'HI, THIS IS FUDGE,' the answering machine whirred. 'Leave a message at the sound of the beep.'

'Fudge, I know you're there,' Joey shouted into the answering machine. 'Pick up, pick up, pic—!'

'Ah, Lady Guinevere, thou doth sing the song of the enchantress,' Fudge crooned, careful not to use Joey's name.

Joey rolled her eyes, refusing to get into it. When it came to cutouts, it was better not to get involved.

'So what can I do for you this evening? Business or pleasure?'

'Do you still know that guy at Omnibank?' Joey asked.

Fudge paused. 'Maybe.'

Joey nodded at the code. That was yes. It was always yes. Indeed, that's what the cutout business was all about: knowing people. And not just any people. Angry people. Bitter people. Passed-over-for-promotion people. In every office, there's someone who's miserable with their job. Those were the ones anxious to sell what they knew. And that's who Fudge could find.

'If I could, what would you be looking for?' Fudge asked.

'Client records . . . but I also need monitors on two accounts. And maybe a few taps on a phone line.'

'Uh-oh, big money talking here . . .'

'If you can't handle it,' Joey warned.

'I can handle it just fine. I know a secretary in Fraud who's still pissed about a snotty comment at an office party with th—'

'Fudge!' Joey interrupted, turning a blind eye to the source. Sure, it made the lawyer in her cringe, but that was what the cutout was there for. Someone else does the dirty work; she gets the product.

THE ELEVATOR DOORS opened and Gallo followed the alphabet round to Apartment 4D. He rang the doorbell.

'Who is it?' a soft female voice asked.

'United States Secret Service,' Gallo said, lifting his badge so it could be seen through the door's eyehole.

There was a pause, then a fast thunking as a totem pole of locks unclicked. The door creaked open, revealing a heavyset woman wearing a yellow cardigan and a pincushion round her left wrist.

'Can I help you?' Maggie Caruso asked.

'Actually, Mrs Caruso, I'm here about your sons . . .'

Her shoulders dropped. 'What's wrong? Are they OK?'

'Of course they're OK,' Gallo promised. 'They just got into a little trouble at work, and, well . . . we were hoping you could come downtown and answer a few questions. It's nothing bad. We just thought you might be able to help us clear it up. You know . . . for the boys.'

'S-Sure . . .' she stammered. 'Let me get my purse.'

'IS THIS EVEN right?' Charlie asks.

'That's what it says,' I point out. I recheck the address, then look up at the numbers stickered to the filthy glass door: 405 Amsterdam. Apartment 2B. Duckworth's last known address.

'No. There's no way, this guy's got three hundred million,' Charlie insists. 'This should be some Upper West Side, snooty doorman snazzfest. Instead, he's living in a scrubby bachelor pad that's tucked above a bad Indian restaurant and a laundromat? Forget it!'

I point to the button for Apartment 2B. 'Should I ring it or not?'

'Sure—what else we got to lose?'

It's not a question I'm ready to answer. I ring the buzzer.

'Yeah?' a man's voice shouts back.

Charlie spots an empty cardboard box in front of the laundromat. 'I got a delivery here for 2B,' he says.

The raspy buzzer explodes, and Charlie pulls on the door. He holds it open; I grab the box. We climb the stairs.

At 2B, I bang on the door. Locks crackle and the door swings open. I'm ready for a fifty-year-old man on the verge of tears—just dying to tell us the full story. Instead, we get a frat boy with a perfectly curved Syracuse baseball cap and oversized lacrosse shorts.

'You got a delivery, yo?' he asks in full white-boy accent.

'Actually, it's for Marty Duckworth,' I say. 'Does he live here?'

'You mean that freaky little guy? Kinda looked like the moleman?'

Flustered, I don't answer.

'That's him,' Charlie jumps in. 'Any idea where he went?'

'Florida, baby. Ocean retirement.'

Retirement, I nod. *That means he's got money.*

'What about a forwarding address?' Charlie asks.

Crossing back through the studio apartment, Frat Boy grabs his electronic organiser from the top of his TV.

From my back pocket, I pull out the letter where we wrote down Duckworth's other address.

'Here you go,' Frat Boy announces, reading from his organiser. '1004 Tenth Street. Sun-shining Miami Beach. 33139.'

It matches. 'Same Bat-time. Same Bat-channel,' Charlie whispers.

Saying our goodbyes, we leave the apartment and hit the stairs.

'What'd you think?' I ask.

'I got no idea—though Frat Boy up there didn't act like Duckworth was dead,' Charlie says.

On the street, I toss the cardboard box back to its home. We head for the payphone on the corner, where I reach for my phone card and quickly dial the number for Florida information.

'In Miami . . . I'm looking for a Marty or Martin Duckworth at 1004 Tenth Street,' I tell the computerised voice that answers.

'Sorry,' the operator finally says. 'That's a nonpublished number.'

'Well?' Charlie asks as I hang up.

'Unlisted.'

'But not disconnected,' he challenges, stepping out of the booth. 'Wherever Duckworth is, he's still got an active number.'

It's a fair point. 'You think we should go to Miami?'

'C'mon, Ollie. Unless we can prove what really happened, Gallo and DeSanctis have a complete hold on reality. And on us. *We* stole the money . . . *we* killed Shep . . . and *we're* the ones who'll pay for it.'

'You know they're going to be watching the airports . . .'

'I've already got a way round it,' Charlie says.

'READY TO GO two-for-two?' Joey whispered into the collar of her shirt as she strolled quietly down Avenue U. Surrounded by commuters returning home from work, she didn't need the red dog leash. For now, she was one of the crowd.

'You never learn, do you?' Noreen mutters.

'Not until we get caught,' Joey said. 'Besides, if they invite you inside, it's not breaking and entering.' Up the block, she eyed the six-storey building that Charlie and his mom called home. A navy-blue sedan was parked illegally across the street. And out front, a broad-chested man was holding the door open for a heavyset woman. Joey recognised Gallo instantly.

'Guess who's here?' she growled, lowering her head. Backing up towards the used bookstore on the corner, Joey ducked into the doorway and poked her neck out just enough to steal a good look.

Up the block, Gallo opened the passenger door to his car and escorted Mrs Caruso into place. As he crossed round to the driver's side, he stared up the block, almost like he was searching for someone. Someone who wasn't there. But would be soon.

'Oh, crap,' Joey added, reading the cocky look on his face.

Gunning his engine, Gallo sped up the block. Joey took off towards the building. 'He's got a crew coming,' she warned Noreen. 'Probably in the next two to ten minutes.' She jerked open the building's front door. As an elderly woman came out from the lobby, Joey caught the interior door, cut inside and flew for the elevator.

'YOU SURE THIS is a good idea?' I ask, keeping lookout as Charlie punches the number into the Excelsior Hotel's payphone. It may not be the best hotel in the city, but it is the closest one with the best selection of phone books.

'Oliver, how else do you plan on getting on a plane? If we use our real IDs, we're fools; if we use our credit cards, they track us.'

'Then maybe we should check out the train?'

'You really wanna spend two days riding Amtrak? Every second we waste lets the Secret Service tighten the thumbscrews.'

I lean in and make him share the receiver. In my ear, the phone rings. 'C'mon . . .' Charlie grumbles. 'Where the hell are y—'

'Law offices,' Bendini answers. 'Whattya need?'

THE FIRST FIFTEEN minutes were supposed to calm her down. No one to yell at, no one to speak to, just her—alone in a room, with nothing but a wooden desk and four chairs. Stark white walls. No pictures, nothing to distract—except for the enormous mirror on the right-hand wall. The mirror was the first thing Maggie Caruso noticed. It was supposed to be. With today's miniaturised video technology, there was no reason to use two-way mirrors. But even when there was no one behind them, they had their own psychological effect.

Maggie told herself that everything was OK. Her sons were fine.

That's what Gallo told her. But if that were the case, what was she doing at the New York headquarters of the Secret Service? The answer came with a sharp rattle and a twist of the doorknob.

'Maggie Caruso?' DeSanctis asked as he stepped inside with a file folder. Gallo followed, nodding a fast hello.

'*Please* . . . when can I see my boys?' Maggie said.

'That's what we were hoping you could help us with,' DeSanctis said. He took the seat on her left; Gallo took the one on her right.

'I don't understand . . .' she began.

Gallo looked at DeSanctis, who slowly slid the folder onto the table. 'Mrs Caruso, last night someone stole a significant amount of money from Greene and Greene Private Bank. This morning, when the thieves were confronted, gunfire was exchanged and—'

'Gunfire?' she interrupted, her voice shaking. 'Was anyone . . .?'

'Oliver and Charlie are fine,' he reassured her. 'But in the process, a man named Shep Graves was shot and killed by the two suspects.'

Maggie turned to Gallo. 'What does this have to do with my sons?'

DeSanctis leaned in close. 'Mrs Caruso, have you heard from Charlie or Oliver in the past few hours?'

'Excuse me?'

'If they were hiding, do you know where that might be?'

'Are you accusing them of—? They'd never do something like that! *Never!*' Maggie insisted.

'I'm not saying they would,' DeSanctis offered, keeping his voice slow and smooth. 'I'm just trying to protect them . . .'

'You sound like someone who's dying to pin them down.'

'We're only trying to help you, Mrs Caruso,' Gallo jumped in. 'You watch the news. When was the last time a fugitive made a safe getaway? It doesn't happen, Maggie. And the longer you keep your mouth shut, the more likely some law enforcement hotshot is going to put a bullet in one of your sons' necks. I know you want to protect them. But do you really want to bury your own children?'

Maggie Caruso watched the world blur in a flood of tears.

OUTSIDE MAGGIE'S apartment building, the Verizon van pulled into an open spot behind a dented black car. The side door of the van slid open and three men in Verizon uniforms got out and unloaded their toolboxes. As physical security specialists all they needed was twenty minutes to turn any home into a perfect soundstage. Heading inside, the tallest of the three shoved a tiny three-pronged tweezer towards the lock. In four seconds, the door was open.

'Phone box in the basement,' the one with black hair called out.

'I got it,' the third said, heading for the stairwell in the corner of the lobby. The other two took the elevator. Eventually, it hiccuped to a halt on the third floor. The door rolled open and Joey was waiting. She took one look at the Verizon uniforms and lowered her head.

'Have a good night,' the taller one said as he stepped out.

'You too,' Joey replied, sliding round him to get in the elevator. He smiled. She smiled right back. And just like that, she was gone.

'I SWEAR, I HAVEN'T heard from them once,' Maggie stammered, wiping her eyes with her sleeve. 'I was home all day but they never—'

'We believe you,' Gallo said. 'But the longer Charlie and Oliver are out there, the more likely they are to check in. And when they do, I want you to keep them talking as long as possible.'

Catching her breath, Maggie tried to picture the moment in her head. So much of it still didn't make sense. 'I don't know . . .'

'I realise it's hard,' DeSanctis added. 'Believe me, I have two little girls myself—no parent should ever be put in this situation. But if you want to save them, this is truly the best . . . for everyone.'

IT TAKES US ALMOST an hour to get from Duckworth's to Hoboken, New Jersey. Following Bendini's instructions, we blow past the bars and restaurants that line Washington Avenue and take a left on Fourth. Coffee shops become town houses, bakeries become brownstones. We're looking for a storefront.

Three blocks later, we see it—a one-storey square brick building with a home-painted MUMFORD TRAVEL sign above it. Inside, the lights are on, but the only one there is a sixty-year-old woman sitting behind an old metal desk and flipping through *Soap Opera Digest*.

A push on the door lets us in.

'Hi,' I say to the woman. 'I'm here to see—'

'I got it!' a screechy voice calls out in a heavy Jersey accent. From the back room, a wiry man in a white golf shirt pushes aside a curtain and steps out to greet us. He's got slightly bulging eyes and a brushed-back receding hairline. He motions us to join him in the back, holding open the drape that leads to the back room.

'Pay no attention to the man behind the curtain,' Charlie says.

'You got that right,' the man agrees. 'But if I'm Oz, who're you—the Cowardly Lion?'

'Nah, *he's* the Cowardly Lion,' Charlie says, pointing my way. 'Me? I see myself more as Toto.'

Oz fights a smile. 'I hear you need to get to Miami,' he says, moving towards his desk in the centre. The dingy back room is the same size as the room out front, but here there's a copier, a shredder and a computer hooked up to a high-tech printer.

'Um . . . can we get started?' I ask.

'That depends,' Oz says, rubbing his thumb against two fingers.

I reach for my wallet. 'Three thousand, right?'

'That's what they say,' Oz replies. Leaning over, he reaches down to the bottom drawer of his desk, pulls two items out and wings them our way. I catch one; Charlie catches the other.

'Clairol Nice 'n Easy Hair Color,' Charlie reads out loud. On the front of his box is a woman with silky blonde hair. On mine, the model's hair is jet black.

Oz immediately points us to the bathroom in the corner. 'If you really want to get lost,' he explains, 'you gotta start up top.'

Twenty minutes later, I'm staring in a filthy mirror, amazed at the magic of a cheap dye job. 'How's it look?' I ask, brushing my newly black hair into place.

'Like Buddy Holly,' Charlie says. 'Only nerdier.'

'Thank you, Carol Channing.'

'You two ready yet?' Oz interrupts. 'Let's go!'

Snapped back to reality, we head out of the bathroom.

'Stand there and pull the shade,' Oz says, pointing to the window at the back of the room. There's a small X taped on the carpet.

Charlie leaps for it and jerks down the shade's cord. 'Blue?' he asks, noticing the pale blue colour on the inside of the shade.

On Oz's computer, a digital image of a blank New Jersey driver's licence blooms into focus. The background for the photo is pale blue. Just like the shade. Oz steps in front of Charlie, digital camera in hand. 'On three, say "Department of Motor Vehicles" . . .'

Charlie says the words, and I squint at the bright white flash.

JOEY PEERED THROUGH the glass doors that led to the lobby of the Upper East Side apartment building. Inside, a doorman was hunched against the front desk, flipping through a newspaper. No uniform; no tie; no problem. Just another daddy's little girl's first apartment.

Painting on a grin, Joey unclipped her cellphone from her belt, held it to her ear and pulled open the door. 'I hate it when they do that!' she whined into the phone. 'Pantihose are *so* middle class.'

'What're you talking about?' Noreen asked.

'You heard me!' Joey shouted. She blew by the doorman without a wave and stormed straight for the elevator. The doorman shook his head. Typical.

Twenty-three floors later, Joey rang the bell for Apartment 23H.

'Who is it?' a female voice answered.

'Teri Gerlach—from the National Association of Securities Dealers,' Joey explained. 'Oliver Caruso recently applied for his Series-7 licence, and since he listed you as one of his references, we were wondering if we could ask you a few questions.'

There was a quiet clink and Joey could feel herself being studied through the eyehole. 'Who else did he list?' the voice challenged.

Joey pulled a small notepad from her bag. 'Let's see . . . a mother by the name of Margaret, a brother, Charles, Henry Lapidus from Greene & Greene Bank and a girlfriend named Beth Manning.'

Chains whirred and locks thunked. As it opened, Beth moved back from the door. 'You'll just have to excuse the mess . . .'

'Don't worry,' Joey laughed as she stepped inside and waved a hand against Beth's forearm. 'My place is fifty times worse.'

'HERE YOU GO,' Oz says, slapping a blue and white Continental Airlines envelope against Charlie's chest. I rip mine open; Charlie does the same. Flight 201—9.50 tonight, nonstop to Miami.

'Twenty-five C,' I tell my brother.

He studies his ticket. 'Seven B.'

Reaching down to the laminating machine, Oz picks up the wrapper and peels it open. He shoves the laminated card at us. It's a perfect New Jersey licence, with my picture and brand-new black hair.

Oz told us to pick easy-to-remember names. Charlie's says Sonny Rollins, jazz master and legend. Mine says Walter Harvey, Dad's first and middle names. Physically and in name, we're no longer brothers.

CHAPTER 6

'Whattya mean, *Wonder Bread*?' Noreen asked through the phone.

'As in *boring*,' Joey replied as she drove back through Brooklyn. 'As in *whiter than white*. Whatever Oliver sees in her—this girl's as exciting as a speed bump. If Oliver's dating Beth, he can't be much of a daredevil.'

'So?'

'So think about how that fits with the other pieces. Here's a twenty-six-year-old kid scrimping and saving with the age-old dream of getting out of Brooklyn. At work, he spends four years as Boy Friday to Lapidus. Clearly, he's got bigger aspirations—but does he break out and start his own company? Not a chance. He applies to business school and decides to take the safe road to riches. Not exactly the type to plan a three-hundred-million-dollar heist.'

'Wait a minute,' Noreen said. 'So now you think they're—'

'They're not innocent,' Joey insisted. 'If they were, they wouldn't be running. But for Oliver to leave his happy little comfort zone . . . there's clearly something else we're not seeing.'

Joey turned onto Bedford Avenue. Even in the darkness, one thing stood out: the telephone company truck in front of Maggie Caruso's building. Joey ducked the car into a driveway and cut the engine. It didn't make sense. If they were still here—

Before she could finish the thought, tyres screeched and a car turned onto the block. Coasting past the van, it bucked to a halt right in front of a fire hydrant.

The doors swung wide and Gallo and DeSanctis stepped into the night air. DeSanctis opened the back door and extended a hand to Maggie Caruso. She stepped out and he led her towards the building. The instant they disappeared, Gallo headed for the van.

The driver rolled down his window and Gallo reached in to shake his hand. The driver handed Gallo a package. Then Gallo's posture tensed and he turned to look straight at Joey.

'What the hell do you think you're doing?' Gallo thundered, storming straight at her car.

Joey thought about starting her car, but it was too late. Thick knuckles rapped against her window. 'Open up,' Gallo demanded.

Knowing the drill, Joey rolled down her window.

'What the hell were you doing inside that apartment?'

'I'm sorry, I don't know what you're talking about.'

'Don't play stupid!' Gallo warned.

'I'm just doing my job,' Joey shot back. She pulled a leather ID case from her pocket and flashed her investigator's licence.

Gallo whipped his hand forward, slapped the ID from her fingertips and sent it flying against the opposite window. 'Listen to me!' he exploded in Joey's face. 'If you interfere with this investigation again, I'll personally drag your ass back across the Brooklyn Bridge!'

Stunned by the outburst, Joey stayed silent. Law enforcement was always territorial about jurisdiction . . . but in the Secret Service . . .

they didn't lose their temper like that. Not without a reason.

'Anything else?' Joey asked.

Gallo tightened his gaze, shoved a closed fist into the car and dumped a Ziploc bag of shattered electronics into Joey's lap. All her bugs and transmitters, wrecked beyond repair.

AS I STAND IN LINE at Newark International Airport, I'm focused on the fidgety woman in front of me, and more important, the security officials I'm thirty seconds away from facing.

If the Service put the word out, this'll be the shortest trip we've ever taken, but as the line shuffles forward, nothing seems out of—

Damn. I didn't even notice him at first. Beyond the conveyor belt. The broad-shouldered guy in the airport security uniform. He's got a metal detector in his hand, but the way he's gripping it like a bat, it's like he's never held one before in his life. As he looks my way, I lower my head, refusing eye contact. Ten people in front of me, Charlie's craning his neck in every direction, anxious for interaction.

'Long day, huh?' he asks the woman running the X-ray machine.

'No bags?' the woman asks as Charlie gets closer to the machine.

'Checked,' he brags, holding up his ticket and single claim check.

In Hoboken, a quick stop at the army-navy store got us a blue gym bag filled with underwear, shirts and a few toiletries. It also got us a miniature lead-lined box that—when stuffed in the bottom of the gym bag—became the perfect hiding spot for Gallo's gun.

No doubt, it's a bad idea—the last thing we need is to be caught with the murder weapon—but these guys are leaping for our throats. Unless we want to wind up like Shep, we need the protection.

A black guard motions Charlie through the detector.

A high-pitched beep rips through the air. Oh, no. I look up to see Charlie forcing a laugh. 'Must be that erector set I ate this morning . . .'

'Man, I used to *hate* those erector sets,' the guard laughs, waving a handheld detector up Charlie's chest and down his shoulders. 'Couldn't build jack with 'em.' In the background, the guard with the square shoulders slowly turns our way.

'That's why you gotta go with Lego,' Charlie adds, unable to stop himself. Spreading his arms, he waves hi to the guard with square shoulders. The guard nods awkwardly and looks away. He wants two brown-haired brothers—not a flaky blond kid travelling alone.

Finding nothing, the black guard lowers his detector. 'Have a safe trip,' he tells Charlie.

'You too,' Charlie adds.

One by one, the rest of the line takes their turn. As I step through the detector, Charlie turns and glances back to make sure I'm OK. Passing the two guards, I keep my mouth shut and glide by.

JOEY WATCHED GALLO walk across the street, back towards the apartment building. Halfway there, he shot a wave to his buddies in the van, who flashed their lights back. With a punch of the pedal, the van pulled out of its spot and disappeared up the block. Gallo stepped inside the apartment building.

'What was that about?' Noreen asked in her ear.

'Nothing,' Joey said, getting out and going round to the back of the car. She opened the trunk, pulled out a metal suitcase and balanced it on the edge of the trunk. Locks popped and flipped open. Joey stuffed what she needed in her pockets and crossed the street.

'You're not going back in the apartment are you?'

'Nope,' Joey said, picking up speed.

'I heard you fidgeting with the goody box. Where are you going?'

Joey stopped in front of Gallo and DeSanctis's car. 'They took all my taps, Noreen—and you know what it's like getting back in while they're listening . . .'

'Wait a minute . . . you're not—' The slam of a car door cut Noreen off. 'Joey, please tell me you're not in the Secret Service's car.'

'Fine, I'm not in their car.' Joey eyed her watch. There wasn't much time. It may've looked like they were helping Maggie back upstairs, but it was probably just Gallo's way of getting another peek round the apartment. Two minutes at the most. Joey reached up for the dome light that lit the inside of the car, snapped off its plastic cover and undid the two screws that held the tiny bulb in place.

'You're bugging the Secret Service! That car's federal property.'

'It's also the only place these bastards are too cocky to look,' Joey pointed out. 'Hell, they're so sure of themselves, they even left the doors unlocked.' She connected a tiny microphone to the red wire that dangled down towards the bulb. The dome light was one of the few places that always had power—even when the car was off.

'Please, Joey—they're gonna come any minute . . .'

'Almost done . . .' Snapping the dome back into place, she ducked down in the back of the car and reached under the driver's seat. Thanks to an upgrade in law enforcement vehicles, Gallo's car was fully stocked with power seats. Feeling around for the wiring that ran up from the floorboard, she clipped onto a red wire and quickly plugged the other end into a small black box.

She lifted her head to glance out of the side window, and a bright light caught her eye. Inside the building. The elevator doors slid open. Here they come. She pulled one last item from her pocket. It was a shiny extendable pointer with a slight hook at the end of it. Opening it to its full three feet, she attached it to the wiry antenna that ran out of the black box and tucked it under the base of the cloth-covered seat. With a sharp shove, she threaded the pointer—and the antenna—straight up the back of the seat. Completely out of sight, but still perfectly angled to send a signal through the moon roof. One homemade global positioning system coming up.

'Joey, get out of there!'

'Call him,' Joey whispered. Stuffing the black box under the seat, she locked it in place with a magnetic thunk. From the back window, she could see Gallo and DeSanctis walking up the block.

A high-pitched ring screamed through the night. Gallo stopped in his tracks. 'This is Gallo,' he answered, flipping open his cellphone. The two agents turned back towards the building. Joey ducked out of the back door and scuttled across the street.

'Sorry, wrong number,' Noreen said in Joey's ear.

Gallo shut his phone and headed back to his car. As he pulled the door open, he squinted up the dark block. Joey was sitting on the hood of her car. 'Any luck up there?' she called out.

Gallo ignored her and drove off.

STEPPING OFF THE PLANE at Miami International Airport, I stick to the crowd and lose myself in the mass of recently arrived passengers being smothered by loved ones. It's not hard to tell the difference between natives and guests—we're in long sleeves and jackets; they're in shorts and T-shirts. As the group fans out towards baggage claim, I scan the terminal, searching for Charlie. He's nowhere in sight.

Racing into baggage claim, I check every corner. Past the rental cars . . . round the conveyor belts . . . still no Charlie.

I rush to the closest door—but the moment I step outside, I'm pummelled by a wave of Florida heat. As a puddle of sweat soaks the small of my back, I realise for the first time I'm still wearing my overcoat. Throwing my arms back, I fight furiously to get it off.

Behind me, someone grabs my shoulder. I tighten my fist. Then I hear the voice. 'Y'OK there, Ahab?' Charlie asks.

I spin round. There he is—dimples and goofy grin. I don't know whether to kill him or hug him, so I settle on a hard shove in the shoulder. 'What the hell is wrong with you? Where were you?'

'Well, no offence, but this was an emergency.'

'What kind of emergency?'

He looks up, but won't answer.

'Oh jeez, Charlie, you called her, didn't you?'

'Don't worry about it—I got it under control. I still live with her, Ollie. If I didn't check in, she'd be having a heart attack.'

'Yeah, well what do you think'll upset her more—missing us for a few nights, or setting up our funerals after the Service hunts us down and buries us? They'll be tracing every call.'

'Really? I didn't think about that—even though it's in, like, every man-on-the-run movie that's ever been done.' Losing the sarcasm, he adds, 'Can you please trust me for once? Believe me, I did it smart. Whoever's listening . . . they're not gonna hear a word.'

'HOW WE DOIN'?' Gallo asked.

'Gimme a sec,' DeSanctis said from the passenger seat. In his lap, his fingers pounded the keyboard of what looked like a standard lap-top. The only working keys, however, were the numbers along the top, which DeSanctis used to adjust the receiver hidden inside.

Onscreen, a window in the bottom left corner blinked to life. As it faded in and the colours became crisp, they had a perfect digital feed of Maggie Caruso bent over the coffee table in the living room, looking like she was about to throw up.

'What's wrong?' Gallo asked. 'Is she sick?'

'Just another second . . .' DeSanctis keyed in one final number and Mrs Caruso's voice echoed from the built-in speakers.

'. . . ank you . . . thank you, God!' she shouted as the tears flooded. She shook her head and unleashed a pained, but unmistakable smile. 'Just take care of them . . . please take care of them . . .'

'They called her!' Gallo exclaimed. 'The bastards just called her!'

Clicking at the keyboard, DeSanctis opened another window on the lap-top. *Caruso, Margaret—Platform: Telephony*. 'That's impossible,' he said, reading from the screen. 'I got everything right here—it's blank—nothing incoming; nothing outgoing.'

'Fax? Email?'

'Not for the seamstress. Doesn't even have a computer.'

'Maybe the brothers called it in to a neighbour.'

DeSanctis pointed to the video picture on the screen. In the background, behind Mrs Caruso, was a clear view of her front door. 'Tech boys were watching since we got here. Even for the two minutes it took to set this up, we'd see someone coming and going . . .'

'Then how the hell did they get to her?'

'I have no idea—maybe—'

'Don't give me *maybes*!' Gallo shouted. 'She's clearly got something that's letting her talk to her boys. Now, I don't care if a neighbour's tapping the radiator in Morse code, I want to know what it is!'

'*I DON'T CARE if a neighbour's tapping the radiator in Morse code, I want to know what it is!*'

Staring up the block at Gallo and DeSanctis's car, Joey sat back in her seat and lowered the volume on her walkie-talkie-sized receiver.

'Sounds like they're already calling in to Mom,' Noreen interrupted through the earpiece.

'Yeah . . . I guess.'

Noreen knew that tone on her boss. 'What's wrong?'

'Nothing,' Joey said. 'It's just . . . if Gallo and DeSanctis are treating this like a real manhunt, why're they the only ones doing surveillance? When the Secret Service sit on a house, they send four people at a minimum. Why's it suddenly two guys sitting alone in a car?'

'Who knows? They could be shorthanded . . . or over budget . . .'

'Or maybe they don't want anyone else around,' Joey challenged.

'When Shep was killed, they lost a former agent,' Noreen pointed out. 'Ten bucks says that's why they're keeping it personal.'

'I hope you're right,' Joey said. 'But if I were Charlie and Oliver, I'd be praying we're the ones who find them first.'

LYING ON MY STOMACH and hiding from the morning sun, I refuse to open my eyes. The futon's about as comfortable as a sack of doorknobs. My left arm's asleep. And just as I blink myself into the day, I swear . . . for the tiniest of seconds . . . I have no idea where I am. That's when I open my eyes.

Rank beige carpet. Stale bug-spray smell. Damn. Shep . . . the money . . . I was hoping it was a bad dream. It's not. It's our life.

Next to me, Charlie's still asleep. I make my way to the shower.

Ten minutes later, it's time for Charlie to do the same.

'Charlie! Get up!' I call from the bathroom.

He finally rolls over to face me. Rubbing the crust from his eyes, he doesn't remember where he is either. Then he looks round and realises we're in the same bad dream. 'Crap,' he mutters.

'There's no hot water,' I tell him, drying my Johnny Cash hair with a fistful of left-behind paper towels.

'I'll be sure to drop a note in the landlord's suggestion box.'

In New York, they call it a studio. Here, it's an efficiency. To me, it's a no-bedroom rathole. But when we were searching the neighbourhood at two in the morning, it was exactly what we needed: on a side street, a FOR RENT sign out front, and a light on in the apartment marked MANAGER. Anywhere else, they would've been suspicious and called the cops. But on the sketchy outskirts of Miami's South Beach, we're business as usual. Between the drug dealers and the illegal foreigners, they're accustomed to tenants who show up at 2.00am.

Stepping back into the main room, I get dressed. Outside, the sun is shining, but we can barely see through the papers that cover the windows. Ripped pages from a Budweiser girls-in-bikinis calendar Scotch-taped to every window. Whoever was here last didn't want to be seen. Neither do we. The calendar stays where it is.

Ten minutes later, Charlie paper-towels himself dry and dresses.

'All set?' I ask.

'Almost . . .' He reaches into the gym bag and feels around inside.

'Relax,' I say. He looks over his shoulder, and I pull up the edge of my untucked shirt. I've got the gun stuffed in the waist of my trousers. Turning round, I head outside. Charlie's a few steps behind. Ready or not, Duckworth—here we come.

'WHAT'RE YOU DOING?' Charlie calls out, as I make a sharp right on Sixth Street. 'I thought we were going to Duckwor—?'

'Trust me,' I cut him off. 'This is just as important.'

I hustle to the corner, where a row of newspaper vending machines stretches up the block. *Miami Herald*, *el Herald*, *USA Today* . . . and the one I fly towards—the *New York Times*. I shove coins in the machine's throat, pull down the door and reach for a paper. I open it and flip through the front section.

'Are we in there?' Charlie asks.

I keep flipping, scouring for any mention of yesterday's events. No money; no embezzlement; no murder. To be honest, I'm not surprised. Lapidus is keeping this on lockdown from the press. Still, some things run every day. I fold the paper back. Right at Obituaries.

'Lemme see,' Charlie says, stepping next to me.

Standing under a dried-out palm tree, I hold the left half of the page; Charlie holds the right. We both find it alphabetically. On most days, I read and he skims. Today it's reverse. 'Graves—Shepard, 37, of Brooklyn . . . Vice President of Security, Greene and Greene . . . survived by wife, Sherry . . . memorial service to be announced.'

'I didn't know he was married,' Charlie says, already lost in Shep's life. But the more he reads on . . . 'Those revisionist bastards,' he grumbles. 'It doesn't even say he was in the Service.'

'Charlie, this isn't about his résumé . . . it's about what's missing from the picture. Three hundred million gets lifted and it doesn't even make the gossip columns? A former Secret Service agent is shot in the chest and no one reports a word? For these guys, a fake obit is the easy part. Whatever they say, people believe it. Whatever really happened, it's being erased. That's what they're gonna do with us, Charlie. They shake the Etch-A-Sketch and the picture disappears. Then they write in whatever they want. *Suspects found with millions—investigation points to murder*. That's the new reality, Charlie. And by the time they're done scribbling, there'll be no way for us to change it.'

We head towards Tenth Street. Duckworth is only blocks away.

WITH $313 MILLION in his account and retirement on his mind, Marty Duckworth could've picked anything. I predicted Art Deco town house; Charlie said Mediterranean bungalow. We couldn't be more wrong.

'I don't believe it,' Charlie says, staring across the street at the one-storey 1960s rambler. Beaten by weather and covered in peeling pink paint, the building is clearly past its prime.

'It's definitely the right address,' I confirm as I check again. I step off the kerb and cross the street. Weaving past the overgrown shrubbery and round the classic blue Beetle that's parked out the front, I race up the path, open the rusted screen door and jam an anxious finger at the doorbell. No answer.

I ring it again, trying to look relaxed. Still no answer.

I press my nose against the diamond-shaped windowpane that's set into the door, trying to get a better view . . . then from inside . . . locks clunk open. I jump back. It's already too late.

'Can I *help* you?' a young woman asks, opening the door. She's got black ringlet hair, thin lips and a tiny, pointed nose. My eyes go straight to her beat-up jeans and spaghetti-strap white top.

'Sorry. I wasn't trying to . . . we were just looking for a friend . . .'

'We're trying to find Marty Duckworth,' Charlie blurts.

The woman's body language shifts—her brow unfurrows; her shoulders sag. 'You're friends of his?'

'Yeah,' I say cautiously. 'Why?'

She pauses a moment. 'Marty Duckworth died six months ago.'

'So he's really dead?' Charlie asks, already starting to panic.

'I'm sorry,' she offers. 'I didn't mean to—'

'Did you know him?' I interrupt.

'No,' she stammers. 'But—'

'Then how do you know he's dead?'

'I remember his name from the deed. It was an estate sale.'

'It's impossible,' I tell her as my voice cracks. 'What abou—'

'He's just upset,' Charlie says. He leans in and pinches my back. 'We should get going,' he adds through gritted teeth. Fake-smiling at the woman, he gives her a quick wave. 'Thanks for all the help . . .'

'I'm really sorry for your loss,' she calls out as we walk away.

'Yeah,' Charlie whispers. 'That makes three of us.'

'WHAT'S WRONG with you?' Charlie asks as we cut back through our courtyard. Checking to see that no one's around, he makes a quick beeline for our new apartment. 'Why'd you go after her like that?'

'She might've known something.'

'Are you really that delusional?' Charlie asks, racing inside. 'Didn't you see her reaction, Ollie—she was floored. Newsflash at eleven: Duckworth's dead. End of story.'

'You think that's all it's about? Duckworth? I couldn't give a crap about Duckworth—I just want my old life back, Charlie! And unless we figure out what's going on, Gallo and DeSanctis are—'

A loud splat smacks against the window. We both duck down. The noise stays loud—rat-a-tat-tatting against the glass—like someone breaking in. I look up to see who, but the only thing there is a starburst of water. Sprinkler . . . just the sprinkler.

'Someone probably tripped on the hose . . .' Charlie says.

I run to the window in the kitchenette, peel back a piece of calendar and peek outside . . . just as a blurred figure darts below the windowsill. I jump back, almost falling over. 'Someone's out there!'

'Are you sure?' Charlie asks.

'I just saw him!' I answer, reaching down and grabbing the gun from my trousers. I cock back the pin and put a finger on the trigger.

Charlie rummages through the kitchen drawers, looking for a weapon. Knives, scissors, anything. Top to bottom, he rips open each drawer. Empty. Empty. Empty. The last one slides out and his eyes go wide. Inside is a rusted machete.

'Blessed are the drug dealers,' he says, yanking it out.

I follow him into the bathroom. Like we worked out last night. Tiny efficiencies may be too small for back doors . . . but they still have back windows. Leaping onto the toilet, he cranks open the window and punches out the screen. I hop up next to him. He steps into my boost. Up and out—he's gone in an instant. I follow.

'Ready to run?' he asks, rechecking the narrow concrete alley created by the building ours backs up to. On our left is a metal gate that leads back to the street; on our right is an open path that snakes round to the main courtyard—right where they're hiding. With a shared glance, we scramble towards the gate . . . and quickly spot the metal chain and padlock that keeps it shut tight.

'Damn,' Charlie whispers, smacking the lock. Without thinking, he takes off towards the other end of the alley.

I grab him by the arm. 'You're gonna run right into them.'

'Not if they're already inside . . . besides, you got a better way out?'

I look around, but there's no arguing with impossibility.

Charlie speeds down the alley. At the edge of the building, he stops and turns my way. *Ready?* I nod, and he peeks round the first corner. *All clear*, he signals, waving me forward. Like burglars in our own back yard, we slip down behind the building, ducking under the windowsills. Around the next corner is where we saw him.

Squeezing in next to Charlie, I check the ground for stray shadows and slowly stick my head out. Around the corner, I scan the courtyard. No one's in sight, Charlie puts up his fist. Counting by fingers, he nods my way. *One . . . two . . .*

We tear out of there at full speed . . .

'Where you off to, Cinderella—late for the ball?' a voice asks from our front steps.

Whirling round, we stop in our tracks. I lift the gun.

'Easy there, cowboy,' she says, hands already in the air. Forget the Service. It's the woman from Duckworth's. 'You want to tell me who you really are?' she asks.

'This isn't about you,' I warn.

'Why were you asking about him?'

'So you *do* know Duckworth?'

'I asked you a question . . .'

'So did I,' I shoot back. I wave the gun to get her attention. She doesn't know us well enough to decide if she should call the bluff.

'How did you know him?' Charlie demands.

She lowers her hands, but never stops staring at me. 'You really don't know?' she asks. 'Marty Duckworth was my father.'

JOEY SAT IN HER CAR across the street from Maggie's building. She was on the phone with her assistant. 'Anything interesting?'

'There is one thing,' Noreen answered. 'Remember that pharmacy you wanted me to check out? Well, I called up, said I was from Oliver's insurance company and asked if they had any outstanding prescriptions for a Mr Caruso.'

'And?'

'Nothing for Oliver but they had one for a Caruso named Charles.'

Joey stopped. 'Please tell me you . . .'

'"Oh, I'm sorry—did I say *Oliver?* I meant *Charles* Caruso."'

'Beautiful, beautiful,' Joey sang. 'So what'd you find?'

'Well, he's got a prescription for something called mexiletine.'

'Mexiletine?'

'I called the office of the prescribing physician, who was only too happy to help out with an ongoing insurance investigation . . .'

'And the final result?' Joey asked.

'Charlie has a heart arrhythmia. He's had it since he was fourteen. That's where all the hospital bills came from. They're in Mom's name because he was a minor at the time. Too bad for them, when the first attack hit, it took a hundred-and-ten-thousand-dollar operation to fix him up. Apparently, he's got some bad electrical wiring in his heart that doesn't let the blood pump correctly.'

'So it's serious?'

'Only if he misses his medication.'

'Aw,' Joey said, shaking her head. 'You think he has it with him?'

'They took off straight from Grand Central—I don't think he has a second pair of socks, much less his daily dose of mexiletine.'

'And how long can he go without taking it?'

'Hard to say—the doctor guessed three or four days under perfect conditions—less if he's running around or under any stress.'

CHAPTER 7

'He's your father?' Charlie blurts.

'So he's alive?' I add.

The woman looks at both of us, but stays with me. 'He's been dead for six months. What'd you want with him?'

'Why'd you lie about who you were?' I ask.

To our surprise, she lets out an amused grin and runs her foot against the top of the grass. It's the first time I realise she's barefoot. 'Funny, I was about to ask you the same thing,' she says.

'You could've said you were his daughter,' Charlie accuses.

'And you could've said why you were looking for him.'

I know a stalemate when I see one. If we want information, we need to give it. 'Walter Harvey,' I say, extending a handshake.

'Gillian Duckworth,' she says, shaking back.

Across the street and up the block, the mailman's making his morning rounds. Charlie hides his machete behind his back and motions my way. 'Uh . . . maybe we should take this inside.'

'Yeah . . . that's not a bad idea,' I say, stuffing the gun back in my trousers. 'Why don't you come in for some coffee?'

'With you two? After you pull a gun and a pirate's knife?' She turns to leave.

'Please, just wait,' I say, reaching out for her arm.

She pulls away. 'Nice meeting you, Walter. Have a good life.'

Knowing we need the info, Charlie goes nuclear. 'We think your father may've been murdered.'

Gillian stops dead in her tracks and turns round, head cocked.

'Just give us five minutes,' I plead. I charge for our front door and never give her a chance to say no. Gillian's right behind me.

As I step into our efficiency, I offer her the foldable chair next to me in the kitchen. But instead of sitting, she props herself up on the white Formica countertop. Her bare feet dangle off the edge.

'So you were telling us about your dad . . .' I begin.

'Actually, I wasn't telling you anything,' she responds. 'I just want to know why you think he was murdered.'

'Up until yesterday, the two of us were living in New York, working at a bank,' I begin hesitantly. 'Then this past Friday, we're going through these old accounts—'

'And we came across one registered to a Marty Duckworth,' Charlie interrupts. I'm about to cut him off, but decide against it. We both know who's the better liar. 'As far as we could tell, your father's account was an old abandoned account in the system. But once we found it, and reported it to the head of Security, well . . . yesterday there were three of us on the run. Today there're only two.'

Charlie looks up at Gillian, who's staring straight at him. Their eyes connect, and just then, she pulls back. Her feet are no longer swinging. She sits on her hands, perfectly still. Whatever she saw in my brother, it's something she knows all too well.

'You OK?' I ask her.

Gillian nods, unable to get the words out. 'I-I knew it . . .'

'Knew what?'

'That something was wrong. I knew it the moment I got the report.' Reading the confusion on our faces, she explains, 'Six months ago, the phone rings. They tell me my dad died in a bicycle accident—that he was riding over the Rickenbacker Causeway when a car veered out of its lane . . . Have you ever seen the Rickenbacker?'

We shake our heads simultaneously.

'It's a bridge that's as steep as a mountain. When I was sixteen, it was a tough ride. My dad was sixty-two. He had trouble tackling the road along the beach. No way was he biking the Rickenbacker.'

We're all silent. Charlie's the first to react. 'Did the cops—?'

'The day after the accident, I drove to his house to pick out the suit he was going to be buried in. The place looked like it was hit by a hurricane. Closets ripped apart . . . drawers overturned . . . but as far as I could tell, nothing was taken except his computer. The best part is, instead of sending the police, the break-in was investigated by—'

'The Secret Service,' I say.

Gillian turns with a sideways glance. 'How'd you know that?'

'Who do you think's chasing us?'

Like she did with Charlie, Gillian locks her gaze on me. I can't tell if she's looking for the truth, or just a connection. Either way, she's found it. Her soft blue eyes stare straight through me.

Charlie lets out a loud, fake cough. 'So what do you think they were looking for?' he asks.

'I never found out,' Gillian explains. 'When I called their Miami office, they had no record of an investigation. I told them I met the agents, but without names there was nothing they could do.'

'So you gave up?' Charlie asks. 'Didn't you think it was a bit odd?'

'You have to understand, when it came to my dad's business, secrets were part of the game. That's just . . . that's just how he was.'

Charlie watches her closely, but I give her a reassuring nod. When it comes to our own jackass dad, I've been able to forgive. Charlie never forgets. 'It's OK,' I say. 'I know what it's like.' As I reach out to touch her arm, Gillian's bra strap falls from under her top and sinks to her shoulder. She lifts it back into place with perfect grace.

'OK, hold on,' Charlie interrupts. 'Your dad died six months ago, right? So was that right after he moved from New York?'

'New York?' Gillian asks, confused. 'He never lived in New York.'

'You sure about that? He's never had an apartment in Manhattan?'

'Not that I know of,' she says. 'He took business trips there once in a while. I know he was scraping cash together for one of them this summer—but otherwise, he's lived in Florida his entire life.'

All this time, we thought we were looking for a New Yorker who made some cash and moved to Florida. Now we find he's a Floridian who could barely afford the few trips he'd taken to New York.

'Can someone please tell me what's going on?' Gillian asks.

I nod to Charlie. He tells her about her father's run-down New York apartment. 'How long was he away last summer?' he asks.

'I-I don't know,' Gillian sputters. 'Two . . . maybe three weeks. I never paid much . . . I barely even saw him when he was here . . .' Her voice fades. 'How much did you say was in that account you found?'

Charlie takes a deep breath. 'Three million dollars.'

Her mouth almost hits the floor. '*What?* In my dad's? There's no way. How could he possibly—?' She cuts herself off and the cogs start spinning . . . whirling through the possibilities. 'You think that's why they killed him, don't you?' she eventually asks. 'Because of something that happened with the money . . .'

'That's what we're trying to figure out,' I explain.

'Do you still have any of his stuff in the house?' Charlie asks.

'Some of it . . . yeah.'

'And have you ever gone through it?'

'Just a little,' she says. 'But wouldn't the Service have—?'

'Maybe there's something they missed,' he tells her.

'Why don't we take a look together?' I add.

With Gillian's hesitant nod, Charlie hops out of his seat, and I follow him to the door. Behind us, Gillian takes a final look round the apartment and studies every detail. The lack of furniture, the papered windows, even the machete. If we were the bad guys, she'd already be dead. She says six words: 'This better not be a trick.'

Charlie and I scramble forward. She steps outside.

'Gillian, you're not gonna regret this,' Charlie says.

GALLO GLARED DOWN at the lap-top balanced between his gut and the base of the steering wheel. For two hours, he'd watched Maggie Caruso make her lunch, clean her dishes and readjust the hems on two pairs of slacks. In that time, she got two phone calls: one from a client and one wrong number. Nothing more.

Gallo opened the feeds from all four digital cameras. Onscreen, he had views of every major room in the apartment. But the only person there was Maggie—hunched over the sewing machine.

'Ready for some relief?' DeSanctis asked as the passenger door popped open.

'Just tell me what you got,' Gallo said. 'Anything useful?'

'Of course it's useful . . .' DeSanctis swung an aluminium attaché case into the front seat. Sliding in next to it, he pulled it onto his lap and flipped the locks. Inside, set into a black foam mould, was what looked like a pudgy camcorder with a wide oversized lens. 'Infrared videocamera with thermal imaging,' DeSanctis explained as he peered through the viewfinder. 'If she's sneaking out late at night, it'll home in on her body heat and spot her down the darkest alley.'

'SO WHERE DO YOU want to start?' Gillian asks as we step into her dad's faded pink house.

'Wherever you want,' Charlie says as I survey the overcrowded living room. The room is set up like an indoor garage sale. Bookshelves crammed with engineering and science-fiction books cover two walls, stacks of papers bury a wicker chair, and throw pillows are tossed across the stained leather couch. In the centre of the room, a coffee table is lost under remote controls, faded photographs, and plastic figures from *Snow White and the Seven Dwarfs.*

'I'm impressed,' Charlie says. 'All this stuff is his?'

'Pretty much,' Gillian replies. 'I've been meaning to go through it, but . . . it's not easy to throw away someone's life. Why don't we start back here,' she suggests, leading us into the room her dad used as an office. Inside, we find an L-shaped black worktop jutting out from the back wall and continuing down the right-hand side of the room. It's covered in paperwork, tools and electronics. Above the desk is a framed picture of Geppetto, from Disney's *Pinocchio*.

'What's with the Disney fetish?' Charlie asks.

'That's where he used to work—as an Imagineer in Orlando.'

'Really? So did he ever design any cool rides?' Charlie asks.

'To be honest, I don't know—I barely knew him growing up. He used to send a Minnie doll every year for my birthday, but that was really it. That's why my mom left—we were just his second job.'

'When did he move back to Miami?'

'I think it was five years ago—said goodbye to Disney and found a job at a local computer game company.'

'He wasn't a bigshot at Disney, was he?' I ask.

'Dad?' she says with a disarming laugh. 'Naw. The closest he got to the action was linking the computer systems so when Disney's weather station sees rain coming, all the gift shops in the park get immediate messages to put out umbrellas and Mickey ponchos.'

'That's still pretty cool.'

'Maybe—though knowing my dad, his role might be overstated.'

'Join the club,' I say with a nod. 'Our dad was a—'

'*Our* dad?' she stops. 'You two are brothers?'

Charlie pummels me with a look, and I bite my tongue.

'What?' Gillian asks. 'What's the big deal?'

'Nothing,' I tell her. 'It's just . . . after yesterday . . . we're trying to keep a low profile.' As I say the words, I watch her weigh each one.

She lets it roll away. 'It's OK,' she says. 'I'd never say a word.'

'I know you wouldn't,' I smile back.

'Can we get on with this?' Charlie interrupts. 'We've still got a house to search.'

Twenty minutes later, we're lost in paper. Charlie has the piles on top of the desk, I've got the drawers below and Gillian's working the filing cabinet in the corner. As far as we can tell, most of it's useless.

'He's got every postcard, thank-you note and birthday card he's ever been sent,' I say. 'Since birth!'

'I don't get it,' Charlie says. 'He keeps everything he ever touched, but doesn't have a single bank statement or phone bill?'

'I'm guessing that's what he kept *here* . . .' I say, pulling open the file drawer. Inside, a dozen empty file folders sway on metal brackets.

'They must've grabbed them when they grabbed the computer,' Gillian says.

'Then we're dead,' Charlie groans. 'The Service took everything?'

'No, they didn't!' I snap. 'Duckworth's got junk everywhere. And since we have no idea what the Service left behind, I'm not leaving until I pick apart every drawer and tear off Happy and Bashful's plastic squeaky heads just to see what might be hidden inside. Now if you have any better options, I'm happy to hear them, but like you said before, we've got a whole house to search!'

'She knows,' Gallo said.

'How could she possibly know?' DeSanctis asked.

'Just look at her,' he said, jabbing a fat finger at the computer. 'Her sons are missing, it's another night alone, but does she cry on the phone to a friend? No—she just sits there, sewing away—'

The chime of a doorbell blared through the lap-top's speakers. Gallo and DeSanctis shot up in their seats.

'She's got a visitor,' DeSanctis said.

'How'd they get past us?' Gallo shouted.

'Could be a neighbour,' DeSanctis pointed out.

'Who is it?' Maggie asked.

The answer was a mumble. Microphones didn't work through doors.

'Sophie! So nice to see you,' Maggie sang as she opened the door. Over her shoulder they saw a grey-haired woman wearing a cable-knit brown cardigan, but no coat.

'Neighbour,' DeSanctis said.

'How have you been?' Sophie asked in a thick Russian accent.

'Fine . . . just fine,' Maggie replied, inviting her inside.

'Watch her hands!' Gallo barked as Maggie reached out and touched Sophie's shoulder.

'You think she's passing something?' De Sanctis asked.

'She doesn't have a choice. No email, no cellphone—her only hope is getting something from outside.'

Crouching down towards the lap-top, the two agents were silent. In the darkness, their faces glowed with the pale light from the screen.

'I took almost an inch off all the sleeves—let me get them off the line . . .' Maggie said as she walked towards the kitchen window. From his bird's-eye view in the smoke detector, Gallo only saw her back, but he studied everything she touched. Hands at her side. Opening the kitchen window. Pulling in the clothes line. Unhooking two women's blouses and angling each onto a hanger.

'You put them out in this weather?' Sophie asked.

'The cold's good for them—makes them crisp.'

'Watch the money change . . .' Gallo warned.

'Uck, where's my head?' Sophie began, searching for a purse that wasn't there. 'I left my . . .'

'Bring it by whenever,' Maggie said. 'I'm not going anywhere.'

'Dammit!' Gallo shouted.

SHUTTING THE DOOR behind Sophie, Maggie made her way back to the kitchen window. She opened it. A blast of cold air shoved its way inside, but Maggie didn't care. With Sophie's shirts gone, there was an open spot on the clothes line. A spot she couldn't wait to fill.

Grabbing the damp white sheet that was draped over the ironing board, she leaned out of the window, took a clothespeg from the pouch in her apron and clipped the corner into place. Inch by inch, she scrolled the sheet out over the alley, slowly pegging more of it to the line. At the edge, she pulled the sheet taut.

She stuffed both hands back into the apron's pouch. Her left hand felt around for a clothespeg; her right searched for the note she had written earlier in the night. Careful to keep her back to the kitchen, she palmed the folded-up sheet of paper. Out of the corner of her eye, she saw the faint glow in Gallo and DeSanctis's car.

She leaned out of the window again, tucked her right hand under the sheet and clipped the note in place. Directly across the way, the window in the building next door was dark—but Maggie could still make out the inky silhouette of Saundra Finkelstein. Hiding in the corner of her window, The Fink nodded. And for the third time since yesterday—under the glare of four digital videocameras, six voice-activated microphones and $50,000 worth of the government's best surveillance equipment, Maggie Caruso tugged at the two-dollar clothes line and, under a cheap, overused, wet sheet, passed a handwritten note to her next-door neighbour.

YOU CAN LEARN a lot about a man by going through his bathroom. Down on my knees under the sink, I snake my arm past the rusted pipes and rummage through random, long-expired toiletries.

'What about the medicine chest?' Charlie asks, squeezing past me and hopping up on the edge of the bathtub.

'I already went through it.'

There's a magnetic click as the medicine cabinet door opens. I lift up my head. Charlie's picking it apart.

'I told you—I already went through it.'

'I know—just double-checking,' he says, quickly scanning the stash of brown prescription vials. 'Lopressor for blood pressure, Glyburide for diabetes, Lipitor for high cholesterol.'

'Charlie, what're you doing?'

'What's it look like? I want to know what medication he was on.'

'What for?'

'Just to see—I want to find out who this guy was—get into his brain—see what he's made of.'

The rambling goes on a beat too long. I give him another look. He quickly starts putting the brown vials back in place.

'You forgot your medication, didn't you?' I say.

'What're you—?'

'The mexiletine—you haven't been taking it.'

He rolls his eyes like a pouty teenager. 'Can you please not overreact—this isn't *General Hospital*.'

'Dammit, I knew something was—' I hear a noise in the hallway and cut myself off.

'What's going on?' Gillian asks, stopping by the door.

'Nothing,' Charlie says. 'Just raiding your dad's medicine chest.' Dancing round me, he slides out of the bathroom—but right now, my eyes are on Gillian as she walks down the hallway.

'Careful, you've got some drool on your lip,' he whispers as he passes. 'I mean, not that I blame you—with all that hippiechick voodoo she's got going, I'm getting all sweaty myself.'

'We'll talk about this later,' I growl.

'I'm sure we will,' he says. 'But if I were you, I'd slow down on buying her a corsage and focus more on the problem at hand.'

By seven o'clock, all we've got left are the kitchen, the garage and the two hall closets. 'I got the kitchen,' Gillian says. As I'm about to turn the corner, I look back. Charlie should be at the hall closets. Instead, he's at the closed door at the end of the hall. Duckworth's bedroom. The only place we haven't been. It shouldn't matter—Gillian said she already went through it—but my brother stares at the door like he's got X-ray vision. After nine hours of picking through this dead man's life, he wants to know what's inside.

'Where're you going?' I ask.

He glances over his shoulder and gives me a mischievous arched eyebrow. With a twist of the doorknob, he disappears into Duckworth's bedroom. I rush towards the closed door. Trying not to make a sound, I turn the doorknob and step inside. As the door shuts behind me, the lights are off, but thanks to some cheap vertical blinds on the window, the room still gets a bath of fading dusk light.

'Welcome to the sanctum sanctorum . . .' Charlie says.

It takes about four seconds for my eyes to adjust, but when they do, it's clear why Gillian checked this room herself. Like the living room and the office, Duckworth's bedroom has the same unapologetic engineer's fashion sense: a plain bed shoved against the off-white wall, an unpainted wooden nightstand holding an old alarm clock, and an almond Formica dresser that looks like it was plucked from the back of a truck. But I realise there's something else: a cream-coloured quilt softens the bed, a vase of burgundy eucalyptus flourishes on top of the dresser, and in the corner, a Mondrian-styled painting leans against the wall. This room may've started as Duckworth's—but now it's all Gillian's. So this is where she lives. A pang of guilt swirls through my gut. This is her private space.

'C'mon, Charlie, let's go . . .'

'Yeah . . . you're right,' he says. 'We're only trusting her with our lives. Why would we ever want to learn anything more about her?'

I go to grab his arm, but he's too fast. 'I'm serious, Charlie.'

'So am I,' he says, sidestepping round me. Moving in further, he searches the floor, the bed and the rest of the furniture, hunting for context clues. Ten steps in, he stops, suddenly confused.

'What? What's wrong?' I ask.

'You tell me. Where's her life?'

'What're you talking about?'

'Her life, Ollie—clothes, photos, books, magazines. Take a look around. Besides the flowers and the art, there's nothing else.'

'Maybe she likes to keep things neat.'

'Maybe,' he agrees. 'Or maybe she's—'

There's a loud clunk as a door slams behind us. I spin round and realise it came from the hallway. I glance at the alarm clock on the nightstand to check the time—and quickly cock my head to the side. That's not an alarm clock. It's an old—

'Eight-track player!' Charlie cries. But as he squints through the darkness of the room, he notices that the slot that usually holds the eight-track looks a little wider than normal. At the edges, the silver-coloured plastic is chipped away. Curious, he moves in, squatting down in front of it. 'Sombitch,' he whispers.

'What now?' Stepping behind him, I lean over his shoulder.

'Here, Ollie.' He points. But what he points at isn't the eight-track player. It's the nightstand underneath. 'Check out the dust.'

I angle my head just enough to see the thick layer of dust that blankets the top of the nightstand.

'It's so perfect, you barely notice it,' Charlie says. 'Like no one's put anything on it, or even touched it . . . in months, even though it's right next to her bed.' He turns back to me and tightens his gaze.

'What's this, a panty raid?' a female voice asks behind us.

Charlie whips round to face Gillian.

She flicks on the lights. 'What're you doing in my room?'

'This is yours?' Charlie asks. 'We were just . . . just checking out this awesome eight-track.' He jabs a thumb over his shoulder to point, but she doesn't bother to look. Her dark eyes lock on his and don't let go. She just stands there, arms crossed against her chest. I don't blame her. We shouldn't have been snooping through her stuff.

'Listen, I'm sorry,' I offer. 'I swear we didn't touch anything.' Locking on me, she puts me through the exact same test. But unlike Charlie, I don't lie, fumble or condescend. I give her the truth and hope it's enough. 'I just wanted to learn more about you.'

As she stares me down, Gillian's arms are still crossed in front of her chest. The free spirit's gone. And then . . . just like that . . . it's back. 'It *is* pretty cool, isn't it?' she says, moving excitedly towards the nightstand. She pushes my brother aside and sits on the bed, right next to me. 'Wait'll you see what he did to it,' she tells me eagerly, flicking the power switch on. 'Just hit pause,' she adds.

Following instructions, I reach down and press the pause button. The ancient machine hums with a mechanical whir, and a plastic CD tray—complete with a shiny compact disc—slides out of the widened opening where you'd normally put the eight-track.

'Pretty cool, huh?' Gillian says.

'Where're you from again?' Charlie asks suddenly.

'Excuse me?'

'Where're you from? Where'd you grow up?'

'Right here,' Gillian replies. 'Just outside Miami.'

'Oh, that's so weird,' Charlie says. 'Because when you just said *Pretty cool*, I coulda sworn I smelt a hint of New York accent.'

Clearly amused, Gillian shakes her head, but she won't take her eyes off my brother. 'Nope, just Florida,' she sings without a care. She turns back to me and the CD/eight-track. 'Check out the disc.'

I reach down and spear it with a finger: *The Collected Speeches of Adlai E. Stevenson*. 'I take it your dad did this?'

'I'm telling you, after he left Disney, he had way too much time—'

'And when did you move in here again?' Charlie interrupts.

'I'm sorry?' she asks. If she's annoyed, she's not showing it.

'Your dad died six months ago—when did you move in here?'

Grinning, she hops up and crosses round to the foot of the bed.

See that? Charlie glares my way. *That's the same trick I use on you. Distance to avoid confrontation.*

'I don't know,' she begins. 'I guess a month or so ago . . . it's hard to say. It took a while to do the paperwork . . . and then to get my stuff over here.' She turns towards the window, but doesn't get flustered. I listen for a New York accent, but all I hear is her short-O Flooorida tone. 'It's still not that easy sleeping in his old bed, which is why most nights I'm curled up on the couch,' she adds. 'Of course, the mortgage is paid, so I got no reason to moan.'

'What about a job?' Charlie asks. 'Are you still working?'

'What do I look like, some trust-fund beach bunny?' she teases. 'Thursday, Friday and Saturday nights at Waterbed.'

'Waterbed?'

'It's a club over on Washington.'

'Let me guess. You bartend in a tight black T-shirt.'

'Charlie . . .' I scold.

She shrugs it off. 'I'm a manager, cutie-pie.' She's trying to make nice, but Charlie's not biting. 'The good part is, it leaves the days free for the paintings, which're really the best release,' she adds.

I scan the canvas in the corner and search for a signature. *G.D.* Gillian Duckworth. 'So this *is* yours,' I say. 'I was wondering if—'

'You painted that?' Charlie asks sceptically.

'Why so surprised?' she asks.

'He's not surprised,' I interrupt, trying to keep it light. 'He just doesn't like the competition.' Pointing to Charlie, I add, 'Guess who used to go to art school—and is still a wannabe musician?'

'Really?' Gillian asks. 'So we're both artists.'

'Yeah. We're both artists,' he says flatly. He quickly checks her fingers—if I had to guess, I'd bet he's looking to see if there's any paint trapped under her nails. Then he takes off for the door.

'Where're you going?' I call out.

'Back to work,' he tells me. 'I've got a closet to rummage through.'

AT MIDNIGHT, Maggie Caruso sat at her dining-room table with the newspaper spread out in front of her and a hot cup of tea by her side. For fifteen minutes, she didn't touch either. *Give it time*, she told herself. *Better to wait the full two hours*. That's how they passed it at nine o'clock, and at eleven. All it took was a little patience.

FIFTY MINUTES LATER, DeSanctis flicked on the thermal imager and aimed it up the block. Through the viewfinder, the world had a dark green tint. Street lamps and house lights glowed bright white. So did the hood of Joey's car, which was now impossible to miss even though it was tucked into an alley. If she wanted the heat to work, the engine had to be at least partially on.

'Guess who's still watching us?' DeSanctis asked.

'I don't wanna hear it,' Gallo rumbled. Pointing to the lap-top, he added, 'Meanwhile, look who's finally ready for bed . . .'

BATTLING EXHAUSTION, Maggie shuffled towards the kitchen and pretended to take a final gulp of tea. But as she tilted her head back, she reached into the pouch of her apron and felt around for her newest note. That was it. Time to get moving. She poured out the full mug of tea. But instead of marching off to her bedroom, she opened the kitchen window, leaned out towards the clothes line and tugged hand over fist to rein in the night's final load.

'CHECK IT OUT—you can see her arms.' DeSanctis flipped open the LCD screen on the side of the camera so Gallo could look. Sticking out of the green-tinted building were two glowing white arms.

'What's that stuff over here?' Gallo asked as he pointed to tiny white splotches on the rope of the clothes line.

'The residue from her touch,' DeSanctis explained. 'Every time she grabs the rope, it holds the warmth and gives us a thermal afterglow.'

Gallo studied the white spots on the glowing conveyor belt. As they scrolled away from Maggie, each spot faded and disappeared.

ONE BY ONE, Maggie inspected each piece of clothing on the line. Dry came in; wet stayed out. By the time she was done, the only thing left was the still damp white sheet. Keeping her head down, Maggie eyed the dark window across the alley. In the shadows, as before, Saundra Finkelstein nodded.

ON THE LCD SCREEN, Gallo and DeSanctis watched Maggie unclip the clothespegs, reach under the sheet and rotate it a half-turn. Her arms glowed faintly under the wet fabric. Replacing the pegs, she gave the rope a final tug and sent the sheet on its way. Once again, the thermal white splotches on the rope faded—but this time, something else remained. Just below the rope, where the peg hit the sheet, a white golfball-sized comet streaked across the alleyway. And disappeared.

'What the hell was that?' Gallo asked.

'What're you talking about?'

'On the sheet! Play that back!'

DeSanctis punched rewind. Onscreen, the picture scrolled in reverse, and Maggie's sheet zoomed back towards her window.

'Right there!' Gallo shouted. 'Hit play!'

The tape whirred back to normal speed. For the second time, Gallo and DeSanctis watched as Maggie readjusted the sheet. Her left hand clipped on the clothespeg. Her right was underneath, holding it all in place. In one quick movement, Maggie pulled her hand out and sent the sheet across the alley—and just like before, there was a fuzzy white dot right below the clothespeg.

'There!' Gallo said, pausing the picture. He pointed at the white dot. 'What could hold a heat signature for that long?'

'If she was hiding it in her hand . . . if her palms were sweaty . . . it could be anything—plastic . . . a piece of clothing . . . even some folded-up paper would—' DeSanctis stopped.

Gallo looked skyward. Across the alley, the window directly opposite Maggie's was black. Without a word, DeSanctis stopped the tape and raised the thermal imager. And as the dark green picture came into focus, there was something new inside the window—a faint, milky-grey silhouette of a woman watching the clothes line.

'*Son of a bitch!*' Gallo shouted, punching the roof of the car. 'Find the neighbour! I want to know who she is, and I want a list of every call in and out of that house in the last forty-eight hours!'

'*SON OF A BITCH!*' Gallo thundered as a high-pitched feedback screech squealed through Joey's receiver. Wincing from the sound, she turned the volume down. She looked up the block as Gallo screamed something at DeSanctis.

Gallo abruptly started the car. Tyres spun angrily against a patch of filthy snow. Finding traction, the car swerved wildly into the street. And as Joey watched the red brake lights turn the corner and disappear, she knew that it was just the start of an even longer night.

CHAPTER 8

'Welcome to Suckville—Population: Two,' Charlie says drily, knee-deep in the sea of cardboard file boxes.

'Can you please stop complaining and check that one over there?'

'I already checked it—it was *yet another* carton of thumbed-through sci-fi novels and outdated computer texts.'

It's been three hours since Charlie joined me in the Warehouse of Useless Garbage doubling as Duckworth's garage. In hour one, we were hopeful. By hour two, we got impatient. Now we're annoyed.

'What about the ones underneath?'

'That's it . . . I'm gone,' Charlie announces, flying towards the door and knocking over one of Gillian's oversized canvases.

'Charlie, wait up!' Chasing him into the living room, I spot Gillian, who's hunched over on her dad's wicker chair. As she looks up, her eyes are all red—like she's been crying.

Charlie blows right by her and disappears into the kitchen.

I can't help but stop. 'What's wrong?' I ask. 'Are you OK?'

She nods silently. In her hands she's holding a wooden picture frame with a Mickey Mouse painted in the bottom right corner. The picture inside is an old photo of an overweight man standing in a swimming pool, proudly showing off his little girl. He's got a crooked-but-beaming smile; she's got a floppy beach hat and bright pink bathing suit. Even the moleman had his day in the sun.

Kneeling down next to her, I do my best to get her attention. 'I'm sorry we're rummaging through his life like this . . .'

She stares at the photo, shaking her head. 'I know it sounds pathetic, but it makes me realise how little I knew him.' Her head stays low and her curly black hair cascades down the side of her neck.

'Gillian, if it makes you feel any better, we've got the exact same photo in our house—I haven't seen my dad in eight years.'

She looks up and our eyes connect. She wipes the tears away with the back of her hand. I reach out and palm her shoulder, but she's already turned away. She buries her face in her hands, and the tears start flowing. But eventually, as I'm learning, we all need to open up. Sagging sideways, she leans her head against my shoulder, wraps her arms round my neck and lets the rest out. With each breathless weep, she barely makes a noise, but I feel her tears soak my shirt. 'It's OK,' I tell her as her breathing slows. 'It's OK to miss him.'

Over her shoulder, I spy Charlie watching us from the kitchen. As Gillian's sobs subside, he circles back towards us in the room.

'Who's up for some TV?' Charlie interrupts. 'We can—' He stops and suddenly acts surprised. 'I'm sorry—I didn't mean to—'

'No, it's OK,' Gillian says, sitting up and pulling herself together.

What're you doing? I ask with a glance. I'm not sure if he's jealous but even I have to admit, she can use the distraction.

'C'mon,' Charlie adds, waving us over to the TV. 'No more heartache—time to relax with some mindless entertainment.' He cruises past us and springboards onto the couch. Gillian follows me to the living room, her fingers holding on to my hand.

'That's it—there's room for everyone—one big happy family,' Charlie teases as he grabs the remote. He clicks it at the TV, but nothing happens. Again, he clicks. Again, nothing. Flipping the remote over, Charlie presses his thumb against the back and shoves open the battery compartment. He looks up at Gillian. 'It's empty.'

'Oh, that's right,' she says. 'I meant to put some new ones in.'

She runs to the closet and returns with a handful of fresh double-As. I have already manually turned on the TV, but Charlie's focused on the remote. He slides the batteries in and gives it another shot. Nothing happens.

'Maybe it's broken.'

'In this house?' Gillian asks. 'Dad fixed everything.'

'Here, give it to me,' I say. Time for the trick I used to use on my old Walkman. Pulling the batteries out of the back, I bring the remote up to my lips and blow a quick puff of air into the empty battery area. To my surprise, I hear a fast, fluttering sound. Cramming two fingers into the battery compartment, I start feeling around for whatever made that noise. Nothing there.

Charlie's out of his seat, anxiously standing over me. 'Break it open,' he says, tossing me a nearby pencil.

I jam it into the battery area and pull hard on the lever. There's a loud crack and the entire back of the remote breaks off. Inside, tacked down by two thick staples, is a sheet of paper folded up so small and tight, it has the length and width of a flattened cigarette.

'What is it?' Charlie asks.

I wedge the staples out with the tip of the pencil. The folded-up paper slowly fans open. I unfold it in a blur of fingertips—and from inside, a glossy, much shorter piece of paper falls to the floor.

Charlie dives for it. Flipping it round, he reveals four photos—headshots. A salt-and-pepper-haired older man, next to a pale mid-forties banker type, next to a freckled woman with frizzy red hair, next to a tired-looking black man with a cleft chin. It's like one of those photo-booth strips, but running horizontally.

'What's yours say?' Charlie asks.

Gripping the legal-looking document, I skim: *Confidentiality . . . Limits on Disclosure . . . Shall not be limited to formulae, drawings, designs* . . . 'I may've never gone to law school, but after four years of dealing with paranoid rich people, I know an NDA when I see one.'

'A what?' Charlie asks.

'NDA—a nondisclosure agreement. You sign them during business deals so both sides'll keep their mouths shut. It's how you prevent a new idea from leaking out.' There's no mistaking the signature at the bottom. Martin Duckworth.

'I don't get it,' Gillian says. 'You think Dad invented something?'

'Oh, he definitely invented something,' I say. 'And from the looks of it, something big. Read the other signature on the contract.'

Charlie grabs my wrist to hold the paper steady. *Signed—Brandt T. Katkin—Chief Strategist, Five Points Capital*. 'Who's Katkin?'

'Forget Katkin—I'm talking about Five Points Capital. With a name like that and a letter like this, I'll bet you my boxers it's a VC.'

'VC?' Gillian asks.

'Venture capital,' I explain. 'They lend money to new companies . . . get entrepreneurs rolling by investing in their ideas. Anyway, when a VC firm signs an NDA we're talking pocketfuls of cash.'

'How do you know?' Charlie asks.

'VCs—they hate nondisclosures. When we took a client to

Deardorff Capital in New York last year, one of the partners said the only way they'd sign an NDA was if Bill Gates himself walked in and said, "I have a great idea—sign this and I'll tell you about it."'

'So the fact that Duckworth got them to sign . . .'

'. . . means that he's got a Bill Gates-sized idea,' I agree. Turning to Gillian, I ask, 'Do you have any clue what he was working on? What he might've been trying to sell?'

'No, I . . . I didn't know he was building anything. What makes you think he was selling it, anyway?'

'You don't go to a VC unless you need some cash.'

'So that's where he got the money?' Charlie asks. 'You think the idea was that good?'

'If they're giving him three million dollars,' Gillian adds, 'it's gotta be major good.'

Charlie wings me a look. *And if it's three hundred million—*

'What about the photos?' Gillian blurts out of nowhere.

'So they're not relatives or anything?' Charlie asks her.

'Never seen 'em before in my life.'

'They could be anyone. Maybe they were his contacts at the VC.'

'Or people he was working with,' Charlie adds.

'Or maybe they were the ones who killed him,' Gillian says. 'They could all be Secret Service . . . So what do we do now?'

'If Five Points Capital made that kind of investment in Duckworth,' I say, 'don't you think they'll want to meet his next of kin . . . ?'

'So you want to go down there?' Charlie asks.

'First thing tomorrow morning,' I say.

'YOU'RE NOT GOING to like it,' DeSanctis warned as he entered Gallo's office in the downtown Field Office of the Secret Service. It was almost two in the morning and the halls were dead-empty, but DeSanctis still shut the door. 'Her name's Saundra Finkelstein, fifty-seven years old. Tax returns say she's been renting there for twenty-four years—plenty of time to become best friends.'

'And the phone records?'

'On average, she spends at least fifteen minutes a day on the horn with Maggie. Since last night, though, not a single call.'

'What about long distance?'

'At one o'clock last night, she accepted her first-ever collect call—from a number identified as a payphone in Miami Airport.'

Gallo slammed the desk with his fist. '*If they're at Duckworth's—*'

'Believe me, I'm well aware of the consequences.'

'Have you looked into flights?'

'Two tickets. They're booking them as we speak.'

'There's nothing to find there,' Gallo insisted as he stood up.

'No one said there was.'

Gallo stormed towards the door. 'When did you say we leave?'

'Next flight out—six o'clock into Miami,' DeSanctis added, chasing behind him. 'We'll be standing on their necks by breakfast.'

SPEEDWALKING BACK to our apartment, Charlie loses himself under the palm trees. Every few steps, he checks anxiously over his shoulder.

'Who're you looking for?' I ask.

'I want to see if she's following,' he hisses.

'Who, Gillian? She already knows where we're staying. Why're you giving her such a hard time anyway?'

'You saw that layer of dust in her bedroom. She's been living there for a month and the place looks like she moved in last week.'

'Oh, so now she's working against us?' I ask.

'All I'm saying is, she's got some random clothes and a few rip-off paintings. Where's the rest of her life? Her furniture, her CDs?'

'I'm not saying she doesn't have her quirks—but that's what happens when you're dealing with an artist . . .'

'Do me a favour. Putting tracing paper on an old Mondrian does not an artist make.'

'Oh, and suddenly you're the authority on all things artistic? You're just mad because she's out-Charlie-ing you at your own game.'

'What're you talking about?'

'You saw how she lives. The fact that she's happy with the bare essentials, that she doesn't need to be in the race. Even when she came after us she doesn't get mad. She just kinda looks through you—like she's not afraid of anything.'

'Axe murderers also aren't afraid of anything.'

'Can you please give it a rest?' I beg as we turn onto our block. 'You're the one always saying I have no sense of adventure.'

'You can have her, Ollie. She's all yours. But just so you know, this is about one thing: divide and conquer. That's what she's gonna do.'

Checking the block one last time, Charlie pushes open the cheap metal gate and races through the courtyard that leads to our apartment. I turn the key and let us inside.

Charlie storms to the futon and hops into bed. Pulling the mangy fuzzy blanket we found in the closet over his head, he calls out, 'Divide and conquer—that's always how it works.'

I CAN'T SLEEP. Staring up at the jagged black fissure in our popcorn-stucco ceiling, I listen to Charlie's laboured breathing. When he was sick, it was much worse—a wet hacking wheeze that used to have me watching over him like a human heart monitor. It's a sound that'll forever haunt me, but as the minutes tick by and his breathing falls into its steady rhythm, I take comfort in the feeling that we're finally getting a break. Between the photos and the nondisclosure agreement and the leads at Five Points Capital, there's actually a pinhole at the end of the tunnel. And then, out of nowhere, it's stolen away by a slight tapping against the front window.

'Charlie, get up,' I whisper.

He doesn't budge.

'*Oliver*,' a voice comes from outside.

I jump out of bed, struggling to be silent.

'*Oliver, are you there?*' the voice asks.

That's not just any voice . . . that's a voice I know. Racing to the door, I ram my eye to the peephole, just to be safe.

'*Oliver, it's me. Open up . . .*'

I twist and unclick the locks. Cracking the door open, I peek out.

'I'm sorry—did I wake you?' Gillian asks with a soft grin.

'What're you doing here?' I whisper.

'I don't know. I just kept thinking about the remote . . . and the photos and . . . and there's no way I was falling asleep, so I figured—' She glances down at my boxers. I blush; she laughs.

'C'mon. Put on some clothes—I'll let you buy me coffee.'

Over her shoulder, I check the empty street. Even at this hour, it's not smart to be strolling in public. 'How 'bout a raincheck?'

Slinking back, she looks like a hurt puppy.

'It doesn't mean you have to go, though . . .' I offer.

She stops and quickly turns back. 'So you want me to stay?'

It's a tease, and we both know it. 'All I'm saying is, I have to be careful.'

'Oh, because of . . . I didn't think . . .' She stumbles in the sweetest way possible, and smiles. 'Of course I want you to be careful, Oliver.'

Suddenly it hits me that I never told her my real name was Oliver. She probably heard it from Charlie. He said my name at least a dozen times in the garage. 'Gillian . . . you said my real name—'

'In the house—your brother said it.'

'I figured . . . but—'

'God! If I thought you didn't trust me, I never would've come.'

I grab her shoulder. 'I trust you, Gillian.'

She shoots me a lasting glance, digesting each word.

'I'm serious,' I quickly add.

Her hand flies out like a dart, grabs me by the back of my neck and reels me in for a soft, smooth kiss.

AT THREE IN THE MORNING, her car blocking the fire hydrant in front of Maggie Caruso's building, Joey promised herself she wouldn't fall asleep. At ten to five, a sharp, shrill beep jolted her awake.

Blinking herself back to the waking world, she chased the sound down to the lit-up screen of her global positioning system. The bright blue triangle was once again moving across the digital map, straight down the West Side Highway. Pulling the screen onto her lap, she watched as Gallo's car weaved its way towards the tip of the city. At first she thought they were headed back to Brooklyn, but when they blew past the entrance to the bridge and shot up the FDR Drive, she felt a flame blaze at the back of her neck. *Aw, don't tell me they're . . .*

Joey cranked the ignition and took off. The most popular 5.00am destination in Queens is La Guardia Airport.

An hour and a half later, Joey was tearing into the USAir parking lot. She screeched into an open spot and cut the engine. Taking one last look at the blue triangle on the electronic screen, she hopped out and scanned the packed-to-capacity lot. There, close to the terminal, Gallo's navy Ford parked illegally in a 'handicapped' space.

Joey yanked her bags from the trunk. With the cellphone earpiece dangling from her ear, she ran towards the terminal. Shoving through the automatic doors, she flew up the escalator.

As she reached the top, her assistant's voice sang in her ear. 'According to USAir's records, Agents Gallo and DeSanctis were booked on the six twenty-seven flight to Miami.'

Joey went right for her watch: 6.31. 'Are they—?'

'Long gone,' Noreen said.

'When's the next—'

'Hour and a half. I already told them to book you a seat.'

Shaking her head, Joey checked the TV screen. *Miami—Flight 412—Departed.* 'How the hell did I miss them?'

'Don't wet your eyes,' Noreen said. 'All they have is a head start.'

'WHAT FLOOR?' Charlie asks early Thursday morning as we step into the elevator.

'Seven,' I say as he pushes the button. I straighten my tie; Charlie licks his hand and flattens his matted blond hair. If we're going to reprise our roles as bankers, we have to look the part. Next to us, Gillian smooths out her long flowered skirt and looks my way. I can't help letting my eyes linger on her legs—that is, until I notice Charlie watching me. I glance at the floor; he shakes his head.

The elevator jerks to a stop and the doors slip open. In the hallway, a silver and gold logo hangs on the wall. Shaped like a star, the silver letters across the bottom tell us we've reached our destination: Five Points Capital—where Duckworth made his deal.

Gillian glides out. Before I can follow, Charlie grabs me by the arm. 'You touched her cookies, didn't you?' he whispers.

'What're you talking about?' I ask, as I step out of the elevator.

'When was it? When you went to get the clothes this morning?'

Pulling out of his grip, I head for the glass doors of the reception area. Charlie is right behind me. I ring the bell.

A receptionist looks up and buzzes us in. Charlie is first in line, ambassador of smiles. Every bigshot needs an assistant. 'Hi, we called this morning,' he says. 'From Greene and Greene—I have Henry Lapidus here to see Mr Katkin.'

'Of course.' She nods at me. 'I'll page him for you, Mr Lapidus.'

You sure this is right? Charlie asks with a glance.

Trust me, I insist. Over the past four years, I've taken tons of clients on the venture capital roadshow. And even in Florida, it takes a big name to open a big door.

'Mr Lapidus, can you sign in for me?' the receptionist asks me. She points to a computer kiosk next to her desk. Onscreen, there's a blank for your name. I type in *Henry Lapidus* and hit enter. Behind the receptionist, a laser printer hums and spits out an ID sticker. *Henry Lapidus—Visitor*. But unlike a normal guest pass, the front of this one has a liquid, almost translucent quality to it. Underneath, if you angle it in the light, the word *Expired* appears in faint red letters.

'What's this?' I ask, rubbing my thumb against the pass.

'Aren't they wild?' the receptionist croons. 'After eight hours, the ink on the front dissolves and the *Expired* part becomes bright red.'

'You guys take security pretty seriously, don't you?' Charlie says.

'We don't have a choice,' the receptionist says with a laugh. 'I mean, considering who we're partners with . . .'

We stare at the woman. She stares right back. We're clueless.

'Oh, I'm sorry,' she adds, 'I thought you knew. It's in all our clippings . . .' She hands me a press kit in a forest-green folder.

I flip it open as Charlie and Gillian read over my shoulder. It's right there on the front page: *Welcome to Five Points Capital, the venture fund of the United States Secret Service.*

Behind us, a door swings open. 'Mr Lapidus?' a baritone voice asks. We turn round and a tall man with military shoulders and thick forearms extends a handshake. 'Brandt Katkin,' he introduces himself as he shakes each of our hands.

'Jeff Liszt,' I say, using another name from the bank. Katkin looks down at my nametag, which says *Lapidus*.

'Sorry . . .' Charlie jumps in, exactly how we practised. 'Mr Lapidus was running late, so we asked Mr Liszt to join us instead . . .'

'Of course,' Katkin says, too polished to show even a hint of annoyance. In the VC world of name-dropping and instant impressions, he's accustomed to the bait-and-switch. Leading us back to his office, he weaves through the corporate grey hallways.

'Has this always been a division of the Secret Service?' Charlie asks.

'I wouldn't call us a division,' Katkin clarifies as we make a sharp left into his office. 'It's more of a partnership.'

Gillian and I take the two seats in front of Katkin's enormous glass-top desk. Charlie steals a space on the contemporary black leather couch. In the corner, there's a framed certificate commemorating Katkin's appointment as a Special Agent in the Secret Service. Charlie is staring straight at it. *Partnership, my big fat behind*, he signals.

I nod in agreement. Secret Service is Secret Service. Still, Katkin doesn't seem to know us—which means, wherever they are, Gallo and DeSanctis are still keeping quiet. 'So how exactly does the fund work?' I stammer, trying not to panic.

'This is just the next step in R&D,' Katkin says. 'With technology whizzing along at lightspeed, government agencies couldn't keep up. As soon as we figured out one security system, another popped up. CIA . . . FBI . . . everyone was at least five years behind the private market. To close the gap, two years ago, we opened Five Points. Every new idea needs money, even the illegal ones. This way, we make it work in our favour. For example, if a guy invents a bullet that slices through Kevlar, instead of letting him go to the black market, we buy it ourselves, figure out what makes it tick and then outfit our agents with the appropriate countermeasures.'

'So the government keeps the profits?' I ask.

'What profits?' Katkin teases. 'We're a 501(c)(3). Nonprofit is our middle name. That way, the politicians are happy, competitors don't see us as a threat and we're still allowed to jump into the world of business. Welcome to the future. Government, Inc.'

'If you can't beat 'em . . .' Charlie begins.

'Eat 'em,' Katkin jokes. 'Now what can I help you with today?'

'It's about my dad,' Gillian says. 'Marty Duckworth . . .'

'Duckworth was your father?' Katkin asks, sounding amused. 'I really liked that guy. How's he doing these days?'

Gillian's gaze drops away. 'Actually, he passed away recently.'

'Oh, I'm sorry, I didn't realise . . .' Katkin offers. I watch closely for his reaction. Eyes wide. Chest sunk. Not shocked, but concerned.

'It's OK,' I say. 'As you might've guessed, we're representing Mr Duckworth's estate and thought there might be a few things you could help us with. You see, when we were going through his effects, we found this . . .' Reaching into my jacket pocket, I pull out the nondisclosure agreement and hand it to Katkin.

Katkin fights a grin. 'There it is—the one that got away . . .'

'So you remember dealing with him?' Charlie asks.

'How could I forget? He was a cold call. Just found our name in the phonebook and walked in. Lap-top under one hand, clipboard in the other. We sent an intern to talk to him. Ten minutes later, they took him to the commercialisation folks. Ten minutes after that, they brought him to me.' Waving the NDA in front of him, Katkin added, 'He downloaded this off some law firm's website. But he wouldn't show us how it worked until we signed it.'

'It was that good?'

'Y'know how many NDAs we signed last year?' Katkin asks. 'Two,' he answers. 'And the other one was for the guy from—' He cuts himself off. 'Let's just say . . . it's someone you've heard of.'

Charlie sits up straight, knowing we're close. 'So you signed it?'

'We signed. But after the first few appointments—I'm guessing it was about eight months ago—we never heard from him again.'

'Wha . . .?' Charlie and I say simultaneously.

'That's exactly what *we* thought. We were all set to go—we had our team—we even flew in our financial crimes expert from New York.'

'New York?' I ask.

'We actually have some friends in the New York office,' Charlie adds. 'What's his name?'

'Oh, he's one of our best,' Katkin says. 'His name's Jim Gallo.'

A sharp pain swoops in between my shoulders, like a vulture gnawing at the back of my neck.

'Jim Gallo isn't the guy we know . . .' Charlie says.

'So my dad took the idea with him when he left?' Gillian asks.

'Happens all the time,' Katkin answers. 'Entrepreneurs come in, they talk it up, and when a better offer gets slapped in front of them, we never hear from them again. And with a moneymaker like this—I just assumed he found a new partner and moved on.'

'See, that's what we're hoping you could help us with,' I interrupt. 'With the lack of documentation in Mr Duckworth's estate, we're having a hard time putting a valuation on his inventions . . .'

'We just want to know what he made,' Gillian jumps in.

'I'm sorry, I'm not permitted to give out that information.'

'But she's Mr Duckworth's only heir,' I insist.

'And that's a nondisclosure agreement,' Katkin shoots back.

'We're not asking for schematics . . .'

'No, you're asking me to violate a binding legal contract—and in the process, open our company up to a mess of liability.'

'Can't you tell us what it has to do with the photos?' Gillian pleads.

'These . . .' From my jacket pocket, I pull out the strip with the four side-by-side headshots. 'Do you know who they are?'

Katkin's face is blank. 'Never seen them before in my life.'

'So it doesn't have to do with the invention?'

'I already told you . . .'

'I know—but this is far more important than a dead man's gag order,' I push. It's one push too many.

Katkin stands and stares down at us. 'I think we're done here.'

'Please . . . you don't understand . . .' I beg.

'It was nice meeting all of you,' Katkin says coldly.

Hopping up, Charlie heads for the door. Gillian follows.

'Let's go,' Charlie calls.

'But it's extremely urgent that we—'

'*Oliver, let's go!*'

Katkin looks my way and the oxygen is sucked from the room. Crap. Fake names. I freeze. Gillian and Charlie just stand there.

Katkin drills us with a stare that's so bitter, it actually burns. 'Son, I don't know who you think you are, but let me give you a nugget of advice—you don't want to pick this fight.'

Charlie puts a hand on my shoulder and pulls me towards the door. In four seconds, we're gone.

'*WHAT DID HE MAKE?*' Charlie moans from the back seat of Gillian's vintage blue Beetle. 'Why'd you have to start blabbing like that?'

'*I* blabbed?' Gillian blasts as she stares him down through the rearview mirror. 'Who's this? *Oliver . . . Oliver— Oops, did I just get us escorted out of the building? I'm sorry—I wasn't thinking. In fact, I wasn't using a* single *brain cell.*'

'Can both of you please stop?' I beg, sitting shotgun as we ride back across the causeway. 'At least now we know what we're looking at.'

'So you think Gallo made Dad a better offer?' Gillian asks.

'You tell me,' I begin. 'Your dad scrounges around for VC money to help with his invention. He brings the idea to Five Points Capital. Gallo is brought in. Your dad suddenly changes his mind, rents a crappy place in Gallo's hometown, and falls off the face of the earth.'

'So Gallo was called into Five Points Capital to consult, but . . .'

'. . . when he saw the invention he realised he could take it to the black market and sell it on his own. He approaches Duckworth: *Why split it with the VC, when we can keep it for ourselves?*'

Charlie leans forward between the bucket seats. 'But if they were working together, why would Gallo turn on him?'

'Because keeping the profits for himself is better than splitting it in two: *Sure, Marty, we'll help you build the prototype . . . Yeah, Marty, it'll be better if you work directly with us . . . Thanks for the help, Marty, now we'll take your idea, stuff all our cash in an account with your name on it, and you can play fall guy*.'

'What about the money itself?' Charlie asks. 'Even if the theory's right, it doesn't tell us how they hid it in the bank.'

'That's why I think they had an inside man,' I say.

'Maybe that's who's in the photos—that's who helped Gallo hide it,' Gillian says.

'I don't know,' I say, grabbing the strip of photos from my jacket. 'The way that account was hidden . . . it takes a bigshot to pull that off.' I stare at the strip. 'I've never seen any of these people before.'

'I think they're people your dad trusted,' Charlie says. 'It's like the nondisclosure agreement—you don't safekeep things that'll get you in trouble—you keep what you want to protect.'

Gillian nods. She knows a good theory when she hears it. 'What if they're people who helped him with the original idea?'

'Or people he confided in,' Charlie suggests.

'What's that game company he worked at after Disney?' I ask.

'Neowerks—I think they're in Broward . . .'

'I saw the address on an old pay stub,' Charlie jumps in. 'In the filing cabinet.'

Gillian pulls a hard right down Tenth Street and lurches to a halt in front of her house.

'How far are we from Broward?' Charlie asks.

'Forty minutes at the most,' Gillian replies.

'I'll make some phone calls—set up an appointment,' I offer, kicking open the car door and helping Charlie squeeze out from the back. Gillian stays put. 'Aren't you coming?' I ask.

'I should check in, make sure I still have a job—I'll be back in ten minutes.' She tosses me the house keys and, with a wave, is gone.

Swiping the keys, Charlie charges up the path and bolts through the front door. Inside, he goes for the files; I head for the phone. But when we hear the door slam behind us, we spin round. That's when we notice all the shades are closed. The whole place is dark. And then . . . a lamp flicks on in the living room.

'Nice to see you, Oliver,' Gallo says from his seat on the sofa.

By the door, a shadow arches, pouncing towards us. Charlie tries to run, but an arm slices the air towards him. Gallo grabs me round the neck. And DeSanctis's fist collides with my brother's face.

'WELCOME TO MIAMI Airport—how can I help you?'

'Hi, I'm here to pick up a car,' Joey said to the blonde at the National car rental counter. 'It should be under the name Gallo.'

The woman typed it into the computer. 'Nothing under Gallo . . .'

'Actually, he probably put it under DeSanctis,' Joey added. Counters for other car companies stretched across the terminal, but Joey went straight for National. When it came to government discounts, there were only three companies the Secret Service travel office listed as 'preferred providers'. National was number one.

Squinting at her screen, the rental agent looked confused. 'I'm sorry . . . but it says here that someone already picked it up.'

'Oh, those enthusiastic *bastards*.' Joey laughed. 'I *knew* they'd jump on the early flight—anything to catch a bad guy.' Flipping open her wallet, she whispered, 'United States Secret Service,' and flashed a gold badge. Sure, she covered the words 'Fairfax County Police' with the tips of her fingers, but as Joey had learned over the years, a badge was more than a badge. Especially when it was her dad's. 'Can I borrow your phone?' she asked. 'I'll try their cell.'

Stretching the cord over the counter, the rental agent punched in the number Joey gave her. Through the receiver, Joey heard her own answering machine pick up. Suddenly serious, she looked up at the rental agent. 'All I'm getting is voicemail . . .'

'I-Is that bad?'

'Do you have any idea where they went?' Joey asked nervously.

'Actually, we're not supposed to—'

'They're my partners,' Joey pushed. 'It's an emergency.'

'They wanted directions to South Beach. That's what I gave them.'

'Anywhere in particular?'
'Tenth Street—they didn't give an address.'
'How fast can you get me a car?' Joey said, grabbing the map.

CHAPTER 9

'*Where is it?*' Gallo roars in my face, winding up for another blow. 'Tell us where it is, Oliver, and we're out of your life!'

It's a simple promise and an absolute lie. The only reason we're still breathing is because we have what they want.

'Don't tell 'em!' Charlie yells, blood dripping down his chin. DeSanctis cranks his arm back and ploughs Charlie in the ear.

'Hit him again and you'll get nothing!' I shout.

'You think we're *negotiating?*' Gallo barks, smashing me into the bookcase. I'm fighting to stay on my feet . . . but I can't get my balance—or the gun that's in the back of my trousers. He wraps his claws round my throat and pins me against the bookcase.

Over Gallo's shoulder, Charlie is on the ground, holding his ear. DeSanctis stands over him. And behind them all . . . I swear, something moves in the kitchen. Before I can react, Gillian tears into the room swinging the glass blender jar. There is a loud thunk as it ricochets against DeSanctis's skull. The impact sends a zigzagging fracture down the jar, even as it sends him staggering forward.

As Gallo turns to follow the sound, I grab a hardcover book from the shelf and crack him in the back of the head. It knocks him off-balance, which is all Gillian needs. She wheels the jar through the air and catches Gallo on the side of the head. There's a loud crash . . . and the glass shatters. In Gillian's hand, all that's left is the handle. On the carpet, Gallo is dazed, but not out.

'*Let's go!*' Gillian shouts as she grabs me by the hand. I go for Charlie. Gillian takes one arm, I take the other. We scoop him up by the armpits and pull him to his feet.

'You OK? Can you hear me?' I ask.

He nods. 'Get us out of here,' he demands.

Gillian leads the way to the bedrooms in the back. Where she snuck in. She's first, then Charlie, then me. But as I fly forward, something grabs me by the ankle. And twists hard. Pain shoots up my leg. I crash to the floor. Behind me, DeSanctis still grips my ankle. He's on his stomach, clawing his way closer. A trickle of blood drips from his hairline, down to his cheek.

I kick wildly, fighting to get free. I can't get him off. '*Charlie!*'

He's already there. My brother's shoe stomps down on DeSanctis's wrist. Howling in pain, DeSanctis lets go and looks up at Gillian.

'What're you—?'

Before DeSanctis can finish, Gillian lets loose with a whirlwind kick that crashes into the side of his head. His neck snaps to the side with a crack. It doesn't slow Gillian down. Lashing out, she kicks him again. And again.

'Enough,' Charlie says, pulling her back. '*Let's go!*' he shouts, reaching down and tugging me to my feet.

He rushes towards the back of the house. I follow. Behind me, Gillian has a hand on my shoulder. We cut through the bedroom, where the sliding glass door that leads to the back yard is wide open.

Bursting outside, we're on a concrete patio. Straight ahead, the wall's too high. On the left, the path runs through the neighbours' back yards—each patio connecting with the one next to it. Charlie is already at the end—leapfrogging off someone's rusted, sun-bleached lounge chair to help him over the wall.

'The car's this way,' Gillian says, yanking me to the right.

'Charlie, wait!' I shout, racing towards my brother. Gillian follows.

'C'mon!' Charlie yells, sliding over the wall.

'Just wait a—' It's too late. He's already gone.

Hopping on the lounge chair, I crane my neck over the wall. But just as I spot Charlie on the other side, a single shot explodes down the block. Two inches to my left, the top of the wall shatters in a violent burst, spraying concrete shards in every direction. Over the wall and down the street, Gallo limps as quick as he can round the corner, his gun aimed right at me.

'*Get down!*' Charlie screams.

A second shot rings out. I duck below the ledge completely off-balance and tumble from the lounge chair to the ground. Flat on my ass, I stare straight at the wall that separates me from my brother.

'Oliver?' Charlie calls.

'*Run!*' I shout back. 'Get out of there, Charlie! *Now!*'

I hear the rumbling of his shoes against the grass as he takes off.

Scrambling to my feet, I stare at the wall as if I could see through it. A third shot rings out. My heart contracts. Holding my breath, I shut my eyes, trying to hear footsteps. There's a muffled tapping in the distance. Please, God, let it be Charlie.

'We should get out of here,' Gillian insists.

'I'm not leaving him.'

'You go back up there, you might as well paint a target on your forehead. Charlie'll be fine—he's got ten times the speed of Gallo.'

'How far is your car?' I ask.

'Follow me.' She grabs my hand and we run back across the open patios to the far end of the back yard. As we reach the wall, it looks like a mirror image of the one Charlie went over—until I glance to my left and see the black metal gate cut into the wall.

Gillian yanks open the gate. It slams with a clang behind us and dumps us in the parking lot of a low-rise apartment complex. We make a left the instant we hit the street. 'Over here,' she says, hopping inside her blue Beetle, which is parked under a tree.

With a flick of her wrist, she starts the car. 'Which way?' she asks.

'Straight ahead. We'll find him.'

Tyres shriek, wheels kick in, and we buck back in our seats. We keep our heads low, just in case we spot Gallo. But as we reach the end of the block—the corner where Charlie was headed—there's no one in sight. Not Gallo . . . not Charlie . . . not anyone. In the distance, there's a faint howl of sirens. Gunshots bring police.

'Oliver, we really should . . .'

'Keep looking,' I insist, scouring every alley next to every pink house we pass. 'He's here somewhere.' But as the car crawls up the block, there's nothing but empty driveways, overgrown lawns and a few palm trees. Behind us, the sirens scream even louder.

Gillian stares in the rearview. She needs a decision. 'Oliver, please!'

Behind us, tyres screech round the corner.

'Go—get us out of here,' I finally give in.

She pumps the gas and the wheels search for traction. A quick right and an ignored speed limit turns the neighbourhood into a pink-and-green blur. Next to me, Gillian reaches out and cups her hand softly on the back of my neck. 'I'm sure he's OK,' she promises.

'Yeah,' I reply as South Beach—and my brother—fade behind us. 'I hope you're right.'

IF SHE'D BEEN ten minutes earlier, Joey would've seen the whole thing: the ruby-red lights of the police car, the uniformed cops as they ran out, even Gallo and DeSanctis as they gave their hastily prepared explanation: Yes, that was us; yes, they got away; no, we can handle it fine by ourselves, thanks all the same. But even with everyone gone, it was still impossible to miss the yellow and black police tape that covered Duckworth's front door.

Jumping out of the car, Joey headed straight for the door and knocked as hard as she could. 'It's me—anyone there?' she shouted, making sure she was alone.

A glance over her shoulder and a flick on the lock's pins did the rest. As the door swung open, she ducked under the police tape. Inside, the living room was wrecked. At the bottom of the bookcase was a stack of old *Wired* magazines. Joey grabbed the top one and scanned the subscription label. *Martin Duckworth*, she read. On a nearby shelf, she noticed a Mickey Mouse picture frame with a photo in it. Joey pulled out the photo and stuffed it in her bag.

Down low, glass shards sparkled against the pale carpet, which had a dark stain by the door. Up the hallway, the blood continued—tiny drops. The further she went, the smaller they got, eventually leading her towards the bedroom and the sliding glass door.

Grabbing her cellphone from her bag, she went for speed-dial.

'How was your flight? You get free peanuts?' Noreen answered.

'Martin Duckworth,' Joey said, staring at the magazine. 'According to Lapidus, he's living in New York—but I'll bet if we put him through the meat grinder, we'll get something more.'

'Give me five minutes. Anything else?'

'I need you to find their relatives,' Joey explained as she walked to the wall. 'Charlie and Oliver—anyone they might know in Florida.'

'C'mon, boss—you think I didn't do that the moment you stepped on a plane for Miami?'

'Can you send me the list?'

'There's only one name on it,' Noreen said. 'But I thought you said they were too smart to hide with relatives.'

'Not any more—from the look of things here, they had a little surprise visit from Gallo and DeSanctis.'

'You think they got nabbed?'

Still picturing the stain on the carpet, Joey walked outside and ran her fingertips against the missing chunk of the concrete wall. 'I can't speak for both of them, but something tells me at least one got away—and if he's on the run . . .'

'. . . he'll be desperate,' Noreen agreed. 'Give me ten minutes.'

'CAN I HELP YOU?' the security guard at the front desk asks. Welcome to the Wilshire Condominium in North Miami Beach, Florida.

'I'm here to see my grandma,' I say, using my nice-boy voice.

'Write your name,' he says, pointing to the sign-in book. Scribbling something illegible, I scan every signature above mine. None of them is Charlie's. Still, we went over this a dozen times. If we ever got lost, go to what's safe. Under *Resident*, I add the words 'Grandma Miller'.

'So you're Dotty's?' he asks, suddenly warming up.

'Y-Yeah, Dotty's,' I say, stepping into the lobby. Sure, it's a lie, but it's not like I'm a stranger. For almost fifteen years, my grandmother lived in this building. Three years ago, she died here—which is why I use the name of her old neighbour to get us in.

Dragging Gillian by the arm, I cut through the lobby and follow the exit signs down the hallway. Pool area, straight ahead. Mom used to send us here for some quality time with the *good* side of the family. Instead, it was two weeks of breath-holding contests and the Condo Commandos complaining we were diving too loud, whatever that meant. Even now, as I step outside, a brother and sister are having a splash fight. Next to the pool, a grandfather with a white shirt, white shorts and long black socks is studying a betting sheet from the race-track. 'I'm sorry to bother you, sir—but can I borrow your clubhouse key?' I ask him. 'My grandmother took ours upstairs.'

He looks up with black button eyes. 'Who you belong to?'

'Dotty Miller.'

He pulls the key from his pocket. 'Bring it right back,' he warns.

'Of course—right away.' I nod to Gillian, and she follows me round the tree-shaded footpath that hides the clubhouse. Once she's inside, I return the key to Mr Black Socks and head back to her.

Inside, the 'clubhouse' is as we left it years ago: two cruddy bath-rooms and a broken sauna. It's never been used. We could stay here for days and no one would interrupt.

'Oliver, are you sure he knows this place?' Gillian asks.

'We talked about it a thousand times. When we were little, we used to hide back here in the sauna. I'd jump inside and—'

'Maybe we should just go to the police,' she interrupts. 'I mean, finding out about my dad is one thing, but when they start shooting at us . . . I don't know . . . maybe it's time to wave the white flag.'

'I can't.'

'Sure you can. All you did was see a bank account on a computer screen—it's not like you did anything wrong . . .'

I turn away as the silence wipes the pulse from the air.

'What?' she asks. 'What are you not saying?'

I don't respond.

'Oliver, you can tell m—'

'We stole it,' I blurt. 'Your dad was dead . . . and the state couldn't find any relatives, so we thought it was a victimless—'

'You *stole* it?'

'I knew we shouldn't—I *told* Charlie that—but when I found out Lapidus was screwing me and Shep said we could pull it off . . . It all seemed to make sense back then. Next thing we knew, we were sitting with three hundred million of the Secret Service's money.'

Gillian coughs like she's about to choke. 'How many million?'

I look her dead in the eye. If she were working against us, there's no way she'd attack Gallo and DeSanctis. But she did. She saved us. It's time I returned the favour. 'Three hundred and thirteen.'

'You stole three hundred and thirteen million dollars?'

'Not on purpose—not that amount. Gillian, I know what you're thinking—I know it's your money—'

'It's not *my* money!'

'But your dad . . .'

'That money got him killed, Oliver! All it's good for now is lining his casket.' She looks up and her eyes are filled with tears. 'How could you not tell me?'

'What was I supposed to say? *Hi, I'm Oliver—I just stole three hundred and thirteen million dollars of your dad's money—want to come and get shot at?*'

'You could've told me last night . . .'

'I wanted to—I swear. I just . . . I knew it would hurt.'

'And you think this doesn't?'

'Gillian, I didn't want to lie—'

'It's not even about the lie,' she cuts me off. 'And it certainly isn't about some truckload of dirty cash. Don't you get it yet, Oliver?' she says angrily. 'I just want to know why they killed my dad!'

'WHAT'RE YOU DOING in there?' an elderly woman asked.

'Sorry—just searching for a lost sock,' Joey replied as she backed out of the laundry room. Turning round in the hallway to face the woman, Joey eyed the TRASH ROOM sign on the nearby metal door.

'Do you even live here?' the woman challenged with her plastic laundry basket and her gold-plated Medic-Alert bracelet.

'Absolutely,' Joey said, stepping round her and peeking into the trash room. No Oliver or Charlie. Rushing away from the woman, Joey pressed the button for the elevator, ran to the doors as they opened and quickly hopped inside. The doors slammed shut.

'Yessiree,' Noreen teased through the earpiece. 'You've once again outsmarted the ninety-year-old retirees in that hotbed of spydom—

the Wilshire Condominium and Communist Lodge.'

'What's your point?'

'All I'm saying is, I don't see the use in scouring some condo just because Charlie and Oliver's grandmother once lived there.'

'Noreen, when it comes to human behaviour, there's only one thing you can absolutely, unquestionably count on . . .'

'*Habit*,' Joey and Noreen said simultaneously

'Don't mock,' Joey warned as the elevator doors opened in the lobby. She followed the sign for the pool area and pushed her way outside. 'When we're in trouble, we run to what's familiar. And that's the most basic habit of all.' She eyed the old man by the swimming pool with the racing form and the black knee-grabbers. Strolling past the pool, Joey studied Oliver and Charlie's old playground. Two kids were chasing each other across the shuffleboard court. Beyond them, to her right, was the clubhouse, obscured by bushes and trees. Joey didn't hesitate. She threaded down the tree-lined path and approached the clubhouse door.

'Excuse me, ma'am . . .' a man's voice called out behind her.

Joey flipped round and faced a young man with bleached blond hair.

'I'm sorry to bother you,' Charlie said, using his hand to block the cut on his lip. 'But can I borrow your clubhouse key? My grandma took ours upstairs.'

CHARLIE STARED at the redhead, knowing something was up. Then he noticed the blood that was all over the back of his hand. Crap. His lip was still bleeding.

'You OK?' the woman asked.

'I'm fine,' he insisted. Realising he'd creeped her out, he forced a laugh. 'It was a bad chewing gum accident. Cherry Bubblicious—a poorly timed bite. Listen, if I can just get that key . . .'

'Of course, of course,' she said, diving in her bag. 'I have it right here . . . Let me just get it for you . . . Charlie.'

Shit. Her hand came out of her bag and she was holding a gun.

'Are you with Gallo?' Charlie asked, hands in the air.

'I swear to you, Charlie, I'm not Secret Service; I'm not law enforcement. All I care about is getting the money back and getting you home safe.' Reading the doubt on his face, she steadied her gun hand, slid her free hand back into her bag and whipped out a white business card, which she flashed like a badge.

Squinting, Charlie read the words *Jo Ann Lemont. Attorney at Law.*

Sheafe International. On the bottom right it said, *Virginia P.I. Licence 17-4127*. A lawyer *and* a private eye. As if one weren't bad enough.

Charlie prayed for a distraction, but they were too well hidden by the trees for anyone to notice. 'What do you want, lady?'

'Please,' she offered, 'call me Joey. Why don't you tell me what's really going on—maybe I can help.'

Charlie didn't answer.

'Believe me, it's not easy to toss your life in the garbage. I did the same thing when I dropped out of college—it took me three months before I realised I had to go back. I know what you're throwing away, Charlie. Forget the job and that other nonsense—there's your music, and your mom . . . and let's not forget your health—'

'We're not thieves,' he told her.

She arched an eyebrow.

'All I'm saying is, we didn't mean to hurt anyone.'

'What about Shep?' she challenged.

'Shep was my friend! You ask anyone at the bank.'

She studied his face, his hands, even his shoes. Charlie knew she was looking for the tell—trying to figure if it was a lie. Still, if she didn't believe him, they wouldn't be talking. 'OK, Charlie, so if you're innocent, who killed him?' she finally asked.

He expected her to lower the gun, but she didn't. 'Why don't you try turning your psych profiles on Gallo and DeSanctis?'

She didn't seem surprised as Charlie said the names. 'You have proof of that?' Joey asked.

'I know what I saw.'

'But do you have proof?'

'We're working on it,' he shot back. 'And while you're at it, you should take a look at Gillian as well.'

Her forehead crinkled. 'Gillian who?'

'Duckworth's daughter. It's her house now.'

Around the corner, there was a shuffling noise on the other side of the clubhouse. Joey assumed it was someone's grandmother, and lowered her gun out of sight. With one eye on Charlie, she stepped back, trying to peek round the edge of the building. But as she poked her head round the threshold, there was a familiar click. Joey's hands went towards the clouds. She took a step back from the corner, a small black gun pressed against the side of her head.

'I swear I'll use it,' Oliver promised as he turned the corner of the clubhouse. He pulled back on the hammer of Gallo's pistol. 'Now drop your gun and get the hell away from my brother.'

'OLIVER, THIS ISN'T the time to be stupid,' Joey warned.

'I'm serious—I'll use it,' Oliver said, his finger flickering against the trigger.

Joey watched the way his hands were shaking. Then she studied his eyes. Unwavering. Frozen and dark. He wasn't joking.

'Joey, what's happening?' Noreen begged through the earpiece. 'Is that them? You want me to call it in?'

'Don't do it . . .' Joey warned and Noreen stopped talking.

'Lose the gun!' Oliver demanded. 'Throw it on the roof.'

Joey lobbed her pistol up towards the edge of the roof.

A car horn beeped twice. Through an opening in the wooden fence that surrounded the pool area, Joey spotted Gillian's blue Beetle pull up to the swinging gate that led out to the parking lot.

Charlie started running. Oliver took another look at Joey. 'Stay the hell away from us,' he warned.

His gun was still on her as he ran backwards towards the car. And before Joey could react, the car door slammed, tyres spun, and Oliver, Charlie and Gillian were gone.

Joey took off for her own car, which was double-parked in front of the building. But as she turned the corner, she spotted the new flat tyres on her two rear wheels.

'Oh, screw me,' she mumbled to herself. 'Noreen, call triple-A.'

'You got it. By the way, did you know the offices of Duckworth's last job are only a few miles away?'

'Beautiful,' Joey said as she ran back to get her gun off the roof. 'And what about his daughter? Any gossip on her?'

'See, that's what doesn't make sense,' Noreen answered. 'I've been digging through birth certificates, driver's licences, even tax records of Duckworth's family and, according to everything I can find, Marty Duckworth doesn't have a daughter.'

FOR THE ENTIRE twenty minutes it takes to get from grandma's old condo to Broward Boulevard, no one—not me, not Charlie, not Gillian—says a single syllable.

From my jacket pocket, I pull out the strip of photos. If we don't figure out who the people are and how they knew Duckworth, this trip is about to get even more uncomfortable.

'There it is,' Gillian says, eventually breaking the silence as she turns into the parking lot of a glass-fronted, four-storey building with a purple and yellow sign above the front door that says it all: *Neowerks Software.*

'SO YOU'RE DUCKY's daughter?' a bushy-haired man with wire-rimmed glasses sings as he grabs Gillian in a both-hands handshake. Dressed in a blue, button-down shirt, wrinkle-free khakis and leather sandals with socks, he's what you get when you cross a fifty-year-old Palm Beach millionaire with a Berkeley teaching assistant. But he's also the only guy who came out to the lobby when we asked if we could speak to one of Duckworth's old colleagues. 'God, I didn't even realise he *had* a daughter . . . And you're friends as well?'

'Yeah,' I say extending a hand. 'Walter Harvey and this is Sonny Rollins,' I add, pointing to Charlie.

'Alec Truman,' he announces, clearly excited to introduce himself.

'Listen, Mr Truman,' Gillian jumps in. 'I appreciate you taking the time to come out and—'

'My honour . . . it's my honour,' he insists. 'We still miss him here. I'm just sorry I can't stay long—I'm right in the middle of this bug hunt, and—'

'Actually, we just had one question we were hoping you could help us with,' I interrupt. Reaching into my jacket pocket, I take out the horizontal photo strip. 'Do any of these faces look familiar to you?'

His face lights up like a kid eating crayons. 'I know *that one*,' Truman says, pointing to the salt-and-pepper-haired older man in the first photo. 'Arthur Stoughton. He used to be with us over at Imagineering—now he runs their Internet group.'

'So you were at Disney too?' Gillian asks.

'How'd you think I met your pop?' Truman says playfully. 'When your dad left and came here, I followed two years later.'

'And what about this guy Stoughton?' I ask, pointing to the picture. 'Did you guys all work together?'

'With Stoughton?' Truman laughs. 'We should be so lucky . . . No, he was the old VP of Imagineering. Even before he went to Disney.com, he didn't have time for grunts like us.'

'What about the other people in the photos?' Charlie leaps in.

Truman takes a long look. 'Sorry, they're strangers to me.'

Gillian's hand reaches out to hold his wrist. 'We found the photos in Dad's drawer . . .' Her voice cracks. 'And now that he's gone . . . we just want to know who they are . . . It's all we have.'

Truman can't help himself. 'If you wait out here, maybe I can take the photos inside and see if anyone knows the other three.'

'Perfect—that'd be perfect,' Gillian sings.

Holding the photos and promising to bring them right back, Truman heads for the main entrance behind the receptionist. There's a small TV screen built into the wall above a security keypad. As Truman approaches, the screen blinks on and nine blue square boxes appear like a telephone touchpad. But instead of numbers, each of the boxes fills with one human face. Even with Truman's shoulder blocking our view, we still see the reflection off the polished black walls.

Touching his pointer finger to the screen, Truman selects the face on the bottom right. The box lights up, the faces disappear and nine brand-new headshots take their place. Like he's entering the password on an alarm, Truman presses the touch-screen and selects the face of the Asian woman on the top left. Once again, the faces disappear; once again, nine new ones take their place.

'You guys really got the whole Buck Rogers thing going, don't you?' Charlie says.

'This?' Truman laughs, motioning to the screen. 'You'll see Passfaces everywhere in the next few years.'

'Passfaces?'

'Ever forget your PIN code at the ATM?' he asks. 'Not any more. There's a reason people don't forget a face—it's embedded in us at birth. It lets us know Mommy and Daddy, and friends we haven't seen for over a dozen years. Now, instead of numbers, they give you random strangers' faces. Combine that with a graphical overlay, and you've got the one password that cuts across every age, language and educational level. Let's see your PIN code do that.'

Tapping the centre square, Truman selects one last face. The box with a blonde woman blinks on and off. Magnetic locks hum, the door clicks open and Truman heads for the back with our pho—

A rush of adrenaline flushes my face. I don't believe it. That's it.

'Did you say Stoughton still works at Disney.com?' I call out.

'I think so,' Truman says. 'You may want to check the web site, though.' The door slams shut and Truman disappears.

Charlie's still lost, but the longer I eye the touch-screen . . .

'Sombitch,' Charlie mutters.

Gillian's mouth drops open. 'You think that's—?'

'Abso-friggin-lutely,' Charlie whispers.

All this time, we've been staring at the inkblot upside-down. We thought the key was to figure out the faces; but now . . . it's clear that the faces are the key. Literally.

Charlie's bouncing on the balls of his feet. *Let's go*, he nods.

As soon as Truman brings back the photos, I nod back. 'I'm sorry to interrupt,' I say to the receptionist as she looks up from a magazine. 'But do you have any idea where we can get some Internet access?'

CHAPTER 10

There are thirty computers on the fifth floor of the Broward County Library. All we need is one and some Internet access.

'Anyone mind if I type?' Charlie asks, sliding his chair up to the keyboard. Gillian and I scoot our chairs next to his.

'Go to www.disney.com,' Gillian says.

'Really? I wasn't sure,' he says sarcastically. He types the address. The computer chugs to the front page of the Disney web site.

Scrolling down, there are three buttons on the Disney Directory: *Entertainment*, *Parks & Resorts* and *Inside the Company*. Charlie hits *Inside the Company*, then clicks the button for *Disney Online.*

As the newest page fills in, there's a box marked *Search*. Charlie types *Arthur Stoughton* into the box and hits enter.

Seconds pass and all three of us glance around, making sure no one's watching.

```
Results for 'Arthur Stoughton': 139 documents
1. Executive Bio for Arthur Stoughton
2. Executive Biographies for Disney.com
```

The list goes on. Charlie clicks on *Executive Bio* and the computer pulls up Stoughton's résumé. Next to it is the official corporate head-shot—identical to the one on the photo strip. Arthur Stoughton. Salt-and-pepper hair, fancy suit, Disney smile.

'Executive vice president and managing director of Disney Online,' Charlie reads but goes straight for the photo.

'Press it,' I agree as he slides the cursor over Stoughton's face. But as he clicks on the photo, nothing happens. He tries again. Still nothing. Knowing we need more faces, he clicks back one screen and hits the button for *Executive Biographies for Disney.com*. Once again, the computer pulls up the same photo of Stoughton. Damn.

'What do we do now?' he asks.

'Scroll down,' Gillian insists. She taps her fingernail against the bottom of the screen, pointing at what looks like the top of another photo. Stoughton's not alone. As Charlie scrolls down the screen, a pyramid of pictures rolls into place. It's the full organisational chart for Disney.com, with Arthur Stoughton in the top spot and the rest spread out below. The pyramid expands to a total of about two dozen: vice presidents and other associates in Marketing, Entertainment, and Lifestyles Content Development, whatever that is.

'There's photo number two,' I blurt. 'Banker guy.'

Sure enough, as I hand Duckworth's photo strip to Charlie, he matches it up with the picture onscreen. There's the second guy . . .

'There's the third,' Gillian points out, pecking her fingernail against the company photo of the frizzy redhead. But none of us sees photo number four: the black man with the cleft chin.

Charlie heads back to the top. Moving the cursor onto Stoughton's photo, he clicks the face. The border of the box moves slightly.

I shoot out of my seat. 'Did that just—?'

'Don't say it,' he warns. 'No jinxes.' He puts the cursor on the pale banker and presses the button. Onscreen, the box once again flinches. Staying with the order on the photo-strip, he clicks on the frizzy redhead. The box blinks and the screen flickers and goes black, like it's clicking to another web page. Then the screen once again hiccups . . . and the Seven Dwarfs appear in front of us. Doc, Sneezy, Grumpy—they're all there—each one standing over a different button, from *Community* to *Library.*

Gillian and Charlie scour the page. I go for the web address at the top of the screen. There's no *www*. Instead, the prefix is *dis-web1*.

'Any idea what we're looking at?' Charlie asks.

'I think we're on their Intranet,' I say. 'Disney's internal network.'

'So what happened to the web site?'

'Forget the web site—that's for the public,' I tell him. 'From here on, we're snooping in the private network for Disney employees.'

'Welcome Cast Members!' it says towards the top of the screen.

'What about the guy with the cleft chin?' Gillian asks.

Charlie raps a knuckle against the screen. There's a red button at the bottom: *Company Directory*. 'If we're looking for employees . . .'

'Reel it in,' Gillian sings.

Another mouse-click takes us to a place marked *Employee Locator*. From there, a new screen pops up and we're staring at dozens of faces. CEO . . . Board of Directors . . . Executive Vice Presidents . . . the list keeps going—tons of photos under each category heading.

'There's gotta be two thousand photos here,' Gillian says.

'Didn't your dad ever do anything easy?' Charlie asks.

'Go to *Imagineering*,' Gillian suggests.

Charlie scrolls as quickly as he can. Imagineers: at the top, the VP of Imagineering; underneath, his first lieutenant; and below them . . .

Marcus Dayal, a black man with an unmistakable cleft chin.

Moving the cursor over Marcus's digital photo, Charlie clicks it. The screen fades to black. Then cascades of images appear, and just as quickly vanish. Web page after web page opens at whirlwind speed, their words and logos fading immediately after they appear: *Team Disney Online . . . Company Directory . . . Employee Locator*— the cursor's moving and clicking in every direction, like it's surfing through the site on fast-forward. The images fly at us, faster and faster, deeper into the website and further down the wormhole. The pages are skimming past us at such high speeds that they merge in a dark purple blur. I'm almost dizzy from staring at it.

And then the brakes kick in. A single, final image slaps the screen. The midnight blue Greene & Greene logo on the top left. The *Est. 1870* sign on the top right. 'A bank statement?' Charlie asks.

I nod. Except for the logo, it doesn't look any different from the monthly statement at any bank: deposits, withdrawals, account number . . . The only difference is the name of the account holder.

'Martin Duckworth,' Charlie reads from the screen.

'This is Dad's account?' Gillian asks.

'Account number 72741342388,' I read out loud. 'This is definitely his—the same as the original one we looked at,' I tell Gillian.

Gillian's eyes are now glued to the screen . . . and to the box labelled *Account Balance:* $4,769,277.44. 'Four million?' she asks, confused. 'I thought you said the account was empty?'

'It's supposed to be,' I insist. She thinks I'm lying. 'I'm telling you, when I called from the bus, they said the balance was zer—'

There's an audible click and all three of us turn to the monitor.

'What was . . . ?'

'There,' I say. I point to *Account Balance: $4,832,949.55*.

None of us says a word.

Click. *Account Balance: $4,925,204.29.*

Click. *Account Balance: $5,012,746.41.*

I shove Charlie out of his seat. Moving the cursor up towards the *Deposits* section, I study the three newest entries to the account:

$63,672.11—wire transfer from Account 225751116.

$92,254.74—wire transfer from Account 11000571210.

$87,542.12—internal transfer from Account 9008410321.

I click on the box marked *Deposits*. A smaller window opens and I'm staring at Duckworth's full account history. 'How the hell did he . . .? It's not possible . . .' I scroll down the digital pages of the account. Deposit after deposit. They don't seem to stop.

'Just say it!' Charlie begs.

'Check out the deposits,' I say. 'Sixty-three thousand . . . ninety-two thousand . . . eighty-seven thousand . . . See the trend? Duckworth's account has over two million dollars moving in every day—but there's not a single deposit over one hundred thousand dollars. One hundred thousand is the threshold where the bank's automatic auditing system kicks in, which means—'

'Anything under a hundred grand doesn't get audited,' Gillian says.

'That's the game,' I reply. 'It's called smurfing—you pick amounts small enough to squeeze under the monitoring threshold. People do it all the time. It's the number one way to keep it below the radar.'

'Keep *what* below the radar?'

I turn back to the screen. 'That's what we're about to find out.'

STUCK IN TRAFFIC on Broward Boulevard, Joey fished through her bag and pulled out the photograph. At first glance, it was Dad and daughter—Duckworth and Gillian, happy as could be. But now that she had it in the light—now that she knew . . .

Holding the photo up close, she didn't know how she missed it before. It wasn't just the bad proportions—even the shadows were skewed. Duckworth had the shade on the left side of his face; the little girl had it on the right.

Joey pumped the gas, and the car flew towards the offices for Neowerks.

'SEE THIS DEPOSIT? The eighty-seven thousand?' I ask, pointing to the most recent addition to Duckworth's account. 'That's from Sylvia Rosenbaum's account. But for as long as I can remember, she's had it set up as a trust with specific beneficiaries.'

'Which means?' Gillian asks.

'Which means once every quarter, the computer automatically makes two internal transfers: a quarter-million-dollar transfer to her son and a quarter-million-dollar transfer to her daughter.'

'So why is this wealthy old woman transferring money to my dad?'

'That's just it,' I say. 'Besides her family and the once-a-year payment to her advisers, Sylvia Rosenbaum doesn't transfer money to *anyone*. But here . . .' I scroll up through Duckworth's records and point to one of the first deposits—another $80,000 transfer from Sylvia's account. This one's dated June. Six months ago. 'See, this shouldn't be here either,' I explain.

'Can you please slow down a second? Whattya mean, *it shouldn't be here*?' Charlie asks. 'How could you possibly know?'

'Because *I'm* the one who handles her account,' I say. 'I've been checking this woman's statements since the first day I started at the bank. And when I checked it last month—I'm telling you—these transfers to Duckworth weren't there.'

'You sure you didn't just miss them?' Gillian asks.

'That's what I was wondering when I first saw it,' I admit. 'But then I saw this one . . .' I highlight another internal transfer that recently came into Duckworth's account: $82,624.00 transferred from Account 23274990007.

'Double-o-seven,' Charlie blurts, reading the last three digits.

'That's the one,' I shoot back. Seeing that Gillian's lost, I explain, 'Double-o-seven belongs to Tanner Drew.'

'*The* Tanner Drew?'

'The man himself—newest member of the Forbes 400. Anyway, last week, he threatened our lives until we transferred forty million dollars into one of his other accounts. All of that happened on Friday at exactly three fifty-nine pm. Now check out the time that Tanner Drew made this transfer to Duckworth . . .'

Gillian and Charlie lean towards the screen. Friday—December 13—3:59:47pm.

'I don't get it,' Charlie says. 'We were the only people accessing the account. How could he be transferring his cash to Duckworth?'

'I *know* he didn't. Once we transferred the money, I checked Tanner Drew's account. The last transfer was the forty mil.'

'Then where did this eighty-two thousand come from?' he asks.

'That's what I'm trying to figure out. But whatever hat Duckworth pulled it out of, it's clear that he had his hand in almost everyone else's business.' I point to all the different account numbers listed under *Deposits*. 'Every one of them is a client of the bank.'

'So Dad was getting cash from all of them?' Gillian asks.

'That's what it looks like,' I say. 'And the money never stopped flowing. But when you look at what he did in the trust account and with Tanner Drew, it's like the transfers shouldn't exist. Forget what it says here. On the bank's system, not a single dollar left any of these accounts. It's almost like this ticking program is convincing the computer to see what's not really—' My chest tightens and I freeze.

'What? What's wrong?' Gillian asks.

'Oh, crap . . .' I point to the screen. 'That's what he invented. It's like a funhouse mirror—it shows you a reality that's not really there.'

'What're you talking about?'

'That's what the Service wanted to invest in . . . and that's what Gallo wanted for himself. The next step in financial crime. Virtual counterfeiting. Why steal money when you can just create it?'

'What do you mean, *create it*?' my brother asks.

'Electronically make it. Convince the computer it exists. Six days ago, Martin Duckworth had three million in his account. Three days ago, the computer said it was three hundred and thirteen million. But when you look at these records, it's clear that didn't happen overnight. These transactions go back six months. Hundreds of deposits. It's like keeping two sets of books. The regular system always said he had three million, but below the surface, his little invention was quietly creating the full three hundred. Then, when the gold-plated nest egg got big enough—wham!—they went to grab it. But we nabbed it first—and as it was sent on its way, the second set of books merged with the first, and every one of his fake deposits now somehow correlated with a real transaction at the bank.'

'Maybe that's how the program works,' Charlie jumps in. 'Like the forty million we transferred to Tanner Drew—it waits for a real transaction to take place, then takes a random amount that's under the audit criteria. By the end, you've got a whole new reality.'

'It's the same thing happening now,' I agree. 'The bank thinks Duckworth's account is empty, but according to this, there's a new five million in there. The crazy thing is, none of the people he took it from is missing any cash. The only proof of what actually happened is right here,' I say, tapping the screen.

Click. *Account Balance: $5,104,221.60.*

The elevator pings behind us. We've been here too long. 'We should print this out and get out of here,' I say.

There's a printer next to the computer. I flip a switch and it grumbles to life. Grabbing the keyboard, Charlie hits *Print*. On screen, a dialogue box pops up: *Please insert copy-card.* At the base of the printer is a card that says: *All copies fifteen cents per page.*

A few computers down, a teenage boy has a copy-card sitting on his desk. 'Hey, young sir,' Charlie calls out. 'I'll give you ten bucks for your card.' The kid slides the card; I pull out a ten.

As I get up to make the trade, Charlie jumps back in the driver's seat. Leaning over his shoulder, I stuff the card into the small machine that's attached to the printer and wait as it whirs into place.

Charlie once again hits *Print*. Like before, a box pops up, but this one's different. The font and type size match the ones on

Duckworth's bank statement: *Warning—To print this document, please enter password.*

'Ask the lady at the reference desk,' Gillian says.

'I don't think this is from the library,' I say, leaning in over Charlie's shoulder. 'This may be a Duckworth precaution.'

'What're you talking about?'

'If you were hiding the smoking gun in the centre of one of the world's most popular websites—wouldn't you bury a couple of land mines just to buy yourself some safety?'

'Wait, so now you think it's a trap?' Gillian asks.

'All I'm saying is we should pick the right password,' I tell her matter-of-factly. 'Try putting in *Duckworth*.'

He hammers the word *Duckworth* on the keyboard and hits *Enter*.

Failure to recognise password—Please reenter.

Crap. If this is like the bank, we've only got two more chances.

'What about *Arthur Stoughton*?' Charlie adds, using the first name from the photos.

As Gillian and I nod, he types *Arthur Stoughton* and smacks the *Enter* key.

Failure to recognise password—Please reenter.

'Try *Gillian*,' I blurt, my voice and confidence already wavering.

Charlie studies Gillian's eyes, searching for the lie. It never comes.

'Try it,' I say.

Charlie types in the word *Gillian* . . . and stops. I reach over and pound the *Enter* key myself.

All three of us squint at the screen, only to see Duckworth's account slowly fade to black. We just jumped on the land mines.

'Charlie, get the web address . . . !' I shout.

Our eyes lock on the address at the top of the screen. I take the first half; he takes the second.

The screen blinks off and a new image clicks into place. It's the Seven Dwarfs, and a red button marked *Company Directory*. Back at the beginning. But at least we're still in the internal employee site.

Charlie anxiously clicks the button for *Directory*. Hundreds of company photos appear on screen. Like before, he scrolls down to the *Imagineering* section. Like before, he finds the black man with the cleft chin. And like before, he clicks on his face. But this time, nothing happens. The photo doesn't even move. 'Ollie—'

'Put in the address.'

Frantically passing me the keyboard, Charlie ducks out of the way as I type in the first half of the memorised address. Then he does his.

The instant he hits *Return*, the screen hiccups. But when the new page appears, the only thing on screen is a plain white background.

Crossing past my brother, I plough towards the nearest computer. Within seconds, I'm at the home page of Disney.com. 'All we gotta do is start over,' I say, clicking through the executive biographies.

'Ollie, it's gone,' Charlie says. 'There's no way you'll find it.'

'Just one more page.' I find the corporate pyramid, and make a beeline for the photo of Arthur Stoughton. I slide the cursor into place, and click. The photo doesn't move. I scroll down to the pale banker. Then I move to the redhead. Nothing happens.

Charlie climbs out of his seat and puts a hand on my shoulder.

I gaze at the screen, hunched over in my chair. Five minutes ago, we had everything that Duckworth had created. Right now—we've got nothing. No bank logo. No hidden account. And no proof.

'DISNEY WORLD reservations—this is Noah. How can I help you?'

'Hi, I'm looking for Information Services,' I say to the over-peppy voice on the other line as I watch Charlie squint in the Florida sun.

'Let me connect you with the switchboard—they'll transfer you from there,' Noah says.

'Thanks,' I tell him as I give the thumbs-up to Charlie and Gillian. Crowded round me by the payphone across the street from the library, they're unconvinced I can pull it off. Still, big companies are big companies. By going through the switchboard, it's now an internal Disney call. We lost our proof once. I'm not losing it again.

'This is Erinn—how may I help you?' the switchboard operator asks.

'Erinn, I'm looking for the IS group that handles the Intranet for Disney cast members.'

'Sir, I'm going to put you through to Steven in the Support Centre,' she announces. 'Extension 2538 if you get disconnected.'

'This is Steven,' a deep voice answers. He sounds young. Perfect.

'*Please tell me I have the right place*,' I beg in his ear.

'I-I'm sorry . . . can I help you?' he asks.

'Is this Matthew?' I say, pouring on the panic.

'No, it's Steven.'

'Steven who?'

'Steven Balizer. In the Support Centre.'

'It doesn't make any sense,' I say. 'Matthew said it'd be on there, but when I went to pull it off, the whole presentation was gone.'

'What presentation?'

'I'm dead . . .' I tell him. 'They'll eat me as an appetiser . . .'

'What presentation?' he repeats, already swinging to my aid. It's Disney training. He can't help himself.

'You don't understand,' I say. 'I've got fifteen people sitting in a conference room, waiting for their first look at our new online subscription service. But when I go to download it off our Intranet, the whole thing is gone. Zip. Nothing. It's not there! Now everyone's looking at me—the lawyers, the creatives, the finance boys . . .'

'Listen, you have to calm down—'

'. . . and Arthur Stoughton, who's sitting red-faced at the head of the table.' All it takes is a single drop of the boss's name. That one I learned from Tanner Drew.

'You said it was on the Intranet?' Steven asks. 'Any idea where?'

I read off the exact address where Duckworth's account was stored. I can hear young Steven jackhammering away at his keyboard. It takes an underling to know one—we're all in this together. 'I'm sorry,' he eventually stammers. 'It's no longer there.'

'Don't say that!' I plead. 'It has to be! I just saw it! This is Stoughton we're talking about! If I don't get his presentation up there . . .' I breathe heavy through my nose, trying to sound like I'm fighting tears. 'There's gotta be some way to get it back. Where do you keep the back-ups?' It's a bluff, but not a risky one. The bank's computer systems run an automatic hourly back-up to protect it from things like viruses and power failures. Then we store the copy somewhere else, for safety purposes. A company the size of Disney has to do the same.

'The DISC building's where they keep all the long-term stuff.'

'Forget long-term—I need what was there three hours ago!'

'The only thing I can think of are the data tapes in DACS. They make a copy every night.'

'And where's this place DACS?'

'In the tunnels.'

'The tunnels?' I ask.

'Y'know, *the tunnels*,' he says, almost surprised. 'The ones below the Magic Kingd—' He stops and there's a pause. 'What department did you say you worked in?' he finally asks.

That's my cue. Abandon ship. I slam the phone in its cradle. 'Let's get out of here,' I say.

'Where to?' Gillian asks.

'Is it far?' Charlie adds.

'That depends how fast we drive,' I reply as I run towards the car. 'How long does it take to get to Disney World?'

'*WHAT?*' GALLO ASKED. Pinching the cellphone between his shoulder and ear, he and DeSanctis raced up I-95. 'Are you sure?'

'Why would I lie?' his associate asked on the other line.

'You really want me to answer that?'

'Listen, I already said I was sorry.'

'Don't bullshit me with sorry,' Gallo hammered. 'Did you really think you could just sneak in without us getting a good look?'

'I wasn't sneaking anywhere. We were just reacting as fast as we could. Once I got in, you were already gone.'

'He still should've dropped word with me—especially when he's just sitting on his ass in New York.'

'No, no, no—not any morc. He flew in first thing this morning.'

'Really?' Gallo asked. 'So he's close?'

'Close as he can get. But if it makes you feel any better, next time we'll send a Hallmark.'

'Actually, you should send it to DeSanctis. He's the one that got gashed in the head.'

'Yeah . . . sorry about that . . .'

'Sure you are,' Gallo said coldly. Turning towards DeSanctis, he pointed to the sign for the Florida Turnpike.

'Listen, I gotta run. I'm in demand these days.'

'So you're sure they're going to Disney World?' Gallo asked.

'That's where the back-up copies are,' she replied. 'The one remaining place where Charlie and Oliver can prove what happened.'

'I still don't see why we don't clip their necks now and save ourselves the headache.'

'Because contrary to what the macho portion of your brain says, torturing them isn't the way to get your hands on the money.'

'And your way is?'

'We'll find out soon enough,' Gillian said.

'YOU SURE WE SHOULDN'T rent a minivan or something more Disney-ish?' Charlie asks as he takes a full whiff of the gas station. He's in the back seat, calling the questions out of the driver's side window. I'm squeezing the nozzle and pumping the car full of gas.

'And how do you plan on renting this van? With what credit card?' I ask as the gas nozzle clicks, telling us the tank is full.

'We ready?' Gillian asks, turning the corner and returning from the minimart bathroom. I nod as I slap the gas tank shut. Gillian hops in the driver's seat and readjusts the rearview. She glances at Charlie in the mirror, but when he catches her eye she looks away, hits the gas, and sends us whipping back in our seats.

According to the guy in the gas station, it's a three-hour drive to Orlando. If we're fast, we'll be there before dark.

Fourteen miles later, we're at a dead stop in traffic.

'This is ridiculous,' I complain as we inch towards the Cypress Creek toll both. 'They've got two hundred cars and four open toll lanes.'

'Welcome to Florida math,' Gillian replies. Swerving to the left, she angles for the one lane that's moving. It's only as we roll towards the shadow of the toll booth that I notice our speed. We're about to blow through the toll booth at thirty miles an hour. 'Gillian . . .'

'Relax, it's SunPass,' she says, thumbing over her shoulder and motioning towards the bar-code sticker on her left rear window.

Charlie stares out of the windshield; I look up to follow. The sign above the toll says *SunPass Only*. Damn.

'Don't go through . . . !' Charlie shouts. It's already too late.

We glide through the toll booth and a digital scanner focuses coldly on the car. 'Dammit!' I shout, pounding the dashboard. 'Do you have any idea how stupid that was?'

'What's wrong? It's just SunPass . . .'

'. . . which uses the same technology as a supermarket scanner!' I blast. 'Don't you know how easy it is for them to trace this stuff?'

'Oliver, I'm really sorry,' Gillian says, grabbing my hand. 'I was only trying to help.' Which is why, as Gillian's fingers braid between mine, I don't hold her hand, but I also don't pull away.

'I'M SORRY I COULDN'T be more helpful,' Truman said as he escorted Joey back into the main lobby of Neowerks.

'You've been great,' Joey said, tapping her notepad against the palm of her hand. On the top sheet, she had written *Walter Harvey* and *Sonny Rollins*—Oliver's and Charlie's fake names. 'So after you spoke to your co-workers, you could still only identify one of the photos?'

'Arthur Stoughton,' Truman agreed. 'It was nice meeting you, Ms Lemont.' He shook hands and scurried back to his office.

As the door shut behind him, Joey went straight for the receptionist. 'Can I ask you a question?' From her bag, she pulled out photos of Charlie and Oliver. She slid them onto the desk, then placed her dad's badge next to them.

'You know they have different colour hair, right?' the receptionist asked, staring at the photos.

'We know,' Joey offered. 'We're trying to figure out where they went from here.'

'You mean *after* the library?'

'Exactly—*after* the library,' Joey replied, nodding like she knew it was coming. 'Which reminds me—what library was that again . . . ?'

HEARING THE FAMILIAR beep as he pulled back onto the Florida Turnpike, he flipped his cellphone open and saw the words *New Message* on the digital screen. He pushed a button on the phone's keypad and waited for the message to play.

'Where are you? Why aren't you picking up?' a female voice asked. The man grinned as soon as he heard Gillian. 'I just spoke with Gallo,' she explained. 'He was happy to hear about Disney, but he's definitely getting suspicious. The man's no moron. Whatever you told him at the start, he sees the chessboard moving. Anyway, I know you wanted to throw him and DeSanctis a bone, but from where I'm standing, it's two against one. So if you really plan on pulling this off, it's time to get your ass up here and help me out. OK? OK.'

He hit delete, slapped the phone shut and put his foot on the gas. He'd tried to stay away as long as he could, but like he always said back at the bank, some things required a personal touch.

'WHATTYA WANT?' Gallo asked as he picked up his cellphone.

'Agent Gallo, this is Officer Jim Evans with the Florida Highway Patrol—we just got a hit on that blue Volkswagen you were looking for, registered to a Martin Duckworth. We put the name in SunPass, just to take a look. Apparently, about forty minutes ago, a pass registered to a Martin Duckworth went through at Cypress Creek.'

'Which direction?'

'Headed north,' Evans said. 'If you want, I can send a few cars—'

'Don't touch 'em!' Gallo shouted. 'Understand? They're confidential informants. I want 'em left alone!'

'Do what you want,' Evans blasted. 'Just remember you're the ones who contacted us.' With a click, the line went dead.

Next to Gallo, DeSanctis shook his head. 'I still don't think you should've called that one in.'

'It was worth it.'

'Why? Just to confirm she was going north?'

'No, to confirm she wasn't going south.'

Nodding to himself, DeSanctis rubbed the back of his head, where a thin white bandage covered the still throbbing cut Gillian had given him earlier. 'You really think she's turning on us?'

'It's definitely a possibility . . .'

'What about you-know-who?'

'She said he flew in this morning.'

'And you believe her?'

'I don't believe anyone after all this,' Gallo said. 'I mean, how does he put her in the house and not even tell us? What the hell is that?'

'I have no idea—I just want to make sure we still get our cash.'

'Don't worry . . . when it's time to split the baby, I guarantee we'll be taking a few extra arms and legs.'

ON THE FIFTH FLOOR of the Broward County Library, Joey walked past the row of computers and approached the one on the far end. The one that—according to the librarian's sign-up sheet—had recently been used by a Mr Sonny Rollins.

Joey sat down in front of the computer. Onscreen was the homepage for the Broward County Library. Wasting no time, she moved the cursor to the button marked *History*, the computer equivalent of looking at an itemised phone bill. She clicked and watched as a full list loaded in front of her. It had every web site the computer had visited in the last twenty days. Starting at the top, she clicked on the most recent.

Mickey and Pluto popped onscreen. *Disney.com—Where the Magic Lives Online*. She clicked the next on the list and found more of the same. *About Disney.com . . . Executive Bios . . . Executive Bios for Arthur Stoughton . . .* Arthur Stoughton?

A high-pitched ring erupted and Joey reached for her cellphone. Every person on the fifth floor turned her way. 'Sorry,' she mouthed to the onlookers as she stuffed her earpiece in place.

'You still at the library?' Noreen asked in her ear.

'What do you think?' Joey whispered.

'Well, get ready to shout, because I just got off the phone with your friend Fudge, who just got off the phone with a woman named Gladys, who is less than satisfied with her boss at the Florida Highway Patrol. For five hundred bucks, Gladys happily put the word *Duckworth* into their computer system and found out that a SunPass registered to Martin Duckworth was last used going north on the Florida Turnpike.'

Directly in front of her, Joey stared at the web site for Disney, the number one tourist attraction in Orlando. North on the Turnpike.

Springing out of her seat, Joey made a mad dash for the elevator.

'What're you doing now?' Noreen asked, hearing the noise.

'Noreen . . . I'm going to Disney World.'

CHAPTER 11

We're stalking Snow White. I lean against the wall. Gillian's next to me, pretending to make chitchat. Charlie flutters in and out of the crowd. Snow White has no idea we're there—and as we stick to the shadows behind Cinderella's Castle, neither do the autograph-seeking kids and photograph-snapping parents who surround her.

From the moment we entered Disney World, we were hunting for characters. Up Main Street, through the castle and straight into Fantasyland. But it wasn't until we heard the six-year-old shriek behind us—'Mom, *look!*'—that we spun round and saw the insta-crowd. There she was at the centre of the storm: Snow White, the fairest of them all. To the kids, she appeared out of nowhere. To us, well . . . that's the whole point. If you want to find the employee tunnel, you have to start with the employees.

One by one, she lets each child have his moment. Some want a signature, others want photos and the smallest ones simply want to hold her skirt and stare. I clock it right from the start. Eight minutes after Snow White appears—just as the crowd hits critical mass—a college-aged kid with a Disney polo shirt arcs round to the back of the mob and gives the signal. Snow White looks up. Stepping back and throwing goodbye kisses to the crowd, she makes it clear it's time for her to go.

'Why's she leaving?' a clearly displeased curly-haired girl asks.

'She's late for her date with Prince Charming,' the college kid announces as pleasantly as possible.

A few flashbulbs go off, a last-second autograph is signed and one final photo is taken. Then, like a movie star waving to her fans, Snow White recedes from the crowd, all of whom are grumbling until . . .

'Winnie the Pooh!' a little boy shouts. Everyone turns. Thirty feet away, the familiar bear magically appears and gets enveloped by tiny hugs. Disney certainly know how to throw a distraction. The crowd runs. We stay. And that's when we see the old wooden door. Snow White and the college kid go straight for it—it's on the back corner of Tinker Bell's treasure shop. The way it's set off from the main path, it almost looks like a bathroom. But it doesn't say MEN or WOMEN. It's just blank. Designed to be overlooked.

The college kid takes a last-minute glance over his shoulder. All three of us look away. Convinced no one's watching, he pulls open the door and escorts Snow White inside. Just like that, they're gone.

I barrel forward, pull open the door and all three of us slide inside. Barely lit by a fluorescent light, the concrete landing is empty.

'Check this out,' Charlie whispers, staring over the metal railing.

I squeeze between him and Gillian to see it for myself: paved stairs that wind down four levels. The entrance to the underground.

Without a word, I head down the stairs. At the bottom, we hit another door. I open it and poke my head into a short corridor. On my right, dozens of people cross back and forth in a bigger, perpendicular hallway. Bright costumes rush by in a flash. Echoed voices ricochet off the concrete.

Slipping out of the stairwell, I march down our corridor and make a sharp left into the main hallway, where I nearly collide with a skinny girl in a Pinocchio costume, minus the Pinocchio head.

'S-Sorry . . .' Catching my balance and cutting round her, I notice Snow White on her right—a different one, with brown hair pinned back, a black wig in her hand and chewing gum in her mouth.

I continue up the hallway. Charlie and Gillian are a few steps behind me. We're swallowed by the rush of Disney employees dressed in everything from the cowboy boots and hats of Frontierland, to the futuristic suits of Tomorrowland, to the simple collared shirts of the janitorial staff. I pull off my tie, stuff it in my pocket and undo the top button of my shirt. Just another Disney employee on his way to a costume change. The problem is, I don't have a clue where I'm going.

The further we go, the more the hallway seems to curve; the more the hallway curves, the more I feel like we're walking in circles. It's clear we need to change strategy.

Up ahead, a woman in a Pilgrim costume steps out of a room marked PERSONNEL. She looks about fifty years old. I motion to Charlie; he shakes his head. The older they are, the more likely they'll ask for Disney ID. And then I see it. Up on the wall: MAP TO THE MAGIC KINGDOM UTILIDOR.

Studying the layout, I go right for the 'You Are Here' sign. The tunnels spread out from Cinderella's castle like spokes on a wheel and weave their way under almost every major attraction.

'Look what's at the far end of the hallway . . .' Charlie points out. He pounds a finger against the top of the map.

DACS. Dead ahead.

WEAVING BETWEEN two princes, Cruella De Vil, a railroad engineer and Piglet, I'm ahead of Charlie, but trail Gillian. On our right, she bolts up a short carpeted ramp that leads to a glass door. 'DACS Central,' it says in bold black letters.

'You sure you want to go alone?' Charlie asks me.

'I'll be fine,' I insist.

As we reach the ramp, Gillian is studying the fingerprint scanner next to the intercom outside DACS. 'Is there anyone left who *doesn't* have one of these?' she asks, pushing some buttons on the scanner.

'Don't touch it,' Charlie warns.

'Don't tell me what to do.'

Charlie knows better than to pick a fight. 'Just ring the bell,' he says.

'I already did!' She rolls her eyes and thumbs the button again.

'*Can I help you?*' a female voice squawks through the intercom.

'Hi—it's Steven Balizer . . . from over in Arthur Stoughton's office,' I say, once again dragging out the big names.

'Extension?' the woman asks.

'Two five three eight,' I say, praying I remember Balizer's direct dial.

Squinting through the translucent glass, I spot the woman staring at me from her desk. I smile and give her my best Mouseketeer wave.

There's a short pause, followed by a croaking buzzer. I step inside.

'So how you doing today?' a sweet maternal voice calls.

Following the sound to the reception desk, I find a petite woman with blue-rimmed glasses and a Little Mermaid shirt.

'Now what can I do for you?' the Little Mermaid asks.

'I called about an hour ago—I'm here to get those back-ups for Arthur Stoughton.'

She flips through a stack of paperwork on her desk. 'And do you remember who you spoke to on that?'

I take another quick scan of the room. There's a closed door on my right. Nameplate says Ari Daniels. Under the door, there's no light. 'It was with an A— Andre . . . Ari . . .'

'Typical Ari,' the woman moans. 'He's already gone for the day.'

'Then how do I—?'

'I'll show you how to sign it out—I just need your ID.'

I pat my chest, then my shirt pocket, then the back of my trousers. 'Oh, don't tell me I—' I pull out my wallet and frantically search through it. 'It's sitting on my desk . . . I swear to you—you can call them right now. Extension two five three eight. It's just . . . when Stoughton loses his cool . . . if we don't get this reloaded, he'll—'

'Relax, darlin', I don't want the migraine either.' Shoving her chair back, she crosses round her desk and heads for the double glass doors in the right-hand corner of the room.

Through the glass, it's a computer nut's dream. Beige lockers filled with state-of-the-art mainframes and servers line the walls. In the centre of the room, a workbench is covered with computers, lap-tops, back-up power supplies and a mess of motherboards and memory chips. As we enter, two tech guys are hunched over a monitor.

Midway down the right-hand wall is a closet marked SUPPLIES. Above the doorknob, I count three locks. The last one is a punch-code. Just like the Cage. Supplies, my foot.

The receptionist pulls out keys and punches in the PIN code.

With a twist of the knob, the door swings wide. Inside, two metal storage racks are filled with hundreds of tapes—all set side by side, so only the spines of the cases are sticking out. At first they look like cassettes, but as we step into the closet, they're more like the digital audiotapes Charlie used to bring back from his recording sessions.

'What was it you were looking for again?' the receptionist asks.

'The Intranet,' I say, trying not to sound overwhelmed.

She runs her fingers across the labels taped to the edge of each shelf. *Alien Encounter . . . Buzz Lightyear . . . Country Bear Jamboree . . .* 'Dis-web1,' she announces, pointing to a collection of seven tapes. The spine of each case is labelled with a different day of the week, Monday to Sunday. 'Which day do you need?'

If I had my choice, I'd take them all, but for now, it has to be one day at a time. 'Yesterday,' I tell her. 'Definitely yesterday.'

She slides out the case marked 'Wednesday', checks to make sure the tape's inside, then unhooks a clipboard that's Velcroed to the side of the storage rack. 'Just fill it out,' she says, handing me both the clipboard and the tape. 'And don't forget to put your extension.'

A high-pitched chime rings from the front room. Doorbell.

'Excuse me one sec,' my guide says, heading out to the front room.

Alone in the closet, I eye the other six tapes. The rest of the proof—and the only way to be absolutely safe.

I take one last look at the tech boys. They couldn't care less. So tape by tape, I work my way through the week, stuffing the tapes in my trouser pockets until they're full. When I'm done, I grab the Wednesday tape and—

'Steven . . . ?' the receptionist calls from the front room.

'Coming!' I answer, racing from the closet. I slow it down through the double glass doors and calmly reenter the main room.

'Just in time,' she says. 'Your friends are here.'

I turn the corner and stop. My hands bunch angrily into fists.

'W-We just wanted to make sure you were OK,' Charlie stammers.

He's standing with Gillian by the receptionist's desk.

'Yeah,' Gillian adds.

And then I see them. They turn the corner and move in close behind Charlie and Gillian. Oh, God.

'There's our boy!' Gallo sings, stepping forward with a dark grin. 'We were getting worried about you.' He envelops me in a huge bear hug, squeezing me tight so I feel his holstered gun against my chest.

'So I guess you got what you needed,' DeSanctis adds, just as jolly.

'Of course he did,' Gallo says, noticing the Wednesday tape in my hand. 'That's why he's Disney's best employee. Isn't that right . . . *Steven*?' He says the name with a smirk, then extends an open hand between us. 'Let's see what you got there, buddy-boy . . .'

Thinking about the gun in the back of my trousers, I turn to Charlie. Behind him, DeSanctis moves in closer. I can't see his hands. Charlie flinches forward—like someone jammed something in his back.

'I don't mean to interrupt,' the receptionist says, clearly unnerved, 'but what department did you say you were with again?'

'Don't worry—we're all friends here,' Gallo teases, still staring at me. 'Now let's take a look at that tape . . .'

I hold on to it. Annoyed, Gallo rips it from my hands. I don't put up much of a fight—not with a gun in Charlie's back.

'Oh, now why'd you go and get Wednesday?' Gallo asks, reading the day on the spine. 'I thought you said we needed the other days as well . . .' Pointing to the receptionist, he adds, 'Can you help us find Thursday through Tuesday?'

Clearly freaked out, the Little Mermaid starts to panic. 'I'm sorry, sir, but I can't do anything until I see your ID.'

'Y'know, I left mine in my other jacket,' Gallo says. 'But you can use our friend Steven's.'

'Actually, I can't,' the woman replies. 'And since this is a restricted area, I'm going to have to ask you to leave.' She reaches for her phone.

Gallo pulls out his Secret Service badge and holds it up. 'Here's my ID. Now please put down the phone and get us the tapes.'

Her eyes go from the badge, to Gallo, then back again. 'I'm sorry, but you're going to have to speak to a supervisor . . .'

'I don't think you understand,' Gallo says. He pulls his gun from his jacket and points it square at the receptionist's face. 'Put the phone down and get us the tapes.'

The receptionist drops the receiver. Her hands tremble as she raises them in the air. 'They're in the back,' she stutters.

'Show us,' Gallo demands. 'Go with her,' he adds to DeSanctis.

Nudging Charlie and Gillian aside, DeSanctis steps between them, holding his gun. He pushes the receptionist towards the glass doors.

'C'mere . . .' Gallo says, grabbing me by the front of my shirt and shoving me. I stumble towards my brother. Our eyes lock.

The tapes aren't there, are they? Charlie asks with a glance.

I brush my hand across my trouser pocket. Gillian sees it and grins along with us.

Gallo points his gun at me, then Charlie, but never at Gillian, who's back to staring silently at the floor.

'You OK?' I whisper to her.

'What'd you say?' Gallo asks.

'I asked if she was OK,' I growl.

Gallo suddenly starts to laugh. 'You still don't know, do you?'

'. . . which brings us to DACS Central—the brain of the entire body,' a cheerful voice announces as the door to DACS swings open. Behind us, a man with a 'Backstage Magic' collared shirt leads a group of twenty tourists into the already cramped reception area.

Gallo ducks his arm behind his back to hide the gun. As the group pours in, a heavy woman in pink shorts and a matching pink sun-visor leads the whole crowd directly between us and Gallo.

Charlie eyes the door. *Go*, I nod to him. Charlie takes off.

'*Don't move!*' Gallo shouts, lifting his gun.

'*Gun!*' a woman screams. The crowd ruptures—everyone's shoving and shouting. We fly for the door as the frenzied crowd follows.

Behind me, Gillian is tucked down and holding on to the back of my shirt. The room empties into the hallway—and the yelling echoes through the concrete tunnel.

'*Keep going!*' I shout, shoving Charlie in the back.

'Up the stairs!' Gillian calls out, as doors whizz by on both sides.

But Charlie just keeps running. It's not until the tunnel starts to curve to the left that I understand what he's doing. Behind us, the screams of the crowd fade—quickly replaced by the echoed footsteps of whoever's chasing us. I turn back to look, but thanks to the arc of the hallway, we can't see them. Which means they can't see us.

'Now . . . !' Charlie says, making a sharp right into a short corridor. At the end, he rips open the metal utility door and holds it open for us. Inside, yellow-painted stairs head straight up. We dart up.

At the top of the landing, we stop in front of a closed metal door. I inch it open and we're overwhelmed by the bright openness of Liberty Square.

'Follow the crowd,' Charlie says, pointing towards the human wave of people flooding towards Frontierland.

We dive into the swarm of people bottlenecked in front of the Diamond Horseshoe Saloon. Gillian lowers her head and matches the pace of the moseying crowd. Wanting no part of it, Charlie runs ahead, weaving his way through the mob.

'Charlie . . . wait . . . !' I call out.

He doesn't even turn round. I take off after him, but he's already four families in front of us. Jumping up for a better view, I follow his blond hair as it swerves through the crowd. As he passes the Country Bear Jamboree, he glances back to make sure I'm with him, but the more I try to catch up, the further Gillian falls behind.

I look over my shoulder at Gillian, who's finally finding some speed. '*C'mon!*' I call out, waving her forward. But as I scope ahead to find Charlie, he's nowhere in sight. '*Charlie!*' I shout, scanning the crowd. Twenty feet in front of me, a familiar blond mop-top juts out from behind a kiosk. '*Charlie!*' I call again.

Get down! he motions, patting the air, palms downward.

He looks back across the street and I follow his gaze—through the mob—to the far corner of the Pecos Bill Café. I spot the two dark suits that stand out amid the Mickey Mouse T-shirt crowd.

And then they spot me. Gallo's eyes narrow into a jet-black glare. He ploughs into the crowd. DeSanctis is right behind him.

'You had to yell, didn't you?' Charlie asks as Gillian and I blow past the kiosk.

'Me? I wasn't the one who—' I cut myself off and focus back on Gallo. Across the street, to our left, he's fighting through the heart of the throng. And we're almost out of running room. In front of us, the road dead-ends at a waist-high wooden gate.

'Down here,' Gillian says, pointing to the right.

Charlie shakes his head. With a sharp tug, he pulls open the gate and runs up what looks like the incline of an asphalt driveway. He's headed straight for a green wooden wall that surrounds the whole park. It has to be at least eight feet high. There's no way we're climbing over this one.

'Charlie . . . stop!' I shout, chasing after him. 'It's a dead end!' But as Gillian and I hit the peak of the driveway, I see what's got his attention—a small sign on the wall that says CAST MEMBERS ONLY.

We couldn't see it from the front gate—the angle was wrong. But as we clear the highest part of the incline, it's obvious that what looks like a single wall is actually two walls that overlap, but never meet. Charlie steps forward, makes a sharp right and disappears. It's not a dead-end—just another optical illusion.

Following Charlie, I zigzag through the gap and run down a long, paved driveway. The park fades behind us and its colours and music are replaced by concrete greys and a creaky silence. Up ahead is an old warehouse with a sign that says MAGIC KINGDOM DECORATING.

A few steps ahead of me, Charlie spins round to check if Gallo's made it through the gate. That's when I see the pain on his face. He's as grey as the concrete, completely drained. Gillian and I catch up. Even *with* his medication, he couldn't keep up this pace.

Just a few more feet, bro—almost there.

Outside the warehouse, fifteen parade floats are parked in three rows under a metal awning. The smell of fresh paint surrounds us, and next to the glittering floats, dozens of empty paint cans tell us where everyone is. It's drying time. No one's around.

We duck into the gaping mouth of the warehouse's enormous door. Inside it's like a giant hangar, but instead of planes it's packed with more floats. Five rows of them fill the righthand side, but unlike the painted ones out front, these are all covered with Christmas lights.

Wasting no time, all three of us scout for hiding spots and—

There's a muffled running in the distance.

Charlie and I lock eyes. He scrambles to the left; Gillian tugs me to the right. I go to fight, but Gallo's too close. Time to get out of sight. Stumbling behind Gillian, I hide behind a huge float that's shaped like Cinderella's coach; Charlie ducks into a storage closet against the wall. He shuts the door behind himself.

Bent down and peeking between the wheels of the coach, I see Gallo's and DeSanctis's tall shadows stretch across the floor of the entrance. Gallo pulls his gun. His partner follows him inside, and they slowly pick apart the room. Gallo flips open a treasure chest. DeSanctis flings open the door of a giant teapot. They circle the warehouse, devouring every detail, trying to figure out where we—

Gallo points to the closet.

I reach under the back of my jacket and pull out the gun we took from him in the train station. I creep forward.

DeSanctis pulls on the closet door, but it barely budges. Charlie's holding it from the inside. 'They're in there,' DeSanctis says. He pulls again and it clamps shut.

'Enough of this,' Gallo says, pushing his partner out of the way. He raises his gun to the doorknob and fires two quick shots.

With a final tug, DeSanctis rips the door open.

'What the hell is this?' Gallo asks, as he stares into the closet.

It's not until DeSanctis steps aside that I see what they're looking at: another door that's already open on the other side. It's not a closet. It's a room that connects to the other half of the building.

DeSanctis and Gallo rush in. I spin round to share the news with Gillian. But as I do, I step on a stray Christmas light that's hanging off the side of the float. There's a sharp crack and I freeze.

'What was that?' Gallo asks.

I duck down and search the aisle for Gillian. She's not there.

'You coming?' DeSanctis asks.

'I'll be there in a sec,' Gallo says as he turns back towards the parade floats. 'I just want to check something out.'

HE DECIDED to wait for the little girl to stop crying. Tucked back on the porch of the Pecos Bill Café, there was no sense calling attention to himself. And as long as the little girl across the street kept screaming—as long as she and her consoling mom were blocking the gate that Gallo and DeSanctis had just ducked behind—he wasn't going anywhere. There was no reason to rush. Oliver and Charlie, Gallo and DeSanctis . . . he found them earlier, he'd find them again. Last time, all he had to do was wait round the corner from DACS. He knew they'd come running by. Just like Gillian had said.

He grinned at the thought of it. *Gillian.* Where'd she get that name anyway? Shrugging it off, he didn't much care about the answer. As long as they got their money, she could call herself what she wanted.

Scanning the crowd, he kept tabs on every stray glance. He didn't like being alone in Disney World. If he were young, maybe, but at his age—without kids—it was a guaranteed way to stand out. And right now, standing out was the last thing he wanted to do. Eventually, he hopped off the porch and calmly headed across the street with the purposefulness of someone rejoining his family. In front of the gate, the little girl had stopped crying. And the crowd had stopped staring.

'I'm sorry—are we in your way?' the mother of the girl asked, kneeling down and wiping her daughter's nose.

'Not at all,' the man said with a friendly nod. Stepping round them, he opened the gate and crossed inside. As it closed behind him, he never looked back.

I SQUAT DOWN behind the Cinderella coach float, and the door to the closet slams shut.

'So who am I with?' Gallo calls out. 'Charlie . . . or Oliver?'

Across the room, three or four aisles down, there's another snap and a quick shuffle of footsteps. Gillian's moving.

'So there're two of you in here?' Gallo asks. 'Am I that lucky?'

Neither of us answers.

'OK, I'll play along,' he says, taking a step in my direction. 'If it's two of you . . . and one's alone in the other room, well . . . I know I don't get Oliver and Charlie. She'd never let that happen. On top of that, I saw who was odd man out in Duckworth's back yard. So whattya say, Oliver? You and Gillian having fun yet?'

The room is dead silent. He takes another step towards me.

'That's the problem with threesomes,' Gallo warns. 'It's always two against one. Isn't that right, *Gillian*?'

I scramble back up the aisle and crouch behind a float shaped like a pirate ship. Gallo leaps into my aisle. But all he sees are two empty rows of abandoned parade floats.

'It's time to make some hard decisions, Oliver—and if you're smart, the first thing you'll ask yourself is: do you trust Gillian?'

'Don't listen to him, Oliver!' Gillian's voice booms through the room. 'He's just trying to confuse you.' I look to my left, hoping to trace the sound, but the acoustics make her impossible to pinpoint.

'All you have to do is use your brain,' Gallo adds. 'You were in the tunnels under Disney World. How do you think we found you?'

His footsteps are close, but he's headed in the wrong direction. I duck under the pirate ship and blanket myself in silence.

'Didn't you ever wonder why you couldn't find any of Duckworth's relatives when you worked at the bank?' Gallo asks. 'He didn't have any, Oliver. Never married. No kids. If he had, we never would've used his name on the account in the first place. That was the whole point.'

'He's a liar!' Gillian shouts.

'Oh, she's getting pissed now, isn't she?' Gallo asks. 'I don't blame her either. I saw what she did to Duckworth's old place—from the photo . . . to the soft-touch bedsheets . . . You have to give 'em the A-plus for effort—they pulled it together pretty quick.'

They?

'Personally, I think the paintings were the nicest touch. I'm betting those were to win over Charlie. Am I right, Gillian?'

For the first time, Gillian doesn't answer. I try to tell myself it's because she doesn't want to reveal her location, but as I'm finally starting to realise, every lie takes its toll. Especially the ones that we tell ourselves.

CHAPTER 12

In a room that felt like a smaller version of the warehouse, DeSanctis stared at row after row of rolling wardrobe racks. In front, a red and white polka-dot dress hung from a hanger labelled 'Minnie'. One rack over, the blue suit and white tail of Donald Duck's butt was hanging in the air. In front of the suit, Donald's head hung upside-down. The heads were the one thing DeSanctis couldn't miss—from Minnie, to Donald, to Pluto, to Eeyore, to all seven of the Dwarfs, the empty heads stared blankly at him.

DeSanctis scanned the aisles. Costumes draped to the floor and blocked every clear view. If he wanted Charlie, he'd have to flush him out. DeSanctis squeezed forward between two sequined butterflies and entered the first aisle of racks. With every step, costumes brushed against both shoulders, but DeSanctis's eyes were locked on the floor, searching for Charlie's shoes. Every few feet, he jabbed his gun into a costume that looked too lumpy, but otherwise nothing slowed him down—not until he reached the end of the aisle and saw the black tuxedo with the bright red shorts, two white gloves clipped to the sleeve. Raising his head, DeSanctis traced the costume up to the top of the rack, which held the head of the world's most famous mouse. Instinctively reaching out, DeSanctis tapped a knuckle against Mickey's smiling face.

'Couldn't help yourself, could you?' a voice asked behind him.

DeSanctis spun round, but it was too late. Wielding an industrial broom, Charlie swung away. The broomstick sliced through the air. There was a loud thud as it collided with DeSanctis's head.

WITH A MECHANICAL CRANK, the turnstile somersaulted as Joey rushed through the main entrance of the Magic Kingdom.

'How's it look?' Noreen asked through the earpiece.

'Like a haystack,' Joey said as she ran under the overpass that housed the railroad station, and found herself in Main Street, USA.

'I'm looking at their online map right now,' Noreen answered. 'It should be directly on your l—'

'Got it,' Joey said, pulling a left. Straight ahead, next to the bright red firehouse, was the main entrance for City Hall. Joey tucked away her earpiece and forced her best panicked look onto her face.

'Oh, no . . .' she began, starting out soft. 'Please don't tell me . . . Help!' she shouted. 'Please, someone . . . help me!' Within seconds, she heard the rumbling of footsteps from inside City Hall.

'What is it, ma'am? What's wrong?' a tall security guard with a crew cut and a silver badge quickly asked.

A black man in a matching blue shirt followed. 'Are you OK?'

'My wallet!' Joey shouted to both men. 'I opened my bag and my wallet was gone! It had all my money . . . my three-day pass . . . !'

'Don't worry—it's OK,' the tall guard said, putting his hand on her wrist. 'She's fine, folks,' he announced to the gawking onlookers. 'Just misplaced her wallet.'

As the crowd broke up and continued on its way, the guards huddled round Joey and helped her to a nearby wooden bench.

'Did it fall out on a ride?' the black guard asked.

'Are you sure this isn't it right here?' the other one asked, pointing to the wallet that stuck out from Joey's bag.

Joey stopped and looked down. 'Oh, God,' she said. 'I'm so embarrassed . . . I could've sworn it wasn't there when I—'

'No worries,' the tall guard said. 'I do the same thing with my keys all the time.'

Standing from the bench, Joey thanked the two men and once again apologised. 'I really am sorry—next time I'll check.'

'Have a nice night, ma'am,' the tall guard said.

The instant the guards had disappeared into the crowd, Joey shoved her earpiece back in.

'Well?' Noreen asked.

'It's like I always tell you . . .' Joey began. She reached into her jacket pocket and pulled out a black police radio with the word SECURITY written on it. 'Whenever you're on vacation, you gotta watch out for those pickpockets.' She turned up the volume and held the radio up to her ear. All she had to do was listen.

'C'MON, OLIVER, you had to know Gillian's background was fishy—or did you never wonder where she got a New York accent? Besides, you've only known the girl two days—how upset could you possib—' Gallo cuts himself off and lets out a throaty laugh. '*Oh*, *Oliver* . . . you really thought she liked you, didn't you? So how'd she get you to bite the hook? Was it the bullshit story, or something more physical?'

From the sound of his footsteps, he's one aisle over. I should run. But I don't.

'What about her age?' Gallo adds. 'What'd she tell you? Let me guess . . . Twenty-six? Twenty-seven? . . . She's thirty-four, Oliver.'

I'm not sure where Gallo is. And I'm not even sure I care.

'And the name—Gillian . . . Gillian Duckworth—pretty good when you consider how quick they had to paste it all together. Of course, if she used Sherry, no one would've known the difference.'

Sherry?

At the front of the aisle, two cheap black shoes turn the corner. Gallo stares straight at me. His gun's up; mine sags at my side.

'To be honest, I didn't think they could pull it off,' Gallo adds. 'But if you never met her before, I guess there's no way you could've known she was his wife.'

'She was *whose* wife?' I blurt, finally breaking my silence.

Gallo smirks. 'Oh, c'mon, Oliver—use your brain for once—how do you think we got Duckworth's program past Securi—'

Behind Gallo, there's a deafening boom. Before I even squint, his chest explodes, spraying tiny flicks of blood up the aisle.

Gallo falls forward. He hits the ground with a thump, but my eyes stay glued straight up the aisle—beyond Gallo. Gillian stares directly at me—her gun still pointed my way.

'Wh-What're you— What the hell are you doing?' I shout.

She lowers the gun and points to the door that leads outside. 'C'mon, Oliver, we should get out of here . . .'

'*Don't move!*' I shout, taking my first step towards her. 'Didn't you hear what Gallo said? It's over, Gillian—no more bullshit!'

'Wait a minute . . .' she begins. 'You don't think—Don't tell me you actually believed him. He was *lying*, Oliver.'

No. 'Tell me who you are,' I demand as I move towards her.

'Don't you see what he was doing—he wanted to pit us against each other. The man was trying to kill us!'

As I charge up the aisle, her words bounce off. 'Your name's not Gillian. You're not Duckworth's daughter. *Tell me who you are!*'

Face to face, she reaches out to touch my arm. With my gun, I backhand her away. She's not getting any closer.

Right there, her expression flips. The soothing smile . . . the innocent blue eyes . . . fade and disappear. I notice a deep crease along her forehead. She shakes her head, like I've made a mistake. Raising her gun, she points it at my chest. 'Just give me the tapes,' she says coldly.

Refusing to answer, I raise my own gun and aim it at her heart.

'I know your feelings got hurt, but if it makes you feel any better, it wasn't all an act,' she says, suddenly playing nice. As she shifts her hips, everything I knew about her evaporates. The barefoot hippiechick . . . the daring free spirit—they're long gone. Like everything else in my life, I saw what I wanted to see. 'I really did have fun with you,' she says, trying to flip back to sincere mode.

'Really? Which part was more fun—lying to my face, or just betraying my trust?'

'Lash out all you want, Oliver. I meant what I said. You can still get out of here—but not with the tapes—and not with our money. So why don't you join us back in reality and put the gun away. We both know who the daredevil is in your family, and just because you want to play the part, doesn't mean it's happening.'

She's hoping to push my buttons. Too bad for her, all it does is focus me more on Charlie. He's next door, alone against DeSanctis. And the only thing stopping me from helping him is Gillian.

I pull back the hammer on my gun. 'Get out of my way.'

'Why don't we start with the tapes . . .?'

'My brother's in there, Gillian. I'm not asking you again.' My gun's aimed at her chest. My finger tightens round the trigger.

'Enough with the outlaw drama, Oliver. I mean, do you honestly think you have the balls to shoot me?'

It's a simple question. He's my brother. 'You really don't know me at all, do you?' I ask her. Without waiting for her answer, I lower my arm, hold the gun to her knee and pull the trigger.

The gun fires with a bright flash and a sharp hiss. But instead of screaming or falling to the ground, Gillian just stands there, a cocky sneer on her face. Confused, I look down at the gun, which is only a few inches from her knee. I pull the trigger again. The gun goes off with a violent bang—and again, Gillian's unharmed.

'Haven't you ever heard of blanks before?' Gillian gloats.

Blanks? It doesn't make sense. All this time . . . The gun isn't even ours—we got it in New York from Gallo—right after he shot—

On my left, a brand-new shadow slides into the warehouse's open garage door. I turn.

'Whatsa matter?' Shep asks with his boxer's grin. 'You look like you seen a ghost.'

'WE'RE ALL CLEAR at Pecos Bill,' a voice squawked through Joey's radio as she weaved her way through the Frontierland crowd.

'Same at Country Bear,' another voice crackled back.

Hidden among the tourists in the street, Joey watched as two clean-cut men in matching blue shirts stepped out onto the porch of the Pecos Bill Café. Another two appeared from the Country Bear

Jamboree. Their walks were the same: strong and purposeful, but never too fast. Never panic the guests.

Out of the corner of her eye, she saw a man and woman moving through the crowd. They weren't wearing matching shirts, but Joey saw it in their walk—more Security. Within seconds, all three groups headed in different directions, checking the surrounding restaurants, storefronts and attractions.

'We'll take Pirates,' a female voice said through the radio as the man and woman team headed towards Pirates of the Caribbean.

Joey didn't follow. Charlie and Oliver were smarter than that. It's one thing to lose yourself in the herd of people; it's quite another to purposely run into a potential dead end like a restaurant or a nearby attraction. She scrutinised the rest of the area. Packed souvenir shops . . . impulse-buy kiosks . . . buzzing tourists. The only calming moment in the whole hurricane was up ahead, where a wooden gate blocked the street. The Disney cops were preoccupied with protecting paying guests, but if Charlie and Oliver were still running, they couldn't afford to be out in the open—they'd need somewhere quiet and tucked away. Joey took another look at the gate. Just visible beyond it was a sign saying: CAST MEMBERS ONLY.

'Quiet and tucked away,' she whispered to herself, heading for the gate and leaving the Disney cops behind.

'WHA . . . H-HOW'RE you . . . ?' My mouth's gaping open as I stare at a dead man. 'What the hell's going on?'

Lumbering towards us, Shep points his gun at me, but he's far more concerned with Gallo, who's got a hole blown through his back. Shep glares at Gillian. She shrugs like she didn't have a choice.

Still in shock, I can't take my eyes off Shep. The sausage forearms. The jagged nose. It's almost like it's not him. But it is. If Gallo shot him with blanks . . . and Shep knew it was coming . . . That's who Gallo was working with. That's how they got Duckworth's worm into the bank. 'You were their inside man.'

'See, now that's why they pay you the big beans.'

My face flushes red and reality slowly settles in like a block of ice melting down the back of my neck. 'So you were there from the start? You knew they'd try to kill us? Or was that the goal from the beginning—invite us in and create some scapegoats?'

'Let's just get out of here and we can—'

'Is that why you brought us in, Shep? To take our heads off?'

'Why don't we—?'

'I want an answer.'

Realising that I'm not moving, he checks the entrance to the hangar. Still clear. 'What did you want me to say, Oliver? *I'm so glad you found our secret. Now let's swipe this three mil, because there's another three hundred million piggybacked on it?* Once you saw the honeypot, I didn't have a choice.'

'You tried to kill us, Shep.'

'If you wanna start calling spades, *you're* the ones who worked one over on *me*,' Shep says.

'What're you—?'

'I checked that Antigua bank Charlie showed me on the Red Sheet. The cash was never there.'

'That's the only thing that saved our lives. If Charlie hadn't done that, we wouldn't even be standing right now.'

'I'm not saying I blame you, Oliver. In fact, I kinda respect it. We all take our opportunities where we find 'em,' Shep explains, his eyes on Gillian. 'Especially when money's involved.'

'So you were never going to share it with anyone, were you?' I ask. 'Not us . . . not Gallo . . . nobody.'

'Gallo may've gotten his mitts on the best idea in the world, Oliver, but it was useless without a bank to put it in.'

'Then I guess that makes it OK to kill everyone along the way.'

'Like I said at the start—there're only two perfect crimes: the crime that never took place, and the job where the criminal dies. But if I was gonna be the body they blamed it on . . . well, to the martyr go the spoils. The only splinter in the eye was when they let you walk out of that train station.'

'And that hatched your great plan? Follow us to Florida, screw over Gallo, and bring in your wife?'

'She fooled you, didn't she?'

I look at Gillian; she stares right back. She has no hesitation facing me. Like Lapidus always taught—business is business. I just can't believe I didn't see it before.

'It's not the end of the world,' Shep says. 'You've still got the golden eggs. Now it's time to decide what to do with them.'

There's a new pitch in his voice. He's back to Big Brother Shep. Sure, he'll show us how to hide the money . . . then, the instant he gets what he wants, he'll slice us at the kneecaps.

'Don't say no yet, Oliver. You haven't even heard the offer.'

'Oh, I haven't? Let me guess—you'll wave your gun in my face and threaten to kill me unless I tell you where the money is.'

'Just hear him out,' Gillian says. 'We can all get what we want.'

'I already know what I want—and I'm not getting it from you.'

'Then who're you getting it from?' Shep asks. 'The police? Lapidus? This is bigger than you and Char—' He cuts himself off and glances around. 'Where's your brother?' he asks me.

'Next door,' Gillian says.

'Go get him,' Shep orders her.

Hiding her gun in the back of her trousers, Gillian heads for the passageway that leads next door. The instant the door opens, I scream the warning as loud as I can. '*Charlie, she's a li—!*'

Shep grabs me by the jaw and clamps his hand over my mouth. I fight to break free, but he's too strong. Gillian enters the closet. She slams the door and the boom bounces against my chest.

Gripping my mouth, Shep holds tight until I stop struggling. 'Listen, Oliver. If you don't calm down, none of us'll get out of here. We've got three hundred million to deal with—we might as well—'

'Do I look that stupid?' I ask as he moves his hand from my jaw to my shoulder. 'You really think we'll help you? It's over, Shep.'

'Nobody move!' a female voice shouts behind us.

Spinning round, we trace the sound to the warehouse door. There's a woman with a gun. The investigator from the condo . . . the redhead . . . Joey . . . She points the gun straight at us.

Flushed with relief, I take a step towards her.

'I said, *don't move!*' she shouts. I raise my hands in the air.

'It's about time,' Shep says. 'I was wondering when you'd get here.'

'Excuse me?' Joey asks.

I expect to see some recognition on her face. Shep's alive—she's smart enough to fill in the rest. But instead, she seems confused. 'Who the hell are you?' she asks.

'Me?' Shep asks with a grin. He scratches at his forearms and lets out a deep, relaxed laugh. 'I'm an investigator—just like you.'

'He's lying,' I blurt. 'It's Shep!'

'Don't let him fool you, Ms Lemont . . .'

'How do you know my name?' Joey asks.

'I told you—I've been investigating this from the start. Call Henry Lapidus—he'll explain everything.' He reaches into his jacket . . .

'Don't even think it!' Joey says.

'It's not a gun, Ms Lemont.' From his chest pocket, he pulls out a black leather wallet. 'Here's my ID,' he says, tossing it at Joey's feet. She reaches down to pick it up, but never lets us out of her sight.

'I swear to you, Joey—his name is Shep Graves . . .'

'Ms Lemont, don't listen to him . . .'

'. . . he faked his death so they'd put the blame on us!'

She glances down at the ID, then slaps it shut.

'And Lapidus'll back up your story?' Joey asks sceptically.

'Absolutely,' Shep croons.

I'm not sure if he's bluffing, or if he's got a whole new card trick up his sleeve. Either way, Joey's come too far to leave without the truth. 'Noreen, are you there?' she says, speaking into the microphone clipped to her shirt. Nodding to herself, she adds, 'Get me Henry Lapidus.'

GILLIAN CUT THROUGH the utility closet and stopped. From the floor to the tops of the costume racks, Minnie, Donald, Pluto and dozens of other character heads stared back at her. Purposefully avoiding their glare, she cautiously stepped deeper into the room.

Straight ahead, at the end of the first aisle of costume racks, DeSanctis was face down on the floor, his arms tied behind his back with what looked like a jump rope. Was he—? No, Gillian realised as she saw his chest rise and fall. Just unconscious.

There was a noise from a few aisles over. Like someone panting. Someone out of breath. She made her way across the back of the aisles. 'Charlie!' she called out. 'It's me—Gillian!'

No response.

'Charlie, you heard the gunshots—Oliver's been hit! He hit Gallo, and Gallo shot him in the thigh—if we don't get him to a doctor—!'

'Gillian, this better not be bullshit,' a voice warned behind her.

She wheeled round as Charlie stepped out from the aisle she'd just passed. He held the broom in his hand, and while he tried to put on a strong face, he was wheezing with each breath. 'You OK?' she asked.

He studied her carefully. Her hands were empty. 'Just show me where Ollie is,' Charlie demanded. Turning his back to Gillian, he headed for the door. There was a muffled click behind him.

'Sorry,' Gillian said as she aimed her gun behind him. 'That's what you get for trusting strangers.'

Charlie wasn't going down without a fight. His fingers tightened round the broom. He spun round as fast as he could.

JOEY'S GOT HER FINGER on the trigger and her eyes on me and Shep, but she's clearly focused on whatever's coming out of her earpiece. My arms are up above my head, but I can still see my watch. It's already past seven. Lapidus is in his car, on his way to Connecticut. There's no way she'll be able to—

'Hello, Mr Lapidus?' she says into the microphone. 'This is Joey calling . . . right, the private investi— No, we haven't found the money yet . . . No, I understand, sir, but I have a quick question I was hoping you could help me with. Do you know anyone named'—she looks down at Shep's ID—'Kenneth Kerr?'

There's a long pause as Joey listens. She watches Shep. He doesn't flinch. He thinks she's bluffing.

'No, I understand,' Joey says. 'Of course. I just wanted to be sure.' She unhooks the cellphone from her belt and pulls out the earpiece. She's got her gun in her right hand and the phone in her left. Holding the receiver, she says, 'Lapidus wants to speak to you . . .'

Shep steps towards her, studying Joey's reaction. Joey studies his, watching for the tell. But Shep's too good to give it.

'Here you go,' she says, reaching out to hand him the phone.

'Thanks,' Shep says as he goes to take it. There's no fear in his voice.

I can see on Joey's face—he's passed her test. But as he reaches for the phone, Shep widens his grip, seizes the phone and Joey's whole hand, and thrusts both their fists and the phone against her face. It's all so fast, I barely realise what's happening. Joey staggers back as the phone cracks against the floor. She tries to lift her gun, but Shep lashes out with another punch, burying his fist in her face. Joey crumbles to the floor, unconscious. Her head hits the pavement with a hollow thunk. Standing over her, Shep reaches for his own gun.

'Get away from her!' I shout, tackling Shep from behind.

He whips around, grabs my neck and plants his whole fist in my left eye. 'Tell me where it is, Oliver!' he growls as he pounds me once more. 'Where's my fuckin' money?'

As Shep's fist crashes towards me, I hear a gun go off in the other room. Then I hear my brother scream.

As Charlie tried to complete his swing, the shot thundered from Gillian's gun. A spurt of blood erupted from Charlie's shoulder blade just as the broom struck Gillian in the hand and sent her gun sliding under the metal clothes rack. Charlie screamed. A snakebite of pain ran down to his elbow.

Gillian reached down to chase the gun, but Charlie wasn't letting her get there. He raised the broom over his head and swung. Jumping back out of the way, Gillian fell back into a row of costumes and tripped on the bar underneath. Feeling light-headed, Charlie tried to raise the stick for another shot, but didn't have the strength. He gasped for air. His shoulder was dead at his side. Gillian kicked the legs of the rack and tipped the whole thing forward. Dozens of character heads—from Mickey to Pluto to Goofy—all rolled to the floor as the rack crashed between them.

Before Charlie could react, Gillian was on her feet, ploughing over the costumes. She tackled him round the waist and knocked him to the floor. He landed on his back. Gillian landed on top of him.

Across the floor, past the wobbling heads, Charlie could see the gun. It was too far. But one thing was closer. With a final burst from his good arm, Charlie reached out, grabbed the leather strap attached to the inside of Pluto's head and swung it towards Gillian. Arcing through the air, the head clipped her on the side of her face like a fifteen-pound cannonball and sent her crashing to the floor.

She quickly climbed to her feet. Searching for balance, so did Charlie, still gripping the leather strap. Gillian rushed towards him in a rabid rage. Charlie arched his arm back and swung for the bleachers. The fifteen-pound head tore through the air. There was a loud pop as it bashed into Gillian's ear. The graphite head cracked on impact, sending a lightning-shaped fissure across Pluto's eyes—and sending Gillian straight to the floor. She crashlanded on the concrete, right at Charlie's feet. This time, she didn't get up. But as Charlie finally took a breath, he felt a familiar ripple inside his chest. He staggered sideways as a needle of pain stabbed him through the heart.

His heart bubbled and thumped. It felt like there was a bag of worms twisting inside his chest. *Please . . . not now . . .* he begged. The worms multiplied, clamping round his windpipe. 'Hhhh—' A sharp wheeze climbed through his throat. 'Hhhhh—' Charlie gasped for air as his heartbeat quickened, then started pounding. Faster and faster, it was a drumroll inside his chest.

Stumbling, he crashed through the utility closet, set his shaking hand on the doorknob and tugged the door open. The worms squirmed, digging and squeezing like a fist round his heart. Charlie tried to breathe, but nothing came in. The fist tightened, gripping his heart. His whole face clenched to fight the pressure. It was about to pop. And then . . . as he sagged to his knees . . . it did.

'Ollie . . .' he stuttered with one last wheeze. He tried to add a goodbye—but as his face hit concrete—it never came.

SHEP GRABS ME by the lapels. 'Last chance,' he warns, his hot breath smothering my face. '*Where. Is. My. Money?*'

My head's ringing like a firehouse. I can barely move it side to side. 'Drop dead, dickhead. You're never getting a dime.'

Enraged, he whips me round and hurls me towards a popcorn cart. I thrust my hands out to protect my face, but as I smash through the glass, my hands are sliced by the shards. Crashing on my stomach inside the cart, I notice a triangular, stray fragment of glass above my chest. There's a polished edge on one side, from where it fitted into the cart.

Shep grabs my legs and yanks me backwards. Shards of glass claw against my stomach. Ignoring the pain, I reach out for the fragment. I clutch it so hard, it almost slices the palm of my hand. And just as my feet hit the ground—before he knows what's happening—I spin round and stab the jagged scalpel straight into his stomach.

His face turns white and he grabs his gut, staring down at the shiny blood that slicks his hands. Reaching inside his jacket, he goes for his gun. I slash at his arm and slice him right above the wrist. Howling from the pain, he can't hold on to the weapon. It drops to the floor and I kick it underneath an enormous rocking horse. I'm not giving him another chance.

I hear a loud wheeze back by the closet that leads next door. I know it like I know myself. To my left—inside the closet. Charlie's holding his chest and gripping on to the wall to stand. 'Ollie . . .' he stutters, his mouth wide open. Gasping for air, he crumples to the ground. I turn for just two seconds. For Shep, it's a lifetime.

As I turn back, he's already barrelling at me. He pummels me like a tackling dummy. I crash on my back onto the concrete.

Shep pulls the jagged blade from my hand, slicing my palm. As I scream out in pain, he doesn't say a word. He's done talking. Sitting on my chest, he pins my biceps back with his knees. I fight to pull my arms free. He weighs too much. I search his eyes, but it's like no one's there. Shep doesn't care any more. Not about me. Not about the money. He raises the blade like a guillotine. His eyes are on my neck. Shutting my eyes, I turn my head and brace for the impact.

But the next thing I hear is a gunshot. Shep's body jerks violently. Blood dribbles out of his mouth. In his hand, the glass blade falls and shatters on the floor. Then his body collapses backwards.

Following the sound, I trace the trajectory. That's when I see her, sitting up on the floor. Not unconscious . . . awake . . . Joey . . .

She climbs to her feet, races for the wall and smashes the butt of her gun against the glass case of the nearby fire alarm. The alarm screams through the silence, and within seconds I hear sirens in the distance. Joey spins round and heads for my brother. Oh jeez . . .

'Charlie!' I shout. '*Charlie!*' I try to sit up, but my arm is on fire.

None of my fingers move. My body's shaking as it goes into shock.

Back by the entrance, half a dozen Disney security guards come streaming into the warehouse. They all come running at me; Joey stays with my brother. 'Please sit still, sir,' one of the guards says, holding my shoulders to keep me from squirming. Next to Charlie, four other guards kneel down, blocking my view.

CHAPTER 13

As I sit in the ground-floor conference room and gaze through the plate-glass window that separates me from my former co-workers, I can't help but feel like the monkey in the zoo. It's been two weeks since the news hit, but this is their first chance to see it for themselves. They're trying to play it cool. But each time one of them passes—each time someone steps off the elevator, or races to the copy machine—they hit me with that stare: part curiosity, part moral judgment.

Lapidus and Quincy finally make their entrance. They don't say anything to me directly. Everything's done through their lawyer. He tells me that they're withholding my final paycheque until the investigation is complete, that my health benefits are terminated effective immediately, that they'll seek legal recourse if I contact any current or former bank clients, and, as a cherry on top, that they'll be contacting the SEC and the banking regulatory agencies with the hope that it'll stop me from working at any other bank in the future.

'Fine,' I say. 'This is for you . . .' I slap a letter-sized envelope onto the desk and slide it across to Lapidus.

Flipping it over, Lapidus notices his own shredded signature across the back flap. He opens the envelope and unfolds my business school recommendation letter.

It's the only reason I came back here today. I wanted to see his face. And let him know I knew.

He keeps his eyes on the letter, refusing to look my way. The discomfort alone makes every second worth it. Folding it up, he stuffs it back in the envelope and heads silently for the door.

The lawyer asks me to wait here while they gather my things.

The door slams behind them, and I look out through the window into the lobby. Two dozen employees once again look away.

Twenty-five minutes later, the door swings open, and Joey hesitantly steps into the room with two cardboard boxes, which she lowers to the table. One's filled with management books and the other's filled with Play-Doh and the rest of Charlie's toys.

'They . . . uh . . . they asked me to bring you these,' she offers. 'I'm sorry they wouldn't let you up there. It's just that after everything that happened, the insurance company asked me to—'

'No, I understand,' I interrupt. 'Everyone has to do their job.'

'Yeah . . . well . . . some jobs are easier than others.'

'No doubt about that.' I look her in the face. Unlike everyone else, she doesn't turn away. 'I just wanted to say thanks for what you did. For me . . . and for Charlie,' I say.

'Oliver, all I did was tell the truth.'

'I'm not talking about the testimony—I meant with Shep . . .'

'I almost got you killed. That bluff about phoning Lapidus . . .'

'. . . was the only way to find out what was going on. Besides, if you hadn't come in when you did—and then with Charlie's medication—'

'Like you said, we all do our jobs,' she adds with a grin. It's the only smile I've seen all day. And means more than she'll ever know.

'So what happens now?' I ask her. 'Did you get the money back?'

'Money? What money?' Joey asks with a laugh. 'It's not money any more—it's just an assortment of ones and zeros on a computer.'

'But the account in Antigua . . .'

'Once you gave us the location, they sent every penny straight back—but you saw how Duckworth designed the worm. The three million . . . the three hundred million . . . none of it was real. But once Gallo brought the program in and Shep unleashed it on the system, the worm burrowed in so deep, it created a whole new reality. The tech boys said it'll take months to purge everything. Trust me, Lapidus and Quincy may be smiling now, but for the next year of their lives, they—and every single client in the bank—are going to be under a magnifying glass the size of Utah.'

She says it to make me feel better. And even though I can picture Tanner Drew's face when he's told about his audit, I'm not sure it works. 'What about Gillian?' I ask.

'You mean Sherry? You know better than I do. You're the one talking to the US Attorney.'

She's right about that one. 'Last I heard, she posted bail just in time to go to the funeral.'

Joey's silent as I share the news. However it happened, she's still the one who pulled the trigger on Shep. Moving for a quick change of subject, she asks, 'So what're you doing after this?'

'You mean, besides five years of probation?'

'Was that the final settlement?'

'As long as we deliver DeSanctis and Gilli—Sherry, the testimony sets us free.'

Joey heads for the door and yanks it open. As she's about to leave, she turns round, 'I really am sorry they had to fire you, Oliver.'

'Trust me, it's for the best.'

She studies me to see if I'm lying—to her and to myself. Unsure, she turns back to the door. 'You ready to go?'

I look down at the two boxes on top of the conference table. The one on the left has how-to-get-ahead textbooks, silver pens and a leather blotter. The one on the right has Play-Doh and Kermit the Frog. The boxes aren't big. I can carry both. But propping Charlie's box against my chest, I leave the other one behind.

Joey motions to it. 'Do you want help carrying th—?'

I shake my head. I don't need it any more.

Nodding slightly, Joey steps back and holds the door wide open.

'SO? WHAT'D THEY SAY? Are we done?' Charlie grills me the instant I set a toe in his bedroom.

'Take a wild guess,' I answer.

Sitting up in bed and readjusting the bandage on his shoulder, he nods to himself. 'Did they say anything about me?' he asks.

At the foot of the bed, I dump the boxful of his desk toys all over his quilt. 'They wanted to make you a partner, but only if they could keep your Silly Putty. Naturally, I told them it was non-negotiable, but I think we can counter with some Matchbox cars.'

As I say the words, he's completely confused. The result, he expected. But not my reaction. 'This isn't a joke, Ollie. Whatta we do now? Mom can't support two apartments.'

'I totally agree.' I leave the bedroom and return two seconds later dragging an enormous army-green duffel bag. With a grunt, I heave it on the bed, next to him. 'That's why we're downsizing to one.'

'So you're moving back in?'

'I hope so—I just spent twenty bucks on my last cab ride.'

Charlie narrows his eyes. 'OK, what's the punch line?' he asks.

'I don't know what you're talking about.'

'No, no, no,' he insists. 'I was there when you moved into your own place. I remember how proud you were that day. So now that you're moving back in, don't tell me you're not devastated.'

'But I'm not.' It may be a temporary move, but it's a good one.

'But you're not,' he agrees, still searching my face.

'So you think this room can still sleep two?' I ask, motioning to the pyramid of speakers where my old bed used to be.

'Two's fine—I'm just happy it's not three,' he says suspiciously.

'What's that supposed to mean?'

'Well, Beth called earlier. She said your phone was disconnected. And she wants to speak to you. She said the two of you broke up.'

This time, I don't respond.

'So who broke up with who?' Charlie asks.

'If it makes you feel any better, I was the one who broke it off—'

'Ohhhh, Lordy, I'm *healed* . . . !' Charlie shouts, raising his shoulder in the air. 'My arm—it works! My heart—it's a-pumpin'!'

I roll my eyes. 'How about helping me move the rest of my stuff?'

He grabs his shoulder. 'Ow, my arm. Cough—I can't breathe.'

'C'mon, you faker—get your butt outta bed—the doctors said you're fine.' I yank the covers aside and see that Charlie's fully dressed in jeans and socks. 'You're really sad, y'know that?' I say.

'No, sad is if I was wearing sneakers.' Hopping out of bed, he follows me into the living room and spots my other duffel bag, two boxes and some milk crates full of CDs, videos and photos.

'Where's your Calvin Kleinish bed?' Charlie asks.

'Mom said she kept my old one in the basement. It'll be fine.'

'*Fine?*' He shakes his head. 'Ollie, I don't care how good an actor you are—I can hear the pain in your voice. We can pawn my speakers. That'll give you at least another month to—'

'We'll be OK,' I interrupt as I grab the other duffel.

'But if you don't have a job—'

'There're plenty of good ideas out there. All it takes is one.'

Charlie looks down at the way I'm bouncing on the balls of my feet. 'OK, so we're past the College Ollie and the Banking Ollie and the Dying-to-Impress Ollie with its very own Removable Soul. So which one's this? Entrepreneur Ollie? Go-Getter Ollie?'

'How about the real Ollie?' I ask.

He likes that one.

Crossing back into the dining room, I can already feel the energy rumbling through my stomach. 'I'm telling you, Charlie—now that I have the time, there's nothing to get in the—'

Cutting myself off, my eyes dart to the torn-open envelope on the edge of the table. Return address says Coney Island Hospital. I know the account cycle. 'They sent us another bill already?' I ask.

'Sorta,' Charlie answers, trying to brush past it.

That's it—something's up. I go straight for the envelope. As I unfold the bill, it's all the same. Total balance is still $81,000, and payment due is still $420. But at the top of the bill, instead of saying 'Maggie', the name above our address now says 'Charlie Caruso'.

'What're you—? What'd you do?' I ask.

'It's not hers,' he says. 'It shouldn't be on her shoulders.'

He's got a calmness to his voice I haven't heard in years. But taking over the hospital bill is one of the rashest things my brother's ever done. That's why I tell him the truth. 'Good for you, Charlie.'

'*Good for you?* That's it? You're not gonna grill me on the details: why I made the change, how'm I possibly gonna afford it?'

I shake my head. 'Mom already told me about the job.'

'She told you? What'd she say?'

'What's to say? It's illustration work at Behnke Publishing. Doing drawings for technical computer manuals—boring—but it pays sixteen bucks an hour. Like I said, good for y—'

Before I can finish, the front door slams behind us. 'I see handsome men!' Mom's voice calls out as we spin round. She's balancing two brown bags of groceries in a double-barrelled headlock. Charlie races for one bag; I race for the other. The moment she's free, her smile spreads wider and her thick arms wrap round our necks.

'Ma, careful of my stitches . . .' Charlie says.

She lets go and he lets her put a wet one on his cheek. She plants one on me and fights her way out of her coat. Noticing the crates and boxes all over the floor, she can barely contain herself. 'Oh, my boys are back,' she coos, following us to the kitchen.

'I saw Randy Boxer's mother in the yarn shop,' she says, turning to Charlie. 'She was so glad you called—it just made her day.'

'Randy Boxer's mom?' I ask. 'What're you calling her for?'

'I was actually trying to get Randy's number,' he explains.

'Really?' I ask. He's not fooling anyone. He hasn't seen Randy in at least four years. 'So why the sudden high school reunion?'

'We were . . . we were thinking of maybe starting a little band . . .'

'A band, huh?' I ask with a wide smile. 'Has this band got a name?'

'How d'ya think we spent our first three hours of practice?'

'So you've already got a name?'

'C'mon, we look like novices? Coming to Shea Stadium next summer—ladies and gentlemen . . . please give a Big Apple welcome to . . . *The Millionaires!*'

I laugh out loud. So does Mom. At the sink, she washes the daily grime from her hands. She's got Band-Aids on four of her fingertips. Behind her, I spot Charlie eyeing the Charlie Brown cookie jar. He reaches out and taps it. 'I don't care how many drawings I have to do,' Charlie whispers my way. 'This sucker's gonna be empty in a year.'

'So you're ready?' Mom interrupts, focused on Charlie.

'Excuse me?' he asks. At first, he takes it as a typical Mom question. But as he reads her face—as I replay it in my head—we both realise it's not a question. *So you're ready*. It's a statement. 'Yeah,' Charlie tells her. 'I think so.'

'Can I come watch you practise?' she adds.

'Forget watching, we need star power like you on stage. Whattya say, Ma—ready to bang some tambourines? We got our first tryouts tomorrow night.'

'Oh, I can't tomorrow night,' she says. 'I have a date.'

'A date? With who?'

'Who do you think, mushmouth?' I jump in. Cutting between them, I slide my arm round Mom. 'You think you're the only one who knows how to cha-cha? Dance lessons wait for no man. Hit it, sweet momma—and a-one, and a-two . . .' Swinging Mom out, I laugh loudly and bounce to my own imaginary beat.

'Did someone actually teach you how to move that awkwardly?' Charlie teases. 'You dance like a fifty-year-old man in a bad wedding conga line.' He's absolutely right. But I don't care.

After years of busting my ass at the nation's most prestigious private bank, I—at this moment—have no job, no income, no savings, no girlfriend, no discernible professional future and not a single safety net to catch me if I plummet off the trapeze. But as I twirl our mom through the kitchen and watch her grey hair spin through the air, I finally know where I'm going and who I want to be. And as my brother angles in for the next dance, so does he.

EPILOGUE

Henry Lapidus stepped into his office, shut the door and headed for his desk. Picking up the phone, he glanced at the Red Sheet in his in-box, but didn't bother to take it out. He learned that lesson years ago—like a magician protecting his tricks, you don't put every number on the sheet—especially the ones you know by heart.

As he dialled and waited for someone to pick up, he stared down at the letter of recommendation he'd written for Oliver, which he was still gripping in his left hand.

'Hi, I'd like to speak with Mr Ryan Isaac, please. This is one of his clients from the private group,' he explained. Lapidus couldn't help but be amused. Sure, his priority had always been to get the money back. Indeed, he'd personally called the bank in Antigua to secure the return of every last cent. But that didn't mean he had to tell the Antigua bank that none of the money was real.

'Mr Isaac, it's me,' Lapidus said the instant Isaac said hello. 'I just wanted to make sure everything got there OK.'

'Absolutely,' Isaac answered. 'It came this morning.'

Three weeks ago, the bank in Antigua was surprised to receive a $313 million deposit. For four days, it was flushed with more cash than it had ever seen. And for four days, in Lapidus's opinion, Oliver had done at least one thing right. It was one of the first lessons Lapidus taught: *Never open a bank account unless you're getting interest*.

Four days of interest. On $313 million.

'One hundred and thirty-seven thousand dollars,' Isaac clarified on the other line. 'Should I put it in your regular account?'

'That'd be perfect,' Lapidus replied. Hanging up the receiver, he swivelled in his seat and stared out at the New York skyline. One hundred and thirty-seven thousand dollars, he thought. Not bad for a day's work.

Lapidus had known that, once the principal was returned, the government would be preoccupied with tracking the worm and figuring out how it worked. Now that they were knee-deep in that, well . . . thanks to a well-placed payment to the Antiguan bank manager, all records of the interest were long gone. Like they never existed.

His eyes still on the skyline, Lapidus crumpled up Oliver's recommendation letter and tossed it into the garbage can. As he took in the shadows of the late afternoon, a ray of sun gleamed off the samurai helmet that was hanging on the wall behind him. Lapidus didn't notice. If he did, he would've seen the twinkle of light just under the helmet's forehead, where a silver object barely peeked out. To the untrained eye, it looked like a nail holding the mask in place . . . or the tip of a fine silver pen. But nothing more.

Except for the occasional glare of sunlight, the tiny videocamera was hidden perfectly. And wherever Joey was, she was smiling.

BRAD MELTZER

Brad Meltzer wrote his first novel, *The Tenth Justice*, while studying to be a lawyer at Columbia University. 'I always wanted to be a writer,' he says, 'but I really didn't expect to be able to earn a living doing it.' By the time he graduated he had a lucrative publishing contract, so the decision to pursue his dream and become a full-time writer was easy. He now has four best-selling thrillers to his name, including *Dead Even* and *The First Counsel*.

The author says that he enjoys researching his novels almost as much as writing them. 'I love digging around for the details. They are the most fun. And, after all, in today's society we have more access to Information than anyone has had at any other time in history. Readers expect writers to know their stuff. And I love taking them into a world where they have never been before. My wife jokes that my next calling is to be an investigative reporter.'

Brad Meltzer spent almost two years researching *The Millionaires* and learned some surprising facts along the way, including how simple it is to get information about other people. He even hired a private eye to look into his own life in order to research the investigative process. 'I gave her my name and asked her to see what she could find. In a minute she had my social security number and a minute after that she had my address and those of all my relatives and neighbours. In no time at all she had my entire life laid out in front of her. It was frighteningly easy.'

While he is writing, Brad Meltzer tries not to read novels in order to ensure that he isn't influenced by the styles of other authors. Instead he reads graphic novels and recently took on the challenge of becoming the writer on DC Comics' *Green Arrow* series. 'It's about a superhero who's a bit like Robin Hood. I'm a huge fan of graphic novels—I eat them like candy. When they offered me the job of writing for *Green Arrow*, I jumped at it.'

And does he ever feel sorry that he gave up law? 'Not a chance. I get to talk to my imaginary friends all day—what's better than that?'

ONLY DAD

Alan Titchmarsh

The smell of fresh herbs on a summer evening; the comfort of holding his wife, Pippa, in his arms; the fierce, protective love he feels for his daughter, Tally. These simple joys are the very bedrock of Tom Drummond's life.

How could he survive without them?

CHAPTER ONE

There are things you ought to know about Tom Drummond. For a start, he never intended to own a restaurant. Well, half of one. Not that there's anything wrong with owning half a restaurant, but it would be a mistake to assume that he had either an obsessive interest in nutrition or a burning desire to entertain. He had neither. He became the owner of half a restaurant entirely by accident. He'd intended to be a farmer. Or, more accurately, his mother had intended him to be one. Tom himself had long harboured dreams of being a writer, but it's difficult to persuade your single parent that you are working when all you do is gaze out of the window wearing a vacant expression. So, partly to please his mother and partly because no other job held any particular appeal, Tom became a farmer.

Now you could argue that looking after sheep on the Sussex Downs isn't exactly on a par with crofting in the Cairngorms, but in spite of their supposedly soft location in the southern half of the country, the rolling slopes above Axbury Minster are often blasted by bitter winds in winter. Tom and old Bill Wilding would regularly feel the bite of the baler twine on their knuckles as they doled out the summer-scented hay to the Southdown sheep. But on a good day in June or July the smooth, soft slopes were framed by a fuzz of woodland and clear blue sky, and Tom shepherded the sheep and worked the land with a song in his heart and a spring in his step.

But the happiness was short-lived. Old Bill Wilding popped his clogs in the dead of winter and the farm came up for sale in spring.

After just two years Tom was out of a job. The following summer his mother departed this life quietly, leaving him with a small legacy, a heavy heart and a clean slate.

It was time to write. Unfortunately, after a year of setting down his finely crafted prose on paper, only two short stories had appeared in print—one in a regional newspaper and the other in the *Lady*. It was a fair way short of the stuff dreams are made of. Tom conceded that it was time to knuckle down. But to what? Over a bowl of soup in a local bistro he scanned the sits-vac column. Difficult to work yourself up into a lather about 'Household insurance: experience essential for liaison and telephone support role'. He was beginning to consider seriously how he could fulfil the role of 'Deputy matron required for full-time day duty' when he fell into conversation with the chef—a fair-haired, fresh-faced youth called Peter Jago. Together they bemoaned their respective fates: Tom, at a loose end with the remains of a modest legacy, and Peter, desperate to strike out on his own. It was foolhardy, really—they didn't know one another—but they pooled their resources and opened a bistro, the Pelican, with Tom running front-of-house and Peter slaving away in his whites over a hot stove.

To everyone's surprise, the venture took off. But then Peter knew his gnocchi from his goulash and Tom, with his easy-going nature, turned out to be a natural host.

Success encouraged the pair to open another bistro, the Albatross, in a nearby village. But it proved to be more appropriately named than either of them could have foreseen. Although they struggled for the best part of five years to make it pay, in the end the seasonality of the business forced them to cut their losses and sell up.

Not that the Albatross was a total failure: Peter had taken on a young cook, a dark-haired girl with a lively wit, a quick mind and a smile that could melt a disgruntled diner three tables away. It melted Tom, too. They had married within the year and Pippa told him, with a warning flash of her nut-brown eyes, that if he was marrying her just for her cooking he had another think coming. Tom was not. He had married her because he had never been so totally in love in his entire life. He had known from their first meeting that there would never be anyone else for him. Which was odd: until then he hadn't even been able to decide if he took sugar in his tea.

Another thing you ought to know is that Tom Drummond had not given much thought to becoming a father, so it came as a bit of a surprise when, a few months after they were married, Pippa broke it to him that the patter of tiny feet was a short time away. Tom was not lacking in the intelligence department, so when Natalie Daisy Drummond—Tally for short—came into his life on May 5, 1985, it took him just seconds to realise that from now on his life would not be his own.

Funded by the sale of the Albatross and partly by Pippa's late parents' legacy, the Drummond family moved from the centre of town to a converted barn that had been one of Bill Wilding's outbuildings. With its acre of land, it suited them down to the ground. Tally grew up among the buttercups and daisies while her mother raised herbs to supply the bistro and other local businesses.

The Drummonds have lived at Wilding's Barn for sixteen years now, with never a cross word. Well, that's if you don't count Tom's exasperated complaints about Tally's loud music when he's making yet another attempt at the now legendary first novel, and his occasional questioning of Tally about the boys in her life. He tries to keep out of her hair as much as he can, but he does find it difficult.

ANY FATHER WHO WANTS to survive the role learns very quickly to recognise the different tones of voice in his offspring. This morning, it was the tone that indicated the need of a favour—what Tom had come to think of as 'the three-note "Dad"'—the middle note being a semitone lower than the first and last.

'Da-a-ad?'

Tom sighed and stuck his head round the corner of Tally's bedroom door. 'Mmm?'

'Are you busy?'

'Do I look busy?'

Tally sized up the fraught, preoccupied expression and worked out, in an instant, that the best approach would be one of hurt bewilderment. 'It's just that Mum said she'd drop me off in town and she's gone without me.'

He looked at her as she zipped up the sides of her short, brown, high-heeled boots, the slender legs encased in white jeans, and wondered where the years had gone. Clichéd though it might be, it really did seem like only yesterday that she had been knee high and pudgy, wrapping her arm around his leg at the approach of any stranger. Now she was sixteen, trim of figure and airily confident yet plagued by insecurities, pretty as a picture yet worried about spots.

She was running a brush through her fine, fair hair in swift, repetitive strokes. Her face, free of make-up except for mascara, wore a troubled expression that only her father could lift. She knew the challenge would be irresistible.

'She's gone without you,' Tom said, 'because it's half past ten. She had to be in Axbury at ten o'clock to drop off some herbs. She told you that yesterday.'

Tally looked suitably contrite. 'Slept in.'

'I'm not surprised. What time did you get home last night?' Tom lowered his head and looked at her from under his frowning brow. 'A quarter past twelve.'

'Was it?' She tried to looked shocked.

Her father nodded.

'Well, you should have been asleep.'

'I'd like to have been. But I wanted to know you were home.'

'But you knew I was with Emma.'

'It doesn't stop me worrying . . .'

She came up to him and hugged him. 'You are sweet.'

'Stop trying to butter me up.' He kissed the top of her head. 'If you're ready in two minutes I'll take you. But I'm off then, whether you're ready or not. I want to meet your mum for a coffee.'

'Thanks, Dad, you're a gem.'

While Tally undertook the finishing touches so vital before the rest of the world could be allowed to see her, Tom grabbed his car keys and crossed the cobbled yard towards the open end of the barn where the Land Rover stood under a mossy pantiled roof. A familiar 'Ooo-ooh!' pierced the clear morning air.

Tom's spirits sank. Maisie Whippingham was a good soul, but of all her deficiencies, an inability to choose the right moment was the most well developed. She waved from behind the hedge of Woodbine Cottage, just across the lane from Wilding's Barn.

'I can't stop, Maisie. I'm running late already.'

'Yes. Of course. Sorry. It's just that I wanted you to know that I've a load of manure coming some time today.' Maisie smiled vaguely from beneath a turban that restrained an explosion of salt-and-pepper hair.

'What do you want manure for, Maisie?'

Maisie's garden was not so much a garden as a conservation area into which she made an annual summer foray with a machete to carve a hole in the brambles for an old pine chair and an easel. She regarded the patch of ground, where Mother Nature had long since gained the upper hand, as a safe haven for wildlife that she hoped one day to commit to canvas. Painting was her passion. Until she was fifty-five she had worked in a bank in London. Then she had retired, sold her London flat, bought Woodbine Cottage and set about being a countrywoman—or her idea of a countrywoman. She dressed like a cross between Edith Sitwell and Vita Sackville-West. Today's turban was multicoloured and sparkled with gold thread, and she wore a navy-blue fisherman's smock topped off with a purple chenille scarf and a pair of brown corduroy trousers tucked into knee-high boots. She was clearly in outdoor mode.

'Want to have a bash at a herb garden,' she said. 'Like Pippa's.'

Tom cast an eye over the low hawthorn hedge that surrounded Pippa's orderly herb garden, where serried ranks of fennel and coriander were surrounded by borders of parsley and chives. Rocket and salad burnet jostled for light and air between orange marigolds and wigwams of sweet peas. It was her passion.

'You've a bit of a job on, then?' Tom nodded at the head-high mattress of brambles and thistles that sprang from Maisie's local landscape.

'Getting help. Mr Poling. Coming soon.'

'Well, good luck. Let us know if you want a hand later.'

Maisie nodded and waved, before ducking back inside Woodbine Cottage.

Tom looked at his watch. There was no sign of Tally. He started up the Land Rover and drove out onto the cobbled yard to wait for his daughter. Still no sign. 'I'm going!' he shouted, and gave a couple of revs on the accelerator. Tally flew out of the front door, a jacket on one arm and a bag over the other. 'Sorry! I forgot my mobile.'

Tom shook his head as she climbed up on to the seat beside him. 'Have you locked the door?'

'Oh! Sorry!' She scrabbled for her keys in her bag.

Tom sighed, and switched off the engine. 'I'll go,' he muttered resignedly. 'I sometimes wonder if you were born in a barn,' he said, when he got back.

'No. I just live in one.'

He looked at her with a mock scowl, then drove off. As always, with her beside him, he felt like a million dollars.

AXBURY MINSTER was the kind of town that Anthony Trollope wrote about, a sort of pocket-sized Oxford with muddy feet. It had once been a market town—still was if you counted the farmers' market on the first Monday of every month—but its days of live-stock auctions had ceased and the sheep pens were now a smart pedestrian precinct coping with well-heeled rather than cloven feet. The Minster was still the heart of the community, and held the town together architecturally, if not spiritually. Just a stone's throw away, The Pelican occupied the ground floor of a Georgian terrace. It was listed, but it was also listing—to the northeast.

Having dropped off Tally outside the Axbury Tearooms, where she fell into the arms of her friend Emma with hugs and girly shrieks, Tom parked the Land Rover in the narrow yard to the rear of the restaurant and let himself in through the kitchen door. The usual scenes of lunchtime mayhem had yet to materialise. It was a quarter to eleven on a Saturday morning, the calm before the storm—they opened at noon. The Pelican was packed most meal-times, Fridays and Saturdays in particular. On Sundays they closed and got their breath back.

Tom walked through to the front of the bistro. He wove his way between scrubbed pine tables and bentwood chairs, towards the bar that ran down one side of the dining area. Peter was behind it restocking cool cabinets with bottles of lager. He looked up. 'Can't keep away?'

'Just parked up here. Everything all right?'

'Funny you should ask. Sam's handed in his notice.'

'What?'

'Says he's found a new job. In Brighton. A partnership. Bastard.'

Tom grimaced. 'Well, you can't blame him. That's what you did.'

'I know, but his timing's not exactly brilliant, is it? Summer coming and all that.'

Peter had taken Sam on as his junior and trained him up. He'd caught on quickly, developing his own creative style, which meant that Peter could have an occasional weekday off—something Tom managed, too, on account of the growing skills of Sally, the head waitress. Sam also took the reins when Peter had one of his 'moments'. All chefs have them: they occur when the relentless provision of finely crafted fodder is at an apparent imbalance with the appreciation of the diners. Sam's departure was bad news.

Peter ran his hands through his fair curly hair. 'Rachel's going to be delirious.'

Rachel Jago was Peter's driving force, or so she liked to think, not that she'd been in the driving seat for very long. They'd married just two years previously—it was Rachel's third attempt. Peter had resisted a long-term relationship for fifteen years or more but buckled under the onslaught of Rachel's determination. She was the only person he'd met whose will overpowered his own and he seemed constantly in awe of her.

Before Rachel's arrival on the scene, Peter and Tom had been good mates who seldom tired of each other's company. Rachel had her own group of cronies and, always keen to be the centre of attention, seemed uncomfortable with Peter's. The friendship between Tom and Peter changed, too, becoming more of a working relationship as Peter, always ebullient and forthcoming in company, began to stand in the shadow of his overpowering wife. It saddened Tom, but he did his best not to dwell on it.

Rachel saw Peter as a sort of Terence Conran and tried to persuade him to become more entrepreneurial. She would have liked him to run a chain of restaurants—Le Caprice and the Ivy, preferably. The Albatross disaster had happened long before her time. 'The climate's different now. People want variety—they don't want to go to the same restaurant week in, week out. Open another. You're too talented to put all your eggs in one omelette.'

Having listened to her argument almost daily for the best part of two years, Peter was beginning to think there was sense in what she said. Rachel had found just the place for the new restaurant—another Georgian town house but of far greater elegance than the tottering pile that was the Pelican. Peter's resistance was crumbling; all he needed now was the final push.

So far, Tom was unaware of Rachel's apparent progress, but he had detected a certain tension when he was in her presence. The truth was that, for once in her life, Rachel had met her match: Tom Drummond might appear gentle and calm on the outside; underneath he was a man of steel. But Rachel Jago was a woman with a mission, and nothing would prevent her getting her own way, not even Tom Drummond.

Now Tom left the Pelican, and a cursing Peter, and walked towards the Minster. Through the window of the Parson's Pantry he saw Pippa, waiting patiently while the prim proprietress wrapped a loaf in a paper bag. As she came through the doorway she saw him and her face lit up. 'I thought you were writing.'

'Taxi driving.'

'She should have caught the bus. You're such a soft touch.'

Tom grinned. 'Fancy a coffee? No words flowing this morning.'

'Come on, then, my literary genius.'

Tom's book had become something of a family joke. Nobody expected him to finish it, least of all Tom himself. But it was taken every bit as seriously as if it were the Bayeux Tapestry or the Forth Bridge, and it kept Tom sane.

Pippa put her arm through his and they set off in the direction of the glass and chrome café across the road from the gloomy Axbury Tearooms patronised by Tally and her mates.

As they sat and sipped their coffee Tom told Pippa about Sam, and Peter's reaction.

'Well, you can see his point,' Pippa said reasonably. 'What a bummer. When's Sam wanting to leave?'

'End of next month.'

'That's a shame, but it's too late to change things now.'

'Too late to change what?' Tom asked.

'Our holiday arrangements.'

'We don't have any.'

'We do now.'

Tom eyed her suspiciously.

'Don't look at me like that. You need a holiday. You said yourself that the words aren't flowing. We *all* need a holiday. It's booked. Two weeks in Tuscany, a little villa in its own vineyard.'

'When?'

'End of the month. Tally will have finished her exams and Peter can cope with the bistro.' He looked at her open-mouthed. 'You're not indispensable, you know.'

'But what about Sam?'

'Advertise for a replacement. You can have it sorted before we go. And, anyway, the kitchen isn't your province. It's Peter's problem.' Pippa drained her cup and smiled. 'Don't you want to come on holiday with two dishy girls?'

'Well, yes, but . . .'

With suspiciously adept timing, a fair-haired head popped through the café doorway. 'How did he take it?'

Her mother turned to her and winked. 'Like a lamb.'

Her father took another sip of his now lukewarm coffee. 'I don't know why I bother.'

But he did, really.

'DO YOU THINK I'm too easy-going?'

They were lying in bed on a Sunday morning, the sun slanting through a chink in the curtains, and Pippa surfaced from a deep sleep and turned to face him, her eyes still tight shut, one arm pulling the covers over her shoulder to keep warm. 'Mmm. What?'

'Sorry. I thought you were awake. I was just thinking about whether or not I'm a pushover.'

She opened one eye. 'What's brought this on?'

'Dunno.' He was lying on his back gazing at the ceiling. 'Midlife crisis, I suppose.'

She pushed out a hand from under the covers and stroked the side of his head. 'Bit early, isn't it?'

'I'm thirty-nine.'

She opened the other eye. 'Well, I'm thirty-seven and I don't intend having mine for a good ten years yet.'

'It's just that sometimes I take stock and I wonder what I've achieved. I wonder if I should have taken charge more, instead of being pushed around by fate.'

The house was silent, but the air outside was filled with birdsong and country sounds: the distant bleating of sheep, a breeze rustling through the leaves of a sycamore, the throaty growl of a tractor.

'You? Pushed around? Fat chance.' She snuggled up to him and put an arm round his waist.

'Well, it took you to organise this holiday.'

'That's because you hadn't time.'

'It's just that I sometimes wonder how I've ended up where I've ended up. I mean, why the heck am I running a restaurant? It's not what I intended.'

'So what did you intend?'

'I don't know, really. I don't suppose I ever have. There's writing, but maybe I'm not driven enough. I just seem to have these distant dreams of something—I'm not quite sure what.'

'And this isn't it?'

He propped himself up and turned to face her. 'Well, no—yes. I mean, you and me, this is what I want but I'm not sure about the rest. Do you see what I'm trying to say?'

'I see exactly what you're trying to say,' she said. 'We're all conditioned from birth to have some sort of life-plan, a career pattern we follow slavishly until we retire.' She kissed his cheek. 'You can't work out why at thirty-nine you're still not in charge of yourself or where you're going. Truth is that nobody is, really. Most people are bored out of their brains.'

'I suppose so.' He wrapped his arms round her and kissed her. There was a tap at the bedroom door. 'Bathroom's empty!'

'Thanks,' Pippa shouted, as she stroked Tom's forehead. 'Better get up, then.'

'Suppose so. What's Madam doing today?'

'Out on the toot. With one of her fellas, I think.'

'One of? How many's she got?'

'Just the two.'

There was a sardonic note in Tom's voice. 'Can't make up her mind?'

'Doesn't want to. Happy playing the field.'

'Is she still going out with whatsisname—Blob?'

'Blip,' Pippa corrected.

'How does a guy come by a name like Blip?'

'His parents already had four children. They hadn't intended to have any more. He was a blip in their birth control.'

'Poor little sod. Seems a bit wet to me.'

'Not really. He's sweet, just a bit shy.'

'But it's not serious?'

'I think Blip would like it to be, but Tally says he's just a friend.'

'So who's the other hunk?'

'Ask her yourself.'

Tom looked hurt. 'I don't like to pry. And I don't want to be one of those interfering dads who disapproves of his daughter's boyfriends.'

'But you will be.'

Tom smiled unwillingly. 'I know.'

'Well, you needn't worry too much. I told you, she's into friendships rather than romance. Doesn't want to get bogged down.'

'We should be grateful while it lasts.'

'SO, ER, WHAT are you doing today?' Tom tried to sound casual as he munched toast and marmalade.

'Going out.' As he had expected, Tally's reply was noncommittal.

'Anyone I know?'

'Dad! Don't be ridiculous.'

Tom took a sip of coffee. 'Only curious.'

Pippa sat down opposite him at the kitchen table, and turned to Tally. 'You know what dads are like, anxious about their children.'

Tally raised her eyes heavenward. 'And you know what daughters are like,' she said. 'Irresponsible and flighty.' She smiled at her father. 'Don't worry, Dad. I'm not a slapper.'

Tom choked on his coffee. 'I should hope not.'

'You're quite safe,' Tally went on. 'As far as I can see the only things that guys are interested in are sleeping, drinking and farting.'

Tom paused, mid-chew, surprised first by his daughter's candour and second by her accuracy.

Tally warmed to her subject. 'It's true. They're children, basically. I'm not ready for children yet.'

'That's a relief. So where are you wanting a lift to today?'

'I'm being picked up.'

'Thank heavens for that. At last, a friend with his own car.' Then concern set in. 'Is he a good driver?'

'Dad! Stop worrying!' She laid a hand on his. 'He's very careful and he knows I won't even get into the car if he drinks. OK?'

Tom sighed. 'Sorry.'

The sound of tyres crunching on gravel signalled the arrival of the beau of the day. The object of his affections got up from the table and took her leave. 'Alex has to go out with his parents tonight so I should be back about six. OK? Bye.' She kissed her mother's cheek, patted her father's head as though he were a favourite dog, and ran out of the front door.

'Well, that's that, then.' Pippa began to clear the table.

Tom gazed out of the window. 'Who's Alex?' he asked casually.

'LIKE THE CAR?'

'It's all right. Not much room for bales of hay.'

Alex Blane-Pfitzer turned to Tally with a look of incomprehension. Then he saw the joke. 'Oh, very funny. Bit faster than a horsebox, though.'

'Mmm.' Tally was determined to seem unimpressed with the black Mazda MX5. After all, people shouldn't be given cars like this on their eighteenth birthday. Even if they were secondhand.

'So where to? The Marina or the Old Harbour?'

'The Old Harbour. It's prettier.'

'OK.' He put his foot down and roared off down the lane.

Enjoying the rush of the wind through her hair, Tally breathed in the fresh early-summer fragrance. Alex kept glancing at her, hoping, since he was wearing a pair of Storm shades, she wouldn't notice.

'Do you like it round here?' he asked.

She nodded. 'It's the best.'

'Better than London?'

'Much. Can't stand the smell. Or the people. They seem so miserable all the time—walking around with long faces.'

'But London's cool.'

'Who cares about cool?'

Alex turned to her and laughed. 'You're funny.'

Tally shrugged and looked sideways at the hedgerow filled with foxgloves, cow parsley and campion. 'Maybe,' she muttered.

Alex squeezed into a parking space alongside the Old Harbour, got out and went round to open Tally's door. He offered her a hand, which she took, then pulled her up. They stood facing each other for a moment, and he pushed his shades onto the top of his head. Then she smiled and said, 'Better lock it. Don't want it pinched.'

'No.' The moment had passed. Alex came to and clipped on the hood, then locked the doors.

They began to walk along the path that led from the harbour round the mouth of the estuary. She was a strange girl. He tried to impress her but every time it seemed he failed. Other girls would be excited by his lifestyle, but not Tally Drummond. And yet there was no one in whose company he would rather be.

It was the perfect June morning—a gentle warmth from the sun, the air still. From the winding estuary path—really just dried and flattened mud between rough tussocks of grass—they could see small boats cruising down the Channel. They rounded a small copse, deep green in its summer livery, and sat down on a peeling bench to look at the view. The sun glinted on the ebbing tidal waters of the Axe, and gulls and oyster-catchers perforated the air with their shrill calls. Alex slipped his arm around her shoulder and leaned back.

Tally spoke first. 'You'd rather have London than this?'

'Oh, I like it here at weekends, but I miss the action and the company. No mates down here, really.'

She turned to face him. 'How long have you been coming here?'

'A couple of years—ever since my parents bought a house down here. Dad works all the hours God sends. We live in Holland Park, but he wanted somewhere to switch off at weekends. What about your dad? What does he do?'

'He runs a restaurant.'

'Can you talk to him?' Alex gazed out across the water.

Tally nodded. 'Always. Sometimes I don't want to, but I know I can if I do want to. He's just . . . well, Dad. How about you?'

'Oh, you know.'

'No, I don't.'

Alex hesitated, unwilling to be disloyal. 'Sometimes I think he'd like to talk more but it's a bit difficult. We haven't seen much of each other because I went away to school and Dad works in the City. Holidays are about the only time we see one another. We go to Salcombe every August. We've a cottage there. Dad likes to sail.'

'And you?'

'Yeah, I like it, too. Till he starts shouting!' He grinned. 'Mum won't sail with him any more. He gets a bit worked up.'

Tally smiled sympathetically. She got up and walked to the water's edge, then looked back at him. 'And what about you? What are you going to do with your life?'

'Depends on my As. I've got a place at Edinburgh if I get my grades.'

'To do what?'

'Economics.' He picked up a stone and skimmed it across the rippling water. 'What about you?'

'Oh, I want to do marine biology. But I've only just done my GCSEs so I'm two years behind you.'

'The perfect age gap.' He saw her colour, and now it was her turn to pick up a stone and throw it into the limpid water.

Tally walked up the bank a little and sat down on the grassy edge of the path, drawing her knees up under her chin and watching him throw stones. It was clear that he was indulged by his parents, but he was not the spoilt brat Tally had assumed he would be. To be truthful, she had only agreed to go out with him because she was flattered he'd asked her rather than Emma when he had seen them in the tea shop. He was tall—a good six foot—and had short fair hair, turned up at the front into a quiff. He wore sturdy deck shoes, jeans that showed off his neat bum, and a baggy pale pink shirt worn outside his trousers. His face, often frowning, was square-jawed, his eyes pale blue. And he had nice hands.

He turned from the water's edge and came up to where she sat. She smiled at him. He sat down beside her, leaned towards her and kissed her. She felt her face moving towards his with a naturalness that surprised her. She closed her eyes as his warm lips pressed against hers. It was a nice kiss. He smelt of soap.

She pulled away from him and they sat quietly for a while. Then he asked, 'Can I see you again?'

She paused and smiled shyly. 'If you like.'

They got up and walked further along the estuary path, he with his arm round her shoulder, and she with her hands in her pockets.

'WE HAVE A PROBLEM.' Tom was standing in the kitchen doorway, jangling his car keys and looking mildly irritated.

'What sort of problem?' Pippa looked up from the basket she was filling with sandwiches and crisps, a bottle of wine and two glasses.

'Where did you fancy going for this picnic.'

'Don't mind. Why?'

'How about the back of the barn?'

'Well, I'd thought we might go a bit further than that. Down to the coast? Up on the Downs?'

'Could be tricky. Maisie's manure has arrived. It's in the middle of the lane. I don't really fancy driving over a mountain of muck.'

Pippa craned her neck to see out of the doorway. 'Why she thinks she needs that amount of manure to grow herbs I've no idea. They'll be six feet tall with no flavour at all. Is she moving it?'

'Oh, she's got Mr Poling beavering away with a barrow but it'll take him a couple of hours.'

'Looks like we're in for a bit of a hike, then. Exercise will do us good.' Pippa grinned. 'Last one up Brindle Hill's a cissy.'

Tom raised his eyebrows. 'Brindle Hill? With that lot? Are you feeling all right?'

'Never better.'

THEY EDGED THEIR WAY round the manure and continued along the lane and over the stile to the right of the cart track, then began the ascent of Brindle Hill across the sheep-dotted meadows.

Soon Wilding's Barn was no more than a matchbox below them and the sky grew—pale blue bordered by clouds stained with primrose. Tom powered his way up the grassy slope with the basket, drawing the rich, clean air into his lungs. Pippa endeavoured to keep up but finally stopped to catch her breath by a stile, holding her side.

Tom turned and looked down at her. 'You all right?'

She nodded, breathless, her cheeks flushed.

His heart swelled at the sight of her—dark brown hair held back in a ponytail, brown shapely legs showing below her dark blue shorts, the contours of her body disguised in a baggy rugby shirt of pink and green. He put down the basket and walked back a few paces to help her, then wrapped his arms round her as she laid her head against his chest, panting. 'Are you sure?'

She laughed through her breathlessness. 'Stitch. That's all.' Then she slapped his bottom and pushed him on. 'Nearly there.'

'No. Let's stop here. No need to go any further.'

They flopped down on the grass and took in the view. Behind them was an amphitheatre of softly rolling hills. Below them they could see the snaking Axe running from the harbour, with its flotilla of boats, into the widening mud-coloured estuary and the glinting silver sea beyond. Around them buttercups wavered in the breeze, and the liquid notes of a soaring skylark floated high above.

Pippa pulled off her hairband and shook out her hair, then fell back into the grass with a sigh. 'Oh, this is the life.'

Tom watched as she closed her eyes, the colour fresh in her cheeks, her hair dark and glossy against the soft green turf. He picked a long-stemmed buttercup and ran it under her chin and across her cheek. 'Just seeing if you like butter.'

She smiled. 'Bad for you.'

'I suppose everything that's nice is bad for you.'

She opened one eye. 'Not everything.'

She closed her eyes again and he ran his hand down her body then inside her shirt, feeling the delicate ridges of her ribs, the softness of her breasts. She sighed as he stroked her skin, and returned the kiss he planted on her lips.

He lay back on the grass next to her and listened to her breathing. He turned to look at her again, then began to unbutton her shorts.

She opened her eyes. 'Tom!'

'Mmm?'

'What are you doing?'

He muffled her words with another kiss, deep and longing this time. The scent of the crushed grass bit into her nostrils, as she felt his hand slide down inside her shorts. She pushed her hands into his shirt, surprised at her willingness to be made love to on top of a hill. Part of her felt she ought at least to glance around to check that they were alone, but the other part did not care. Her breathing began to quicken and Tom enfolded her in his arms. 'I do love you,' he said.

CHAPTER TWO

It was Tuesday morning. The holiday was four days away, exams were over, and Tally had a day off school. She decided that it was time for her and Pippa to go shopping. It was the sort of outing Pippa loved—even though her daughter would persuade her to buy clothes that were far too young for her.

Pippa tried on cotton skirts that came down to her ankles; Tally held up tiny strappy tops that she considered perfect for Pippa's trim figure. Then garment after garment was held up against Tally's slender frame, and a bargaining ensued, in which one unsuitable item of clothing was traded off against something sensible. Finally, weary, yet excited at the prospect of two weeks in Tuscany, the pair flopped down in Tally's favourite teashop and ordered lunch.

'Do you think he'll like them?' asked Pippa, tentatively.

'Course he will. You look gorgeous.'

'I'm not sure about that top.'

'It looks great.'

An anxious look. 'Not too young?'

'Oh, Mum! You're not that old . . . Dad is, but you're not.'

'Don't be mean.'

'Is he OK?' Tally asked lightly.

'Yes. Why?'

'Oh, I don't know. He just seems preoccupied.'

'A lot on his mind, with Sam going and everything.' She paused. 'He's been rather thoughtful lately. I think he's feeling a bit restless.'

'Probably just his age.'

Pippa made to reprimand her, but Tally continued, 'No, I don't mean . . . well . . . I mean I'm not being unkind . . . it's just that I suppose Dad's never really done what he wants to do, has he?'

Pippa sighed. 'Not really. I think part of him loves his life, but he doesn't think he's achieved much.'

'And what do you think?'

Pippa looked wistful. 'I think he's achieved a lot, but maybe he feels he hasn't explored his full potential—he might have been more adventurous if he didn't have us to look after. I also think he's a very good man.'

'What a lovely thing to say.' Tally beamed and took a bite of her toasted sandwich, then muttered, 'I hope it rains.'

'What?' Pippa frowned.

'There's no point in going away somewhere hot when it's hot here. It's a waste.'

Pippa smiled. 'Don't worry. Storms are on the way. I heard it on the news this morning.'

As if on cue, the door of the teashop opened and Rachel Jago, with a couple of chums in tow, breezed in and set about loudly installing her party at the table in the window, to the irritation of other customers intent on a quiet lunch.

It was some moments before she noticed Pippa and Tally. When she did, she excused herself to her smartly dressed companions, and crossed to where mother and daughter sat. 'Pippa! Tally! How lovely to see you!' She kissed the air to the side of their cheeks, and motored on. 'You must be getting ready for the holiday? Lovely!

What a time to go! But I expect we'll cope. The boys are interviewing a new under-chef today.'

Under the table Tally slid her hand over her mother's and squeezed it: colour was rising in Pippa's cheeks. Before either of them could say anything Rachel continued, 'And I see you've been shopping. I hope you found something. I find it impossible to shop here in Axbury. Peter's very sweet and lets me go up to London once a month. Bless him! Still, I suppose it doesn't really matter who sees you in holiday wear. Anyway, must dash.' She rejoined her friends.

Pippa darted a look at Tally and murmured, 'Don't say anything.'

Tally's face was bright pink. 'She's such a bitch. How do you put up with it?'

'I think pleasant thoughts.'

'Poor Dad. How does he put up with it?'

'He thinks unpleasant thoughts.'

AT THE PELICAN the kitchen was pulsating with life. Pans clattered from hob to hob, and Peter had extracted an enormous salmon from a fish kettle and was laying pieces of it on plates.

'Table twenty-three!' He banged his hand on the hot cabinet to attract the attention of a young waiter. 'Come on, come on! Twenty-three!' The red-faced youth lifted the plates onto a tray then made his way back out through the swing door into the restaurant. Sam, beavering away at four plates of scallops, kept his head down and dribbled some sauce over them.

Out front, Tom was meeting and greeting. He seated diners, took their orders, suggested a suitable wine and cleared the tables while still finding time to chat to regulars. It was, he thought, no job for a grown man. Peter was the important one—the restaurant rose or fell in people's estimation on account of his culinary skills. But perhaps the success of the Pelican was as much down to his own easy-going manner, he reflected, and it was that, more than anything, that kept him going. Some people were destined to be movers and shakers, surgeons and nurses, teachers and airline pilots, and others, like himself, were suited to work in life's amusement arcade. Dining out was an amusement, and he had an important role in helping people to lead brighter lives. Sometimes he almost believed it.

It was a lunchtime much like other lunchtimes. There were unexpected arrivals who swore they had booked when they hadn't, there were couples who looked furtive, and businessmen who talked loudly and drank too much. But as the last diner departed and the blind was pulled down on the door, Tom was left with his usual feeling of quiet satisfaction. He left Sally and the two other waitresses to clear up, and sauntered through to the kitchen, slackening his tie.

Peter was washing his hands. 'All right, squire?' he asked.

'Fine,' Tom replied. 'One handbag that we didn't have when we started, but Sally's checked the contents and put in a call.'

Peter dried his hands and unbuttoned his whites. 'So, when's the great white hope coming?'

Tom checked his watch. 'Four o'clock.'

'That gives us under an hour to get our act together.'

The two men walked from the kitchen to a freshly cleaned corner table at the back of the restaurant, and studied the letter of the sole respondent to the advert in the *Axbury Gazette*.

Dear Sir,

I am writing in response to your advertisement for a sous-chef. I have had several years' experience in the restaurant trade and would like to apply for the position. I enclose my CV for your consideration and look forward to hearing from you.

Yours sincerely,

K. Lundy

'Keith or Kevin?' asked Peter, scrutinising the letter for clues.

'Doesn't say. Might be Karen.'

'She should say so, then. And where's the CV? It says, "I enclose my CV"?' Peter made great play of examining the inside of the empty envelope.

'Must have forgotten to put it in.'

'Pathetic.'

'Oh, you don't know. We all make mistakes.'

Peter shook his head. 'Always ready to think the best of someone.'

'Until I know the worst.'

TOM DRUMMED HIS NAILS on the table. Four fifteen. Still no sign. Then at twenty past four came the knock they had been expecting. Tom went to open the door.

Standing before him was a slight woman with close-cropped fair hair, aged between thirty-five and forty. Her pale green eyes were glistening with what looked like a mixture of anger and sorrow. A canvas bag hung over her shoulder.

'Mr Jago?' she asked, her voice trembling with emotion.

'Drummond,' said Tom.

The woman thrust out her hand and Tom took it. 'Kate Lundy. I'm so sorry I'm late. Not a very good start.' She tried to smile.

Tom beckoned her in, curious to know why she was so distraught. 'It really doesn't matter. Come in. Tea? Coffee?'

'Water, please. Tap.'

Tom pointed towards the table at which Peter was pulling out a chair, then went to fill a glass from the tap at the back of the bar.

Kate shook hands with Peter and sat down.

When Tom returned, she smiled gratefully at him and took a sip of water. Peter looked at Tom and raised his eyebrows.

Tom tried to break the ice. 'We weren't sure whether you'd be a Kevin or a Keith.'

She put down the glass. 'Sorry. With some chefs you don't even get an interview if you're female. Some would rather swear at a man than a woman.' She was calming down.

Peter took the bull by the horns. 'Do you mind being sworn at?'

'Used to it.'

Tom butted in. 'What sort of experience have you had? Only there was no CV.'

'God! I'm sorry. I thought I'd put it in.' She rummaged in the canvas bag, saying, 'One fish restaurant . . .'

'Cod and chips?' Peter asked cuttingly.

'Turbot and rösti.'

Peter tried to look unimpressed. Tom suppressed a smile.

'Here it is.' She handed a folded piece of paper to Peter and continued, 'I did twelve months at Brian Turner's restaurant in Kensington. Then six months at Claridge's.'

Peter tried to keep the upper hand. 'Not long.'

'Long enough to know I preferred small restaurants where the work was more rewarding.'

Peter scanned the CV. 'You don't seem to have worked for a few years.'

'No.'

The two men looked at her, waiting for an explanation.

'Domestic problems.'

Peter leaned back. 'What sort of problems?'

Tom butted in, 'Would you be able to work six days a week? Up to a hundred covers every lunch and evening?'

'No problem.'

Peter looked at the floor and folded his arms. 'I'm losing a guy who knows all my funny little ways.'

'I'll do my best to get used to them,' Kate responded.

'We haven't offered you the job yet,' Peter said. 'And what I've heard so far isn't exactly encouraging.'

'Peter . . .' Tom sensed unpleasantness brewing, but Kate cut in, 'No. You're right. I turn up late, looking a wreck, I forget my CV, and tell you I haven't worked for a few years. Why should you take me on? I'll tell you why. Because I'm bloody good.' She raised her voice, which took the two men by surprise. 'I'm good under pressure, I'm a fast learner and, in spite of what you might think from my appearance, I'm reliable. If you want a creative prima donna I'm not your woman. If you want a doormat I'm not your woman. But if you want a reliable sous-chef who knows her stuff and can keep cool, then you're looking at her. I won't let you down.'

Peter's mouth hung open.

Kate picked up her bag from the floor. 'I'm sorry. You've probably got a lot of people to see.' She got up, and the two men followed suit. She managed a brief smile. 'Just ring to let me know.' And then, resignedly but with good humour, 'I won't hold my breath.' With that she took her leave. Tom and Peter stood silently, staring at the swinging 'closed' sign on the door.

'WE'D BE MAD to take her on.' Peter was levering the cap off a bottle of Beck's. 'If she gets into that sort of state when she's had a bad journey and turns up fifteen minutes late, what the hell's she going to be like in the kitchen? It'll be tears every five minutes.'

'You don't know that.'

'Oh, come on, Tom. We've had enough sous-chefs like her in the past. You know what a bastard I am when I'm working. How's she going to cope with that?'

'I thought she coped quite well, actually. It was the first time she'd met you and you were a bit hard on her. But she refused to be browbeaten.'

'We should see more people before we make up our minds.'

'There *are* no more people. She's the only one who applied,' Tom reminded him. 'I reckon she's better than she seemed. There was something about her, a sort of inner strength.'

Peter took a gulp from the bottle. 'Sometimes I don't understand you. You've gone soft. You used to be dynamic and go-ahead and look at you now. Where's your sense of adventure?'

Tom was surprised. 'What do you mean? It's me who's saying we should take her on.'

'Oh, I don't mean with her, I mean with the Pelican. Why don't you want to go for it with another place?'

He should have sensed that this was coming, Tom thought. He'd realised that Peter had been brooding again, but had put it down to worry over Sam's imminent departure.

'We've tried that before. We know it doesn't work.'

'*Didn't* work. The climate's different now. Rachel reckons we should have another go.'

'Ah.' Tom nodded slowly. 'I see. So, what's the plan?'

Peter had gone further than he had intended and tried to back down. 'No plan. I just think we should consider it again, that's all.'

Tom was unwilling to tackle the hoary old chestnut that had raised its head regularly since Rachel had come on the scene. He changed the subject. 'And in the immediate future are we giving Ms Lundy a chance?'

'Well, on your head be it. But the first time we have tears in there,' Peter pointed towards the kitchen, 'she's outa here.'

TOM MADE THE PHONE call that evening from the back of the bar. A soft voice answered the phone, quite different from the one he had heard that afternoon.

'Kate Lundy, please.'

'Speaking.'

'It's Tom Drummond.'

'Oh, yes.' Apprehension crept into her voice.

'Just to say that we'd be happy to have you in the kitchen if you still want the job.'

Silence.

'Hello? Are you there?'

'Yes. It's just that . . . I thought . . . well . . .'

'Probably not a good start, really.' His tone was friendly. 'We'd had a bit of a day and I guess you had, too. Well, anyway, there we are. If we could have a couple of references it would be useful.'

'Fine, yes, I'll get it sorted.'

'Can you start on Monday? Ten o'clock.'

'Of course.' There was disbelief in her voice. She pulled herself together. 'Thank you, Mr Drummond.'

'Tom.'

'Yes. Thank you. Well, I'll see you Monday.'

Then he remembered. 'You won't, actually. I'm on holiday for a couple of weeks. But Sam will still be there—he's the guy you're replacing—so you won't have to cope with Chef on your own.'

'Right.'

'Good luck, then, and I'll see you when I get back.'

Tom put the phone down. What a time to go on holiday. Still, what could he do if he stayed, other than give Kate Lundy moral support? It was Peter she had to impress.

TOM WOKE TO FIND the bed empty—as usual. He was the owl, Pippa the lark. He went to the window and threw up the sash. Sooty storm clouds were gathering, and a low rumble of thunder broke the still air. The foliage of the kitchen garden was bathed in a strange and threatening light: the blue-green cabbages seemed almost luminous. Then he saw Pippa, on her hands and knees among the parsley, snipping at stems and putting them in small polythene bags. 'You'll have to hurry,' he called. 'Have you nearly finished?'

'I've got the mint and coriander still to do.'

Tom realised that both she and the herbs were in for a soaking. 'I'll be down.'

'Thanks.' She didn't like to get him up early when he had come back late from the restaurant, but today she was glad of his help.

He came out in a pair of jeans and a sweatshirt. She rose and pecked him on the cheek. 'Saviour.'

He worked alongside her, slipping herbs into their bags as she cut, breathing in the fresh scent of the mint as the downy leaves brushed against his skin.

A splat on a rhubarb leaf heralded the start of the downpour. As the heavens opened they rushed to the barn for shelter, leaning back against the old stone wall as the heavy rain beat down on the herbs, releasing an ever-changing mixture of fragrances—fruity basil, aniseedy fennel, the sweet summer scent of rosemary.

He put his arm round her and breathed deeply. 'Lovely smell.'

'The best. We'll be able to smell them in the wild next week,' she said, 'with warm sun on them.'

'Yes.' Tom tried to think of two weeks in Italy, but his mind was still on work. He told Pippa of the previous day's events. 'You think I was right to go for her? She was in a bit of a state.'

'Yes, I do. There was probably a reason.'

'She didn't tell us what it was.'

Pippa looked up at him. 'You should be grateful. If she'd given you a long explanation you'd have known you'd got a moaner on your hands.'

'But *we* tell one another our problems.'

'We're married. It comes with the territory.'

He laughed briefly. 'Yes. I suppose so.' He kissed the top of her head. 'Anything you want to get off your chest?'

'Not really. Except that I wish we had more time together. These past couple of days have been so lovely . . . Just made me realise . . .' She stopped and he saw that she was fighting back tears.

'Hey!' He put both arms round her as the rain clattered about them. 'What's the matter?'

'Just a bit tired, I suppose. Need a holiday. Like you. Sorry.' He brushed the tears off her cheek with his fingers, then began to hum. She laughed as she recognised the tune—'Night and day . . . you are the one . . . Only you beneath the moon and under the sun.'

'Come on.' He pulled a clean handkerchief from his pocket. 'Wipe away the tears and show me what you've bought for the trip.'

She blew her nose loudly, then looked at him sideways. 'What do you mean?'

'That shopping trip you had in Axbury yesterday. I can sniff out a carrier bag from half a mile away.'

By the time they reached the house she was laughing, and within half an hour she had tried on all that Tally had chosen for her. Tom raised his eyebrows only once, at a skimpy top, which she confessed was Tally's.

Over coffee he watched as the Pippa he knew returned—strong-willed and good-humoured, annoyed only when she thought he was selling himself short or allowing himself to be walked over. He waved as she drove off to Axbury, feeling a protective surge of love for his wife. Then he climbed the stairs and stopped outside his study. He pushed open the door and walked to the table in front of the window. To one side of the laptop sat a red file, marked 'Making Waves'. He felt the thickness of the manuscript—about an inch. One hundred and forty-nine pages. He had intended to write a thriller, but it seemed to be turning into a gentle romance. Life mirrors art. He sighed, and went for a shower.

THE THREE-THIRTY bell came and Tally walked out of school and into town with Emma. They had a Coke and a tea cake in their favourite haunt.

'Are you seeing him again?'

Tally sipped her drink slowly, keeping Emma waiting for a reply. 'Might do.'

'Did you . . . er . . .' Emma's eyes were wide with anticipation.

'Emma!' Tally tutted, then took pity on her friend. 'He's a great kisser.' She frowned as she broke off a piece of tea cake and popped it into her mouth. 'But what about Blip?'

'What about him? Alex is much better-looking.'

'I'm not going out with Alex because of his looks. Alex is fun.'

'And Blip isn't?'

'Yes, of course. Well . . . it's different. Oh, I don't know. Alex is far too spoilt. I mean, look at that car. He's everything I hate in a guy—self-assured, too much money, up himself. Except that he's not. He's sweet. And I enjoyed his company.'

'And his kisses.'

'Sssh!' Tally looked around anxiously in case they were being overheard, but the usual coterie of elderly ladies seemed indifferent to anything but their own ill-health and the weather.

Emma looked at her friend searchingly. 'There's something funny about you. You look different. Especially when you talk about him.'

Tally blushed. 'Don't be silly.'

'You do. See? You're blushing. Are you in love?'

''Course not. I've only been out with him once.'

Emma grinned, then looked thoughtful. 'Do you think it's OK to do it? I mean if it's serious?'

'Do what?'

'Make love. Have sex. You know.'

Tally stopped chewing her tea cake. 'I don't know. Not yet. Why are you asking?'

'Pressure from . . . you know.'

Tally fixed Emma with an unwavering eye. 'And have you?'

'Got pretty near it yesterday.'

Tally took hold of her hand. 'You don't have to, you know.'

Emma nodded. 'I know. It's just that half of me wants to and the other half is scared. You know?'

'I didn't know you and Toby were that serious. But if you do . . . you will take precautions?'

'Oh, don't worry. Toby was already pulling it on when I backed out last night.'

They stared at each other for a moment before collapsing in a fit of laughter. Their hilarity was short-lived.

'Hi!'

Tally and Emma looked up to see a slender youth with dark, cropped hair. He wore a navy-blue school blazer, but his tie had been loosened and his off-white shirt was hanging out of his trousers. A Manchester United bag was slung over one shoulder.

Tally coloured. 'Hi, Blip!'

'Do you want another Coke?' he asked.

'No, thanks. I'm fine.'

'Emma?'

Emma shook her head.

Tally regained her composure. 'Sit down. How've you been?'

'OK.' Blip looked uneasy, but lowered himself into the chair opposite the two girls and dropped his bag on the floor. 'Wondered if you wanted to come and see that new Brad Pitt film tonight.'

Tally blustered, 'Oh! I'm sorry, I can't tonight. Got to pack.'

'I thought you weren't going until Saturday?'

'I'm not but . . . you know . . . lots to do.'

'I see.' Blip looked crestfallen. 'I've been looking up the place you're going to—in Tuscany. I couldn't find it on the map.'

'It's very small. Quite near Florence,' she added.

'I see. That's nice.'

Tally offered him a smile, but the conversation ground to a clumsy halt. Blip ran a hand through his spiky hair then stood up and picked up his bag. 'Maybe I'll see you when you get back?'

'Maybe.' And then, feeling that she was being a little too cool, 'That would be nice.'

He nodded at Emma, waved to Tally, and left.

'Poor Blip,' said Emma.

ON FRIDAY EVENING the Drummonds prepared their final supper before departure.

'I still think we could have had this meal on our own.' Tom was laying the table.

'But we haven't seen her for ages. And she hasn't seen Tally for even longer.'

'I suppose.'

Tally's footsteps came thumping down the stairs. 'She's here! She's here!'

Pippa turned from the sink and dried her hands, and the three went to the door to greet their guest.

The filthy Golf GTi ground to a halt on the gravel, and the figure inside it waved madly. Janie Giorgioni emerged from her car with a broad grin and her arms spread wide. 'Hello, my little blessings! It's been bloody ages!'

Tally ran towards her and gave her a hug. 'It's *sooo* lovely to see you, Janie.'

Janie squeezed her godchild in her arms. 'Oh, and you, my love. How've you been? Any boys? Any decent ones?'

'One or two.'

Janie turned to Pippa—'Lovely to see you, darling'—and kissed her on both cheeks before rounding on Tom. 'And you, Mr Drummond, are you looking after my girls?'

Tom scowled. 'No. I beat them daily. It's the only way to keep them in check.'

'Bastard!' She grinned and kissed him. 'You don't deserve them.'

'I know. Funny how they keep coming back for more. Must be my natural charm.' He kissed her cheek, and said, 'Nice to see you, Janie, even if we are going on holiday tomorrow.'

'Oh, I'm sorry. But it's the only time I've got before I go back up to the frozen north.'

Janie Giorgioni had an Italian father and a Scottish mother. She was tall and dark and ravishingly good-looking, but had remained steadfastly single, claiming that to marry was folly. She regarded Tom and Pippa's happy marriage as a rare aberration.

She and Pippa had met at catering school. Since those days Janie had changed jobs a dozen times and was now something in the travel business. She went through men like most women go through tights.

Tom gazed at her standing before him in black trousers and sweater, her thick raven hair brushing her shoulders, and wondered how she'd managed to come this far in life without getting attached, though he couldn't for the life of him imagine the sort of man that would ever be the other half of Janie. He thought he detected, just occasionally, the merest hint of wistfulness, though Janie didn't really do wistful. At least, not in company.

She opened the boot of her car, and threw aside clothes and glossy carrier bags in a frantic search. Ah! Here we are.' She pulled out two bottles and thrust them at Tom. 'For you. Open them. I'm gasping!'

Tom grinned. 'Come on, then, you old dragon. Let me pour you a glass.'

'Less of the old.' She slapped his bottom. 'I can give you a good three years.' She turned back to the car. 'Just a minute.' She held out a scarlet designer carrier bag to Tally. 'Here you are, sweetheart. Something for the holiday.'

Tally peeped inside the bag. 'Wow! Oh, wow!' She lifted out a triangle of black, silky fabric.

'What is it?' asked Tom, screwing up his eyes as if to focus. 'A handkerchief? A headscarf?'

Tally raised her eyes heavenward. 'It's a top!' She kissed her godmother, '*Stupendo! Grazie!*'

Janie murmured, '*Prego*. It'll look great with a tan.'

IN THE EVENT Janie's company did them all good. Pippa put to one side her fear of flying, Tom forgot his preoccupations, and Tally listened, wide-eyed, to her godmother's exploits.

Janie was only too happy to regale them with the saga of her most recently departed combatant, Jason. 'Completely unreasonable. Expected me to do everything for him. He couldn't even book a car in for servicing without asking me to look up the phone number.'

'So what made you take up with him?' asked Tom.

'Matchless in bed. Unbelievable staying power.'

Tom choked on his wine.

'Only kidding. Oh, I don't know, he seemed fairly kind. Quite a looker. In the end I just got bored, I suppose. I do like a bit of life in my men. I mean, look at you, Pippa. Why haven't you got rid of this drone yet?' She jerked her head in Tom's direction.

'Don't know, really. Never got round to it. But he can take the car in for a service without my help, so I suppose that's something.'

Tom helped himself to more of Pippa's fish pie. 'You just can't hack it, can you, Janie? If we were at each other's throats the whole time you'd be happy.'

'Yes. But I wouldn't enjoy coming here so much. Mind you, if you could manage the occasional spat it would make me feel better. Don't you ever fall out?'

Pippa shot a look at Tom. 'Sometimes.'

'About stupid things,' said Tom.

Tally tutted. 'Like whose turn it is to take the bins down to the end of the road.'

'Only because your mother always forgets.'

'I do not forget,' chipped in Pippa. 'It's just that I don't take them down as early as you do.'

'But if you leave it until too late you miss them.'

'When did I last leave it until . . .?' She stopped, her eyes on Janie, who was beaming broadly.

'How wonderful!' Janie said. 'At last I think I see signs of a crumbling marriage. Anyway,' she said, raising her glass, 'here's to you and your holiday. *Alla Salute!*'

It was eleven o'clock before Janie took her leave, with Tom enquiring if she was OK to drive and Janie assuring him that her limit was five glasses and she'd only had three. He looked doubtful. Janie kissed Pippa and Tally then turned to Tom. 'You know, there are times, you old goat, when I really do quite fancy you.' She kissed his cheek.

Tom frowned. 'What are we going to do with you?'

'Find me a decent man. No. Find me an indecent man—they're more fun.' She looked at him with a serious expression. 'Usually.'

As Tom walked Janie to her car, she said, with uncharacteristic tenderness, 'Look after them, Tom. They're very precious.'

'I will.'

'And tell Pippa I'll be in touch as soon as she gets back.'

'OK. You take care too, you old boot.'

'Bastard!' She flashed him a reassuring smile, started up the car and careered off down the rough gravel.

Tom stared after her. He wondered what Janie was really looking for in life, and decided that he was unlikely to find out. He couldn't even decide what he wanted for himself. He walked to the five-barred gate that led from the yard into an acre of paddock. The scent of newly dampened meadow filled his nostrils and the sounds of Pippa and Tally talking in the kitchen drifted out on the still night air. He leaned against the gate, looking towards the kitchen. He watched them together, easy, relaxed and joking, and realised, in a moment of clarity, that his feelings of futility were, as Pippa had suggested, due to nothing more than tiredness. At this moment, he could think of nowhere else he would rather be, and no one else he would rather be with than the two women who shared his life.

EARLY SATURDAY MORNING at Wilding's Barn found the Drummonds packing clothes into suitcases. Well, Tom was packing: Pippa and Tally had done the majority of theirs before Janie's arrival. Tom, as ever, was hurling in an assortment of whatever he could find at the last moment.

He was mining the contents of a sock drawer when the two women put their heads round the bedroom door.

'What are you wearing to travel?' asked Tally.

'Don't know. Haven't thought.'

Pippa and Tally looked at each other, then Pippa's hand appeared from behind the door with a coat hanger bearing a white cotton short-sleeved shirt and a pair of navy-blue chinos, the labels still attached.

'What's this?' asked Tom, puzzled.

'Couldn't let you go in old clothes, could we?' Pippa grinned.

'Or shoes.' Tally brought into view a pair of suede loafers.

'But I thought . . .'

'That we'd only been shopping for us? Oh, no. Didn't want you letting us down.' Tally tossed the shoes at her father, who caught one in each hand and perched on the bed.

Pippa remained by the door. 'Do you think we might go to any smart restaurants?' she asked.

'Well, I hope so.' Tom was trying on his new shoes.

'Good. This should come in handy, then.' She brought her other arm into view, on which was draped a pale blue linen suit.

'What? That's outrageous!'

'You don't know till you've tried it on.'

'Come on, Dad. Give us a fashion show.'

'I don't know. I leave you two alone for a day and what happens? You spend all my money on blue suits.'

'Not quite all. There's a bit left over for treats.'

Five minutes later he was standing in front of them wearing the suit with a cream polo shirt and his new loafers. 'How do I look?'

'Scrummy.' Tally's eyes gleamed.

Pippa looked at him with a critical eye. 'Very smart. Quite fanciable, really.' She went up to him and pecked him on the cheek. 'Very fanciable.'

'I'm outa here.' Tally made a beeline for the door, calling, 'How long before we leave?' as she bounded down the stairs.

'An hour,' Pippa shouted after her.

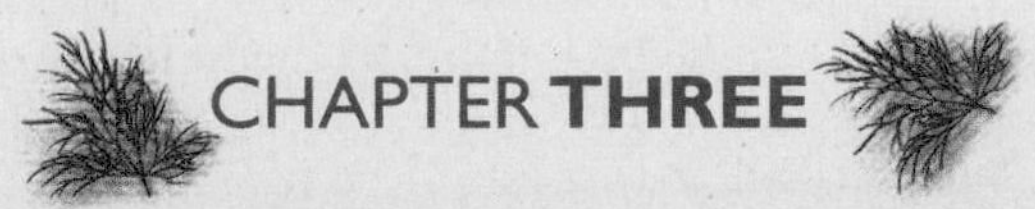

CHAPTER THREE

'Look at the sky—it's pink!' Tally's voice held a note of awe. 'I think I'm going to like Italy.'

Tom smiled to himself. At sixteen Tally could be both the sophisticated young woman and the wide-eyed child. At the moment she was in the second mode, and through her eyes he saw Italy as he had first seen it himself, in the company of Pippa. They had honeymooned in Siena and loved it—so much that they'd never been back. 'It would never be the same again,' said Pippa. But to come again to the country where their love had blossomed, where they had time only for each other, reminded them both of things that were sometimes too easily forgotten, too readily taken for granted.

Tom glanced at Pippa, and saw on her face a look of contentment that he had not seen in a while. Suddenly, home seemed worlds away. They had picked up the hire car at Pisa airport and had driven north into the hills. The road was narrower now and dusty, bordered by slender cypresses of deep, dusky green, and fringed by sturdy pines. Tally had unplugged herself from the Walkman and was peering out of the window. Every so often the undergrowth would clear to reveal a view of a vineyard in a valley, or pale grey and purple hills beyond. The evening air smelt of dust and rosemary, as Pippa had known it would, and Tally's 'Wow!' came at increasingly frequent intervals.

'Is that all you can say? Wow?'

'No. I can also say, "*Dove é la stazione di servizio piu vicina?*"'

Tom swerved to avoid a goat on the road. 'What was that?'

'I said, "Where is the nearest petrol station?"'

Pippa turned to her daughter. 'Where on earth—?'

'And I can say, "*La doccia non funziona*"—the shower doesn't work, and "*Non c'e carta igienica in bagno*"—there's no toilet paper in the bathroom, and "*Ci porta la lista dei vini?*"—could we see the wine list?'

'Have you been talking to your godmother?' Tom asked.

Tally grinned. '*Solo un pó.*'

They were now in a land of olive groves and citrus trees, and valleys dotted with pumpkin plants and mulberries. A low, pantiled roof hove into view among a stand of slender cypresses.

'Is that it?' Tally leaned forward from the back seat so that her head was between her father's and mother's.

Pippa looked at the map on her lap. 'It might be. There should be a turning just round this corner, and a sign saying "Villa Bartolo".'

'There! There it is!'

Tom turned into a rough gravel drive flanked by two crumbling stone gateposts and rough grass verges. Slowly they drove up a potholed drive. The roof of the villa was a dusky shade of terracotta, the walls washed a dark ochre, and a ramshackle framework of timber and wire supported a vine on one side. The evening sun slanted through the pale green leaves onto a stone terrace, where half a dozen wooden chairs surrounded a plank table.

Tom pulled up alongside the terrace and switched off the engine. An electric chirruping filled the air.

'What's that?' asked Tally.

'Cicadas,' answered Pippa.

'Wow! Can I get out? I want to see. This is just so cool!'

Pippa climbed out and lifted the seat to allow Tally to escape. She squeezed out and stood taking it all in. 'It's so . . . Italian.'

'That's a relief.' Tom was getting out now. 'What about a key?'

Pippa looked at the letter that accompanied the map. 'The letter says it's in a wooden box on the terrace.'

'That's trusting.'

Pippa grinned at him. 'Welcome to Tuscany.'

'And you.' He walked round the car, took her in his arms and kissed her forehead. 'Have a lovely time.'

Tally disappeared on the other side of the terrace, but her voice cut through the evening air. 'Oh, wow!'

Tom cast a sideways glance at Pippa. 'Her Italian's impressive, but I wish her English was more ambitious.'

They followed her, crisp vine leaves crunching under their feet. Where the ground fell away in front of them, a small turquoise pool was cut into the hillside. The softly rolling vineyards below them were perforated at intervals by cypresses and isolated farm buildings. Pale grey olive groves encroached on their boundary, and the view was framed by mountains flushed purple, copper and vibrant orange in the dying sun. It was close to perfection.

Pippa gasped. 'Oh, my goodness. How beautiful.'

The letter instructed them that a maid would appear in the morning, that they would find milk and bread in the fridge. A box of basic provisions would be in a cool room just off the kitchen.

Pippa and Tally hung the contents of the suitcases in tall wardrobes, while Tom heated a pizza and opened the bottle of Chianti that had been left for them. They ate under the stars as darkness fell, then slid between cool white sheets and fell asleep to the fading chorus of cicadas in the warm fragrance of the Tuscan night.

TALLY WOKE FIRST. The morning light was clear and strong. Her watch told her it was a quarter to seven. Far too early. But the light had a coruscating brilliance that defied her attempts at sleep. She slipped out of bed, went across to the window and pushed out the old brown shutters, which clattered against the walls.

The sights and sounds of an Italian morning greeted her eyes and ears. A cock crowed. The tall, slender cypresses, which the night before had seemed such a dark green, were almost lavender blue in the morning light. The sky was clear and pale as a bunch of forget-me-nots, and she could feel the warmth of the sun on her face.

She slipped out of her pyjamas and into shorts and a fresh white T-shirt before tiptoeing out of the house and onto the terrace. She breathed in deeply. She had never smelt anything like it before: the crisp, fresh, fruity air was rich with the scent of rosemary and sage, rosy red earth and vine leaves, cypress bark and pine needles. She walked to the low wall that surrounded the terrace and looked again at the view of the Tuscan valley. The clear pool, its surface broken by gentle ripples, glittered and gleamed in the morning sun.

She skirted the edge of the terrace and walked down the steps towards the water, where she crouched down and dipped in her hand. It was warm. She pulled off her T-shirt, and felt the gentlest of breezes on her skin. She undid her shorts and stepped out of them. For a moment she stood naked by the water, her head lifted to the sun, her eyes closed. Then she dived into the water and surfaced only when she had swum the full length of the pool.

She threw back her head to clear her hair from her eyes, and looked about her at the landscape through the shimmering haze that made the cypress trees dance. She had never felt so free, so . . . happy.

She swam to the ladder, climbed out and slipped her clothes on over her wet skin. Then she walked up the steps to the terrace and sat in the dappled light beneath the vine, waiting for her parents to come to life.

WHILE THE MAID, Maria, swept the terrace, made the beds and checked the towels, the three holidaymakers went shopping. The *supermercato* on the road to Pistoia was much more fun than the one at home. There was a certain thrill in buying *latte* rather than milk and *vino* rather than wine. Pippa got a kick out of choosing olives and melon, Parma ham and pasta, while Tom filled a trolley with Chianti and Vino Nobile di Montepulciano.

By early afternoon they were grouped round the table on the terrace having lunch. 'So what does everybody want to do?' asked Tom.

Pippa and Tally looked at one another then spoke in unison: 'Very little.'

Tom grinned. 'Right answer.' He put his hands behind his head and leaned back in his chair.

Tally got up. The sun was high in the sky now and the paving baking beneath her feet. 'I think I'll go for a swim.'

'Make sure you've got some sun-block on,' her mother said.

'Oh, Mum!'

'I'm not nagging, Tal. I just don't want you burning. Skin like yours cooks in this heat.'

Tally frowned. 'What about Dad?'

'He'll need it, too.'

'Don't worry about me. My skin's like leather.'

Pippa threw him a sideways look. 'I've heard that before. Last time you couldn't sleep on your back—remember?'

Tally went indoors and Tom moved his chair alongside Pippa's, then closed his eyes and enjoyed the warmth of the sun, stretching out his hand to find hers. She linked her fingers through his and sighed contentedly before a sharp click caused them both to open their eyes. Their daughter was standing in front of them, camera in hand. 'Ah! What a sweet picture. Two lovebirds asleep together!'

'We weren't asleep, we were sunbathing.'

'Without these?' She held up a tube of cream and a bottle of lotion. 'You'll burn, you know. And I don't want you coming to me and moaning when you can't lie on your back.'

At which point Tom leaped out of his chair and chased Tally down the terrace steps. Her screams of terror were short-lived. In seconds her father had whisked her off her feet, scooped her into his arms, and with a cry of triumph leaped high into the air. They hit the water with an almighty splash.

Pippa slipped off her shorts to reveal a bikini and dived silently into the water to surface just feet away from them. She brushed her dark hair from her eyes and enquired, 'Can anyone join in?'

ON THE EVENING of their first day, as the sun sank behind the olive grove, the three dined on spaghetti alle vongole and sipped Tom's Gaioli '94 as they chatted in the flickering candlelight on the terrace. Tom saw the new colour in Tally's cheeks and the glow in Pippa's eyes, her shoulders delicately flushed after their first day in the sun.

'Does the food always taste this good over here?' asked Tally.

'Always,' confirmed Tom. 'Especially when your mum cooks it.'

Pippa protested. 'I think it's the sun. The olives are different, the bread is different, even the pasta tastes better.'

'More of the same tomorrow?' asked Tom.

'Oh, I think so,' Pippa answered.

'By the pool for me. Reading,' said Tally and, seeing that her mother was about to draw breath, 'with sun block on my nose, factor fifteen on my arms and legs and very little else.'

Tom raised an eyebrow. 'I see the handkerchief has come out.' He nodded at the triangle of black silk that was Tally's top, the gift from Janie, and tried to appear disapproving.

'It's so cool and comfortable,' said Tally.

'It looks stunning,' Pippa remarked. 'Trust Janie.'

'Talking of which,' said Tom, 'when did you learn all this Italian? You haven't seen Janie for nearly a year.'

'We talk on the phone and she writes me letters.'

'Did you learn how to say "my father wouldn't approve"?'

''Fraid not.'

Tally got up and cleared away the remnants of supper.

Pippa had seen that her daughter's eyelids were heavy, and said, 'Time for bed, Tal. Go on.'

Tally grinned beatifically, stretched and yawned. She kissed her father, then her mother.

'Sleep well, sweetheart.'

Tally wove her way across the terrace to bed, leaving Tom and Pippa alone.

'Happy?' he asked.

'Very. You?'

'Blissfully.'

'Bed?'

'Bed.' Tom rose and held out his hand. Pippa took it and he folded his arms round her.

'Seems like yesterday,' she murmured.

'I know.'

'It smells the same and sounds the same.'

'That's because it is the same.'

'Are we, do you think?'

'Oh, yes.'

Italy was their place, the place where they had their happiest times. She eased away from him. 'I'm glad. I'm so glad I met you, Tom Drummond.' Eight words that would live with him for ever. He put his arm round her shoulder and walked her slowly along the length of the dark terrace to their room.

THE FOLLOWING MORNING Tom woke first. He looked across to where Pippa lay, still sleeping, then eased himself out of bed. He dressed and crept quietly out onto the terrace, where the sight that had greeted Tally the previous day worked its magic on him, too.

He went to the kitchen and made coffee, then took a mug out

onto the terrace. There, in the ripening morning, he sat and waited for his family.

Tally appeared first, rubbing her eyes and asking what time it was.

'Nine o'clock. Early for you.'

'I was up before seven yesterday,' she murmured.

Tom sipped his coffee. 'Do you want to go and see if your mum's awake? She was fast asleep when I left her. Ask her if she wants a cup of tea or coffee.'

'OK.' Tally tottered off, and Tom heaved a contented sigh as he gazed at the landscape.

'Dad!'

He looked round. Tally was standing on the terrace. There had been a catch in her voice. 'What is it?'

'It's Mum.' He got up and saw the fear in her eyes. Quickly he ran along the terrace to their bedroom door and went in. Pippa was lying where he had left her earlier. Still and silent. He sat on the edge of the bed. Only then did he notice that her eyes were wide open.

He rushed out onto the terrace, shouting, 'Fetch a doctor!' then realised the impossibility of his request. Tally was shaking.

'Where's Maria?' he bellowed. 'Where does she live?' Tally pointed to a cottage a few hundred yards along the track. 'Go and get her.'

Tally began to cry.

'Quickly!' He ran back to the bedroom.

AS THE AMBULANCE sped to Pistoia, Tom knew the race was futile. When they arrived, the doctor, who spoke good English, was kind and thoughtful, as well as practical. Then he left them in a waiting room. Tom wrapped an arm round Tally, who leaned into him, trembling. They said little.

When the doctor called for them he explained that the likely cause of Pippa's death was heart failure. There would have to be a post-mortem. They would endeavour to complete the formalities quickly, but it might take a few days. Would they care to go back home immediately or wait and travel with the body? The word brought Tom up short, but he did not need time to think: they would not leave without her.

They returned to the villa to pack and moved into a hotel in Pistoia—it seemed impossible to stay in what for them had been paradise without Pippa.

Two days passed in an agonising haze of visits to the British Consulate and the hospital. Everyone was sympathetic and helpful, but the end result was the same: Tom had lost the love of his life, and Tally her mum.

Tom watched Tally carefully. There were moments of frenzied questioning—Why had it happened? Why had there been no warning signs? He could not answer her, much though he wanted to. Then anger and disbelief were replaced by a quiet reserve. He found it more worrying than if she had continued sobbing uncontrollably—it was as if she didn't want to let him down in his hour of need. All he wanted to do was tell her that everything would be all right, but he knew it would not be.

ON THEIR RETURN home an eerie silence filled Wilding's Barn. Tom thanked the taxi driver, who nodded uncomfortably and drove off. For a few moments the two stood on the gravel, unable to move. Then Tom touched Tally's shoulder. She swung round and buried her face in his chest. He wrapped his arms round her.

'I know. I know.' He rocked her gently as though she were a baby, and as he did so, the enormity of his loneliness began to dawn, its vastness engulfing him. He swallowed hard. 'Come on.' He led her to the door and ushered her into the hollow stillness of the house. 'I think you should go and have a shower,' he said. She looked up at him as though he were speaking a foreign language. 'You'll feel better.' She said nothing. He had never seen her looking so desolate, so lost. In that moment, the weight of his burden settled on him. He knew he must find something inside himself to bring her through. Failure was not an option. She was all he had left.

HE SAT ON HER bed as she showered. He was there, but not there. He floated in a sea of unreality, but nothing was more real.

She came into the room in a bathrobe and sat beside him. She looked into his eyes. 'It's so unfair.'

He nodded. All the words in his head seemed so inadequate. How do you explain that life must go on, when you don't believe it can? He tried to say the right thing without being too sentimental or too unfeeling, the whole time finding it impossible to take in what had happened. It was Pippa they were talking about, Pippa—who had been younger than he was. Heart failure was something that affected older people, wasn't it? Panic gripped him. He wanted to be the best support Tally could have, and at the same time he wanted to scream, 'No! Not me! It's not fair! I need her!'

He sat beside his daughter until the light faded, then brought her a cup of tea. When finally she fell asleep he quietly left her room. He walked along to his and Pippa's room. It smelt as it always had—a mixture of clean linen overlaid with the faint suggestion of her perfume. He glanced at the table on Pippa's side of the bed and saw a folded piece of paper. He picked it up. It was the bill for his pale blue suit. He crumpled it in his fist. Then he sat on the bed and wept.

THE NEXT FEW DAYS passed like some blurred hallucination. The local vicar had been kind, the undertaker matter-of-fact, and the locals as supportive as he could have hoped, though solitude was all he really wanted.

He phoned Janie, who said she was on her way. He was half glad: perhaps Janie's irreverence would help them through. He was worried about Tally. Over the past few days she had gone deeper inside herself, unable to cry.

Peter had been devastated, then supportive, insisting that Tom stay at home where he could do most good.

Janie arrived and he surprised himself by breaking down. They cried openly together, which surprised Janie, too. But she pulled herself together quickly. 'Have you eaten?' she asked, as she lugged her case into the hall.

Tom pushed his hanky into his pocket then picked up her case. 'Not since breakfast.' He began to stagger up the stairs. 'What have you got in this? A body?' Then he realised what he had said.

'I should laugh if I were you,' said Janie. 'Otherwise you'll cry again.' She wiped away her tears with her hand. 'Where's Tal?'

'In the garden, I think.'

Janie walked through the house and out of the back door. It was a warm afternoon, dull, oppressive. She saw Tally sitting on a wooden bench at the far end of the garden.

'Hello,' she said quietly, and dropped a kiss on the top of Tally's head. 'Oh, my love, what an absolute bugger.'

Tally nodded. 'Did you know that Mum had a weak heart?'

'No.'

'Nor me. Nor Dad. She'd had a few pains. She got a stitch sometimes when she walked. Perhaps that was something to do with it.' Tally looked questioningly at Janie. 'Maybe it's better if you don't know when death is going to come.'

'Maybe.' Janie sat beside her. 'You get a chance to say your goodbyes if death comes slowly, but in a way that makes it all the more difficult to bear. It's hard to watch a friend suffer. But if it comes without warning you feel robbed, cheated, angry.' She stroked Tally's arm. 'Are you coping?'

'Not really.' Tally forced a flicker of a smile.

'Get tomorrow out of the way. God! I hate funerals, don't you?'

'Never been to one.'

Janie saw the ineptitude of her remark but soldiered on. 'Look, I'm going to say all the wrong things over the next few days because I'm useless at this sort of thing, OK? But I'll do my best because I loved your mum. She was my best friend. I don't know how I'm going to manage without her. But neither does your dad. So you and me, we've got to look after him too.'

Tally's eyes were brimming with tears.

'I know I take the piss out of your dad, and I know that he thinks I'm a cynical old cow, but he loves me, really, and I love him. He's that rare thing in life, a good man. Your dad's a star.' Janie sniffed back the tears. 'You remember that night when we had supper and I teased your mum and dad about never arguing?'

Tally nodded.

'Jealousy, that's all.'

'No,' Tally said.

'Oh, they knew it was a joke. Knew it was only envy.' Janie turned to face her. 'And that's the truth of it. And now I've got to sort you two out. Because if I don't your mum will never forgive me.'

THE DAY OF THE FUNERAL dawned with a stark inevitability. The sun shone, the birds sang, and a soft breeze rustled the leaves of the sycamore. Tally put on a long black skirt and jacket, and pinned back her hair. Janie tapped lightly on her door. 'OK?'

Tally nodded.

Tom came out of his bedroom and ushered the two women down to where the hearse was waiting in the drive. As they motored slowly down the lane, Tally gripped the hands to either side of her, and never once took her eyes off the coffin with the single spray of summer flowers and herbs that she and her father had made.

The journey to the Minster took less than ten minutes, and as the coffin was raised to the shoulders of the undertaker's men, Janie slipped aside, leaving Tally and her father to walk behind it.

They sang 'Praise, My Soul, the King of Heaven' and 'Love Divine'. The vicar said some kind words, then Janie stepped up to the lectern. Tom squeezed Tally's hand.

Janie took out a single sheet of paper, then began, 'It's hard to think of this as a celebration of a life, because it was a life that we wanted to go on celebrating together—all of us who knew and loved Pippa. We thought she'd always be there, because she always was there when we needed her. I first met her at catering college. She was cheerful, outgoing, and good at all the things I wasn't—gardening, cooking and making friends. She proved that by quietly becoming the best friend I ever had.'

Janie paused. 'She was also very good at marriage, which I didn't believe in. I was with Pippa the week she met Tom. She couldn't stop going on about him. I tried to tell her to take her time, that it was stupid to fall in love, that she'd only get hurt. Do you know what she said? "I've no choice." When Pippa met Tom, she became a whole person. Tom and Pippa Drummond were the most perfect couple I've ever known.

'We might think that Pippa's gone, but she hasn't. She's still here—in our memories and in our hearts.' Janie's voice wavered. 'I hope I can go on being annoyed by bits of her, because that way she'll stay real. Pippa spent her life unconsciously undermining me. But it did me good. It proved I wasn't always right, and discovering that you're not always right reminds you that you still have a lot to learn. But in one particular area I know that I was right and Pippa was wrong. She always thought that she was just an ordinary person, and I knew she was not. She was the kindest, funniest, most loving friend I've ever known. And like Tom and Tally, I'll miss her so very much.'

Janie went back to her seat. The Minster fell silent. Then the faintest sound of strings swelled from the loudspeakers and the Temptations began singing 'Night and Day'. With tears streaming down their faces, Tally and Tom followed the coffin out into the clear and sunny day.

CHAPTER FOUR

'Are you going to finish this or not?' Janie was standing in the doorway of the kitchen, a plate of toast in her hand.

'No, thanks.'

She crossed to where he stood. 'You ought to, you know. You need your strength.'

He looked her in the eyes.

She sighed. 'Yes, all right, I know.' She went back into the kitchen and somewhere, in the depths of himself, he heard dishes being washed up. He wanted to move. No. He did not want to move. What was the point?

JANIE GLANCED at the figure leaning against the window frame, her own grief sidelined by her worry for him and his daughter. She glanced at the clock. A quarter to eleven. Tally had still not emerged. Janie climbed the stairs and tapped on her door. No sound. She tapped again. A low murmur. She opened the door and went in. She pulled back the curtains and let the daylight flood the room.

A tousled head appeared. 'What time is it?'

'Probably time to get up. Only if you want to.'

'Not really.' Tally sighed. 'It's hard.'

'I know.' Janie perched on the bed.

'I can't believe it. I keep thinking of things to tell her. I nearly got out of bed this morning to go and tell her something. Then I remembered. It's horrible.'

'Have you had a good cry?'

'Only in church. When I heard their song. Why can't I cry? It's wrong. I must be awful.'

'Don't be silly. It takes us all different ways. It doesn't make you any less of a person because you can't let go.'

'But what must Dad think?'

'Right now he's still in shock. He doesn't know what to think.'

'That's why I've got to be strong.'

Janie pushed strands of fair hair from Tally's face. 'Don't take the weight of the world on your shoulders, sweetheart.'

'But you can see the state he's in. Supposing he can't cope?'

'He will. Eventually. He's just got to work through it.'

'But he'll be hopeless without Mum.'

'He's still got you.'

'Exactly. That's why I can't let him down.'

Janie knew she had walked right into it. She got up, took a towel off the radiator and tossed it at Tally. 'Come on—up you get. Have a shower and come down for breakfast.'

TOM DRAGGED HIMSELF up the stairs and caught sight of his face in the landing mirror—bleak, unshaven, gaunt. It reflected the inner man. He turned away and went into his study, sat down and gazed out of the window across the herb garden to Brindle Hill. He remembered the day of their picnic, Pippa having to stop to catch her breath. A stab of realisation. Had it really been just a stitch? He would never know.

He looked down at the folder containing *Making Waves*. He picked it up and put it in a drawer, then looked out of the window again.

Halfway through the afternoon Janie interrupted him. 'Tom?'

He carried on staring into the distance.

'Tom!' She put a hand on his shoulder. 'I'm going to go home.'

He came to. 'Yes. Sorry. What?'

'Look. I've been thinking. It's probably better if I go.'

He nodded.

'I'd stay but I really think you two need to be with each other. I don't want to be in the way.'

Good manners overrode his preoccupation. 'You're not in the way. We couldn't have managed without you.'

'You're very sweet, but I've done all I can. Look, you know where I am. You must ring me if you need anything. OK?'

'Yes. Of course.' And then, trying to find some inner resource, 'I'm sorry about this. It just that . . . well . . . I can't take it in.' He had turned to face her now. And then he started to shake. She put her arms round his shoulders as the tears fell down his cheeks. 'Oh, Janie, what am I going to do? What am I going to do?'

'Come on, it's all right, it's all right.' She raised her voice to get through to him, and to give herself confidence.

'I can't live without her. I don't want to.'

'No, Tom! Come on!'

'Why did it have to be her? Why not me?' And then she held him as he cried the agonised tears of a broken man.

She did not go home that afternoon.

THE FOLLOWING MORNING the two of them waved Janie off. They watched as the Golf wound its way down the lane and out of sight. Tally was the first to speak. 'What are you doing today?'

Tom was surprised at the question. 'Don't know.'

'Shall we go out? Just you and me?' She realised what she had said and made to cover it up. 'I mean—'

He butted in, 'Do you know what I think? I think you should give Emma a call and go and see her.'

'I'm not sure I can face her yet.'

'Got to do it some time.'

'I know. But she might not be in.'

'Won't know until you try.'

She looked up at him. 'Only if you're sure you'll be OK.'

Tom smiled at her reassuringly. 'I'm sure. Just don't be late back, that's all.'

'I won't. I'll be back to tuck you in.' She stood on tiptoe and kissed him. 'You really are the best dad in the world, you know.'

He promised himself that he had cried for the last time. Apart from anything else, he was exhausted.

THEY SAT at the kitchen table in Emma's house and Emma listened as her friend related the events of the past week. She was amazed at Tally's calm.

'How's your dad?'

'Not very good. He doesn't know what to do with himself.'

'Has he been back to work?'

'Not yet. I'm worried about him. He's in such a terrible state.'

'And what about you? How do you feel?'

'I don't know. I mean sad. So sad. But I can't . . . let dad . . .' She stopped short.

Emma put her hand on Tally's shoulder. 'I don't think this is a good idea.'

Tally winced. 'I'm a bit short on good ideas,' she said.

'We could go away for a few days?'

Tally got up from the table and walked over to the kitchen window. 'I can't leave him yet.'

'No, I suppose not.' Emma made one last effort. 'But will you keep coming out? Just to give yourself a break?'

'Of course.'

'And what about . . . you know . . . him?'

'I can't think about that right now.'

'Do you want to see him again?'

No response.

'Only I thought you were . . .'

Tally's pale blue eyes flashed. 'No, I don't think so. And, anyway, he hasn't rung.'

'I THINK YOU'RE MAD to go. Rachel's an old cow and I can't think why she's invited you.'

'Thanks very much.' Tom was straightening his tie in the mirror.

'You know what I mean.'

'Yes, I do. But they've been very good, coping with the Pelican.'

'She hasn't coped with it. Peter has. And, anyway, you know you'll only get cross.'

He turned from the mirror and smiled at her. She saw the tiredness in his face. 'It'll get me out of the house. I can't stand Rachel any more than you can—I just feel that I should go and say thank you.'

'Well, you be careful. She eats men for breakfast.'

He narrowed his eyes. 'Not this one.'

'Just you make sure that's true. And don't be late back,' Tally said, brushing some dust from the sleeve of his jacket.

'Thank you.'

'What do you mean?'

'Nothing. Just thank you.'

As he drove down the lane he was aware of a glimmer of pride under the heavy blanket of sadness.

TOM HAD BEEN GONE only half an hour when the doorbell rang. Tally opened the door. Blip Butterly smiled nervously and held out a bunch of cottage-garden flowers. 'I just wanted to say . . . you know.'

Tally took the bunch of larkspur and marigolds from him. 'Thanks.' She hesitated, then kissed his cheek and held open the door, inviting him in.

Blip followed her into the kitchen and sat at the table while she put the flowers in water.

'Would you like a beer?'

'Thanks.'

Tally took two Budweisers from the fridge, levered off the caps and pushed one across the table towards him, before sitting down opposite. 'Cheers.'

'Cheers.'

They sat in an uneasy silence for a few moments, and then he spoke again. 'I just wanted to say that if you need, you know, to talk . . .'

'Thanks. I seem to have done nothing else.'

'Does it help?'

'Not much.' She took a sip from her bottle.

Blip pushed his finger around in a drop of beer that had fallen on the table. 'Look, I kind of get the feeling you've been avoiding me.'

Tally looked surprised. 'I've had other things on my mind.'

'I know. But it was happening before that, wasn't it?'

Tally got up. 'How can you bring it up now?'

'I didn't want to. I've been trying not to. But I just want to know if I'm wasting my time.'

'Well, the answer is yes. I think you are wasting your time.'

Blip stared at her. He had not intended to come out with it, and now she was upset. 'I think I'd better go.'

'Yes. That's it. Walk away. Don't face up to things.'

He looked crestfallen. 'I didn't—'

'No. You didn't, and nobody else does either . . .' She tried to carry on, but failed, blinking back tears.

Blip came up and put his hands on her shoulders, and she slumped against him and sobbed uncontrollably. 'I'm so sorry. It's just— I can't—'

He stroked the back of her head, trying desperately to find something to say, and failing abysmally.

Eventually the tears subsided, and Tally sniffed. 'I'm sorry. Been bottling it all up too long. Looking after Dad.'

'You must miss her so much.'

Tally wiped away tears. 'The silly things most. Shopping, tea not being on the table, the house being quiet, things not moving from where I leave them. That sort of thing.'

'I know. Football kit not being washed, bed not being made . . .'

Tally looked at him. 'Oh, I'm so sorry. I forgot. How long now?'

'Three years.'

'Does it get better?'

'A bit. You learn how to . . . well . . . get on.'

'I'm sorry. I didn't mean to—'

'No, it's all right. I know. You can't think of anything else when it happens.'

'No. But thank you—for listening and for coming round.'

'It's OK. Look, if you change your mind, or you just want . . . you know . . . a friend or to talk or anything, just let me know.'

'I will.'

'I'd better be going.' He walked towards the door. 'It will get better. I mean, I'm living proof.'

She was touched at his attempt at a joke. Blip, who always seemed so serious and so earnest.

He closed the door quietly behind him.

'TOM . . . DARLING. How lovely to see you.' Rachel kissed the air beside his cheeks, then wrapped her arms round him and gave him a peremptory hug. He would rather have been embraced by a boa constrictor. She showed him through to the sitting room of the elegant town house—all oak floors and linen curtains.

The rest of the company, all six of them, greeted him with muted voices, nodding their sympathy.

Peter came over and gave him a manly hug, put a glass of champagne into his hand and muttered, 'All right, mate?'

Tom made an effort to appear cheerful.

Rachel's voice rose above the soft conversation: 'Now, we're not going to dwell on sadness this evening. Tom's come out to cheer himself up and we're here to help. So here's to Pippa. We all miss her very much.' Rachel raised her glass, accompanied by polite murmurs.

Tom knew no one well. These were Rachel's friends, ladies in expensive sweaters and trousers, men who were clearly in trading or law. But he must be polite, see the evening through. God, he wished he hadn't come.

A couple came over to him. She was in a cream two-piece, with pearls at the neck, the red-faced husband in a blazer and open-necked shirt. 'Rotten luck. So sorry,' he said.

'Dreadful,' the wife agreed. 'Are you planning to stay where you are? It's such a big house for the two of you.'

Tom felt himself become irritated. 'Not really.' He took a sip of champagne. The woman's voice became an echo, rattling away nineteen to the dozen. Then he was aware of silence. He looked at her face. She must have asked a question. 'I'm sorry?'

'What about the Pelican?'

He had no time to answer. Rachel's voice cut in, 'I think we'll go in and eat now.'

They went into the dining room. He was seated between Rachel and the woman with the pearls. Opposite him was a painfully thin woman with a long neck and heavy gold jewellery, her hair swept up into a walnut whip of blonde froth.

Peter had cooked an entire henhouse full of guinea fowl, which he placed in the middle of the table, along with a dish of green beans tied into neat, faggot-like bundles with chives.

Tom wished he felt like eating, then breathed deeply and told himself to get a grip. He spoke to the thin, gilded woman opposite, who turned out to have a shop specialising in interior design and soft furnishings. Anodyne conversation followed. The absurdity of it all struck him like a slap in the face and he leaned back in his chair.

Rachel seized the moment. 'I've got some news to cheer you up, Tom. Peter and I have been busy while you've been away.'

'Oh?'

At the other end of the table Peter looked up nervously. He picked up the bottle of *premier-cru* Chablis and carried it towards Tom. Tom intercepted it with a single finger laid across the top of his glass. His gaze never left Rachel and he listened attentively.

Peter accepted the futility of his intervention and retreated.

'You know we've been talking about branching out?' Rachel continued. 'Well, we've found somewhere. A Georgian town house in Portland Street. Perfect for the new restaurant.'

'What sort of restaurant?' Tom asked calmly.

Rachel looked wrong-footed. 'One that serves Peter's food.'

'I rather gathered that.'

'Aren't you pleased?'

'It's not really anything to do with me.'

'Of course it is. We're in partnership. It will be like the Albatross.' Rachel realised her mistake. 'I mean in that we'll both own it. It will be much more successful than the Albatross, obviously. Because there's much more of a demand for new places to eat now.'

'I see.'

The atmosphere around the table became uneasy. The cold note in Tom's voice had been audible to everyone. Except Rachel.

'And it will help to take your mind off things.'

Tom took a deep breath. 'Why should I want to take my mind off things?'

Rachel looked discomfited. 'Well. You know. It's been a ghastly time—still is, I know—but you've got to move on.' She laid her hand over his. He let it lie there. If Pippa had been here, she would have nudged him under the table and tried to suppress her laughter at Rachel's interference. But now he was on his own.

He nodded. 'Yes. You're right. It's time to move on. Time for a change.'

'I'm glad you understand.' She patted his hand. 'So you're up for it, then?'

'No. Not at all.'

'I'm sorry?'

'I'm up for a change. Not for another restaurant. I'm selling my share in the Pelican. You can buy it if you want. Or I can sell it to somebody else.'

Peter's face drained of colour. 'But . . .' Rachel struggled for words. 'But if you don't . . . we can't . . .'

Tom shrugged. 'Sorry. Other plans.'

'What sort of plans?'

Tom wiped the corners of his mouth with his napkin. 'I have

absolutely no idea. No idea at all.' He got up from the table. 'Thanks so much for supper. Please excuse me. I have to go and see to my daughter. It's not been an easy time.'

Peter looked as though he was about to be sick.

'I'll be in tomorrow and we'll talk about the financial arrangements. I'm sure everything will be all right. Sally's mastered the front-of-house bit now, and you've got—what was her name? Kate Lundy. How's she been by the way?'

Peter replied as though he were talking to a ghost: 'Fine. Absolutely fine.'

'That's good. Glad we made the right decision. You can never be sure—but then you can never really be sure about anything, can you?'

WHEN HE LOOKED in on her, Tally was fast asleep. He perched on the edge of her bed, and stroked a stray wisp of hair from her temple. She stirred but did not wake.

What to tell her? She would think he'd lost it. Sometimes it seemed that Tally was sixteen going on forty-two. Over the past few days the roles of adult and child had alternated between them. She would make a juvenile remark and he would look at her with an admonishing fatherly eye. Or he would do something she considered irrational, and she would assume the parental role. He stared at her, the only woman in his life—his daughter, his friend, his guardian. Why should she be expected to fulfil all these roles at sixteen. Where was the justice of it? And now he had burned his boats. Well, one of them. What would she think?

For the first time since Pippa's death the pinched look on her face had gone. He stroked her cheek with the back of his hand, then got up and walked along the landing to his bedroom. The bed now seemed absurdly large—a massive island in the middle of the oak-beamed room. An island on which he was marooned with little hope of rescue. He sat at the foot of the bed and took off his shoes. Then leaned forward and held his head in his hands. He could still smell her, still feel her presence in the air. He shivered and got up to take off his clothes. The wardrobe was full of her things. What was he meant to do? Clear them out and send them to the charity shop? He didn't want to think about it.

He slid between the sheets. The sounds and silences of the dinner party were still reverberating in his head. He lay back, saw the ice-white moon shining in at the window and felt as though he were frozen in time. How he wished he could turn back the clock, say the things he had never said, do the things he had never done. Why hadn't they taken those holidays together instead of working so hard and trying to fit things in? He could see, oh-so-clearly now, how happy they had been, how perfect their relationship, how lucky.

Sleep was a long time coming. It was gone three before he finally drifted off into a fitful doze, and by half past seven he was wide awake again and at the beck and call of another unwelcome day.

HE WAS SURPRISED to find Tally already sitting at the breakfast table. She looked up as he came in. 'You look terrible!'

'Thanks.' He ran a hand through his tousled hair. 'Not a very good night.'

She nodded. 'No. I woke early.' She was munching a slice of toast and holding a glass of orange juice. 'How did it go?' she asked.

'Dreadful.' He sat down at the table opposite her. 'Rachel wants to open another restaurant.'

'Not that again. What did you say?'

'I told Rachel and Peter that I wanted out. That I didn't want to stay at the Pelican. That it was time for a change.'

'Good for you, Dad.'

This was not what he had expected. 'You're not cross? You don't think I'm stupid?'

Tally shook her head.

He looked out of the window at the brightening morning. 'What would your mum have said?'

'I don't know. But if it's what you want she'd have been glad.'

'Do you think so?'

'I know so.'

'But I'm supposed to be a responsible parent, looking after you, making sure you're cared for and that there's enough money coming in to give you an education. I don't want you having a student loan round your neck if you go to university.' The kettle whistled and he rose from the table. 'I'd better go in and tell them I was too hasty.'

Now it was Tally's turn to get up. 'You will not.'

He was astonished at the anger in her voice.

'You've never been really happy there,' she said. 'And If I thought you were doing it just for me I'd hate it. I want you to do something that makes you happy.' She came and put her arms round his waist while he made coffee. 'You've always wanted to write. Why don't you?'

'Because I'm probably no good at it.'

'You don't know until you try. Anyway, you've got your novel.'

'I don't think I can get stuck in . . . just yet.'

Her voice lowered. 'No.' She paused. 'But that doesn't mean you won't be able to . . . some time. When . . . you know . . .'

'I know.'

She brightened again. 'Why don't you write short pieces for newspapers? You could write about . . . I don't know. Life. Things.'

'I think I've had enough of life and things for a while.'

'Oh, Dad! What am I going to do with you?'

He looked up from his coffee to the scrap of a girl he was meant to be bringing up. 'I don't know, Tally. I really don't know.'

HE WAS NOT LOOKING forward to the meeting with Peter. He felt guilty at having made a spur-of-the-moment decision that would affect Peter's life as much as his own. He peered anxiously into the kitchen at the Pelican. There was no sign of Peter, just a fair-haired figure pulling pans out of a cupboard.

'Hello,' he said.

Kate Lundy spun round and a smile flashed across her face, to be replaced in an instant with a look of sympathy. 'I'm so sorry.'

'Thanks.' There was an awkward silence. Then he asked, 'How are you getting on?'

'Fine. Well, you know, learning fast. Would you like a coffee? I'm just making some.'

'Yes, please. Just milk.'

She poured coffee from a jug into two mugs.'Look, I must thank you for getting me this job. I know you had to convince Peter. He's told me so. I hope I've convinced him.'

'I think you have, from what he said last night.'

'Look, if there's anything I can do, you only have to ask . . .'

'Thanks.'

'It's funny, really. When we met my life was at rock bottom. Then you took me in. A couple of weeks later and things have changed, for both of us, in different ways.'

Tom picked up his mug. 'Why were you in such a state?'

'My divorce papers had just come through.'

'Oh God! I'm so sorry.'

'Don't be. I wasn't. It had been going on so long. When the papers arrive you suddenly realise the finality of it all. No going back. But at least my separation was out of choice.'

'Yes,' he agreed sadly.

'This is terrible. Talking about me and my problems when—'

They were interrupted by Peter's hurricane-like entrance. 'Somebody hold this bloody door open! I can't get these crates in on my own.'

'Coming, Chef.' Kate walked to the door and took its weight as three crates of fresh vegetables rounded the corner, with only a pair of legs visible beneath them.

'God knows what we're going to do for herbs now.'

The remark was as wounding to Tom as any knife.

Kate cut in, 'Not a problem. I know someone in West Chortle who grows them.'

Then Peter saw Tom. 'Ah. Hello.'

'Hi.'

'Take these, will you?' he said to Kate. 'Tom and I need to talk.'

Kate relieved him of the vegetables. Tom held open the door of the restaurant and the two men walked through.

FOR HALF AN HOUR she could hear them in earnest conversation, Peter's voice occasionally rising in volume. When they returned to the kitchen, Peter said nothing, but grabbed a jacket from the back of the kitchen door and stormed out.

'My fault, I'm afraid,' said Tom. 'I'm leaving the restaurant. Bit of a bombshell.'

'Oh God!'

'It's good of you to be concerned but there's no need. Peter will be fine when he's calmed down. He just needs to have a stomp around and get it out of his system.'

She stared at him. 'Is it because of what's happened?'

'Yes. Just need a change. Rachel—Peter's wife—wants to open another restaurant and I couldn't face it. Been there before. And not just that. I want to move on. They'll get over it. They might even go ahead. I'm not sure.'

'But what will you do?' Kate came over to him and leaned against the table beside him.

Tom shrugged. 'I don't know. My daughter Tally thinks I ought to write. I've always dabbled, but never done anything about it.'

'How is she?'

'She's a great help. I just keep telling myself I should be helping her.'

'Same here. I have a son. He's at university. I tell myself that I'm supposed to be the one supporting him—well, I do, financially—but he seems to look after me most of the time.'

'Role reversal?'

Kate nodded. 'I think that's what happens when you're a single parent. The usual rules don't apply. It's almost like a marriage, in a funny sort of way.' She looked reflective, then changed her tone. 'Come over for supper. I'll ring you.'

Tom was surprised at the offer. 'Thanks.'

DURING THE WEEKS after her mother's death Tally had watched her father carefully. He had been to the solicitor, muttered about insurance polices and probate and she had wished that he could be allowed to get through without being tied up by legalities.

At night, when he went to bed alone, she grieved for him. She thought, too, of Alex and wondered when she would see him again—*if* she would see him again. Then one day he called out of the blue and asked if he could take her out for the evening. She had hesitated, but in the end agreed. She said nothing about her mother on the phone. He said he would pick her up at six, if that was all right.

'WOULD YOU MIND if I went out?'

Tom was washing up the tea things and looking out of the kitchen window, reminding himself that he must weed the herb garden. 'What?'

'Only Alex has asked me out and I'd like to go.'

'Is he the one with the fast car?'

'Yes. But I make him go slow.'

'As long as you do. Where will you go?'

'Dad!'

He looked contrite. 'Sorry. Just . . . well . . .'

'I think we're going to Nutley marina. For a bite to eat at the Spinnaker—the bar there.'

'Fine. Sorry. I sound like an old woman.'

'Glad you care.' She came up and kissed him.

'Does he know?'

'Not yet,' she murmured. 'Thought I'd tell him face to face, not on the phone.'

ALEX HAD THE ROOF down and the evening was warm, although lumpy clouds were gathering in the west. He watched her get into the car—elegantly in spite of her short skirt. Her slender legs were golden brown, her hair held back in a single, short plait. She looked stunning, but thinner than he remembered.

They swapped pleasantries on the twenty-minute journey, and finally drew up in the marina car park. He got out and came round to open the door. 'You hungry?'

'A bit. Could we walk for a minute?' she asked.

''Course.' He opened the car door and let her out, then locked it.

They walked along the edge of the marina, where sailboats and cruisers bobbed gently alongside the pontoons. When they came to a wooden jetty Tally stopped. She leaned on a handrail and looked out over the water. 'I've lost my mum.'

For a moment he was silent. Then the reality of the statement struck him. 'Oh, God! Oh, I'm so sorry. But when . . . what happened?'

Tally spoke quite calmly. 'She died when we were on holiday—in her sleep. Heart failure.'

He put his arm round her. 'Why didn't you ring me?'

'I haven't got your number.'

Alex slipped his hand into hers, then turned her round to face him. He looked down at her, then bent and kissed her lips. Tally felt herself melt into him.

When he raised his head her eyes were full of tears. She managed a shy smile, then turned and brushed them away.

TALLY COULD NOT remember feeling like this before. She had little appetite, but managed a plate of smoked salmon and scrambled egg and a glass of mineral water. Alex had plaice and French fries, helped down by a bottle of Beck's.

They talked easily now—he about his weekend in Salcombe with the family. He made her laugh with a tale of picking up a buoy—he leaning over the bows of the tiny sailing boat and trying to secure the painter while his father fought to stop the boat in the right position, finally tipping his son into the water.

He listened attentively as she spoke about her mother, explaining that there had been times when they were more like sisters, especially when it came to shopping and coping with her dad. There was concern and love in her voice when she talked about him.

Over coffee Alex wrote on a paper napkin, which he passed to her. 'My phone number—if you still want it.'

Tally slipped it into her bag. 'Thanks.' Then, she looked at her watch. 'Better be getting back. I don't want Dad to worry.'

'No.' Alex got up and went round to where she sat, easing away her chair as she stood up.

Tally grinned.

'What is it?'

'It's just that you're the only person I know who does that, apart from my dad.'

ALEX SWITCHED OFF the engine and Tally turned to face him. 'Thank you for tonight.'

'No. Thank you. I'm just so sorry . . .'

She lifted a finger and laid it lightly across his lips. 'Thank you for being there. You know, when I first met you I thought you were so cool, with your fast car and your shades and all that.'

He looked disappointed. 'But I am cool . . . aren't I?'

'In the nicest possible way.' She leaned over and kissed him. After a few minutes she eased away.

'Can I see you again?' he asked.

'Just give me a couple of days.'

Alex touched her face. 'How did you get so brown?'

'Sitting in the back garden, thinking.'

'Don't think too much. Mmm? At least, not about sad things.'

That night she lay awake again, but not all her thoughts were sad, and when she finally drifted off to sleep she could still smell the fragrance of his aftershave.

'DAMN!' TOM WAS LOOKING out of the window at the rain.

'What's the problem?' asked Tally.

'I wanted to weed the herb garden and it's peeing down.'

'Good. That means you'll have to stay in and start writing.'

'Look, sweetheart, I'm not sure about this writing thing. I haven't an idea in my head and I've no confidence either. The two things don't make for a winning combination.'

'You won't know until you try.'

Tom came and sat beside her. 'You look different.' Then a dawning realisation crept over him. 'Ah. Last night. How did it go?'

'Fine, thanks.'

'Only fine?'

'Yes. Isn't that enough?'

'I suppose so. Is he . . . nice?'

'No, he's horrible. Of course he's nice.'

Tom shrugged. 'Just curious, that's all.'

Tally sighed. 'His name's Alex Blane-Pfitzer, he's eighteen, he's just finished school at Sherborne and he goes to uni in the autumn—if he gets a place.'

'Blane what?'

'Pfitzer. It's a bit of a mouthful, isn't it?'

'Is he aristocratic?'

'No. He's not. Quite well off but just . . . lovely.'

Tom saw the glow in her eyes. 'Well, that's all right, then. Only . . . Be careful. Don't get hurt.'

'I'll try not to.'

Tom watched as Tally walked towards the stairs, a dreamy far-away look in her eyes. He was glad that she had something to take her mind off Pippa's death. He just hoped she wouldn't shut him out. He felt a sudden stab of deep loneliness, isolation. Then he told himself he was feeling sorry for himself and went upstairs into his bedroom and stared out of the window at the miserable day.

Above the splashing sound of the water in the bathroom he heard his daughter humming: a Westlife song. A few days ago such a display of happiness would have been unimaginable. He knew it would help her get through. He just wished he could hum, too, but right now he couldn't even bear to hear music on the radio.

THE CALL CAME sooner than Tom had expected. Kate Lundy had said she would phone, but he had assumed it was just a kind gesture.

'Would you like to come round on Saturday night?' she asked. 'Peter's given me the night off.' He could not think of any good reason to decline so he accepted.

Getting ready that evening he was irritable and nervous. Tally watched, curled up on the bed, as he changed into navy trousers, suede loafers and a blue polo shirt. 'You look handsome,' she said lightly, intending to boost his confidence. She was startled by his reaction.

'I'm not trying to look handsome, just clean.' Then he regretted his churlishness. 'Sorry. It's just that it seems all wrong, getting dressed up, and not for your mum.'

'You're only going out to be friendly.'

'Yes. I know. Stupid, really. It just feels odd.' Tom sat down on the bed beside her. 'How do you think we're doing?'

'As well as we can . . . considering.'

'It's a bugger, isn't it?'

'Yep. A bugger. I remember when you'd have told me off for saying that.'

Tom sighed. 'More important things to worry about now.'

She pushed him in the middle of his back. 'Like getting you out of here. Come on. Just go and have a nice time.'

Tom grabbed a bottle of something red from the wine rack in the kitchen. When the door slammed behind him, Tally switched on the television in the corner of the kitchen. Then she switched it off again. She had never liked *Blind Date*.

KATE LUNDY'S DIRECTIONS were easy to follow. She lived on the outskirts of Portsmouth, a good forty-five minutes from Axbury Minster. Tom found the modest block of flats and pressed the button on the entryphone. A whirring buzz, followed by a click, opened the door, and he climbed three flights of lino-covered stairs to flat six.

He rounded the corner and saw her standing in the doorway. Her face was relaxed, her smile welcoming. 'You found it?'

'I guess so. Good directions.' He offered her the bottle. 'Nothing terribly exciting, but not bad for summer evenings.'

Kate motioned him to a fat sofa decorated with a bright red throw and held up the bottle. 'Some of this or what I've already opened?'

'Oh, what you've opened will be fine.'

Tom looked about him as she poured. The small flat had clearly been furnished on a shoestring, but the wall sported bright prints of John Miller seascapes, and the worn carpet was cheered up with Indian rugs. He felt comfortable as he took the glass from her.

'It's all a bit simple, I'm afraid.'

'It's lovely.' He raised his glass. 'Cheers!'

'Cheers!' Kate took a sip, then leaped up and put down her glass. 'God! I've forgotten the vegetables.'

He got up, walked over to the kitchen door and stood there as she cut up broccoli and topped and tailed mangetouts. She wore a baggy white cotton shirt and black trousers, her feet were bare and her face was free of make-up apart from mascara. Her cheeks were flushed and she was prettier than he had remembered.

Above the worktop he noticed the photograph of a young man, dark-haired and smiling. 'Yours?' he asked.

'Yes. All nineteen years of him. Harry. At Bangor studying marine biology.'

'That's funny. Marine biology is what Tally wants to do. I don't think she's thought where to do it yet, though.'

'It was there or Edinburgh. Both seem to be a million miles away, but you've got to let them go, haven't you?'

'Yes.' He looked reflective. 'I think mine is on her way already. Just found her first real boyfriend.'

'I shouldn't worry. She'll still need you, you know.'

He looked thoughtful, then brightened. 'I didn't think you were old enough to have a son of nineteen.' As soon as he said it he realised how like a chat-up line it must have sounded.

Kate laughed. 'I'll take that as a compliment. I'm thirty-nine. I married young.'

He felt ill at ease, and at that moment he wished he hadn't come. It seemed there were reminders everywhere just waiting to trip him up. Kate read his discomfort. 'Come on. Let's go and sit down for a bit.' She ushered him back into the sitting room.

Tom sat on the sofa, Kate in an armchair opposite. As they sipped the wine they swapped notes on children, restaurants and the relative merits of Portsmouth and Axbury Minster. Eventually Kate said, 'Time to eat.' She returned to the kitchen, and Tom listened to the soft music playing in the background. For the first time since Pippa's death, he didn't want to switch it off.

Kate returned with two dishes of vegetables and two plates of Dover sole. Tom helped himself to vegetables.

'Have you decided what to do yet?' she asked gently.

'Not really. I'm finding it a bit difficult to concentrate.'

'It's hardly surprising, is it?'

'No, but I can't go on like this. Rudderless. I must sort myself out.'

Kate looked agitated. 'Look, I hope you don't think my timing's all wrong.'

Tom looked up from his fish. 'Sorry?'

'Well. It's the Pelican. Are you set on pulling out?'

'Yes.'

She took a sip of wine to bolster her courage. 'Would you sell your half of the business to me?'

He was taken aback. 'But you—'

'I know. I've only just arrived and I hardly know either of you. I've no reason to expect you to agree.'

'But what about—?'

'The money?'

'Well, yes.'

'At the moment I haven't a bean. It's just that now my divorce has come through I should be able to get my half of the proceeds. It may take a few months, though.'

'Have you asked Peter what he thinks?'

'No. I wanted to talk to you first.'

'Right.' Tom stared straight ahead. It had not crossed his mind that Kate would be a potential buyer. 'It's a hell of a risk.'

'After what I've been through over the past few years it seems like security. I'm prepared to take a chance. I thought very carefully about it and the more I thought about it the more I knew it was what I wanted. I know Peter can be a shit, but he's a good chef and I can cope with the fireworks.'

Tom could not think what to say next.

'Don't say anything now. Just promise me you'll give me first refusal,' Kate said.

Tom nodded slowly.

'And I'm sorry to bring it up now. It's not a good time, I know, but I didn't know when would be a good time. I thought at least if I asked you quietly, in private, you could tell me where to get off.'

'No. Not at all.' Tom was dazed. It was so unexpected. He didn't know whether to be pleased that someone wanted to buy his share in the Pelican, or sad that he really was leaving the place.

When he left Kate's flat at a quarter to midnight he stopped in the doorway to thank her. She kissed his cheek. Without thinking he kissed her back and she smiled.

'Let me know. And thank you for coming. It was fun.'

'Yes, it was. Thanks for getting me out of the house.'

'You're welcome.'

He drove home, hardly noticing the journey, and pulled into the drive of Wilding's Barn at half past twelve. The light was on in the kitchen, but there was no sign of Tally. He climbed the stairs, noticing the faint glow from her bedroom. He stuck his head around the door and found her propped up in bed reading *Cosmopolitan*.

'How did it go?' She put down the magazine.

'Fine.'

'Only fine?'

'Where have I heard that before?'

'Well? What's she like?'

'She's very nice. But she did drop a bit of a bombshell. She wants to buy my share in the Pelican.'

'Wow!'

'Precisely.'

'So how did you leave it?'

'I said I'd give her first refusal.'

'Well, there you are, then. Sorted.'

'Yes, but . . . I can't believe it's that easy.'

'Pessimist.'

'Realist.' Tom bent down and kissed her.

HE WAS DEEPLY ASLEEP when she woke him. As his eyes focused, he saw her standing at the foot of his bed with her hands by her sides. She was shaking.

He got out of bed and went to her. 'What on earth's the matter?'

Tally tried to hold back the tears. 'I couldn't see her—Mummy. I tried to see her face and I couldn't see her.'

The words sliced into him. He pulled her into his arms and held her close. 'Oh, sweetheart.' He disengaged one hand and switched on the lamp. 'There you are, there she is.' He pointed to the photo on his bedside table.

Tally looked at it. 'Tell me it doesn't mean I've forgotten.'

'No. Of course it doesn't. It's just your mind playing tricks.'

'Only I thought it might be because of Alex and things.'

'No. You mustn't think that.'

She sobbed now, and he was grateful for the release of her emotion, letting his own tears splash into his daughter's hair. 'Oh dear. Just when you think it's getting better, eh?'

Tally nodded, her face buried in his pyjama jacket.

'We'll get there, poppet, but it might take a bit of time.'

CHAPTER **FIVE**

Tom had not seen Maisie for the best part of a fortnight and felt guilty. She had probably been trying to stay out of the way but he wanted her to know that he was grateful for her restraint.

She met him at the door of Woodbine Cottage and threw her arms round him. 'Oh, Tom! Wonderful to see you! Missed you both so much. Didn't want to interfere. Come in for a coffee?'

He nodded. 'Thanks. But I can't stay long, I have to go into town—sort things out.'

Maisie busied herself with kettles and jugs. 'What sort of things?'

'The Pelican. I'm selling up.'

Maisie turned to face him. Her turban today was orange and puce, her trousers and cardigan black. 'Goodness. Are you sure?'

Tom nodded. 'Time to move on.'

'But what will you do?'

'Tally wants me to write. I'm not sure.'

'The arts, yes. I can tell a fellow artist a mile off. Body language. Aptitude. Impossible to disguise. What you need is a shed.'

'Sorry?'

'All the best writers have a shed. Bernard Shaw had one that revolved. So it could always face the sun.' Maisie decanted the coffee from an earthenware jug into two lopsided pottery beakers. 'We need to set you up with some kind of sanctuary.'

Tom was anxious that she should not get too carried away. 'I have a room in the house, Maisie, I think that'll do to start with. Anyway, I don't know what I'm going to write.'

'Good God! Yes. Just the thing. Here somewhere.' She leapt up from the kitchen table, dived into a drawer and pulled out a fistful of letters. She plucked one from the pile. 'Here we are. It's from an old school chum. Works for that glossy magazine . . . What's it called?' She screwed up her eyes. 'Can't really see.'

Tom pointed at the half-moon spectacles, fastened to a chain and resting on her bosom.

'Oh, yes.' She put them on. 'That's better. Yes, here we are . . . The *Metropolitan*—that's it. They need . . . now, how did she put it? Yes, "someone who can write about country life without sounding twee or sentimental". Preferably someone who understands about farming and wildlife but who can write "readable and provocative articles on life out of town", she says.' Maisie took off her glasses and looked up. 'She thought I might be interested. But words . . . not my thing. I'm more into the physical arts. I should have replied and said sorry, but I haven't yet. So, shall I introduce you?'

'Well, it isn't really what I intended.'

'It would start you off. At least you could talk to them.'

'I suppose so.'

'Good.' She brightened. 'What fun. So glad I've been able to help. A little rung on the ladder.'

PETER WAS SITTING outside the back door of the Pelican drinking coffee when Tom arrived. 'What are you doing here?' he asked. Then he felt guilty at his abruptness. 'I mean, I thought you'd be busy writing or whatever.'

'Not yet. I just wanted a chat. Fancy a walk?'

'If you like.' Peter put down his mug, then shouted behind him into the kitchen, 'Back in a few minutes.'

The two men made their way out into the street, eventually crossing to the expanse of grass that flanked the Minster.

'I just wanted to sound you out. About my share.' Tom came straight to the point. 'Kate's interested.'

Peter stopped walking. 'Bloody hell! She didn't waste any time.'

'No. But what do you think?'

'Do you care?'

Tom sighed. 'Of course I care.'

Peter looked apologetic. 'Sorry, mate. It's just a lot to take in, you know?' He struggled for words. 'It was all a bit of a shock. After all this time. Look, you do what you need to do. I don't mind. You were right, you know. Kate's really the business.' He met Tom's gaze. 'Yes. OK. Sell to her. If that's what you want.'

Tom nodded. 'Yes. I think so.'

The two sat down on a bench. 'You OK?' asked Peter.

'I'm not sure what to say when people ask that. "Yes, fine," or "No, I'm bloody not." I worry that people will start avoiding me because I'm a sad old sod who ought to be moving on, but right now I just want to go away and hide.'

'It'll take time.'

'The way I feel now it will take for ever.' He looked up at the Minster spire, silhouetted against a pale blue sky, the rays of sunlight spearing through its crenellations. 'I miss her so bloody much, Pete. I can't think why I should bother carrying on—except for Tally.'

Peter put his arm round Tom's shoulder. 'You've got to give yourself something to think about, Tom, start living for yourself. Then you'll be of more use to Tally. Look, I know it sounds callous but it's not. It's a way of making sure you survive. It doesn't make Pippa any less important, it just means that you'll be able to find a way out of all this. Right?'

'Yeah, I guess.'

'Anyway, pity me.'

Tom turned to face him. 'Why?'

'I'll have to tell Rachel that our new partner is female.' He slapped Tom on the back. 'Go on, off to your writing. I've got a hundred lunches to cook.'

'WELL? HOW DID IT GO?' Tally demanded a few days later, throwing her arms round him. 'Tell me! *Tell me!*'

Tom flopped down on a kitchen chair. 'I got the job.'

'*Yes!* Well done! Gosh! That means you're a writer. Wow!'

'Not yet it doesn't. Not until I write something. They said they'd give me three months' trial.'

'Wow! And what about the money? Can we live on it?'

He was touched by her concern. 'Sweetheart, I don't think it will keep you in the manner to which you've become accustomed, but by the time the sale of the restaurant goes through and with insurance policies and stuff'—he swallowed hard—'we'll be OK. And it won't take up too much time so I think I'll be able to start writing—'

'The novel?'

'Maybe.'

'Great! Come on, then.' She got up and walked across the kitchen. 'Time for a celebration.'

'Oh, Tal, I don't think—'

'No buts. We need things to celebrate, you and me, and this is our first step.' She opened the fridge and took out a bottle of Laurent Perrier.

'Where did that come from?'

'Never you mind.'

'What would I do without you?'

'You'd have more money for a start.'

'Ah. Did I pay for that?'

Tally nodded.

'I see what you mean. Come on.' He opened the bottle and poured the fizz into the two flutes Tally passed him. He handed one to her and took one for himself. 'Here's to us, my love.'

'Here's to us.' She chinked her glass against his. 'And the future.'

Tally wrinkled her nose and spluttered as the champagne went down the wrong way.

He patted her on the back. 'You're not used to it.'

'No, but if you do well I could get used to it.'

'Cheeky monkey! Develop a taste for this and you'll need a richer man than I am to look after you.'

He wondered why her face had taken on a glazed expression. She did not tell him that two hours earlier she had rung Alex Blane-Pfitzer. She had worried over it for days, but finally something inside her snapped. She could not go on longing to travel in one emotional direction with Alex but being pulled in quite another by her concern for her father. It was better that she end it . . . wasn't it? For a while anyway. Then at least she could get her head round things. She told Alex that she needed time to herself for a while. When he asked how much time, she was unable to say.

TALLY'S GCSE RESULTS arrived in the middle of August. Tom hoped with all his heart that they would be good enough to encourage her rather than set her back. He need not have worried. Three As, five Bs and two Cs saw her jumping up in the air.

'I'm so proud of you,' he said, hugging her tightly and fighting back the tears. They drank champagne, and Tom allowed himself to say how proud Pippa would have been.

Tally thought wistfully of Alex and longed to call him, but instead she set about cooking a celebratory meal for herself and her father.

Tom waited for the OK from Kate to proceed with the sale of the Pelican, but things moved more slowly than expected. Whenever he bumped into Peter in town, he prevaricated, but Peter always changed the subject anyway.

As summer turned to autumn, father and daughter began to notice changes in one another, nothing too marked at first, just an easing of tension and the slenderest lightening of sorrow.

The most difficult time was Christmas, when the jollity of the rest of the world seemed to be at odds with their own sense of loss. Tom even suggested a holiday abroad, but Tally insisted that they had to get through the festivities as best they could. And they did, with Janie dropping in on Boxing Day.

Blip had arrived on their doorstep on Christmas Eve, a small, neatly wrapped present in his hand. 'I brought you this,' he said.

Tally tore away the wrapper to reveal a small leatherette box. She opened it, gasped, then laughed and asked, 'What's it for?'

'For when you need me. Just blow it.'

She lifted the shiny football referee's whistle and cradled it in her hand. 'You're very kind.'

Blip looked at the floor. 'I just wanted you to know that I'm here when you need me.'

Tally bit her lip, then said, 'Thank you,' softly. She gave him a hug. 'I'll keep it with me all the time.'

WINTER TURNED TO SPRING and spring to early summer. Tally had set aside thoughts of marine biology, and plumped, instead, for A levels in English and Italian. Tom was surprised, having worried that the tragic Italian holiday would have far-reaching consequences. He was proud that Tally had grasped the nettle. He'd done it himself to a degree, by battling on with his novel.

When a year's worth of anniversaries had passed, and just when they were both wondering what would happen next, Janie telephoned at the start of the summer holidays and invited herself over. 'I'll only come for the weekend on condition that you let me cook.'

'Are you expecting me to refuse?'

'You'd be the first man who did.'

'So I've heard.'

'Cheeky bastard—you're certainly back on form.'

'Almost.'

She spoke more softly. 'I know. Look, I'll be with you late afternoon on Friday. I'll bring all the stuff—just get some wine in, OK?'

'The best of my cellars will be at your disposal, madam.'

'I should bloody well think so.'

Tom shook his head. She was all bluster, as usual. It rather cheered him up.

He put down the phone, smiling to himself, then turned to see Tally standing in the doorway, her face pale.

'What on earth's the matter?'

'It's Alex. The boy I went out with . . . for a bit.'

'What's happened.'

'He's just rung. He wondered if we could meet up again.'

'Well? Do you want to?'

'I think so.'

'You don't sound very sure.'

She hesitated. 'It's just that I'm surprised he's rung. After all this time.'

'Shows he's got stamina.'

Tally had convinced herself that she had blown it—sent Alex away just when their relationship was about to develop. How could any male ego recover from such humiliation? And yet he had called back. It must mean he was desperate, unable to find anybody else and so happy to settle for her. For the time being. Either that or . . . She stopped herself from going any further. Life had moved on. She would move on, too. It had taken the best part of a year.

It was Friday afternoon and Tally had been closeted in her bedroom with her mobile for nearly an hour. Eventually she came downstairs and exercised her best wheedling voice: 'Da-a-ad?'

'What do you want?' He was at the sink, washing up.

'How do you know I want something?'

'Years of experience.'

'Oh. Well, it's just that Mr and Mrs Blane-Pfitzer have asked me if I'd like to go on holiday with them to Devon. The first two weeks in August. They'll be there for the whole month but they've asked if I could go for a fortnight. Can I?'

Tom turned from the stubborn remains of a lasagne he was trying to scrape off a Pyrex dish. He was temporarily lost for words. 'When do they need an answer?'

'Well, now, really. Mrs Blane-Pfitzer said if you'd like to give her a ring she'd be happy to talk about it with you.'

'Oh, did she?'

His loss of cool surprised her. 'I just thought . . .'

'I don't think you did think. That's the trouble. How can I let you go off with someone who's had nothing to do with you for a year then suddenly decides he'd like to take up with you again?'

'It was my decision to end it—not his.'

'Well, why did you pack up with him if he was so special?'

'Because of . . . things.' She wanted to say, 'Because of you,' but she couldn't. Why did he have to make such an issue of it?

Tom was well into his stride now. 'And he's someone I don't even know from a family I've never met.'

Tally was hurt. 'I just thought I'd ask, that's all, but you're clearly not keen so I'll say no.'

'Thank you.'

Tally's lip trembled and she fought to control herself. 'I didn't think you'd mind.' She stormed out of the room.

Her father shouted after her, 'There's no need to get a strop on. How can you expect me to agree when I don't even know them?'

He heard the slam of her bedroom door. He threw the tea towel into the sink, where it landed with a splash. 'Bugger!' He sat down at the table. Janie would be arriving within the hour and they were in the middle of a family row. 'Oh, shit!' He pulled the soggy tea towel out of the greasy water and wrung it out, then tossed it into the washing machine to join a waiting heap of coloureds.

Why had nothing prepared him for all this? He'd worked in the catering trade, was used to dishes, pots, pans, glasses, organising meals. But organising a household was a different matter. Meals, washing, shopping, cleaning. Sometimes it seemed that there was hardly enough time to write, what with organising Tally's timetable and keeping the garden going. He'd been determined that the herb garden should be just as good as it was when Pippa looked after it.

Perhaps now it was all coming to a head. Since Pippa's death he and Tally had had hardly a cross word. There had been tensions, certainly, but never a full-blown row. He wasn't being overprotective, just cautious, so why was she being so unreasonable?

He walked to the bottom of the stairs. 'Janie will be here soon.'

No answer. He was clearly *persona non grata*. Well, tough. If she wanted to be childish that was her problem. She was far too young to be allowed to go on holiday with people he didn't know.

It stung him like a bee. Was he being selfish? No. He was genuinely concerned for her, didn't want to let her out into a world he didn't trust. Who were the Blane-Pfitzers anyway? He stomped up to his study and pulled the copy of Debrett's *People of Today* from the shelf. He found the entry: 'Blane-Pfitzer, David. Chairman and chief executive of Unicorn Holdings.' Clearly a high flyer. Sherborne and Cambridge, patron of a couple of charities. Not that that made him fit to take care of Tom's daughter.

He heard Janie's car in the drive and went out to welcome her.

'God! What a journey!' she said.

Tom kissed her cheek. 'Give me a hug, I'm in need of TLC.' He put his arms round her and squeezed.

'What's up, then?'

'Oh, we've just had our first row since . . .'

'It had to happen. Real life and all that.'

'I'm just sorry it happened now—spoilt your entrance.'

'Doesn't matter. What was it all about?'

'Tally wants to go to Devon with her new boyfriend.'

'Oh, I see. And Dad's not too keen?'

'Exactly.'

Janie opened the back door of the car and proceeded to drag out crates of food. 'Can you grab these?'

'Good God! How many are you expecting to feed?'

Their conversation was interrupted by the appearance of Tally at her bedroom window.

Janie looked up. 'Hello, lovely! I gather he's being a bastard. Are you coming down to help?'

Tally smiled and disappeared from the window.

'Do you mind not taking sides?' said Tom irritably.

'I'm not taking sides, just helping to clear the air.' She dug him in the ribs with her elbow. 'SOHB.'

'What?'

'Sense of Humour Breakdown.'

'Janie, it's serious.'

'Of course it is. Very serious. Otherwise she wouldn't be asking to go on holiday with him.'

'That's not what I meant.'

'I know.' Janie winked at him. 'Come on, there's stuff that needs to go in the fridge before it goes off. Leave the car windows open, will you? Bit of a pong. Hello, sweetheart!' She greeted Tally on the doorstep. 'I gather I've arrived at just the right time.'

THEY ATE IN THE GARDEN at an old oak table covered with a gingham cloth. Candles flickered in tin lanterns. It was a warm evening, and Tom steered the conversation away from holidays.

As he went indoors to make coffee, Janie turned to Tally. 'Don't worry. He'll come round. He's just being protective, that's all.'

'Well, why can't he ring them up and talk to them? Then he'd see it's all right. It's so annoying.'

'Look, leave it to me. I'll have a chat with him.'

'No. I don't want him to think I've gone behind his back.' She looked at Janie with wide, pale blue eyes. 'It's just that I really would like to get to know Alex better—*and* have a bit of fun. Dad and I have been looking after each other for a year now. I just think we should both start to live our own lives again.'

'Have you told him this?'

'No. Half of me thinks it's wrong but the other half . . .'

'I know. Just be patient.'

'But I have to let them know by the end of the weekend, otherwise Alex's brother is taking a friend.'

Janie looked sympathetic. 'I'm sure he'll come round.'

Tom emerged from the kitchen with a tray of coffee.

'Anyway, I've got a present for you both,' Janie said. 'Something to cheer you up. Inspiration for your father and company for you.'

Janie walked over to the car and lifted the tailgate. She returned through the gloom carrying a cardboard box tied with string.

'What is it?' Tally asked excitedly.

Janie put it on Tally's knee. 'Open it and see.'

Tally pulled off the rough string and eased open the top of the box. 'Oh! Oh—how wonderful! He's lovely!'

'He's a she.'

Tally lifted out a tiny white and buff kitten.

Tom was horrified. 'What the—?'

'Now, before you start, I thought it was time you both had something to think about.'

'But it will need looking after.'

'Animals usually do, but most people manage.'

'But—'

'Oh, stop butting, Tom. All these writers who do columns in newspapers and magazines have an animal to write about.'

'That's ridiculous.'

'Well, I think she's gorgeous.' Tally was cradling the kitten in her hands. 'What's her name?'

'That's up to you,' said Janie.

Tally deposited the kitten in Tom's lap thoughtfully, and watched as her father stroked the little animal. 'Wendy,' she said. 'I won't be long. I have to make a phone call.'

Tom watched her go. 'What a name. Why Wendy?' he asked Janie.

'You remember *Peter Pan*, don't you? Well, who was Wendy?'

'She looked after the Lost Boys.'

Janie smiled. 'So she did.'

MRS BLANE-PFITZER—'Call me Helen'—had seemed very pleasant. 'You must be worried but please don't be. We can keep a close eye on them and there are plenty of rooms in the house.'

Tom assumed she had said this to reassure him, but he felt like saying, 'Yes, and who's going to make sure they don't tiptoe into each other's at dead of night?' But he checked himself. He trusted Tally implicitly, and her common sense. But how could he trust the boy? He had been one and he knew.

'Why don't you come down yourself for the middle weekend? There's plenty of room.'

'Oh, no, that's all right.'

'You must. We'd be really happy to see you.'

'Well, if you're sure . . .'

'Absolutely. Look, we'll pick Tally up on the Saturday morning around eleven and you can meet us all then.'

How could he object? The Blane-Pfitzers were being so reasonable and considerate. Tally would be going to Devon and he'd have to get used to the idea. Janie had started it—asked him how he could refuse. It wasn't long before he realised that he didn't have a leg to stand on.

A couple of days later he had told Tally over breakfast. He felt bad when she flung her arms round him and kissed him. 'I'm sorry I was so foul,' she said, and he felt worse.

'Oh, don't worry. Just promise me you'll be careful.'

'I will.'

'There is one thing. The Blane-Whatsits have invited me down for the middle weekend.'

'Great!'

'You don't mind?'

'Of course I don't mind—as long as you don't cramp my style!'

'I'll try not to.'

He watched her running upstairs, doubtless to phone her beau and tell him the good news. August was just a fortnight away, and then what? The prospect of being in the house alone did not appeal one bit. He went out into the garden to pull weeds from among the herbs and try to think of something else. It didn't work.

'SO, WHAT MADE you ring me after all that time?' she asked.

'I had to find out if you really didn't want to see me again or if you did just need a break. I thought you'd need a year to get through all the anniversaries and stuff.'

'Yes.' She was surprised by this thoughtfulness. 'And what about Edinburgh?'

'I didn't go. I thought I needed a gap year.'

By the end of the call her head was reeling. She felt a mixture of pleasure and guilt that perhaps she could have affected him as much as he had affected her. And now she would be with him for a fortnight. The prospect was exciting, but scary. What if they didn't get on? She could always go back with her dad if things got a bit sticky. She had not admitted that this was one of the reasons why she was pleased he would be joining them. But it would be good to see him, too, to check that he was all right.

She leaned on her windowsill and watched her father in the herb garden. He worked at it daily now. He would weed for a bit, then sit on the grass and gaze into the distance, then work again.

Sometimes she felt so sad that she ached, while on other days she seemed to find strength and optimism from somewhere deep inside herself. She could never predict which of the two states of mind would prevail. She would often sit by her window, the kitten in her lap, looking out over the rolling Sussex Downs. In the first few months after her mother's death she'd been able to settle to nothing, but slowly her ability to concentrate had returned and she began to pick up the threads. Some things still hurt. Most of all she missed her mum's physical presence. Sometimes she wished that she had been buried, rather than cremated. Then at least she would have had something on which to focus. But that was silly, she told herself. Her mum was still with her in spirit—what did it matter that her ashes were scattered on the grass in some distant part of Sussex? She tried not to think about it. It was still too frightening.

THE OFFER FROM KATE LUNDY came with the morning post. It was couched in legal terms and it was a good one. He would not haggle. He rang her at home.

'Kate? It's Tom Drummond. I've just got your letter.'

'Is it all right? I'm sorry it's taken so long.'

'Not at all. And, er, I think that'll be fine. I'll contact my solicitor and get something drawn up.'

'Oh, that's fantastic.'

'I'm glad you're pleased. Have you said anything to Peter?'

'No, I didn't want to count my chickens'

'OK. I'll give him a call and tell him we're going ahead.'

There were a few more pleasantries, and then she said goodbye. He had done it. Tom's relief was tinged with sadness, although he had not set foot inside the Pelican for more than a year.

What pleased him was that he had managed to make headway with the novel. There were days when it seemed as though he was trying to spoon treacle with a feather, but the manuscript was growing thicker. Writing allowed him to escape into another world, and gave him a brief respite from his loneliness. Tally was with him, yes, but he was conscious that he had nobody with whom he could share those things that required intimacy on a different level from that of father and daughter. Tally was there to be steered, watched over and guarded, not dumped on—she had her own row to hoe.

HE PHONED PETER. The response was brief, accepting but not joyous. Half an hour later Peter called back. 'Look, mate, I think we might have a bit of a problem. You see, Rachel's got a couple of friends interested. You met them at our place last year, Sarah and Richard—you know, the guy with the red face and the woman with the jewellery. They want to buy your share of the Pelican and come in with us on the new place. I haven't mentioned it because . . . well because I thought you had enough on your plate. But it's not too late, is it? I mean you can tell Kate you've had a better offer, can't you?'

'I've already accepted.'

The silence at the other end of the phone was epic. Finally Peter responded: 'Tell her you can't. We've been together for years. You owe it to me.'

'But you didn't say anything when we talked last year. I told you about Kate and you agreed it was a good idea.'

'That was then. This is now. You haven't signed a contract.'

Tom felt a germ of irritation. 'Just because you've changed your mind, Pete, I can't go and change mine.'

'But . . . the thing is Rachel desperately wants Sarah and Richard on board.'

'Ah. I see. Sorry, Pete, your problem. I've given Kate my word and

I'm not going to let her down. I'm sorry, but that's that.'

'I wish it were. I bloody well wish it were.' Peter put the phone down without saying goodbye.

Tom replaced his handset and exhaled deeply. He suspected he had not heard the last of this.

'NOW HAVE YOU got plenty of underwear?'

'I bet you say that to all the girls!'

'Don't be facetious.' Tom looked at his daughter meaningfully. 'I can get some more washed quickly, if you want.'

'Dad, I've got underwear coming out of my ears.'

'What you call underwear and what I call underwear are two different things.'

'I should hope so. I wouldn't want to see you in lace.'

'Oh, very funny.'

'Lighten up, Dad! I'll be fine. I won't talk to any strange men—only the one I know.' Tally walked over to him. He was standing by the airing cupboard on the landing, his arms full of towels, his face careworn and weary. 'Are you sure you're going to be all right without me?' she asked.

He shrugged. 'Probably not.' He pushed the towels into the cupboard and closed the door. 'What about your time of the month?'

'Just had it.' Tally put her arms round him and gave him a hug. 'You are funny.'

'What do you mean?'

She sighed. 'Oh, nothing.' She looked up into his eyes. 'Thanks for being there.'

Tom ruffled her hair. 'Oh, I'll always be there.'

CHAPTER SIX

By eight thirty, Tally had still not risen. Tom tapped gently on her door, eased it open and regarded the mound huddled under the Winnie-the-Pooh duvet. She might be leaving to go on holiday with a man, but she still clung to childhood comforts. 'You awake?'

A grunt.

'They'll be here in an hour and a half.'

A groan. Then her face blinked into view. 'What time is it?'

'Half past eight.'

Her head dropped back onto the pillow. 'Oh, no. I don't want to go. Supposing they're awful?'

'They won't be awful.'

'They might be.'

'Who's trying to convince who? I thought you wanted to go.' Tom went across the room and pushed the hair out of Tally's eyes. 'Come on, silly girl, into the shower. You'll feel better when you're clean.'

'Bet I don't.'

'Well, you needn't go. You can stay here and cook for me.'

'All right, I'm going.' She swung her legs out of bed and staggered towards the bathroom.

Tom looked at her open suitcase, piled high with the things a girl might need on holiday, and wondered how she would get it shut. In one corner he saw a tiny teddy bear, and in another, a neatly folded triangle of black silk. It took a supreme effort of will-power to leave the case exactly as she had packed it.

THE BLANE-PFITZERS' Mercedes estate, filled with cases and bags, cut a graceful arc in the gravel outside the barn. Father and daughter heard its approach from Tally's bedroom.

'Well, here we are, then,' said Tom. A sickening feeling churned inside him.

'Yes.'

He put his arm round her. 'Have a great time. Just—'

'Yes, I'll be careful. And don't worry.' She stood on tiptoe and kissed him. 'I'll be fine.'

'Maybe that's what worries me.'

'I still need you, you know. You're still my dad.'

'Only your dad.'

'No. Not only my dad. Lots more than that.' She took his hand, and without looking at him said softly, 'I love you.'

With his forefinger he turned her head to face him. He wanted to say, 'And you.' In the event, all he could do was nod. He sniffed and took a deep breath, then looked at the suitcase—bulging but closed. 'I'll carry it down for you.'

They stepped out of the front door to be greeted by the Blane-Pfitzers. As the parents exchanged pleasantries, Tally went and stood by Alex. Mrs Blane-Pfitzer lifted up the tailgate of the car and came over for Tally's suitcase. She took one look at it and summoned her husband. 'David, I think you'd better lift this one.'

'Oh, don't worry.' Tom hurried over and carried it towards the car. 'In here?'

Then they all climbed into the Mercedes, Tally sandwiched between Alex and his brother on the back seat.

Tom lip-read his daughter's valediction as the car eased out of the yard . 'Be careful,' she said, and gave him a little wave. It would have been funny, if it had not hurt so much.

AFTER THEY HAD GONE, Tom tried hard to settle to something. He cut the grass, even though the dew had not yet burned off. He pulled flower heads off the rhubarb and fought with the apple mint, forcing it to retreat back into the border where it belonged.

Then he sat down at the laptop, but he could think of nothing except Tally. Where were they now? Poole? Exeter?

The phone rang at two o'clock. They had made it. The house was wonderful, looking out over the harbour, and the sun was shining. She seemed happy.

She was on her own now—till next weekend. He told himself he was being overprotective, neurotic even. For God's sake, the girl was seventeen. She had to have a bit of independence.

The trouble was, he missed her.

THE JOURNEY TO SALCOMBE had been tense. The traffic had irritated Alex's father, resulting in an uncomfortable tension between him and his wife, and Alex's brother, Henry, had been glued to his Gameboy, his elbow digging into Tally's side as he punched away at the buttons. She'd tried to talk to him but had received only a scowl in return.

Alex had once squeezed her hand tentatively and smiled at her, but their conversation was constrained by the atmosphere. When they pulled into the drive of the long, low cottage at the top of the hill, she had feared the worst, but as the journey ended the tension evaporated. Even Henry flung his Gameboy onto the car seat and charged out of the car, cheering.

'Welcome to Salcombe,' whispered Alex in her ear. 'It'll get better now.'

And it did.

Alex's father, so grumpy in the car, stretched his arms and legs and said, 'Thank God for that!' then smiled at her and said, 'Sorry. A bit tense. Better now. Alex, you go and show Tally the view.'

Alex took her round the back of the cottage to a stone-flagged terrace fringed by orange-flowered montbretia and dumpling-shaped hebes. A low stone wall ran round it and, beyond, the land fell away to reveal a view of the harbour, glittering in the afternoon sun like dark blue velvet sprinkled with sapphires. Above it rose the soft green domes of the Devon hills. Boats bobbed on their buoys, pleasure craft ploughed across the water, and the green swords of montbretia rustled in the sea breeze.

'Oh, wow! It's beautiful!'

'Thought you'd like it. Do you want to see your room?'

He pulled her through the French windows into the sitting room, with its chintz-covered armchairs and sofa, and up a lopsided staircase to the first floor. The ceilings were low, with dark oak beams. At the end of the landing he lifted the iron latch on a particularly low doorway and guided her in.

The small room contained a single bed covered in a rose-patterned quilt, a small white-painted wardrobe, a dressing-table stencilled with flowers, and a washbasin. But the most striking thing of all was the view: through the tiny dormer window, its thin white curtains floating in the warm breeze, she could see the harbour laid out before her. She leaned out to get a better look. 'It's stunning. Thank you so much for asking me.'

'Thank you for coming.' He bent down and kissed her. There was the slightest moment of awkwardness, and then he said, 'I'd better get your case.'

She watched him go, in his white polo shirt, dark green shorts and ancient deck shoes, then turned back to the view. It was just heavenly. A stab of sadness seared into her. She was on holiday for the first time without her mother and father. She rested her head on the window frame and breathed deeply to steady herself. Then she looked once more at the glittering bay below, her emotions a tangled web of sorrow and delight. How she wished her dad could see it. She rang him to say she had arrived safely.

THE PHONE RANG AGAIN. It was five o'clock. The day had flown by, and although it had once looked as though Tom would have nothing much to show for it except a half-tidied border and a washed Winnie-the-Pooh duvet cover, he now had a healthy pile of manuscript pages on his desk.

'Tom? It's Janie.'

He was surprised. 'Hello, you. How are you?'

'More to the point, how are you?'

'Bloody.'

'Thought so. Fancy some company?'

'If you'd asked me this morning I'd have said no. I was drowning in self-pity. Right now I'd love some.'

'I'll be there in an hour.'

'I thought you were with your mum.'

'I can take just so much Scottish common sense before I need to run kicking and screaming. I'm in a service station near Andover. I'm desperate to get drunk and swear.'

'Well, come here then, and I'll drink and swear with you.'

Tom was laughing as he put down the phone. Thank God for Janie. The belligerent voice of reason in a confusing, worrying world.

HE GREETED HER on the doorstep with a hug and a kiss. 'You look nice.'

'Steady. Don't flatter a girl too much. Mind you, you clean up pretty well yourself.'

Tom was wearing a white linen shirt and navy chinos, and his face and arms were tanned from weeks of therapeutic weeding in the herb garden.

'Mind you, your hair needs cutting.'

He was opening a bottle of chilled white wine. 'I haven't thought about it—I don't need to look smart for anyone now. The restaurant, I mean, not . . .'

'I know. Well, you look pretty good to me.'

'Chicken all right? A bit boring I know, but I wasn't expecting you.'

'Fine. Sorry to ring so late.' Janie sat at the kitchen table, watching him prepare the meal. 'Was it hard seeing her off?'

Tom nodded. 'Stupid, really. I know she's growing up but I don't want her to get taken advantage of.'

'All part of it, I'm afraid.'

'I guess so.'

'I know so. I've made an art form of it, sweetheart.'

Tom grinned. 'And survived?'

'By the skin of my teeth.'

Tom could never understand why Janie had not managed to hold on to a man. She was strikingly attractive. Her eyes were dark brown—black when she was angry or excited—her skin a soft shade of olive, and her teeth white and even. Tonight, her glossy dark brown hair was swept up into a French plait, and she wore a pale blue linen shirt that did not quite meet the waistband of her white jeans, and flat Italian shoes.

While the chicken cooked they moved outside, and sat under the branches of an old apple tree at the gingham-covered table where they had dined before. Janie felt something soft and warm brushing past her leg. She looked down. 'Hello, you, where've you been?'

'Where she shouldn't have been. Tally's bedroom.'

'Oh dear! Making the boss cross, are you?' Janie looked from the cat to Tom. 'How's she getting on?'

'Too well. I'd like to complain but I hardly see her. Well, until now. I expect I'll have to take over now that her mistress is away.'

The kitten curled herself round a table leg and proceeded to do battle with it until suddenly it closed its eyes and fell asleep.

'She's supposed to be your cat as much as Tally's. You're to take care of her and she'll take care of you.'

'Oh, I think I'm past being taken care of.'

A SECOND BOTTLE of wine relaxed them both, as they sat, one on each side of the table, enjoying their supper, the candles flickering in the lanterns. When they had finished eating, Janie leaned back on the bench and took a large sip of wine. 'So, what of the future, Tom?'

'Can't really think that far. Some days I don't seem to have one. Other days I don't want one. Then, very occasionally, I have this yearning to get up and get on. Like today. But it doesn't last long. I feel I can't let it last long.'

'But you must. Otherwise you'll just waste your life.'

'It seems as though that's happened already.'

Janie got up, walked round the table and sat down next to him on the bench. 'You mustn't believe that. If you do, you're finished.'

Tom lowered his head.

Janie lifted his chin with her finger. 'You're a lovely man and you mustn't let it happen.'

'You're very kind. It's just that I get so bloody low. There's only Tally to think and worry about. And it won't be long before she goes, university or whatever. She's slipping away now, really. I know I have to let her, but it's hard.'

Janie put her arm round his shoulder, and pulled him towards her so that he lay across her lap. 'You'll cope. You're tough.'

'I don't really want to be tough, Janie. I just want to let go.' He was looking up at the stars now, his eyes distant.

'I know, I've been there—but only through my own fault. I can't begin to imagine what it must be like when things are taken away from you.'

He sighed a long, deep sigh. 'It sounds so selfish, and I feel so guilty to admit it . . . but I do so miss having someone to love.'

Janie said nothing, but ruffled his tousled hair. For several minutes they were silent, Tom with his head in her lap, she stroking his hair. Then she spoke, slowly and softly. 'Oh, Tom,' she said, gazing upwards to avoid his eyes, 'this is so bloody hard, and you can tell me to shut up and go away . . . but I do love you so very much.'

He said nothing. Her heart pounded in her chest and she knew that she had blown it. Then she looked at him and discovered that he was fast asleep.

'I'M SORRY IF I GOT a bit maudlin last night.' They were sitting at the kitchen table, Tom, unshaven, in an old shirt and a pair of shorts, Janie in a long, baggy white T-shirt, her hair scraped back into a clip. 'That's not why I said yes to your coming round. Just so I could moan at you.'

'I know that. And that's not why I came round—just to listen to you moaning.' Janie sipped her orange juice.

'So why did you come?' he asked lightly, hardly expecting a serious answer.

'You really want to know?'

'Yes.' He bit off a mouthful of toast.

She put down her orange juice and looked across the table at him. 'I came because I wanted to make sure you were OK.'

'What?' He chewed. 'Me and Tally?'

'No. Just you.'

He swallowed, then grinned. 'Steady. I might take that the wrong way.'

Janie shrugged.

Tom looked puzzled. 'What are you saying?'

She smiled, ruefully. 'Don't worry, Tom. I'm not going to do anything stupid. Last night I nearly did. I so desperately wanted to take you to bed, to hold you and tell you that everything would be all right.'

'Oh, Janie.' He shook his head. 'It's very kind of you but there's no need . . .'

'Come off it, Tom. I'm not kind, I'm selfish.' She took another sip of juice and looked out of the window. 'I'd just love to spend some time with you, that's all.'

'What?'

'I'm sorry. I shouldn't have said anything.'

Tom stood up and leaned against the sink. He took a deep breath. 'You're not serious!'

'Oh, I am.'

'But you've never said . . . I didn't know . . .'

'Why should you? Pippa was my best friend. You were her husband.'

'But you were always so . . . rude?'

Janie smiled. 'Just a front. Fancied you like mad.'

Tom rubbed his chin.

'Oh, Tom! There really is no reason to worry. I won't make a nuisance of myself. I've never felt so guilty in my life. It feels as if I must have wished her ill. I didn't for one moment. I loved her so much. You know how they say that the worst thing that can happen to you is that your dreams come true?"

Tom said nothing.

'Well. That's me.' She drained her juice. 'I'd better go.' She got up from the table.

'No. Look. Don't go.' He reached up and held her by the wrist.

Janie turned her head away and he saw that she was fighting back tears. 'Christ, look at me. Miss Tough Cookie. Sorry.'

'No. Don't apologise. I'm very flattered. And . . .' He looked thoughtful. 'Stunned. And confused. It's only been a year and a bit.'

'But how long can you go on mourning?'

Tom drew a deep breath.

'No. Don't. I'm sorry. That was a dreadful thing to say. But I'm not asking you to do anything dramatic. Just think about it, that's all. I just want you to know that if you fancy a bit of company then I'd rather it were me than anyone else.'

'I can't believe this.' He looked around, as if searching for reinforcements. 'I'm sorry. It's just that I'm having trouble letting myself go. I'm moving on slowly, but it's not that easy. Pippa's still here, everywhere I look. Still in every cupboard and drawer. In the garden.' He turned to the window. 'I see her out there sometimes, clear as day, kneeling among the herbs. Then she's gone, and I'm on my own again.'

'And you're happy to be like that?'

'No, I'm not. But I need to be sure I know what I'm doing.'

'Are we ever sure?'

He shrugged.

Janie moved towards the door. 'I think I'd better go before the neighbours start to talk.'

Tom reached out and put his arms round her. 'You are funny. All these years you give me hell and now this.'

'I'm sorry.'

He held her at arm's length. 'Will you stop saying you're sorry? It's just a bit of a shock. And you know, I'm really not your type.'

'Isn't that for me to decide?'

'I think I have a say in it, too, don't I?'

She lowered her eyes. 'Yes. Stupid of me not to have realised.'

STANDING IN THE DOORWAY of the house, he watched her drive away, and wondered if it had all been a dream. Distractedly he picked up the post: two bills, one circular and a letter in a crisp cream envelope. The writing looked vaguely familiar. He opened it and sat down at the breakfast table:

Dear Tom,

I am sorry to have to write this letter, but it seems that it is the only course open to us. Peter and I really do feel that we must be given the chance to buy your share of the Pelican, rather than let it go to an outside party or someone who is new to the business. Peter has explained your unwillingness to sell to us and so we therefore have no alternative but to seek legal advice.

If you have second thoughts and think that this would be unnecessary we will be only too pleased to negotiate with you and sort this out amicably.

Please do let me know at your earliest convenience.

Yours sincerely,

Rachel

Tom folded the letter and placed it back in the envelope. Then he went to the telephone and called his solicitor.

ABOVE SALCOMBE HARBOUR, Tally was watching Alex and his father pull out a small sailing boat from the garage.

At dinner the night before, the conversation had been friendly and easy. But she had detected a tension between Alex and his father, even though she could not put her finger on the reason for it.

They had gone to bed at eleven, and there had been that tricky moment outside her bedroom door when she was sure that Alex had wanted to kiss her good night, but instead just smiled as his parents and younger brother went in and out of the bathroom in a seemingly endless choreographic routine.

In the morning she had flung the window wide to let in the fresh air. There had been little activity on the bright, ice-blue water, but she could hear the distant *ting* of halyards on masts, and could feel the sun on her face. The cries of squabbling gulls echoed around her.

She had put on a pair of shorts and a T-shirt, and had fastened her hair back from her face with a band. She looked at herself in the dressing-table mirror, craning her neck to see how her legs looked. She hoped she would do.

Alex had not seemed to notice her much over breakfast. He seemed intent only on locating the Shreddies and the milk. But after a while he came to and smiled at her. Maybe he wasn't a morning person.

Alex's father had said that they would get the boat onto the water together and Alex and Tally could take it out on their own, if they were careful and wore life jackets. Tally would have been happy to go for a walk and discover the town, but she did not want to disappoint either father or son so she smiled and said, 'Lovely.'

Getting the boat onto the water resulted in a few sharp words from father to son. 'No! Watch the centreboard! Alex, grab that painter! Quickly!' Tally did her best not to get in the way.

Then they were out on the water and alone.

Alex sighed a deep sigh. 'Thank God! He's always a bit of pain with his boat. I'm sorry it's been a bit tricky.'

'It's all right.'

'It'll be better when we've all relaxed—and Henry's got over not being able to bring his friend.'

'I thought you said there was no room. There seems to be plenty.'

'Yes. Only Mum doesn't much like Eddie, so she says that to Eddie's parents.'

'But you told me I had to make up my mind quickly or Henry's friend would come instead.'

Alex blushed and looked guilty. 'I said that to hurry you up. I just wanted you to come.'

Tally grinned. 'You wicked boy.'

Alex grinned back. 'I know. Do you mind?'

Tally shook her head, and for the first time she knew exactly why she was there.

TOM GAZED AT THE WORDS 'The End', then added the final twelve pages to the fat manuscript of *Making Waves* and slid it into the desk drawer. It was finished. Done. Now he could start on a new one. The thought surprised him. He had concentrated on *Making Waves* for so long that he had never imagined writing another. But the title was already in his head. It meant a fresh start.

He swivelled in his chair and looked out of his study window at the full-blown summer garden and the distant Downs. He had heard nothing since that first call. But Tally would have rung if things were not going well . . . wouldn't she? He must stop worrying about her. And about Janie. He had hardly dared ask himself how he felt about her. He was still raw from the shock of Pippa's death, and yet . . . for the first time since he had lost her he felt a deep warmth inside him. It was comforting to know that he was wanted.

How *could* he be thinking like this after just a year? But, as Janie had said, how long does a man have to mourn? How long would he have to wait before he inhaled the scent of someone's perfume, found bags of shopping dumped on the worktop, felt a soft, warm body beside him in bed and heard laughter in the house?

A shed, that's what he needed. Maisie was right. He looked out across the herb garden. In the far corner was a clear patch of grass—perfect for a shed. He could run electricity to it from the house and it would be a new place. It would not burden him with memories. He would be able to move on. A little.

A phone call to a local firm was all it took. Yes, they had a variety of sheds. Yes, he could come and look. Yes, they could supply and deliver it within the week. He was on his way.

CHAPTER SEVEN

Tally had deliberately avoided ringing her father. She had come close to it on several occasions but was determined to stand on her own two feet. She wanted to be independent. Sort of.

By the second day Alex had made sure that he and Tally could operate independently of the rest of the household by asking his parents if they could have breakfast in the summerhouse that overlooked the harbour. She had been worried that his parents might think they were being rude but, to Tally's surprise, they didn't object.

Early that morning she had got dressed and tiptoed downstairs, out into the garden and down across the small sloping lawn. When she reached the bleached wooden summerhouse it was empty. She was about to go back to the house, when a low voice at her shoulder said, 'Hello!' She spun round, and found Alex beside her with a packet of cornflakes in one hand and a pint of milk in the other. His fair hair was tousled, and glinted like golden thread where the early-morning sun caught it. He wore a faded red and white striped rugby shirt and a pair of shorts.

Tally blushed. 'Hi!'

'Hi!' He nodded at the door of the summerhouse. 'Can you . . .?'

'Oh. Yes. Of course.' She opened the door. Alex placed the packet and the bottle on an old plywood table flanked by two even older Lloyd Loom chairs. She watched as he moved across to a small cupboard in one corner, opened the door and took out two bowls and two spoons, a carton of orange juice and two glasses.

'How did you know . . .?'

'Put them there last night.' He smiled, and walked up to her. 'You look lovely.'

Tally grinned. 'You look as though you've just woken up.'

'I have.' He put his arms round her. 'Been dreaming about you, though.'

She felt herself blushing. 'Nice dreams, I hope.'

He nodded, then bent down and kissed her. Tally felt the fluttering sensation in her stomach again. She put her arms round him and felt his tongue slide into her mouth. Slowly his hands slipped up from her waist until they almost reached her breasts. She lifted her own hands to intercept them.

Alex eased away and spoke softly. 'Sorry.'

Tally smiled and lowered her eyes. 'No need.' Then she looked up at him and said brightly, 'Breakfast?'

ALL DAY SHE FELT as though she were walking on air. That morning they messed about in the boat, taking it up the estuary and pulling it up on small patches of beach. They sat on the sand, watching other boats butting through the gentle waves, and talked about everything and nothing.

In the heat of the afternoon she slipped off her T-shirt to reveal a Lycra bikini top and Alex exclaimed, 'Wow!'

'Too much?' she asked, concern in her voice.

'No. Just right.' And then, seeing her raised eyebrows, 'It's all right. I'll try to control myself.'

'I don't want you to think . . .'

'Ssssh! It's hot.' He took off his own T-shirt, to reveal his broad but trim torso, the honeyed skin dusted with freckles. She turned away, embarrassed, and watched the boats.

He put his arm round her. 'What are you thinking?'

'Just how lucky I am.'

'Not sad?'

'A bit, but not too much.'

'I'm glad.' There was a moment of silence, then, 'I've a few friends down here. I wondered if you'd like to meet them tonight.'

'Oh.' At first Tally was disappointed at the prospect of having to share him, but it would be unkind to refuse. 'Fine. I'd love to.'

She was lying. Inside she felt nervous and taut, where moments ago she had felt relaxed. For the rest of the afternoon the prospect of an evening with strangers hung over her like a dark cloud.

WHEN THE PHONE RANG, Tom was convinced that it must be Tally, but it was Peter, asking if he could come round.

'Look, I'm sorry,' Tom said, 'only I really don't want—'

'I just want to clear things up.'

'What, about Rachel's letter?' Tom's solicitor had said to hold fire on the matter of Rachel's threatened lawsuit, and to await developments.

'Oh, fuck the letter. And fuck Rachel.'

Tom was surprised—he was used to Peter swearing, but he had never heard him apply it to Rachel. He told Peter to come round, then the phone rang again. That would be Tally. At last.

'Tom?'

'Janie.'

'I thought I'd better ring.'

'Oh?' He was pretty sure of what was coming.

'It's just that I didn't want you to think . . .'

'That you really meant it?'

'No. That I didn't mean it.'

Tom stood perfectly still, his powers of speech suspended.

Janie continued, 'I did mean it, but I shouldn't have said it. I'm so sorry. There are some things one should keep to oneself and that was probably one of them. You've enough on your plate without me adding to life's complications. I think it's probably a good idea if I stay away for a while.'

'I don't know what to say.'

'Don't say anything. Look, I'll call you in a while.'

Tom searched for the right words, but failed to find anything suitable. 'OK. Only . . .'

'No. Don't say any more. I'll be thinking of you, you know that. Take great care, you old sod.'

Before he had time to reply she was gone. He put down the phone and saw Peter storming up to the front door with a face like thunder.

TOM WENT TO THE FRIDGE and took out a bottle of Beck's, flipped off the cap and handed it to his soon-to-be-former partner. Then he leaned back against the worktop as he watched Peter drink from the neck. 'Now, look . . .' he said, as the bottle was lowered. Then he saw Peter's face properly. He looked almost frightened, and the hand holding the beer was shaking. 'What the hell's the matter?'

'I've left her.'

'What?'

'Rachel. I've had enough.'

Tom stared at him.

'It's just impossible. I've tried reason, I've tried agreeing with her, I've even tried arguing, which comes very easily.' He took a gulp from the bottle. 'I just can't hack it any more, Tom.'

Finally Tom managed to speak. 'When did this happen?'

Peter looked at his watch. 'Seventeen minutes ago.'

'I see. Any particular reason?'

'That letter to you. That was the last straw. I mean, what the fuck did she think she was doing writing to you like that? It was as if we didn't know each other. I've come round to say I'm sorry for what's happened. I never wanted that other bloody restaurant.' He looked out of the window. 'When I think what I was stuck with.'

'But you were besotted with her.'

'Until I found out what she was really like. No wonder she'd been through two husbands.' Peter drained the bottle.

Tom walked up and put his hand on his friend's shoulder. 'Sorry.' He had never expected to see him in such a state—Peter, the confident, arrogant but good-hearted chef, he of the bolshy temperament, looking crumpled and desolate. 'So, what will you do now?'

'Stick a bed in the attic at the Pelican for a bit. I kept the restaurant in my name, but I expect it'll be ages before I can get any money off her—if ever. What a state, eh? You and me both on our own again, but for different reasons.'

'Yes.'

Peter opened the door to leave. 'Look mate, I'm, sorry,' he said. 'You've got enough on your plate right now without me. Anyway, you know where I am. The company will be better now—just me.'

Peter walked across the yard to his car and Tom stood at the doorway enveloped in an uneasy kind of emptiness. He had never liked Rachel, yet he felt sad for both her and Peter.

TALLY TOOK LONGER than usual to get herself ready for the evening out. She took ages over her make-up and even longer deciding what to wear. When she emerged, in a pale blue and white striped cotton dress with pencil straps, Alex greeted her with 'Wow!' He looked about him to make sure the coast was clear, then kissed her lightly. 'Can't wait to show you off.'

'Is that what this is all about?'

'Of course.'

'We haven't seen much of your parents,' she said as they left.

'Never do. Mum's off visiting friends, and Dad's looking at boats. He wants something bigger. A yawl, I think.'

Tally hesitated. 'I haven't talked to him much yet.'

'He doesn't say much.'

'I've noticed. Why is that, do you think?'

Alex struggled. 'He doesn't know how to, I guess. His dad died when he was tiny. Maybe he didn't see how it's done.'

'Neither did my dad, but at least he talks to me.'

'Mine talks to me. Sometimes. It's just . . . tricky, that's all.'

She left it there. It seemed that Alex was unwilling, or unable, to take the subject further.

'So where to?'

'I said we'd meet them at the Jolly Sailor.'

'Who are they?'

'Right, well, there's two school chums. Mark with ginger hair and Raife—he's dark-haired, and a dark horse, too, bit of a wheeler-dealer. Then there's Anna, you'll like her—she's Mark's sister. She's tiny with short dark hair. Clee, short for Cleone, is a blonde who's had an on-off relationship with Raife for about three years You'll like them, I promise. They're good fun.'

'Where do they stay?'

'In Mark's parents' house in East Portlemouth—just the other side of the harbour. They have to get home by boat at eleven thirty otherwise they're stuck over here.'

THE JOLLY SAILOR was seething with bodies. Loud conversation drifted out of the open windows onto the narrow, thronged street, along with the smell of beer and cigarette smoke.

Alex called out to the two young men coming down the front steps with a tray of glasses and crisps. 'Hi, you guys!'

His greeting was returned by a fresh-faced, towering figure with a mop of ginger hair, and a slightly shorter one with dark, spiky hair and sunglasses.

'We're round the back. On the quay. Walk this way,' instructed the taller of the two.

They followed as instructed and sat down at a combined bench and table of the sort regularly found in pub gardens.

Alex went through the introductions. 'This is Tally. Tally, this is Mark, and Raife and Clee and Anna.'

Mark said, 'Hi,' with a warm grin.

Raife said, 'Hi,' coolly, trying to impress and not look impressed. Clee managed a brief smile, and Anna said, 'Hello, lovely to see you. We've heard all about you.'

Tally smiled nervously.

'All good,' added Mark, 'and there's no need to be shy. We're a perfectly acceptable bunch, if you don't count the fact that these two had a row this afternoon and aren't speaking to one another.'

Raife said, 'Shut up,' and Clee raised her eyes heavenward.

Anna attempted to make Tally feel more at home. 'Give them a few minutes and half a glass of lager and they'll be fine.' And then, noticing that Tally and Alex lacked glasses, 'Guys, you haven't bought Alex and Tally a drink.'

Mark cut in, 'Yes, we have. Here you are, squire, a pint of Mr Foster's best, and, for the lady, a Smirnoff Ice. OK?'

'Thanks.' Tally was a little unsettled. She wondered if they knew her age. Clearly they were all a couple of years older than she was, more sophisticated, worldly.

'So, Alex,' said Raife softly, 'where did you find this babe?'

Alex brushed off the implied sarcasm. 'We met in Axbury.'

'Ah, the country retreat.' Raife turned to Tally. 'And you fell for the fast car and the smooth talk.'

Alex attempted to cut in, but Tally beat him to it. She said sweetly, 'No. I thought he was a jumped-up little shit, actually, when I met him, but then I discovered otherwise.'

The table fell silent. Anna threw back her head and laughed. 'Good for you, Tally.'

Tally felt ashamed that she had been so crude and, at the same time, empowered. She had guessed that unless she stood her ground at the outset there would be little chance of her holding her own.

Raife pushed his glasses back onto the top of his head. 'First hit to Tally, then.'

'How nice to see you put in your place, Raife,' Clee retorted.

Mark, sensing it was time to move on, opened up the conversation: 'So, what have you two done today?'

Alex, with occasional contributions from Tally, told them about the boat and about their plans for the next few days.

While the boys were in conversation, Anna leaned over and whispered in Tally's ear, 'Well done. They take a bit of mastering, these guys, but I think you've sorted them.'

'Thanks. I'm a bit nervous.'

'I'm not surprised.'

THEY ATE—EVENTUALLY—at a fish bar, by which time Mark was pleasantly sloshed, Raife silent and brooding, and Anna glassy-eyed. Clee could not stop talking, about boys, shoes and handbags. Tally began to find her rather funny.

The drinks had helped her to relax a little, but she had moved on to orange juice after the third Smirnoff Ice, much to the barely veiled disgust of Raife. She noticed that Alex lurched from side to side a little and that his S's were over-enunciated. Her reverie was cut short by Anna shrieking, 'God, look at the time! We'll miss the boat.'

'Same time tomorrow night?' mumbled Raife.

There was muttered agreement from the rest of the group.

Raife hurried towards the door, saying, 'I'll go and ask it to wait.' Then he was clearly struck by another thought. He lumbered over to Tally, beamed and said, 'See you again, Princess,' then kissed her hand and bowed his way out of the door backwards.

Clee scowled at him, then turned to Tally. 'He's mine,' she whispered, before picking her way through the tables in Raife's alcoholic slipstream.

Quite suddenly they had all disappeared, leaving Tally and Alex among the remains of a fish supper.

'I think we'd better go,' she said.

Alex nodded. 'Suppose so. Up the wooden hill to Bedfordshire.'

She helped him up the road to the house, his arm draped round her as he tried to walk in a straight line.

They climbed the stairs together, with difficulty, and at his bedroom door they stopped. She expected to have difficulty in persuading him to go into his own room, but he smiled beatifically, said, 'Good night, Tally-Wally,' and almost fell through the door. She closed it quietly behind him and murmured, 'Good night, Alex.'

As she lay in bed, she wondered what her mum would have said if she could have seen her now.

'HOW MUCH?'

'Four hundred and ninety-five, sir. That's including the VAT.'

'But I could buy a house for that, in a remote part of Lancashire.' Tom scratched his head. 'It's only shiplap, with a bit of felt on the roof. Supposing I made it myself?'

'Plenty of timber, sir.' The man at the timber yard gestured over his shoulder with his thumb, to tall stacks of wood.

Tom took the bull by the horns. 'Right. You any good at quantity surveying? I want a shed eight foot by ten with windows down one side and a door at one end.'

'Right, then, we'll sort you out.'

And they did. Tom arrived home with timber sticking out of the back of the Land Rover. He unloaded the planking, the timber supports, the glass and two rolls of roofing felt, and stacked them in the barn, then went to survey the potential building site in the corner of the herb garden.

The familiar 'Oooh-ooh!' greeted him from across the lane.

He turned round. 'Hello, Maisie.'

She was pushing a wheelbarrow containing an easel and a chair. 'Hello, Tom. How goes it? Everything tickety-boo?'

'Not too bad, Maisie. How's the garden coming along?'

'Not terribly well, I'm afraid. I think I underestimated the power of the manure last year. Now I can't see anything for nettles and buttercups. Perhaps there's more to it than I thought.' She spotted the timber stacked against the wall of the barn. 'Something new?'

'I'm taking your advice, Maisie. Building myself a shed.'

Maisie clapped her hands. 'Oh, I'm so glad. You'll find it a real plus, I know. And perhaps it will help to give you a fresh start.'

'That's what I thought. So, if you'll excuse me, I'd better get cracking.'

'Yes, yes, of course. Glad it's all starting to work out. My friend who wrote about the magazine job says they love your stuff.'

Suddenly he felt guilty at having tried to extricate himself from the conversation. 'Oh. That's nice.' Then, with feeling, 'I'm really enjoying it. Gets me thinking about . . . well, other things, you know. I couldn't have done it without you. Thanks, Maisie.'

She looked like a blushing schoolgirl. 'Happy to help out. Must get on. I've a painting to finish. Bye!' She backed away in the direction of Woodbine Cottage.

Tom went to look for his tools. A bit of sawing and hammering was just what he needed to get a heap of things out of his system.

AT THE END of the day he was surprised by what he had achieved. The floor was down, much of the superstructure was in place, and he had cut the timber to length for two of the sides.

He ran a bath, poured himself a glass of white wine and lowered his weary body into the soothing water. His mind wandered over all-too-familiar terrain: he could see Pippa, and hear her, but her voice seemed more distant, almost like the memory of an old film. He saw Janie, too, and found himself smiling. He sipped his wine, and tried to clear his mind of a jumble of thoughts. Then he wondered, as he wondered at almost every minute of the day, what his daughter was doing. He could always ring her on her mobile and find out, but he guessed that that would not go down well. She would ring him when she was ready. He would just have to come to terms with that.

IF ANYTHING, Tally's day had been even better than the previous one. The sun had shone all morning. They had climbed the steep path to Bolt Head, where they had sat among the scrubland and grasses and looked out to sea.

'What did you make of last night?' Alex had asked.

'I liked Mark and Anna. The other two'll take getting used to.'

'But you don't mind going out again tonight?'

'As long as we get some evenings on our own.'

'We will. I just thought you might be a bit bored if it's always you and me.'

She cocked her head on one side. 'And I used to think you were so confident and cool.'

'All a front, I'm afraid. I'm as unsure as the next man.'

'But a bit of a smoothie when it comes to cars.'

'Only because my dad bought me one.'

She looked thoughtful. 'Why does he buy you an expensive sports car, yet not spend much time with you?'

'I told you, he finds it difficult. I suppose the car is his way of showing me he loves me. Anyway, can we stop talking about my relationship with my dad, and get on with our own?'

'Sorry. Just curious. I've never really known anybody else's dad except my own. I suppose they're all different.'

They had walked down towards the harbour, had a snack lunch at a quayside café, then made their way back up to the cottage. Alex had pulled a pair of ancient sun-loungers from the summerhouse, then he and Tally lay by a low stone wall, reading books.

Once, she caught him looking at her over the top of his book. 'I can see you,' she said.

'Well, you shouldn't look so gorgeous.'

The sun had caught her arms and legs, but thanks to the good sense instilled by her mother she had been generous with the sun cream and had turned a gentle shade of golden brown. He had been less cautious, and she noticed the reddening on his shoulders. 'You're beginning to burn. You should put some more cream on.'

'Do it for me?'

She smiled. 'Only on your shoulders.'

'Spoilsport.' He threw her the bottle of Ambre Solaire. She poured some into her hands then rubbed it into his neck and shoulders. She was surprised at how taut he felt, and how smooth his skin was. She felt slightly guilty at enjoying the sensation. He leaned forward as she massaged him. 'That's nice.'

'Just don't get too used to it.'

He took off his Storm shades. 'Do you want me to do your back?'

'No, thanks, I've done it.'

'Double spoilsport.'

She felt almost sorry for him, sitting there with his tousled fair hair and perfect body, trying his best to behave. She wondered if he would be put off by her reluctance to be too intimate, wondered how long she could resist his advances. She picked up her book and tried not to think about it. She did not notice, for a few moments, that it was upside-down.

THAT NIGHT THEY ALL met up again at the Jolly Sailor. Mark and Anna were as friendly as the previous evening, Clee seemed to have got over her fit of pique, and even Raife was less surly, giving Tally a sly wink in greeting. Anna was in a little black number, Clee was in a long linen dress, and Tally had on a short white skirt and strappy top that showed off her tan.

'Look, guys, how about a beach party?' suggested Mark. 'I've blagged the keys of the putt-putt from Dad so we can get up the river a bit then be back in time for the ferry.'

'Are you sure that you'll be in a fit state to bring the boat back?' asked Alex.

'Well, I might have a couple but I'll be careful.'

'The deli is still open,' said Anna. 'We can get some food there. You guys sort out the booze, and we'll meet you at the boat in twenty minutes. OK?'

So they went their separate ways, Tally with Clee and Anna, Alex with the guys.

They found the deli, and bought ready-boiled quails' eggs, smoked-salmon sandwiches, shortbread and peaches, then walked down to the harbour. The boys were waving from a small blue and white dory named *Miss Isle*, in the bottom of which lay several carrier bags filled with assorted bottles and cans.

The dory tilted a little as Tally put one foot on the side to step aboard. Alex took her hand and helped her in. While he did the same for Clee, Tally slipped off her shoes and took Raife's outstretched arm to steady herself. She felt his hand brush lightly across her bottom. She glanced at him and saw him smile, the shades pushed back on his head, his dark brown eyes glistening in the early-evening sun. She half smiled, unsure whether he was flirting or teasing. She sat down next to Alex, who took her hand and held it.

Mark started up the engine. 'OK, cast off, Raife. Up the river for a bit of fun, boys.'

They moved off slowly between assorted boats moored at bobbing white and orange buoys, then out into the centre of the river.

All conversation stopped under the roar of the outboard, until fifteen minutes later when Mark pointed the dory towards a small apron of deserted beach. 'This should do.' He turned off the engine as the boat nosed in towards the sand and shingle, and with a sliding crunch came to rest. When everyone was safely on the beach the three men manhandled the dory out of reach of the tide.

'So, where are the cans?' asked Raife. 'Let's get stuck in.'

Anna, Tally and Clee pulled out the contents of the two carrier bags. Mark threw them a couple of car rugs, and they spread the food in a corner before sitting back on the rug to admire the view.

'Do you do this sort of thing every year?' asked Tally.

'Most years,' said Anna.

Raife came over with a tin tray, clearly 'borrowed' from the Jolly Sailor, loaded with three Smirnoff Ices poured into plastic glasses. 'Your drinks, ladies.' He handed them out with mock servility.

Tally smiled and took a sip of her drink. After a hot day in the sun it tasted wonderful, and the more she sipped at it, the more relaxed she became.

Alex cracked open quails' eggs for Tally and fed them to her. He put his arm round her, and once or twice his hand lightly brushed against her breast.

As dusk fell, the conversation became more riotous, and Tally was aware that she was talking rather a lot. But they were all laughing, so it must be all right. When Mark suggested they play hide and seek she volunteered to hide.

While they counted, she sneaked away from the beach up through gorse bushes and long grass, between waving willowherb and faded foxgloves, finally pulling herself behind a gnarled hawthorn and leaning into the trunk. She felt dizzy, but pleased with her hiding place. In the fading light she was convinced that she would be invisible. She had forgotten that she was wearing white.

'Coming, ready or not.' Laughter followed, then the sound of rustling foliage and snapping twigs, way down below her. She breathed deeply, pulling the fragrant sea air into her lungs. It was a rich mixture and her head spun. She clung to the hawthorn trunk for support. Her head cleared a little and she scanned the path below her for moving figures. Nothing. They must have missed her. She leaned back against the tree trunk.

'Found you!' She nearly leaped out of her skin. She turned to see Raife beaming at her.

She laughed nervously. 'You made me jump.'

'Sorry.'

'That's OK. Now we'd better go and find the others.'

'What about my reward?' His eyes were glazed, his smile lopsided.

'What do you mean?'

'A kiss for finding a princess.'

She had no time to say anything, or even to move. He had her backed up against the hawthorn tree. She felt him press against her, and as she drew breath to cry out, his lips were on hers and his tongue forced its way into her mouth. She brought up her arms to push him off, but he was stronger and pinned them to her sides by putting one arm round her. Then he moved his other hand up inside her top until it reached her left breast and squeezed it as she fought for breath. She began to feel a hardness at the front of his body, but felt powerless to move.

Suddenly she saw Alex with his hand on Raife's collar, then on top of Raife on the ground hitting him. She could do nothing but sob.

'Hey, man! Hey!' Raife cried, between punches. 'It was just a bit of fun.' The final punch landed on his jaw, and the fun ended.

THE BOAT JOURNEY back was undertaken in silence, Raife looking outboard and holding his jaw, Clee sitting with her head in her hands. Tally did her best to stifle her sobs as Alex cradled her in his arms. No one said anything as she and Alex stepped onto the pontoon in the harbour, but she saw the look of distress on Anna's face as she turned to leave.

When they arrived the house was dark and quiet. Alex opened the front door, led Tally up the stairs, along the landing and into her room, where she sat on the edge of the bed, shaking.

'I'm so sorry, so bloody sorry,' he said. 'I really don't think he meant to harm you, just got a bit carried away.'

Tally sniffed back tears. 'Not your fault.'

'Yes, it is. I should have noticed what he was doing.'

'But you couldn't see.'

'Not when you went to hide, no. But I should have seen what he was doing to your drinks.'

'What do you mean?'

'He was lacing your glass with more vodka. I found it when we were clearing up.'

She fell back on the bed. 'Oh, God! I'm so stupid. I've been allowed away on holiday on my own because I persuaded my dad that I could be trusted and look what happens—I get groped by some guy in the bushes, and if you hadn't been there, God knows what would have happened.'

'Well, it didn't. Here.' He tore a bunch of tissues from a box on the bedside table and handed them to her.

'Thanks.' She blew her nose. 'I must look a sight.'

'You do a bit. But you're still gorgeous.' He put his arm round her. 'I suppose you'll want to go home now.'

She looked up at him. 'I'm not sure. I really want to ring my dad, but I don't want to give in. Don't want to be a failure.'

He squeezed her hand. 'You'd better get some sleep, and so had I. I'll see you in the morning and we can decide what to do. You sure you're OK?'

She nodded amid the fistful of tissues.

He kissed her forehead lightly and walked towards the door, then turned to face her. 'You won't say anything to Mum and Dad about what happened, will you? Only I'd rather we sorted this out ourselves if that's OK?'

She nodded again, and he left the room.

It was too late for a shower. She might wake the rest of the household. Instead, she washed herself from head to toe with the flannel at the washbasin, cleaned her teeth, put on a clean T-shirt and slipped between the sheets.

Suddenly she wished she were at home, with her dad sitting on the bottom of her bed, ruffling her hair in that infuriating way he had when she'd just brushed it, and telling her everything would be all right. She fell asleep eventually, a thousand drums beating in her head.

SOMEONE HAD CLEANLY sliced off the top of her head. That was the only thing that could account for the pain. She lifted her head from the pillow, tilted her face forward, rested it in her hands and said softly but with great feeling, 'Owwwww!'

It took her a few moments to discover that if she moved very slowly she could just about retain her equilibrium, so she slid off the bed and crept to the washbasin. It was half an hour before she emerged into the garden, squinting, even though her eyes were protected by the peak of a baseball cap and sunglasses. The garden was empty of people so she made her way to the kitchen in search of something to stop the pounding in her head.

'Hello? You're late up.'

She peered above the sunglasses, and found herself face to face with Alex's father.

'Oh dear! Hard night?' he asked.

She nodded, then regretted it as the percussion section of the orchestra played overtime. She winced.

David Blane-Pfitzer smiled understandingly. 'Sit over there on that lounger, in the shade, and I'll make you something that will sort you out.'

She did as she was told.

Within a few minutes Alex's dad was back with a glass in his hand. 'Here you are. All down in one. It tastes revolting, but it always does the trick.'

Tally took the glass, looked at the yellow and brown mixture, and drained it, grimacing as she handed it back.

Alex's dad sat on the lounger next to hers. 'We haven't seen much of each other since you arrived. Are you having a good time?'

'Yes, thank you. Very nice.' It hurt less when she didn't nod.

'I've been out looking at boats.'

'Alex said.'

'I thought it was time he had the little one to himself. He gets fed up with me shouting at him. Funny, really. I'm not a shouter—except on the water.' He grinned. 'Oh, yes, I asked Alex to help his mum with the shopping. He should be back any time now.'

She had not imagined him to be like this. From Alex's explanation she had expected a dour, humourless man. He was tall and dark with a tanned, creased face, attractive rather than handsome, and wearing a polo shirt with shorts and deck shoes of similar vintage to his son's..

'Is this your first time away on your own?'

'Yes.'

'Well, it's only a couple of days till your dad comes down. Will you go back with him or stay on?'

She was surprised at his question. 'I'm not sure. I mean, I'm having a lovely time . . . It's just that . . .'

'Too much too soon?'

'Yes. In a way.'

'And missing your dad, I expect?'

'Yes.'

He spoke more quietly now. 'I think daughters do.'

'Not sons?'

'Oh, in a different sort of way.'

'How different?'

He shrugged. 'Sons aren't really allowed to miss their fathers. They have to get on. Conditioned to do their own thing.'

'That sounds a bit hard.'

'Oh, it is.' He became more reflective. 'It's funny being a dad—especially with a son. You're never quite sure how much they need you, and they never let on.'

Tally listened attentively, slightly uncomfortable, but at the same time flattered that he should confide in her.

'I suppose you can be more obviously protective of a daughter.'

'But daughters have to stand on their own two feet as well.'

'Yes, but you can be forgiven for trying to stop them. It's seen as being a good father. More difficult with a lad, somehow. You're always conscious of letting them be their own person. Tricky, really, getting the balance right. I'm not sure that Alex and I have cracked it. I try to stay out of his way as much as I can, let him get on. But I do enjoy his company.' He slapped his knees and stood up. 'Listen to me going on. And you with a hangover. Now just you stay there until that brew takes effect. As soon as you feel hungry, go inside and have two slices of dry toast. You'll be right as rain then. OK? I have to nip up to the City, I'm afraid. Back in a day or two.'

And he was gone, leaving Tally to look out over a silvery harbour.

WITHIN HALF AN HOUR, Alex had returned. He came straight out into the garden. 'You OK?' he asked.

'Just about. Your dad sorted me out.'

The colour drained from his face. 'Did you tell him about last night?'

'I'm afraid it was pretty obvious from the state I was in.'

'I mean . . . about . . . you know?'

Tally shook her head. It was the first time she had been able to do so without it hurting.

Alex sat down beside her. 'So, how do you feel about staying on?'

'Not sure . . . only . . . can we have some time together now? Just you and me?'

''Course.'

TOM SLID THE SECOND roof panel into place, then set about fitting the felt. Soon his shed would have a door and windows. There was enough of it now, after two days of working from dawn till dusk, to show that it would serve its purpose nicely.

He felt something brush past his legs. He looked down to see Wendy take a tentative step up onto the floor and pad slowly forward. Tom stood, hands on hips, watching. 'What do you think, then?'

Wendy looked back at him, climbed into the cardboard box filled with timber offcuts in one corner of the shed.

'That's not very comfortable, is it? Come here.' He picked up the old sweater he had been wearing until he had got too hot, and slid it underneath her. She kneaded it with her claws, then sank into it, purring loudly.

'Well, I guess that's you sorted. Room for two, I suppose.'

He looked at his watch. A quarter to seven. Time for a bath. It had become a daily ritual that he half looked forward to and half dreaded. He would lie back in the water and think of Pippa. Go over things. Remember things said. And then would come the emptiness—the aching blackness—and the realisation that she had gone.

She was still with him deep inside. Yet something seemed to be getting in the way, an invisible barrier that numbed his senses and prevented him feeling the rawness of their previous intimacy. He found himself talking out loud. 'Why can't I *feel* you like I could. I can remember what it was like seeing you smiling at me. I can still smell you, touch you. I can remember kissing you. I can remember exactly how it felt but . . . I can't feel it. *Properly*. I don't want it to slip away. I still want you so much . . .'

THAT EVENING after supper Tally rang her dad.

'How is it? What have you done? Are you OK? Is he behaving?'

Tally laughed. 'It's fine. We've boated, and eaten out. They're very nice and Alex has been the perfect gentleman. But how are you? What are you doing?'

'Oh, I've been very busy.' She noticed that his voice had a forced jollity about it. 'I've finished *Making Waves*.'

'That's great! Well done! Are you pleased?'

'Oh, I think so. But I've put it away. I'm starting on another. And I've decided that I need somewhere else to write, so I've been building a writing shed. On that patch of grass next to the herb garden. To give myself a fresh start—fresh surroundings.'

'Wow!'

'Yes, wow!'

'And how's Wendy? Is she behaving?'

'I have to admit, grudgingly, that she is. She moved into the shed before I'd even got the door on. She spends most of the day sleeping on top of my old sweater.'

'You've built a Wendy house. I'll have to call you Peter Pan.'

Tom laughed. 'I'll settle for Dad.'

There was a pause. 'I miss you.'

'I miss you, too, sweetheart.'

'When are you coming down?'

'I'm leaving here first thing on Saturday morning, and I should be with you around lunchtime. Do you think that will suit the Blane-Whatsits?'

'Yes, I'm sure. It's all very relaxed here.' She looked back at the house from her perch on the garden wall, just to check that she was not being overheard. 'I've hardly seen Alex's mum—she visits friends the whole time, with Henry—but I spoke with his dad today.'

'Nice?'

'Very nice. Have you spoken to Janie?'

'Not recently. She's gone away for a while. Working. Not sure where she is.'

'But you can ring her on her mobile.'

'Oh, I've been busy and I don't like to bother her.'

Tally was puzzled. There was something odd in his tone, but she could not put her finger on it. Maybe he was just busy, with his shed and everything. 'Well, anyway, I'm looking forward to seeing you.'

'And I you, my love. It's been lovely to hear your voice.'

'I'll see you Saturday, then. I can't wait. Love you.'

'Love you, too, Tal.'

She put her mobile into the pocket of her shorts, then looked out over the water. She hadn't told her father that her intention was to go home with him. Maybe she was just keeping her options open.

TOM WAS STARING at Janie. She was smiling at him, her shiny dark hair brushing her brown shoulders. He stretched out to touch her and awoke, covered in perspiration. He leaned over and looked at the clock on the bedside table. It was 3.00am. He flopped back onto the pillow. The dream had been so real. He felt reluctant to admit that he had feelings for her. But he felt guilty, too, that he had been so cold when she had said that she loved him.

What a mess. He was mourning the woman he had loved for seventeen years, yet turning away another woman for whom he felt a growing love. But how could he ever love her as much or as well as Pippa? Not yet, surely. It couldn't be love. Maybe it was just need.

He could not keep going round in emotional circles, he had to strike out in a different direction. He would pour himself into work. He would try to forget it all. Get stuck into the new novel.

He got up, dressed and went down to the shed. Maisie's ability to sleep long and deep came in handy that night. She did not hear the sounds of hammering that rang out from behind Wilding's Barn, and by morning the writing shed was finished.

BY FRIDAY EVENING grey weather had settled over Salcombe like a shroud. Earlier in the week the family had been sweltering in shorts and T-shirts, but now they were in long trousers and fleeces. Heavy showers sent them scuttling for cover in the house, where Tally and Alex pulled out the Scrabble board.

At around eight thirty a gap appeared between the clouds. Alex looked up. Henry was now glued to the television, his mother was in the kitchen and his father had still not returned. Alex walked to the French windows and called to Tally, 'Look at the sun on the water.'

She came and stood beside him. 'Wow!'

He turned to her. 'I love your wows!'

'Sorry. My dad says it's a sign of a poor vocabulary.'

'Mine, too. But your wows are more expressive than most.' He opened the windows. 'Fancy a walk?'

Tally looked up at the approaching clouds. 'We might have to make it a quick one.'

'Come on, then.'

He walked with her to the far corner of the garden. They looked out across the water, streaked with fiery copper in the dying evening light. 'Doesn't it look wonderful? Like it's on fire,' she said. Then she looked up as the first spots of rain began to fall. 'Oh dear.'

'Quick, in here.' He pulled her inside the summerhouse.

She looked at him and her face creased into a grin. 'This was just a ploy to get me in here, wasn't it?'

'Do you think I'd do something like that?'

'I hope so.' She put her arms round him, tilted her head upwards and kissed his lips. He responded, running his fingers through her fine fair hair.

She eased away from him.

'Are you really going home tomorrow?' he asked.

She nodded.

'Why?'

'Because it's so lovely. Because I'm frightened it might be too much, too soon.'

He looked hurt. 'But if it's so good, how can you go away?'

'Because that way it stays good and it can't go wrong. You're my first proper boyfriend and I want it to go on and on.'

He looked serious. 'Am I really your first?'

'The first real one. There was another for a while.'

'Blip?'

She looked up. 'How did you know?'

'Girls talk. What was he like?'

'He's very nice. But sometimes being nice isn't enough.'

'No. Can I tell you something?'

'Depends what it is.'

'I've never felt like this before.'

'Neither have I.'

She moved towards him and looked up into his face.

He bent down to kiss her, gently, sensuously, so different from Raife's clumsy attempts. She whimpered slightly as his hands stroked her breasts, her skin tingled and she felt the strength of his body pressed against hers.

They were both breathing heavily now. He pulled the fleece and T-shirt over her head in one, then held her to him, running his hand down her smooth back.

Her hands began to unbutton his thick shirt. The heat of his naked flesh took her breath away, and he began to kiss her more passionately, on her neck and breasts, his hands running over her back then down to her bottom and, finally, between her legs. She gasped and let out a cry. 'Sorry,' he murmured.

She smiled and shook her head. 'Not yet.'

They held each other close until their breathing became slow and even. Then he helped her back into her clothing.

'Do you mind?' she whispered.

Now it was Alex's turn to shake his head.

'You might have to wait a while.'

'Don't care.'

Tally looked searchingly into his eyes.

'What is it?' he asked.

'I don't know whether to say it.'

'What?' He looked down at her, half hoping, half scared.

'You see, the only other man I've ever said it to was my dad.'

He saw the tears spring into her eyes, and carefully tilted her face towards him. He whispered softly, 'I do love you.'

She lowered her eyes and nodded, then whispered, 'And I love you.'

CHAPTER **EIGHT**

Tally got through to Tom on his mobile while he was *en route* to Salcombe.

'Dad? Promise you won't be cross with me?'

'Why? What have you done?'

'Nothing. Only . . . do you think you could take me home?'

'Why? What's wrong? What's the matter?'

'Absolutely nothing. It's been fine. Only . . . I think I'd rather quit while I'm ahead. And, anyway, I miss you.'

She heard the sigh. 'OK, my little love, I'll bring you back if you want. But why didn't you tell me before?'

'Oh, I just didn't want to worry you. You'd have thought I was unhappy and I'm not.'

'OK, sweetheart. Look, I'll have to go now. I'll see you soon, all right?'

'Thanks, Dad. You're a wonder.'

Tally sat on top of her suitcase and tried to force down the lid. It would need greater pressure than her slender frame could provide. She went in search of Alex for a bit of muscle power.

David Blane-Pfitzer had returned late the night before. Now he was down in the kitchen with his family. 'You ready for the off?' he asked, as Tally came in.

'Almost. Just need a strong arm on my case.'

'That'll be you, then, Alex.' His father smiled at him.

Alex looked up. 'Yes, of course.'

He tramped up the stairs after her to her room. It took only a few seconds to fasten down the lid.

'Sure you won't stay?'

She nodded. 'Can I ask you something? This is really none of my business, and I shouldn't be interfering . . .'

'What is it?'

'Would you ask your dad to go sailing with you? In the little boat?'

'What on earth for?'

'Oh . . . I just think he might like to.'

He shook his head and smiled. 'I shall miss you . . . Tal.'

WITHIN THE HOUR, her father had arrived, and thanked the Blane-Pfitzers for looking after his daughter. He was sorry she had to leave; he hoped they wouldn't mind. Tally looked anxious, Alex and his father smiled understandingly.

While the families exchanged pleasantries—'She's been no trouble, we've hardly seen her'—Tally said goodbye to Alex at the bottom of the garden. They kissed tenderly.

'You will ring me?' She squeezed his hand and looked at him searchingly. 'Promise you'll ring me.'

'Yes. Every day.'

'Well, text me at least.'

'At least.'

She let go of his hand, and began to walk up the garden, then stopped, turned to face him once more. '*Arrivederci, amore mio*.'

He smiled at her. '*Prenditi cura di te*.'

Her heart missed a beat. 'How did you know . . .?'

Alex shrugged. 'Granny lives in Florence.'

THE JOURNEY HOME was uncharacteristically quiet. Tom was keen to find out all about her week away, but he soon realised that now was not the time to ask. He caught glimpses of Tally from time to time, looking out of the window, a million miles away.

It wasn't until they were home and she was unpacking that he felt able to enquire how the week had gone.

'It was lovely.'

'But you came home?'

'Yes.' Tally realised that some sort of explanation was only fair. She flopped on the edge of the bed and looked up at him. 'We got on really well. I didn't want to risk it all going wrong. Simple as that.'

'And I needn't worry.'

'No. He's lovely and . . . I'm very fond of him.'

'Good.' Tom was leaning in the doorway, trying to appear casual.

'Da-a-ad?'

'Mmm?'

'Do you think there's a difference between being a father to a girl and being a father to a boy?'

'Yes. Tons. Why?'

'What sort of difference?'

'Well, I think with fathers and sons there's always that undercurrent of . . . succession, I suppose you might call it. The leader of the tribe knows that one day he'll be knocked off his perch by a young upstart. It's instinctive rather than conscious. Then you have all that stuff about a son achieving his father's unfulfilled ambitions, the father not wanting to lose face in front of his son, the son not wanting to let his father down. It's a lot of baggage when you think about it.'

'Do you think some fathers are better with daughters than sons?'

'Most, I should think. But there are different problems in being a father to a daughter.'

'What sort of problems?'

'I think by now, my little love, you probably know every last one of them.' He turned to leave. 'Oh, by the way. Did you wear that little triangular thing? The one made of black silky stuff.'

'No.'

'Oh. Good.'

ALEX WAS TRUE to his word. He called her every day and texted her morning and evening. She felt wanted, cared for, loved in a way she had not experienced before, yet she was aware of the fragility of any relationship.

Tom tapped away daily at his laptop in the shed, and Tally read, dared to dream, and even started to pull a few weeds from among the mint and parsley in the herb garden, conscious of its importance to her father. She realised, now, why he had cared for it so assiduously. It was another way of showing that he cared for her mum.

He seemed happier now that he was writing somewhere other

than in his study, happier that he had started a second novel. But there was still an air of preoccupation about him.

She considered how best to cheer him up. What he really needed was company—new company. Tally sometimes let herself think about the prospect of him finding someone else. It was not easy. She determined to ready herself for it, but not just yet.

It was during a trip to Axbury, when she picked up her holiday snaps, that she thought about Janie. She sat on a bench in the shadow of the Minster and rang her on her mobile.

'Janie? It's Tally.'

'Sweetheart, how on earth are you?'

Tally explained about the holiday, with Janie anxious for details about 'that man'. 'I was wondering if you'd come for supper. We haven't seen you for ages and I think Dad could do with cheering up.'

'Have you asked him?'

Tally wanted to make Janie welcome. 'Of course.'

'And he doesn't mind?'

'Of course he doesn't.'

Janie assumed that Tom had been consulted. 'Well, only if you're sure your dad's happy with that.'

'Perfectly. I know he's dying to see you.'

A date was fixed for two nights hence and Tally rang off, feeling pleased with herself. Then she met Emma for a tea cake and Coke. It was not the happy reunion she had expected. Emma sat across the table, looking haunted.

'What on earth's the matter?'

Emma bit her lip.

Tally recognised the problem. 'Did you . . .?'

Emma cast her eyes down.

'Oh, God!' Then, after a pause, 'Not very good?'

'Awful.'

Tally put her hand across the table and laid it on top of Emma's. 'Want to talk about it?'

'Not really. Just wish I could go back and start again.' Emma changed the subject. 'How did you get on?'

Tally looked apologetic. 'Fine. It was lovely.'

'And he didn't try it on?'

'A bit.'

'But you . . .?'

'No. I was tempted, though.'

'You've got more sense.'

'Not really. Just more scared.'

'Well, you keep being scared. It's a good defence mechanism.' Emma slurped at her Coke. 'When will you see him again?'

'I don't know. He's still down in Devon.'

'Why didn't you stay?'

'I don't know, really. I just know it was right to come away. I do love him . . . but I've got exams and he's going to uni in Edinburgh, and then when will we see each other?'

'So Little Miss Sensible walked away?'

'No. I'm just terrified of getting hurt, if you want the truth. I've had enough hurt to last me for a long time.'

'YOU'VE DONE WHAT?'

'Asked her to supper. We haven't seen her for ages.'

Her father seemed irritated. 'You should have asked me.'

Tally looked surprised. 'I thought you'd be pleased.'

Tom needed to find an excuse not to meet Janie. 'What about food and stuff?'

'Dad, that's pathetic. I can do the shopping if you're busy writing. Don't you want to see Janie?'

'Yes, yes, of course I do . . . It's just that . . .' There was nothing he could do without making Tally suspicious.

'Look, Dad, I think you need a bit of female company.'

Her candour surprised him. 'I've got female company. You.'

'That's different.'

'In any case, why Janie?'

'You get on so well together. And she makes you laugh.'

He wondered if somehow she knew. Dear old Tal, doing her best to sort her dad out. Perhaps she was paving the way for . . . what? No. He tried to put the thought out of his head. 'Did she seem happy to come?'

'Of course. I'll do the cooking, if you like. My treat.'

This was all a bit unnerving, but he said, 'Great, I'll leave it to you, then.'

THAT EVENING Kate Lundy rang. 'Just to say that my solicitor is ready to exchange contracts and he'll be talking to your solicitor in the morning, if that's OK?'

'Fine.'

'Look,would you mind if I came round? It's just that there's something I want to talk over with you.'

'I'll be here.'

Tally was upstairs in her room when Kate arrived—Tom had said he needed half an hour to discuss business. Tom let Kate in and returned her kiss on the cheek.

'How are you getting on?' he asked.

'Very well.' She looked a little uneasy. Embarrassed, even.

He tried to make her feel more at home. 'Glass of wine?'

'No, thanks, I won't. I just wanted to tell you before you heard it anywhere else . . . Pete and I . . . we're moving in together.'

Tom could not help but look surprised. 'I see.'

'Oh, I know I've only just got divorced—but, we just found that we like being together.'

'I see. Er . . . how long?'

'Oh, the chemistry was there before the break-up with Rachel, I think we both knew that, but we didn't do anything about it. We're going to buy a flat in Axbury.'

Tom half laughed. 'This is all so sudden.'

'Oh, it's quite mad. I must be barmy. But you don't meet someone you get on with like a house on fire every day, do you? Got to take your chances while you can, I suppose. And I've been hurt once, so I'm going into it with my eyes open. Pete, too. But we both want to give it a bash. When you like being with someone it's wrong not to be with them just because of respectable intervals and all that sort of thing. Who does that please? Only the gossips.'

'I suppose so.'

'Anyway, are you managing OK?'

'Oh, yes, I'm being well looked after.' He raised his eyes in the direction of Tally's bedroom.

'Don't get used to it. She'll have flown the nest before you know where you are.'

'I hope not. Look, are you sure you won't have a glass of wine?'

'I'd love one. I wasn't sure how you'd take it about me and Pete. I thought you might think me a bit of a schemer.'

'Oh, I'm past making judgments.' He opened a bottle and poured two glasses of white wine. 'Well, here's to you and Pete.'

She smiled. 'Cheers.' She took a gulp of wine. 'I needed that. You've no idea how nervous I was coming here to tell you.'

'Am I such an ogre?'

'No, not at all. It's just . . . well . . . circumstances, I suppose.'

'Oh, I shouldn't worry about those. Can't be helped.' He hoped she might change the subject. His luck was out.

'Tom? I'm not sure how to ask this . . . Do you . . . I mean would you be interested . . . I have a friend who's on her own. Another divorcee.'

Tom fumbled for a way out. 'Oh, I'm OK at the moment.'

'Too soon?'

He sighed. 'Yes. Well, no, I suppose not. I don't know, Kate. There is somebody, but I'm not sure . . .'

'Tom, don't feel bad.'

'But I do.'

'There's no need. It happens.'

'Yes, but . . .'

'They do say that the more someone loved the partner they have lost, the more likely they are to fall in love again. If you've loved a lot you don't suddenly stop having all that love inside you. It seems to me that holding back when you know that your love is returned is wasteful. And that's putting it mildly.'

'Especially if the reason you're holding back is respectability?'

'And misplaced guilt, yes.'

Tom took another sip. 'Well, thanks for your concern.'

'I've spoken out of turn. I'm sorry.'

'No, not at all. It's good to talk it through.'

Kate turned in the doorway. 'You're a good man, Tom. Nobody will begrudge you a bit of company.' She got into her car and motored off down the drive.

THE FOLLOWING DAY Tom could settle to nothing. He tried to write but the words came out in a jumble. He made a sortie into the herb garden, but the coriander and parsley were running to seed and the mint was making a takeover bid for the marjoram. The battle for male supremacy was lost. Pippa would have fared much better.

Half of him was longing to see Janie, the other half was apprehensive. Would she be standoffish? It must have taken courage for her to admit her feelings, and he had brushed them off. Now she figured largely in his dreams. And still he felt riddled with guilt.

At six he bathed, put on smart chinos and a clean shirt, then paced up and down the sitting room. Tally had laid the kitchen table and was beavering away preparing her smoked-salmon starter.

When the sound of car wheels crunched up the drive, Tom felt as nervous as a schoolboy outside the headmaster's study. He took a deep breath, and went to the door to greet her. Janie stepped out onto the drive, her skin more than usually tanned, her figure slender in navy-blue trousers and a white shirt. She closed the car door and said, 'Hello, you.'

'Hello, you, too,' he replied. She walked up to greet him, kissed his cheek and squeezed his arm. 'Nice to see you,' he said.

'And you.'

He waited for the sobriquet, but it never came. There was no 'old sod' or 'bastard', just a simple 'And you'.

Tally came racing out of the front door. 'Janie!'

'Hello, my little angel, how've you been?'

'Very well.'

'And what about your pa?' Janie enquired.

'Better. Still room for improvement. I thought you could help.'

AT THE KITCHEN TABLE, decorated with fat, stubby candles that cast an orange glow over their faces, the three talked about Tally's holiday, Tom's shed and the general state of the nation. Both Tom and Janie became more relaxed, even cast each other knowing glances during the meal, while Tally served up the smoked salmon, then pasta with bacon and herbs, and finally raspberries and cream. There was even a brief moment when Tom laid his hand over Janie's and smiled into her eyes. She returned his smile, then slid her hand away when Tally returned with coffee.

'Well, I have to say, miss,' she said, 'that was the best meal I've had in ages.'

'Glad you came?' asked Tom.

'Very glad.'

Maybe he was reading too much into things, but she seemed to say it with more feeling than he had expected.

Tally rose from the table. 'Back in a minute. Just going upstairs.'

Tom waited until she was out of earshot, then said softly, 'How have you really been?'

'Pretty grim. How about you?'

'The same. I'm sorry. I thought you might be upset. About my reaction, I mean. I wasn't exactly encouraging, was I?'

'No.' She smiled ruefully. 'But, then, it was my fault, really.'

He hesitated. 'I wanted to say . . . Well, I don't want you to think that I don't feel . . . well . . .'

'It's OK. Really it is. Do you think Tally . . .?'

'I'm not sure.'

They heard her coming downstairs and turned as she came into the kitchen.

She had her hands behind her back and spoke to her father. 'I've got something for you. Promise you won't be upset?'

'Why should I be upset?'

'Well, because you might. Only I thought you'd like to have it.'

'Have what?'

'This.' She handed him a photograph. It was of him and Pippa lying side by side on sun-loungers, holding hands.

TALLY WENT TO BED at eleven, leaving Tom and Janie sitting either side of the kitchen table.

Janie looked thoughtful. 'Do you think it was a warning shot?'

'No. No way. That's not Tally's style at all. She'd suddenly have remembered getting it from Boots and knew I'd love it and acted on impulse. Whatever else Tally may be she's not calculating—and she's not cruel, either.'

'I suppose.'

'You know, there are two ways of looking at this.'

'That's one more than I can see.' Janie took a large sip of wine.

'Either we go back to where we were, or we grit our teeth and get on with it from where we are now.'

Janie put down her glass. 'What?'

'I can't work magic, Janie, but I don't want to lose you.'

Janie ran a hand through her hair. 'What are you trying to say, Tom? And please be bloody careful how you answer.'

'I'm trying to say rather a lot of things and they might not come out in the right order.'

Janie stared at him. He had never seen her look scared before.

'You think far too much when you've been through what I have. Your mind goes over and over and over the same things, but you can't stop. It's some kind of rite of passage, something you have to go through. There seems no earthly point in it, yet you do it because you know you *have* to do it.'

Janie was listening attentively, unsure where he was going.

'It's even harder when the faintest glimmer of hope appears, because then you tell yourself you're giving way, losing your resolve. What you've been doing to get yourself through it all suddenly becomes a way of life in itself. You've clung on to it so hard and for so long that you can't see a way forward without it. The grief, in its way, is your only source of comfort.' He paused. 'Is this making sense?'

She spoke steadily. 'Go on.'

'Letting go of misery is scary, because at least it's constant. You can't believe or trust in happiness ever again.'

'But that's wrong.'

'I can see it is now, but it's taken me so long to get there and I'm not confident of never having a relapse.'

'But you won't have a relapse, provided that the source of the happiness doesn't let you down.'

'Yes, but what about other things? Outside agencies.'

'Death, you mean?'

'Yes.'

'You can't legislate for that one, Tom. That's the risk you take.'

'I know. I took it. I'd be mad to take it again.'

'So?'

'I guess I'm asking you how serious you are.'

Janie looked at him and said nothing for a few moments. Then, very softly, her voice lacking any drama, she said, 'I've never been more serious in my life.'

Tom sighed. 'Isn't that a bit frightening?'

'Scares the shit out of me.'

'Me, too.'

'But you seemed so surprised . . . when I said.'

'I was. Too frightened to admit it to myself.'

Janie leaned back in her chair. 'Well, what a night this has turned out to be. Look!' She held up her hand. It was shaking.

'Come here.' He stood up and held out his arms.

She got up and walked towards him. 'This is so silly.'

'What?'

'Feel.' She took his right hand and laid it on her left breast. He could feel the thumping of her heart through the white linen of her shirt. He felt the soft warmth of her breast, and bent down to kiss her. When he broke off and looked into her eyes, he saw they were glistening with tears.

JANIE SPENT THE NIGHT in the spare room. For hours neither slept, both staring at the ceiling, separated by a wall. All Tom could think of was how to break the news to Tally. All Janie could think of was how Tom would break the news to Tally.

THEY WERE BOTH downstairs and dressed by seven. There was no sign of Tally. Tom had been making coffee when he heard Janie's footsteps coming towards the kitchen. Anxiously he looked round.

Would she look worried, would she have changed her mind?

She seemed anxious, too. He feared the worst. 'Are you OK?'

She smiled. 'Yes. As long as you haven't changed your mind.'

'Thank God for that.' He walked over to her and gave her a hug. 'I was so worried that I'd wake up this morning and find you gone.'

'No chance.'

They kissed tenderly and his heart beat faster. 'Oh, you feel so good,' he whispered.

'And you. Oh, and you.'

'You mean I'm not an old sod or an old bastard any more?'

'Oh, you'll always be an old bastard to me,' she said.

'That's all right, then.' He held her silently for a few moments. 'So we can either go on pretending nothing has happened, or broach the subject gently and see what her reaction is.'

'Yes.'

'Any suggestions?'

'Absolutely none.'

The discussion was interrupted by the sound of Tally coming down the stairs.

'Morning!'

Tom busied himself with coffee-making. 'Hello, sweetheart. Sleep well?'

'Not really. Too many things to think about.'

'What sort of things?' asked Janie.

'Oh, you know. This 'n' that.'

'Coffee?'

'No, just cereal, thanks.'

As she spooned up her cereal she asked, 'And what are you two doing today?'

Janie and Tom spoke in unison. 'What do you mean?'

Tally laughed at their chorus. 'I mean, what are you doing? It's Saturday. Start of the weekend, you know? Time off!'

'Oh, hadn't thought,' blustered Tom.

Janie shrugged. 'Dunno.'

'Oh. Well, I thought I'd go out for the day with Emma. She needs cheering up.'

Tom did his best to sound casual. 'OK.'

'Would it be all right if I stayed the night?'

'Er, yes. I suppose so.'

'Fine.' She finished her cereal and began to climb the stairs. 'Only I don't want to cramp your style.'

'CAN I JUST ASK you something?' Tom was driving Tally into Axbury. 'Last night, when you gave me that picture . . .'

'Yes. I'm sorry. The timing was wrong. I realised the moment I'd done it. I felt so stupid. I should have kept it for later.'

'So this morning, when you said . . .'

'Yes?'

'What did you mean?'

'Oh, I think you know.'

'I don't!'

'Dad, I can see it even if you can't. You and Janie, you're good together.'

'Yes, but . . .'

'Mum?'

'Yes.'

She looked across at him. 'You're too good to waste, Dad.'

He pulled up at the side of the road. 'But what about you?'

'I'm your daughter.'

'That's what I mean.'

She leaned across and kissed him lightly on the cheek. 'And I'll always be your daughter.'

Tom put his arm round her shoulders and pulled her close to him. He took a deep breath, then sniffed loudly.

'But only on one condition,' said Tally.

'What's that?'

'That you'll always be my dad.'

ALAN TITCHMARSH

During the past two decades Alan Titchmarsh's down-to-earth, light-hearted style as the presenter of BBC television's *Gardener's World* and *Ground Force* has won him a devoted following. And four years ago, when his first novel, *Mr McGregor*, vaulted into the best-seller charts, he also became one of Britain's best-loved writers. An OBE followed in the wake of these achievements, and as the Queen presented him with his award she is said to have remarked, 'You've given a lot of ladies a lot of pleasure.' It's a tribute that Alan Titchmarsh says he wants to have engraved on his tombstone.

Even as a boy, growing up in Yorkshire, he had a passion for gardening, inheriting, it seems, the genes of his paternal grandfather and great-grandfather, both of whom were gardeners. Young Alan loved to potter about on his grandfather's allotment, and in his own parent's garden, where his father, a plumber, was only too happy to hand over the spade. At fifteen, with one O level to his name, he went to work as an apprentice for Ilkley Parks Department while also studying for his City and Guilds in horticulture. Stints at Oaklands College in Hertfordshire and at the Royal Botanic Gardens in Kew followed, before he moved into journalism, eventually becoming deputy editor of *Amateur Gardening* magazine and then a regular guest on various television shows.

Barleywood, Alan Titchmarsh's Hampshire home, boasts over an acre of organically cultivated land from where he regularly presents *Gardener's World*. He and his wife Alison share this patch of English countryside with their two daughters, two cats, and an assortment of chickens and ducks. 'Sometimes I just can't believe my luck,' he says. 'To be able to spend my life in a garden with plants and to write and broadcast about them is, for me, simply the best life there is.'

GONE FOR GOOD

Harlan Coben

Eleven years ago, Ken Klein disappeared, fleeing from accusations that he had murdered his brother's ex-girlfriend.

Everyone believes he's gone for good. Almost certainly dead. Until the day Will Klein hears his mother whisper on her death bed: 'He's alive.'

Suddenly it seems Ken's story is far from over.

Chapter 1

Three days before her death, my mother told me—these weren't her last words, but they were pretty close—that my brother was still alive.

That was all she said. She didn't elaborate. She said it only once. And she wasn't doing very well. Morphine had already applied its endgame heart squeeze. Her eyes had sunk deep into her skull. She slept most of the time. She would, in fact, have only one more lucid moment—and that would be a chance for me to tell her that she had been a wonderful mother, that I loved her very much, and goodbye. We never said anything about my brother. That didn't mean we weren't thinking about him.

'He's alive.'

Those were her exact words. And if they were true, I didn't know if it would be a good thing or bad.

WE BURIED MY MOTHER four days later.

When we returned to the house to sit shiva, my father stormed into the living room. His face was red with rage. I was there, of course. My sister, Melissa, had flown in from Seattle with her husband, Ralph. Aunt Selma and Uncle Murray paced. Sheila, my soul mate, sat next to me and held my hand.

Dad kept glancing out of the bay windows and muttered under his breath, 'Sons of bitches.' Then he'd turn round and think of someone else who hadn't shown up. 'For God's sake, you'd think the

Bergmans would have at least made an appearance.' Then he'd close his eyes and look away as the anger consumed him anew.

One more betrayal in a decade filled with them.

I needed air. I got to my feet. Sheila looked up at me with concern. 'I'm going to take a walk,' I said softly.

'You want company?'

'I don't think so.'

Sheila nodded. We had been together nearly a year. I've never had a partner so in sync with my moods. She gave my hand another I-love-you squeeze, and the warmth spread through me.

I stepped outside and strolled up Downing Place. The street was lined with numbingly ordinary split-levels, *circa* 1962. I still wore my dark grey suit. It itched in the savage heat. An image of my mother's light-the-world smile—the one before it all happened—flashed in front of my eyes. I shoved it away.

I knew where I was headed, though I doubt if I would have admitted it to myself. I was drawn there, pulled by some unseen force. Some would call it masochistic. Others would note that maybe it had something to do with closure. I thought it was probably neither.

I just wanted to look at the spot where it all ended.

The sights and sounds of summer suburbia assaulted me. Kids squealed by on their bicycles. Mr Cirino, who owned the Ford dealership on Route 10, mowed his lawn. The Steins—they'd built up a chain of appliance stores—were taking a stroll hand in hand.

A lawn sprinkler did the slow wave in front of Eric Frankel's house at 23 Downing Place. Eric had a space-travel-themed bar mitzvah at the Chanticleer in Short Hills when we were both in seventh grade. The ceiling was done up planetarium style—a black sky with star constellations. My seating card told me that I was sitting at 'Table Apollo 14'. Cindi Shapiro and I had sneaked into the chapel room and made out for over an hour. It was my first time. I didn't know what I was doing. Cindi did. I remember it was glorious.

When Cindi and I returned to Table Apollo 14, ruffled and in fine post-smooch form, my brother, Ken, pulled me to the side and demanded details. I, of course, too gladly gave them. He smiled and slapped me five. That night, as we lay on the bunk beds, Ken on the top, me on the bottom, the stereo playing Blue Öyster Cult's 'Don't Fear the Reaper' (Ken's favourite), my older brother explained to me the facts of life as seen by a ninth-grader. When I think back to that night, I always smile.

'He's alive . . .'

I shook my head and turned right at Coddington Terrace by the Holders' old house. Maybe it was just my imagination, but people began to stare. The bicycles, the dribbling basketballs, the cries of touch footballers—they all seemed to hush as I passed. Some stared out of curiosity because a strange man strolling in a dark grey suit on a summer evening was something of an oddity. But most, or again so it seemed, looked on in horror because they recognised me and couldn't believe that I would dare tread upon this sacred soil.

I approached the house at 47 Coddington Terrace. I jammed my hands in my pockets and toed the spot where kerb met pavement. Why was I here? I saw a curtain move in the den. Mrs Miller's face appeared at the window, gaunt and ghostlike. She glared at me. I didn't move or look away. She glared some more—and then to my surprise, her face softened. It was as though our mutual agony had made some sort of connection. Mrs Miller nodded at me. I nodded back and felt the tears begin to well up.

YOU MAY HAVE seen the story on *20/20* or *PrimeTime Live*. For those who haven't, here's the official account: On October 17 eleven years ago, in the township of Livingston, New Jersey, my brother, Ken Klein, then twenty-four, brutally raped and strangled our neighbour Julie Miller. In her basement. At 47 Coddington Terrace.

That was where her body was found. The evidence wasn't conclusive as to if she'd actually been murdered there, but that was the assumption. My brother escaped capture and ran off to parts unknown—at least, again, according to the official account.

Over the past eleven years, Ken has eluded an international dragnet. There have, however, been 'sightings'.

The first came about a year after the murder from a small fishing village in northern Sweden. Interpol swooped in, but somehow my brother evaded their grasp. Supposedly he was tipped off.

The next sighting occurred four years later in Barcelona. Ken had rented—to quote the newspaper accounts—'an oceanview hacienda' with—again I will quote—'a lithe, dark-haired woman, perhaps a flamenco dancer'. A vacationing Livingston resident, no less, reported seeing Ken and his Castilian paramour dining beachside, but yet again he slipped through the law's fingers.

The last time my brother was purportedly spotted he was skiing down the black runs in the French Alps (interestingly enough, Ken never skied before the murder). Nothing came of it, except a story on *48 Hours*, probably when the programme was low on material.

I naturally hated television's coverage of 'suburbia gone wrong' or whatever similar cute moniker they came up with, which always featured the same photographs of Ken in his tennis whites—he was a nationally ranked player at one time—looking his most pompous. I can't imagine where they got them. In them Ken looked handsome in that way people hate right away. Haughty, Kennedy hair, suntan bold against the whites, toothy grin, he looked like one of those people of privilege (he was not) who coasted through life on his charm (a little) and trust account (he had none).

Anyway, that was the official account of what happened.

I've never believed it. I'm not saying it's not possible. But I believe a much more likely scenario is that my brother is dead—that he has been dead for the past eleven years.

More to the point, my mother always believed that Ken was dead. Her son was not a murderer. Her son was a victim.

'He's alive . . . He didn't do it.'

The front door of the Miller house opened. Mr Miller stepped through it. His fists rested on his hips in a pitiful Superman stance. 'Get the hell out of here, Will,' Mr Miller said to me.

And I did.

THE NEXT BIG SHOCK occurred an hour later.

Sheila and I were up in my parents' bedroom. We sat on the king-size bed with my mother's most personal items—the stuff she kept in her bloated nightstand drawers—scattered over the duvet. My father was still downstairs by the bay windows, staring out defiantly.

I don't know why I wanted to sift through my mother's things. It would hurt. I knew that. But I needed to do it, I guess.

I looked at Sheila's lovely face—tilted to the left, eyes down and focused—and I felt my heart soar. It was not just her beauty—hers was not what one would call classical anyway, her features a bit off centre from either genetics or, more likely, her murky past—but there was an animation there, an inquisitiveness, a delicacy too, as if one more blow would shatter her irreparably. Sheila made me want to—bear with me here—be brave for her.

She looked up and saw my expression. 'What?' she asked.

I shrugged. 'You're my world,' I said simply.

'You're pretty hot stuff yourself.'

'Yeah,' I said. 'Yeah, that's true.'

She feigned a slap in my direction. 'I love you, you know.'

'What's not to love?'

She rolled her eyes. Then her gaze fell back onto the side of my mother's bed. Her face quieted.

'What are you thinking about?' I asked.

'Your mother.' Sheila smiled. 'I really liked her.'

We started going through the laminated yellow newspaper clippings. Birth announcements—Melissa's, Ken's, mine. There were articles on Ken's tennis exploits. His trophies, all those bronze men in miniature in mid serve, still swarmed his old bedroom. There were photographs, mostly old ones from before the murder. Sunny. It had been my mother's nickname since childhood. It suited her. Sunny was the favourite grown-up among my friends. They liked it when she drove the car pool. They wanted the class picnic at our house. Sunny was parental cool without being cloying, just 'off' enough, a little crazy perhaps, so that you never knew exactly what she would do next. There had always been an excitement—a crackle if you will—around my mother.

'She was so lovely,' Sheila said.

It's an awful cliché to say that a part of her died when they found Julie Miller's body, but the thing about clichés is that they're often dead-on. My mother's crackle quieted, smothered. After hearing about the murder, her whole manner became flat, monotone—passionless would be the best way to describe it.

I remember the first time the windows had been shot out with a BB gun, not long after the murder—the way Dad shook his fist with defiance. Mom, I think, wanted to move. Dad would not. Moving would be a surrender in his eyes. Moving would be admitting their son's guilt. Moving would be a betrayal.

Dumb.

Sheila had her eyes on me. Her warmth was almost palpable, and for a moment I just let myself bathe in it. We'd met at work about a year before. I'm the senior director of Covenant House on 41st Street in New York City. We're a charitable foundation that helps young runaways survive the streets. Sheila had come in as a volunteer. She was from a small town in Idaho, though she seemed to have very little small-town-girl left in her. She told me that many years ago, she too had been a runaway. That was all she would tell me about her past.

'I love you,' I said.

'What's not to love?' she countered.

I did not roll my eyes. Sheila had been good to my mother towards the end, when she was in the St Barnabas Medical Center. I had seen

Sheila with my mother. And it made me wonder. I took a risk.

'You should call your parents,' I said softly.

Sheila looked at me as though I'd just slapped her across the face. She slid off the bed. 'This isn't the time, Will,' she said.

I picked up a picture frame that held a photo of my tanned parents on vacation. 'Seems as good as any.'

'You don't know anything about my parents.'

'I'd like to,' I said.

She turned her back to me. 'You've worked with runaways,' she said. 'You know how bad it can be.'

I did. I thought again about her slightly off-centre features—the nose, for example, with the telltale bump—and wondered. 'I also know it's worse if you don't talk about it.'

She turned to face me. 'Not now, OK? Please.'

I had no response to that one, but perhaps she was right. My fingers were absently toying with the picture frame. And that was when it happened.

The photograph in the frame slid a little.

I looked down. Another photograph started peeking out from underneath. My finger found the clips on the back. I slid them to the side and let the back of the frame drop to the bed. Two photographs floated down behind it. One—the top one—was of my parents on a cruise, looking happy and healthy and relaxed. But it was the second photograph, the hidden one, that caught my eye.

The red-stamped date on the bottom was from less than two years ago. The picture was taken atop a field or hill or something, with snow-capped mountains in the background. The man in the picture wore shorts and a backpack and sunglasses and scuffed hiking boots. His smile was familiar. So was his face, though it was more lined now. His beard had grey in it. But there was no mistake.

The man in the picture was my brother, Ken.

MY FATHER WAS ALONE on the back patio. Night had fallen. He sat very still and stared out at the black.

I slipped through the sliding glass door. 'Hey,' I said to him.

He spun round, his face already breaking into a wide smile. He always had one for me. 'Hey, Will,' he said, the gravel voice turning tender. Dad was always happy to see his children. Before all this happened, my father was a fairly popular man. He was friendly and dependable, if not a little gruff, which just made him seem all the more dependable. But while my father might smile at you, he didn't care a lick. No one else mattered to him. His world was his family.

I sat in the lounge chair next to him, not sure how to raise the subject. I took a few deep breaths and listened to him do the same. I felt wonderfully safe with him. He might be older and more withered—and by now I was the taller, stronger man—but I knew that if trouble surfaced, he'd still step up and take the hit for me.

'Have to cut that branch back,' he said, pointing into the dark.

I couldn't see it. 'Yeah,' I said.

The light from the sliding glass doors hit his profile. The anger had dissolved now, and the shattered look had returned.

'You OK?' he asked me. His standard opening refrain.

'I'm fine. I mean, not fine but . . .'

Dad waved his hand. 'Yeah, dumb question,' he said.

We fell back into silence. He lit a cigarette. I folded my hands and put them on my lap. Then I dived in. 'Mom told me something before she died.'

His eyes slid towards me.

'She said that Ken was still alive.'

Dad stiffened, but only for a second. A sad smile came to his face. 'It was the drugs, Will.'

'Did Mom say anything to you?'

Dad shrugged. 'She told me pretty much what she told you,' he said. 'That Ken was alive, that he didn't kill Julie. She said he'd be back by now except he had to do something first.'

'Do what?'

'She wasn't making sense, Will. She was dying.'

'Did you ask her?'

'Of course. But she was just ranting. She couldn't hear me any more. I shushed her. I told her it'd be OK.'

He looked away again. I thought about showing him the photograph of Ken but decided against it. I wanted to think it through before I started us down that path.

'I told her it'd be OK,' he repeated, getting to his feet. 'I'll be right back,' he said.

I watched him walk until he thought he was out of sight. But I could see his outline in the dark. I saw him lower his head. His shoulders started to shake. I don't think that I had ever seen my father cry. I didn't want to start now.

I turned away and remembered the other photograph, the one still upstairs of my parents on the cruise looking tanned and happy, and I wondered if maybe he was thinking about that too.

WHEN I WOKE late that night, Sheila wasn't in bed.

I sat up and listened. Nothing. At least, not in the apartment. I could hear the normal late-night street hum drifting up from three floors below. I looked over towards the bathroom. The light was out. All lights, in fact, were out.

I slipped out of bed and padded towards the living room. Sheila was there. She sat on the windowsill and looked down towards the street. I stared at her back, the swan neck, the wonderful shoulders, the way her hair flowed down the white skin, and again I felt the stir. Our relationship was still on the border of the early throes, the gee-it's-great-to-be-alive love, that wonderful run-across-the-park-to-see-her stomach-flutter that you know, *know*, would soon darken into something richer and deeper.

'Hey,' I said.

She turned just a little, but it was enough. There were tears on her cheeks. I could see them sliding down in the moonlight. She didn't make a sound—no cries or sobs. Just the tears. I wondered what I should do.

'Sheila?'

On our second date, Sheila performed a card trick. It involved my picking two cards, putting them in the middle of the deck while she turned her head, and her throwing the entire deck save my two cards onto the floor. She smiled widely after performing this feat, holding up the two cards for my inspection. I smiled back. It was—how to put this?—goofy. Sheila was indeed goofy. She liked card tricks and cherry Kool-Aid and boy bands. She sang opera and read voraciously and cried at Hallmark commercials. And most of all, Sheila loved to dance. She loved to close her eyes and put her head on my shoulder and fade away.

'I'm sorry, Will,' Sheila said without turning round.

'For what?' I said.

She kept her eyes on the view. 'Go back to bed. I'll be there in a few minutes.'

I wanted to stay to offer up words of comfort. I didn't. She wasn't reachable right now. Words or action would be either superfluous or harmful. At least, that was what I told myself. So I made a huge mistake. I went back to bed and waited. But Sheila never came back.

THE NOTE SHE LEFT me was short and sweet.

Love you always, S.

She hadn't come back to bed. I assume that she'd spent the entire evening staring out of the window. I heard her slip out at around five in the morning. The time wasn't that odd. Sheila was an early riser, so I was more confused by her behaviour than worried.

I showered and dressed. The photograph of my brother was in my desk drawer. I took it out and studied it for a long time. There was a hollow sensation in my chest. My mind whirled and danced, but coming through all that was one pretty basic thought:

Ken had pulled it off.

Chapter 2

You may have been wondering what'd convinced me that he'd been dead all these years. Part of it, I confess, was old-fashioned intuition mixed with blind hope. I loved my brother. And I knew him. Ken was not perfect. Ken was quick to anger and thrived on confrontation. Ken was mixed up in something bad. But Ken was not a murderer.

But there was more to the Klein family theory than this bizarre faith. First off, how could Ken have survived on the run like this? He'd only had $800 in the bank. Where did he get the resources to elude this international manhunt? And what possible motive could there have been for killing Julie? How come he never contacted us during the past eleven years? Why was he so on edge when he came home for that final visit? Why did he tell me that he was in danger? And why, looking back on it, didn't I push him to tell me more?

But most damaging—or encouraging, depending on your viewpoint—was the blood found at the scene. Some of it belonged to Ken. A large splotch of his blood was in the basement, and small drips made a trail up the stairs and into the Millers' back yard. The Klein family theory was that the real murderer had killed Julie and seriously wounded (and eventually killed) my brother. The police's theory was simpler: Julie had fought back.

There was one more thing that backed the family theory—something directly attributable to me, which was why, I guess, no one took it seriously.

That is, I saw a man lurking near the Miller house that night.

Like I said, the authorities have pretty much dismissed this—I am, after all, interested in clearing my brother—but it is important in understanding why we believe that whatever mess he had got himself into, Ken had somehow been set up.

Some people did give credence to our family's theory, but most were conspiracy nuts, the kind who think Elvis and Jimi Hendrix are jamming on some island off Fiji. As time went by, I grew quieter in my defence of Ken. Selfish as this might sound, I wanted a life. I wanted a career. I didn't want to be the brother of an infamous murderer on the run.

Covenant House, I'm sure, had reservations about hiring me. Who would blame them? Even though I'm the senior director, my name is kept off the letterhead. My job is strictly behind the scenes. And most of the time, that's OK with me.

I looked again at the picture of a man so familiar yet totally unknown to me. Had my mother been lying from the beginning? Had she been helping Ken, sneaking him money, while telling my father and me she thought he was dead? Had Sunny known where he was from the start? Questions to ponder.

I wrested my eyes away and opened a kitchen cabinet. I'd already decided that I wouldn't go out to Livingston this morning—the thought of sitting in that coffin of a house for another day made me want to scream—and I really needed to go to work. My mother, I was sure, would not only understand but encourage. So I poured myself a bowl of cereal and dialled Sheila's work voicemail. I told her I loved her and asked her to call me.

My apartment—well, it's *our* apartment now—is on 24th Street and Ninth Avenue. I usually walk the seventeen blocks north to Covenant House, which is on 41st Street, not far from the West Side Highway. This used to be a great location for a runaway shelter in the days before the cleanup of 42nd Street, when this stretch of stench was a bastion of in-your-face degradation. Forty-second Street had been a sort of Hell's Gate, a place where commuters and tourists would walk past prostitutes and dealers and pimps and porno palaces and movie theatres, and when they'd reach the end, they'd either be titillated or they'd want to take a shower and get a shot of penicillin.

The city's cleanup, in a sense, made our jobs harder. The Covenant House rescue van had known where to cruise. The runaways were out in the open, more obvious. Now our task wasn't as clear-cut. And worse, the city itself wasn't really cleaner—just cleaner to look at. Because sleaze like this never really dies. Sleaze is a cockroach. It survives. It burrows and it hides. I don't think you can kill it.

The first honk didn't make me turn round. It was not until I heard the familiar voice yell 'Hey, asshole' that I turned round. The Covenant House van screeched alongside me. Squares lowered the window and whipped off his sunglasses. 'Get in,' he said.

I opened the door and hopped into the passenger seat. Squares kept his eyes on the road. 'What the hell are you doing?'

'Going to work.'

'Why?'

'Therapy,' I said.

Squares nodded. He'd been up all night driving the van—an avenging angel searching for kids to rescue. He didn't look worse for wear, but then again, he hadn't started out too sparkly anyway. His hair was long, parted in the middle and on the greasy side. I don't think I'd ever seen him clean-shaven, but I'd never seen him with a full beard or even a nifty-neat *Miami Vice* growth either. His jeans looked like they'd been trampled in a prairie by buffalo. A pack of Camels was rolled up in his sleeve.

'You look like shit,' he said.

'That means something,' I said, 'coming from you.'

He liked that one. We called him Squares, short for Four Squares, because of the tattoo on his forehead. It was, well, four squares, two by two, so that it looked exactly like a four squares court you still see on playgrounds. Now that Squares was a big-time yoga instructor with videos and a chain of schools, most people assumed that the tattoo was some sort of significant Hindu symbol. Not so.

At one time, it had been a tattoo of a swastika. He'd just added four lines. Closed it up.

It was hard for me to imagine this. Squares is probably the least judgmental person I've ever known. He's probably also my closest friend. When he first told me the origins of the squares, I was appalled and shocked. He never explained or apologised, and like Sheila, he never talked about his past. Others have filled in pieces.

'Thanks for showing up at the funeral,' I said. He had brought a group of Covenant House friends in the van. They'd pretty much made up the entire non-family funeral brigade.

'Sunny was great people,' he said.

'Yeah.'

A moment of silence. Then he said, 'But what a shitty turnout.'

'Thanks for pointing that out. You're quite the comfort, Squares. Thanks, man.'

'You want comfort? Know this: People are assholes.'

Silence. Squares stopped for a red light and sneaked a glance at me. His eyes were red. He unrolled the cigarette pack from his sleeve. 'You want to tell me what's wrong?'

'Uh, well, see, the other day? My mother died.'

'Fine,' he said, 'don't tell me.'

The light turned green. The van started up again. The image of my brother in that photograph flashed across my eyes. 'Squares?'

'I'm listening.'

'I think,' I said, 'that my brother is still alive.'

Squares didn't say anything right away. He withdrew a cigarette from the pack, put it in his mouth and lit it. Then he said, 'So why the sudden change of heart?'

He pulled into the small Covenant House lot, but neither of us moved to get out.

'Let me ask you a question,' I said eventually.

He waited.

'You've never given me your take on what happened to my brother,' I said.

Squares shrugged. 'You never asked.'

'We talked about it a lot.'

Squares shrugged again.

'OK, I'm asking you now,' I said. 'Did you think he was alive?'

'Always.'

Just like that. 'So all those talks we had, all those times I made convincing arguments to the contrary . . .'

'I wondered who you were trying to convince, me or you.'

'You never bought my arguments?'

'Nope,' Squares said. 'Never. You thought your bro didn't have the resources to hide, but you don't need resources. Look at the runaways we meet every day. If one of them really wanted to disappear, presto, they'd be gone.'

'There isn't an international manhunt for any of them.'

'International manhunt,' Squares said with something close to disgust as we stepped out of the van. 'You think every cop in the world wakes up wondering about your brother?'

He had a point—especially now that I realised he may have got financial help from my mother. 'He wouldn't kill anyone.'

'Bullshit,' Squares said.

'You don't know him. He would never rape and murder an innocent woman.'

'Some yoga schools teach mantras,' Squares said. 'But repeating something over and over does not make it true.'

'You're pretty deep today,' I said.

'And you're acting like an asshole.' He stubbed out the cigarette. 'You going to tell me why you've had this change of heart?'

We were near the entrance.

'In my office,' I said.

We hushed as we entered the shelter, because when we are in our house, all our focus, all our concentration, is aimed at the kids. They deserve nothing less. For once in their often sad lives, they are what matters most. We love them hard in here, totally and without conditions. Every day we do that. Or we just go home. It doesn't mean that we are always successful. We lose a lot more than we save. They get sucked back down into the streets. But while here, in our house, they will stay in comfort. While here, they will be loved.

When we entered my office, two people—one woman, one man—were waiting for us. Squares stopped short. He lifted his nostrils and sniffed the air, hound dog style.

'Cops,' he said to me.

The woman smiled and stepped forward. 'Will Klein?'

'Yes?' I said.

She unfurled her ID with a flourish. The man did the same thing. 'My name is Claudia Fisher. This is Darryl Wilcox. We're both special agents for the Federal Bureau of Investigation.'

'The Feds,' Squares said to me, thumbs up, like he was impressed I ranked such attention.

She frowned at Squares and slid her eyes back to me. 'We'd like a few words with you.' Then she added, 'Alone.'

We are naturally suspicious of law enforcement here. I have no desire to protect criminals, but I do not want to be a tool in their apprehension either. Cooperating with law enforcement would cripple our street cred—and really, our street cred is everything.

'I'd rather he stayed,' I said.

'This has nothing to do with him.'

'Think of him as my attorney.'

Claudia Fisher took Squares in—the jeans, the hair, the tattoo. He pulled on imaginary lapels and wriggled his eyebrows.

I moved to my desk. Squares flopped into the chair in front of it.

I spread my hands. 'What can I do for you, Agent Fisher?'

'We're looking for one Sheila Rogers.'

That had not been what I expected.

'Can you tell us where we might find her?'

'Why are you looking for her?' I asked.

Claudia Fisher gave me a patronising smile. 'Would you mind just telling us where she is?'

'Is she in trouble?'

'Please just tell us where we might locate Sheila Rogers.'

'I'd like to know why.'

She looked at Wilcox. Wilcox gave her a very small nod. She turned back to me. 'Earlier today, Special Agent Wilcox and I visited Sheila Rogers's place of employment on 18th Street. Her employer informed us that she had called in sick. Her current place of residence was listed as yours, Mr Klein, on 378 West 24th Street. We visited there. Sheila Rogers was not present.'

Squares pointed at her. 'You talk real purdy.'

She ignored him. 'We need to question Sheila Rogers. Right away. We can do it the easy way. Or, if you choose not to cooperate, we can travel an alternate, though less pleasant, avenue.'

Squares rubbed his hands together. 'Ooo, a threat.'

'What's it going to be, Mr Klein?'

'I'd like you to leave,' I said.

'How much do you know about Sheila Rogers?'

This was turning weird. My head started aching.

'Are you aware,' Fisher said, 'of Ms Rogers's criminal record?'

I tried to keep a straight face, but even Squares reacted to that one.

Fisher started reading from a sheet of paper Wilcox had handed her. 'Shoplifting. Prostitution. Possession with intent to sell.'

Squares made a scoffing noise. 'Amateur hour.'

'Armed robbery.'

'Better,' Squares said. 'No conviction on that one, right?'

'That's correct.'

'So maybe she didn't do it.'

Fisher said, 'This must all seem a little déjà vu, Mr Klein.'

'What the hell is that supposed to mean?'

'Covering up. First for your brother. Now your lover.'

'Go to hell,' I said.

'You're not thinking this through,' she said. 'How do you think the Covenant House donors would take it if you were arrested for, say, aiding and abetting?'

Squares took that one. 'You know who you should ask?'

Claudia Fisher crinkled her nose at him, as if he were something she'd just scraped off her shoe.

'Joey Pistillo, top gun for the FBI on the East Coast,' Squares said. 'I bet Joey would know.'

Now it was Fisher and Wilcox's turn to rock back on their heels.

'You got a cellphone? You can ask him right now,' Squares said. Then: 'Oh, wait, you probably don't know his private line.' Squares stretched out his hand and wiggled his finger at her in a give-me gesture. 'You mind?'

She handed him the phone. Squares pressed the number pad and put the phone to his ear. 'Joey? Hey, man, how are you?' Squares listened for a minute and then he burst out laughing. He schmoozed a bit and I watched Fisher and Wilcox turn white. Normally I'd enjoy this power play—between his chequered past and current celebrity status, Squares was one degree of separation from almost everyone—but my mind was reeling.

After a few minutes, Squares handed Agent Fisher the cellphone. 'Joey wants to talk to you.'

Fisher and Wilcox stepped out into the corridor and closed the door.

'That's something, huh,' Squares said. 'I mean, about Sheila having a record. Who'd have guessed?'

Not me.

When Fisher and Wilcox came back, the colour had returned to their faces. Fisher handed the phone to Squares with a smile.

Squares put it to his ear and said, 'What's up, Joey?' He listened for a while. Then he said, 'OK,' and hung up.

'What?' I said.

'Joey wants to see you in person,' Squares said. He looked away. 'I don't think we're going to like what he has to say.'

ASSISTANT DIRECTOR IN CHARGE Joseph Pistillo not only wanted to see me in person, but alone.

'I understand your mother passed away,' he said.

'How do you understand?'

'Pardon?'

'Did you read the obituary in the paper?' I asked, feeling the old anger creep in. 'Did a friend tell you? Or did you have an agent watching us? Watching her. At the hospital. At her funeral.'

We looked at each other. Pistillo was a burly man, bald except for a close-cropped fringe of grey, gnarled hands folded on his desk.

Neither one of us broke eye contact.

'I'm sorry for your loss,' Pistillo said.

'Thank you.'

He leaned back. 'Why won't you tell us where Sheila Rogers is?'

'Why won't you tell me why you're looking for her?'

He sighed. There was a computer monitor on his desk. He turned the screen so that I could see it. Then he pressed some buttons. A colour image came up, and something inside me clenched.

An ordinary-looking room. Tall lamp in the corner overturned. Beige carpet. Coffee table on its side. A mess. Like a tornado aftermath. But in the centre of the room, a man lay in a puddle of what I assumed was blood. The man lay face-up, his arms and legs splayed.

As I looked at the image on the monitor, I could feel Pistillo's eyes on me, gauging my reaction.

He pressed the keyboard. Another image replaced the blood-soaked one. The same room. The lamp was out of sight now. Blood still stained the carpet—but there was another body now, this one curled up in the foetal position.

Panic rose up in me. Ken, I thought. Could one of them be . . .?

But then I remembered their questions. This wasn't about Ken.

'These pictures were taken in Albuquerque, New Mexico, over the weekend,' Pistillo said.

I frowned. 'I don't understand.'

He smiled at me. 'The crime scene was something of a mess. Someone had wiped the place pretty good, but the crime-scene people still lifted a set of fingerprints—one clean set that didn't belong to either of the victims. We ran them through the computer and got a hit early this morning.' He leaned forward and the smile was now 'You want to make a guess?'

I saw Sheila, my beautiful Sheila, staring out of the window.

'I'm sorry, Will.'

'They belong to your girlfriend, Mr Klein. The same one with a criminal record. The same one we're having a lot of trouble finding.'

THEY WERE in Elizabeth, New Jersey, and the cemetery.

Philip McGuane sat in the back of his Mercedes limousine—a stretch model equipped with armour-reinforced sides and bullet-proof one-way windows at a cost of four hundred thou—and stared out at the blur of fast-food restaurants, tacky stores and strip malls.

'You OK, Mr McGuane?'

McGuane turned to his companion. Fred Tanner was huge, the approximate size and consistency of a city brownstone. His gaze was one of supreme confidence. Old school, Tanner was—still with his shellac-shiny suit and the ostentatious pinky ring. Tanner always wore the ring, an oversized gold thing, twisting and toying with it whenever he spoke. 'I'm fine,' McGuane lied.

The limousine exited Route 22 at Parker Avenue. Tanner was fifty, a decade and a half older than his boss. His face was a weathered monument of harsh planes and right angles. McGuane knew that Tanner was very good—a cold, disciplined and lethal son of a bitch for whom mercy was about as relevant a concept as feng shui.

'Who is this guy anyway?' Tanner asked.

McGuane shook his head. In another era, McGuane might have been called a consigliere or capo or some such nonsense. But that was then, this was now. Gone were the days of back-room hangouts and velours sweats. Now you had offices and a secretary and a computer-generated payroll. You paid taxes. You owned legit businesses.

But you were no better.

'And why we driving way out here anyway?' Tanner went on. 'He should come to you, no?'

McGuane didn't reply. Tanner wouldn't understand.

If the Ghost wants to meet, you meet. To refuse would mean that the Ghost would come and find you.

A block away from the cemetery, the limousine pulled to a stop.

'You understand what I want,' McGuane said.

'I got a man in place already. It's taken care of.'

'Don't take him out unless you see my signal.'

'Right, yeah. We've gone over this.'

'Don't underestimate him.'

Tanner gripped the door handle. Sunlight glistened off the pinky ring. 'No offence, Mr McGuane, but he's just some guy, right? Bleeds red like the rest of us?'

McGuane was not so sure. Even though he was one of the most powerful men in New York, right now, more than anything, he wanted to run away. Just pack what he could and simply disappear.

Like his old friend Ken.

Tanner got out, and the car started moving again. They turned left and slid past the gates of Wellington Cemetery. Tyres crunched loose gravel. McGuane told the driver to stop. The driver obeyed. McGuane stepped out and moved to the front of the car.

'I'll call you when I need you.'

The driver nodded and pulled out.

McGuane was alone. He pulled up his collar. His gaze swept over the graveyard. No movement. He wondered where Tanner and his man had hidden themselves. Probably closer to the meet site. In a tree or behind a shrub. If they were doing it right, McGuane would never see them. He found the path and headed east. Not far now. His eyes scanned the surroundings. Still no movement. It was quieter back here—peaceful and green. He veered left, and moved down the row until he arrived at the right grave.

McGuane stopped. He read the name and the date. His mind travelled back. He wondered what he felt and realised that the answer was, not much. He didn't bother looking around any more. The Ghost was here somewhere. He could feel him.

'You should have brought flowers, Philip.'

The voice, silky with a hint of a lisp, chilled his blood. McGuane slowly turned to look behind him. John Asselta approached, flowers in his hand. McGuane stepped away. Asselta's eyes met his. 'It's been a long time,' the Ghost said.

Asselta, the man McGuane knew as the Ghost, moved towards the tombstone. McGuane stayed perfectly still. The temperature seemed to drop thirty degrees when the Ghost walked past.

McGuane held his breath.

The Ghost knelt and gently placed the flowers on the ground. He stayed down there for a moment, his eyes closed. Then he stood, reached out with the tapered fingers of a pianist and caressed the tombstone with too much intimacy.

McGuane tried not to watch. 'What do you want?' he asked.

The Ghost looked up at him. He had skin like cataracts, milky and marshlike. His eyes were shale, almost colourless. His head, too big for his narrow shoulders, was shaped like a light bulb. The sides of his skull were freshly shaved, a sprout of mud-brown hairs sticking up from the middle and cascading out like a fountain. There was something delicate, even feminine, in his pale features—a nightmare version of a Dresden doll.

'What do you want, John?' McGuane repeated.

'I think you know.'

McGuane did, but he said nothing.

'The two men you sent to New Mexico,' the Ghost continued. 'They failed, correct?'

'Yes.'

The Ghost whispered, 'I won't.' He looked at the tombstone, and for a moment McGuane thought he saw something almost human there. 'Are you sure he's back?'

'Fairly sure,' McGuane said.

'How do you know?'

'Someone with the FBI. The men we sent to Albuquerque were supposed to confirm it.'

'They underestimated their foe.'

'Apparently.'

'Do you know where he ran to?' the Ghost asked.

'We're working on it.'

'But not very hard.'

McGuane said nothing.

'You'd prefer that he vanish again. Am I right?'

'It'd make things easier.'

The Ghost shook his head. 'Not this time.'

'The FBI picked up his brother an hour ago. For questioning. Maybe Will knows something.'

That got the Ghost's attention. His head popped up. 'That might be a good place for me to start,' he said softly.

McGuane managed a nod. And that was when the Ghost stepped towards him. He put out his hand. McGuane didn't move.

'Afraid to shake an old friend's hand, Philip?'

He was. The Ghost took another step closer. McGuane's breathing was shallow. He thought about signalling Tanner.

One bullet. One bullet could end this.

'Shake my hand, Philip.'

It was a command, and McGuane obeyed it. Almost against his will, his hand rose from his side and slowly reached out. The Ghost, he knew, killed people. Lots of them. With ease.

McGuane averted his eyes.

The Ghost quickly closed the gap between them and clasped McGuane's hand in his own. McGuane bit back a scream. He tried to pull away from the clammy trap. The Ghost held on.

Then McGuane felt something—something cold and sharp digging into his palm.

The grip tightened. McGuane gasped in pain. Whatever the Ghost had in his hand speared into a nerve bundle like a bayonet. The grip tightened a little more. McGuane dropped to one knee.

The Ghost waited until McGuane looked up. The two men's eyes met. The Ghost loosened his grip. He slipped the sharp something into McGuane's hand and folded his fingers over it. Then he stepped back. 'It could be a lonely ride back, Philip,' he said.

McGuane found his voice.

'What the hell's that supposed to mean?'

But the Ghost turned and walked away. McGuane looked down and opened his fist. In his hand, twinkling in the sunlight, was Tanner's gold pinky ring.

Chapter 3

After my meeting with Assistant Director Pistillo, Squares and I hopped in the van. 'Well, I'm listening,' he said.

I recounted my conversation with Pistillo.

'Albuquerque. Hate that place, man.' Squares shook his head. 'So when did Sheila go there?'

'I don't know,' I said.

'Think. Where were you last weekend?'

'I was at my folks'.'

'And Sheila?'

'She was supposed to be in the city.'

'You called her?'

I thought about it. 'No, she called me.'

'Anybody who can confirm she was in the city?'

'I don't think so.'

'So she could have been in Albuquerque,' Squares said.

I considered that. 'There are other explanations,' I said.

'Like?'

'The fingerprints could be old,' I said. 'Maybe she went out to Albuquerque last month or hell, last year.'

Squares adjusted his sunglasses. 'Reaching.'

'But possible.'

'Yeah, sure.'

A taxi cut us off. We made a right turn, nearly clipping a group of people standing three feet off the kerb.

'You know Sheila,' I said. 'Do you really think she could be a killer?'

Squares was quiet. He pulled the van to a stop at a red light and looked at me. 'Starting to sound like your brother all over again.'

'All I'm saying, Squares, is that there are other possibilities.'

'Are you for real, Will? Last night Sheila cried and told you she was sorry—and in the morning, poof, she's gone. Now the Feds tell us her fingerprints were found at a murder scene. What could it mean?'

'It doesn't mean she killed anyone.'

'It means,' Squares said, 'that she's involved.'

I let that one sink in. I sat back and looked out of the window and remembered our first full night together, lying in bed, Sheila's head on my chest, her arm draped over me. There was such contentment there, such a feeling of peace, of the world being so right. We just stayed there. I don't know how long any more. 'No past,' she said softly, almost to herself. I asked her what she meant. She kept her head on my chest. And she said nothing more.

'I have to find her,' I said.

'Yeah, I know.'

'You want to help?'

Squares shrugged. 'You won't be able to do it without me.'

'So what should we do first?'

'To quote an old proverb,' Squares said, 'before we go forward, we have to look back.'

'You just make that up?'

'Yeah.'

'Guess it makes sense, though.'

'Not to state the obvious or anything, but if we look back, you may not like what we see.'

'Almost assuredly,' I agreed.

SQUARES DROPPED ME by the door and drove back to Covenant House. I entered the apartment and tossed my keys on the table. The apartment felt empty, drained of energy. The place I'd called home for the past four years seemed somehow different to me, foreign.

So now what?

Search the place, I guess. Look for clues, whatever that meant. But what struck me immediately was how spartan Sheila had been. She had very few possessions—she'd always been one of those people who lived by that 'possessions own you, not the other way round' philosophy. Now I wondered about that, about the fact that possessions don't so much own you as bind you down, give you roots.

My XXL Amherst College sweatshirt lay over a chair in the bedroom. I picked it up, feeling a pang in my chest. We spent homecoming weekend at my alma mater last fall. There's a hill on Amherst's campus, a steep slope that starts a-high on a classic New England quad and slides towards a vast expanse of athletics fields. Most students, in a fit of originality, call this hill 'the Hill'.

Late one night Sheila and I walked the campus, hand in hand. We lay on the Hill's soft grass, stared at the pure fall sky and talked for hours. I remember thinking that I had never known such a sense of peace, of calm and comfort and, yes, joy. It was that night, on that hill, when I first realised, really realised with an almost supernatural certainty, that she was the one, that we would always be together, that the shadow of my first love, my only love before Sheila, the one that haunted me and drove away the others, had finally been banished.

I looked at the sweatshirt and, for a moment, I could smell the honeysuckle and foliage all over again. And I wondered for the umpteenth time since I'd spoken to Pistillo, Was it all a lie?

No. You can't fake a connection like ours.

Whatever had happened, Sheila must have her reasons. She loved me. I knew that. My task now was to find her, to help her, to figure a way back to . . . I don't know . . . us. I would not doubt her.

I checked the drawers. Sheila had one bank account and one credit card—at least, that I knew of. But there were no papers anywhere—no old statements, no receipts, no bankbooks, nothing.

The computer screensaver disappeared when I moved the mouse. I signed on, switched over to Sheila's screen name, clicked Old Mail. Nothing. Not one. Odd.

I clicked Filing Cabinet. Empty too. I checked under Bookmarked Web Sites. More nothing. I checked the history. *Nada.*

I sat back and stared at the screen. A thought floated to the surface. I considered it for a moment, wondering if such an act would be a betrayal. Squares had been right about looking back in order to figure out where to go next. And he was right that I might not like what I found.

I logged on to switchboard.com, a massive on-line telephone directory. Under Name I typed Rogers. The city was Mason, Idaho. I knew that from the form she'd filled out when she volunteered at Covenant House.

There was only one listing. On a slip of scrap paper, I jotted down the phone number. Yes, I was going to call Sheila's parents. If we were going to go back, we might as well go all the way.

Before I could reach the receiver, the phone rang. I picked it up, and my sister, Melissa, said, 'What are you doing?'

I thought about how to put it and settled for 'I have something of a situation here.'

'Will,' she said, and I could hear the older-sister tone, 'we're mourning our mother here.'

I closed my eyes.

'Dad's been asking about you. You have to come.'

I looked around the stale, foreign apartment. No reason to hang here. And I thought about the picture still in my pocket—the image of my brother on the mountain.

'I'm on my way,' I said.

MELISSA GREETED ME at the door and asked, 'Where's Sheila?'

I mumbled something about a previous commitment and ducked inside.

We actually had a real-life non-family visitor today—an old friend of my father's named Lou Farley. Lou and my father traded stories from long ago. Something about an old softball team, and I had a vague recollection of my father suiting up in a maroon uniform of heavy polyester. So long ago. He and Lou Farley laughed. I hadn't heard my father laugh like that in years. His eyes were wet and far away. My mother would sometimes go to the games too. I can see her sitting on the benches with her sleeveless shirt and tanned arms.

I glanced out of the window, still hoping Sheila might show up, that this could still all somehow be one big misunderstanding. While my mother's death had long been expected—Sunny's cancer had been a slow, steady death march with a sudden downhill plunge at the end—I was still too raw to accept all that was happening.

Sheila.

I had loved and lost once before. We all have that first love. When mine left me, she blew a hole straight through my heart. After she dumped me, I was convinced that I was doomed to either settle for someone . . . lesser . . . or be for ever alone. And then I met Sheila.

I thought about the way Sheila's green eyes bore into me, about the silky feel of her red hair. I thought about how the initial physical attraction—and it was immense, overwhelming—had spread to all corners of my being. I thought about her all the time. I could feel my heart do a little two-step when I first laid eyes on that face.

We talked about everything but the past. I see that a lot in my line of work. It didn't trouble me much. Now, in hindsight, I wondered, but back then it had added, I don't know, an air of mystery maybe.

Yeah, I know.

Melissa sat next to my father. I saw them both in profile. The resemblance was strong. I can't help but remember when Melissa was going through her wild stage, sneaking around with local bad boy Jimmy McCarthy. What a gleam in her eye there had been back then. How spontaneous and outrageously, even inappropriately, funny she could be. I don't know what happened, what changed her. People claim that it was just maturity. I don't think that's the full story. I think there was something more.

Melissa—we'd always called her Mel—signalled me with her eyes. We slid into the den.

'Ralph and I are leaving in the morning,' she told me.

'Fast,' I said.

'What's that supposed to mean?'

I shook my head.

'We have children. Ralph has work.'

'Right,' I said. 'Nice of you to show up at all.'

Her eyes went wide. 'That's a horrible thing to say.'

It was. I looked behind me. Ralph sat with Dad and Lou Farley, downing a messy beefburger. Ralph was middle-manager America, a good ol' boy with a firm handshake, slicked hair, limited intelligence. I wanted to tell her that I was sorry for what I'd said. But I couldn't. Mel was the oldest of us, three years older than Ken, five years my senior. When Julie was found dead, she ran away. She upped with her new husband and baby and moved across the country to Seattle. I still felt the anger of what I perceived as abandonment.

I thought again about the picture of Ken in my pocket and made a sudden decision. 'I want to show you something.'

We moved a little farther away until we were near the door leading to the garage.

'Sheila and I were going through Mom's things yesterday,' I began.

Her eyes narrowed a little as I reached into my pocket, plucked out the photograph and held it up in front of her face.

It didn't take long. Melissa turned away as if the photo could scald her. She gulped a few deep breaths and stepped back. I moved towards her, but she held up a hand, halting.

'It's Ken,' I said stupidly. 'He's alive. Mom knew it. She had this picture.'

Silence.

'Mel?'

'Is there anything else?' Melissa asked.

'What . . . that's all you have to say?'

'What else is there to say, Will?'

'Oh, right, I forgot. You have to get back to Seattle.'

'Yes.'

The anger resurfaced. 'Tell me, Mel. Did running away help?'

'I didn't run away. Ralph got a job out there.'

'Bullshit,' I said.

'How dare you judge me?'

I flashed back to the time Tony Bonoza spread rumours about Mel, how Ken's face had turned red when he heard, how he'd taken Bonoza on, even though he gave up two years and twenty pounds.

'Ken is alive,' I said again.

Her voice was a plea. 'And what do you want me to do about it?'

'You act like it doesn't matter.'

'I'm not sure it does. Ken's not a part of our lives any more.'

'He's your brother.'

'Ken made his choices.'

'And now—what?—he's dead to you?'

'Wouldn't it be better if he was?' She shook her head. I waited. 'Maybe I did run away, Will. But so did you. Our brother was either dead or a brutal killer. Either way, yes, he's dead to me.'

'He doesn't have to be guilty, you know.'

Melissa looked at me. 'Come on, Will. You know better.'

'He defended us. When we were kids. He looked out for us. He loved us.'

'And I loved him. But I also saw him for what he was. He was drawn to violence, Will. You know that. Yes, he stuck up for us. But don't you think part of that was because he enjoyed it? You know he was mixed up in something bad when he died.'

'That doesn't make him a killer.'

Melissa closed her eyes. I could see her mining for some inner strength. 'For crying out loud, Will, what was he doing that night?'

Our eyes met and held. A sudden chill blew across my heart.

'Forget the murder, OK?' she continued. 'What was Ken doing having sex with Julie Miller?'

My voice, when I finally found it, was tinny, far away. 'We'd been broken up for over a year.'

'He betrayed you, Will. Face it already. At the very least, he slept with the woman you loved. What kind of brother does that?'

'We broke up,' I said, floundering. 'I held no claim to her.'

She wouldn't take her eyes off mine. 'Now who's running away?'

My face dropped into my hands. I put myself together a piece at a time. It took a while. 'He's still our brother.'

'So what do you want to do? Find him? Hand him over to the police? Help him to keep hiding? What?'

I had no answer.

Melissa started to head back into the den. 'Will?'

I looked up at her.

'This isn't my life any more. I'm sorry.'

WE NEVER FORGET our first love. Mine ended up being murdered.

Julie Miller and I met when her family moved onto Coddington Terrace during my freshman year at Livingston High. We started dating two years later. We were pretty much inseparable.

Our breakup was surprising only in its predictability. We went off to separate colleges, sure our commitment could stand the time and distance. During our junior year, Julie called me on the phone and said that she wanted to see other people, that she'd already started dating a senior named—I'm not kidding here—Buck.

I should have got over it. And I probably would have. Eventually. I mean, I dated. It was taking time, but I was starting to accept reality.

Then Julie died, and it seemed as though a part of my heart would never break free of her grip from the grave.

Until Sheila.

I DIDN'T SHOW the picture to my father.

I got back to my apartment at ten o'clock at night. Still empty, still stale, still foreign. No messages on the machine. If this was life without Sheila, I wanted no part of it.

The scrap of paper with her parents' phone number was still on the desk. What was the time difference in Idaho? One hour? Maybe two? That made it either eight or nine o'clock at night. Not too late to call.

A woman answered on the third ring. 'Hello?'

I cleared my throat. 'Mrs Rogers?'

There was a pause. 'Yes?'

'My name is Will Klein.'

I waited, seeing if the name meant anything to her. If it did, she wasn't letting me know.

'I'm a friend of your daughter's.'

'Which daughter?'

'Sheila,' I said.

'I see,' the woman said. 'What can I do for you, Mr Klein?'

That was a good question. I didn't really know myself, so I started with the obvious. 'Do you have any idea where she is?'

In a tired voice, she said, 'I haven't seen or spoken to Sheila in years.'

I opened my mouth, closed it, tried to see a route to take, kept running into roadblocks. 'Are you aware that she's missing?'

'The authorities have been in touch with us, yes.'

'Then do you have any idea where she might have gone? Where she'd run away to? A friend or a relative who might help?'

'Mr Klein, Sheila has not been a part of our life for a long time.'

'Why not?' I just blurted that out. I imagined a rebuke, of course, but again she fell into silence.

'It's just that'—I could hear myself begin to stammer—'she's a wonderful person.'

'You're more than a friend, aren't you, Mr Klein?'

'Yes. I love her very much.'

'But she never told you about her past.'

I wasn't sure how to respond to that one, though the answer was obvious. 'I'm trying to understand,' I said.

'Let me ask you something, Mr Klein.'

Her tone made my grip on the receiver tighten.

'The federal agent who came by,' she went on. 'He said they don't know anything about it.'

'About what?' I asked.

'About Carly,' Mrs Rogers said. 'About where she is.'

I was confused. 'Who's Carly?'

There was another long pause. 'Let me give you a word of advice, Mr Klein. Get on with your life. Forget you ever knew my daughter.'

And then she hung up.

I GRABBED A BROOKLYN LAGER from the fridge and slid open the glass door. I stepped out onto what my real estate agent had optimistically dubbed a 'verandah'. It was the approximate size of a baby crib. One person, perhaps two if they stood very still, could stand on it at one time. But it was air and night and I still liked it.

My brain slipped into numb. I didn't know what was happening. I didn't know what to do next. My call to Sheila's mother raised more questions than it answered. Melissa's words still stung, but she'd raised an interesting point. Now that I knew Ken was alive, what was I prepared to do about it?

I was raising the bottle to my lip when I noticed him.

He stood on the corner, maybe fifty yards from my building. He wore a trench coat and what might have been a fedora, under which his face looked like a featureless white orb. I couldn't see his eyes, but I knew he was looking at me. I could feel it, the weight of his stare. It was palpable. Something about him was familiar.

I didn't want to take that too far. We were at a pretty good distance and it was night-time and my vision is not the best. But the hair on the back of my neck rose like on an animal sensing danger.

I stared back to see how he reacted. He didn't move. I didn't look away. And neither did the featureless face.

The phone rang.

I wrested my vision away. My watch said it was nearly 11.00pm.

Late for a call. Without a backward glance, I stepped back inside and picked up the receiver.

Squares said, 'Want to take a ride?'

He was taking the van out tonight. 'You learn something?'

'Meet me at the studio. Half an hour.'

He hung up. I walked back to the terrace and looked down. The man had gone.

THE YOGA SCHOOL was simply called Squares. It was located in a six-storey block on University Place. The beginnings had been humble. The school had toiled in happy obscurity. Then a certain celebrity, a major pop star you know too well, 'discovered' Squares. She told her friends. A few months later, *Cosmo* picked it up. Then *Elle*. Somewhere along the line, a big infomercial company asked Squares to do a video. Squares, a firm believer in selling out, delivered the goods. *The Yoga Squared Workout* took off. Hey, Squares even shaved on the day they filmed. The rest was history.

Suddenly, no Manhattan social event could deem itself 'a happening' without everyone's favourite fitness guru. Squares rarely had time to teach any more. If you want to take any of the classes the waiting list is at least two months. He charges twenty-five dollars per class. He has four studios. The smallest holds fifty students. The largest close to two hundred. As I approached the school now it was eleven thirty at night and three classes were in session. Do the maths.

The gift shop greets you first, filled with incense and books and lotions and tapes and videos and CD-ROMs and DVDs and crystals and beads and ponchos and tie-dye. Behind the counter were two anorexic twentysomething-year-olds dressed in black.

'I'm here to see Squares. I'm Will Klein.'

The name meant nothing to them. Must be new. 'He's finishing up a class,' one of the twentysomethings said. 'Pranayama breathing.'

I nodded and walked down the corridor to Squares's office.

Five minutes later the door opened. Squares leaned his unshaven mug into the doorway and gave me the thumb. 'Let's rock'n'roll.'

We didn't speak until we were safely ensconced in the Covenant House van. Many of our kids are rescued in this van. The job of outreach is to connect with the community's seedy underbelly—meet the runaway kids, the street urchins, the ones too often referred to as the 'throwaways'. We lose a lot of these kids. More than we save.

'The Feds exaggerated Sheila's record,' Squares said.

'Go on.'

'The arrests. They were all a long time ago. Want to hear this?'

'Yes.'

We started driving deep into the gloom. Tonight the hookers were out in force. Squares gestured with his head. 'Sheila could have been any one of them.'

'She worked the street?'

'A runaway from the Midwest. Got off the bus and straight into the life.'

I'd seen it too many times to shock me. But this wasn't a stranger or street kid at the end of her rope. This was Sheila.

'A long time ago,' Squares said as though reading my thoughts. 'Her first arrest was age sixteen.'

'Prostitution?'

He nodded. 'Three more like that in the next eighteen months, working, according to her file, for a pimp named Louis Castman. Last time she was carrying two ounces and a knife. They tried to bust her for both dealing and armed robbery, but it got kicked.'

I looked out of the window. The night had turned grey, washed out. You see so much bad on these streets. We work hard to stop some of it. I know we succeed. I know we turn lives around. But I know that what happens here, in the vibrant cesspool of night, never leaves them. The damage is done. You may work around it. You may go on. But the damage is permanent.

The street veterans—by veterans, I mean anyone over the age of eighteen—greeted Squares warmly. They knew him. They liked him. They were a bit wary of my presence. It had been a while since I'd been in the trenches. Still, some of the old-timers recognised me and, in a bizarre way, I was glad to see them.

Squares approached a hooker named Candi. She pointed with her chin at two shivering girls huddled in a doorway. I looked at them, no more than sixteen years old, their faces painted like two little girls who'd found Mommy's make-up case, and my heart sank. They were dressed in shorter-than-short shorts, high boots with stiletto heels, fake fur. I often wondered where they found these outfits, if the pimps had special hooker stores or what.

'Fresh meat,' Candi said.

Squares frowned, nodded. Many of our best leads come from the veterans. The reason was that—and please don't think me naive here—they want to help. They see themselves, know it's too late for them. They can't go back. I used to argue with the Candis of the world. I used to insist that it was never too late, that there was still time. I was wrong. Here again is why we need to reach them quickly. There is a certain point that once passed, you cannot save them.

'Where's Raquel?' Squares said.

'Working a car job,' Candi said.

Squares nodded and turned to the two new girls. One was already leaning into a Buick Regal. You cannot imagine the frustration. You want to step in and pull the girl away. Or at least chase the john away. But you don't do that. If you do that, you lose the trust. You lose the trust, you're useless. It was hard to do nothing.

I watched the passenger door open. The Buick seemed to devour the child. She disappeared slowly, sinking into the dark. Feeling helpless, I looked at Squares. His eyes were focused on the car. The Buick pulled away. The girl was gone as though she'd never existed.

Squares approached the remaining new girl. I followed, staying a few steps behind him. The girl's lower lip quivered as though holding back tears, but her eyes blazed with defiance. Squares stopped about a yard away, careful not to invade her space.

'Hi,' he said.

She looked him over and muttered, 'Hey.'

'I was hoping you could help me out.' Squares took another step and pulled a photograph out of his pocket. 'I'm wondering if you've seen her.'

The girl did not look at the picture. 'I haven't seen anyone.'

'Please,' Squares said with a smile. 'I'm not a cop.'

She tried to look tough. 'Figured that,' she said. 'You talking to Candi and all.'

Squares moved a little closer. 'We, that is, my friend here and I'—I waved on cue—'we're trying to save this girl.'

Curious now, she narrowed her eyes. 'Save her how?'

'Her pimp is after her. He's a bad guy. See, we work for Covenant House. You heard of that?'

She shrugged.

'It's a place to hang out,' Squares said, downplaying it. 'No big deal. You can stop in and have a hot meal, a warm bed to sleep in, whatever. Anyway, this girl'—he held up a school portrait of a white girl in braces—'her name is Angie.' Always give a name. It personalises it. 'She's been staying with us. She's a really funny kid. And she got a job too. Turning her life around, you know?'

The girl said nothing.

Squares held out his hand. 'Everyone calls me Squares,' he said.

The girl sighed, took the hand. 'I'm Jeri.'

'Nice to meet you.'

'Yeah. But I haven't seen this Angie. And I'm kinda busy here.'

Here was where you had to read. If you push too hard, you lose them for ever. All you want to do now is plant the seed. You let her know that there is a haven for her, a safe place where she can get a meal and find shelter. Once she gets there, you show the unconditional love. But not now. Now it chases them away.

As much as it ripped you apart inside, you could not do any more. That's why few people could do Squares's job for very long.

Squares hesitated. He has used this 'missing girl' gig as an icebreaker for as long as I've known him. The girl in the picture, the real Angie, died fifteen years ago, out on the street, from exposure. Squares found her behind a Dumpster. At the funeral, Angie's mother gave him that photograph. I've never seen him without it.

'OK, thanks.' Squares took out a card and handed it to her. 'If you do see her, will you let me know? You can call any time.'

She took the card, fingered it. 'Yeah, maybe.'

Another hesitation. Then Squares said, 'See you around.'

'Yeah.'

We then did the most unnatural thing in the world. We walked away.

RAQUEL'S REAL NAME was Roscoe. At least that was what he or she told us. I never know if I should address Raquel as a he or a she. I should probably ask him/her.

Squares and I found the car parked in front of a sealed-off delivery entrance. A common place for street work. The car windows were fogged up, so we kept our distance.

The door opened a minute later. Raquel came out. As you may have guessed by now, Raquel was a cross-dresser, hence the gender confusion. With transsexuals, OK, you refer to them as 'she'. Cross-dressing is a bit trickier.

Raquel rolled out of the car, and it pulled away.

Many transvestites are beautiful. Raquel was not. He was black, six foot six, and comfortably on the north side of 300 pounds. He had biceps like giant hogs wrestling in sausage casing, and his six o'clock shadow reminded me of Homer Simpson's.

Raquel claimed to be twenty-nine years old, but he'd been saying that for the six years I'd known him. He spotted us and started tottering in our direction on stiletto heels. Men's shoes size fourteen. No easy task, I assure you. Raquel greeted Squares with a hug and peck on the cheek, then he turned his attention to me. 'You looking good enough to eat, Sweet Willy,' he said.

'Gee thanks, Raquel,' I said. 'I've been working out. Makes me extra yummy.'

Raquel threw an arm round my shoulder. 'I could fall in love with a man like you.'

'I'm flattered, Raquel.'

'Man like you, he could take me away from all this.'

'Ah, but think of all the broken hearts you'd leave in these sewers.'

Raquel giggled. 'Got that right.'

I showed him a photograph of Sheila. 'You recognise her?' I asked.

Raquel studied the picture. 'This your woman,' he said. 'I seen her at the shelter once.'

'Right. She's run off, Raquel. I'm looking for her.'

Raquel studied the picture some more. 'Can I keep this?'

I'd made some colour copies at the office, so I handed it to him.

'I'll ask around,' Raquel said.

'Thanks.'

He nodded.

'Raquel?' It was Squares. Raquel turned to him. 'You remember a pimp named Louis Castman?'

Raquel's face went slack. He started looking around. 'I gotta get back to work, Squares. Bidness, you know.'

I stepped in his way. 'She used to work for him,' I said.

'Your girl?'

'Yes.'

Raquel crossed himself. 'A bad man, Sweet Willy. The worst.'

'How so?'

He licked his lips. 'Girls out here. They just a commodity, you know what I'm saying. Merchandise. It bidness with most folk out here. But Castman, he was different. He'd damage his own merchandise. Sometimes just for fun. And he got them hooked on drugs too.'

Squares said, 'You keep referring to him in the past tense.'

'That's 'cause he ain't been around in, oh, three years.'

'He alive?'

Raquel became very quiet. He looked off. Squares and I waited.

Raquel just shook his head. 'I just heard rumours.'

'What kind of rumours?'

He shook his head again. 'I told you. He ain't been around in years.' Raquel walked away then, steadier on the stiletto heels. A car drove up, stopped, and again I watched a human being disappear into the night.

Chapter 4

Squares and I did not discuss what Raquel had told us about Louis Castman. But it didn't stop me from thinking about Sheila, about what she'd been, about what Castman might have done to her. I reminded myself that once she had fallen into his clutches, she was the victim here, that nothing she had done had been her fault. I should not view her any differently. But this clear-headed and obvious rationale would not stick.

And I hated myself for that.

It was nearly four in the morning when Squares dropped me off at my building. Back in my apartment, I checked my phone messages before turning in. One message knocked me back a step. I checked the time on the LCD. It had been left at 11:47pm. Awfully late. I figured it had to be family. I was wrong.

I hit the play button and a young woman said, 'Hi, Will. It's Katy. Katy Miller.'

I stiffened.

'Long time, right? Look, I, uh, sorry I'm calling so late. You're probably asleep. Listen, Will, could you give me a call as soon as you get this? I don't care what time it is. I just, well, I need to talk to you.'

She left her number. I stood there, dumbstruck. Katy Miller. Julie's little sister. The last time I'd seen her . . . she'd been six years old or so. Now she'd be, what, seventeen or eighteen.

Why after all these years, was she calling me?

THE RING HIT ME like a cattle prod. I jolted upright, heart racing. I checked the digital clock: 6:58am.

I groaned and leaned over to pick up the phone. 'Hello?'

'Uh, Will Klein?'

'Yes?'

'It's Katy Miller.' Then, as if an afterthought, 'Julie's sister.'

'Hi, Katy,' I said.

'I left a message for you last night.'

'I didn't get in until four in the morning.'

'Oh. I guess I woke you up then.'

'Don't worry about it,' I said.

Her voice sounded sad and young and forced. I remembered when she was born. I did a little maths. 'You're, what, a senior now?'

'I start college in the fall. Bowdoin. It's a small college in Maine.'

'I know it. It's an excellent school. Congratulations,' I said.

'Thanks.'

I sat up a little more, trying to think of a way to bridge the silence. I fell back on the classics: 'It's been a long time.'

'Will?'

'Yes?'

'I'd like to see you.'

'Sure, that would be great. Where are you?' I asked.

'I'm in Livingston,' she said. 'But I can come to the city.'

'No need,' I said. 'I'll be out visiting my father today. How about we hook up before that?'

'Yeah, OK,' she said. 'But not here. You remember the basketball courts by the high school?'

'Sure,' I said. 'I'll meet you there at ten.'

'OK.'

'Katy,' I said, switching ears. 'Do you mind telling me what you want to see me about?'

'What do you think?' she replied.

I did not answer right away, but that did not matter. She was already off the line.

WILL LEFT HIS APARTMENT. The Ghost watched.

The Ghost remembered Julie Miller. He remembered her naked body in that basement. He remembered the purple-yellow of her face, the pinpoints of red in the bulging eyes, her features contorted in horror and surprise. He remembered the neck, the unnatural bend in death, the way the wire had actually slashed deep into her skin, nearly decapitating her. All that blood.

Strangulation was his favourite method of execution. He had visited India to study the Thuggee, the cult of silent assassins who'd perfected the art of strangulation. Over the years, the Ghost had mastered guns and knives and the like, but when possible, he still preferred the cold efficiency of strangulation.

Will disappeared from view.

The brother.

The Ghost thought about all those kung fu movies, the ones where one brother is murdered and the other lives to avenge the death. He thought about what would happen if he simply killed Will Klein.

No, this was not about that. This went way beyond revenge.

Still he wondered about Will. He was the key, after all. Had the years changed him? He would find out soon enough.

Yes, it was almost time to meet Will and catch up on old times.

The Ghost crossed the street towards Will's building.

Five minutes later, he was in the apartment.

I TOOK THE BUS out to Livingston. I hopped off the bus and headed down Livingston Avenue towards Livingston High School, the huge brick edifice where I had spent my high-school years, one of 600 kids in my graduating class.

I found the basketball courts and stood under a rusted rim. The town tennis courts were on my left. I played tennis in high school. I was actually pretty good too, though I never had the heart for sports. I lacked the competitive spirit to be great.

'Will?'

I turned and when I saw her, I felt my blood turn to ice. The clothes were different—hip-hugging jeans, a too-tight too-short shirt that revealed a flat, albeit pierced, belly—but the face and the hair . . . I looked away for a moment.

'I know,' Katy Miller said. 'Like seeing a ghost, right?'

I turned back to her.

'My dad,' she said, jamming her tiny hands into the tight jeans pockets. 'He still can't look at me straight on without crying.'

I did not know what to say to that. She came closer to me. We both faced the high school. 'You went here, right?' I asked.

'Graduated last month.'

'Like it?'

She shrugged. 'Glad to get out.'

The sun shone, making the building a cold silhouette, and for a moment, it looked a bit like a prison.

'I'm sorry about your mother,' Katy said.

'Thank you.'

She took a pack of cigarettes out of her back pocket and offered me one. I shook her off. I watched her light up and resisted the urge to lecture. 'I was an accident, you know,' she said. 'I came late. Julie was already in high school. My parents were told they couldn't have more children. Then . . .' She shrugged again.

'It's not like the rest of us are well planned,' I said.

She laughed a little at that, and the sound echoed deep inside me. It was Julie's laugh, even the way it faded away.

'Sorry about Dad,' Katy said. 'He just freaked when he saw you.'

'I shouldn't have done that.'

She took too long a drag and tilted her head. 'Why did you?'

I thought about the answer. 'I don't know,' I said.

'I saw you. From the moment you turned the corner. It was weird, you know. I remember as a little kid watching you walk from your house. My bedroom. I mean, I'm still in the same bedroom, so it's like I was watching the past or something. It felt weird.'

I looked to my right. The drive was empty now, but during the school year, that was where the parents sat in cars and waited for their kids. I remember my mom picking me up there in her old red Volkswagen. She'd be reading a magazine and the bell would ring and I'd walk towards her and when she'd spot me, her smile, that Sunny smile, would burst forth from deep in her heart, that blinding smile of unconditional love, and I realised now with a hard thud that nobody would ever smile at me that way again.

Too much, I thought. Being here. The visual echo of Julie on Katy's face. The memories. It was all too much.

'You hungry?' I asked her.

'Sure, I guess.'

She had a car, an old Honda Civic. We drove to a classic New Jersey diner on Route 10 without speaking.

A man with a heavy beard and heavier deodorant asked us how many. We told him that we were two. Katy added that we wanted a smoking table. As soon as we sat, she pulled the ashtray towards her, almost as if for protection.

'After you came by the house,' she said, 'I went to the graveyard. I had to get out of the house. My dad was raging. My mom was crying. I just had to get out.'

'I didn't mean to upset anyone,' I said.

She waved my words away. 'It's OK. It's good for them in a weird way. Most of the time we tiptoe around it, you know. It's creepy.' Katy leaned forward. 'You want to hear something totally freaky?'

I gestured for her to go ahead.

'We haven't changed the basement. That old couch and TV. That ratty carpet. That old trunk I used to hide behind. They're all still there. And we still have to walk through that room to get to our laundry room. You understand what I'm saying? That's how we live.'

She stopped and sucked on the cigarette as if it were an air hose. I sat back. I'd never really thought about Katy Miller, about what the murder of her sister had done to her. I thought about her parents, of course. I thought about the devastation. I often wondered why they'd stayed in the house, but then again, I never really understood why my parents had not moved either.

But I'd never really considered the case of Katy Miller, about what it must have been like growing up with your sister's lookalike spectre forever at your side. I looked at Katy again, as if for the first time, and saw the tears in her eyes. I reached out and took her hand, again so like her sister's. The past came at me so hard I nearly fell back.

'This is so weird,' she said.

Truer words, I thought. 'For me too.'

'It needs to end, Will. My whole life . . . whatever really happened that night, it needs to end.'

I had no idea where she was going with this. I just sat and looked at her and tried to let her know that I was here to listen.

'You don't know how much I hated your brother—not just for what he did to Julie, but for what he did to the rest of us by running away. I prayed they'd find him. I had this dream where he'd be surrounded and he'd put up a fight and then the cops would smoke him. I know you don't want to hear this. But I need you to understand.'

'You wanted closure,' I said.

'Yeah,' she said. 'Except.'

'Except what?'

She looked up and for the first time our eyes locked. 'I saw him,' she said.

I thought that I heard wrong. I grew cold again.

'Your brother. I saw him. At least I think it was him.'

I found my voice enough to ask, 'When?'

'Yesterday. At the graveyard.'

The waitress came over then. She withdrew the pencil from behind her ear and asked what we wanted. Katy ordered some sort of salad. The waitress looked at me. I asked for a cheese omelette. She asked, did I want home fries or French fries with that? Home fries. And nothing to drink, thank you. The waitress finally left.

'Tell me,' I said.

Katy stubbed out the cigarette. 'It's like I said before. I went to the graveyard. Just to get out of the house.'

'Tell me what happened.'

'He looked pretty different. Your brother, I mean. I don't remember him much. Just a little. And I've seen pictures.' She stopped.

'Are you saying he was standing by Julie's grave?'

'Maybe a hundred feet away. By a willow tree. See, I didn't come in the front gate. I hopped a fence. So I came up from the back and I saw this guy staring in the direction of Julie's stone. He never heard me. I tapped him on the shoulder. He jumped like a mile in the air and when he turned round and saw me . . . well, you see what I look like. He nearly screamed. He thought I was a ghost or something.'

'And you were sure it was Ken?'

'Not sure, no. I mean, how could I be?' She took out another cigarette and then said, 'Yeah. Yeah, I know it was him.'

'But how could you be sure?'

'He told me he didn't do it.'

My head spun. My hands fell to my sides and gripped the cushion. When I finally spoke, my words came out slowly. 'What did you do?'

'I told him he was a liar. I told him I was going to scream.'

'Did you?'

'No.'

'Why not?'

'Because I believed him,' she said. 'Something in his voice, I don't know. I'd hated him for so long. You have no idea . . . But now . . .'

'So what did you do?'

'I stepped back. I was still going to scream. But he came and took my face in his hands and looked me in the eye and said, "I'm going to find the killer, I promise." That was it. He let go and ran off.'

'Have you told—'

She shook her head. 'No one. Sometimes I'm not even sure it happened. Like I imagined the whole thing.' She looked up at me. 'Do you think he killed Julie?'

'No,' I said.

'I've seen you on the news,' she said. 'You've always thought he was dead. Do you still believe that?'

'No,' I said. 'I don't believe that any more.'

'What made you change your mind?'

I didn't know how to reply to that. 'I guess,' I said, 'I'm looking for him too.'

'I want to help.'

She'd said want. But I know she meant need.

'Please, Will. Let me help.'

And I said OK.

SPECIAL AGENT CLAUDIA FISHER stiffened her spine and knocked on the door.

'Come in.'

She turned the knob and entered the office of Assistant Director in Charge Joseph Pistillo. Aside from the director in Washington, an ADIC was the most senior agent in the FBI.

Pistillo looked up. 'What?'

'Sheila Rogers was found dead,' Fisher reported.

Pistillo cursed. 'How?'

'She was found on a roadside in Nebraska. No ID. They ran her prints through the National Crime Information Center and got a hit.'

'Damn.'

Pistillo chewed on a cuticle. Claudia Fisher waited.

'I want a visual confirmation,' he said.

'Done.'

'What?'

'I took the liberty of emailing the local sheriff the mugshots of Sheila Rogers. She and the medical examiner confirmed it was the same woman. The height and weight match too.'

Pistillo leaned back. He grabbed a pen, raised it to eye level, and studied it. Fisher stood at attention. He signalled for her to sit. 'We need to contact Sheila Rogers's parents. They live in Idaho.'

Fisher nodded. 'The local police are on standby. The chief knows the family personally.'

Pistillo nodded. 'OK, good. How was she killed?'

'Probably internal bleeding from a beating. The autopsy is still under way.'

'Jesus.'

'She was tortured. Her fingers had been snapped back, probably by a pair of pliers. There were cigarette burns on her torso.'

'How long has she been dead?'

'She probably died some time last night or early in the morning.'

Pistillo looked at Fisher. 'Fast,' he said.

'Excuse me?'

'If, as we were led to believe, she ran away, they found her fast.'

'Unless she ran to them.'

Pistillo leaned back. 'Or she never ran at all.'

'I'm not following.'

He studied the pen some more. 'Our assumption has always been that Sheila Rogers fled because of her connection to the Albuquerque murders, right?'

Fisher tilted her head back and forth. 'Yes and no. I mean, why come back to New York just to run away again?'

'Maybe she wanted to go to the mother's funeral, I don't know,' he said. 'Either way, I don't think that's the case any more. Maybe she never knew we were on to her. Maybe—stay with me here, Claudia—maybe someone kidnapped her.'

'How would that have worked?' Fisher asked.

Pistillo put down the pen. 'According to Will Klein, she left the apartment at five in the morning. Someone grabbed her right away. As soon as she left the apartment. They flew her to Nebraska where she was tortured, then dumped.'

'Or they drove like a demon.'

'Or . . .?'

Fisher looked at her boss. 'I think,' she said, 'that we're both coming to the same conclusion. The time line is too close. She probably disappeared the night before.'

'Which means?'

'Which means that Will Klein lied to us.'

Pistillo grinned. 'Exactly.'

Fisher's words started coming fast now. 'OK, here's a more likely scenario: Will Klein and Sheila Rogers go to the funeral of Klein's mother. They return to his parents' house afterwards. According to Klein, they drive back to their apartment that night. But we have no independent confirmation of that. So maybe'—she tried to slow down—'maybe they don't head home. Maybe he hands her over to an accomplice, who tortures and kills her and dumps the body. Will meanwhile drives back to his apartment. He goes to work in the morning. When Wilcox and I brace him at his office, he makes up this story about her leaving in the morning.'

Pistillo nodded. 'Interesting theory. Do you have a motive?'

'He needed to silence her.'

'For?'

'Whatever happened in Albuquerque.'

They both mulled it over in silence.

'I'm not convinced,' Pistillo said.

'Neither am I.'

'But we agree that Will Klein knows more than he's saying.'

'For certain.'

Pistillo let loose a long breath. 'Either way, we need to give him the bad news about Ms Rogers's demise. Call that local chief out in Idaho. Have him inform the family. Then get them on a plane for official identification.'

'What about Will Klein?'

Pistillo thought about that. 'I'll reach out to Squares. Maybe he can help us deliver the blow.'

KATY DROPPED ME off on Hickory Place, maybe three blocks from my parents' house. We did not want anybody to see us together.

'So what now?' Katy asked.

I had been wondering that myself. 'I'm not sure. But if Ken didn't kill Julie—'

'Then someone else did.'

'Man,' I said, 'we're good at this.'

She smiled. 'So I guess we look for suspects?'

It sounded ridiculous—who were we, the Mod Squad?—but I nodded.

'I'll start checking,' she said.

'Checking what?'

She gave me a teenager shrug, using her whole body. 'I don't know. Julie's past, I guess. Figure out who'd have wanted to kill her.'

'The police did that.'

'They only looked at your brother, Will.'

She had a point. 'OK,' I said, again feeling ridiculous.

'Let's hook up later tonight.'

I nodded and slid out. Nancy Drew sped off. I stood there and soaked in the solitude. I was not all that eager to move.

When I arrived at our house, there were no cars out front and no mourners inside. No surprise there. I called out to my father. No answer. I found him alone in the basement with a cutting razor in his hand. He stood perfectly still in the middle of the room, surrounded by old wardrobe boxes. The sealing tape had been sliced open. He did not turn round when he heard my footsteps.

'So much already packed away,' he said softly.

The boxes had belonged to my mother. My father reached into one and plucked out a thin silver headband. He turned to me and held it up. 'You remember this?'

We both smiled. Everyone, I guess, goes through fashion stages, but not like my mother. There was her Headband Era, for example. She'd grown her hair out and worn the multihued bands like an Indian princess. When the headbands were retired, the Suede-Fringe Period began. That was followed by the Purple Renaissance—not my favourite, I assure you, like living with a Jimi Hendrix groupie.

The fashion stages, like so many other things, ended with Julie Miller's murder. My mom—Sunny—packed the clothes away and stored them in the dingiest corner of the basement.

Dad flipped the headband back into the box. 'We were going to move, you know.'

I hadn't.

'Three years ago. We were going to get a condo in West Orange. But when we found out your mother was sick, we put it all on hold.' He looked at me. 'You thirsty?'

'Not really.'

'How about a Diet Coke? I know I could use one.'

Dad hurried past me and towards the stairs. I turned away from the old boxes and followed him. When we reached the kitchen, he opened the refrigerator door.

'You want to tell me what happened yesterday?' he began.

'I don't know what you mean.'

'You and your sister.' Dad pulled out a two-litre bottle of Diet Coke. 'What was that all about?'

'Nothing,' I said.

He nodded as he opened a cabinet and took out two glasses. 'Your mother used to eavesdrop on you and Melissa,' he said.

'I know.'

He smiled. 'She wasn't very discreet. I'd tell her to cut it out, but she'd just tell me to hush, it was a mother's job.'

'You said, me and Melissa.'

'Yes.'

'Why not Ken?'

'Maybe she didn't want to know.' He poured the sodas. 'Very curious about your brother lately.'

'It's a natural enough question.'

'Sure, natural. And after the funeral, you were asking me if I think he's still alive. And then the next day, you and Melissa have an argument about him. So I'll ask you once more: What's going on?'

The photograph was still in my pocket. Don't ask me why. I'd made colour copies with my scanner, but I couldn't let go of it.

When the doorbell rang, we both jumped, startled. We looked at each other. Dad shrugged. I told him I'd get it. I trotted to the front door. It was Aunt Selma and Uncle Murray, with their grieving smiles in place. Selma came in and took over the kitchen. Murray busied himself with a loose wall plate he'd spotted yesterday.

And my father and I stopped talking. In fact, we carefully avoided each other. I love my father. I think I have made that pretty clear. But a small part of me irrationally blames him for my mother's death. I don't know why I feel that way, but from the moment she first became ill, I looked at him differently. As though he hadn't done enough. Or perhaps I blamed him for not saving her after Julie

Miller's murder. He hadn't been a good enough husband. Couldn't true love have helped Mom recover, salved her spirit?

Like I said, irrational.

When I got back to my apartment I found the door was ajar. It was only open a crack, but it made me pause. I always lock it—hey, I live in a doorman-free building in Manhattan—but then again I had not been thinking straight of late. Perhaps in my haste to meet Katy Miller I'd just forgotten.

I frowned. Not likely.

I put my hand on a door panel and pushed. I waited to hear the door creak. It did not. I heard something. Faint at first. I leaned my head through the opening and immediately felt my insides turn to ice.

Nothing I saw was out of the ordinary. The lights were out, as a matter of fact. The blinds were drawn. No, nothing out of the ordinary—or again, nothing that I could see. But I could hear music.

Again, that alone would not cause too much alarm. I confess to a major streak of absent-mindedness. I could have left my CD player on. That alone would not chill me like this.

What did chill me, however, was the song selection.

That was what was getting to me. The song playing was 'Don't Fear the Reaper'. I shuddered.

Ken's favourite song. By Blue Öyster Cult, a heavy-metal band, though this song was subdued, almost ethereal. Ken used to grab his tennis racket and fake-guitar the solos. And I know that I do not have a copy of that song on any of my CDs. No way. Too many memories.

What the hell was going on here?

I stepped into the darkened room, feeling awfully stupid. Hmm. Why not just flick on the lights, numbnuts?

As I reached for the switch, another inner voice said, Better yet, why not just run? That was what we always yelled at the movie screens, right? The killer is hiding inside the house. The stupid teenager, after finding her best friend's decapitated corpse, decides that this would be the perfect time to stroll through the darkened house instead of, say, fleeing and screaming like a mad animal.

The song faded down in a guitar solo. I waited for the silence. It was brief. The song started up again. The same song.

What the hell should I do? Call the police? I could just see that. What seems to be the problem, sir? Well, my stereo is playing my brother's favourite song so I decided to start running down the hall screaming. Can you rush over here with guns drawn? Uh-huh, sure, we're on our way. How dorky would that sound?

My heart picked up a beat as my eyes began to adjust to the dark. I decided to leave the lights off. If there was an intruder, there was no reason to let him know I was standing there, an easy target.

OK, fine, let's play it that way. Lights stay off. Now what?

The music. Follow the music. It was coming from my bedroom. I turned in that direction. The door was closed. I stepped towards it. Carefully. I was not going to be a total idiot. I opened the front door all the way and left it like that—in case I had to make a run for it.

I moved forward in a sort of spastic slide, leading with the left foot but keeping the right toes firmly pointed towards the exit. I slid a yard. Then another. Blue Öyster Cult's Buck Dharma—the fact that I remembered not only that name, but that his real name was Donald Roeser said a lot about my childhood—sang how we can be like they are, like Romeo and Juliet. In a word: dead.

Reaching the bedroom door, I pushed against the frame. No go. I'd have to turn the knob. My hand gripped the metal. I looked over my shoulder. The door was still wide open. My right foot stayed pointed in that direction. I turned the knob as silently as possible, but it still sounded like a gunshot in my ear.

I pushed just a little, just to clear the frame. I let go of the knob. The music was louder now. Crisp and clear.

I stuck my head in, just for a quick look. And that was when someone grabbed me by the hair. I barely had time to gasp. My head was tugged forward so hard, my feet left the ground. I flew across the room, my hands stretched out Superman style, and landed in a thudding belly flop.

The air left my lungs with a whoosh. I tried to roll over, but he—I assumed it was a he—was already straddled on top of me, an arm snaked round my throat. I tried to struggle, but his grip was impossibly strong. He pulled back and I gagged. My eyes bulged. I pawed at my throat. Useless. My fingernails tried to dig into his forearm, but it was like trying to penetrate mahogany. The pressure in my head was growing unbearable. I flailed. My attacker did not budge. Then I heard the voice: 'Hey, Willie boy.'

That voice. I placed it instantly. There are certain sounds, voices mostly, that get stored in a special section of the cortex, on the survival shelf if you will, and as soon as you hear them, your every fibre tenses, sensing danger.

He let go of my neck—suddenly and completely. I collapsed to the floor, gagging. He rolled off me and laughed. 'You've gone soft on me, Willie boy.'

I flipped over and scooted away in a back crawl. My eyes confirmed what my ears had already told me.

'John?' I said. 'John Asselta?'

He smiled that smile that touched nothing. I felt myself drop back in time. The fear—the fear I hadn't experienced since adolescence surfaced. The Ghost—that was what everyone called him, though not to his face—had always had that effect on me. I wasn't alone in that. He terrified pretty much everyone, though I had always been protected. I was Ken Klein's little brother. For the Ghost, that was enough.

I have always been a wimp, a coward. I am deathly afraid of violence. That might be normal—survival instinct and all—but it still shames me. My brother, who was, strangely enough, the Ghost's closest friend, had the enviable aggression that separated the wanna-bes from the greats. His tennis, for example, reminded some of a young John McEnroe in that take-on-the-world, pit-bull, won't-lose, borderline going-too-far competitiveness. I was never like that.

I scrambled to my feet. Asselta rose straight up, like a spirit from the grave, and before I could react, he embraced me. He was pretty short, what with that strange long-torso, short-arms build. His cheek pressed my chest. 'Been a long time,' he said.

I was not sure what to say, where to start. 'How did you get in?'

'What?' He released me. 'Oh, the door was open. I'm sorry about sneaking up on you like that but . . .' He smiled, shrugged it away. 'You haven't changed a bit, Willie boy. You look good.'

'You shouldn't have just . . .'

He tilted his head, and I remembered the way he would simply lash out. John Asselta had been a classmate of Ken's, two years ahead of me at Livingston High School. He captained the wrestling team and was the Essex County lightweight champ two years running. He probably would have won the states, but he got disqualified for purposely dislocating a rival's shoulder. I still remembered Asselta's small smile as they carted his opponent away.

My father claimed that the Ghost had a Napoleon complex. That explanation seemed too simplistic to me. I don't know what it was, if the Ghost needed to prove himself or if he had an extra Y-chromosome or if he was just the meanest son of a bitch in existence.

Whatever, he was definitely a psycho. No way round it. He enjoyed hurting people. You never met his eye, never got in his path, because you never knew what would provoke him. He would strike with no hesitation. There were rumours that the Ghost, at the tender age of ten, stabbed a kid named Daniel Skinner with a kitchen knife.

Supposedly Skinner, who was a couple of years older, picked on the Ghost, and the Ghost had responded with a knife to the heart.

I tried to push the past away. 'What do you want, John?'

I never understood my brother's friendship with him. My parents had not been happy about it either, though the Ghost could be charming with adults. His almost albino complexion—ergo the nickname—belied gentle features. He was almost pretty, with long lashes and a cleft in the chin. I had heard that after graduation he had gone into the military, enlisted in something clandestine involving Special Ops or Green Berets, something like that.

The Ghost did the head-tilt again. 'Where's Ken?' he asked in that silky, pre-strike voice.

'I don't know.'

He put his hand up to his ear. 'Excuse me?'

'I don't know where he is.'

'But how can that be? You're his brother. He loved you so.'

'What do you want here, John?'

'Say,' he said, and he showed the teeth yet again, 'whatever happened to your high-school hottie Julie Miller? You two get hitched?'

I stared at him. He held the smile. He was putting me on, I knew that. He and Julie had, strangely enough, been close. I never understood that. I once joked that she must have pulled a thorn from his paw. I wondered now how to play it.

This was creeping me out big-time.

'So when was the last time you saw Ken?' I said.

He feigned deep thought. 'Oh, must have been, what, twelve years ago? I've been away a long time. Overseas. Haven't kept up.'

'Uh-huh.'

He narrowed his eyes. 'You sound like you're doubting me, Willie boy.' He moved closer. I tried not to flinch. 'You afraid of me?'

'No.'

'Big bro's not here to protect you any more, Willie boy.'

'And we're not in high school either, John.'

He looked into my eyes. 'You think the world's so different now?'

I tried to hold my ground. 'Get out,' I said.

His reply was sudden. He dropped to the floor and whipped my legs out from under me. I fell hard on my back. Before I could move, he had me wrapped up in an elbow lock. Then he lifted up against my triceps and the elbow started bending the wrong way. A deep pain knifed down my arm.

I tried to move with it. Give way. Anything to relieve the pressure.

The Ghost spoke in the calmest voice I've ever heard. 'You tell him no more hiding, Willie boy. You tell him other people could get hurt. Like you. Or your dad. Or your sister. Or maybe even that little Miller vixen you met with today. You tell him that.'

His hand speed was unearthly. In one move, he released my arm and shot his fist straight into my face. My nose exploded. I fell back against the floor, my head swimming, only half conscious.

When I looked up again, the Ghost had vanished.

Chapter 5

Squares handed me a freezer bag of ice and said, 'Yeah, but I oughta see the other guy, right?'

'Right,' I said, putting the bag on my rather tender nose. 'He looks like a matinée idol.'

Squares sat on the couch and threw his boots up on the coffee table. 'Explain.'

I did.

'Guy sounds like a prince,' Squares said.

'I don't get it.' I lowered the bag. My nose felt like it was jammed with crushed-up pennies. 'Why would the Ghost be looking for my brother?'

'Hell of a question.'

'You think I should call the cops?'

Squares shrugged. 'Give me his full name again.'

'John Asselta.'

'And he grew up in Livingston?'

'Yes,' I said. 'Fifty-seven Woodland Terrace.'

'You remember his address?'

Now it was my turn to shrug. That was the way Livingston was. You remembered stuff like that. 'His mother, I don't know what her deal was. She ran away or something when he was very young. His dad lived in a bottle. Two brothers, both older. One—I think his name was Sean—was a Vietnam vet. He had this long hair and matted beard and all he'd do was walk around town talking to himself. Everyone figured he was crazy.'

Squares wrote down the info. 'Let me look into it.'

I put the ice back on my nose, wincing when it touched down.

That made him snigger. Then he stopped, gnawed on the inside of his cheek, said, 'Something's come up.'

I did not like the tone of his voice.

'I got a call from our favourite Fed, Joe Pistillo.'

Again I lowered the ice down. 'Did they find Sheila?'

'Don't know. He wouldn't say. He just asked me to bring you in.'

'When?'

'Now. He said he was calling me as a courtesy.'

'Courtesy for what?'

'Damned if I know.'

'MY NAME IS CLYDE SMART,' the man said in the gentlest voice Edna Rogers had ever heard. 'I'm the county medical examiner.'

Edna Rogers watched her husband, Neil, shake the man's hand. She settled for just a nod in his direction. The woman sheriff was there. So was one of her deputies. They all, Edna Rogers thought, had properly solemn faces.

Clyde Smart moved to the table. Neil and Edna Rogers, married forty-two years, stood next to each other and the medical examiner pulled back the sheet.

When Neil Rogers saw Sheila's face, he reeled back like a wounded animal and let out a cry that reminded Edna of a coyote when a storm is brewing. She knew then that there would be no reprieve, no last-minute miracle. She summoned the courage and gazed at her daughter. She reached out a hand—the maternal desire to comfort, even in death, never let up—but she made herself stop.

Edna continued to stare down until her vision blurred, until Edna could almost see Sheila's face transforming, the years running backwards, until her first-born was her baby again, her whole life ahead of her, a second chance for her mother to do it right.

And then Edna Rogers started to cry.

'WHAT HAPPENED to your nose?' Pistillo asked me.

I was back in his office. Squares stayed in the waiting room. I sat in the armchair in front of Pistillo's desk. Claudia Fisher, the agent who'd visited me at Covenant House, stood behind me.

'I fell,' I said.

Pistillo didn't believe me, but that was OK. He put both hands on his desk. 'We'd like you to run through it again for us,' he said.

'Through what?'

'How Sheila Rogers disappeared.'

'Have you found her?'

'Just bear with us, please.' He coughed into his fist. 'What time did Sheila Rogers leave your apartment?'

'Why?'

'Please, Mr Klein, if you could just help us out here.'

'I think she left around five in the morning.'

'Why aren't you sure?'

'I was asleep. I thought I heard her leave.'

'At five?'

'Yes.'

'You looked at the clock?'

'Are you for real? I don't know.'

'How else would you know it was five?'

'I have a great internal clock. I don't know. Can we move on?'

He nodded. 'Ms Rogers left you a note, correct?'

'Yes.'

'What did the note say exactly?'

'That's personal.'

'Mr Klein—'

I sighed. 'She told me that she'd love me always.'

'Do you still have the note?'

'I do.'

'May we see it?'

'May you tell me why I'm here?'

Pistillo sat back. 'After leaving your father's house, did you and Ms Rogers head straight back to your apartment?'

The change of subjects threw me. 'What are you talking about?'

'After your mother's funeral, you and Sheila Rogers returned to your apartment. Correct?'

'That's what I told you.'

'Did you stop on the way home?'

'No.'

'Can anyone verify that?'

'Verify that I didn't stop?'

'Verify that you two went back to your apartment and stayed there for the remainder of the evening.'

'I don't know.' I looked over my shoulder at Claudia Fisher. 'Why don't you canvass the neighbourhood?'

'Why was Sheila Rogers in New Mexico?'

I turned back round. 'I don't know that she was.'

'She never told you that she was going?'

'I know nothing about it.'

'Do you know anyone in New Mexico, Mr Klein?'

'I don't even know the way to Santa Fe.'

'San Jose,' Pistillo corrected him, smiling at the lame joke. 'We have a list of your recent incoming calls.'

'And that's legal? You having my phone records?'

'We got a warrant.'

'I bet you did. So what do you want to know?'

Claudia Fisher moved for the first time. She handed me a photocopy of what appeared to be a phone bill. One number—an unfamiliar one—was highlighted in yellow.

'Your residence received a phone call from a payphone in Paradise Hills, New Mexico, the night before your mother's funeral.' He leaned in a little closer. 'Who was that call from?'

I studied the number, totally confused yet again. The call had come in at six fifteen in the evening. It'd lasted eight minutes. I did not know what it meant, but I didn't like the whole tone of this conversation. I looked up.

'Should I have a lawyer?'

That slowed Pistillo down. He and Claudia Fisher exchanged another glance. 'You can always have a lawyer,' he said carefully.

'I don't know what the hell is going on, but I don't like these questions. I came down because I thought you had information for me. Instead, I'm being interrogated.'

'Interrogated?' Pistillo spread his hands. 'We're just chatting.'

A phone trilled behind me. Claudia Fisher snapped up her cellphone and said, 'Fisher.' After listening for about a minute, she hung up and nodded some kind of confirmation at Pistillo.

I stood up. 'I've had enough of this bullshit, Pistillo. I'm tired of—'

'Sit down, Will.'

He'd used my first name. First time. I did not like the sound of it. I stood where I was and waited.

'We were just waiting for visual confirmation,' he said.

'Of what?'

He did not reply to my query. 'So we flew Sheila Rogers's parents in from Idaho. They made it official, though the fingerprints had already told us what we needed to know.'

His face grew soft. My knees buckled, but I managed to stay upright. He looked at me now with heavy eyes. I started to shake my head, but I knew there was no way to duck the blow.

'I'm sorry, Will,' Pistillo said. 'Sheila Rogers is dead.'

DENIAL IS AN AMAZING THING.

Even as I felt my stomach twist and drop, even as I felt the tears push hard against my eyes, I somehow managed to detach. I nodded while concentrating on the few details that Pistillo was willing to give me. She'd been dumped on the side of a road in Nebraska, he said. I nodded. She'd been murdered in—to use Pistillo's words—'a rather brutal fashion'. I nodded some more. She had been found with no ID on her, but the fingerprints had matched and then Sheila's parents had flown in and identified the body. I nodded again.

I did not sit. I did not cry. I felt something inside me press against my rib cage, making it almost impossible to breathe. I flashed to a simple moment: Sheila reading on our couch, her legs tucked under her, the sleeves of her sweater stretched too long. I saw the focus on her face, the way her eyes narrowed during certain passages, the way she looked up and smiled when she realised that I was staring.

Sheila was dead.

I was still back there, with Sheila, back in our apartment, when Pistillo's words cut through my reverie.

'You should have cooperated with us, Will.'

I surfaced as if from a sleep. 'What?'

'If you told us the truth, maybe we could have saved her.'

NEXT THING I REMEMBER, I was out in the van.

Squares alternated between pounding on the steering wheel and swearing vengeance. My reaction had been just the opposite. It was like someone had pulled out my plug. Denial was still holding, but I could feel reality start hammering against the walls. I wondered how long before the walls collapsed under the onslaught.

'We'll get him,' Squares said yet again.

For the moment, I did not much care.

We parked in front of the apartment building. Squares jumped out.

'I'll be fine,' I said.

'I'll walk you up,' he said. 'I want to show you something.'

I nodded numbly.

When we entered, Squares reached into his pocket and pulled out a gun. He swept through the apartment, gun drawn. No one. He handed me the weapon. 'Lock the door,' he said. 'If that creepy asshole comes back, blow him away.'

I kept my eyes on the gun.

'If you need me, I got the cellphone. Twenty-four, seven.'

'Right. Thanks.'

He left without another word. I put the gun on the table. Then I looked at our apartment. Nothing of Sheila was here any more. Her smell had faded. The air felt thinner. I wanted to close all the windows and doors, try to preserve something of her.

Someone had murdered the woman I love.

For the second time?

No. Julie's murder had not felt like this. Not even close. Denial was, yep, still there, but a voice was whispering through the cracks: nothing would be the same ever again. And I knew that I would not recover this time.

I would never be with Sheila again. Someone had murdered the woman I love. I thought about her past, about the hell she had gone through. I thought about how valiantly she'd struggled, and I thought about how someone—probably someone from her past—had sneaked up behind her and snatched it all away.

The wall of denial began to buckle and crack. Grief spread over me, ripping the breath from my lungs. I collapsed into a chair and hugged my knees against my chest. I rocked back and forth and started to cry, really cry, gut-wrenching, soul-tearing cries.

IT WAS NEAR MIDNIGHT. I was still sitting in the dark with my knees up against my chest. I was screening calls. Normally I would have turned off the phone, but the denial was still potent enough to make me hope that maybe Pistillo would call and tell me it was all a big mistake. The mind does that. It tries to find a way out. It makes deals with God. It makes promises. It tries to convince itself that maybe there is a reprieve, that this could all be a dream, the most vicious of nightmares, and that somehow you can find your way back.

I had picked up the phone only once and that was for Squares. He told me that the kids at Covenant House wanted to have a memorial service for Sheila tomorrow. Would that be all right? I told him that I thought Sheila would have really liked that.

I looked out of the window. The van circled the block again. Yep, Squares. Protecting me. He had been circling all night. I knew that he would not stray far. The phone rang again. I waited for the answering machine to pick up. After the third ring, I heard a click and then my voice said to leave a message at the beep. When the beep sounded I heard a semifamiliar voice.

'Mr Klein?'

I sat up. The woman on the answering machine stifled a sob.

'This is Edna Rogers. Sheila's mother.'

My hand shot out and snatched the receiver. 'I'm here,' I said.

Her answer was to cry. I started crying too.

'I didn't think it would hurt so much,' she said after some time had passed. 'She wasn't my daughter any more. I had other children. She was gone. For good. It's not what I wanted. It was just the way it was.'

I said nothing. I just listened.

'And then they flew me out here. To Nebraska. They said they had her fingerprints already, but they needed a family member to identify her. So Neil and me, we flew here. They brought me into this office and there was this . . . this lump on the table covered with a sheet. And then this man pulled back the sheet and I saw her face . . .'

She lost it then. She started crying and for a long time there was no letup. I held the receiver to my ear and waited.

'Mr Klein,' she began.

'Please call me Will.'

'You loved her, Will, didn't you?'

'Very much.'

There was a pause. 'I'm flying to New York tomorrow morning.'

'That would be nice,' I said. I told her about the memorial service.

'Will there be time for us to talk afterwards?' she asked.

'Of course.'

'There are some things I need to know,' she said. 'And there are some things—some hard things—I have to tell you.'

'I'm not sure I understand.'

'I'll see you tomorrow, Will. We'll talk then.'

I HAD ONE VISITOR that night.

At one in the morning, the doorbell rang. I figured it was Squares. Then I remembered the Ghost. I glanced at the table. The gun was still there. The bell sounded again.

I shook my head. No. I was not that far gone. Not yet anyhow. I moved towards the door and looked through the peephole. But it wasn't Squares or the Ghost. It was my father.

I opened the door. We stood and looked at each other as if from a great distance. His eyes were swollen and tinged with red. I stood there, unmoving, feeling everything inside me collapse away. He nodded and held out his arms and beckoned me forward. I stepped into his embrace. I pressed my cheek against the scratchy wool of his sweater. It smelt wet and old. I started to sob. He stroked my hair and pulled me closer. I felt my legs give way. But I did not slide down. My father held me up. He held me up for a very long time.

Chapter 6

The memorial service was held in the Covenant House auditorium. Squares sat on my right, my father on my left. Dad kept his arm behind me, sometimes rubbing my back. It felt nice. The room was packed, mostly with the kids. They hugged me and cried and told me how much they'd miss Sheila. The service lasted almost two hours. Terrell, a fourteen-year-old who'd been selling himself for ten dollars a pop, played a song on the trumpet that he'd composed in her memory. It was the saddest, sweetest sound I'd ever heard. I pushed away the pain and listened closely because these kids deserved that. They were not cuddly. Most were hard to love, but that did not mean you gave up. It meant just the opposite, in fact. It meant we had to love them all the more. Unconditionally. Sheila had known that. It had mattered to her.

Sheila's mother—at least, I assumed it was Mrs Rogers—came in about twenty minutes into the ceremony. She was a tall woman. Her face had the dry, brittle look of something left too long in the sun. Our eyes met. She looked a question at me, and I nodded a yes. She sat perfectly still throughout the service, listening to the words about her daughter with something approaching awe.

Squares spoke last. He was eloquent and funny and brought Sheila to life in a way I knew I never could. He told the kids how Sheila had been 'one of you', a struggling runaway who'd fought her own demons. He remembered watching Sheila bloom here. And mostly, he said, he remembered watching her fall in love with me.

I felt hollow, and again I was struck with the realisation that this grief would forever be my constant companion.

When the ceremony ended, no one knew exactly what to do. We all sat for an awkward moment, no one moving, until Terrell started playing his trumpet again. People rose. They cried and hugged me all over again. I don't know how long I stood there. I was thankful for the outpouring, but it made me miss Sheila all the more.

Someone announced that there was food in the cafeteria. The mourners slowly milled towards it. I spotted Sheila's mother standing in a corner. She looked drained, as if the vitality had leaked out from a still-open wound. I made my way towards her.

'You're Will?' she said.

'Yes.'

We did not hug or kiss cheeks or even shake hands.

'Where can we talk?' she asked.

We found an empty dorm room and stepped inside. I closed the door. 'It was a beautiful service,' she said.

I nodded.

'What Sheila became.' She stopped, shook her head. 'I had no idea. I wish that she'd called and told me.'

I did not know what to say to that.

'Sheila never gave me a moment of pride when she was alive.' Edna Rogers tugged a handkerchief out of her bag and gave her nose a quick, decisive swipe. 'I know that sounds unkind. She was a beautiful baby. And she was fine in elementary school. But somewhere along the way'—she looked away, shrugged—'she changed. She became surly. Always complaining. Always unhappy. She stole money from my bag. She had no friends. The boys bored her. She hated school. She hated living in Mason. Then one day she dropped out of school and ran away. She never came back.'

She looked at me as if expecting a response.

'You never saw her again?' I asked.

'Never.'

'I don't understand,' I said. 'What happened?'

'You think there was some big event, right? Her father must have abused her. Or maybe I beat her. Something that explains it all. But there was nothing like that. It wasn't our fault.'

'I didn't mean to imply—'

'I know what you were implying.'

Her eyes ignited. She pursed her lips and looked a dare at me. I wanted off this subject. 'Did Sheila ever call you?' I said.

'The last time was three years ago.'

She stopped. She began to circle the room and look at the beds and the dressers. She fluffed a pillow. 'Once every six months or so, Sheila would call home. She was usually stoned or drunk or high, whatever. She'd get all emotional. She'd cry and I'd cry and she'd say horrible things to me.'

'Like what?'

She shook her head. 'Downstairs. What that man with the tattoo on his forehead said. About you two falling in love. That true?'

'Yes.'

She looked at me. Her lips curled into what might pass for a smile. 'So,' she said, 'Sheila was sleeping with her boss.'

'She was a volunteer,' I said.

Edna Rogers curled the smile some more. 'And what exactly was she volunteering to do for you, Will?'

I felt a shiver down my back. 'Maybe I'm beginning to understand why she ran away,' I said.

She blinked and then glared at me. 'You didn't know her. You still don't.'

'In all due deference, I'm really not in the mood to hear you trash her any further.'

Edna Rogers stopped pacing and closed her eyes. The room grew very still. 'That's not why I came here.'

'Why did you come?'

Edna Rogers looked me straight in the eye. 'I'm here about Carly.'

I waited. When she did not elaborate, I said, 'I don't know anyone called Carly.'

She showed me the cruel, curled smile again. 'You wouldn't be lying to me, would you, Will?'

I felt a fresh shiver. 'No. Who is she?'

'Carly is Sheila's daughter.'

I was struck dumb. Edna Rogers seemed to enjoy my reaction. 'She never mentioned she had a daughter, did she?'

I said nothing.

'Carly is twelve years old now. And no, I don't know who the father is. I don't think Sheila did either.'

My head began to spin.

'The last time Sheila called me was on Carly's ninth birthday,' she said. 'And I spoke to her myself. Carly, that is.'

'So where is she now?'

'I don't know,' Edna Rogers said. 'That's why I'm here, Will. I want to find my granddaughter.'

WHEN I STUMBLED back home, Katy Miller was sitting by my apartment door, her knapsack between her splayed legs.

She scrambled to her feet. 'I called but . . .'

I nodded.

'My parents,' Katy told me. 'I just can't stay in that house another day. I thought maybe I could crash on your couch.'

'It's not a good idea,' I said, putting the key in the door.

'It's just that I've been trying to put it together, you know. Like we said. Who could have killed Julie. And I started wondering. How much do you know about Julie's life after you two broke up?'

We stepped into the apartment. 'Now is not a good time.'

She finally saw my face. 'Why? What happened?'

'Someone very close to me died.'

'You mean your mother?'

I shook my head. 'My girlfriend. She was murdered.'

Katy gasped and dropped the knapsack.

'Did you love her?'

'Very much.'

She looked at me.

'What?' I said.

'It's like someone murders the women you love.'

The same thought I'd earlier pushed away. Vocalised, it sounded even more ridiculous. 'Julie and I broke up more than a year before her murder.'

'So you were over her?'

I did not want to travel that route again. I said, 'What about Julie's life after we broke up?'

Katy fell onto the couch the way teenagers do, as if she had no bones. 'I started thinking,' she said, 'if Ken didn't kill her, someone else did, right?'

'Right.'

'So I started looking into her life. You know, calling old friends, trying to remember what was going on with her, that kind of thing.'

'And what did you find?'

'That she was pretty messed up.'

I tried to focus on what she was saying. 'How so?'

She sat up. 'Did you know Julie dropped out of Haverton?'

That surprised me. 'You're sure?'

'Senior year,' she said. 'When did you last see her, Will?'

I thought about it. It had indeed been a while. I told her so.

'So when you broke up?'

I shook my head. 'She ended it on the phone.'

'Cold,' Katy said. 'And you just accepted that?'

'I tried to see her. But she wouldn't let me.'

Katy looked at me as though I'd just spouted the lamest excuse in history. Looking back on it, I guess maybe she was right. Why hadn't I gone to Haverton? Met her face to face?

'I think,' Katy said, 'Julie ended up doing something bad.'

'What do you mean?'

'I don't know. Maybe that's going too far. I remember she seemed happy before she died. I hadn't seen her that happy in a long time. I think maybe she was getting better, I don't know.'

The doorbell rang. My shoulders slumped. I wasn't in the mood for more company. Katy, reading me, jumped up and said, 'I'll get it.'

It was a deliveryman with a fruit basket. Katy brought it into the room. She dropped it on the table. 'There's a card,' she said.

'Open it.'

She plucked it out of the tiny envelope. 'It's a condolence basket from some of the kids at Covenant House. A Mass card too.'

Katy kept staring at the card. Then she looked up at me. 'Your girlfriend's name was Sheila Rogers?'

'Yeah, why? What is it?'

Katy shook her head and put the card down. 'Nothing,' she said.

'Don't give me that. Did you know her?'

'No.' Katy's voice was firmer this time. 'Just drop it, OK?'

The phone rang. I waited for the machine. Through the speaker I heard Squares say, 'Pick it up.'

I did.

Without preamble, he said, 'Raquel just called me. He may have come up with a serious lead on how Sheila ran. You game for a ride?'

'Pick me up,' I said.

PHILIP MCGUANE SAW his old nemesis on the security camera. His receptionist buzzed him.

'Mr McGuane?'

'Send him in,' he said.

'Yes, Mr McGuane. He's with—'

'Her too.'

McGuane kept flicking the remote on the security camera, keeping up with his federal antagonist Joe Pistillo and the female underling he had in tow. McGuane spent a lot on security. It was worth it. Every person who entered the private elevator to his office was digitally recorded from several angles, but what made the system stand out was that the camera angles were designed to shoot in such a way that anyone entering could be made to look as though they were also leaving. Both the corridor and elevator were painted spearmint green. The effect was rather hideous, but to those who understood digital manipulation, it was key. An image on the green background could be plucked out and placed on another background.

McGuane pulled out an old photograph from his top drawer. It was a picture of three seventeen-year-old boys—Ken Klein, John 'the Ghost' Asselta and McGuane. They'd grown up together in the suburb of Livingston, New Jersey. Ken Klein had been the fiery tennis player, John Asselta the psycho wrestler, McGuane the wow-'em charmer and student council president. They had hooked up in high school, drawn to each other, noticing—or perhaps this was giving them all too much credit—a kinship in the eyes.

The office door opened. Joseph Pistillo and his young protégée entered. McGuane smiled and put away the photograph.

'Ah, Javert,' he said to Pistillo. 'Do you still hunt me when all I did was steal some bread?'

'Yeah,' Pistillo said. 'Yeah, that's you, McGuane. The innocent man hounded.'

McGuane turned his attention to the female agent. 'Tell me, Joe, why do you always have such a lovely colleague with you?'

'This is Special Agent Claudia Fisher.'

'Charmed,' McGuane said. 'Please have a seat.'

'We'd rather stand.'

McGuane shrugged a suit-yourself and dropped into his chair. 'So what can I do for you today?'

'You're having a tough time, McGuane.'

'Am I?'

'Indeed.'

'And you're here to help? How special.'

Pistillo snorted. 'Part of me wants to sit back and watch you get eaten alive, McGuane.' He swallowed, tried to hold something deep inside him in check. 'But a bigger part of me wants to see you rot in jail for what you've done.'

McGuane turned to Claudia Fisher. 'He's very sexy when he talks tough, don't you think?'

'Guess who we just found, McGuane?'

'Who?'

'Fred Tanner.'

'Who?'

Pistillo smirked. 'Don't play with me. Big thug. Works for you.'

'I believe he's in my security department.'

'Not any more. We found him in the Passaic River.'

McGuane frowned. 'How unsanitary.'

'Especially with two bullet holes in the head. We also found a guy named Peter Appel. Strangled. He was an ex-army sharpshooter.'

Only one strangled, McGuane thought. The Ghost must have been disappointed that he'd had to shoot the other.

'Yeah, well, let's see,' Pistillo went on. 'We have these two men dead. Plus we have the two guys in New Mexico. That's four.'

'And you didn't use your fingers. They're not paying you enough, Agent Pistillo.'

Pistillo leaned over the desk so that their faces were inches apart. 'Are you aware,' he said, 'that Sheila Rogers is dead too?'

'Who?'

Pistillo stood back up. 'Right. You don't know her either. She doesn't work for you.'

'Many people work for me. I'm a businessman.'

Pistillo looked over at Fisher. 'Let's go,' he said.

'Leaving so soon?'

'I've waited a long time for this,' Pistillo said. 'What do they say? Revenge is a dish best served cold.' He smirked again. 'Have a nice day, McGuane.'

They left. McGuane did not move for ten minutes. What had been the purpose of that visit? Simple. To shake him up. He hit line three, the safe phone, the one checked daily for listening devices.

The Ghost answered on the first ring with a drawn-out 'Hello?'

'Where are you?'

'Just off the plane from Nebraska.'

'Learn anything?'

'Oh yes. There was a third person in the car with them.'

McGuane shifted in his seat. 'Who?'

'A little girl,' the Ghost said. 'No more than twelve years old.'

KATY AND I WERE on the street when Squares pulled up. She leaned over and kissed me on the cheek.

'I thought you were staying on my couch,' I said to her.

Katy had been distracted since the fruit basket's arrival. 'I'll be back tomorrow. I just need to do a little research.'

'On?'

She shook her head. I did not press it. She gave me a quick grin before taking off. I got in the van.

Squares said, 'And she is?'

I explained as we headed uptown. There were dozens of sandwiches and blankets packed in the bag. Squares handed them out to the kids. The sandwiches and blankets, in the same vein as his rap about the missing Angie, made excellent icebreakers, and even if they didn't, at least the kids would have something to eat and something to keep them warm.

I reached back and took a sandwich. 'You working again tonight?'

He lowered his head and looked at me above his sunglasses. 'No,' he said drily, 'I'm just really hungry.'

We cut across town and took the Harlem River Drive north. When we passed a group of kids huddled under an overpass, Squares pulled over and shifted into park.

'Quick work stop,' he said.

'You going to use the sandwiches?'

Squares examined his potential help-ees and considered. 'Nah. Got something better.'

'What?'

'Phone cards.' He handed me one. 'I got TeleReach to donate over a thousand of them. The kids go nuts for them.'

They did too. As soon as they saw them, the kids flocked to him. Count on Squares. I watched the faces, tried to separate the smeared mass into individuals with wants and dreams and hopes. Kids do not survive long out here. Forget the physical dangers. They can often get past that. It is the soul, the sense of self, that erodes out here. Once the erosion reaches a certain level, well, that's the ball game.

Sheila had been saved before reaching that level.

Then someone had killed her.

I shook it off. No time for that now. Focus on the task at hand. Action kept the grief at bay. 'You haven't told me where we're going,' I said, when Squares returned to the van.

'Corner of 128th and Second Avenue. Raquel will meet us there.'

We exited the highway and passed a sprawl of housing projects. From two blocks away, I spotted Raquel. This was not difficult. Raquel was the size of a small principality and was dressed like an explosion at the Liberace museum in pink pumps with a green dress. Square parked the van in front of a storefront with a faded sign that read GOLDBERG PHARMACY. When I stepped out, Raquel came forward and wrapped me in an embrace.

'I'm so sorry,' he whispered.

'Thank you.'

He released me, and I was able to breathe again. He was crying.

'Abe and Sadie are inside,' Raquel said through the tears. 'They're expecting you.'

Squares nodded and we headed into the pharmacy. A ding-dong sounded when we entered. The store shelves were high and packed and tight. I saw bandages and deodorants and shampoos and cough medicines, all laid out with seemingly little organisation.

An old man with half-moon reading glasses appeared. He wore a sleeveless sweater over a white shirt. His hair was high and thick and white, and bushy eyebrows gave him the look of an owl.

'Look! It's Mr Squares!'

The two men hugged, the old man giving Squares's back a few hard pats. 'You look good,' the old man said.

'You too, Abe.'

'Sadie,' he shouted. 'Sadie, Mr Squares is here.'

Sadie, an older woman who would never see five feet even in Raquel's highest pumps, stepped down from behind the pharmacy stand. She frowned at Squares and said, 'You look skinny.'

'Leave him alone,' Abe said.

'Shush you. You eating enough?' She smiled conspiratorially. 'I got kugel. You want some?'

'Maybe later, thanks.'

'I'll put some in the Tupperware.'

'That would be nice, thank you.' Squares turned to me. 'This is my friend, Will Klein.'

The two old people showed me sad eyes. 'He's the boyfriend?'

'Yes.'

They inspected me. Then they looked at each other.

'You can trust him,' Squares said.

'We talk, we could be killed.'

'No one will know. I give you my word.'

The old couple looked at each other some more.

Squares stepped towards them. 'We need your help.'

Sadie took her husband's hand in a gesture so intimate I almost turned away. 'She was such a beautiful girl, Abe.'

'And so nice,' he added. Abe sighed and looked at me. The door opened and the ding-dong chimed again. A dishevelled black man walked in and said, 'Tyrone sent me.'

Sadie moved towards him. 'I'll take care of you over here,' she said.

I looked at Squares. I didn't understand any of this.

Squares took off his sunglasses. 'Please, Abe. It's important.'

Abe held up a hand. 'OK, OK, just stop with the face, please.' He waved us forward. 'Come this way.'

We walked to the back of the store. He lifted the counter flap, and we walked under. We passed the pills, the bottles, the bags of filled prescriptions and headed down into the basement. Abe flicked on the light. 'This,' he announced, 'is where it all happens.'

I saw very little. There was a computer, a printer, and a digital camera. That was about it. I looked at Abe and then at Squares.

'Does someone want to clue me in?'

'Our business is simple,' Abe said. 'We keep no records. If the police want to take this computer, fine, go ahead. They'll learn nothing. All the records are located up here.' He tapped his forehead. Then he spotted my confusion. 'Fake IDs,' he said.

'Oh.'

He lowered his voice. 'You're in trouble? Poof, I'll make you disappear. Like a magician, no? You need to go away, really go away, you don't go to a travel agent. You come to me.'

'I see,' I said. 'And there's a big need for your services?'

'You'd be surprised. It's often just parole jumpers. Or bail jumpers. We service a lot of illegal immigrants too. They want to stay in the country, so we make them citizens.' He smiled at me. 'And every once in a while we get someone nicer.'

'Like Sheila,' I said.

'Exactly. You want to know how it works?'

Before I could answer, Abe had started up again. 'It's not like on the TV,' he said. 'On the TV they always look for a kid who died and then they send away for his birth certificate or something like that. They make up all these complicated forgeries.'

'That's not how it's done?'

'That's not how it's done.' He sat at the computer terminal and started typing. 'First of all, that would take too long. Second, with the Net and the Web and all that nonsense, dead people quickly become dead. You die, so does your social security number.'

'So how do you create a fake identity?' I asked.

'Ah, I don't create them.' Abe smiled. 'I use real ones.' He paused. 'You saw that man upstairs? The one who came in after you.'

'Yes.'

'He looks unemployed, no? Probably homeless?'

'I guess.'

'But he's a person. He has a name. He was born in this country. And'—he waved his hands theatrically—'he has a social security number. As long as he has that number, he exists. You follow?'

'I follow.'

'So let's say he needs a little money. What he doesn't need is an identity. He's out on the street, so what good is it doing him? It's not like he has a credit rating or owns land. So we run his name through the computer to see if he has any outstanding warrants against him. If he doesn't—and most don't—then we buy his ID. Let's say his name is John Smith. And let's say you, Will, need to be able to check into hotels or whatever under a name other than your own.'

I saw where he was heading. 'You sell me his social security number and I become John Smith.'

Abe snapped his fingers. 'Bingo.'

'But suppose we don't look alike?'

'There's no physical descriptions associated with your social security number. Once you have it, you call up any bureau and you can get whatever paperwork you need.'

'Suppose our John Smith gets rousted and needs an ID?'

'He can use it too. Heck, five people can use it at the same time. Who's going to know? Simple, am I right?'

'Simple,' I agreed. 'So Sheila came to you?'

'Yes. Two or three days ago.'

'Did she tell you where she was going?'

Abe smiled. 'Does this look like an ask-a-lot-of-questions business? Like I said upstairs, loose lips can get you killed. In fact, when Raquel first put out feelers, we didn't say boo. Discretion. That's what this business is about.'

'So what made you change your mind?'

Abe looked sad. 'We heard what happened to that poor, lovely girl. Mr Squares tells me there's a child involved, too. It isn't right.' He threw up his hands. 'But what can I do? I can't go to the police. Thing is, I trust Raquel and Mr Squares. They're good men. They dwell in the dark but they shine a light. Like my Sadie and me, see?'

The door above opened, and Sadie felt her way down the stairs and stood next to Abe, their bodies touching, somehow fitting together.

'You want to know something?' Sadie said to me.

I nodded.

'Your Sheila. She had'—she raised two fists in the air—'a special something. A spirit about her. She was beautiful, of course, but there was something more. The fact that she's gone . . . we feel lessened. She came in and she looked so scared. And maybe the identity we gave her didn't hold up. Maybe that's why she's dead.'

'So,' Abe said, 'we want to help.' He wrote something down on a piece of paper and handed it to me. 'The name we gave her was Donna White. That's the social security number. The real Donna White is a homeless crack addict.'

I stared down at the scrap of paper.

Sadie moved towards me and put a hand on my cheek. 'You look like a nice man,' she said. 'Find that little girl.'

I nodded once and then again. Then I promised that I would.

Chapter 7

Katy Miller was still shaking when she arrived at her house. This can't be, she thought. It's a mistake. I got the name wrong.

'Katy?' her mother called out. 'I'm in the kitchen.'

'I'll be there in a little while, Mom.'

Katy headed for the basement door. When her hand reached the knob, she stopped. The basement. She hated to go down there.

You would think that after so many years, she'd be desensitised to the threadbare couch and water-stained carpet and so-old-it's-not-even-cable-ready television. She wasn't. She flicked the light switch and then crept down the stairs. She kept her line of vision up and over the couch and carpet and television. Why did they still live here? It made little sense to her.

She found Julie's trunk in the corner. Her father had put some kind of wooden crate under it in case of a flood. Katy flashed back and saw her sister packing for college. She remembered crawling into the trunk as Julie packed, pretending that her big sister might pack her up too, so that they could go to college together.

Katy examined the trunk's lock. There was no key, but all she needed was a flat edge. She found an old butter knife with the stored silver. She stuck it into the opening and turned. The lock fell open.

It took her nearly half an hour, but she found it.

And it changed everything.

WHEN WE WERE back in the van, I asked Squares what we should do.

'I have a source,' he said, a true understatement if ever I've heard one. 'We'll run the name Donna White through the airline computers, see if we can figure out when she flew out or something.'

We lapsed into silence.

'What are you trying to do here, Will?' Squares said eventually.

'Find Carly,' I said too quickly.

'And then what? Raise her as your own?'

'I don't know.'

'You realise, of course, that you're using this to block.'

I looked out of the car window. The neighbourhood was full of rubble. We drove past housing projects that housed mostly misery. I looked for something good. I didn't see any.

'I have to keep searching,' I said, 'because I'm not sure what I'll do if I don't. I'm not suicidal or anything, but if I stop running'—I stopped, tried to think how to say this— 'it'll catch up to me.'

'It's going to catch you eventually, no matter what.'

'I know. But by then, maybe I'll have saved her daughter. Maybe, even though she's dead, I'll have helped her.'

'Or,' Squares countered, 'you might find out that she was not the woman you believed her to be. That she fooled us all.'

'Then so be it,' I said. 'You still with me?'

'To the end, Kemosabi.'

'Good, because I think I have an idea. Drop me off at home. I think I need to do a little Web surfing.'

YES, I HAD A PLAN.

I figured that as Sheila's fingerprints were found at a murder scene in New Mexico, that had something to do with Carly, too. It stood to reason that the FBI were not the ones to discover those two bodies. Probably a local cop did. Or maybe a neighbour. Which meant the crime had probably been reported in the local paper.

I surfed to refdesk.com and clicked on national newspapers. They had thirty-three listings for New Mexico. I tried the ones in the Albuquerque area. I sat back and let the page load. Found one. OK, good. I clicked on to the archives and started searching.

It took almost an hour, but I finally nailed it:

TWO MEN FOUND MURDERED

by Yvonne Sterno

Late last night, the Albuquerque suburb of Stonepointe was reeling from news that two men were both shot in the head and found in one of the community's homes. The two men remain unidentified. Police had no comment other than to say that they were investigating. The homeowner is listed as Owen Enfield. An autopsy is scheduled for this morning.

That was about it. I searched the next day. Nothing. I searched the day after. Still nothing. I searched for all the stories written by Yvonne Sterno. There were pieces on local weddings and charity events. Nothing, not another word, about the murders.

I sat back. Why weren't there more stories?

One way to find out. I picked up the phone and began to dial the number for the *New Mexico Star-Beacon*.

The switchboard was one of those machines that ask you to spell your party's last name. I had dialled the S-T-E-R when the machine cut in and told me to hit the pound key if I was trying to reach Yvonne Sterno. I followed orders. Two rings later a woman answered.

'Hello?'

'Yvonne Sterno?'

'Yes, speaking.'

'My name is Will Klein. I wanted to talk to you about that double murder you wrote about recently.'

'Uh-huh. And what's your interest in the case?'

'I just have a few questions.'

'I'm not a library, Mr Klein.'

'Please, call me Will. And bear with me for just a moment. How often do double murders occur in places like Stonepointe?'

'This would be the first that I'm aware of.'

'So,' I said, 'why didn't it get more coverage?'

'And again I will ask you: What's your interest in the case?'

I knew enough reporters to know that the way to their hearts is through their by-line. 'I may have some pertinent information.'

'Pertinent,' she repeated. 'That's a good word there, Will. Where you calling from anyway?'

'New York City,' I said.

There was a pause. 'So what will I find pertinent?'

'First I need to know a few basics.'

'That's not how I work, Will.'

'I looked up your other pieces, Yvonne. You mostly do features. You cover weddings and society dinners. A story like this doesn't fall in your lap every day. Take a chance. Who knows, maybe I'm legit.'

When she did not respond. I pushed ahead.

'You land a big murder story like this. But the article doesn't list victims or suspects or any real details.'

'I didn't know any,' she said. 'The report came in over the scanner late at night. We barely made it in time for the morning edition.'

'So why no follow-up? Why was there only that one piece?'

'I was closed down,' she said softly. 'We were lucky to get even that much into the paper. The next morning there were Feds all over the place. The head Fed in the area got my boss to shut the story down. I tried a little on my own, but all I got was a bunch of no-comments.'

'Is that odd?'

'I don't know, Will. I haven't covered a murder before. But yeah, I'd say it sounds pretty odd.'

'What do you take it to mean?'

'From the way my boss has been acting?' Yvonne took a deep breath. 'It's big. Bigger than a double murder. Your turn, Will.'

I wondered how far I should go. 'Are you aware of any fingerprints found at the scene?'

'No.'

'There was one set belonging to a woman. That woman was found dead yesterday in a small town in Nebraska.'

'Whoa, Nelly. Murdered?'

'Yes.'

'Her name?'

I leaned back. 'Tell me about the homeowner, Owen Enfield.'

'Oh I see. Back and forth. I give, you give.'

'Something like that. Was Enfield one of the victims?'

'I don't know.'

'What do you know about him?'

'According to neighbours, he moved in alone, three months ago. A woman and a young girl have been hanging around the last few weeks.'

A tremor started in my heart. I sat up. 'How old was the girl?'

'I don't know. School age. Maybe ten or twelve.'

'Where are they now?'

'I don't know. Like I said, I'm off the case.'

'Can you find out where they are?'

'I can try. I have a few good sources,' she said. 'You want to tell me your interest in all this?'

I thought about that. 'You up for rattling cages, Yvonne?'

'Yeah, Will. Yeah, I am.'

'Are you any good?'

'Want a demonstration?'

'Sure.'

'You may be calling me from New York City, but you're from New Jersey. My bet is you're the brother of an infamous murderer.'

'An alleged murderer,' I corrected her. 'How did you know?'

'I have Lexis-Nexis on my computer. I plugged in your name and that's what came up.'

'My brother had nothing to do with any of this.'

'Sure, and he was innocent of killing your neighbour too, right?'

'That's not what I mean. Your double murder has nothing to do with him.'

'Then what's your connection?'

I let loose a breath. 'Someone else who was very close to me.'

'Who?'

'My girlfriend. Her fingerprints were those found at the scene.'

'So it was your girlfriend who was found dead in Nebraska?'

'Yes.'

'And that's your interest in this?'

'Part of it.'

'What's the other part?'

I was not prepared yet to tell her about Carly. 'Find Enfield,' I said.

'What was her name, Will? Your girlfriend.'

'Rogers,' I said. 'Her name was Sheila Rogers.'

I heard her typing. 'I'll do my best, Will,' she said. 'I'll call you.'

I SHUT DOWN the computer and slept.

Far away, I heard the phone ring. A deep voice on the answering machine penetrated my dream. 'This is Lieutenant Daniels of the Livingston Police Department. I am trying to reach Will Klein.'

In the background, behind Lieutenant Daniels, I heard the muffled laugh of a young woman. My eyes flew open. As I reached for the phone, I heard the young woman whoop another laugh. It sounded like Katy Miller.

I picked up the phone. 'This is Will Klein.'

Lieutenant Daniels said, 'Hi, Will. This is Tim Daniels. We went to school together, remember?'

Tim Daniels. He'd worked at the local gas station. He used to wear his oil-smeared uniform to school, complete with his name embroidered on the pocket. I guessed that he still liked uniforms.

'Sure,' I said, totally confused now. 'How's it going?'

'Good, thanks.' His voice grew grave. 'I, uh, read about your mother in the *Tribune*. I'm sorry.'

'I appreciate that, thanks,' I said.

'Look, the reason I'm calling is, well, I guess you know Katy Miller?'

'Yes.'

Silence. He was probably remembering that I'd dated her older sister and what fate had befallen her. 'She asked me to call you.'

'What's the problem?'

'I found Katy in the Mount Pleasant playground with a half-empty bottle of Absolut. Totally blitzed. I was going to call her parents—'

'Forget that!' Katy shouted again. 'I'm eighteen!'

'Right, whatever. Anyway, she asked me to call you instead. Hey, I remember when we were kids. We weren't perfect either, you know what I mean?'

'I do,' I said.

And that was when Katy yelled something, and my body went rigid. I hoped that I'd heard wrong.

'Idaho!' she yelled. 'Am I right, Will? Friggin' Idaho!'

I gripped the receiver, sure I heard wrong. 'What is she saying?'

'I don't know. She keeps yelling out something about Idaho.'

My breath had gone shallow.

'Look, Will, can you come down and get her?'

I found my voice enough to say, 'I'm on my way.'

I RENTED A CAR at a twenty-four-hour place on 37th Street and drove out to Livingston police station. Detective Tim Daniels greeted me with too firm a handshake. I noticed that he hoisted his belt a lot. He jangled—or his keys or cuffs or whatever did—whenever he walked.

I filled out some paperwork and Katy was released into my custody. She had sobered up in the hour it took me to get there. There was no laugh in her now, just the classic teenage-sullen posture. I thanked Tim again. Katy did not even attempt a wave. We walked towards the car.

'You want to tell me why you were drinking alone?'

Katy kept walking. Her breathing grew deeper. 'I was thirsty.'

'Uh-huh. And why were you yelling about Idaho?'

She looked at me but didn't break stride. 'I think you know.'

I grabbed her arm. 'What kind of game are you playing here?'

'I'm not the one playing games here, Will.'

'What are you talking about?'

'Idaho, Will. Your Sheila Rogers was from Idaho, right?'

Her words hit me like a body blow. 'How did you know that?'

'Where did your Sheila go to college?' she asked.

'I don't know.'

'I thought you two were madly in love?'

'It's complicated.'

'You bet it is. Sheila Rogers went to Haverton, Will. With Julie. They were in the same sorority.'

I stood, stunned. 'That's not possible.'

'I can't believe you don't know. Sheila never told you?'

I shook my head. 'Are you sure?'

'Sheila Rogers of Mason, Idaho. Majored in communications. It's all in the sorority booklet I found in Julie's trunk in the basement.'

'I don't get it. Do you remember the name of everyone in Julie's sorority?'

'No, Will,' Katy said. 'Sheila and Julie were room-mates.'

SQUARES ARRIVED at my apartment with bagels and spreads. It was 10.00am, and Katy was sleeping on the couch. Squares lowered his head and looked at me over his sunglasses. 'That bad?'

'Worse,' I said.

Katy stirred on the couch and stumbled towards the shower.

'How does your nose feel?' he asked.

'Like my heart moved up there and is trying to thump its way out.'

He nodded and took a bite out of a bagel.

'Sheila lied to me,' I said.

'We knew that already.'

'Not like this. She and Julie Miller were sorority sisters in college. Room-mates even.'

He stopped chewing. 'Come again?'

I told him what I'd learned. The shower stayed on the whole time. Katy would ache from the alcohol aftereffects for some time yet.

When I finished filling him in, Squares leaned back and said, 'I don't get it, man.' He started spreading another bagel. 'Your old girlfriend, who was murdered eleven years ago, was college room-mates with your most recent girlfriend, who was also murdered?'

'Yes.'

'And your brother was blamed for the first murder?'

'Yes again.'

'OK, yeah.' Squares nodded. Then: 'I still don't get it.'

I tried to shrug. 'It must have all been a set-up. A lie.'

He made a yes-and-no gesture with his head. His long hair fell onto his face. He pushed it back. 'To what end?'

'I don't know.'

'Then let's go through the possibilities,' Squares said. He raised his finger. 'One, it could be a giant coincidence.'

I just looked at him.

'Yeah, OK, let's forget that,' he agreed. 'Possibility two'—Squares raised another finger, looked up in the air—'hell, I'm lost here.'

'Right.'

We ate. He mulled it over some more. 'OK, let's assume that Sheila knew exactly who you were from the beginning . . . I still don't get it, man. What are we left with here?'

'I've been thinking about it all night,' I said. 'And I keep coming back to New Mexico.'

'How so?'

'The FBI wanted to question Sheila about an unsolved double murder in Albuquerque.'

'So?'

'Years earlier, Julie Miller was also murdered.'

'Also unsolved,' Squares said, 'but they suspect your brother.'

'Yes.'

Squares nodded. 'OK, I see point A and I see point B. But I don't see how you get from one to the other.'

'Neither,' I said, 'do I.'

We grew silent. Katy peeked her pallid face through the doorway. She groaned and said, 'Where's my clothes?'

'The bedroom closet,' I said.

She gestured an in-pain thank you and closed the door. I looked at the couch, where Sheila liked to read. How could this be happening? The old adage 'Better to have loved and lost than to never have loved at all' came to me. I wondered about that. But more than that, I wondered what was worse—to lose the love of a lifetime or to realise that maybe she never loved you at all. Some choice.

The phone rang. I lifted the receiver and said hello.

'Will, it's Yvonne Sterno. I've been up all night working on this.'

'And?'

'And it keeps getting weirder. I got my contact to go through the deeds and tax records and it turns out the murder-scene house was leased by a corporation called Cripco.'

'And they are?'

'Untraceable. It's a shell. They don't seem to do anything.'

I thought about that.

'Enfield also had a car. A Honda Accord. Also leased by Cripco.'

'Maybe he worked for them.'

'Maybe. But the interesting thing is that the police found the car abandoned in Lacida. Two hundred miles east of here.'

'So where is Owen Enfield?'

'My guess? He's dead. For all we know, he was one of the victims.'

'And the woman and little girl? Where are they?'

'No clue. Hell, I don't even know who they are.'

'Did you talk to the neighbours?'

'Yes. It's like I said before: no one knew much about them. But the woman was in her mid-thirties, attractive, and a brunette. That's about as much as any of the neighbours could tell me. No one knew the little girl's name. She was around eleven or twelve with sandy-brown hair. Mr Enfield was described as six foot with a grey crew cut and goatee. Forty years old, more or less.'

'Then he wasn't one of the victims,' I said.

'How do you know?'

'I saw a photo of the crime scene when I was being questioned by the FBI about my girlfriend's whereabouts.'

'You could see the victims?'

'Not clearly, but enough to know that neither had a crew cut.'

'Hmm. Then the whole family has up and vanished.'

'Yes.'

'There's one other thing, Will.'

'What's that?'

'Well, one of the neighbours swore she saw Owen Enfield at the local QuickGo store at three o'clock on the day of the murders.'

'I'm not following you, Yvonne.'

'Well,' she said, 'the thing is, all the QuickGos have security cameras.' She paused. 'You following me now?'

'Yeah, I think so. If we can get the tape for that day,' I began, 'we might be able to get a good view of Mr Enfield.'

'Big if, though. I went to see the store manager. He was firm. There was no way he was going to turn anything over to me.'

'There has to be a way,' I said.

'I'm open to ideas, Will.'

Squares put his hand on my shoulder. 'What?'

I covered the mouthpiece and filled him in. 'You know anyone connected to QuickGo?' I said.

'Incredible as this might sound, the answer is nope.'

Damn. We mulled it over for a bit. Yvonne started humming the QuickGo jingle, a torturous tune sung by a big-time pop star simply known as Sonay.

Hold the phone. Sonay.

Squares looked at me. 'What?'

'I think you may be able to help me after all,' I said.

Chapter 8

Sheila and Julie had been members of Chi Gamma sorority. I still had the rent-a-car from my late-night jaunt to Livingston, so Katy and I decided to take the two-hour drive up to Haverton College in Connecticut and see what we could learn.

Earlier in the day, I called the Haverton registrar's office to do a little fact-checking. I'd learned that the sorority's housemother back then had been one Rose Baker. Mrs Baker had retired three years ago and moved into a campus house directly across the street. She was to be the main target of our pseudo-investigation.

As we approached her door, I heard a familiar song wafting through the wood: Elton John's 'Candle in the Wind' from the classic *Goodbye Yellow Brick Road* double album. I knocked on the door.

A woman's voice chimed, 'Just a minute.'

A few seconds later, the door opened. Rose Baker was probably in her seventies and dressed, I was surprised to see, for a funeral. Her wardrobe, from the big-brimmed hat with matching veil to the sensible shoes, was black.

'Mrs Baker?' I said.

She lifted the veil. 'Yes?'

'My name is Will Klein. This is Katy Miller.'

The saucer eyes swivelled towards Katy and locked into position.

'Is this a bad time?' I asked.

She seemed surprised by the question. 'Not at all.'

I said, 'We'd like to speak with you, if that's OK.'

'Katy Miller,' she repeated, her eyes still on her. 'Julie's sister.'

It was not a question, but Katy nodded anyway. Rose Baker pushed open the screen door. 'Please come in.'

We followed her into the living room. Katy and I stopped short, taken aback by what we saw.

It was Princess Di. She was everywhere. The entire room was sheathed, blanketed, overrun with Princess Di paraphernalia. There were photographs, of course, but also tea sets, commemorative plates, lamps, figurines, books, thimbles, a toothbrush (eeuw!), sunglasses, salt-'n'-pepper shakers, you name it. I realised that the song I was hearing was not the original Elton John–Bernie Taupin classic, but the more recent Princess Di tribute version.

Rose Baker said, 'Do you remember when Princess Diana died?'

I looked at Katy. She looked at me. We both nodded yes.

'Do you remember the way the world mourned?'

She looked at us some more. And we nodded again.

'For most people, the grief, the mourning, it was just a fad. But for some of us, well, she really was an angel. Too good for this world maybe. We won't ever forget her. We keep the light burning.'

She dabbed her eye. A sarcastic rejoinder came to my lips, but I bit it back and started right in.

'Mrs Baker,' I said, 'you remember Katy's sister, Julie?'

'Yes, of course. I remember all the girls. My husband, Frank—he taught English here—died in 1969. We had no children. That sorority house, those girls, for twenty-six years they were my life.'

'I see,' I said.

'And Julie, well, late at night, when I lie in bed in the dark, her face comes to me more than most. Not just because she was a special child—oh, and she was—but because of what happened to her.'

'You mean her murder?' It was a dumb thing to say, but I was new at this. I just wanted to keep her talking.

'Yes.' Rose Baker reached out and took Katy's hand. 'Such a tragedy. I'm so sorry for your loss.'

Katy said, 'Thank you.'

'Mrs Baker, do you remember another sorority sister named Sheila Rogers?' I asked.

Her face pinched up. 'Yes.' She shifted primly. 'Yes, I do.'

From her reaction, it was obvious that she had not heard about the murder. I decided not to tell her yet. If she knew that Sheila was dead, she might sugar-coat her answers. Before I could follow up, Mrs Baker said, 'May I ask you a question?'

'Of course.'

'Why are you asking me all this now?' She looked at Katy. 'It all happened so long ago.'

Katy took that one. 'I'm trying to find the truth.'

'The truth about what?'

'My sister changed while she was here.'

Rose Baker closed her eyes. 'You don't need to hear this, child.'

'Yes,' Katy said, and the desperation in her voice was palpable enough to knock out a window. 'Please. We need to know.'

Rose Baker kept her eyes closed for another moment or two. Then she nodded to herself and opened them. 'In many ways Julie reminds me of Diana herself. Both of them were beautiful. Both of them were special—almost divine.' She smiled and wagged a finger. 'Ah, and both had a wild streak. Julie was a good person. Kind, smart as a whip. She was an excellent student.'

'Yet,' I said, 'she dropped out. Why?'

She turned her eyes on me. 'College changes people. Your first time away, your first time on your own . . .' She drifted off for a moment, then continued. 'I'm not saying this right. Julie was fine at first, but then she, well, she started to withdraw. From all of us. She cut classes. She broke up with her home-town boyfriend. Not that that was unusual. Almost all the girls do first year. But in her case, it came so late. Junior year, I think. I thought she really loved him.'

I swallowed, kept still.

'Earlier,' Rose Baker said, 'you asked me about Sheila Rogers.'

Katy said, 'Yes.'

'She was a bad influence.' Her eyes were moist now. 'I don't want to sound melodramatic, but Sheila Rogers brought something bad to Chi Gamma. I should have thrown her out. I know that now. But I had no proof of wrongdoing.'

'What did she do?'

She shook her head.

I thought about it for a moment. Junior year, Julie had discouraged me from coming down to Haverton, setting up a quiet getaway at a bed and breakfast in Mystic instead of having us stay on campus. At the time, I'd thought it romantic. Now, of course, I knew better. Three weeks later, Julie called and broke it off with me. But looking back on it now, I remembered that she had been acting both lethargically and strangely during that visit. She blamed it on her studies, said that she'd been cramming big-time. I bought it because, in hindsight, I wanted to.

When I now added it all together, the solution was fairly obvious. Sheila had come here straight from the streets and drugs. That life is not so easy to leave behind. It does not take much to poison the well. Sheila arrives at the start of Julie's junior year, Julie begins to act erratically. It made sense.

I tried another tack. 'Did Sheila Rogers graduate?'

'No, she dropped out too.'

'The same time as Julie?'

'I'm not even sure either of them officially dropped out. Julie just stopped going to class towards the end of the year. When I confronted her'—her voice caught—'she moved out.'

'Where did she move to?'

'An apartment off campus. Sheila stayed there too.'

'So when exactly did Sheila Rogers drop out?'

Rose Baker kept her eyes down. 'I think Sheila left after Julie died.'

'Do you know where Sheila went?' I asked.

'No. She was gone. That was all that mattered.'

She would not look at us any more. I found that troubling.

'Mrs Baker?' I tried again. 'Mrs Baker, what else happened?'

'Why are you here?' she asked.

'We told you. We wanted to know—'

'Yes, but why now?'

Katy and I looked at each other. She nodded. I turned to Rose Baker and said, 'Two days ago, Sheila Rogers was found murdered.'

I thought that maybe she had not heard me. Rose Baker kept her gaze locked on a black-velvet Diana, a grotesque reproduction.

'Mrs Baker?'

'Was she strangled like the others?'

'No,' I said. And then I stopped. 'Did you say others?'

'Yes.'

'What others?'

Her shoulders slumped. Our visit had unleashed demons she had maybe buried beneath the Di accoutrements. 'You don't know about Laura Emerson, do you?'

Katy and I exchanged another glance. 'No,' I said gently. 'Who is Laura Emerson? What happened to her?'

'Laura was another sorority sister. She was a year behind Julie. She was found dead near her home in North Dakota eight months before Julie. She'd been strangled too.'

Icy hands were grabbing at my legs, pulling me back under. Katy's face was white. She shrugged at me, letting me know that this was new to her, too.

'Did they ever find her killer?' I asked.

'No,' Rose Baker said. 'Never.'

I tried to process this new data, get a grip on what this all meant. 'Mrs Baker, did the police question you after Julie's murder?'

'Not the police,' she said. 'Two men from the FBI.'

'Did they ask you about Laura Emerson?'

'No. But I told them anyway.'

'How did they react to that?'

'They told me that I should keep that to myself. That saying something could compromise the investigation.'

Too fast, I thought. This was all coming at me too fast. It would not compute. Three young women were dead. Three women from the same sorority house. That was a pattern if ever I saw one. A pattern meant that Julie's murder was not the random, solo act of violence that the FBI had led us—and the world—to believe.

And worst of all, the FBI knew it. They had lied to us all these years. The question now was, why.

MAN, I HAD a good head of steam going. I wanted to explode into Pistillo's office. I wanted to burst in and grab him by the lapels and demand answers. But real life does not work that way. Route 95 was littered with construction delays. I leaned on the horn and swerved in and out of lanes, but in New York that just raises you to average.

When we finally reached Pistillo's office, his secretary smiled with the genuineness of a politician's wife and asked us to take a seat. Katy looked at me and shrugged. I would not sit. I paced like a caged lion.

Fifteen minutes later, the secretary told us that Assistant Director in Charge Joseph Pistillo would see us now. She opened the door. I blasted into the office.

Pistillo was standing at the ready. He gestured at Katy. 'Who is this?'

'Katy Miller,' I said.

He looked stunned. He said to her, 'What are you doing with him?'

But I was not about to be sidetracked. 'Why didn't you ever say anything about Laura Emerson?' I demanded.

Pistillo waited a beat. Then he said, 'Why don't we all sit?'

'Answer my question.'

He lowered himself into his seat, his eyes never leaving me. 'You're in no position to make demands,' he said.

'Laura Emerson was strangled eight months before Julie.'

'So?'

'Both of them were from the same sorority house.'

Pistillo steepled his fingers. He played the waiting game and won.

I said, 'Are you going to tell me you didn't know about it?'

'Oh, I knew.'

'And you don't see a connection?'

'That's correct. We looked into it at the time, of course. I think the local media picked up on it too. But in the end none of us saw a true connection.'

'And the fact that they both belonged to the same sorority?'

'A coincidence.'

'You're lying,' I said.

He did not like that, and his face reddened. 'Watch it,' he said, pointing a beefy finger in my direction. 'You have no standing here.'

The rage was building back up again. 'Sheila Rogers was a member of that sorority too. Is that another coincidence?'

That caught him off guard. He leaned back, trying to get some distance. Was it because he didn't know or because he didn't think I'd find out about it?

'You knew,' I said. 'And you knew that my brother was innocent.'

He shook his head. 'I knew—correction: know—nothing of the sort.'

But I did not believe him. He had been lying from the start. Of that I was now certain. To my surprise, my voice grew suddenly soft.

'Do you realise what you've done?' I said, barely a whisper. 'The damage to my family. My father, my mother . . .?'

'This doesn't involve you, Will.'

'Like hell it doesn't.'

'Please,' he said. 'Both of you. Stay out of this. For your own sakes. You won't believe this, but I'm trying to protect you.'

'From?'

He did not reply.

'From?' I repeated.

He slapped the arms of his chair and stood. 'This conversation is over,' he said, moving towards the door.

'What do you really want with my brother, Pistillo? Why are you trying to frame him?'

Pistillo stopped and turned round. 'You want to get into truths, Will?' he said.

I did not like his change of tone. I suddenly wasn't sure of the answer. 'Yes.'

'Then,' he said slowly, 'let's start with you, Will. Who do you think killed Julie Miller?'

'I don't know.'

'Well then, let's examine what you think happened, shall we?' Pistillo strode towards me. There was fire in his belly now, and I had no idea why. 'Your dear brother, the one you were so close to, had sexual relations with your old girlfriend the night of the murder. Isn't that your theory, Will?'

I might have squirmed. 'Yes.'

He made a tsk-tsk noise. 'That must have infuriated you.'

'We'd broken up,' I said, though even I could hear the whiny weakness in my own voice.

He gave a small smirk. 'Sure, that always ends it, doesn't it?'

'That's right.'

Pistillo smiled and spread his hands. 'So what were you doing there that night, Will?' He said it in a casual, almost singsong voice.

'I was taking a walk,' I said quickly.

Pistillo paced, pressing his advantage. 'Uh-huh. So your brother is having sex with the girl you still loved. You happen to be taking a walk by her house that night. She ends up dead. And you, Will, know that your brother didn't do it.'

He grinned. 'So if you were investigating, who would you suspect?'

A large stone was crushing my chest. I could not speak.

'If you're suggesting . . .'

'I'm suggesting you go home,' Pistillo said. 'That's all. Go home, both of you, and stay the hell out of this.'

Pistillo offered to find Katy a ride home. She declined and said that she would stay with me. He didn't like that, but what could he do?

We drove back to the apartment in silence. Once inside, I showed her my impressive collection of take-out menus. She ordered Chinese. I ran downstairs and picked it up. We spread the white boxes out on the table. I sat in my usual seat. Katy sat in Sheila's. I flashed back to Chinese with Sheila—her hair tied back, fresh out of the shower and smelling sweet, in that terry-cloth robe . . .

It was odd what you would always remember.

I dumped some fried rice on my plate and followed it up with a dash of lobster sauce. We pretended to eat.

'I didn't kill Julie,' I said.

'I know.'

We pretended to eat some more.

She finally asked, 'Why were you there that night?'

I put down the chopsticks. I wondered how to explain. 'I guess that maybe I wasn't really over Julie.'

'You wanted to see her?'

'Yes.'

'Did you know your brother was there?'

I moved the food around the plate.

'You knew,' Katy said. 'You knew Ken was there. With Julie.'

'I didn't kill your sister.'

'What happened, Will?'

I folded my arms across my chest. I leaned back, closed my eyes. I did not want to go back there, but what choice did I have? Katy deserved to know.

'It was such a strange weekend,' I began. 'Julie and I had been broken up over a year. I hadn't seen her in all that time. I'd tried to bump into her on school breaks, but she was never around.'

'She hadn't been home in a long while,' Katy said.

I nodded. 'The same with Ken. That was what made it all so bizarre. All of a sudden, all three of us are back in Livingston at the same time. I can't remember the last time that happened. Ken was acting strangely too. He was up to something. I don't know what. Anyway, he asked me if I was still hung up on Julie. I told him no. That we were history.'

'You lied to him.'

'It was like . . .' I tried to figure out how to explain this. 'My brother was like a god to me. He was strong and brave and . . .' I shook my head. I didn't know how to say this right. 'The point is, Ken always defended me. Sure, we fought the way brothers do. He'd tease me mercilessly. But he'd step in the way of a freight train to protect me. And me, I never had the courage to reciprocate.'

Katy put her hand to her chin.

'What?' I said.

'It's odd, that's all.'

'What is?'

'That your brother would be insensitive enough to sleep with Julie.'

'It wasn't his fault. He asked me if I was over her. I told him I was.'

'You gave him the green light,' she said.

'Yes.'

'But then you ended up following him.'

'You don't understand,' I said.

'No, I do,' Katy said. 'We all do stuff like that.'

I FELL into such a deep sleep that I never heard him sneak up on me.

I had found fresh sheets and blankets for Katy, made sure she was comfortable on the couch, taken a shower, tried to read. The words swam by in a murky haze. I'd go back and reread the same paragraph over and over again. I signed on to the Internet and surfed. I did not want to stop, to let the grief catch me unawares.

I was a worthy adversary, but eventually sleep managed to corner and take me down. I was out, falling in a totally dreamless pit, when I felt a jerk on my hand and heard the click.

Something metallic dug into my wrist.

My eyelids were fluttering open when he leapt on top of me. He landed hard, whoever he was, knocking the wind out of my lungs. He straddled my chest, his knees pinning down my shoulders. Before I could mount any sort of serious struggle, my attacker yanked my free hand to the side above my head. I didn't hear the click this time, but I felt the cold metal close around my skin.

Both of my hands were cuffed to the bed. The bedroom was dark. My assailant was no more than a shadow to me. He wore a mask of some sort, something dark.

My veins flooded with ice. I opened my mouth, about to scream or at least say something, but my attacker grabbed the back of my head and covered my mouth with a piece of duct tape, which he wound round the back of my skull and over my mouth, maybe ten times.

I could no longer speak or cry out. Breathing was a chore—I had to suck the air through my broken nose. It hurt like hell. My shoulders ached from the cuffs and his body weight. I tried to buck him off me which was totally futile.

And that was when I thought about Katy alone in the other room.

As I watched in helpless horror, he headed out of the bedroom door and into the room where Katy was sleeping. He closed the door behind him. My eyes bulged. I tried to scream, but the tape muffled any sound. I bucked like a bronco. I kicked and flailed. No progress.

Then I stopped and listened. For a moment there was nothing. Pure silence in the dark room. And then Katy screamed.

Oh Christ. I bucked some more. Her scream had been brief, cut off midway, as though someone had turned off a switch. Panic took full flight now. I jerked hard on both cuffs. Nothing.

Katy screamed again.

The sound was fainter this time—the gasp of a wounded animal. No way anyone would hear it, and even if they did, nobody would react. Not in New York. Not at this time of night.

My sanity felt as though it were being torn in two. I went nuts. I thrashed around, seizure style. My nose hurt like hell. I swallowed some of the fibres from the duct tape. I struggled some more.

But I made no progress.

Oh God. OK, calm down. Be cool. Think a second.

I tried to curl up my body, tried to lift myself off the bed so hard that, I don't know, maybe the bed would lift up too. Just an inch or two and then maybe it'd break on the way down. I bucked some more. The bed did indeed slide a few inches out. But it was no good.

I was still trapped.

I heard Katy scream again. And in a scared, panic-filled voice, she shouted, 'John—' And then she was cut off again.

John, I thought. She'd said John. Asselta?

The Ghost . . .

Oh no, please God, no. I heard something muffled. Voices. A groan maybe. Like something being smothered by a pillow. The fear struck at me from every angle. I flung my head from side to side, looked for something, anything. The phone.

Could I . . .? My legs were still free. Maybe I could swing them up, grab the phone with my feet, drop the receiver into my hand. From there I could, I don't know, maybe dial 911 or 0. My feet were already on the rise. I lifted my legs, swung them to the right. My weight teetered to the side. I lost control of my legs. I pulled back up, trying to regain balance, and when I did, my foot hit the phone.

The receiver clattered to the floor. Damn.

Now what? My mind snapped—I mean, I totally lost it. I thrashed to exhaustion, at my wits' end and about to give up, when I remember something Squares had taught me. Plough pose.

That's what it was called. You usually do it from a shoulder stand. You lie on your back and flip your legs over your head until your toes touch the floor behind your head. I did not know if I could go that far, but it didn't matter. I crunched my stomach and swung my legs up as hard as I could. I threw them back behind me. The balls of my feet thudded against the wall and I pushed against it with my legs. The adrenaline kicked in. The bed slid away from the wall. I pushed some more, got enough room. Ok, good. Now for the hard part.

I let my legs fall towards the floor. I was doing, in effect, a back somersault off the bed. The weight of my legs gave me the momentum and—in a stroke of luck—my wrists turned in the cuffs. If they hadn't I would have dislocated both shoulders as my feet landed hard on the floor. When I finished, I was standing up behind the bed. My hands were still cuffed. My mouth was still taped. But I was standing. I bent my knees. I lowered my shoulder to the back of the headboard and I drove the bed towards the door as if I were an offensive lineman and the bed was a tackle sled. The bed crashed into the door.

The collision was jarring. Pain knifed down my shoulder, my arms, my spine. Something popped and hot pain flooded my joints. Ignoring it, I pulled back and rammed the door again. Then again. The third time, I pulled extra hard on both cuffs at the precise moment the bed made contact with the wall.

The bed rails gave way and I was free.

I tried unwrapping the tape from my mouth, but it was taking too long. I grabbed the doorknob and turned it, then flung open the door and leapt into the darkness.

Katy was on the floor. Her eyes were closed. Her body was limp. The man was straddling her chest. He had his hands on her throat. He was choking her. Without hesitation, I launched myself at him. He saw me coming—had plenty of time to prepare—but it still meant that he would have to release her throat. He turned and faced me. I couldn't see anything but a black outline. He grabbed hold of my shoulders, put his foot into my stomach, and using my own momentum, he simply rolled back.

I flew across the room. My arms windmilled in the air. But I lucked out again. Or so I thought. I landed on the soft reading chair. It wobbled for a second. Then it toppled over from my weight. My head bounced hard against the side table before banging to the floor.

I fought off the dizziness and tried to get to my knees. When I started rising for a second offensive, I saw something that terrified me like nothing before ever had.

The black-clad assailant was up too. He had a knife now. And he was heading towards Katy with it.

I was too far away to reach him. I knew that. Even through the dizziness, through the blow from hitting my head on the table . . .

The table.

Where I'd placed Squares's gun.

Was there time to reach it and turn and fire? My eyes were still on Katy and her assailant. No. Not enough time.

The man bent over and grabbed Katy by the hair.

As I went for the gun, I pawed at the tape on my mouth. The tape shifted enough for me to shout, 'Freeze or I'll shoot!'

His head turned in the dark. He saw immediately that I was unarmed and turned back to finish what he had started. My hand found the gun. No time to aim. I pulled the trigger.

The man startled back from the sound.

That bought me time. I swung round with the gun, already pulling the trigger again. But the man had rolled back like a gymnast and I could barely make him out, he was just a shadow. How many bullets did this thing hold? How many had I fired?

He jerked back, but kept on moving. Had I hit him?

The man jumped towards the door. I considered firing into his back, but something, perhaps a fly-through of humanity, made me stop. He was already out of the door. And I had bigger worries.

I looked down at Katy. She was not moving.

Chapter 9

Another officer—the fifth, by my count—came to my hospital room to hear my story.

'I want to know how she is first,' I said.

'Just answer my question,' the cop said.

This had been going on for two hours now. The adrenaline had died down, and the ache was starting to gnaw on my bones. I'd had enough.

'Yeah, OK, you got me,' I said. 'First, I put cuffs on both my hands. Then I broke up some furniture, fired several bullets into the walls, choked her nearly to death in my own apartment, dislocating my shoulder and cutting my hands in the process. Then I called the police on myself. You got me.'

He gave a classic cop-shrug. 'So how come none of your neighbours saw anyone running out of your apartment?'

'Because—and this is just a wild stab in the dark—it was two in the morning?'

I was still sitting up on the examining table. The doctor had stopped working on me.

The door opened, and Pistillo entered. He gave me a look as heavy as the ages. I closed my eyes and massaged the bridge of my nose with my forefinger and thumb. Pistillo signalled to the officer to leave. I was alone now with Pistillo.

He did not say anything at first. Pistillo circled the room, studying the glass jar of cottonwool balls, the hazardous-waste disposal can.

'Tell me what happened,' he said eventually.

'I want to know how Katy is first.'

He weighed my request for a second or two. 'Her neck and vocal cords will be sore, but she'll be fine.'

I closed my eyes and let the relief flow over me.

'Start talking,' Pistillo said.

I told him what happened. He stayed quiet until I got to the part about her shouting out the name 'John'.

'Any idea who John is?' he asked.

'Maybe.'

'I'm listening.'

'A guy I knew when I was growing up. John Asselta.'

Pistillo's face dropped. 'What makes you think she was talking about Asselta?'

'He's the one who broke my nose.'

I filled him in on the Ghost's break-in and assault. Pistillo did not look happy. 'Asselta was looking for your brother?'

'That's what he said.'

His face reddened. 'Why the hell didn't you tell me this before?'

'Yeah, it's weird,' I said. 'You've always been the guy I could turn to, the friend I could trust with anything.'

He stayed angry. 'He's one of the most dangerous wackos out

there,' Pistillo said. 'He lives overseas, no one knows where exactly, and has worked for government death squads in Central America and Africa.' Pistillo shook his head. 'If Asselta wanted her dead, we'd be tying a toe tag on her right about now.'

'Maybe she meant another John,' I said.

'Maybe.' He thought about that. 'One other thing I don't get. If the Ghost or anyone else wanted to kill Katy Miller, why not just do it? Why go to the trouble of cuffing you down?'

That had troubled me too, but I had come up with one possibility. 'Maybe it was a set-up. The killer cuffs me to the bed. He chokes Katy to death. Then'—I could feel a tingle on my scalp—'maybe he'd set it up to make it look like I did it.' I looked at him.

Pistillo frowned. 'You're not going to say "Like my brother", are you?'

'Yeah,' I said. 'Yeah, I think I am.'

'That's horseshit.'

'Think about it, Pistillo. One thing you guys could never explain: why was my brother's blood at the scene?'

'Julie Miller fought him off.'

'You know there was too much blood for that.' I moved closer to him. 'Ken was framed eleven years ago and maybe tonight someone wanted history to repeat itself.'

He scoffed. 'Don't be melodramatic. And let me tell you something. The cops aren't buying your Houdini-cuff-escape story. They think you tried to kill her. And so does her father.'

'You know I didn't do it, Pistillo. And despite your theatrics yesterday, you know I didn't kill Julie.'

'I warned you to stay away.'

'And I chose not to heed your warning.'

Pistillo let loose a long breath and nodded. 'Exactly, tough guy, so here's how we're going to play it.' He stepped closer and tried to stare me down. 'Right now you're going to be shipped off to jail.'

'Fine, I want a lawyer.'

He looked at his watch. 'Too late for that. You'll spend the night in lockup. Tomorrow you'll get arraigned. The charges will be attempted murder and assault two. The DA's office will claim that you're a flight risk—case in point: your brother—and they'll ask for the judge to deny bail. My guess is, the judge will grant it.'

I started to speak but he held up a hand. 'Save your breath. I don't care if you did it or not. I'm going to find enough evidence to convict you. And if I can't find it, I'll create it. Go ahead, tell your lawyer about this chat. I'll just deny it. Who do you think they'll believe?'

I looked at him. 'Why are you doing this?'

'I told you to stay away. You didn't listen. Now your girlfriend is dead and Katy Miller just barely escaped with her life.'

'I never hurt either one of them.'

'Yeah, you did. You caused it. If you listened to me, you think they'd be where they are now?'

His words hit home, but I pushed on. 'And what about you, Pistillo? What about your burying Laura Emerson's connection—'

'Hey, I'm not here to play point-counterpoint with you. You're going to jail tonight. And make no mistake, I'll get you convicted.'

He headed for the door.

'Pistillo?' He turned round. 'What are you really after here?'

He stopped and leaned so that his lips were only inches from my ear. He whispered, 'Ask your brother,' and then he was gone.

I SPENT WHAT WAS LEFT of the night in the precinct holding pen at Midtown South on West 35th Street. The cell reeked of urine and vomit and that sour-vodka smell when a drunk sweats. I had two cell-mates. One was a cross-dressing hooker who cried a lot and the other was a black man who slept the whole time. The night was uneventful.

My one call had been to Squares. I woke him up. When I told him what happened, he said, 'Bummer.' Then he promised to find me a good lawyer and see what he could learn about Katy's condition.

'Oh, the security tapes from that QuickGo,' Squares said. 'Your idea worked. We'll be able to see them tomorrow.'

'If they let me out of here.'

'Yeah, I guess,' Squares said. Then he added, 'If they don't give you bail, man, that would suck.'

In the morning, the cops escorted me to central booking at 100 Center Street. Squares was there when I stood before the judge. So was my new attorney, a woman named Hester Crimstein. I recognised her from some famous case, but I could not put my finger on which one. She introduced herself to me and never looked my way again.

The young DA rose and said, 'We request that Mr Klein be held over without bail. We believe that he is a serious flight risk.'

'Why's that?' the judge asked, boredom perspiring from every pore.

'His brother, a murder suspect, has been on the run for the past eleven years. Not only that, Your Honour, but his brother's victim was this victim's sister.'

That got the judge's attention. 'Come again?'

'The defendant, Mr Klein, is accused of trying to murder one Katherine Miller. Mr Klein's brother, Kenneth, is a suspect in the eleven-year-old murder of Julie Miller, the victim's older sister.'

The judge, who'd been rubbing his face, stopped abruptly. 'Oh, wait, I remember the case.'

The young DA smiled as if he'd been given a gold star.

The judge turned to Hester Crimstein. 'Ms Crimstein?'

'Your Honour, we believe that Mr Klein should be released on his own recognisance. Mr Klein has no criminal record at all. He has a job working with the poor in this city. He has roots in the community. As for that ridiculous comparison to his brother, that's guilt by association at its worst.'

'You don't think the people have a valid concern, Ms Crimstein?'

'Not at all, Your Honour. I understand that Mr Klein's sister recently got her hair permed. Does that make it more likely that he will do the same?'

There was laughter.

The young DA flushed. 'Your Honour, with all due deference to my colleague's silly analogy—'

'What's silly about it?' Crimstein snapped. 'The sole reason they're making this claim is because they believe his brother fled—and no one is even sure about that. He may be dead. But either way, Your Honour, the assistant district attorney is leaving out one crucial element.'

Hester Crimstein turned to the young DA and smiled.

'Mr Thomson?' the judge said.

Thomson, the young DA kept his head down.

Hester Crimstein waited another beat and then dived in. 'The victim of this heinous crime, one Katherine Miller, claimed this morning that Mr Klein was innocent.'

The judge did not like that. 'Mr Thomson?'

'That's not exactly true, Your Honour. Ms Miller claimed that she did not see her assailant. It was dark. He wore a mask.'

'And,' Hester Crimstein finished for him, 'she said that it wasn't my client.'

'She said she did not *believe* it was Mr Klein,' Thomson countered. 'But, Your Honour, she's injured and confused. She didn't see the attacker, so she really couldn't rule him out—'

'We're not trying the case here, Counsellor,' the judge interrupted. 'But your request for no bail is denied. Bail is set at thirty thousand dollars.'

The judge banged the gavel. And I was free.

I WANTED TO HEAD up to the hospital and see Katy. Squares shook his head and told me that would be a bad idea. Her father was there. He refused to leave her side. He had hired an armed guard to stand outside the door. I understood. Mr Miller had failed to protect one daughter. He would never let himself do that again.

Squares drove his own car, a 1968 venetian-blue Coupe de Ville that was about as inconspicuous as our cross-dressing friend Raquel/Roscoe at a Daughters of the American Revolution gathering, through the Lincoln Tunnel.

'Smart thinking,' Squares said, as the traffic crept through the tunnel.

'What?'

'Remembering that Sonay was a devout practitioner of Yoga Squared.' Sonay was the big-time pop star who performed the jingle for QuickGo's latest commercial campaign.

'So how did it work?'

'I called Sonay and told her about our problem. She told me that QuickGo was run by two brothers, Ian and Noah Muller. She called them, told them what she wanted, and . . .' Squares shrugged.

I shook my head. 'You are amazing.'

'Yes. Yes, I am.'

QuickGo's offices were housed in a warehouse off Route 3 in the heart of northern New Jersey's swamps.

We headed into the warehouse. The Muller brothers were worth close to $100 million each, yet they shared a small office that sat in the middle of a hangarlike room. Their desks were pushed together facing each other. There were no computers or fax machines or photocopiers, just the desks, tall metal filing cabinets and two phones. All four walls were glazed. The brothers liked to look out at the cargo boxes and fork-lifts. They did not much care who looked in.

The two of them looked alike and were dressed the same. They wore what my father called 'charcoal slacks' with white button-downs. Together they rose and aimed their widest smiles at Squares.

'You must be Ms Sonay's guru,' one said. 'Yogi Squares.'

Squares replied with a serene, wise-man head nod.

They both rushed over and shook his hand.

'We had them overnight the tapes,' the taller of the brothers said, clearly looking for approval. Squares deigned another nod at him. They led us to a windowless room with a TV and VCR on a counter.

The taller one turned on the TV and stuck a tape in the VCR. 'This tape covers twelve hours,' he said. 'You told me the guy was in the store around three o'clock, right?'

'That's what we were told,' Squares said.

'I have it set at two forty-five. The tape moves pretty quickly since it only captures an image every three seconds. Just press the play button right here whenever you're ready. We figured you'd want privacy so we'll leave. Take your time.'

'Thank you.'

Then we were left alone. I approached the VCR and pressed play.

The images were in black and white. The camera pointed at the cash register from above. A young woman with blonde hair worked it. Her moving in jerky, every-three-second clips made me dizzy.

'How are we going to know this Owen Enfield?' Squares asked.

'We look for a forty-year-old guy with a crew cut, I guess.'

Watching now, I realised that this task might be easier than I'd first thought. The customers were all elderly and in golf-club garb. It seemed Stonepointe catered mostly to retirees.

At 3:08.15, we spotted him. His back anyway. He wore shorts and a short-sleeved shirt. We could not see his face, but he had a crew cut. He headed past the register and down the last aisle. We waited. At 3:09.24, our potential Owen Enfield headed back towards the check-out. He carried a half-gallon of milk and a loaf of bread. I put my hand near the pause button so I could stop it and get a better look.

But there was no need.

I stood there, unmoving. I did not know if I should celebrate or cry. I turned towards Squares. His eyes were on me instead of the screen. I nodded at him, confirming what he already suspected.

Owen Enfield was my brother, Ken.

Chapter 10

The intercom buzzed. 'Joshua Ford and Raymond Cromwell are here, Mr McGuane,' said the receptionist, part of his security force.

Joshua Ford was the senior partner at Stanford, Cummings, and Ford, a firm that employed more than 300 attorneys. Raymond Cromwell would thus be the note-taking underling. Philip watched them both on the monitor. Ford was a big guy, six foot four, 220 pounds. He had a reputation for being tough, aggressive, nasty, and, fitting that profile, he worked his face and mouth as though he were chomping on either a cigar or a human leg. Cromwell, in contrast, was young, soft, manicured and waxy smooth.

McGuane looked over at the Ghost. The Ghost smiled, and McGuane felt another cold gust. Again he wondered about the intelligence of bringing Asselta in on this. In the end, he had decided that it would be OK. The Ghost had a stake in this too.

Still keeping his eyes on that skin-crawling smile, McGuane said, 'Please send in Mr Ford alone. Make sure that Mr Cromwell is comfortable in the waiting room.'

'Yes, Mr McGuane.'

When Joshua Ford opened the door, the Ghost had the iron baton ready. It was the approximate length of a baseball bat, with a powerful spring that helped it snap with the force of a blackjack.

Joshua Ford entered with a rich-man's swagger. He smiled at McGuane. 'Mr McGuane.'

McGuane smiled back. 'Mr Ford.'

Sensing someone to his right, Ford turned towards the Ghost, his hand outstretched for a customary shake. The Ghost had his eyes elsewhere. He aimed the metal bar for the shin and hit it flush. Ford cried out and dropped to the floor like a marionette with its strings cut. The Ghost hit him again, this time in the right shoulder. Ford felt his arm go dead. The Ghost smashed the baton against the rib cage. There was a cracking sound. Ford tried to roll into a ball.

From across the room, McGuane asked, 'Where is he?'

Joshua Ford swallowed and croaked, 'Who?'

Big mistake. The Ghost snapped the weapon down on the man's ankle. Ford howled, put up a hand, pleading for mercy.

Over the years, McGuane had learned that it was best to strike before you interrogate. Most people, when presented with the threat of pain, will try to talk their way out of it. They'll search for angles, for half-truths, for credible lies. They are rational, the assumption goes, and thus their opponents must be the same.

You need to strip them of that delusion.

'He stopped in Las Vegas,' McGuane explained. 'That was his big mistake. Ken visited a doctor there. A doctor who couldn't keep his mouth shut. We checked the nearby payphones for out-of-state calls made an hour before and an hour after Ken's visit. There was only one call of interest. To you, Mr Ford. He called you, his lawyer.'

Joshua Ford said, 'But—'

McGuane held up his hand to stop him. 'If you deny or pretend you don't know what I'm talking about,' McGuane said, 'my friend here will stop the love taps and start to hurt you. Do you understand?'

Ford took a few seconds. When he finally looked up, McGuane was surprised by the steadiness of the man's gaze. Ford looked at the Ghost, then at McGuane. 'Go to hell,' Ford spat out.

The Ghost looked at McGuane. He arched an eyebrow, smiled, and said, 'Brave.'

'John . . .'

But the Ghost ignored him. He whipped the iron bar across Ford's face. Blood squirted across the room. Ford fell back.

'Where is he?' McGuane asked again.

This time Ford shook his head.

McGuane walked over to the monitor. He swivelled it so that Joshua Ford could see the screen. Cromwell was sitting cross-legged, sipping coffee. McGuane pointed at the young associate.

'How old is he?' McGuane asked.

Ford tried to sit up, fell back. He did not reply.

The Ghost lifted the bar. 'He asked you—'

'Twenty-nine.'

'Married?'

Ford nodded.

McGuane studied the monitor some more. 'Tell me where Ken is, Ford, or he dies.'

The Ghost carefully put down the metal bar. He reached into his pocket and pulled out a Thuggee strangulation stick. The handle portion was made of mahogany, with deep grooves cut into it, making it easier to grip. There was a braided rope attached to either end. The rope was made of horsehair.

'He's got nothing to do with this,' Ford said.

'Listen to me closely,' McGuane said. 'I'm only going to say this once.'

Ford waited.

'We never bluff,' McGuane said. He waited a beat, his eyes on Ford. Then he hit the intercom button. The receptionist responded.

'Yes, Mr McGuane.'

'Bring Mr Cromwell here.'

'Yes, sir.'

They both watched the monitor as a security guard waved towards Cromwell. Cromwell rose, and followed the security guard out of the door. Ford turned to McGuane. Their eyes met and locked.

'You're a stupid man,' McGuane said.

The Ghost regripped the wooden handle and waited.

The security guard opened the door. Raymond Cromwell entered with his smile at the ready. When he saw the blood and his boss crumpled on the floor, his face dropped. 'What the—?'

The Ghost stepped behind Cromwell and kicked the back of both legs. Cromwell let out a cry and fell to his knees.

The rope dropped over the younger man's head. When it fully circled his neck, the Ghost jerked back violently while simultaneously putting his knee against Cromwell's spine. As the rope tightened, the Ghost twisted the handle, cutting off blood flow to the brain.

'Stop!' Ford shouted. 'I'll talk!'

But McGuane merely shook his head and repeated his earlier statement: 'We never bluff.'

I HAD TO TELL my father about the security tape.

Squares dropped me off at a bus-stop near the Meadowlands. I had no idea what to do about what I'd just seen. Part of me was ecstatic. There was a chance at redemption, a chance to be with my brother again, a chance—dare I even think of it?—to make this all right.

But then I thought about Sheila.

Her fingerprints had been found in my brother's house, along with two dead bodies. How did Sheila fit into all this? I had no idea, or maybe I just didn't want to face the obvious. She had betrayed me—the only scenarios I could come up with involved betrayal of one form or another. So I plodded on with one thought in mind: closure. My brother and my lover had both left me without warning. I knew that I could never put any of this behind me until I knew the truth. Maybe now, finally, it was my turn to be brave. Maybe now I would save Ken instead of the other way round.

So that was what I'd focus on: Ken was alive. He was innocent—if I had been subconsciously harbouring any doubts before, Pistillo had erased them. I could see and be with him again. I could—I don't know—avenge the past. Let my mother rest in peace.

On this, the penultimate day of our official mourning, my father was not at the house. Aunt Selma was in the kitchen. She told me that he'd taken a walk. I watched her cleaning out the sink. Selma, Sunny's quiet sister, laboured quietly. I had always taken her for granted. But as I stood and looked at her, as if for the first time, I saw yet another human being struggling every day to do right.

'Thank you,' I said to her, and gave her a hug. At first she seemed startled by my aberrant display of affection, but then she relaxed.

'It'll be OK,' she told me.

I knew my father's favourite walking route. I crossed Coddington Terrace, carefully avoiding the Miller house, and then took the path that led to the town's Little League fields. The fields were empty, the season over, and my father sat alone on the top row of the metal stands. I remembered how much he loved coaching with Mr Bertillo and Mr Horowitz, his two best friends, beer buddies. Both men were dead of heart attacks before sixty, and I know that as I sat next to him now, he could still hear those clapping hands and that repetitive banter and smell that sweet Little League clay-dirt.

He looked at me and his eyes widened when he saw the bruises.

'What the hell happened to you?'

'It's OK,' I said.

'Did you get in a fight?'

'I'm fine, really. I need to talk to you about something.'

He was quiet. I wondered how to approach this, but Dad took care of that. 'Show me,' he said.

I looked at him.

'Your sister called this morning. She told me about the picture.'

I still had it with me. I pulled it out. He took it in his palm, as though it was a small animal he was afraid that he might crush. He looked down and said, 'Your mother never said anything until, you know.' His eyes began to glisten. His wife, his life partner, had kept this from him, and it hurt.

'There's something else,' I said.

He turned to me.

'Ken's been living in New Mexico.' I gave him a thumbnail sketch of what I'd learned. Dad took it in quietly and steadily, and when I'd finished, he said, 'How long had he been living out there?'

'Just a few months. Why?'

'Your mother said he was coming back. She said he'd be back when he proved his innocence.'

'Did you ever suspect Ken was alive, Dad?'

He took his time. 'It was easier to think he was dead.'

'That's not an answer.'

He let his gaze roam again. 'Ken loved you so much, Will.'

I let that hang in the air.

'But he wasn't all good.'

'I know that,' I said.

He let that settle in. 'When Julie was murdered,' my father said, 'Ken was already in trouble.'

'What do you mean?'

'He came home to hide.'

'From what?'

'I don't know.'

I thought about it. I again remembered that he had not been home in at least two years and that he'd seemed on edge, even as he asked me about Julie. I just didn't know what that all meant.

Dad said, 'Do you remember Phil McGuane?'

I nodded. Ken's old friend from high school, the 'class leader'.

'What about him?'

'Ken was mixed up with McGuane.'

'How?'

'That's all I know.'

I thought about the Ghost. 'Was John Asselta involved too?'

My father went rigid. I saw fear in his eyes. 'Why do you ask?'

'The three of them were all friends in high school,' I began—and then I decided to go the rest of the way. 'I saw him recently.'

'Asselta?'

'Yes.'

Dad closed his eyes.

'What is it?'

'He's dangerous,' my father said.

'I know that.'

He pointed at my face. 'Did he do that?'

Good question, I thought. 'In part, at least.'

'In part?'

'It's a long story, Dad.'

He closed his eyes again. When he opened them, he put his hands on his thighs and stood up. 'Let's go home,' he said.

I wanted to ask him more, but I knew that now was not the time. I followed him down the rickety steps and when we reached the gravel, we turned towards the path. And there, smiling patiently with his hands in his pockets, stood the Ghost.

For a moment I thought it was my imagination, as if our thinking about him had conjured up this horrific mirage. But I heard the sharp intake of air coming from my father. And then I heard that voice.

'Ah, isn't this touching?' the Ghost said.

My father stepped in front of me as though trying to shield me. 'What do you want?' he shouted.

The Ghost looked up at the sky, closed his eyes, took a great big sniff of air. 'Ah, Little League.' He smiled again and lowered his gaze to my father. 'Say, Mr Klein, do you remember coaching that all-star team in the state finals?'

My father said, 'I do.'

'Ken and I were in, what, fourth grade, was it?'

Nothing from my father this time.

The Ghost snapped, 'Oh wait.' The smile slid off his face. 'I almost forgot. I missed that year, didn't I? Jail time, don't you know.'

'You never went to jail,' my father said.

'True, true, you're absolutely right, Mr Klein. I was'—the Ghost made quote marks with his skinny fingers—'hospitalised. You know what that means, Willie boy? They lock up a child with the most depraved whack-jobs that ever cursed this wretched planet, so as to make him all better.'

'That was a long time ago,' my father said softly.

The Ghost's eyes narrowed as if he were giving my father's words very special attention. Finally he nodded and said, 'Yes, yes, it was. And it wasn't like I had a great home life to begin with. You could almost look at what happened to me as a blessing: I could get therapy instead of living with a father who beat me.'

I realised then that he was talking about the killing of Daniel Skinner, the bully who'd been stabbed with the kitchen knife.

'Hey, Willie boy?'

'What?' I said.

'You know I was'—again with the finger quotes—'hospitalised again, don't you?'

'Yes,' I said. 'I remember.'

'I had only one visitor the whole time I was there. Do you know who it was?'

I nodded. The answer was Julie.

'Ironic, don't you think?'

'Did you kill her?' I asked.

'Only one of us here is to blame. And that's you, Willie boy.'

I was confused. 'What do you mean?'

'That's enough,' my father said.

'You were supposed to fight for her,' the Ghost went on. 'You were supposed to protect her.'

The words pierced my chest like an ice pick.

'Why are you here?' my father demanded.

'The truth, Mr Klein? I'm not exactly sure.'

'Leave my family alone. You want someone, you take me.'

'No, sir, I don't want you.' He considered my father, and I felt something cold coil in my belly. 'I think I prefer you this way.'

The Ghost gave a little wave goodbye then and stepped into the wooded area. We watched him move deeper into the brush, fading away until, like his nickname, he vanished. We stood there for another minute or two. I could hear my father's breathing, hollow and tinny, as if coming up from a deep cavern.

'Dad?'

But he had already started down the path. 'Let's go home, Will.'

Chapter 11

When I got back to the apartment there were two phone messages on my voicemail. The first was from Sheila's mother, Edna Rogers. Her tone was stiff and impersonal. The funeral would be in two days, she stated, at a chapel in Mason, Idaho. Mrs Rogers gave me times and addresses and directions. I saved the message.

The second was from Yvonne Sterno. She said it was urgent that I call her. Her tone was one of barely restrained excitement, and I wondered if she'd learned the true identity of Owen Enfield.

Yvonne answered on the first ring.

'What's up?' I asked.

'Got something big here, Will.'

'What's that?'

'Put the pieces together. A guy with a pseudonym living in a quiet community. The FBI's strong interest. All the secrecy. You with me?'

'Not really, no.'

'Cripco was the key,' she went on. 'As I said, it's a dummy corporation. So I checked with a few sources. Truth is, they don't try to hide them that hard. The cover isn't that deep. The way they figure it, if someone spots the guy, they either know or they don't know.'

'Yvonne?' I said. 'I don't have a clue what you're talking about.'

'Cripco, the company who leased the house and the car, traces back to the United States marshal's office.'

Once again I felt my head teeter and spin. 'What are you saying? That Owen Enfield is an undercover agent?'

'No, I don't think so. I mean, what would he be investigating at Stonepointe—someone cheating at gin rummy?'

'What then?'

'The US marshal—not the FBI—runs the witness protection programme. I think that the government was hiding Owen Enfield here. They gave him a new identity. The key, like I said before, is that they don't take the background that deep. If, say, Gotti were searching for Sammy 'the Bull', they'd either recognise him or not. They wouldn't bother checking his background to make sure. Know what I mean?'

'I think so.'

'So the way I figure it, for some reason this Owen Enfield murders these two guys and runs off. The FBI doesn't want that out. Think how embarrassing it would be—the government cuts a deal with a guy and then he goes on a murder spree.'

I didn't say anything.

'Will?' There was a pause. 'You're holding out on me, aren't you? Come on,' she said. 'I give, you give, remember?'

I don't know what I would have said—if I would have told her that my brother and Owen Enfield were one and the same—but the decision was taken from me. I heard a click and the phone went dead.

There was a sharp knock on the door.

'Federal officers. Open up now.'

I recognised the voice. It belonged to Claudia Fisher. I reached for the knob, twisted it, and was nearly knocked over. Fisher burst in with a gun drawn. She told me to put my hands up. Her partner, Darryl Wilcox, was with her.

'What the hell is this?' I said.

'Hands up now!'

I did as she asked. She took out her cuffs, and then, as though thinking better of it, she stopped. Her voice was suddenly soft. 'You'll come without a hassle?' she asked.

I nodded.

'Then come on, let's go.'

I DID NOT ARGUE. I did not call their bluff or demand a phone call or even ask them where we were going. Such protestations at this delicate juncture would, I knew, be either superfluous or harmful.

We pulled up to a row of houses in Fair Lawn, New Jersey. Everywhere I looked I saw the same thing: tidy lawns, overdone flowerbeds. We approached a house no different from any other. Fisher tried the knob. It was unlocked. They led me through a room with a pink sofa and console TV to the kitchen. Pistillo sat at the Formica table with an iced tea. A woman stood by the sink. Fisher and Wilcox made themselves scarce. I stayed standing.

'You have my phone tapped,' I said.

Pistillo shook his head. 'A tap just tells you where the call originated. What we're using here are listening devices. And just so we're clear, they were court ordered.'

'What do you want from me?' I asked him.

'The same thing I've wanted for eleven years,' he said. 'Your brother.'

The woman at the sink turned on the tap and rinsed out a glass. Pistillo turned to her and said, 'Maria?'

The woman shut off the water and turned towards him.

'Maria, this is Will Klein. Will, Maria.'

The woman—I assumed that this was Pistillo's wife—dried her hands on a tea towel. Her grip was firm. 'Nice to meet you,' she said.

I mumbled and nodded, and when Pistillo signalled, I sat on a metal chair with vinyl padding.

'Would you like something to drink, Mr Klein?' Maria asked me.

I accepted a glass of iced tea. When she put it in front of me she said, 'I'll wait in the other room, Joe.'

'Thanks, Maria.'

She pushed through the swinging door.

'That's my sister,' he said, still looking at the door she'd just gone through. He pointed to some snapshots on the refrigerator. 'Those are her two boys. Vic Junior is eighteen now, Jack is sixteen.'

'Uh-huh.' I folded my hands and rested them on the table. 'You've been listening in on my calls.'

'Yes.' He took a sip of the iced tea, but he was still staring at the refrigerator; he head-gestured for me to do likewise. 'You notice anything missing from those pictures?'

'I'm really not in the mood for games, Pistillo.'

'No, me neither. But take a longer look. What's missing?'

I did not bother to look because I already knew. 'The father.'

He snapped his fingers and pointed at me like a game show host. 'Got it on the first try,' he said. 'Impressive.'

'What the hell is this?'

'My sister lost her husband, Victor, twelve years ago. The boys, well, you can do the maths on your own. They were six and four. Vic was murdered, Will. Shot twice in the head, execution style.' He drained his iced tea and then added, 'Your brother was there.'

My heart lurched. 'What do you mean, my brother was there?'

Pistillo stood up and opened the freezer, took out an ice tray, broke it open in the sink. He fished some cubes out and started to fill his glass with more iced tea. 'I want you to make a promise.'

'What?'

'It involves Katy Miller.'

'What about her?'

'She's just a kid. I don't want her getting hurt again.'

'Neither do I.'

'So we agree then,' he said. 'Promise me, Will. Promise me you won't involve her any more.'

I looked at him and I knew that point was not negotiable. 'OK,' I said. 'She's out. Now tell me about my brother.'

He finished pouring the iced tea and settled back into his chair. 'You read in the paper about the big busts,' Pistillo began. 'You read about how the Fulton Fish Market's been cleaned up and you think the mob is gone. The cops have won.'

My throat suddenly felt parched, as if it might close up altogether. I took a deep sip from my own glass. The tea was too sweet.

'Do you know anything about Darwin?' he asked.

I thought the question was rhetorical, but he waited for an answer. I said, 'Survival of the strongest, all that.'

'Not the strongest,' he said. 'That's the modern interpretation, and it's wrong. The key to Darwin was not that the strongest survive—the most adaptable do. See the difference?'

I nodded.

'So the smarter bad guys, they adapted. They moved their business out of Manhattan. They sold drugs, for example, in the less competitive 'burbs. For your basic corruption, they started feeding on the Jersey cities. Camden, for example. Three of the last five mayors have been convicted of crimes. Newark and all that revitalisation bullshit. Revitalisation means money. Money means kickbacks and graft.'

I shifted in my chair. 'Is there a point to this, Pistillo?'

'Yeah, asshole, there's a big point.' His face reddened. 'My brother-in-law—the father of those boys—tried to clean the streets of these scumbags. He worked undercover. Someone found out. And he and his partner ended up dead.'

'And you think my brother was involved in that?'

'Yeah. Yeah, I do.'

Pistillo took a breath. He needed time. I could see that. His face was surprisingly matter-of-fact, composed even, but that was because he was jamming the rage back in the closet.

'Your brother worked for Philip McGuane. I assume you know who he is.'

I was giving him nothing. 'Go on.'

'McGuane is more dangerous than your pal Asselta. He's smarter. The OCID considers him one of the top guns on the East Coast.'

'OCID?'

'Organised Crime Investigation Division,' he said. 'McGuane is the ultimate survivor. He works all the classics—drugs, prostitution, loan-sharking—but he specialises in graft and kickbacks and setting up his drug trade in less competitive spots away from the city. He killed my brother-in-law and his partner. Your brother was involved. We arrested him but on lesser charges six months before Julie Miller was murdered.'

'How come I never heard anything about it?'

'Because Ken didn't tell you. And because we didn't want your brother. We wanted McGuane. So we flipped him.'

'Flipped him?'

'We gave Ken immunity in exchange for his cooperation.'

'You wanted him to testify against McGuane?'

'More than that. McGuane was careful. We didn't have enough to nail him for murder. We needed an informant. So we wired him up and sent him back in.'

'You're saying that Ken worked undercover for you?'

Something flashed hard in Pistillo's eyes. 'Don't glamorise it,' he snapped. 'Your low-life brother wasn't a law enforcement officer. He was just a scumbag trying to save his own skin.'

I nodded, reminding myself that this could all be a lie. 'Go on,' I said again.

'McGuane found out. You have to understand. McGuane is a brutal son of a bitch. Killing someone is always an option for him, a matter of convenience, nothing more. He feels nothing.'

I saw now where he was heading with this. 'So if McGuane knew that Ken had become an informant—'

'Dead meat,' he finished for me. 'Your brother understood the risk. We were keeping tabs, but one night he just ran off.'

'Because McGuane found out?'

'That's what we think, yes. He ended up at your house.'

'And then?'

'By now you must have guessed that Asselta was working for McGuane too. Well, your brother told us that Asselta had murdered Laura Emerson, the other sorority sister who was killed. According to Ken, Laura Emerson had found out about the drug trade at Haverton and was set to report it.'

I made a face. 'And they killed her for that?'

'Yeah, they killed her for that. These are monsters, Will. Get that through your thick head.'

I remembered Phil McGuane coming over and playing Risk. He always won. He was quiet and observant, the sort of kid who makes you wonder about still waters and all that. He was student council president, I think. I was impressed by him. The Ghost had been openly psychotic. I could see him doing anything. But McGuane?

'Somehow they learned where your brother was hiding. Maybe the Ghost followed Julie home from college, we don't know. Either way, he catches up with your brother at the Miller house. One theory is that he tried to kill them both. You said you saw someone that night. We believe you. We also believe that the man you saw was probably Asselta. His fingerprints were found at the scene. Ken was wounded in the assault—that explains the blood—but somehow he got away. The Ghost was left with the body of Julie Miller. So what would be the natural thing to do? Make it look like Ken did it.'

He stopped and started nibbling on a cookie. Now it was my turn to fight back the rage.

'So all this time'—I stopped, swallowed, tried again—'so all this time, you knew that Ken didn't kill Julie.'

'No, not at all.'

'But you just said—'

'It was just a theory, Will. It's just as likely that he killed her.'

'What could possibly be Ken's motive for killing Julie?'

'Your brother was a bad guy. Make no mistake about that.'

'That's not a motive.' I shook my head. 'Why? If you knew Ken probably didn't kill her, why did you always insist he had?'

He chose not to reply. But, maybe he didn't have to. The answer was suddenly obvious. I glanced at the snapshots on the refrigerator. They explained so much.

'Because you wanted Ken back at any cost,' I said, answering my own question. 'Ken was the only one who could give you McGuane. If he was hiding as a material witness, the world wouldn't really care. There would be no press coverage. No major manhunt. But if Ken murdered a young woman in her family basement—the story of suburbia gone wrong—the media attention would be massive. And those headlines, you figured, would make it harder for him to hide.'

He kept studying his hands.

'I'm right, aren't I?'

Pistillo slowly looked at me. 'Your brother made a deal with us,' he said coldly. 'When he ran, he broke that deal.'

'So that made it OK to lie? Do you know what it did to us?'

'You know something, Will? I don't give a damn. You think you suffered? Look in my sister's eyes. Look at her sons.'

'That doesn't make it right—'

He slammed his hand on the table. 'Don't tell me about right and wrong. My sister was an innocent victim.'

'So was my mother.'

'No!' He pounded the table, this time with his fist, and pointed a finger at me. 'There's a big difference between them, so get it straight. Vic was a murdered cop. He didn't have a choice. He couldn't stop his family's suffering. Your brother, on the other hand, chose to run. That was his decision. Don't you dare compare what your family went through with what my sister went through. Don't you dare.'

I met his eye. Arguing with him would be useless—and I still did not know if he was telling the truth or twisting it for his own purposes. Either way I wanted to learn more.

'So what happened next?' I asked him.

'It was a stroke of luck actually. One of our agents was vacationing in Stockholm. He spotted your brother on the street.'

I blinked. 'Wait a second. When was this?'

Pistillo did a quick calculation in his head. 'Four months ago.'

I was still confused. 'And Ken got away?'

'Hell no. The agent tackled your brother right then and there, and he was extradited back to the United States.'

'So how come it wasn't in the papers?' I asked.

'We kept it under wraps,' Pistillo said.

'Because you still wanted McGuane,' I said. 'And my brother could still deliver.'

'He could help.'

'So you cut another deal with him. Put him in the witness protection programme?'

Pistillo nodded. 'Ken hired a big-time lawyer, and we worked out a deal. We found him a place in New Mexico. He had to report to one of our agents on a daily basis until we needed him to testify. Any break in that deal, and the charges, including the murder charge from Julie Miller, could be reinstated.'

'So what went wrong?'

'McGuane found out and sent out two goons to kill your brother.'

'The two dead men at the house,' I said.

'Yes. They underestimated your brother. He killed them and ran.'

'And now you want Ken back again.'

His gaze wandered back to the photographs. 'Yes.'

'But I don't know where he is.'

'I know that, but he'll reach out to you eventually.'

'What makes you so sure?'

He sighed and stared at the glass. 'Because he called you already.'

A block of lead formed in my chest.

'There were two calls placed from a payphone near his house in Albuquerque to your apartment,' he went on. 'One was made just before the two goons were killed. The other, right after.'

I should have been shocked, but I wasn't. Maybe it finally fitted, only I didn't like how.

'You didn't know about the calls, did you, Will?'

I swallowed and thought about who, besides me, might answer the phone if Ken had indeed called. Sheila.

'No,' I said. 'I didn't know about them.'

He nodded. 'We didn't know that when we first approached you. We'd figured you were the one who answered the phone.'

I looked at him. 'How does Sheila Rogers fit into this?'

'Her fingerprints were found at the murder scene. We figured that Sheila was your go-between, that you'd been helping your brother out. And when Ken ran off, we figured you two knew where he was.'

'But now you know better.'

He nodded. 'I'm telling you all this, Will, because I was afraid you were about to do something stupid.'

'Like talk to the press,' I said.

'Yes—and because I want you to understand. Your brother had two choices. Either McGuane and the Ghost find him and kill him, or we find him and protect him.'

'Right,' I said. 'And you guys have done a bang-up job so far.'

'We're still his best option,' he countered. 'And don't think McGuane will stop with your brother. That attack on Katy Miller was no coincidence. For all your sakes, we need your cooperation.'

I said nothing. I could not trust him. I knew that. I could not trust anyone. That was all I had learned here. But Pistillo was especially dangerous. He had spent eleven years looking into his sister's shattered face. That kind of thing twists you. He had made it clear that he would stop at nothing to get McGuane. He would sacrifice my brother. He had jailed me. Most of all, he had destroyed my family. I thought about my mom, the Sunny smile, and realised that the man sitting in front of me, this man who claimed to be my brother's salvation, had smothered it away. And now he wanted me to help him.

I did not know how much of this was a lie. But I decided to lie right back. 'I'll help,' I said.

'Good,' he said. 'I'll make sure the charges against you are dropped.'

I did not say thank you. As I stood up to leave, he said, 'I understand that Sheila's funeral is coming up. Now that there are no charges against you, you're free to travel.'

I said nothing.

'Are you going to attend?' he asked.

This time I told the truth. 'I don't know.'

Chapter 12

I couldn't stay at home waiting for I-don't-know-what, so in the morning I went to work. Entering Covenant House—I can only compare the experience to an athlete strapping on his 'game face' when he enters the arena. These kids, I reminded myself, deserve nothing less than my best. Cliché, sure, but I convinced myself and faded contentedly into my work.

This is not to say I no longer wanted to pursue where my brother was or who killed Sheila or the fate of her daughter, Carly. But today there was not much I could do. I had called Katy's hospital room, but the blockade was still in place. Squares had a detective agency run Sheila's Donna White pseudonym through the airline computers and thus far, they had not got a hit. So I waited.

I volunteered to work the outreach van that night. Squares joined me—I had already filled him in on everything—and together we disappeared into the dark. The children of the street were lit up in the blue of the night. Squares handed me a stack of phone cards to hand out. We hit a dive on Avenue A known for its heroin and started our familiar rap. We talked and cajoled and listened. I saw the gaunt eyes. I saw the way they scratched away at the imaginary bugs under their skins. I saw the needle marks and the sunken veins.

At four in the morning, Squares and I were back in the van. We had not spoken to each other much in the last few hours. He looked out of the window. The children were still out there. More seemed to come out as though the bricks bled them.

'You know, we should go to Sheila's funeral,' Squares said.

I did not trust my voice.

'You ever see her out here?' he asked. 'Her face when she worked with these kids?'

I had. And I knew what he meant.

'You don't fake that, Will.'

'I wish I could believe that,' I said.

'How did Sheila make you feel?'

'Like I was the luckiest man in the world,' I said.

He nodded. 'You don't fake that either,' he said.

'So how do you explain it all?'

'I don't.' Squares shifted into drive and pulled into the street. 'But we're doing so much with our heads. Maybe we just need to remember the heart now.'

I frowned. 'That sounds good, but I'm not sure it makes sense.'

'How about this then: we go pay our respects to the Sheila we knew.'

'Even if that was just a lie?'

'Even if. But maybe we also go to understand what happened.'

'Weren't you the one who said we might not like what we find?'

'Hey, that's right.' He wriggled his eyebrows. 'Damn, I'm good.'

I smiled.

'We owe it to her, Will. To her memory.'

He had a point. I needed answers. Maybe someone at the funeral could supply some—and maybe the funeral in and of itself would help the healing process. I was willing to give anything a shot.

'And there's still Carly to consider.' Squares pointed out of the window. 'Saving kids. That's what we're all about, isn't it?'

THE EARLY-MORNING flight from LaGuardia to Boise was uneventful. Squares sat on my right. He was reading an article on himself in *Yoga Journal*. Every once in a while he would nod at something he read about himself and say, 'True, too true, I am that.' He did that to annoy me. That was why he was my best friend.

Squares had rented a Buick Skylark. We got lost twice on the trip, but eventually we found the chapel. Edna Rogers was standing outside by herself, smoking a cigarette. Squares pulled to a stop. I felt my stomach tighten. I stepped out of the car and started towards her. Squares stayed by my side. I felt hollow, far away. Sheila's funeral. We were here to bury Sheila.

Edna Rogers kept puffing on the cigarette, her eyes hard and dry. 'I didn't know if you'd make it,' she said to me.

'I'm here.'

'Have you learned anything about Carly?'

'No,' I said, which was not really true. 'How about you?'

She shook her head. 'The police aren't looking too hard. They say there is no record of Sheila having a child.'

The rest was a fast-forward blur. Squares interrupted and offered his condolences. Other mourners approached. They were mostly men in business suits. Listening in, I realised that most worked with Sheila's father at a plant that made garage-door openers. I shook more hands and forgot every name. Sheila's father greeted me with a bear hug and moved towards his coworkers. Sheila had a brother and a sister, both younger, both surly and distracted.

We all stayed outside, almost as though we were afraid to begin the ceremony. Squares drew stares, but he was used to that. He still had on his dust-ridden jeans, but he also wore a blue blazer and grey tie.

Eventually the mourners started to filter into the small chapel. Edna Rogers slid next to me and put her arm through mine, forcing a brave smile. I still did not know what to make of her.

We entered the chapel last. There were whispers about how 'good' Sheila looked, how 'lifelike', a comment I always found creepy in the extreme. I am not a religious fellow, but I like the way we of the Hebrew faith handle our dead—that is, we get them in the ground fast. We do not have open caskets.

Did I want my final memory of Sheila to be here, lying with her eyes closed in a well-cushioned box of fine mahogany? As we got closer, Edna's knees buckled. I helped her stay upright. She smiled at me again, and this time, there seemed to be genuine sweetness in it. 'I loved her,' she whispered. 'A mother never stops loving her child.'

I nodded, afraid to speak. Squares stood behind us, last in line. I kept my eyes diverted, but as we moved forward, there was that unreasonable hope again knocking at my chest. It happened at my mother's funeral, the idea that it was all somehow a mistake, a cosmic blunder. Maybe that was why some people liked open caskets. Finality. You see, you accept. I was with my mother when she died, yet I was still tempted to check the casket that day, just in case maybe God changed his mind.

Many bereaved, I think, go through something like that. Denial is part of the process. So you hope against hope. I was doing that now. I was praying for a miracle—that somehow Sheila was alive, that she had not been murdered and dumped on the side of the road.

But that, of course, did not happen.

Not exactly anyway.

When Edna Rogers and I arrived at the casket, I made myself look down. And when I did, the floor beneath me fell away. I started plummeting.

'They did a nice job, don't you think?' Mrs Rogers whispered.

She took my arm and started to cry. But that was somewhere else, somewhere far away. I was not with her. I was looking down. And that was when the truth dawned on me.

Sheila Rogers was indeed dead. No doubt about that.

But the woman I loved, the woman I'd lived with and wanted to marry, was not Sheila Rogers.

I did not black out, but I came close. A hand shot out and gripped my forearm. Squares. I looked at him. His face was set. His colour gone. Our eyes met and he gave me the slightest of nods.

It hadn't been my imagination. Squares had seen it too.

We stayed for the funeral. What else really could we do? I sat there, unable to take my eyes off the stranger's corpse, quaking, but nobody paid any attention. I was, after all, at a funeral.

After the casket was lowered into the ground, Edna Rogers wanted us to come back to the house. We begged off, blaming the airlines for the tight flight schedule. We slipped into the rental car and drove straight to the airport, and all the while I was muffling the possible euphoria. I didn't want hope clouding my thinking. Not yet.

ON THE PLANE, Squares said, 'If our Sheila is not dead, she's alive.'

I looked at him.

'Hey,' he said, 'people pay big bucks for this kind of wisdom.'

'And to think I get it for free.'

'So what do we do now?'

I crossed my arms. 'Donna White—the pseudonym she bought from the Goldbergs—can you get the agency to widen their search now? Not just the airlines.'

'Sure, I guess.'

The flight attendant gave us our 'snack'. My brain kept whirring. This flight was doing me a ton of good. It gave me time to think.

'It explains a lot,' I said. 'Like her secrecy. Her not wanting her picture taken. Her having so few possessions. Her not wanting to talk about her past.'

Squares nodded. 'So the real Sheila Rogers,' he said, looking up, 'I mean, the one we just buried, she dated your brother?'

'So it seems.'

'And her fingerprints were at the murder scene.'

'Right.'

'So we assume the woman with Ken in New Mexico, that was the dead Sheila Rogers?'

'Yes.'

'And they had a little girl with them,' he went on.

Silence.

Squares looked at me. 'Are you thinking the same thing I am?'

I nodded. 'That the little girl was Carly. And that Ken might very well be her father.'

'Yeah.'

I sat back and closed my eyes.

'Will?'

'Yeah.'

'The woman you loved. Any idea who she is?'

With my eyes still closed, I said, 'None.'

SQUARES WENT HOME. He promised to call me the moment they got anything on the Donna White pseudonym. I headed home, bleeding exhaustion. When I reached my apartment door, I put the key in the lock. A hand touched my shoulder. I jumped back, startled.

'It's OK,' she said.

Katy Miller.

Her voice was hoarse. She wore a neck brace. Her face was swollen. Where the brace stopped under the chin, I could see the deep purple and yellow of bruising. 'Are you OK?' I asked.

She nodded.

I hugged her gingerly, too gingerly, for fear of hurting her further. 'When did you get out?' I asked.

'A few hours ago. I can't stay. If my father knew where I was—'

I held up a hand. 'Say no more.'

We pushed open the door and stepped inside. She grimaced in pain as she moved. We made our way to the couch. I asked her if she wanted a drink or something to eat. She said no.

'Are you sure you should be out of the hospital?'

'They said it's OK, but I need to rest.'

'How did you get away from your father?'

She tried a smile. 'I lied.'

'No doubt.'

She looked away with just her eyes—she could not move her head—and her eyes welled up. 'Thank you, Will.'

I shook my head. 'I can't help but feel it was my fault.'

'That's crap,' she said.

I shifted in my seat. 'During the attack, you yelled out the name John. At least, I think that's what you said.'

'The police told me.'

'You don't remember?'

She shook her head. Tears pushed into her eyes. 'I only remember the hands on my throat.' She looked off. 'I was sleeping. And then someone was squeezing my neck. I remember gasping for air.' Her voice fell away.

'Do you know who John Asselta is?' I asked.

'Yeah. He was friends with Julie.'

'Could you have meant him?'

She considered that. 'I just don't know, Will. Why?'

'I think'—I remembered my promise to Pistillo about keeping her out of it—'that maybe he had something to do with Julie's murder.'

She didn't blink. 'When you say have something to do with—'

'That's all I can say right now.'

'You sound like a cop.'

'It's been a weird week,' I said.

'So tell me what you got.'

'I know you're curious, but I think you should listen to the doctors. You need to rest.'

'You want me to stay out of this?'

'Yes. We're on dangerous ground right now.'

'And what have we been on up to now?'

Touché. 'Look, I need you to trust me here.'

Katy slid closer to me. 'I need to see this through. You, more than anyone, should understand.'

'I do. But I promised I wouldn't say anything.'

'Promised who?'

I shook my head. 'Just trust me, OK?'

She stood up. 'Not OK.' She headed for the door.

'Wait a second,' I said.

'I don't have time for this now,' she said shortly. 'My father will be wondering where I am.'

I stood. 'Call me, OK?' I gave her the cellphone number. I'd already memorised hers.

She slammed the door on her way out.

THE PHONE RANG. I rubbed my eyes and was surprised to see it was morning. I must have fallen asleep on the couch the previous night. I checked the caller ID. It was Squares. I fumbled for the receiver.

'Hey,' I said.

He skipped the pleasantries. 'I think we found our Sheila.'

Half an hour later, I was entering the lobby of the Regina Hotel.

It was less than a mile from my apartment. We had thought she had run across the country, but Sheila—what else was I supposed to call her?—had stayed that close.

The detective agency Squares used had little trouble tracking her down. She had deposited money in a First National and taken out a debit Visa card. You cannot stay in this city—hell, almost anywhere—without a credit card. The days of signing into motels with a false name and paying cash are pretty much over.

She probably assumed that she was safe and that was understandable. The Goldbergs had sold her an ID. No reason to believe that they would ever talk—the only reason they had was because of their friendship with Squares and Raquel, plus the fact that they in part blamed themselves for her theoretical murder.

The credit card had been used to withdraw funds from an ATM yesterday in Union Square. From there it was just a question of hitting the nearby hotels. This was easy. Just call the hotels and ask to speak with Donna White. You do that until one hotel says 'Please hold' and connects you. And now, as I took the steps into the lobby of the Regina Hotel, I felt the jangle. She was alive. I couldn't let myself believe that—would not believe it—until I saw her with my own eyes. Hope does funny things to a brain. It can darken as well as lighten. Where before I had made myself believe that a miracle was possible, now I feared that it might all be taken away from me again.

I approached the front desk. The receptionist was on the phone. I leaned against the desk, feigning relaxed, until she replaced the receiver and gave me her undivided attention. 'May I help you?'

'Yes,' I said. 'I'm here to see Donna White. Could you give me her room number?'

'I'm sorry, sir. We don't give out our guests' room numbers.'

I almost slapped myself on the forehead. How stupid could I be? 'Of course. I'll call up first. Do you have a house phone?'

She pointed to the right. Three white phones, none with keypads, lined the wall. I picked one up and listened to the ring. An operator came on. I asked her to connect me to the room of Donna White, and seconds later I heard the phone ring.

My heart crawled up my windpipe.

Two rings. Then three. On the sixth ring, I was transferred into the hotel's voicemail system. I hung up. Now what? Wait, I guess. What else was there? I bought a newspaper at the stand and found a spot in the corner of the lobby where I could see the door.

An hour passed without incident. My cellphone rang.

'You see her yet?' Squares asked.

'She's not in her room. At least she's not answering the phone.'

'Where are you now?'

'I'm staking out the lobby.'

Squares made a sound. 'Did you really say "staking out"?'

'Give me a break, OK?'

'Look, why don't we just hire a couple of guys from the agency to do it right? They'll call us as soon as she gets in.'

I considered that. 'Not yet,' I said.

And that was when she entered.

My eyes widened. My breathing starting coming in deep swallows. My God. It was really my Sheila. She was alive.

'I have to go,' I said.

I clicked off the power. My Sheila—I'll call her that because I don't know how else to refer to her—had changed her hair. It was cut shorter now and she had curls too. The colour had been darkened to an Elvira black. But the effect . . . I saw her and it was like someone had punched my chest with a giant fist.

Sheila kept moving. I started to rise. The dizziness made me pull up. She walked the way she always walked—no hesitation, head high, with purpose. The elevator door was already opened, and I realised that I might not make it in time.

She stepped inside. I was on my feet now, hurrying across the lobby. I did not want to make a scene. Whatever was happening here—whatever had made her vanish and change names and Lord knows what else—needed to be somewhat finessed. I could not just yell out her name and sprint across the lobby.

My feet clacked on the marble. The sound echoed too loudly in my own ears. I was going to be late. I watched the elevator doors shut.

Damn.

I pressed the call button. Another elevator opened immediately. I started towards it but pulled up. Wait. I didn't know what floor she was on. I checked the lights above my Sheila's elevator. Floor five, then six. Had she been the only one in the elevator? I thought so.

The elevator stopped on the ninth floor. OK, fine. Now I pushed the call button. The same elevator was there. I hurried inside and pressed nine, hoping that I would get there before she entered her room. The doors closed. I leaned against the back until the ninth floor. As the doors opened, I dashed out. The corridor was long. I looked to my left. Nothing. I looked to my right and heard a door close. Like a hunting dog on point, I sprinted towards the sound. Right-hand side, I thought. End of the corridor. I followed the audible scent, if you will, and deduced that the sound had come from either room 912 or 914.

I knocked on both doors. I stood between them and waited.

Nothing.

I knocked again, harder this time. Movement. I was rewarded with some kind of movement emanating from room 912. I slid in front of the door and braced myself. The knob turned and the door began to swing open.

The man was burly and annoyed. He wore a V-neck vest and striped boxers. He barked. 'What?'

'I'm sorry. I was looking for Donna White.'

He put his fists on his hips. 'Do I look like Donna White?'

'Uh, sorry,' I said.

He slammed the door shut.

OK, let's rule out room 912. At least, I hoped I could. I raised my hand to knock on 914, when I heard a voice say, 'Can I help you?'

I turned and at the end of the corridor, I saw a no-neck buzz cut wearing a blue blazer. The blazer had a small logo on the lapel. He puffed out his chest. Hotel security and proud of it.

'No, I'm fine,' I said.

He frowned. 'Are you a guest of the hotel?'

'Yes.'

'What's your room number?'

'I don't have a room number.'

'But you just said—'

I rapped the door hard. Buzz Cut hurried towards me.

'Please come with me,' he said.

I ignored him and knocked again. There was still no answer, so I yelled, 'I know you're not Sheila.' That confused Buzz Cut. We both stopped and watched the door. Nobody answered. Buzz Cut took my arm. I did not put up a fight. He led me downstairs and through the lobby.

I was out on the sidewalk. I turned. Buzz Cut puffed his chest again and crossed his arms. Now what?

I looked for a safe place, as close to the building as possible. I huddled near a plate-glass window. My Sheila was inside. The thought made me light-headed.

OK, fine, so what did that mean exactly? Had she spotted me? Was that why she hurried to the elevator? When I followed her, had I made a mistake about the room number?

I didn't know. I couldn't go home, that was for sure. I took a deep breath and watched the pedestrians race by, so many of them, one bleary mass. And then, looking through the mass, I saw her.

My heart stopped.

She just stood there and stared at me. I felt something inside me give way. I put my hand to my mouth to stifle a cry. She moved towards me, reaching out to me, and pulled me close. 'It's OK,' she whispered.

I closed my eyes. For a long while we just held each other. We did not speak. We did not move. We just slipped away.

Chapter 13

'My real name is Nora Spring.'

We sat together in the lower level of a Starbucks on Park Avenue South, in a corner near an emergency fire exit. No one else was down here. She kept her eyes on the stairs, worried I'd been followed. She held an iced latte between both hands. I went with the frappuccino.

She sipped at the latte. 'I'm sorry,' she said.

I squeezed her hand.

'To run out like that. To let you think'—she stopped—'I can't even imagine what you must have thought.' Her eyes found mine.

'I'm OK,' I said.

'How did you learn I wasn't Sheila?'

'At her funeral. I saw the body.'

'I wanted to tell you, especially after I knew she'd been murdered.'

'Why didn't you?'

Nora turned away. 'Ken told me it might get you killed,' she said.

My brother's name jarred me. For a long time neither of us spoke. I broke the silence. 'How long have you known my brother?'

'Almost four years,' she said.

I nodded through my shock, trying to encourage her to say more, but she still had her face turned away. I gently took hold of her chin and turned her to me. I kissed her lightly on the lips.

She said, 'I love you so much.'

I felt a soar that nearly lifted me off the chair. 'I love you too.'

'I'm scared, Will.'

'I'll protect you.'

She studied my face. I don't know what she was looking for. 'I'm married, Will.'

I tried to keep my expression blank, but it was not easy. Her words wrapped around me and tightened, boa-constrictor-like. I almost pulled my hand away. 'Tell me,' I said.

'Five years ago, I ran away from my husband, Cray. Cray was'—she closed her eyes—'incredibly abusive. I don't want to go into details. They're not important anyway. We lived in a town called Cramden. It's not far from Kansas City. One day, after Cray put me in the hospital, I ran away. That's all you need to know, OK?'

I nodded.

'I don't have any family. I had friends, but I really didn't want to get them involved. Cray is insane. He wouldn't let me go. He threatened . . .' Her voice trailed away. 'Never mind what he threatened. But I couldn't put anyone at risk. So I found a shelter that helps battered women. They took me in. I told them I wanted to start over. But I was afraid of Cray. You see, Cray is a town cop. You have no idea . . . It's impossible to explain.'

I scooted a little closer, still holding her hand. I had seen the effects of abuse. I understood.

'The shelter helped me escape to Europe. I lived in Stockholm. It was hard. I got a job as a waitress. I was lonely. I wanted to come back, but I didn't dare. One day I met an American woman. There was something about her. I guess we both had that on-the-run look. She at least had a husband and daughter. They were in hiding too.'

'This woman,' I said. 'It was Sheila Rogers?'

'Yes.'

'And the husband?' I swallowed. 'That was my brother?'

She nodded. 'They have a daughter named Carly.'

It was beginning to make sense.

'Sheila and I became close friends, and while it took him a little longer to trust me, I grew close to Ken too. I moved in with them, started helping them take care of Carly. Your niece is a wonderful child, Will. Smart and beautiful.'

My niece. Ken had a daughter. I had a niece I had never seen.

'Your brother talked about you all the time, Will. He might mention your mother or your father or even Melissa, but you were his world. He knew all about your working at Covenant House. He had been in hiding for what, seven years? He was lonely too, I guess.'

I blinked and looked down at the table.

'Are you OK?' she asked.

'I'm fine,' I said. I looked up. 'So what happened next?'

'I got in touch with a friend back home. She told me that Cray had hired a private detective and that he knew I was in the Stockholm area. I panicked. I needed a deeper ID, in case Cray kept hunting. Sheila was in the same boat. Her fake ID was all surface, just a name change. And that was when we came up with a simple plan.'

I nodded. This one I knew. 'You switched identities.'

'Right. She became Nora Spring and I became Sheila Rogers. This way, if Cray came after me, he'd only find her. And if the people searching for them found Sheila Rogers, well it adds another layer.'

I considered that, but something still did not add up. 'OK, so that's how you became Sheila Rogers. And'—here was the part I was having trouble with—'somehow we happened to meet. Here in New York City.'

Nora sat back and sighed. 'I'm not sure how to explain this, Will.'

I just held her hand and waited.

'OK, you have to understand. I was so lonely overseas. I spent all that time hearing your brother rave about you, and it was like . . . The truth is, I think I was half in love with you before we ever met. So I told myself when I came to New York that I'd just meet you, see what you were really like. Call it destiny or fate or whatever, but the moment I saw you, that day I walked into Covenant House, I knew that I would love you for ever.'

I was scared and confused and smiling.

'What?' she said.

'I love you.'

She put her head on my shoulder. There was more. It would come in time. For now, we just enjoyed the silence of being with one another. When she was ready, she started up again.

'A few weeks ago, I was sitting at the hospital with your mother. She was in such discomfort, well, you know.'

I nodded.

'I loved your mother. I couldn't stand just sitting there doing nothing. So I broke my promise to your brother. Before she died, I wanted her to know that her son was alive and that he loved her and that he hadn't hurt anybody.'

'You told her about Ken?'

'Yes.'

I froze. I saw it now. What had started it all. The visit to the bedroom after the funeral. The picture hidden behind the frame. I turned to her. 'And you gave my mother that photograph of Ken?'

Nora nodded.

'And you told her he was coming back?'

'Yes.'

'Were you lying?'

She thought about that. 'It wasn't an outright lie. You see, Sheila contacted me when they captured him. Ken had always been very careful. He had all sorts of provisions set up for Sheila and Carly. So when they caught him, Sheila and Carly ran off. The police never knew about them. Sheila stayed overseas until Ken thought it was safe. Then she sneaked back in.'

It was all adding up. 'And she called you from New Mexico when she arrived?'

'Yes.'

That would be the first call Pistillo was talking about—the one from New Mexico to my apartment. 'So then what happened?'

'It all started going wrong,' she said. 'I got a call from Ken. He was in a frenzy. Someone had found them. He and Carly had been out of the house when two men broke in. They tortured Sheila to find out where he'd gone. Ken came home during the attack. He shot them both. But Sheila was seriously wounded. He called and told me that I had to run now. The police would find Sheila's fingerprints. McGuane would also learn that Sheila had been with him.'

'They'd all be looking for Sheila,' I said.

'Yes.'

'And that was you now. So you had to disappear.'

'I wanted to tell you, but Ken was insistent. If you didn't know anything, you'd be safer. And then he reminded me that there was Carly to consider. These people tortured and killed her mother. I couldn't live with myself if anything happened to Carly.'

'How old is Carly?'

'She'd be close to twelve by now.'

'So she was born before Ken ran away?'

'I think she was six months old.'

Another sore point. Ken had a child and never told me about her. I asked, 'Why did he keep her a secret?'

'I don't know.'

I was about to ask a follow-up question when my cellphone

chirped. I glanced at the caller ID. Katy Miller. I pressed the answer button. 'Katy?'

'Oooo, no, sorry, that's incorrect. Please try again.'

The fear flooded back. Oh Christ. The Ghost. I closed my eyes. 'If you hurt her, so help me—'

'Come, come, Will,' the Ghost interrupted. 'Impotent threats are beneath you.'

'What do you want?'

'We need to chat, old boy.'

'Where is she?'

'Who? Oh, you mean Katy? Why, she's right here.'

'I want to talk to her.'

'You want proof she's alive?' the Ghost began in his silkiest hush. 'I can make her scream for you. Would that help?'

I closed my eyes again. 'Please don't hurt her,' I said. 'She has nothing to do with this.'

'Where are you?'

'I'm on Park Avenue South.' I gave him a location two blocks away.

'I'll have a car there in five minutes. Get in it. Oh, and Will?'

'Yes.'

'Don't call anyone. Don't tell anyone. Katy Miller has a sore neck from a previous encounter. I can't tell you how tempting it would be to test it out.' He whispered, 'Still with me, old neighbour?'

'Yes.'

'Hang tight then. This will all be over soon.'

CLAUDIA FISHER BURST into the office of Joseph Pistillo.

Pistillo lifted his head. 'What?'

'Raymond Cromwell didn't report in.'

Cromwell was the undercover agent they'd assigned to Joshua Ford, Ken Klein's attorney. 'I thought he was wired?'

'They had an appointment at McGuane's. He couldn't wear a wire in there.'

'Christ.'

Pistillo was already up and moving. 'Get every available agent. We're raiding McGuane's office now.'

TO LEAVE NORA ALONE like that—I had already got used to the name—was beyond heart-wrenching, but what choice did I have? The idea that Katy was alone with the sadistic psycho gnawed straight into my marrow.

Nora made an effort to stop me, but she understood. Our goodbye kiss was almost too tender. I pulled away. The tears were back in her eyes. 'Come back to me,' she said.

I told her I would and hurried out.

The car was a black Ford Taurus with tinted windows. There was only the driver inside. He handed me an eye-shade, the kind they give out on planes, and told me to put it on and lie flat in the back. I did as he asked. He started the car up and pulled out.

I used the time to think. I ran it all through in my mind and here was what I semiconcluded: eleven years ago, Ken was involved in illegal activities with his old friends, McGuane and the Ghost. My big brother might have been a hero to me, but there was no way round the fact now: Ken had done wrong.

Somewhere along the way, Ken was captured and agreed to help bring down McGuane. He risked his life. He went undercover. McGuane and the Ghost found out. Ken ran. He came home, though I'm not sure why. I'm not sure how Julie fitted in here either. Did the Ghost follow her, knowing that she would lead him to Ken?

I don't know any of that. Not yet anyhow.

Whatever, the Ghost found them, probably in a delicate moment. He attacked. Ken was injured, but he escaped. Julie was not so lucky. The Ghost wanted to put pressure on Ken, so he framed him for the murder. Ken ran. He picked up his steady girlfriend, Sheila Rogers, and their infant daughter, Carly. The three of them disappeared.

Years pass. Ken and Sheila stay together. Then one day, Ken is captured. He is brought back to the States, convinced, I imagine, that they'll hang him for the murder of Julie Miller. But the authorities have always known the truth. They don't want him for that. They want McGuane. And Ken can still help deliver him.

So they strike a deal. Ken hides out in New Mexico. Once they believe it's safe, Sheila and Carly join him. But McGuane learned where they were. He sent two men. Ken wasn't home, but they tortured Sheila to find out where he was. Ken surprises them, kills them, packs his injured lover and daughter in the car, and then he runs again. He warns Nora, who is using Sheila's ID, that the authorities and McGuane are going to be on her tail. She is forced to run too.

That pretty much covered what I knew.

The Ford Taurus came to a stop. I heard the driver shut off the engine. I pulled the eye-shade off and checked my watch. We had been driving for an hour. Then I sat up.

We were in the middle of thick woods. There was a watchtower of sorts, a flimsy aluminium structure that sat on a platform about ten feet off the ground.

The driver turned round. 'Get out.'

I did as he asked. My eyes stayed on the structure, a sort of oversized toolshed. The door opened, and the Ghost stepped out. He had something in his hand. A rope of some kind. A lasso maybe. I froze. 'Katy looks so much like her sister, don't you think?'

I tried to keep the quake from my voice. 'Where is she?'

He blinked. 'She's dead, Will.'

My heart sank.

'I grew bored waiting and—' He started laughing then. The sound echoed in the stillness, ripping through the air. He pointed and shouted, 'Gotcha! Oh, I'm only joshing, Willie. Katy is just fine.' He waved me forward. 'Come on and see.'

I hurried towards the platform, my heart firmly lodged in my throat. There was a rusted ladder. I climbed it. I pushed past him and opened the door to the aluminium shack.

Katy was there.

The Ghost's laugh was still ringing in my ears. I hurried over to her. Her eyes were open, though several strands of hair blocked them. Her arms were tied to the chair, but she look uninjured.

I bent down and pushed the hair away. 'Are you OK?' I asked.

'I'm fine.' Her voice shook. 'What does he want with us?'

'Please let me answer that one.'

We turned as the Ghost entered. He kept the door opened. The floor was littered with broken beer bottles. There was an old filing cabinet in the corner. A laptop computer sat closed in another corner. Three metal folding chairs, the kind used for school assemblies, were out. Katy sat on one. The Ghost took the second and signalled for me to take the one on his left. I remained standing.

The Ghost sighed and stood back up. 'I need your help, Will.' He turned towards Katy. 'And I thought having Miss Miller here join us, well'—he gave me the skin-crawling grin—'I thought she might work as something of an incentive.'

I squared up. 'If you hurt her, if you so much as lay a hand—'

The Ghost did not wind up. He did not rear back. He merely snapped his hand from his side and caught me under the chin. I staggered and turned away, choking. The Ghost took his time. He bent low and used an uppercut. His knuckles landed flush against my kidney. I dropped to my knees, nearly paralysed by the blow.

He looked down at me. 'Your posturing is getting on my nerves,

Willie boy. We need to contact your brother. That's why you're here.'

I looked up. 'I don't know where he is.'

The Ghost slid away from me. He moved behind Katy's chair. He gently, almost too gently, put his hands on her shoulders and stroked the bruises on her neck with his index fingers.

'I'm telling the truth,' I said.

'Oh, I believe you,' he said.

'So what do you want?'

'I know how to reach Ken.'

I was confused. 'What?'

'Have you ever seen one of those old movies where the fugitive leaves messages in classified ads?'

'I guess.'

'Ken is taking that one step further. He uses an Internet newsgroup to leave and receive messages on something called rec.music.elvis. It is, as you might expect, a message board for Elvis fans. So, for example, if his attorney needed to contact him, he would leave a date and time and post with a code name. Ken would then know when to IM said attorney.'

'IM?'

'Instant message. It's like a private chat room. Totally untraceable.'

'So what do you need me for?' I asked.

'Your brother would not agree to meet his attorney,' the Ghost said. 'I believe he suspected a trap. We set up another IM appointment, though. We hope that you can persuade him to meet with us.'

'And if I can't?'

He held up the rope lasso. There was a handle attached to the end. 'Do you know what this is?'

I did not reply.

'It's a Punjab lasso,' he said. 'The Thuggees used it. They were known as the silent assassins. From India.' He looked at Katy and held the primitive weapon up high. 'Need I go on here, Will?'

I shook my head. 'He'll know it's a trap.'

'You must convince him otherwise. If you fail'—he looked up, smiling—'well, you'll see how Julie suffered all those years ago.'

I could feel the blood leaving my extremities. 'You'll kill him.'

'Oh, not necessarily. Your brother made tapes, gathered incriminating information,' he said. 'But he has kept it from the Feds all these years. That's good. It shows cooperation. And'—he stopped, thinking—'he has something I want.'

'What?' I asked.

He shook me off. 'Here's the deal: if he gives it all up and promises to disappear again, we can all go on.'

A lie. I knew that. He'd kill Ken. And he'd kill us all. I had no doubt about that. 'And if I don't believe you?'

He dropped the lasso round Katy's neck. She let out a small cry. The Ghost smiled. 'Does it really matter?'

I swallowed. 'I'll cooperate.'

He let go of the lasso; it hung from her neck like the most perverse necklace. 'Don't touch it,' he said. 'We have an hour. Spend the time staring at her neck, Will. And imagine.'

Chapter 14

McGuane had been caught off guard.

He watched the FBI storm inside. He had not foreseen this. Yes, Joshua Ford was important. Yes, his disappearance would raise eyebrows, though he had made Ford call his wife and tell her he'd been called out of town. But this forceful a reaction? It seemed like overkill.

No matter. McGuane was always prepared. The blood had been cleaned with a newly developed peroxide agent, so that even a blue-light test would reveal nothing. And if a few hairs and fibres were found, so what? He would not deny that Ford and Cromwell were here. And he could offer proof that they had departed. His security people had already replaced the real surveillance tape with the digitally altered one that would show both Ford and Cromwell departing the premises of their own accord.

McGuane pressed a button that automatically erased and reformatted the computer files. Nothing would be found. McGuane automatically backed up via email. Every hour, the computer sent an email to a secret account. The files thus stayed safely in cyberspace. Only McGuane knew the address. He could retrieve the back-up whenever he wanted.

He rose and straightened his tie as Pistillo burst through the door with three other agents. Pistillo pointed his weapon at McGuane.

McGuane spread his hands. No fear. Never show fear. 'What a pleasant surprise.'

'Where are they?' Pistillo shouted.

'Who?'

'Joshua Ford and Special Agent Raymond Cromwell.'

McGuane did not blink. Ah, that explained it. 'Are you saying that Mr Cromwell is a federal agent?'

'I am,' Pistillo barked. 'Now, where is he?'

'I'd like to file a complaint then. Agent Cromwell presented himself as an attorney,' McGuane said, his voice even. 'I trusted that representation. I confided in him, assuming that I was protected by attorney–client privilege. Now you tell me that he is an undercover agent. I want to make sure that nothing I said is used against me.'

Pistillo's face was red. 'Where is he, McGuane?'

'I don't have the slightest idea. He left with Mr Ford.'

'What was the nature of your business with them?'

McGuane smiled. 'You know better than that, Pistillo. Our meeting would fall under attorney–client privilege.'

Pistillo wanted so very much to pull the trigger. 'Search the place,' he barked. 'Box and tag everything. Place him under arrest.'

McGuane let them cuff him. He would not tell them about the surveillance tape. Let them find it on their own. It would have that much more impact that way.

THE GHOST STEPPED into the woods, leaving Katy and me alone. I sat in my chair and stared at the lasso round her neck. It was having the desired effect. I would cooperate.

Katy looked at me and said, 'He's going to kill us.'

It was not a question. It was true, of course, but I still denied it. I promised her that I would find a way out. My eyes moved about the room. Think, Will. And think fast.

Katy whispered, 'I know where we are.'

I turned to her. 'Where?'

'We're in the South Orange Water Reservation,' she said. 'We used to come here and drink. We're not far from Hobart Gap Road.'

'You know the way? I mean, if we make a run for it, would you be able to lead us out?'

'I think so,' she said with a nod. 'Yeah, I could lead us out.'

OK, good. That was a start. I looked out of the door. The driver leaned against the car, smoking a cigarette. The Ghost stood with his hands behind his back, his gaze was turned upwards, as if birdwatching. I quickly scoured the floor and found what I was looking for—a big hunk of broken glass. I peeked out of the door again. Neither man was looking. So I crept behind Katy's chair and started sawing back and forth.

'Are you out of your mind? If he sees you—'

'We have to try something,' I said. 'There'll be a chance to escape somewhere down the line. We have to take advantage of it.'

It was slow work and I was about halfway through the rope when I felt the platform shake. I stopped. Someone was on the ladder. I made it back to my seat just as the Ghost entered.

'You're out of breath, Willie boy,' he said.

I slid the broken glass to the back of my seat, almost sitting on it. The Ghost frowned at me. I said nothing. My pulse raced. The Ghost looked towards Katy. She stared back defiantly. But when I looked towards her, the terror struck me again.

The frayed rope was in plain sight.

'Hey, let's get on with this,' I said.

It was enough of a distraction. The Ghost turned to me. Katy adjusted her hands, giving the frayed rope some cover. Not much if he looked closely. But maybe enough. The Ghost went for the laptop. The computer was already on. The Ghost did some typing. He got on-line with a remote modem. He clacked some more keys and a textbox appeared. He smiled at me and said, 'It's time to talk to Ken.'

My stomach knotted. On the screen, I saw what he had typed:

You there?

We waited. The answer came a moment later.

Here.

The Ghost smiled. He typed some more and hit the return.

It's Will. I'm with Ford.

There was a long pause.

Tell me the name of the first girl you made out with.

The Ghost turned to me. 'He wants proof it's really you.'

I said nothing, but my mind raced.

'I know what you're thinking,' he went on. 'You want to warn him. You want to tell him an answer that's close to the truth.' He moved over to Katy. He picked up the stick end of the lasso. He pulled just a little. The rope coiled against her neck.

'Here's the deal, Will. I want you to stand up, go over to the computer and type in the correct answer. But if you play any games I won't stop tightening this until she's dead. Understand?'

I nodded.

He tightened the lasso a little. Katy made a noise. 'Go,' he said.

I hurried to the screen. Fear numbed my brain. I put my fingers on the keys and typed: Cindi Shapiro.

The Ghost smiled. 'For real? Man, I'm impressed.'

He let go of the lasso. Katy released a gasp. He moved back over to the keyboard. I moved quickly back to my seat. We waited for the response.

Go home, Will.

The Ghost rubbed his face. 'Interesting response,' he said. He thought about it. 'Where did you make out with her?'

'What?'

'Cindi Shapiro. Were you at her house, your house, where?'

'Eric Frankel's bar mitzvah.'

The Ghost smiled. He typed again.

You tested me. Now it's your turn. Where did I make out with Cindi?

Another long pause. I was on the edge of my seat too. It was a smart move by the Ghost, because we really didn't know if this was Ken or not. This answer would prove it one way or another.

Thirty seconds passed. Then:

Go home, Will.

The Ghost typed some more.

I need to know it's you.

A longer pause. And then finally:

Frankel's bar mitzvah. Go home now.

Another jolt. It was Ken . . .

I looked over at Katy. Her eyes met mine. The Ghost typed again.

We need to meet.

The answer came fast: *No can do, Will. Not safe.*

Where R U?

There was another long pause.

I heard about Mom. Was it very bad?

The Ghost did not consult me for this one. Yes.

How's Dad?

Not good. We really need to see you. Please.

I love you, Will. Go home.

Again, as if he were inside my head, the Ghost typed: Wait.

Signing off now, Bro. Don't worry.

The Ghost let out a deep breath. 'This isn't working,' he said.

He typed: Sign off, Ken, and your brother dies.

A pause. Then: *Who is this?*

The Ghost smiled. Hint. Casper the Friendly.

No pause this time.

Leave him alone, John. He has nothing to do with this.

You know better than to play with my sympathies. You show up, you give me what I want, I don't kill him.

Let him go first, then I'll give you what you want.

The Ghost laughed and clacked the keys: Oh please. The yard, Ken. You remember the yard, don't you? Be there in three hours.

Impossible. I'm not even on the East Coast.

The Ghost muttered, 'Bull.' Then he typed frantically: Then you'd better hurry. Three hours. If you're not there, I cut off a finger. I cut off another every half-hour. Then I get creative. Three hours.

The Ghost disconnected the line and stood up. 'Well,' he said with the smile, 'I think that went rather well.'

NORA CALLED SQUARES on his cellphone. She gave him an abbreviated version of the events surrounding her disappearance. Squares listened without interruption, driving towards her all the way. They met up in front of the Metropolitan Life building on Park Avenue.

She hopped into the van and hugged him. 'I'm scared, Squares. Will's brother told me about these people. They'll kill him, for sure.'

Squares mulled it over. 'How do you and Ken communicate?'

'Via a computer newsgroup.'

'Let's get him a message. Maybe he'll have an idea.'

THE GHOST KEPT HIS DISTANCE.

Time was growing short. I palmed the broken glass. If there was an opening, any opening, I was going to risk it.

I glanced at Katy. She was holding up well. I thought again about what Pistillo had said, how adamant he had been that I leave Katy Miller out of this. He was right. This was my fault.

I had to find a way to save her.

The Ghost's cellphone rang. For the first time, I saw something that might have been confusion cross his face. I tensed, though I did not dare reach for the broken glass. Not yet. But I was ready.

He flicked on the cell and put it to his ear. 'Go,' he said.

He listened. I studied his face. His expression remained calm, but something was happening here. He did not speak for nearly two full minutes. Then he said, 'I'm on my way.'

He rose and walked towards me. He lowered his mouth towards my ear. 'If you move from this chair,' he said, 'you'll beg me to kill her. Do you understand?'

I nodded.

The Ghost left, closing the door behind me. There were no windows in the front, so I had no way of knowing what they were doing.

'What's going on?' Katy whispered.

I put a finger to my lips and listened. An engine turned over. A car started up. I thought about his warning. Do not leave this seat. The Ghost was someone you wanted to obey, but then again, he was going to kill us anyway. I bent at the waist and dropped off the chair.

I looked over at Katy. Our eyes met and again I signalled her to remain silent. She nodded.

I stayed as low as possible and crawled carefully towards the door, trying not to cut myself on the shards of glass on the floor.

When I reached the door, I put my head against the floorboard and peeked through the crack at the bottom of the door. I saw the car drive off. I moved round to get a better angle and bang, there he was. The driver. But where was the Ghost?

I did the quick calculation. Two men, one car. One car drives off. I am not much with maths, but that meant that only one man could be left. I turned to Katy. 'He's gone,' I whispered. 'The Ghost drove off.'

I moved back towards my chair and picked up the large piece of broken glass. Stepping as gently as possible, fearing that even the slightest weight change could shake the decrepit structure, I made my way back behind Katy's chair. I sawed at the rope.

'What are we going to do?' she whispered.

'You know a way out of here,' I said. 'We'll make a run for it.'

'The other guy,' she said. 'He could be armed.'

'Yeah, but would you rather wait for the Ghost to come back?'

She shook her head.

Finally the rope cut through. She was free. She rubbed her wrists as I said, 'You with me?'

She nodded.

I pressed my eye against the crack again. I saw the driver. He sat on a tree stump, smoking a cigarette. His back was turned.

I put the glass shard in my pocket and signalled with a lowering palm for Katy to bend down. I reached for the knob. It turned easily. The driver was still not looking. I had to risk it. I pushed the door open more. Enough to squeeze through.

My plan, as it were, was to shimmy down the pole in the back corner. She would go first. If he heard her, a seemingly likely event, well, I had a plan of sorts for that too.

I pointed the way. She nodded and moved towards the pole. She slid off and held on to the pole, firefighter style. The platform lurched as a beam underneath gave way. I stared helplessly as the platform swayed some more. There was a noise not unlike a groan.

'What the hell are you two—?'

The driver was moving towards us. Still holding on, Katy looked up at me.

'Jump down and run!' I shouted.

She let go and fell to the ground. She looked back at me, waiting.

'Run!' I shouted again.

The man now: 'Don't move or I'll shoot.'

'Run, Katy!'

I threw my legs over the side and let go. I landed hard. When I stood up, I saw the man coming at us, maybe fifteen yards away.

'You don't stop, you're dead.'

But he didn't have a gun in his hand.

'Run!' I shouted to Katy again. 'I'm right behind you! Go!'

My job now was to slow down our adversary—slow him down enough so that Katy could escape. 'You can get help,' I urged. 'Go!'

She finally obeyed, leaping over the roots and high grass. I was already reaching into my pocket when the man levelled me with a tackle. The blow was bone-jarring, but I still managed to wrap my arms round him. We tumbled down together. I gave him a bear hug, squeezing him as tight as I could, taking some hits. I knew I was not really hurting him. Didn't matter. It would slow him down. Every second counted. I held on tight. He struggled. I would not let go.

That was when he landed the head butt.

He reared back and struck my face with his forehead. It felt as though a wrecking ball had smashed into my face. My eyes watered up. My grip went slack. I fell away. He wound up for another blow, but something instinctive made me turn away, curl into a ball. He rose to his feet. He aimed a kick at my ribs.

But it was my turn now.

I prepared myself. I let the kick land and quickly trapped his foot against my stomach with one hand. With the other, I jammed the shard of glass into the fat of his calf. He screamed as it sliced deep into his flesh. I pulled it out and stabbed again, this time in the hamstring area. I felt the warm gush of blood.

The man dropped and began to flail, fish-on-the-hook style.

I was about the strike again when he said, 'Please. Just go.'

I looked at him. His leg hung useless. He would not be a threat to us now. And we needed to get away before the Ghost came back.

So I turned and ran.

After twenty yards I heard Katy's voice call, 'Will, over here!'

I turned and spotted her.

'This way,' she said.

We ran the rest of the way. Fifteen minutes later, we headed out of the woods and onto Hobart Gap Road.

WHEN WILL AND KATY emerged from the woods, the Ghost was there. He watched from a distance. Then he smiled and stepped back into his car. He drove back and began the cleanup. There was blood. He had not expected that. Will Klein continued to surprise and yes, impress him. That was a good thing.

When he was done, the Ghost drove down South Livingston Avenue, then stopped at the mailbox on Northfield Avenue. He hesitated before dropping the package through the slot. It was done.

The Ghost took Northfield Avenue to Route 280 and then the Garden State Parkway north. It would not be long now. He thought about how this had all begun, and how it should end. He thought about McGuane and Will and Katy and Julie and Ken.

But most of all, he thought about his vow and why he had come back in the first place.

Chapter 15

A lot happened in the next five days.

After our escape, Katy and I naturally contacted the authorities. We led them to the site where we'd been held. The shack was empty. A search found traces of blood near where I'd stabbed the guy in the leg. But there were no prints or hairs. No clues at all. Then again, I'm not sure it mattered. It was nearly over.

Philip McGuane was arrested for the murder of an undercover federal officer named Raymond Cromwell and a prominent attorney named Joshua Ford. This time, however, he was held without bail. When I met with Pistillo, he had the satisfied gleam in the eye of a man who had finally conquered his own Everest.

'It's all falling apart,' he said gleefully. 'We got McGuane nailed on a murder charge. The whole operation is ripping at the seams.'

I asked him how they finally caught him. Pistillo was only too happy to share.

'McGuane made up this phoney surveillance tape showing our agent leaving his office. This was supposed to be his alibi, and let me tell you, the tape was flawless. That's not hard to do with digital technology—at least, that's what the lab guy told me.'

'So what happened?'

Pistillo smiled. 'We got another tape in the mail. Postmarked from Livingston, New Jersey, if you can believe it. The real tape. It shows two guys dragging a body into the elevator. Both men have already flipped and turned state's evidence. There was a note, too, telling us where to find the bodies. And to top it off, the package also had the tapes and evidence your brother gathered all those years ago.'

I tried to figure it out, but nothing came to me. 'Who sent it?'

'Don't know,' Pistillo said, and he did not seem to care.

'So what happens to John Asselta?' I asked.

'We have an APB out on him.'

'You've always had an All Points Bulletin out on him.'

He shrugged. 'What else can we do? The Ghost was just hired muscle, anyway.'

'He killed Julie Miller.'

'Under orders. Look, Will, I'd love to nail the Ghost, but I'll be honest. It won't be easy. We know he's out of the country already. He'll get work with some despot who will protect him. But in the end the Ghost is just a weapon. I want the guys who pull the trigger.'

I did not agree but I did not argue either. I asked him what this all meant for Ken. He took a while before answering.

'The truth is, I don't know if we need Ken any more. But he's safe now, Will.' He leaned forward. 'I know you haven't been in touch with him'—and I could see in his face that this time he did not believe that—'but if you somehow manage to reach him, tell him to come in from the cold. It's never been safer. And OK, yes, we could use him to verify that old evidence.'

Like I said, an active five days.

Aside from my meeting with Pistillo, I spent that time with Nora. We talked about her past but not very much. The fear of her husband remained enormous. Only time would help that.

Nora told me about my brother, how he'd had money stashed away in Switzerland, how he spent his days hiking, how he seemed to seek peace out there and how peace eluded him. Nora talked about Sheila Rogers too, who found nourishment in both the international chase and her daughter. But mostly, Nora told me about my niece, Carly, and when she did, her face lit up. Abandoning the child had been the hardest part for Nora.

Katy Miller kept her distance. She had gone away—she didn't tell me where and I didn't push it—but she called almost every day. She knew the truth now, but in the end, I don't think it helped much. With the Ghost still out there, there would be no closure.

We were all living in fear, I guess.

But I just needed to see my brother, maybe now more than ever. I thought about his lonely years. I thought about those long hikes of his. That was not Ken. Ken was not one for hiding in shadows.

Katy and I had kept our contact with Ken a secret from Pistillo so that Ken and I could keep our lines of communication open. What we eventually arranged was an Internet newsgroup switch. I told Ken not to let death scare him, hoping he'd pick up the clue. He did. Again it harps back to our childhood. Don't Fear Death a.k.a Ken's favourite song, Blue Öyster Cult's 'Don't Fear the Reaper'. We found a board that posted information on the old heavy-metal band. There were not many posts, but we managed to set up times to IM each other. And then, one day, Ken and I set up a family reunion.

SQUARES OWNED an up-market yoga retreat in Marshfield, Massachusetts. We agreed that it would be the perfect reunion spot.

Melissa flew in from Seattle. Because we were extra-paranoid, we had her land in Philadelphia. She, my father and I met at a rest stop on the New Jersey Turnpike. The three of us drove up together. No one else knew about the reunion, except Nora, Katy and Squares. The three of them were travelling up separately. They'd meet with us tomorrow because they, too, had an interest in closure.

But tonight, the first night, would be for immediate family only.

I handled the driving duties. Dad sat in the passenger seat next to me. Melissa was in the back. No one did much talking. The tension pressed against our chests—mine, I think, most of all. Until I saw Ken with my own eyes, until I hugged him and heard him speak, I would not let myself believe that it was finally OK.

The ride took an agonising five hours. We pulled up to the red farmhouse Squares had had built, complete with fake silo. There were no other cars. That was to be expected. We were supposed to arrive first. Ken would follow. He, I knew, would be coming alone. Carly was somewhere safe. I did not know where. We rarely mentioned her during our communications. Ken might risk himself by attending this reunion. He would not risk his daughter. I, of course, understood.

We paced about the house. Nobody wanted anything to drink. We were all thinking about Mom. She should have been here, too. She should have had the chance to see her son one more time. The grandfather clock's tick-tocking was maddeningly loud in the still room. Dad finally sat down. Melissa moved towards me. She whispered, 'Why doesn't it feel like the nightmare is about to end?'

I didn't even want to consider that.

Five minutes later, we heard an approaching car.

We all rushed to the window and peered out. It was dusk now. The car was a grey Honda Accord, a totally inconspicuous choice. My heart picked up a step. I wanted to rush out, but I stayed where I was.

The Honda came to a stop. I saw a foot hit the ground. And then someone slid out of the car and stood.

It was Ken.

He smiled at me, the Ken smile, that confident, let's-kick-life's-ass smile. That was all I needed. I let out a yelp of joy and broke for the door. I threw it open, but Ken was already sprinting towards me. He burst into the house and tackled me. The years melted away. Just like that. We were on the floor, rolling across the carpet. I giggled like I was seven. I heard him laugh too.

The rest of it was a wonderful blur. Dad jumped on. Then Melissa. I see it now in fuzzy snapshots. Ken hugging Dad; Dad grabbing Ken round the neck and kissing the top of his head, holding the kiss, his eyes squeezed shut, tears streaming down his cheeks; Ken spinning Melissa in the air; Melissa crying, patting her brother as if to make sure he was really there.

Eleven years.

I don't know how long we acted like that, but somewhere along the way we calmed down enough to sit on a couch. Ken kept me close.

'You took on the Ghost and survived,' Ken said, laughing. 'Guess you don't need me covering your back any more.'

And pulling away, I said in a desperate plea, 'No, I do.'

DARKNESS FELL. We all went outside. The night air felt wonderful in my lungs. Ken and I walked ahead. He started telling me the story. It pretty much matched what I already knew. He had done some bad things. He had made a deal with the Feds. McGuane and Asselta had found out.

He skittered round the question of why he had returned home that night, why he had been at Julie's house. But I wanted it all out in the open. So I asked him, 'Why did you and Julie come home?'

Ken took out a pack of cigarettes. 'Julie and I thought it would be a good place to meet up.'

I remembered what Katy said. Like Ken, Julie had not been home in more than a year. I waited for him to go on. He stared at the cigarette, still not lighting it. 'I'm sorry,' he said.

'It's OK.'

'I knew you were still hung up on her, Will. But I was taking drugs back then. I was a total shit.'

'It doesn't matter,' I said. And that was true. It didn't. 'But I still don't understand. How was Julie involved?'

'She was helping me.'

'Helping you how?'

Ken lit the cigarette. I could see the lines on his face now. His features were chiselled but weathered now, making him almost more handsome. His eyes were still pure ice. 'She and Sheila had an apartment in Haverton. They were friends.' He stopped, shook his head. 'Look, Julie got hooked on the stuff. It's my fault. When Sheila came up to Haverton, I introduced them. Julie fell into the life. She started working for McGuane too.'

I had guessed that it was something like that. 'Selling drugs?'

He nodded. 'But when I got caught, when I agreed to go back in, I needed a friend—an accomplice to help me take down McGuane. We all saw it as a way out. A way to find redemption, you know?'

'I guess.'

'Anyway, they were watching me closely. But not Julie. She helped me smuggle out incriminating documents. When I made tapes, I'd pass them on to her. That was why we met up that night. We finally had enough information to give to the Feds.'

'But then the Ghost found out where you were.'

'Yes.'

'How?'

We reached a fence post. Ken put his foot up. 'I don't know, Will. Look, Julie and I were both so scared. Maybe that was part of it. Anyway, we were reaching the endgame. We were in the basement, on that couch, and we started kissing . . .'

'And?'

'Suddenly there was a rope round my neck.' Ken took a deep drag. 'I was on top of her, and the Ghost had sneaked up on us. Next thing I knew, I was being strangled. I thought my neck would snap. I'm not even sure what happened next. Julie hit him, I think. That's how I got loose. He punched her in the face. I pulled away and started backing up. The Ghost took out a gun and fired. The first shot hit my shoulder.' He closed his eyes.

'I ran then. God help me, I just ran.'

We both soaked in the night. Ken worked on his cigarette some more. I knew what he was thinking. Ran away. And then she died.

'He had a gun,' I said. 'It's not your fault.'

'Yeah, sure.' But Ken did not appear convinced. 'You can probably guess what happened from there. I ran back to Sheila. We grabbed Carly and we took off. It wasn't until a few days later, when the papers started listing me as a suspect in Julie's murder, that it hit me that I was not just running from McGuane but the whole world.'

I asked the question that had been bothering me from the start. 'Why didn't you tell me about Carly?'

His head snapped away as if I'd connected with a right on his jaw.

'Ken?'

He would not face me. 'Can we skip that for now, Will? It's no big secret.' His voice was strange now. I could hear the confidence start coming back, but it was somehow different, a shade off maybe. 'I was in a dangerous spot. The Feds captured me not long before her birth. I was afraid for her. So I didn't tell anybody she even existed. I didn't even live with them. Carly stayed with her mother and Julie. I didn't want her connected to me in any way. You understand?'

'Yeah, sure,' I said. I waited for him to say more.

'The Feds were lucky to catch me. Though sometimes I think that maybe I wanted to be caught. Living like we were, always in fear, never putting down solid roots . . . it wears on you, Will. I missed you all so much. You most of all. Maybe I just got careless.'

'So they extradited you?'

'Yeah.'

'And you cut another deal.'

'I thought they were going to pin Julie's murder on me for sure. But when I met up with Pistillo, well, he still wanted McGuane so badly. And they knew I hadn't killed Julie. So . . .' He shrugged.

Ken talked then about New Mexico, about how he had never told the Feds about Carly and Sheila, still protecting them. 'I didn't want them to come back that early,' he said, his voice softer now. 'But Sheila wouldn't listen.'

Ken told me about how he and Carly had been out of the house when the two men came by, how he came home and found them torturing his beloved, how he killed both men, and once again, how he ran. He told me how he called Nora at my apartment—that would be the second call the FBI knew about. 'I knew that they would come after her. So I told her she had to hide.'

It took a couple of days for Ken to find a discreet doctor in Las Vegas. The doctor had done what he could, but it was too late. Sheila died the next day. Not sure what else to do—and hoping it would take pressure off Nora—he put the body of his lover of eleven years on the side of a road and drove away with Carly in the back of the car.

Melissa and Dad hovered closer now. We all let in a little silence. 'What then?' I asked softly.

'I dropped Carly off with a friend of Sheila's. A cousin actually. I knew she'd be safe there. Then I started making my way east.'

And when he said that, when those words about making his way east left his mouth . . . that was when it all started to go wrong.

Have you ever had one of those moments? You are listening, you are nodding, you are paying attention. Everything seems to be making sense, and then you see something, something small, something seemingly irrelevant—and you realise with mounting dread that everything is terribly wrong.

'We buried Mom on a Tuesday,' I said.

'Right,' Ken said, looking confused.

'You were in Las Vegas that day, right?'

He thought about it. 'That's right.'

I played it over in my head. 'I don't get something.'

'What?'

'On the afternoon of the funeral'—I stopped, waited for him to face me—'you were at the other graveyard with Katy Miller.'

Something flickered across his face. 'What are you talking about?'

'Katy saw you at the cemetery. You were standing under a tree near Julie's tombstone. You told Katy you were innocent. You told her you were back to find the real killer. How did you do that if you were on the other side of the country?'

My brother did not respond then. We both stood there. I felt something inside me start shrinking.

'I lied about that.'

We all turned as Katy Miller stepped out from behind the tree. I looked at her and said nothing. She moved closer.

Katy had a gun in her hand.

It was pointed at Ken's chest. My mouth dropped open. Katy looked directly at me, trying to tell me something I could never understand. I shook my head.

'I was only six years old,' Katy said. 'Easy enough to dismiss as a witness. I saw your brother that night. But I saw John Asselta too. Maybe I mixed them up, the cops could say. How would a six-year-old know the difference between cries of passion and agony anyway? It was easy for the Feds to finesse what I told them. They wanted McGuane. To them, my sister was just another junkie.'

'What are you talking about?' I said.

Her eyes turned to Ken. 'I was there that night, Will. Hiding behind my father's old army trunk. I saw everything.' She looked at me again and I am not sure I ever saw such clear eyes.

'John Asselta didn't murder my sister,' she said. 'Ken did.'

My support beams started giving way. I started shaking my head again. I looked at Melissa. Her face was white. I tried my father, but his head was down.

Ken said, 'You saw us making love.'

'No.' Katy's voice was surprisingly steady. 'You killed her, Ken. You chose strangulation because you wanted to pin it on the Ghost—the same way you strangled Laura Emerson because she threatened to report the drug selling at Haverton.'

I stepped forward. Katy turned to me. I stopped.

'When McGuane failed to kill Ken in New Mexico, I got a call from Asselta,' she began. 'He told me how they had already captured your brother in Sweden, but because he could still deliver McGuane they were keeping it quiet. I was in shock. After all this time, they were going to let Julie's murderer just walk away? I couldn't allow that. Not after what my family had been through. Asselta knew that, I guess. That was why he contacted me.'

I was still shaking my head, but she pressed on.

'My job was to stay close because we figured that if Ken contacted anybody, it would be you. I made up that story about seeing him at the graveyard, so you would trust me.'

I found my voice. 'But you were attacked,' I said. 'In my apartment. You even called out Asselta's name.'

'Think about that, Will.' Her voice was so even, so confident. 'Why were you cuffed to the bed like that?'

'Because he was going to set me up, the same way he set up—'

Now she was the one shaking her head. Katy pointed the gun at Ken. 'He cuffed you because he didn't want you to get hurt.'

I opened my mouth, but nothing came out.

'He needed to get me alone. He needed to find out what I'd told you—to see what I'd remembered—before he killed me. And yes, I called out John's name. Not because I thought it was him behind the mask. I called out to him for help. And you saved my life, Will. He would have killed me.'

My eyes slowly slid towards my brother.

'She's lying,' Ken said. 'Why would I kill Julie? She was helping me.'

'That's almost true,' Katy said. 'And you're right: Julie had agreed to help bring McGuane down. It was her chance for redemption. But your brother took it a step too far.'

'How?' I asked.

'Ken knew that he had to get rid of the Ghost too. No loose ends. So he framed Asselta for Laura Emerson. Ken figured that Julie would have no problem going along with that. But he was wrong. Julie cared about John. I think she was the only one who ever did. She would gladly bring down McGuane. But she would never hurt John Asselta.'

I couldn't speak.

'That's bull,' Ken said. 'Will?'

I did not look at him.

Katy continued. 'When Julie found out what Ken was going to do, she called the Ghost to warn him. Ken came to our house to get the tapes and files. She tried to stall him. They had sex. Ken asked for the evidence, but Julie refused to give it to him. When he finally realised what was up, he snapped and strangled her. The Ghost arrived seconds too late. He shot Ken as he ran away. I think he would have gone after him, but when he saw Julie dead on the floor, he just lost it. He fell to the floor. He cradled her head and let out the most anguished, inhuman wail I've ever heard.'

'But the Ghost,' I said, flailing. 'He kidnapped us . . .'

'We set that up,' she said. 'He let us escape. We had no idea you'd hurt that driver so badly.'

'But why?'

'Because the Ghost knew the truth.'

'What truth?'

She again gestured towards Ken. 'That your brother would never show just to save your life. That something like this'—she lifted her free hand—'was the only way he'd ever agree to meet you.'

I shook my head again.

'We had a man wait at the yard that night. Just in case. No one came.'

I stumbled back. I looked at Melissa. I looked at my father. And I knew that it was all true. Every word that she said. It was true.

Ken had killed Julie.

'I never meant to hurt you,' Katy said to me. 'But my family needs closure. The FBI had set him free. I had no choice. I couldn't let him get away with what he did to my sister.'

My father spoke for the first time. 'So what are you going to do now, Katy? Are you just going to shoot him?'

Katy said, 'Yes.'

And that was when all hell broke loose again.

My father made the sacrifice. He dived towards Katy. She fired the gun. My father staggered and continued towards her. He knocked the weapon from her hands. He also went down, holding his leg.

But the distraction had been enough.

When I looked up, Ken had whipped out his own gun. His eyes were focused on Katy. He was going to shoot her, no hesitation.

I jumped towards him. My hand hit his arm just as he pulled the trigger. The gun went off, but the shot was wild. I tackled my brother. We rolled on the ground again, but this time he elbowed me in the stomach and winded me. He rose. He pointed the gun at Katy.

'No,' I said.

'I have to,' Ken said.

I grabbed him. We wrestled. I told Katy to run. Ken quickly gained the advantage. He flipped me over. Put the barrel of the gun against my forehead.

I heard Melissa scream. I told her to stay back. In the corner of my eye, I saw her take out a cellphone and start dialling.

'Go ahead,' I said. 'Pull the trigger.'

'You think I won't?' he said.

'You're my brother.'

'Didn't you hear anything Katy said? Don't you understand what I'm capable of—how many people I've hurt and betrayed?'

'Not me,' I said softly.

He laughed, his face inches from mine, the gun still pressed against my forehead. 'Not you?' he said. He lowered his lips towards me.

'You,' he whispered in my ear, 'I've hurt and betrayed more than anyone.'

His words hit me like a ton of bricks. I looked up at him. His face tensed and I was sure he was going to pull the trigger. I closed my eyes and waited. There were shouts and commotion, but all of that seemed very far away. What I heard now—the only sound that really reached me—was Ken crying. I opened my eyes. The world faded away. There was just the two of us.

I can't say what happened exactly. Maybe Ken looked down and saw me vulnerable, helpless, and something instinctive took over.

Maybe that was what shook him. I don't know. But as our eyes met, his face began to soften, started shifting in degrees.

And then it all changed again.

I felt Ken's grip on me loosen, but he kept the gun against my forehead. 'I want you to make me a promise, Will,' he said.

'What?'

Ken closed his eyes now, and I saw genuine anguish. 'I want you and Nora to take care of Carly. Promise me.'

'But what about—?'

'Please,' Ken said, his voice a desperate plea. 'Promise me.'

'OK, I promise.'

He was crying hard now. Tears ran down his cheeks, wetting both our faces. 'Promise me, dammit. You raise her as your own. Never let her visit me in prison. Promise me that, Will. Or I'll start firing.'

'Give me the gun first,' I said, 'and I'll promise.'

Ken looked down at me. He pushed the gun into my hand. And then he kissed me hard. I wrapped my arms round him. He cried into my chest like a small child. We were like that for a long time, until we heard the sirens.

I tried to push him away. 'Go,' I whispered to him, pleading. 'Please. Just run.'

But Ken did not move. Not this time. Ken stayed in my arms. He held on to me until the police came over and pulled him away.

FOUR DAYS LATER. Carly's plane was on time.

Squares drove us to the airport. He, Nora and I headed towards Newark Airport's Terminal C together. Nora walked up ahead. She knew the child and was anxious and excited to see her again. Me, I was anxious and scared. I was about to raise a twelve-year-old girl I did not know. I would do my best, but I could never be Carly's father. I had come to terms with a lot about Ken, but his insistence on never seeing his daughter again gnawed at me. He wanted, I assume, to protect his child. He felt, again I assumed, that the girl was best off without him.

I say 'assumed' because I could not ask him. Once in custody, Ken had refused to see me too. I did not know why, but his whispered words . . . *You I've hurt and betrayed more than anyone* . . . kept echoing inside me, shredding with razor talons, inescapable.

Squares stayed outside. Nora and I rushed in. We found the arrivals gate and hurried down the corridor.

We sat and held hands and waited. Melissa had decided to stay in town for a little while. She was nursing my father back to health. Yvonne Sterno had, as promised, got the exclusive story. I don't know what it will do for her career.

As for Katy, no charges had been filed following the shooting. I thought about how much she needed closure, and I wondered if that night had helped her or not. I think maybe it did.

I had, of course, been crushed to learn the truth about my brother, and yet—this is going to sound odd—it was somehow OK. The ugliest truth, in the end, was still better than the prettiest of lies. My world was darker, but it was back on its axis.

Nora leaned over. 'I love you,' she said. 'Carly will love you too.'

The Continental Airlines gatekeeper picked up the microphone and announced that Flight 672 had landed. Carly's flight. I turned to Nora. She smiled and gave my hand another squeeze.

I let my eyes travel then. My gaze floated across the waiting passengers, the men in suits, the women with carry-ons, the families heading for vacation, and that was when I saw him looking at me. My heart stopped.

The Ghost. A spasm ripped through me.

The Ghost beckoned me towards him. I stood as if in a trance.

Nora said, 'Where are you going?'

'I'll be right back,' I said. 'I just need to run to the bathroom.'

I kissed the top of Nora's head gently. She looked concerned but I knew that running would be futile.

I had to face him.

I started walking in the direction where he'd been. When I passed a long row of abandoned payphones, I heard him.

'Will?'

I turned and he was motioning for me to sit next to him. I did.

'I didn't come back for your brother,' the Ghost said. 'I came back for Carly.'

His words turned me to stone. I said, 'You can't have her.'

He smiled. 'You don't understand.'

'Then tell me.'

The Ghost shifted his body towards me. 'You want people lined up, Will. You want the good guys on one side, the bad on the other. It doesn't work like that. Love, for example, leads to hate. I think that was what started it all. Primitive love. Your father. He loved Ken too much. I look for the seed, Will, and that's where I find it. In your father's love.'

'I don't know what you're talking about.'

'What I'm about to say,' the Ghost continued, 'I've only told one other person. Do you understand?'

I said that I did.

'You have to go back to when Ken and I were in the fourth grade,' he said. 'You see, I didn't stab Daniel Skinner. Ken did. But your father loved him so much that he protected him. He bought off my old man. Paid him five grand. Believe it or not, your father almost saw himself as charitable. My old man beat me all the time. The way your father saw it, I would either get off on self-defence or end up getting therapy and three square meals a day.'

I was stunned into silence.

'I only told one person the truth,' he said. 'Any guesses?'

Something else fell into place. 'Julie,' I said.

He nodded. The bond. It explained a lot.

'So why are you here?' I asked.

The Ghost sighed. 'There is no easy way to tell you this, Will, but maybe science can help.'

He handed me a folder. I looked down at it. 'Open it,' he said.

I did as he asked.

'It's the autopsy report of one Julie Miller.'

The cold spread inside me. He flipped it open and pointed to an entry and started reading, 'Pubic scars, changes in the microscopic architecture of the breast and uterine tissues,' he said. 'And the trauma was recent. See here? The scar from the epislotomy was still pronounced.'

I stared at the words.

'Julie did not come home just to meet up with Ken. She was finding herself again after a bad spell. She wanted to tell you the truth.'

'What truth?'

'Julie had a baby six months before she died,' the Ghost said. 'She and the child, a girl, lived with Sheila Rogers in that apartment. Sheila loved the child too. When Julie was murdered and your brother needed to escape, Sheila wanted to keep it as her own. And Ken, well, he saw how useful a baby could be to give cover to an international fugitive. He had no children. Neither did Sheila. It would be better than the best disguise.'

Ken's whispered words came back to me. *You I've hurt and betrayed more than anyone*.

The Ghost's voice cut through the haze. 'Do you understand, Will? You're not a substitute here. You're Carly's real father.'

I don't think I was breathing any more. I stared out at nothing.

Hurt and betrayed. My brother. My brother had taken my child.

The Ghost stood up. 'I didn't come back for revenge or even justice,' he continued. 'The truth is, Julie died protecting me. I failed her. I made a vow that I would save her child. It took me eleven years.'

I stumbled to my feet. We stood side by side. Passengers were pouring off the plane. The Ghost jammed something in my pocket. A piece of paper. I ignored it.

'I sent that surveillance tape to Pistillo, so McGuane won't bother you. I found the evidence in the house that night and kept it all these years. You and Nora are safe now.'

More passengers disembarked. I stood up and waited and listened.

'Remember that Katy is Carly's aunt, that the Millers are her grandparents. Let them be a part of her life. Do you hear me?'

I nodded, and that was when Carly came through the gate. Everything inside me shut down. The girl walked out with such poise. Like . . . like her mother. Carly looked around and when she spotted Nora, her face broke into the most amazing smile. My heart shattered, right there and then. That smile, you see, belonged to my mother. It was Sunny's smile, like an echo from the past, a sign that not all of my mother—nor all of Julie—had been extinguished.

I choked back a sob and felt a hand on my back.

'Go now,' the Ghost whispered, gently pushing me forward.

I glanced back, but he was already gone. So I did the only thing I could. I made my way towards the woman I loved and my child.

LATER THAT NIGHT, after I kissed Carly and helped her to bed, I found the piece of paper he'd jammed into my pocket. It was just the first lines of a newspaper clipping:

KANSAS CITY HERALD

Man Found Dead in Car

Cramden, Missouri—Cray Spring, an off-duty police officer with the Cramden force, was found strangled in his car, apparently the victim of a robbery. His wallet was reportedly missing. Police chief Evan Kraft said that there were no suspects at this time, and that the investigation was ongoing.

HARLAN COBEN

Harlan Coben is the author of a critically acclaimed mystery series featuring sports agent Myron Bolitar, but it was only in 2001, when *Tell No One* was published, that he hit the best-seller lists. Following hard on the heels of this success, his new novel, *Gone for Good,* is full of the author's trademark twists and turns. His philosophy as a writer is simple. 'I want to make the pulse pound and the heart stir,' Coben explains. 'I always keep the readers in mind, thinking about what will keep them turning the pages. I try to write suspense. If I'm boring you I'm in big trouble.'

The author lives with his wife and family in a small town in New Jersey and says that he finds suburban life a rich subject for fiction. 'In *Gone For Good* I wanted to write a suspenseful story involving a suburban family—the ties, the bonds, the betrayals. And I wanted to write from the viewpoints of both the victim's and the suspect's families. Evil acts ripple. Julie's murder in the novel destroys more than one family. I wanted to show that.'

One of the most powerful aspects of the novel is Will Klein's work among the street children and homeless of New York. Covenant House, where Will is based, is a real place and Coben was able to obtain inside information. 'My wife is medical director for Covenant House in Newark, so I had incredible access to the work they do. It's a wonderful organisation that saves runaways every single day. I took some liberties as a writer, of course, but it was a great place to set a story.'

In the novel Harlan Coben has created a memorable sidekick for Will Klein in the form of a yoga guru called Squares. Coben enjoyed creating a character whose image is so different from his personality. 'I love sidekicks,' he says. 'And one of the things I've noticed in both life and books is that no one is exactly what you think they might be. The schoolmarm might be a nymphomaniac and the politician might be telling the truth. You never know.'

BLACK ICE

MATT DICKINSON

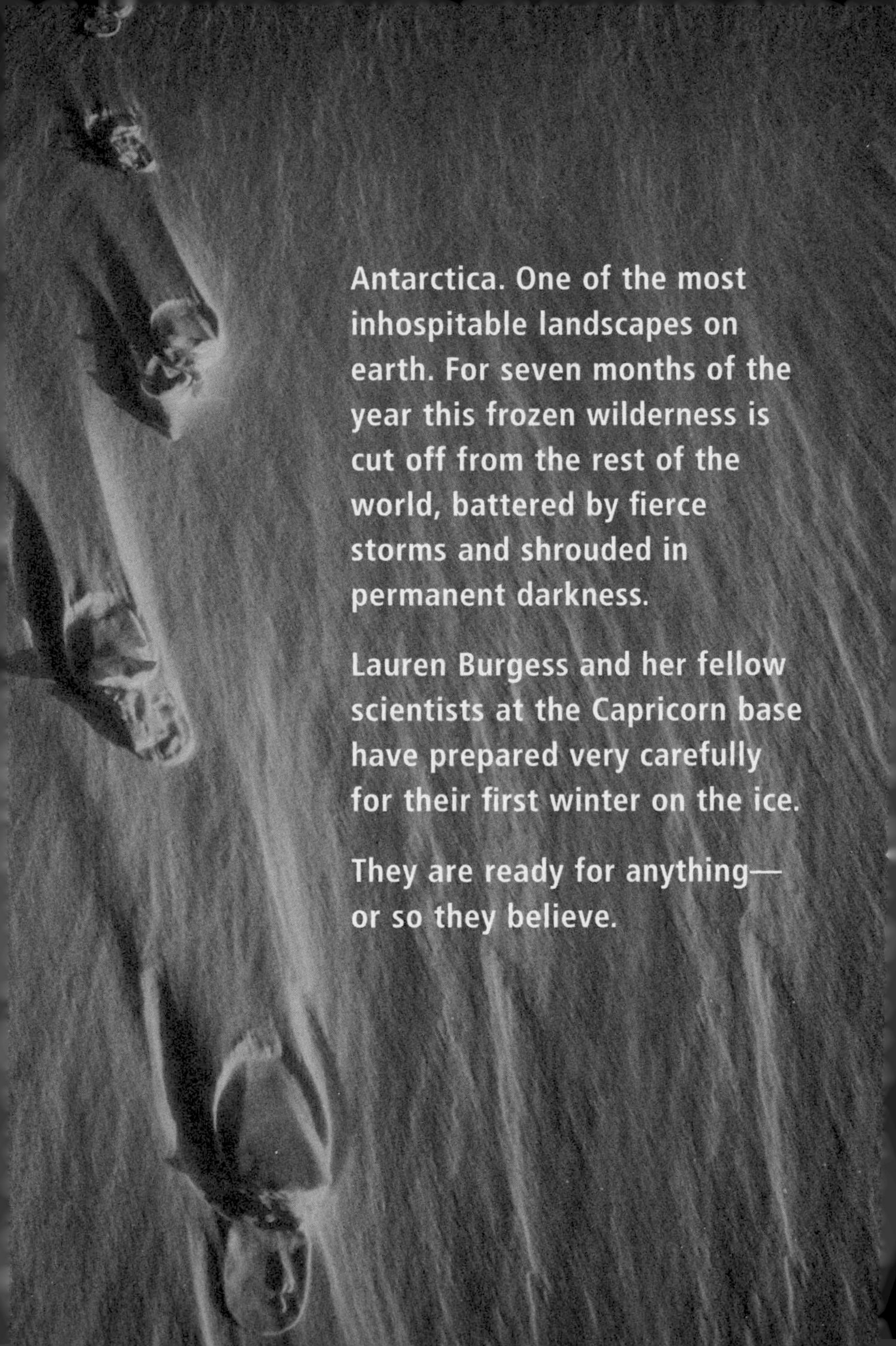

Antarctica. One of the most inhospitable landscapes on earth. For seven months of the year this frozen wilderness is cut off from the rest of the world, battered by fierce storms and shrouded in permanent darkness.

Lauren Burgess and her fellow scientists at the Capricorn base have prepared very carefully for their first winter on the ice.

They are ready for anything—or so they believe.

1 ANTARCTICA

Enchanted as a child by tales of the last unexplored continent on earth, Carl Norland had fallen in love with Antarctica. Now, not far short of his twenty-seventh birthday, the Norwegian explorer was beginning to appreciate that it was a love affair that might—quite soon—end with his death.

He turned his face to the north. Somewhere beyond that dark horizon there was a world of warmth, of light, and the love of a wife and daughter. But if he didn't act fast, he was never going to see that world again.

Carl crawled into the tent and pulled the emergency beacon from the side pocket of the rucksack. He cradled the device in his hands, ignoring the searing pain in his fingers, the crackle of the frostbite blisters as his skin flexed and broke. Many days earlier the last battery on their main radio had failed, leaving this transmitter as their final lifeline. This box of tricks had to work, he prayed, or no one would ever find them.

The casing was yellow plastic, a stubby black rubber aerial protruding for six inches or so from the top. Next to it, protected by a plastic seal, was a red switch marked *Activate only in emergency*. Once activated, the beacon would emit a constant radio pulse on the international distress frequency of 121.5 megahertz, which would be picked up by a passing satellite. Their position would be fixed and a rescue plane would be despatched from Tierra del Fuego—the landmass closest to Antarctica.

More than anything he had ever desired before, Carl wanted to rip open that seal and throw the switch.

He stumbled out of the tent and stood swaying on his swollen feet as a bitter gust of wind ran through the camp. What were they trying to prove here? Carl squinted at the immensity of the landscape that surrounded them and realised he was no longer sure.

Three and a half months earlier, he and one other had set out from the far side of this continent. Their plan was an audacious one—a crossing of Antarctica at its widest point—a trek of more than 2,000 miles, which would establish their names alongside the great legends of Antarctic exploration.

They were manhauling, each starting out with a sledge carrying 500 pounds of gear. The weight had been crucifying, the straps chafing running sores into their flesh, their bodies deteriorating with every passing day until they were on the point of collapse.

Now—eighty miles short of their objective—they had failed. There was no food left. The rolling ocean of ice had sucked the flesh from their bones, supped the very essence of sinew and muscle away until they were reduced to the stumbling progress of a child.

Winter was closing in on them. Daylight was down to just a few gloomy hours a day. Soon, the permanent night of the Antarctic winter would fall across the ice, and then there would be no escape.

It was time to get out. And fast.

Before him, slumped in a despondent heap against his sledge, was Julian Fitzgerald—crosser of continents, planter of flags, conqueror of the heights and depths, and member of that elite band of media-friendly explorers whose faces are as familiar on TV chat shows as they are in the hallowed corridors of the Royal Geographical Society of London and the Explorers Club of New York. The fact that a significant number of Fitzgerald's expeditions had ended in failure never seemed to diminish the media appetite for more of the same.

Fitzgerald had his fans, but they wouldn't have recognised the faded figure lying on the ice in front of Carl. He was staring into the white beyond, his face devoid of expression.

Carl sat down, easing the pain in his legs, wondering if he had the courage to tell Fitzgerald what he had decided, and wondering, also, how this adventure had ever gone so wrong.

The two men had met a year before—a chance encounter at the Alpine Club, where Fitzgerald was holding a launch party for the publication of his latest expedition book. Fitzgerald was initially offhand, but on learning that Carl had recently skied across the

Greenland ice cap in record time, his attitude changed, and they agreed to meet for lunch at Fosters, where traditional English fare, such as jugged hair and spotted dick, was treated with due gastronomic reverence.

'This is my favourite restaurant,' Fitzgerald confided. 'I dream of it while I'm out on the ice.'

He went on to tell Carl of his planned Antarctic journey and asked the Norwegian—quite bluntly—to explain his background.

Carl told Fitzgerald about his home town of Trondheim, on Norway's western shore, and about his role as fisheries researcher on a three-year postgraduate attachment to London University. He told him of his English wife, Sally, about his six-month-old daughter, Liv, but mostly he talked about what Fitzgerald was really interested in—his passion for polar travel and overland expeditions. His crossing of the Greenland ice cap had been a great triumph, and now he had his sights set on bigger things. If he was offered the opportunity to go south, Carl told Fitzgerald, he would jump at the chance.

Fitzgerald had been impressed with the Norwegian's enthusiasm, and proposed—straight out—that they team up for the attempt.

'Just one thing,' he'd told Carl. 'Even though there'll only be two of us out there, I'm still the leader of this expedition. You accept that my decisions will be final?'

'Yes, sir.' Carl gave a mock salute in an attempt to make the moment a humorous one. But Fitzgerald did not smile.

'I CAN'T TAKE ANOTHER STEP,' Carl told Fitzgerald.

Fitzgerald stared right at him for long moments before he spoke, the booming, operatic voice of which he was so proud reduced to a plaintive croak. 'You want to quit? When we're so close?'

'I don't want another fight,' Carl told him quietly. 'We're talking life and death now, and I think you know it.'

Fitzgerald pulled a map from his pocket and stabbed it with a finger. 'Eighty miles, Carl, and the widest crossing is ours. Write our names in the history books once and—'

'You think anyone gives a damn?' Carl felt the familiar frustration well up inside him. 'And if the weather closes in? We haven't eaten for a week. Winter is just around the corner. If that plane can't get to us, we'll both starve to death.'

'I should have gone solo.' Fitzgerald retreated to his habitual mantra. 'I'd have been faster without you.'

They sat in silence for many minutes, looking out across the unending expanse of ice, while Carl pondered the manner in which his relationship with Fitzgerald had deteriorated.

Fitzgerald's hoped-for balancing act of the master and his apprentice had been way off the mark. The concept of Carl deferring to Fitzgerald's greater range of experience had been sorely tested by a number of bitter arguments between the two men: rows over navigation, over food, over Fitzgerald's use of the radio for endless media interviews even when their battery supply was dwindling fast.

On an emotional level, Fitzgerald had been reserved, taciturn even, giving little away. The one subject on which he could get emotional was his past failings—whether imagined or real. Criticism of any of his previous expeditions, particularly by the media, could leave the explorer apoplectic with fury. When he heard on the radio that an investigative reporter was putting a damning documentary together about his recent disastrous Tierra del Fuego Youth Expedition—a trip that had ended with several of the participants hospitalised with serious injuries—Fitzgerald went ballistic, going into a sulk that lasted for weeks.

Faced with a virtually silent travelling companion, Carl sought solace with his diary. He wrote for hours in the tent each night, venting his frustration at what he saw as Fitzgerald's increasingly irrational decision-making, and his growing fears that the trip would end in disaster.

The crux had come at the South Pole—the halfway point and effectively the moment of no return. According to Carl's calculations, their food would run out before the challenge was over. He had been tempted to call a halt. But now it was too late. As Carl sat there, he knew that he should never have continued beyond the Pole.

'The saddest thing of all,' Carl told Fitzgerald, 'is that I used to love this place. Now I think of it as the enemy.'

'We can still do it,' said Fitzgerald. 'Your mind is letting you down.'

'Look at me,' Carl pleaded. 'I've lost too much weight. I can taste ammonia in my mouth . . . Do you know what that means? Our bodies are consuming themselves.'

Fitzgerald turned away in disgust. 'If you're so desperate to get out, why didn't you just push the ruddy switch anyway?'

Carl sighed. 'We should take all the important decisions together.'

'Very noble, I don't think.'

They sat in strained silence for a while, both exhausted by the expenditure of nervous energy.

'Do it if you want,' Fitzgerald told him, finally, 'but I want it to be understood between us that it's you who is calling the expedition to a halt, not me. It's not in my nature to quit.'

Carl took the emergency beacon and ripped the protective seal away. 'I'm doing this for both of us. In time you'll appreciate that.'

He clicked the switch to ON. A faint bleep could be heard emitting from the tiny loudspeaker.

RICHARD LEIGHTON was in his hotel room in Ushuaia when the telephone rang. It was Julian Fitzgerald's radio operator, Irene Evans, calling from the expedition control room at the airport.

'We just got a call. They let off the beacon. Get down here fast.'

'Thank heavens for that. I'll be right with you.'

Please God, Richard thought as he packed his kitbag, don't let this be a false alarm. Kicking his heels in Tierra del Fuego wasn't what he'd expected when he was offered the job of his dreams.

Just a month earlier, he had walked into the offices of the *Daily Mail* and been given his first foreign assignment, the royal tour to Brazil. He filed his reports, stayed awake during interminable official meals and slipped easily into the reporters' 'club' that followed the British royals around the globe. Then the bad news, as he was packing his bags for the flight home: the call from his editor in London.

'Ever heard of a place called Ushuaia?'

'Can't say I have.'

'I want you down there as soon as possible. Seems that the explorer Fitzgerald has gone missing in Antarctica. They haven't had any radio contact for ten days.'

When he reached Ushuaia, Richard had made contact with Irene, Fitzgerald's stressed-out radio operator, who filled him in on the nuts and bolts of the story. The two explorers, Fitzgerald and Norland, had been out there for well over three months and should have been making radio contact every day or two. In fact, there had been silence for eleven days.

That was the beginning of the wait, the beginning of Richard Leighton's forced exile at the southernmost tip of South America. The days had dragged so slowly he actually began to believe that time had a different pace to it down here in nowhere land.

Now Irene's call had broken the spell, and the waiting was over. Richard bustled into the tiny expedition-control room at the airport, where the radio operator and a local pilot were consulting a large map.

'What's the news?' Richard asked.

'They're here,' Irene told him, tapping a position on the map, 'at the far end of the Blackmore Glacier. I'm discussing the rescue with Captain Villanova here.'

Richard shook the captain's hand. 'Think you can get them out?'

'There are many crevasses in that area,' Villanova told him, 'but we can try.'

'How about the weather?'

'There's a big storm front coming in from the west, but that's normal for Antarctica. We'll try and get in and out before it hits.'

Richard made a quick call home to his fiancée, Sophie, then the copilot, Juvenal Ariza, escorted him out to the aircraft.

Finally, some action, Richard thought as he buckled himself into his seat. Desperate explorers, tales of derring-do, skeletons on the ice: maybe this story would get his by-line on the front page.

THE TWO MEN LAY side by side in their sleeping-bags, suspended in that miserable hinterland between sleep and despair.

Carl was astonished at how painful starving to death was proving to be. After seventeen days without a scrap of food, every cell of his body was putting out chemicals that were causing him pain. His kidneys ached, and urination had become a dreaded event. His head pulsed constantly with a brilliant, sharp pain, his teeth had loosened and fractured, tiny infections in their roots flaring into abscesses. Carl had done his research. He knew in perfect detail what was happening, how his systems were breaking down. There would be a point at which he would not recover. Carl was terrified he was already there.

'We have to put out the flares,' he said, switching his thoughts to the rescue. 'The pilots will need a landing strip to be marked out.'

Fitzgerald grunted. 'You do it. I'll melt down some ice.'

Carl slowly unzipped himself from his sleeping-bag and dressed in his cold-weather gear. He found the flares and went out onto the glacier, scanning the terrain for an area to mark out a strip. His progress was erratic as he wandered backwards and forwards, looking for a good enough site. Each time he found a possible stretch of ice, he would slowly pace its length, counting his steps laboriously before coming to the next obstacle and realising that it was not enough. The Twin Otter needed a minimum of 400 yards. Carl reckoned that was about 650 of his shuffling steps.

So far he had failed to find any strip of ice longer than half that. The area was more fractured with crevasses than he had thought, and where there were no fissures; the ice was ridged and pocked with sastrugi—rock-hard ridges like miniature dunes of ice.

He scrunched up his eyes, viewing the glacier with increasing frustration, trying to remember the pilots' briefing back in Ushuaia. 'It doesn't have to be flat,' he recalled them telling him, 'but it has to be smooth. We can land on a slope but we can't land with too many sastrugi.'

He forced his body to move, this time skirting the end of a huge crevasse and exploring the area west of the tent. Finally, one possibility emerged: a long, slightly curving swath of ice between two parallel crevasses. It was wide enough, he was sure, but was it long enough? Carl rested, then began to pace it out. He had reached 610 steps by the time he came to the end of the available ice. It was an uncompromising fall into one of the biggest crevasses he'd ever seen.

Making his way back to the front end of the strip, Carl found another problem; there were two large sastrugi, each more than three feet high, directly in the line the pilot would have to take as he landed. Carl kicked at one with his boot, but the impact didn't leave a mark. There was nothing he could do to remove them.

Perhaps there was a better place. Groaning with pain, Carl managed to climb up onto one of the sastrugi to give himself a better vantage point over the surrounding terrain.

The answer was what he expected: no matter where he looked he could see no run of ice that offered more than this one. Carl knew the strip he had found was far from perfect, but what else could he do? They certainly couldn't move out of the crevasse field—neither he nor Fitzgerald had the strength for the two or three days' effort that would involve.

He didn't feel good about it, but Carl made the decision, putting in the first of the flares, twisting the sharpened base into the ice. Then he stumbled for 150 paces and placed the second. Thirty minutes later he had completed the task . . . the four flares in as straight a line as he could achieve.

He put in a ski pole to mark the spot and tied a scarf to it so it could be seen from a distance. When they heard the aircraft approach, one of them would have to find the strip and light the flares.

He took one last look at the landing place, a mixture of hope and dread filling his heart. Then he began to pick his way back through the maze to the tent.

AFTER SEVERAL HOURS in the air, Captain Villanova left his copilot alone at the controls and joined Richard in the passenger cabin.

'Are you hungry?' he asked the reporter.

Villanova fetched some things from the back of the plane. 'Cheese sandwich and cake,' he told Richard. 'Not exactly British Airways business class, but we do our best.'

Richard smiled and ate the contents of the cardboard box. Later, Villanova produced a flask and poured them both a cup of coffee.

'You see that?' The pilot pointed out of the window.

Richard looked hard but could see nothing but the grey ocean.

'We are crossing the Antarctic convergence,' Villanova told him. 'Can you see how the sea ahead is a different colour?'

Then Richard could see it—the ocean was changing colour as he watched. Beneath them all was grey, a silty-looking sea like most he had seen. But in front was a different colour: darker, denser—the type of blue-black water that speaks of serious depth.

'This is the point where the Southern Ocean meets the Atlantic. They don't mix; the Southern Ocean is much colder.'

'How long would we survive if we had to ditch?' Richard asked.

Villanova considered the question. 'A few minutes at most.'

'Not very good odds then?'

'Let's put it this way. I know of at least fifteen planes that have ditched in the Southern Ocean. I have never heard of a survivor.'

From then on, Richard's heart tripped a beat every time the engine pitch varied.

Villanova went back to the cockpit and Richard slept for a while. When he awoke, the scene had changed once more. The sea was filled with chunks of ice, each one the size of a small car, he guessed.

The sea solidified, almost turning to ice before his eyes. There were cracks and faults that looked like they had been forced open by passing ships. Then the sea ice ended abruptly, great mountains began, and they were flying over the Antarctic continent itself.

THE DRONE OF THE APPROACHING aircraft seemed to Carl to be the most beautiful sound he had ever heard. Contained within that reassuring buzz was the promise of salvation . . . of a continued life . . .

There had been false alarms in the hours before: whistles of wind that had tricked them cruelly. It is astonishing how the human ear can hear what it wants to hear when the truth is merely a guy rope vibrating in a light breeze.

But this time the engine noise was too persistent. This time it was real. Carl crawled out of the tent in time to see the aircraft enter its first great arc. Where were they going? Couldn't they see the tent?

Fitzgerald got the flares running.

Carl watched, his heart soaring, as the pilot flew directly over them. They'd been seen!

The pilot came in for a pass at the strip. The engine note cut stronger as the pilot climbed over the tent and circled round once more. This time his approach was slower, and for a second or two Carl held his breath as the skids kissed lightly against the polished surface of the glacier.

A test, Carl realised. Testing the ground. The pilot was right to be cautious. Carl hoped he had liked what he had discovered.

Slowly, so slowly it seemed it should fall out of the sky, the pilot brought his craft round and straightened up on the strip. Judging from the angle, they were planning to glide in with the landing skids just inches above the sastrugi. They were obviously hoping to maximise the strip available to them, and with that monster crevasse at the far end it wasn't hard to understand why.

Just as it seemed they would skim above the ice mounds with a hair's-breadth to spare, the Twin Otter seemed to be gripped by a new force as a sudden rip of wind raced across the strip. As it did so, the port wing seemed to dip as the aircraft lost height. Carl saw the tip of one of the skids smash into the ice mound.

There was only a few inches in it, but luck was not on the pilots' side. The leading edge of the port-side skid crumpled as it impacted into the iron-hard ridge of ice, the starboard wing swinging round immediately as the aircraft slewed out of true.

The Twin Otter belly-flopped onto the glacier with a sickening crunch, the engines screaming as the pilots applied reverse thrust. But the four-and-a-half-ton aircraft was still travelling at more than 100 miles an hour. The plane spun in a fast pirouette, the port-side wing sending a shower of ice crystals into the air as it ploughed a furrow into the glacier. Eighty miles an hour—the entire engine was ripped off and flung to one side with a rending shriek of metal.

Still the aircraft did not stop. It had too much momentum for that.

Carl saw the face of a man—one of the pilots—pressed against the glass in a silent scream.

Then the Twin Otter fell headlong into the crevasse.

There was a muffled impact from the depths.

Carl walked to the lip, numb with shock. Fitzgerald, ashen-faced, was soon beside him. They could hear an electronic buzzing from the crevasse, like a swarm of bees heard far away. A light cloud of acrid blue smoke was lingering in the fissure. The two men stood looking down into a void in which they could see nothing but black depth.

2 CAPRICORN BASE

On first inspection, Capricorn base seemed small, feeble even. Home to just five personnel, this collection of huts, anchored to the ice on a desolate plateau of Antarctica, promised little enough protection against the savage forces that played around it. In total it was just five buildings: three interconnected modular units and two shedlike structures some fifty yards to one side. From one of the sheds a rhythmic thud-thud-thud spoke of a large engine at work.

Lauren Burgess was Capricorn base commander, at twenty-eight the youngest occupant of such a post in the history of the continent. This was not her first Antarctic posting; in fact, she had spent a total of seven years at other bases, working in her research speciality of glacial biology. But Capricorn was different, Capricorn was hers. This newly built drilling station was not merely Lauren's brainchild, it was the beginning, middle and end of her universe. This was the manifestation of a lifelong dream, and home to a scientific programme which—if it worked—would pull off an astonishing coup.

That morning—as every morning of the seven weeks in which the base had been operational—Lauren was in the place she loved best, the laboratory, analysing samples of the ice cores that drilling engineer Sean had delivered from the overnight bore session.

Lauren was absorbed in the work, the knowledge that a storm was raging outside not worrying her one bit, and by midday the tasks were done, the log books completed and the newly discovered data inputted into the computer.

Lauren picked up her empty coffee mug and walked the carpeted corridor towards the mess room. To her right was the small gymnasium. She put her head round the door, finding, as she had expected, the Capricorn medic, Mel, halfway through her morning fitness session. Mel was from Auckland. She had a perennially cheerful personality and rarely got depressed—a perfect qualification for surviving the rigours of an Antarctic winter.

'Morning, Mel.'

Mel didn't break her bench presses. 'Hi,' she puffed. 'Four hundred and ten . . . four hundred and fifteen . . . '

Lauren continued to the mess room, where she joined radio operator Frank at the breakfast table.

Murdo poked his head out of the galley. 'What are you having, boss?'

'My conscience says muesli . . . ' Lauren hesitated.

'But your belly says "Murdo's bacon and egg special"?'

'Add a sausage to that and I'll love you for ever.'

'At this rate we're going to ship half a ton of rabbit food back home,' Murdo observed, his rich Scottish vowels accentuated in mock indignation. 'Unless we can find some penguins to feed it to.'

Lauren smiled as she turned to the weather fax. She loved the morning banter of the mess room—the cosy epicentre of their world. It wasn't particularly big but it was welcoming, with bright rugs and two huge sofas on which the team could relax. In one corner was a small library, packed with paperbacks; in another was a television and video. Evening films were one of their few entertainments.

This was a happy team, she reflected with some satisfaction: a small but cohesive unit of five committed individuals who—so far—had been getting along just fine. But winter was almost upon them, the days had already diminished to a few gloomy hours of half-light. Winter, Lauren knew, was when the team dynamics would be put to the real test; for seven months they would be locked into the darkest and most intimidatingly cold place on earth.

'That front is quite something, don't you think?' Frank observed, nodding to the weather fax.

'Ninety-six millibars,' Lauren noted as she looked out of the window into the storm. 'Doesn't get much worse. Not the type of conditions to be out on a field trip.'

Lauren finished her breakfast

'Where's the grease monkey?' she asked.

'Where do you think?'

'That boy works too hard. I'll take him out some coffee.'

Frank was whistling the theme from *Love Story* as Lauren filled up Sean's thermal mug. She pretended not to notice—the team teased her mercilessly about the imagined chemistry between her and the roustabout who was in charge of the Capricorn drilling rig.

Her duck-down wind suit was hanging on the hook by the door. Lauren zipped the quilted wind protector over the top, donned a woollen hat and pulled on her 'bunnyboots'—the plastic boots that had been invented by oil-line workers in Alaska and were still the warmest footwear in the world. Lastly, on went the gloves; Lauren was ready to commit herself to the frigid exterior, into a wind that was going to try its hardest to whip her off her feet.

It took her breath away every time, the crisp bite of superchilled air sending a shock into the centre of her head as she breathed in.

Lauren leaned into the wind, trying not to spill a drop of coffee as she made her way to the drilling shed. Inside, Sean was swarming all over the massive Perkins diesel engine and the rig that stood in a tripod above it.

Sean Lowery had proved to be a brilliant addition to the team, coming to Lauren's attention after a series of sparkling recommendations by several colleagues at the Scott Polar Research Institute.

Lauren had flown the American engineer across from his Colorado home for an interview at her London laboratory. He was younger than she'd expected, still weatherbeaten from his recent Greenland contract, his blond hair tied back in a ponytail that made him look more like a climber than an engineer. Lauren liked him instantly: there was something in his nomadic existence that echoed her own restless progression from one base to another.

Sean had watched her carefully as she made him coffee that first day, deciding that his previous theory regarding the undesirability of female scientists was now blown firmly out of the water. Dressed in a simple white T-shirt and a pair of faded denim jeans, Lauren had the type of un-made-up beauty—and certainly the figure—of a model. With her dark, naturally curly hair and her earnest brown eyes, she looked a bit like a young Sigourney Weaver, he had decided.

'Tell me about the expedition,' Sean said. 'Are you drilling a core like the Greenland team?'

'Drilling a core . . . with a twist,' Lauren told him, wincing at her own pun. 'At the far end of the core is a lake. I want to pull up a water sample, and it has to be completely sterile.'

'A lake? Beneath Antarctica? I thought it was frozen.'

'So did scientists,' she told him, 'until the early 1970s. That's when aircraft from various scientific missions began running airborne sounding radar over certain stretches of Antarctica. That type of radar can penetrate ice and find a reflection off the underlying rock or whatever's beneath it.'

'I got you.'

'They found something pretty staggering in Eastern Antarctica. A freshwater lake about the size of Lake Ontario, and twice as deep, was sitting beneath the ice. They called it Lake Vostok, after the Russian base situated above it.'

Sean leaned forward, his attention caught. 'Why doesn't it freeze?'

'We believe it's because it's sitting in a tectonic rift—the type of fault that Lake Baikal and the Red Sea occupy. The heat from the earth's interior is sufficient to melt down the lake, and there it is, perfectly locked away from the rest of the planet—a source of pristine water, and potentially a source of new life forms.'

'So you want to drill down and explore that lake?'

'Not Vostok. Vostok has too many problems. To reach it, we'd have to drill a colossal two miles or more through the ice.'

'Two miles!' Sean was astounded. 'But that's impossible.'

'Exactly. That's why I've got a different proposal. About a thousand miles from Vostok there's a volcano locked beneath the ice.'

'How do you know it's there?'

'It was discovered by British scientists back in 1956. But since there are plenty of under-ice volcanoes in Antarctica, no one paid this discovery much attention.'

'So how come you're so interested in this one?'

'Firstly, because my father was one of the scientists who discovered it, and secondly, because this volcano is the one closest to the surface. The crater is just over two thousand feet beneath the ice. Much better chance of getting a probe down into the lake.'

'Wait a second. I'm confused. Why should there be a lake connected with this volcano?'

'It has a true crater—we can deduce that from echo location. And it's an active volcano. There has to be heat. Where there's heat, ice becomes water, and where there's water . . . there's life. We may be talking about life forms that have evolved completely independently. That's the challenge for science: these lakes are like time capsules—we can push our knowledge of how life forms far beyond where it is now if we can just get to them.'

'What are the practicalities?'

'I want to set up a tiny independent base, perhaps no more than a handful of personnel. I want to get a drilling rig and put two thousand, two hundred and fifty feet of probe down into that lake and find creatures no one has ever dreamed of before.'

Sean laughed at her raw enthusiasm. 'When you say creatures, are we talking things big enough to see?'

'Almost certainly not. But just because they're microscopic doesn't mean they're any less important. Some of the greatest advances in life sciences have come from studying creatures that can only be seen through an electron microscope.'

'I like the project,' Sean told her. 'I've been looking for a chance to get down to Antarctica for years. You can count me in.'

THE MONEY for setting up Capricorn had been tough to find, particularly as the project was regarded as risky by many of the bigger grant-giving scientific organisations. But by sheer power of persuasion, allied with her fast-growing reputation for getting results, Lauren pulled it together.

There was £300,000 from the Scott Polar Research Institute, and a quarter of a million from the National Foundation for Science. Charitable trusts came in with a further £150,000, and Lauren won grants from several leading scientific publications who were keen to gain first access to the expedition findings.

There was still a one-million-pound hole in the budget when Lauren got a call from Alexander De Pierman, chief executive of Kerguelen Oils. De Pierman was a billionaire oil prospector with a serious image problem. His company had encountered the wrath of the green lobby for its oil prospecting in the waters around the Falkland Islands, and his share price was suffering. His PR advisers had decided to look around for a worthy project to 'adopt' as sponsor and—luckily for Lauren—had stumbled across her expedition.

Lauren was uneasy with the association, but she agreed to meet De Pierman to discuss the idea. To her surprise, the two of them got on extremely well. De Pierman immediately grasped the scientific objectives of the base and impressed her with his insight into some of the technical problems the drilling operation would face.

De Pierman, likewise, was very happy with the meeting. Lauren was a winner, he decided, and he agreed to back her project.

With the money in place, and Sean on board, Lauren had selected her team. Frank was her first recruit. Lauren had worked with him on three different Antarctic bases and he'd become a friend, even a father figure in some ways. Lauren liked his unflappable personality and his gentle sense of humour, and his experience of constructing bases in the field was second to none.

Murdo was an obvious choice, too, mainly because, in addition to being the best base chef Lauren had ever known, he had skills in plumbing and electrics that would be invaluable when it came to the rapid construction of Capricorn. Mel was—like Sean—a new face for Lauren, but the Kiwi doctor had come highly recommended.

And that was Lauren's famous five—but for the design stage it was really Frank that she depended on. Together, they devised a computer-aided design program that would enable them to create a three-dimensional computer model of the proposed base, a virtual blueprint that would produce the final construction plan.

The two of them spent many hundreds of hours poring over the options, designing the base in a series of different modules—heavily insulated against the cold yet lightweight enough to be air-transportable. Five personnel would need to live in Capricorn for one year; they would have to be fed, they would need hot water to shower, they would need a relaxation area. There had to be a laboratory for Lauren, a clinic for Mel, a radio room and more.

The program allowed them to enter the three-dimensional graphic and explore the rooms and corridors of the base. Problems could be rapidly resolved. A click of a mouse moved the accommodation quarters so they would be further from the cooking smells of the galley, a further click installed triple-glazed windows in every room.

Finally, in January, the middle of the Antarctic summer, precisely one year after De Pierman had delivered his cheque, Capricorn was boxed up and flown to Antarctica.

Seven weeks later they had it built: bolted together, anchored against the wind and ready for work. Lauren was pleased with the design: it was warm, functional and sturdy enough to resist the ferocity of the elements. The official opening ceremony was simple: a red ribbon pinned across the door frame of the mess hut, a magnum of champagne in an insulated bag to prevent it from freezing.

Lauren cut the ribbon with the scissors on her Swiss army knife.

'I declare Capricorn base well and truly open,' she said with a beaming smile as the others looked on proudly. 'It may be small but from here we're going to do great things.'

'I BROUGHT YOU A COFFEE.' Lauren had to shout to be heard above the engine noise that filled the drilling shed.

Sean's oil-stained face turned to her as he heard the shout, his face lighting up as he saw the drink.

'How's she going?' Lauren handed him the mug.

Sean consulted the screen that sat beside the rig, the green display registering the progress of the bit.

'Four hundred and sixty feet and sounding sweet.'

'No breaks?'

'Nothing. She's running fine.'

Less than 1,800 feet to go. Lauren felt a delicious shiver of excitement at the thought. Five years of planning and dreaming and now they were really making progress.

A call came from the doorway. 'Lauren! Radio call. Urgent!'

Curious to know what could possibly be important enough to

make the normally placid Frank sound so stressed, Lauren followed him out into the storm and back to the main block, where she hurried to the radio room. There was interference on the connection and Lauren had to concentrate to hear the woman's voice.

'This is Trans-Antarctica expedition control. We have an emergency, Capricorn. I repeat, an emergency. Do you read me? Over.'

Lauren stared at the radio handset in surprise, wondering if she was hearing right. Who could possibly be reporting an emergency and why on earth were they calling Capricorn?

'Who are you and what is the nature of this emergency? Over.' Lauren said.

'My name is Irene Evans,' came the reply. 'I'm the coordinator for Julian Fitzgerald's Trans-Antarctica expedition. I'm up in Ushuaia. Forty-eight hours ago we got a signal from their radio beacon. I sent a Twin Otter down to the Blackmore Glacier to pick them up . . . it had a reporter on board as well. But the plane hasn't returned and we think it may have crashed. Over.'

'I hear you, Irene, but why don't you send down a second plane to check out the situation? Over.'

'That's what we're trying to arrange, but the weather's too unstable. As soon as they get a window, they'll go down, but unless this storm drops off, they won't be able to land. Over.'

'I understand,' Lauren told her. 'We're sitting in the same storm here. Tell me, how many people are involved? Over.'

'In total, five. The two pilots, a British journalist, and the two expedition members.' Irene hesitated, fearing perhaps in advance what response her question would illicit. 'I suppose what I'm really asking,' she continued, 'is what your state of readiness would be if a land rescue was the only option? You are the nearest base. Over.'

Lauren looked at the massive map of Antarctica that was pinned to the wall of the radio room, her heart sinking as she contemplated the implications of such a rescue.

'Where are they, Irene? Give us the coordinates. Over.'

There was a pause as Irene checked some papers, then the figures for fixing latitude and longitude came down the radio link.

Frank scribbled the coordinates on his pad, making a quick calculation. He consulted the huge map, stabbing a point with his pencil. 'They're here,' he told Lauren.

Lauren paled. 'How many miles from here to their location?'

'More or less three hundred miles, I'd say, and a bloody dangerous three hundred miles at that. Each way.'

Lauren resumed the radio communication. 'Irene, every instinct inside me wants to help, but a rescue at that distance would stretch our resources to the limit. I still think an air rescue is your best option. Over.'

'I've already told you,' Irene replied, 'they don't think they'll be able to put down. Winter's too close and the temperature is already too low. A land rescue is probably the only answer. Capricorn is our only hope. Over.'

Lauren took a deep breath as she considered her options. 'Irene? All right. It will take us twenty-four hours to organise a rescue expedition. In that time I think you should try every avenue to find out what has happened to the plane. I'm not giving the rescue the green light until I have confirmation from Antarctic Air Service that it has crashed or is incapacitated. Otherwise I might risk my people's lives and get down there to find it was just waiting out the storm and has flown happily back with your team. Is that clear? Over.'

'Affirmative. I'll put as much pressure as I can on them to fly down and recce the site. Over.'

'We need some more details before you sign off,' Lauren continued. 'Give us the names of everyone involved and what you know about their condition. Over.'

Lauren scribbled the information down, and terminated the call.

'This is the last thing we need,' she told Frank.

'They might still get a plane in.'

Lauren gestured to the window, to an exterior world that was black with the raging storm.

'In this?' she asked him. 'I wouldn't hold your breath. I think it looks like I'm going on a little trip. I'll take Sean with me. We have to keep this rescue small or the logistics will get ridiculous.'

'And the drilling?'

'The drilling?' This time Lauren couldn't disguise her misery. 'For the moment, the drilling will have to stop.'

José Antonio Romero and Claudio Vargas flew the second AAS Twin Otter out of Ushuaia some fourteen hours after the radio call that had alerted Capricorn to the situation. It was a full three days since Villanova had disappeared. They were hoping to exploit a predicted lull in the storm.

Conditions were bad, the freezing storm still raging across the northern flanks of Antarctica. Both pilots knew they were in for a rough journey, but they could not delay this reconnaissance flight any longer. The thought that their fellow pilots were waiting, perhaps injured, with a wrecked plane, was enough to make the two men volunteer.

They flew at midnight, over Cape Horn and out across the Drake Passage, a tail wind chasing them at eighty miles an hour.

Just before nine that morning they reached the target area where the storm was raging ever stronger. Thick, near-black clouds were obscuring the ground, giving them just the occasional frustrating glimpse of the glacier surface.

For fifty minutes the two pilots doggedly maintained their search. Then, as the grey mass briefly parted, Vargas cried out. 'I saw something! Go around.'

The clouds held back, both pilots could see it: a solitary tent with a waving figure beside it. Next to it, etched into the ice in uneven black lines, were three large letters: *SOS*.

As clouds ran across, obscuring the scene, Romero saw something else—a black object perhaps a hundred yards from the tent. It was large—a boulder perhaps? No. An engine.

'That's what he's used to write the letters,' he told Vargas. 'Engine oil. Villanova crashed on landing.'

They came around once more, but now the clouds had engulfed the glacier. Two circuits later and the decision was made for them. Unless they could land, there was no assistance they could give the survivors . . . and in those conditions such a landing was completely out of the question.

'There's nothing more we can do,' Romero said, his voice choking as he spoke. 'It'll have to be a land rescue. Let's go home.'

LAUREN SUMMONED the team to the mess room.

'All right,' she told them. 'This rescue has to happen, so let's make it good. Every day Sean and I are away from base is a day of drilling lost, so I want this to be as fast and painless as possible.'

She referred to a clipboard in her lap. 'I've split the logistics into five categories: communications, transport, provisions, medical and special equipment. Frank, what can you do for us on comms?'

'I'm going to pack you up with two hand-held transmitters and plenty of back-up batteries.'

'Should we take an aerial? We'll be six thousand feet lower once we get down onto the Blackmore.'

Frank nodded. 'Fair enough. I'll throw in an aerial and an extension pole.'

Lauren turned to Sean. 'What do we need for the snowcats, Sean?'

'How many miles are we talking about?'

'Six hundred and ten, give or take.'

Sean scribbled some figures down on a scrap of paper. 'If we throw in a contingency for deviations, getting lost and so on, we should be packing a hundred and fifty litres of petrol per machine. Minimum.'

'Very well. I want you to sort that out as soon as you can, please. Now, Murdo, how about provisions?'

'How many days? How many people?' he asked.

Lauren thought quickly. 'Sean and myself for six days max. Plus a maximum of five more on the return trip if by some miracle the pilots and journalist are still alive. That's an extra fifteen man-days.'

Murdo sucked on his pipe. 'No problem. I'll pack you up with four propane/butane gas stoves and the pans and cutlery. I'll give you fifty man days of high-energy rations plus a ten per cent contingency. That way you've got enough whatever happens.'

'Thank you. Moving on to medical. What can you spare, Mel?'

Mel read from her list. 'I'm not expecting that you can do much more than the basics out there in the field, so the whole operation is geared to keeping the victims alive and as free from pain as possible until you can get them back to the base. We're talking saline drips, sterile swabs and bandages, excision kit with syringes and gloves, iodine, broad-spectrum antibiotics, painkillers, stretchers, inflatable splints and, finally, medical oxygen.'

Lauren nodded. 'Now, how about special equipment?'

'I'll throw in some ropes, ascenders and pulleys in case we need to perform a crevasse rescue at some stage,' Sean told her.

Frank raised a hand. 'Sorry to be a pain, but no one has talked about the possibility of laying down a couple of depots en route. Being a natural pessimist, how about you lose both snowmobiles, both radios and all your supplies in a crevasse fall? Then you're completely stuffed. But if you lay down a barrel of supplies every fifty miles on the outward leg, then you've at least got a fighting chance of survival until we can get out and find you.'

'What would you propose the barrels contain?' Lauren asked him.

'Keep it simple. A tent or two, a few days of emergency rations, cooking gear, medical supplies, a couple of sleeping-bags.'

Sean looked doubtful. 'It's going to make the snowcats awful slow. How about we lay one depot at the hundred-mile marker and another at two hundred miles? That's easier on the machines and it still gives us a margin.'

Lauren nodded. 'That sounds like a good compromise. You happy with that, Frank?'

'Yep. I'll supervise the preparation of the barrels for you.'

Lauren scanned the room. 'Anyone got anything to add?'

No one spoke.

'Go to it. Sean and I leave in one hour. I want everything packed and stowed on the sledges by then.'

THE FIRST THIRTY miles were straightforward enough—a flat run of ice with little in the way of obstructions. Lauren stayed in front, navigating by way of the compass she had mounted on the front of the snowmobile and checking constantly in her mirror to confirm that the yellow beam of Sean's headlight was still following.

The conditions were diabolical, visibility down to twenty or thirty feet at most, ice collecting on their goggles so rapidly that they were forced to stop and clear them every mile or two. Lauren kept the speed slow, throttling back and fixing her attention on the terrain ahead, ever alert for any change in the surface texture that would indicate a trough or crevasse.

Thirty-seven miles from base, two and a half hours into the journey, the ground began to change, the flat surface breaking up into something much less predictable. There were sudden dips, the snowmobiles crashing down without warning into holes that threatened to rip off a belt. Lauren called a halt.

'It gets a little rougher from here,' she shouted to Sean. 'Stay as close as you can and watch my back light.'

Lauren had an insulated pack strapped on top of the petrol tank. She pulled out a Thermos flask and poured sweet coffee into a mug.

'Sure wish we could see some scenery,' Sean told her, raising his face visor so he could get at the fluid. 'It gets a bit wearing on the nerves, driving into this whiteout.'

They set out again, Sean tailing Lauren as close as he dared, staring hard into the gloomy light as the blizzard—and the lateness of the hour—conspired to reduce the world to black. It was a rough ride, the snowmobiles bucking and sometimes becoming airborne as they hit hidden ridges and pits.

They pushed themselves on, tensing fingers and toes inside their gloves and boots to try to prevent them from freezing. Lauren knew from bitter experience how painful frostbite could be.

Now they hit sastrugi, roughing up the ride even more. Sometimes they were small, creating a surface like the furrows of a newly ploughed field; more frequently they were big enough to bring the riders to a halt. One area they got into was sculpted by the forces of wind so that every sastruga resembled a breaking wave. Like a frozen sea, Sean thought, a force ten tempest frozen in midflow.

The place was like a maze, one dead end leading to another. Lauren patiently explored every possibility, detouring round the impassable obstacles, revving the machine over the lighter ridges, always keeping an eye on the faithful glow of the compass.

At 9.00pm she came to a stop. 'We're getting near to the mountains,' she told Sean. 'This mess is getting worse. What do you say we set up camp, have some food and sleep? We can leave at first light.'

'I'll go with that,' he told her. 'We should rest up the snowmobiles.'

Lauren found the dome tent in one of the kitbags and they worked together to thread the Kevlar poles through the loops. It was no easy task—the wind threatened to rip it from their hands at any moment.

Finally they had it constructed. Lauren crawled inside to weigh the tent down while Sean banged ice stakes into the glacier to anchor the guy lines.

Lauren unpacked the cooking gear while Sean put the canvas covers over the snowmobiles to protect them from freezing in the night. When he was finished, he threw in the kitbags with their sleeping-bags and crawled in after them to join her.

That first night camping was an awkward one, both Lauren and Sean experiencing the natural self-consciousness of two relative strangers forced into a space not much bigger than a refrigerator.

Since arriving at Capricorn, they had had little contact—Sean locked as he was in the drilling shed for ten hours a day and Lauren wrapped up in the lab work and the thousand small administrative tasks that were part of running an Antarctic base. Now the rescue had thrown them together and Lauren realised, as they tried to get the tent into some semblance of order, that she didn't know much about Sean at all. She was attracted to him, her Capricorn colleagues had got that right, but Lauren had seen how messy base relationships could get—a complication she wanted to avoid at all costs.

'I suppose I should ask you—you being the boss—do you like sleeping on the left or the right side?' Sean asked with a cheeky smile.

'I'll take the left side,' she told him. 'That way you get the cold wind.'

'Thanks a lot.'

They unpacked the things they would need for the overnight stop, fumbling in a clumsy ballet as they clashed shoulders and hips in their efforts to unroll the unwieldy sleeping-bags out of their stuff sacks.

'We've got to warm this place up. I'll get the cooker going.' Lauren kneeled in the entrance and sparked the little canister stove into life, the blue flame licking round the bottom of the aluminium pan as she poured in water from a Thermos flask.

They drank hot chocolate, then boiled up some prepacked meals of casserole and potatoes. The warm food was gone in minutes, the heat it conveyed seeping quickly and welcomingly into their bodies.

'So what more can you tell me about this Fitzgerald character?' Sean asked her as he lay back in his sleeping-bag.

'You really want to know?' Lauren asked him. 'I'm almost reluctant to tell you in case you decide to head back for base.'

'Come on,' Sean responded. 'He can't be as bad as all that.'

'Well,' Lauren told him earnestly, 'that would depend on who you talked to. In the UK, he's a legend. An exploration superstar. A successor to Scott and Shackleton . . . at least in his own eyes.'

'We're talking about someone with a big ego?'

'Ego?' Lauren snorted with laughter. 'He's got an ego the size of Antarctica. He's got charm too, coming out of his ears.'

'Do you know him?'

'When I was young he used to be a sort of idol of mine, embarrassing though it is to admit it. Maybe I even had a crush on him. I can remember going to a few of his lectures when I was a child.'

'You can? So he's pretty old?'

'He has to be in his mid-fifties.'

'Isn't that a touch ancient for crossing the Antarctic on foot?'

'He's still fantastically strong. Everyone who's ever been on an expedition with him says the same thing. He's got that type of natural fitness that means he can just keep going and going.'

'So how come he's failed on this one?'

'Oh, I imagine the same reason just about half of his other expeditions have failed. He's got the dream, but he hasn't always got the attention to detail that these things require.'

'But he still gets sponsorship?'

'Sure. He's a genius when it comes to getting press attention. He's everyone's favourite tame explorer. Or he was until last year.'

'What happened?'

'He put a trip together called the Tierra Del Fuego Youth Expedition—there was a girl from Senegal, a boy from Siberia, a few Europeans and Americans. The purpose was to cross the Patagonian ice cap on foot—a sort of international peace expedition. He got the UN and all sorts of other foundations to fund it.'

'Sounds OK,' Sean replied. 'A bit holy for my tastes, but I guess the kids had a great time.'

'His critics say it wasn't really about the kids,' Lauren told him. 'That he was in it for the reflected glory, for the kudos of flying this great humanitarian flag. But things went seriously wrong. They got halfway up this mountain, the kids were already exhausted and badly scared, when a storm ripped in. Fitzgerald was the only one with a compass, the only one who knew where the camp was, and the only one with any real idea of how to get off the mountain. The whole thing was caught by a documentary camera team.'

'You've seen the film?'

'Sure, it's pretty strong stuff. They ended up wandering through this ice fall, the kids almost on their last legs, a few of them already suffering from frostbite and exposure. It went on for hours, right into the night, with Fitzgerald screaming at them to keep up. In the end he forced the camera team to stop filming. By the time they finally found the camp, three of those kids were in a serious state. The girl from Senegal lost a hand to frostbite, one of the American kids lost both his feet . . . can you imagine the horror of that when you're sixteen? Fitzgerald was deeply fortunate no one got killed.'

'What was the response when he got back to London?'

'Initially he was fêted as a hero. As far as the media saw it, he'd saved those children's lives in the face of a potentially fatal storm.'

'So how did things go sour?'

'A couple of the kids' parents began to look a little closer at the story, started to piece together what had really happened that day. As far as they were concerned, the whole incident was Fitzgerald's fault from start to finish: he deliberately led the kids up the mountain when he knew that a storm was on the way.'

'Why on earth would he do that?'

'The parents reckoned he did it to pump up the film. He needed some drama along the way so he could end up being the great all-conquering hero of the moment.'

'That's a pretty serious allegation. How did Fitzgerald react?'

'He did a big damage-limitation job. He spun the press a story about how it was a freak storm—conditions beyond his control.'

'They swallowed that?'

'At first, but the tide's turning against him. There was a critical radio documentary about him last month. I caught a review of it on the BBC's Internet news site.'

'How about you? You still got a soft spot for your childhood hero?'

'I think his heart's in the right place, but I think he's losing the plot. This Antarctic expedition is a case in point: he's bitten off more than he can handle and now it's us—and Capricorn—who are having to bail him out at the cost of precious time and resources.'

Lauren and Sean brewed up a final cup of hot chocolate and fell silent as they drank it, lost in their own thoughts as they listened to the wind ripping at the outer shell of the tent.

NEXT MORNING they saw the mountains before them, revealed suddenly as the clouds parted in a rare moment of calm. Sean and Lauren paused as they took in the scene, awestruck at the imposing ramparts of the Heilman Range soaring many thousands of feet out of the glacier. The peaks were sharp, the frost-shattered rocks jutting like the shoots of early spring flowers from beds of winter ice.

Lauren pulled her map from her wind-suit pocket and folded it to the relevant section. 'We've got two choices here,' she told Sean. 'We can continue parallel to the range for another eighty miles or so and sneak round the far end onto the glacier. Or we can tackle it head on.'

'I say we go for it,' Sean told her after he'd scanned the route with the binoculars. 'That pass doesn't look like it'll give us any problems.'

Lauren smiled. 'OK. We'll go for it. But don't forget we have to put down the first depot before we hit the mountains.'

JUST AFTER 3.00pm, Sean checked his milometer and gave his snowmobile a burst of speed to catch up with Lauren.

'That's a hundred miles since we left the base,' he called over as she slowed. 'This would be a good place for the depot, on that sastruga.'

Lauren considered the terrain. 'You're right. Not much in the way of landmarks, so we might as well make it as high as possible.'

They untied the first of the emergency barrels from the back of Lauren's sledge, rolled it to the top of the sastruga and set it upright. Sean screwed two ice anchors into the walls of the mound and Lauren fetched the marker pole, the red pennant at its top fluttering in the wind at the end of the six-foot aluminium pole.

They viewed their handiwork from the snowmobiles. The finished result was about as good as they could hope for, as visible as they could make it under the circumstances.

Lauren brought out her mobile GPS unit, switched it on and waited for the transmitter to lock on to the satellites that would give the precise latitude and longitude. She wrote down the figures on her pad and replaced the precious unit back inside her jacket.

'Sure hope we don't need to rely on finding this depot without the GPS,' Sean said. 'All it needs is a real good blow and that pole could snap like a twig. Then we could end up like Scott, wandering round in circles trying to find the damn thing while we starve to death.'

'Don't talk like that,' Lauren told him. 'There's no reason we should ever need this depot. And no reason why we should end up in a situation where we haven't got the GPS.'

She pressed the starter on the snowmobile and drove off across the plateau, trying to clear Sean's words from her mind.

The Heilman Range was waiting for them ahead, the peaks jutting through the swirling storm. The sooner they were through it, the happier she would be.

CROSSING THE RANGE was largely a matter of following the natural weaknesses in the terrain, the valleys and cwms that glaciers had eaten into the mountains over millenniums of passage.

With every thousand feet of height gained, they lost another degree of temperature. Soon Sean was shivering inside his layers of protective clothing, his fingers beginning to freeze even though the gauge in front of him indicated the heated grips were still working.

He put the discomfort to the back of his mind, knowing that only by the highest level of concentration would they beat a trail through these mountains without an accident. In front of him, Lauren was driving with considerable skill, rising from the seat to throw her centre of gravity forward on the steepest parts of the ascent and never failing to take the best line through the many dangerous ice-falls that littered the route.

There was one truly heart-stopping section: a polished face as smooth as glass, on which the incline was working against them, tipping the snowcats—and the sledges—out to the point where it seemed likely they would roll. Beneath the slope, revealed from time to time when the clouds allowed, was a thousand-foot fall to a plateau littered with sharp rocks.

Both were painfully aware that if one of the sledges lost its grip and began to slide sideways there would be little they could do to recover the situation. But the runners held. They reached the better gradient of the far side and celebrated with a bar of chocolate.

Lauren showed Sean the altimeter. 'We're nearly at the high point.'

It was a dramatic view: banks of rushing cloud scudding across the horizon as the black heart of the storm front continued on its path. Here and there individual snow clouds burst out from the mass. Beneath the cloud they could see small patches of the glacier they were now to cross.

'The Blackmore. Biggest glacier on earth,' Lauren told Sean. 'You could fit France and Germany into the space this thing occupies. Which way do you think we should take for the descent?'

Sean considered the options. 'I think we should keep to the left.'

'What about the smooth gully down the middle?'

Sean shook his head. 'That's an avalanche chute. See where the icefall at the tops feeds into it? Not a good place to be caught if something decides to come down.'

They committed to the descent, using the inherent braking potential of the snowcat engines to keep the pace down to walking speed. Many times they were forced to try their luck on another trajectory, but by eight o'clock they were down, stiff and bruised after thirteen hours of almost continuous driving.

'Camp?' Lauren asked Sean. That was the only word she needed to utter. He was as ready to rest as she was.

They had the tent erected in less than twenty minutes, a meal cooked and eaten in just an hour. Then they put up the radio aerial for the nightly call back to Capricorn, the calm voice of Frank a reassuring presence as they gave him an update on progress.

'How about tomorrow?' Sean asked as he helped Lauren pack the radio away.

'Tomorrow,' Lauren replied, 'will make today look like a picnic. We're heading for one of the most evil crevasse fields in Antarctica.'

'That's nice to know,' Sean mumbled before falling asleep.

IT WAS THE UNCERTAINTY that was so wearing, the never-quite-sure of whether a snow bridge was going to hold, the will-it-or-won't-it of the process that shredded even the steeliest of nerves in the end.

'The technique is pretty simple,' Lauren had told Sean when they reached the first of the big ones. 'You take a good look at the snow bridge, pick what you think is the strongest part and drive as fast as you can across it before it collapses.'

'How do they form?' Sean asked.

'By the wind. Imagine it blowing hard from the south. Snow gets impacted against that far wall there and it begins to stick together. Over the years it congeals and hardens, growing outwards to the other wall until eventually it forms a seal—like an arch—over the top. Some crevasses get covered completely.'

'So how many of these are we going to have to deal with?'

Lauren squinted into the distance, trying to assess the scale of the crevasse field they were about to weave through.

'Hundreds certainly,' she told him. 'Maybe even thousands.'

By the halfway stage, Sean had taken over the lead, quickly assessing each crevasse crossing as it came along and invariably choosing the same route that Lauren would have done. Gradually she relaxed, secretly pleased that he was taking the responsibility for a while.

They came to a smooth section of crisp, even snow offering maximum purchase for the snowmobile tracks. Sean pushed the speed up to fifteen, twenty miles an hour.

Then Lauren saw it.

'Stop!' Her scream was loud enough to cut through the rip of the engines. Sean did as she said and she pulled up by his side.

'You see that?' she said.

Ahead of them was the merest hint of shadow, a long line which they were about to cross, something so subtle that Sean could not be sure it was there at all.

'I'm . . . I'm not sure,' he told her. 'I think it's solid. It looks like a fault line from an old pressure ridge.'

'But look how wide it is,' Lauren told him.

Sean looked again. Then he saw what Lauren was saying: it really *was* wide—the darker shadowed area was a good thirty yards across. Looking to each side he could see it snaking for hundreds of yards, perhaps even miles in each direction. A cold shadow of terror crossed him as he recognised its true scale.

'You think there's a crevasse under there?' Sean asked.

Lauren shrugged. 'I don't know, but I think we should check it out before we try and drive over it.'

She took a snow probe from her rucksack, a thin section of aluminium with a sharpened tip normally used for locating buried avalanche victims. She used it to test the solidity of the snow on the lip of the shadowed area. To her horror, the probe slipped into the snow as easily as a hot knife through butter. She put her fist into it and moved it around, easily creating a hole. Whatever she had found, it was hollow, there was no doubt about that.

Lauren bent her face to the snow and looked into the hole. 'No way!' she whispered in awe. 'Sean, you are not going to believe what I'm looking into here.'

Sean inched forward to join her, bending down to look into the hole. His eyes took a while to register the scale, but when they did he could hardly comprehend what he was seeing. It was the biggest crevasse he had ever looked into, a cobalt crack that might have plunged down to the true surface of the continent, for all he could guess.

'You think that snow would have held if I'd kept going?'

Lauren chose not to answer verbally but instead broke a piece of ice off a nearby sastruga.

Sean watched as Lauren tossed it right into the middle of the snow bridge, the area around the impact immediately caving in to create a hole about three feet in diameter. The ice was swallowed out of sight, and an instant later it plummeted to the depths of the crevasse.

They listened, like two children waiting for a stone to hit the bottom of a well, for any sound from the interior, but there was none.

'This one has to be named,' Sean said. 'I'll christen it Deep Throat.'

They remounted the snowcats and found a route round the giant crevasse, Lauren leading the way. The detour was a big one, but when it was over she felt they had overcome the worst.

Although they never discussed it formally, Sean let Lauren lead the way from that moment on.

THAT AFTERNOON they hit the 200-mile point, the agreed position for the second depot. This time the location was an easier choice, a huge black boulder that sat, incongruous and alone, on the surface of the glacier.

They placed the barrel in the lee of the boulder and lashed it down. Lauren made a note of the GPS position in her pad and they had some food while they checked the map.

'We've got another fifty miles of flat ground, then we're into the next crevasse field,' Lauren told Sean. 'And it's bigger than the last.'

'What I don't understand,' Sean said, 'is why the hell Fitzgerald and his buddy kept going when they hit more crevasses. They must have known by then that they'd have to call in a plane . . . so why didn't they do it here, where it could land realistically?'

Lauren shrugged. 'That's Fitzgerald for you. The man just doesn't know when to quit.'

Three hours later they were driving the snowcats into the labyrinth, progressing cautiously as huge drops fell away beneath them on every side. The transit passed without incident, and they found themselves in the middle of the crevasse field.

'This is it,' said Lauren. 'According to my calculations we're right on top of the coordinates for the spot where the beacon was fired.'

Sean looked around. 'I see nothing. How accurate do you think that beacon is?'

Lauren thought. 'Maybe accurate to within five hundred yards each way, or more.'

They looked out over the glacier, realising the task of finding the tent was going to be no easy feat in that minefield of crevasses.

They began the search, keeping together for safety, slowly crossing and recrossing the glacier in a grid pattern, stopping every ten minutes to scan the surrounding terrain with binoculars. The weather conditions were fickle and changeable—for ten minutes it might snow heavily, preventing them from moving at all. Then it would clear without warning, giving them another chance to see.

Suddenly, Sean spotted the tent. 'There's someone standing next to it! He's heard the engines.'

The lone figure raised a hand as he saw them approach, a gaunt spectre of a man standing by the half-collapsed tent. Not far off, odd-shaped bits of metal were strewn across the ice field—the remains of the crashed aircraft, partly covered in snow.

They killed the engines as the man stumbled forward.

If Lauren hadn't known she was looking at Julian Fitzgerald, she would not have guessed it was him. Fitzgerald was proud and erect with a ramrod back, well built, almost stout; this creature was stooped and hunched, emaciated and hollow.

'We're from Capricorn base,' Lauren told him. 'We came overland.'

'Welcome to our camp,' he said, and fell forward onto his hands and knees.

Lauren and Sean helped him to sit and gave him hot chocolate to drink from a flask.

'Have you got food?' he asked them urgently. 'We don't seem to have eaten for some time.'

'We've got everything you need,' Lauren told him. 'But what happened here? Why did the rescue plane crash?'

'The landing site was too small,' Fitzgerald replied. 'They tried to bring it in but it was just too tight. They hit that sastruga at the far end and lost control. That big lump out there is one of the engines.'

'Where's the rest of the plane?'

'Down here.' Fitzgerald stood with some difficulty and led them to the edge of the nearby crevasse. 'And it's not a pretty sight I can tell you. The fuselage is broken in two.'

'Those poor men.' Lauren was distraught. 'They wouldn't have stood a chance.'

Sean spotted a red rope dangling over the edge of the lip. 'You've been down there?' he asked Fitzgerald.

Fitzgerald unclipped the rope from its anchor. 'Of course I've been down there. How do you think I got the journalist out?'

Sean was astounded. 'You pulled a man out of there on your own?'

The explorer shrugged. 'Not the first time I've carried out a crevasse rescue. We had a pulley with us.'

'What type of condition is he in?'

'In a lot of pain. Both legs broken I think.'

Sean was expecting the explorer to pull up the rope, but instead Fitzgerald tossed the end of the rope into the crevasse.

'Won't be needing that again. Both the pilots are dead. Nothing we can do for them now.'

Lauren went to the tent to check on the condition of the other men. The interior was squalid, reeking of human waste.

The man on the left was the Norwegian Carl Norland, she imagined, the more skeletal of the two. His condition looked bad, his nose damaged by frostbite, his mouth bleeding. He appeared to be close to coma, unconscious, starving and extremely dehydrated. In his right hand he held the emergency transmitter, his bony fingers locked round the yellow casing.

Lauren prised the unit from his grasp and deactivated the switch. There was no point in having the emergency bleeper sounding into the airwaves with the land rescue under way. She tossed the transmitter to the back of the tent and turned to the other man. This was the journalist, she realised, awakening from sleep as she bent over him.

'I heard a noise,' he croaked. 'Is there another plane?'

'We're here to rescue you,' Lauren told him. 'You're going to be all right now. We've got drugs and food. What's your name?'

'Richard. My legs . . . you've got to do something about my legs.'

Lauren pulled back the sleeping-bag, trying not to retch at the stench. His legs were in a terrible state. Lauren shuddered to think of the pain the reporter must have gone through.

'You need morphine,' she told him. 'I'm going to give you an injection now.'

'Thank you.' The reporter looked at her with such gratitude, Lauren thought for a moment that she would cry.

'I'll go and get my medical kit,' she told him and left the tent.

'How are they?' Sean asked her.

'Worse than I hoped. The reporter has two nasty fractures on his legs. The other man is extremely weak. I'm going to do what I can to stabilise them both, but the priority has to be to get them back to the base, where we can look after them properly.'

Lauren assembled the radio and raised Capricorn base. She confirmed that they had found the explorers and gave Frank an accurate account of the survivors' conditions to pass on to Irene Evans at Ushuaia. Then she signed off and turned to Sean.

'I want you to get these machines refuelled and ready to leave as soon as possible.'

'Sure. Don't you think I should go down and check the wreckage?'

Fitzgerald stepped up to him. 'What do you want to do that for? Can't you see every second counts in getting those two men to medical attention?'

Sean was surprised at Fitzgerald's tone. 'Well I was just thinking that either Lauren or myself should see the wreck. There's obviously going to be an inquiry into the crash and the deaths . . . Perhaps we can help the investigators.'

'I can tell an inquiry anything they need to know,' said Fitzgerald.

'Did you take any photographs?'

Fitzgerald stepped closer still to Sean. 'Photographs? There are two men dead down there. You think I'm going to go snapping holiday pictures, desecrating the dead?'

Lauren stepped in. 'Sean. Maybe Fitzgerald is right: we don't have time to lose now. Forget about the plane, stick to the snowcats.'

Sean held up his hands. 'Anything you say. I'll have them ready.'

They turned to their tasks. Sean serviced and refuelled the two machines and Lauren administered painkillers, putting Richard's legs in splints, and boiling water to begin the process of rehydrating the three men.

Fitzgerald made himself useful, warming up soup on the small gas stove and helping Richard to drink before feeding himself.

'What about your gear?' Lauren asked the explorer, gesturing to the tent. 'We're running overweight, so be selective.'

'Just our personal packs,' Fitzgerald told her. 'The rest of the stuff's beyond repair anyway.'

Sean entered the tent and found the two small rucksacks. He left the soiled sleeping-bags and the jumble of harnesses and cooking gear that was scattered at the back. Then he spotted the yellow emergency transmitter.

'What about the transmitter?' he called to Fitzgerald.

'Leave it,' the explorer told him. 'It's dead weight. The suppliers give me a new one for every expedition.'

Sean left the transmitter in the tent and helped the others as they loaded up. They put the two sicker men into clean sleeping-bags.

Sean arranged the kitbags so that they could lie in relative comfort on the sledges, and tied both men on.

They made slow progress through the crevasse field, weaving their way carefully to avoid the harder bumps. Fitzgerald rode pillion behind Sean.

As the effects of the morphine faded, Richard began to cry out with every shudder of the sledge. No matter how delicately Sean drove, the rough surface was transmitting shocks to his shattered legs.

'He needs more drugs,' Lauren decided. 'We'll pitch camp for a few hours' sleep. We could all do with some rest anyway.'

By the early hours of the morning they had their three tents erected and had melted down enough ice to hydrate some more food. Richard ate like a man possessed, but Carl Norland had to be spoonfed and still showed little sign of recovery.

Lauren put in a radio call to base, then—utterly exhausted—fell into a deep sleep as soon as her head touched her inflatable pillow.

Sean lay awake by her side—there was too much running through his mind. Finally he dressed quietly and went out onto the glacier.

He looked back at the tents. All was quiet. He climbed onto the snowmobile and fired up the engine, letting the machine idle as he arranged his balaclava and gloves.

Suddenly a hand gripped his arm. Fitzgerald was next to him, standing on the ice in just his socks. 'Where are you going?'

'I lost one of the kitbags off the back of the sledge,' Sean told him, easy with the lie. 'I'm going to backtrack and see if I can find it.' He shrugged off the explorer's hand.

'Wait! I'll go with you. It's not safe on your own.'

'I'll be fine,' Sean told him. 'Get some sleep.'

SEAN PUSHED the snowmobile hard, squinting through his goggles as the headlight picked out the tracks that were his guide.

Unladen, the machine was fast. By 2.00am he had located the crevasse. It wasn't going to be a problem identifying where the Twin Otter was—the skidding aircraft had cut a trench a foot deep into the glacier as it crashed, ending right at the crevasse lip.

Sean snapped his crampons onto his boots and walked carefully to the crevasse edge. He leaned as far as he dared over the lip, shining his head torch down into the abyss. But the Twin Otter was too deep to be seen.

He pulled a rope from the rucksack and uncoiled it as he looked for a suitable anchor point. He found a patch of unbroken ice and scraped it clean with his axe. Next, he twisted an ice screw into place, snapped on a carabiner and secured the rope to it.

A few steps away, a glint of metal caught his eye: another ice screw. Fitzgerald's belay was still in place. Sean inspected the device, noting that the explorer had done a good job.

But why had Fitzgerald tossed his rope into the crevasse like that? It went against the grain to waste any resource out here.

Sean clipped his descendeur onto the line and stepped off the lip backwards into the frigid green interior of the crevasse. He began to lower himself cautiously down, abseiling in one continuous movement into the dark chasm below and shivering involuntarily from the rapid drop in temperature.

About 130 feet down, he began to pick out the broken outline of the Twin Otter, the shattered wreckage shining dimly in the light of his head torch. Sean let himself down gently onto the flattest section of metal and checked on his line. He had descended 145 feet—almost the entire length of the rope.

He took stock, sweeping the twisted debris with the head-torch beam, each breath sending a puff of frozen vapour to catch the light, the sharp smell of aviation fuel still detectable in the air.

The aircraft was tilted on an angle, the nose down, the fuselage crushed by the vicelike jaws of the glacier. Directly beneath it the crevasse narrowed dramatically, becoming little more than a three-foot-wide slit falling away to an unknown depth.

Sean walked down the fuselage, still holding the rope for safety. He saw that one of the wings had been ripped off to a fractured stump, the control wires and cables spewing out like the nerve endings of a sawn-off arm. The other wing had been folded down beneath the plane. Both engines had been lost.

One thing was certain: the Twin Otter was not broken in half as Fitzgerald had described. As far as Sean could determine, the only major part of the structure that had been severed was that wing.

He swung down further and found the gaping hole where the door had been ripped from its hinges. He entered the passenger area, wondering how the reporter had survived. Almost all the seats had been torn from their anchoring points and were jumbled in the front end.

There was a pool of frozen black blood near the front. Close to it, two dark green boxes lay among the debris. Sean read the labels: *Fuerzas Aéreas Argentinas: Comida de Emergencia.*

The plane had been carrying emergency food, he realised. Sean checked the boxes, finding them empty, as were the many tins and wrappers scattered all around. This was how Fitzgerald and the others had kept alive while they waited for rescue.

There was a medical supply box too, and to Sean's surprise he found it had barely been touched.

Then he noticed a small packet of biscuits, wrapped in green paper. Sean put it in his pocket to eat on his way back to the camp.

Next he pushed through the gap in front of the fuselage and entered the cockpit. The head-torch beam picked out the two pilots. The scene was not as he had imagined it. He had expected the stench of death, but there was none: both victims had been frozen where they sat before decomposition could set in.

Suddenly a loud crack cut through the silence. The wreckage shifted slightly. Sean's heart beat wildly as he realised that the walls of the crevasse must be closing in, crushing the plane ever tighter.

What should he do? Sean was overcome with a terrible sadness at the fate of these two men and for the families who must be grieving for them. There was no way he could extricate their bodies for a proper burial. He took out his compact camera and switched on the flash. He took photographs of the bodies and their wounds—maybe a crash investigation would need this evidence later.

Another loud crack. The aircraft fuselage gave a metallic groan.

Time to go. Sean clambered out of the wreck, taking a couple of photographs of the passenger area as he scrambled through it. Then he began the ascent. An image flashed in to his mind as he climbed—Fitzgerald manhandling that reporter out of the plane, using the crevasse pulley to winch him to the surface.

My God, he must be strong, Sean thought, marvelling at the feat.

One hour later he was back at the camp. He covered up the snow-cat and crawled quietly into the tent he shared with Lauren.

'You went down to the plane?' she asked him sleepily.

'Yeah. Not a sight I want to see again in a hurry.'

'Get some sleep,' Lauren told him. 'We're leaving at six to try to get these men back to Capricorn.'

'Going to be a tough one towing these guys on the back of the sledges. They're going to go through hell.'

'I think they've already been there,' she told him. 'And there's a different kind of hell waiting for them back at the base. Tomorrow we're officially into winter. No flight will be able to reach us until September at the earliest.'

'These guys are going to be stuck with us for the whole winter?'

'I'm afraid so.'

'But that's going to be a nightmare. What if the mix doesn't work? We don't know them at all.'

'There's nothing we can do, Sean, so we'll have to accept it. Maybe it won't be so bad.'

Even as she spoke the soothing words, Lauren knew that she didn't believe them for a moment. She knew too much about the unique pressure the Antarctic winter exerts on the human psyche.

Nightmare might not be a strong enough word.

3 THE BIG EYE BLUES

Frank raised the binoculars to his eyes and began a sweep of the northern horizon. It was the fifth or sixth time this morning that he'd forsaken the warmth and security of the base to venture out onto the ice, scanning for the headlights of the two snowcats.

The previous searches had revealed nothing, but this time he locked on to two crystal pinpricks of light.

He rapped on the window of the mess room, where the others were enjoying their midmorning coffee break. 'Incoming! Lauren and Sean on the horizon!'

The inhabitants of Capricorn waited in a state of nervous anticipation as the two specks of brilliance gradually crept towards them. It was an hour before the first of the machines came roaring up.

'Welcome back and well done!' Frank gave Lauren a big hug as, stiffly, she dismounted the snowmobile. 'I can't say how delighted we all are to have you back!'

The second machine pulled in, Sean driving with Fitzgerald riding pillion behind him. The two men dismounted. Sean was greeted and hugged by the team members, Fitzgerald warmly welcomed with handshakes and smiles.

Carl and Richard were the obvious priority, and they were transported into the clinic, where both were rapidly assessed by the doctor.

'You patched them up pretty good,' Mel told Lauren, as she examined the temporary splints and dressings. 'I'll deal with the journalist first. Why don't you take some rest?'

But Lauren refused to leave, staying to assist Mel through the hour-long operation to X-ray, administer anaesthetic and then set and plaster Richard's two broken legs.

'He was lucky these weren't compound fractures,' Mel observed. 'He's escaped serious infection by the looks of it, but I'll still put him on a course of penicillin to be sure.'

The skeletal Carl was next, his frostbitten face and hands bandaged and treated before he collapsed without a word into a bunk.

'He's lost a dangerous amount of weight,' Mel observed, 'and he seems in shock. Has he been like that since the rescue?'

'He hasn't said a word,' Lauren told her. 'It's like his mind has closed down with the stress and trauma.'

Lauren made sure both men were given soup and tea, then made her way to the mess room, where she flopped into one of the sofas. The sensation of sitting on the soft fabric was heaven after the six days of constant jarring on the snowmobiles.

Fitzgerald was pouring himself tea from a flask. Lauren couldn't help noticing that he poured his drink into Mel's personal mug—clearly marked with her name—even though Murdo had put out plastic cups for the new arrivals. Then he crossed to the long table and began to demolish the huge plate of sausages and potatoes Murdo had served him.

'You really should come and join me, my dear,' Fitzgerald called over to her. 'This is simply delicious.'

'I'll hang on for Sean.'

'Coffee?' Frank broke her reverie, standing before her with the percolator steaming in his hand.

'You bet.'

Lauren supped the coffee slowly. 'So,' she asked Frank, 'what's new?'

Frank handed her a sheath of papers. 'Calls from the press while you've been away. Your little rescue mission has stirred up more media interest than you'd believe.'

'I'll deal with these in the morning.'

Sean came in and flopped down next to Lauren. 'Now we're back, I guess we're going to start with the drilling right away?'

'If you're up to it,' Lauren told him. 'I'd like to fire up the plant this afternoon. I want to try to claw back the days we've lost, so it might mean some twenty-four-hour sessions, if that's all right.'

'Fine by me,' Sean told her.

'Thanks.' Lauren handed Sean a coffee. 'You want some food?'

A stab of memory hit Sean. He still had that packet of emergency biscuits from the plane. He patted the right hand pocket, feeling the bulge. 'Hey . . . I've got some biscuits. I clean forgot about them.'

Sean pulled out the distinctive military-green packet, gave one of the biscuits to Lauren, and then began to eat one himself, only then noticing that Fitzgerald had fixed his attention on him with unusual intensity. Sean tried to ignore the stare but it quickly became irritating.

'What's up?'

'Nothing . . . ' Fitzgerald returned to his normal inscrutable smile as he watched Sean toss the green wrapper into a wastebasket.

'YOU'D BETTER TALK to De Pierman,' Frank told Lauren. 'Our sponsor's getting a little hot under the collar, I'm afraid.'

Lauren followed Frank through to the radio room, where he patched her through to De Pierman in London.

'Alexander, it's Lauren calling from Capricorn.'

'Lauren! I've been waiting for you to get in contact.'

'Sean and I got back this morning. The rescue was a complete success. We brought back three survivors, namely Julian Fitzgerald, Carl Norland and Richard Leighton, the *Daily Mail* journalist. How's it been your end?'

'It was fine to begin with—then the lack of news set the media looking for a spin on the story . . . and the spin happened to be me and my oil operations.'

'Oh.' Lauren could hear the clipped anger in De Pierman's voice.

'This is rapidly becoming a pain in the neck, Lauren. I've got press men camped—and I mean literally camped—outside my offices here. Listen to this little gem from *The Times* at the weekend; it's only a diary piece, but you can't imagine what trouble it's caused me: "Oil man Alexander De Pierman is treading on thin ice with his latest venture, a drilling operation in the very heart of Antarctica. According to the Antarctic Treaty, only genuine scientific bases may be established, but some scientists have already questioned the objectives of Capricorn commander Lauren Burgess, suggesting that her project has only a slender chance of success. De Pierman is no fool; he knows that Antarctica is the last great reserve of mineral wealth. If Capricorn's scientific objectives prove to be a front, De Pierman could find himself in contravention of the Antarctic Treaty and looking at a fine of up to fifty million dollars." '

'God, I'm so sorry, Alexander. The last thing I ever wanted was for your name to be dragged through the dirt.'

'When are we likely to get some results? Something to put these rumours to rest?'

Lauren sighed. 'We can't hurry it, Alexander. If we push the drilling too hard, we run the risk of screwing it up completely. We're scheduled to reach the lake some time in August, and even that is assuming we don't get any technical glitches.'

'August? That's months away.' De Pierman was despondent. 'Look. Give me some good news to play with, a progress report in a few weeks' time, anything positive. I need ammunition to keep the environmental lobby off my back.'

'We'll do our best. And thank you for hanging with this, Alexander. It will all be worth it when we break through to the lake.'

The radio line went dead.

Lauren stretched her arms in the air, turning her head to try to ease some of the stiffness in her neck.

The radio signalled an incoming transmission.

'This is Sarah Armitage at Reuters in London. Can you give us an update on the rescue of Julian Fitzgerald?'

'I can do better than that,' Frank told her as he saw Fitzgerald arrive at the doorway. 'The man himself has just arrived at the base.'

'Marvellous! Just fantastic! Are we the first to speak to him? Has Associated Press talked to him yet? Put me onto him now!'

The explorer hastily took the handset from Frank and sat at the transmission desk. 'This is Julian Fitzgerald speaking.'

'Good morning, sir. I'm delighted to hear you are alive and well after your ordeal. Can you tell us more about the rescue?'

'The rescue?' Fitzgerald found his voice cracking with emotion. 'I only did what anyone would have done under the circumstances . . . '

'Let me stop you there . . . ' The journalist's voice was confused. 'I was thinking about the rescue that has just been carried out to bring you back to Capricorn base.'

'That? A simple matter of driving a snowmobile . . . a bit like tootling round the M25, my dear. No, the rescue I'm talking about was the one in which I managed to retrieve the *Daily Mail* journalist when his plane crashed down the crevasse.'

'Well, that *does* sound dramatic. Tell me more about that.'

'It will be a pleasure.'

Lauren couldn't listen to any more, she went to her room, suddenly feeling more tired than she could ever remember.

One thing was for sure, Lauren reflected as she lay in her bed—Capricorn wasn't going to be the same place now. The three new additions would have to remain at the base for the duration of the winter; there was simply no way a plane could get in and rescue them during the following months. A base in winter was like a pressure cooker, a slowly simmering, human melting-pot waiting for someone to snap. Antarctic veterans called it 'Big Eye': the gradual retreat of an individual into a dark—and sometimes violent— world of their own. That was why she had worked so hard to choose the right mix of people. And that was why she was beginning to worry now, as she contemplated what this winter would bring.

'CAN'T WE TRY one last time,' Richard pleaded, his voice desperate. 'There *must* be a way to get out of this place. I've got too much to do, there's so many things I'll miss . . . I don't even know if my job will still be there waiting for me after all that time.'

'Let alone your girlfriend,' Fitzgerald added.

'Precisely.' Richard's gloomy expression took on extra seriousness.

'These two know the reality,' Lauren told him, referring to Carl and Fitzgerald. 'Once winter strikes in Antarctica there really is no way in . . . and no way out. Capricorn is going to be completely unreachable by air for at least two hundred days and maybe more.'

'Because there's no daylight?'

'Partly, and there's the complication of gale-force winds or blizzards. But the real clincher is the temperature. Hercules C130s have an operating range down to a minimum of sixty below freezing. Twin Otters can only handle forty below. We're already below that, and this winter will take us down to minus eighty or worse.'

'That's it then.' The journalist blinked back tears. 'We're trapped.'

'I'm sorry,' Lauren told him, gently. 'I know this is going to be tough on you. We'll give you all the support we can.'

'And you're not the only one,' Fitzgerald reminded him. 'This is just as much of a disaster for me.'

Carl said nothing, just rocked back and forth in his bed.

'Anyhow, you're all part of Capricorn now, so Mel and I will take you on a quick tour and give you some of the base rules.'

They lifted Richard into a wheelchair, then turned to Carl.

'Are you coming with us?' Mel asked him.

Carl's response was to pull the covers over his head.

'It's OK,' Lauren told him. 'We'll take you on the tour when you're feeling stronger.'

They wheeled Richard into the mess room, Fitzgerald shuffling behind in a pair of slippers he had borrowed from Frank.

'This is the heart of the base,' Lauren told them. 'It's our meeting place, playroom and dining hall all in one. There's always coffee on tap here, and Murdo keeps these cookie jars full when he's not hung over. Meal times are set so that we all eat together. Unless you're sick, we really want you there at every meal; often it's the only time we get to see each other.'

Lauren opened the television cabinet. 'Mondays and Fridays are movie nights. Don't blame me for the selection, that was down to Mel. There's chess, backgammon and plenty of packs of cards here, and the dartboard's open to all comers.'

They crossed to the bar, where Murdo was busy cleaning the previous night's beer stains off the Formica top.

'This is the sacred temple,' he told them, 'and it opens from eight to eleven sharp every night. No alcohol at any other time or we'll run out of booze.'

'Everyone chose their alcohol allocation before we left Europe,' Lauren explained. 'So if you want to drink you'll be dependent on the generosity of your fellow man.'

Back in the corridor they stopped at the notice board.

'This is the duty rota.' Lauren read down the list. 'Laundry, bathrooms, galley, drilling shed, ice cutting for the water maker. As soon as you're both fit enough, I want you signed on and sharing it with us. It gives you one task a day.'

She showed them into the laboratory, the microscopes neatly dressed with their dustsheets, the shelves lined with research manuals.

'This is where the real work happens,' she told them happily. 'But the serious drama's going to come later in the winter when we break through to the lake that's sitting over two thousand feet beneath us.'

'A lake?' Richard asked, not quite sure if he'd heard right.

'Don't get her going,' Mel warned him. 'She'll never stop.'

'I'll tell you another time,' Lauren said, as they left the lab.

She opened the door to one of the bathrooms. 'You can take two showers a week, but never more than three minutes at a time. Every litre of water we use in this base has to be melted down from ice, and that takes precious energy, so go easy on it.'

They continued down the corridor to the next room, where a sunbed occupied most of the space.

'This is the sun room. You have to spend two hours a week in here, on doctor's orders.'

'It's compulsory?' Fitzgerald asked.

'Certainly is,' Mel told him. 'If you don't, you'll end up the far side of winter looking like a cave-dwelling lizard, with anaemia and vitamin D deficiency thrown in.'

Lauren pointed out a red alarm button on the wall. 'The one thing we can't take a chance on here is fire,' she continued. 'We'll be running fire drills every week through the winter, and you'll be required to participate.'

'Every week?' Richard questioned. 'Isn't that overkill?'

'Fire is the biggest single cause of loss of life in Antarctica,' Lauren told him. 'There have been six major bases burned down in the last three decades, so we can't afford to take any chances.'

At the radio room they found Frank manning the machines.

'Good timing,' he told Fitzgerald. 'There's another newspaper wanting to talk to you.'

He gave the handset to the explorer, who gladly quit the tour. Lauren and Mel wheeled Richard to the dressing area and explained the importance of the thermal weather gear.

'You *never* leave the base unless you're properly dressed,' Mel told him. 'Take a look out there and you'll see why.'

Richard peered out of the window into the pitch-black world that surrounded them. Ice granules were flying through the air at surprising speed. A small way distant he could see two sheds, each spilling light out of frosted windows. A rope connected each shed to the base via a series of waist-high poles.

'The shed on the left is the drilling operation and the generator. That's Sean's department. The right one holds all our fuel supplies. When you're fitter, you'll be helping him out as part of the rota.'

'How many days did you say we'll be trapped here?' Richard asked.

'Two hundred. At least.'

Mel and Lauren watched a tear roll down his cheek.

'I'm supposed to be getting married in July. How the hell do you think I'm going to tell my fiancée?'

THE DAYS THAT FOLLOWED were a period of adjustment, a shakedown stage in which Lauren and Sean got back into the rhythm of the base and the new arrivals began the monumental task of adjusting to a fate that was, in effect, not far from a prison sentence.

Richard had broken the news to his fiancée in a radio call. Then—partly to distract himself—he set about writing an account of the plane crash and the rescue.

'I have to file my story,' he told Lauren stubbornly. 'My editor will be waiting for it, and it's a type of therapy.'

They took him into the radio room and kept him stoked up with tea and painkillers as he recounted his incredible tale via satellite to the waiting editor. Later he got the news that his story had been run on the front page of the next day's edition.

'That was my first front-page byline,' Richard told the others at the evening meal. 'That's something at least.'

Carl was not so quick to recover; in fact, Mel confided in Lauren that she was deeply worried about his mental state.

'It's almost like he's lost the will to fight back,' she observed. 'He shows no interest in eating, no interest in fighting the infections he's got. It's as if the ordeal he's been through has put him into a state of deep shock. He just lies in his bed, sleeping twenty hours a day.'

'Let's patch a call through for his family to talk to him,' Lauren suggested. 'His wife's been on the radio several times wanting to make contact. That might snap him out of it.'

'I'd rather not,' Carl told them weakly when Lauren proposed the plan. 'It's easier on my mind not to think about them.'

'I can see your point,' Lauren told him gently, 'but I think it's worth doing. It will remind you there's a world out there that's waiting for you.'

But no amount of cajoling could change Carl's mind.

Fitzgerald, meanwhile, was spending his time in the way he liked best, virtually living in the radio room as he conducted one interview after another. The passing days did not seem to have diminished the media's interest in the story, and a week after they had returned to Capricorn, it was still going strong. In ten days, Fitzgerald managed to rack up more than $2,000 of satellite time.

Lauren waited for an opportunity to speak to the explorer alone. 'We've got to get some things straight,' she told him.

'Go on . . . ' Fitzgerald was wary.

'It's about your radio use. It's costing a fortune. And your stories are getting more and more sensational. We are a serious scientific base, Julian, but at the moment we're not much more than a sideshow to the Fitzgerald media circus.'

'I don't see what that has to do with you,' Fitzgerald retorted. 'I'll tell my story how I want. And if you think this publicity is bad for Capricorn, then you're wrong. All publicity is good publicity.'

'That's not true,' Lauren objected. 'I want the world to be focused on the science, and not on the exploits of Julian Fitzgerald.'

'I'll use the radio as and when I bloody well like!' With that, the explorer stormed off to his room.

SEAN WENT BACK to his room for a shower at the end of a long session in the drilling shed, happy that the operation was going well. He'd left Frank in charge and announced he was taking half a day off.

In the sixteen days since returning from the rescue mission, his time had been devoted to the drilling operation, but he could now afford some time for the personal tasks he'd had to postpone. The film he'd taken on the rescue, for example, was waiting to be processed.

He took the canister of film to the darkroom and prepared the chemicals for processing. Working under the infrared developing light, he extracted the film and wound it onto a spindle, which he slid into the processing bath—a lightproof cylindrical chamber. He agitated the chamber to ensure the film was evenly coated, then screwed on the lid and left the film to soak.

Half an hour later, he was back, ready to extract the film, wash off the outer residue of chemicals and dry the emulsion.

But as soon as he unscrewed the lid of the chamber, Sean knew that something had gone wrong. He held the film up to the light, hoping he was mistaken. He was not. The film was blank.

Sean swore beneath his breath, wondering how the hell he had made such a mistake. Perhaps the film had never engaged on the sprocket inside the camera? But he could clearly remember the tension as he had rewound it before extracting the film. Or maybe the camera shutter had a fault?

He checked his camera. The shutter seemed fine. So what on earth had gone wrong? Perhaps he'd processed the wrong film.

Sean examined the canister itself, looking for the tiny cross he habitually scratched with his knife into the bottom of the casing when he took the film out of the camera. It was an old habit, learned from a professional photographer, a trick to ensure that an exposed film would never be mistaken for a fresh one.

The cross wasn't there. The bottom of the canister was unmarked. Sean shook his head, totally perplexed, then decided he must have made a mistake somewhere along the line.

'Midwinter madness already,' he told himself, turning to other tasks.

LAUREN BURST INTO the generator shed in a state of high excitement.

'Sean. You have to see what's happening in the sky.'

Sean shucked on his outerwear and walked out to join her.

'Come away from the base,' she said. 'We have to get away from the lights and the engine noise.'

Lauren took Sean's hand, and they walked together for a while, their rubber bunnyboots squeaking on the fresh snow.

When his eyes had adjusted, Sean whistled in amazement. The platinum moon was surrounded by concentric circles of coloured light that shimmered and pulsed like a rainbow, each bangle a fusion of iridescent reds and greens.

'Moon halo,' Lauren whispered. 'But wait, there's more.'

The luminous rings began to fade as a new phenomenon superceded them: a coppery curtain of luminescence that stretched in a languid spider's web of light from horizon to horizon. To Sean the light looked liquid, metallic, like a shower of mercury droplets.

'I've never seen anything more wonderful,' he whispered.

They stood for many minutes, watching the lights play across the deep black of the sky. Then Sean took Lauren in his arms.

'You know, this winter would be a hell of a lot warmer if we were together,' he told her.

'We are together. With six other people.'

'You know what I mean. If I kiss you now, do you think our lips would freeze together?'

'Try.' Lauren laughed. 'I bet no one else has at minus sixty-four.'

They slowly kissed, the warmth of their mouths shocking in the freezing temperature, then Lauren pulled away.

Suddenly, Sean was laughing. 'I just got this vision of the two of us creeping into the doc with our faces welded together. You think we'd get any sympathy?'

'We'd never live it down.'

They turned their attention back to the night sky, but the southern lights had melted away.

'How do you feel about it?' he asked her.

Lauren kissed him again. 'There's nothing I want more . . .'

Sean looked at her quizzically. 'And I sense an Antarctic-sized "but" coming along.'

'This base is everything I've ever wanted,' she told him softly, 'and being the commander brings special responsibilities. I definitely can't be seen to be having a relationship with one of my crew. It would change the whole dynamic.'

'I see. So the dynamic's what's important is it? More important than what I might feel for you? Or what you might feel for me?'

'Hey, Sean, I didn't mean that . . . '

'Forget it ever happened,' Sean said, as he set off for the engine shed.

MEL AND LAUREN WERE out on the glacier, cutting ice, on the sixty-fourth day of winter. This duty was the toughest of the daily tasks, slicing into the specially created ice quarry and carving chunks for transport back to the water-maker in the generator shed.

'I'm still dead worried about Carl,' Mel confided as they lifted a suitcase-sized block of ice into the wheelbarrow. 'We're only two months into this winter and he's going downhill fast.'

'Don't think I haven't noticed. I haven't seen him in the mess room for weeks. How's his medical condition?'

'That's the perplexing bit. There's nothing clinically wrong with him. All the medical problems he had when you brought him back here have cleared up, but he still isn't getting any better. It's definitely a mental thing—he's just deeply depressed.'

'We've got to take action on this,' Lauren said. 'I want him out of that medical room and into the mess room as much as possible.'

Each morning, Lauren and Mel would bully Carl out of his bed and take him for a shaky walk to the mess room, where he would spend the day lying listlessly on the sofa beneath layers of blankets.

At mealtimes he reluctantly took his seat, pushing food around the plate with a fork but eating little.

The only time he became animated was when Fitzgerald was in the room at the same time. Then he would make a point of sitting as far away from the explorer as he could.

Finally Lauren found an opportunity to talk to him alone.

'This winter is going to be hard on all of us, Carl, but it'll be much worse for you if you carry on like this. I suggest you find something to occupy you over the next five months.'

'That's easy for you to say,' Carl told her bitterly, 'but I never asked to be locked up here for the winter. This is a bloody nightmare for me and nothing you can say is going to make it any easier.'

Lauren had a sudden brainwave. 'What if I gave you a laptop?' she proposed. 'That's what keeps Julian busy.'

Carl's interest was spiked. 'Fitzgerald's got a laptop?'

'Sure. He asked to borrow one at the start of the winter.'

'Writing his fictional account of our great expedition, no doubt.'

'Can you possibly be doubting the veracity of the greatest explorer on earth?' Lauren smiled as she faked indignation.

Carl returned the smile, the first time Lauren had seen his face register anything other than despondency.

'He'll do his normal whitewash,' Carl told her, dropping his voice so they couldn't be heard out in the corridor, 'and he'll probably blame me for the fact we failed.'

'But why would he do that? Surely you share the responsibility?'

'No, no. It was his blundering that screwed our chances. If he'd planned the whole thing properly, we could have pulled it off. And what sickens me the most is that he'll fool the public with his official book, make out I was the weak link.' With that, Carl reached into the bedside drawer and brought out his diary. 'This is what the public should be reading. I've got the real story here.'

Lauren took the battered notebook and flipped through a few of the pages. 'This is a lot of work.'

'Yeah. Not that I'll ever be able to publish any of it.'

'Why not?'

'Fitzgerald made me sign a pre-expedition contract.'

'Well, if I gave you a laptop at least you could get all this down. It would be worth it just for your own records.'

Carl thumbed through the diary as he thought about the offer.

'All right. I'll do it. It'll keep me busy at least.'

The next day, Carl was up from his bed under his own steam, making his way to the mess room without assistance and amazing Murdo by requesting fried eggs and toast. Then he returned to the medical room, locking himself away with the computer.

RICHARD DREW a ring round the date and snapped his diary shut with a sigh. Today was going to be a psychological endurance test, he already knew—even more of an endurance test than Capricorn days normally were. It was ninety-two days since he'd entered the base, with so many weeks of winter left to run that Richard preferred not to think about it.

He quit his room and went to the rota board to see what tasks he'd been allocated today. Getting the casts off his legs had been a huge boost, and a daily two-hour physio session with Mel had got them feeling—almost—as good as new.

Standing on his own two feet had been a turning point. It meant he could participate in the thousand-and-one physical tasks that were on the rota through the Capricorn week. It was therapeutic, this mundane cycle of essential tasks; it voided his mind and seemed to banish the tick-tick-tock of the clock that was so slowly marking the hours of winter in his head.

And it gave him a break from thinking about Sophie.

Breaking the news that he wasn't going to get home at all for the next seven months hadn't made things easy between them, and meant that their wedding in her parents' home village in Suffolk—a full church affair with a 300-guest reception—had had to be postponed.

After his chores, Richard made his way to the mess room, where he sat at the bar for a beer.

'What's up, Rich?' Murdo asked. 'Got the blues?'

'Kind of.' Richard toyed with his glass. 'Today's the day I should be getting married.'

'Oh dear.' Murdo cracked open a Guinness. 'Try and put it out of your mind,' he told the journalist. 'If you dwell on what's happening fourteen thousand miles away, you'll end up talking to the pixies.'

'But it's here. It's in my head. It doesn't matter how far away I am. How about you? You got someone back home?'

'Oh, aye. Got a girlfriend called Jan, she works in the kitchens at one of the big hotels in Aberdeen. We're both saving at the moment, getting psyched up for a big trip round the world. Twelve months on the road, no responsibilities, just the two of us living out of rucksacks on the quest for the perfect beach. That's what keeps me going when I get blue down here in nowhere land.'

LAUREN WENT to the sun room and stripped off to her underwear for her session on the sunbed. She stretched out luxuriously beneath the buzzing brilliance of the ultraviolet tubes, enjoying the tingling sensation as her skin soaked up the rays. She let her body relax, putting all thoughts of work aside and thinking instead of the party organised for that evening—the team's 100th day without sun, and the halfway point of the winter night.

After the sunbed, Lauren showered and dressed in a light blue silk shirt and clean jeans—the nearest thing she had to party wear.

The meal was a triumph. The knowledge that they had successfully reached the halfway stage of winter had put the entire crew in an excellent frame of mind, and there was a contented buzz of laughter around the table as the champagne bottles emptied one by one. As the last of the desserts were finished, Lauren chinked a spoon on her glass and got the room quiet.

'I just wanted to say thanks,' she told them, 'for the first hundred days. I know there's been tension, and a bit of conflict here and there. But I want everyone to put that behind them and concentrate on making the next hundred days as positive and productive as we can. We're halfway through, guys. Let's raise our glasses to Capricorn!'

'And the sun!' Frank added. 'Wherever the hell it's gone!'

'To the sun!' They raised their glasses and downed their champagne.

Then Julian Fitzgerald stood up. 'I wanted to add a brief word,' he told them. 'More in the way of an announcement, I suppose. I've been thinking about the way that my Trans-Antarctica expedition failed, and I've decided I'm going to give it another try at the end of the winter. Go back to the place where I was forced to postpone the expedition, and set off—solo this time—to try to reach the edge of the continent. That way, I will still become the man to have crossed the Antarctic continent at its widest point!'

Fitzgerald raised his champagne glass. 'To adventure!' he exclaimed, and sat back as muted applause went round the table.

Cigars were circulated, and the base's single bottle of vintage port breached and distributed. Then it was over to the dartboard for a tournament that was destined to last into the early hours.

Lauren stayed at the table, and so did Fitzgerald.

'I don't want to pour cold water on your plans, Julian,' she told him, 'but how are you planning to get back to where you left off on the trek?'

'Snowmobile, of course. Simply drive back down to Blackmore.'

'And if I can't spare a snowmobile?'

'You've got four, haven't you? I'll pay you back when we all get back to Europe.'

Lauren was furious. 'Don't you think it would have been better to *ask* me first? You're talking about using the base's resources as if they're your own. Well, they're not, and they're in limited supply.'

'It's to the greater good,' Fitzgerald told her. 'I'm surprised you can't see the merit in the idea.'

'There's another thing,' Lauren continued. 'We've already put massive resources into one rescue; how do I know you won't screw up again and call us out for a second time?'

Fitzgerald's face puckered up with anger. 'That's one step short of slander,' he hissed. 'It was Carl who decided to quit.'

'That's not what he says.'

'Oh yes,' Fitzgerald leaned towards her, his eyes glittering. 'What does he say exactly?'

'Maybe you should read his book.' Lauren regretted the words as soon as they had left her mouth.

Fitzgerald's eyes narrowed. 'So that's what he's doing in that sick bay all day? He's writing a book?'

'He's transcribing his diary. I gave him a laptop to get him interested in something. When I said a book, I mean he's copying his diary down . . . nothing more as far as I know.'

'As far as you know . . . '

For a while they sat in silence at the table, then Fitzgerald broke the pause. 'I know about you and Sean,' he told her. 'You thought you'd kept that one quiet, didn't you?'

Lauren felt all the blood drain from her face. 'What are you talking about?'

'Very romantic . . . but not terribly professional to embark on a sexual relationship with one of your crew. The sort of thing that causes friction, don't you think? I do hope the others don't find out.'

'LAUREN, CAN WE TALK?'

Lauren turned away from the microscope and gave Sean her attention. 'Sure. What's up?'

'Carl showed me a section of his expedition manuscript yesterday. He's written this really graphic chapter describing in pretty gruesome detail the pain his body was going through, and the starvation he was suffering after the rescue plane crashed.'

'And?'

'So what about the food and drugs that were in the plane? They must have been eating pretty well after Fitzgerald found that stuff.'

Lauren shook her head. 'What are you talking about?'

'In the back cabin there were the remains of two big emergency food boxes. Everything had been eaten. There was a medical kit too, with morphine and bandages and so on—most of that was still intact.'

'Really? Why didn't you mention it to me?'

Sean looked a little shamefaced. 'I just assumed they'd been sharing the stuff between them and anything left down there was excess to requirements. There's another thing,' he continued quietly. 'You remember how strange Fitzgerald was about me going down the crevasse . . . to see the plane?'

Lauren nodded.

'Maybe there was something down there he wanted to hide. Maybe that's also why he was giving me such a weird look when he saw me with a packet of biscuits I picked up at the crash site . . . that confirmed to him that I *had* been down to the plane . . . and confirmed that I knew about the food.'

'You think he kept it all for himself,' Lauren asked, incredulous, 'and let the others starve?'

'Well . . . yeah. I don't see what else could have happened.'

A flash of fear crossed Lauren's face. 'You didn't mention this to Carl or Richard, did you?'

'I've got a mind to. Don't you think they deserve to know?'

'No, I don't! We'll run the risk of a row that could go on all winter. I'll find another way to check this out. Stay here.'

Ten minutes later Lauren was back, her expression even more

disturbed than before. 'I told Richard I was compiling a chart of his daily calorific intake to put on his file. He confirmed that from the moment of the crash to the time we arrived he ate absolutely nothing. Nor did Fitzgerald give him any medical supplies.'

Sean whistled. 'How could Fitzgerald deliberately let those two men starve while he set about saving his own life?'

'Hold on,' Lauren said. 'If Fitzgerald was stocking himself up with calories, how come he was so weak when we arrived?'

'Maybe it was an act. He wasn't *that* weak—he'd just been down to the aircraft. We can't let him get away with this, Lauren.' Sean went to the door. 'We have to tell them what he did. Its going to eat away at me all winter if we don't.'

Lauren stood, her voice low and insistent. 'Please, Sean. This place is on a hair trigger as it is. Let it go, for the sake of the base.'

'All right. But it's not the type of secret I relish keeping.'

MEL AND LAUREN were peeling potatoes in the galley on the 125th day of winter, the doctor obviously itching to get some gossip off her chest. She waited until Murdo was out of earshot.

'You're a dark horse,' Mel told Lauren with a sly smile.

'What do you mean?'

'There's a rumour going round the base that you and Sean are doing some drilling practice of your own, if you know what I mean. Not that I'd blame you, of course; he is pretty gorgeous.'

'Who told you that?' Lauren asked, knowing the answer already.

'Just a little bird,' Mel said coyly, 'but a juicy titbit like that doesn't stay secret for long.'

'The whole base knows?' Lauren was aghast.

'So you admit it! And I had you down for a number-one ice queen. So much for all your stuff about discipline, eh?'

Lauren threw a half-peeled potato into the pail and ran to Fitzgerald's room.

'Are you in there Julian?' She tried the handle but the door was locked. 'I don't appreciate your lies,' Lauren shouted through the door. 'You've gone a step too far. Come out here!'

But there was no response.

FITZGERALD WAS BUILDING up his stash, little by little, night by night. The opportunities were not difficult to exploit, for none of the Capricorn stores was ever locked. For six to eight hours every night he could cherry-pick the provisions he needed, package by package, tin by tin, which he then hid carefully in a small crevice in the ice, away from the base. This was a good insurance, he reasoned—a hedge against the certainty that Lauren would refuse to supply him when it came to the crunch.

The base commander's reluctance to back his bid to restart his Trans-Antarctica trek had struck Fitzgerald as particularly unfair. That, and the way she had given Carl a laptop. That was even worse.

It was a conspiracy, of course. She wanted Carl's lies to be made public; she wanted Fitzgerald humiliated and cowed. No doubt she had encouraged Carl, egged him on, tempted him with tales of massive publishing advances: that was why he had decided to start typing.

Everything was under threat, but soon it would be time to go.

LAUREN COULD FEEL the muscles in her shoulders tense up as she waited in the drilling shed for the 794th extension to come up the bore on the wireline. The critical phase of the drilling operation was about to commence—the day on which they would break through to the under-ice lake and attempt to extract a precious water sample.

In the next hour they would de-rig the conventional cutting tool, fit the custom-built final extraction head and send it into the black depths of the ice cap on its one and only journey.

'Here she comes. And not a single break on the line,' Sean said with pride as the cutting head came smoothly up the bore.

'Don't speak too soon,' Lauren warned. 'The show's not over yet.'

Sean cut the power to the wireline winch and hitched the cutting head to the block and tackle suspended from the drill shed's main gantry. Lauren and Frank put on their thin leather work gloves and helped him with the bolts, working as fast as they could to minimise the exposure of their hands to the frozen metal. When they had the cutting head free, they swung it to one side and onto a wheeled trolley that was stowed in the storage area.

'Time for Big Boy,' Sean said.

'Big Boy' was the nickname Sean had given to the next piece of equipment to go down the bore: a one-off, $200,000 piece of drilling innovation, which they now lifted from its protective flight case.

Back in London, Lauren and Sean had spent months agonising over the design for the extractor, consulting with mining engineers all over the world, until someone came up with the comment: 'What you need is not a drill extractor; you need a giant biopsy needle.'

The throwaway remark had led Lauren and Sean into fruitful new terrain. They borrowed the biopsy technology, adapted it, and commissioned a specialist drill-bit manufacturer in Norway to turn the designs into reality. The result was Big Boy, 300 pounds of titanium and chrome, which would shortly be sent down to the bore end, where it would be less than three feet from the roof of the lake.

When they were sure it was in position, the hydraulic 'needle'—several inches in diameter—would be spun out of the cutting head and slowly rammed through the ice. A radio echo sounder was built into the device, and, connected to a screen at the surface, it would enable an operator to judge the instrument's proximity to the lake.

Then came the fine judgment. Inches before the final breakthrough, the sterile inner probe—less than a quarter of an inch in diameter—would be fired into the lake itself, where it would suck out no more than a litre of fluid and snap back into the sleeve in less than a second.

'Let's get it down there,' Sean said.

They rigged up the extractor and Sean sent it down the wire. Lauren felt her stomach turn as she watched it descend, and, as she sat at the radio echo monitor with Frank, she noticed that her hands were shaking.

They waited, Lauren watching the seconds tick past on her wristwatch, knowing that if the next stage failed they would be going home empty-handed. And if they contaminated the lake, things would be even worse—tainting a hitherto pristine reservoir of life would make future fundraising virtually impossible.

'I think the honour's yours,' Sean told her.

Lauren held her breath and pressed the button that would release the final stage of the probe. There was a hiss of compressed air as the hydraulic ram was activated. Seconds later a green light came on on the instrument panel.

Frank checked the gauge that monitored the contents of the probe's sterile internal tank. 'Acquisition confirmed,' he told her.

'That's it!' Sean shouted in joy. 'We reached the lake!'

Lauren stared at the instrument panel in delight. 'It worked!' she cried. 'It really worked! Now get that thing back up here quickly before the whole unit freezes in.'

Four minutes later the unit was swinging free from the gantry, the inspection hatch on the side opened to reveal the titanium container in which the lake sample was stored. Lauren unscrewed the specimen container and held it reverently in her hands, lost for words.

Sean smiled as he took a rag to wipe away her tears. 'Hell of a lot of effort to get your hands on a litre of water!'

JULIAN FITZGERALD LAY BACK on the bench and wrapped his hands round the rubber grips of the weight bar suspended above him. He devoted anything up to six hours of his day to honing his body back into shape. It was a familiar business, this test of pain, a way of blocking the frustrations that were growing inside him day by day.

Carl, his expedition partner, was still an unresolved problem. As was the question of the rival book that Lauren had clumsily revealed to him. What were Carl's plans? Had he emailed a publisher already? Fitzgerald let the weight bar down and rubbed the sweat from his face with a towel. It was time for a confrontation, he knew—time to find out from Carl what the hell he thought he was up to.

Fitzgerald made his way to the medical bay, where he found Carl sitting up in his bed, the laptop positioned on his knees.

'How are you feeling?' Fitzgerald asked him.

Carl stopped typing and looked at the explorer suspiciously. 'What do you want?'

Fitzgerald sat on the bed and tapped the back of the laptop with his hand. 'Working on anything in particular?' he asked.

'Just some correspondence.'

'You're not writing a book about our expedition?' he asked.

'I don't have to answer that question, Julian, so I'm not going to.'

'Because you know you can't. By law. You signed a contract with me before we set out, remember?'

'What's wrong, Julian? What are you scared of?'

'I'm not scared of anything. I just wouldn't want there to be any misunderstanding between us.'

'Misunderstanding?' Carl managed a bitter laugh. 'Oh, you needn't worry about that.'

'You are, aren't you? That's what you're doing in here, all day every day. You're writing a bloody book!'

Carl said nothing, but resumed his typing.

'You won't find a publisher,' Fitzgerald told him. 'My lawyer will see to that.'

'You're talking about your precious gagging clause? That pathetic so-called "contract" you forced me to sign? Well, I no longer agree to it. It's a fundamental breach of my rights of freedom of speech.'

'It's enforceable by law.'

'There is no law here, Julian, or hadn't you noticed that?'

There was a pause in the conversation while Carl continued to type. Fitzgerald sat on the bed, itching to rip the laptop from his hands and only restraining himself with some difficulty.

'Is it a question of money?' Fitzgerald asked after a while. 'Because, if it is, I think I can propose a compromise.'

'No deal,' Carl told him. 'This isn't about the money, Julian, and you know it . . . although I dare say my account might attract a bigger advance than your own.'

The two men stared at each other until Fitzgerald broke the silence.

'The law is on my side, Carl. I'll take out an injunction if I need to.' With that, he stood up to go. As he reached the door, the tap-tap of Carl's fingers on the laptop keyboard had already begun again.

LAUREN CALLED MEL into the laboratory, where she had been analysing the samples. When she spoke, her voice was unsteady.

'Mel. Can you take a look at this, please? I want to be sure I'm not imagining these.'

Mel put her eye to the viewer on the compound microscope, her reaction immediate. 'What the hell are they?'

'Well, they don't exist in any textbook I've seen, that's for sure.'

Mel watched the organisms twist and turn. 'They're beautiful.'

'They're more than beautiful,' Lauren laughed. 'They're exquisite; they're gorgeous. We did it, Mel: we found life!'

'We have to tell the others,' Mel said. 'Do you want me to go and fetch them?'

Within minutes the team had assembled in the laboratory.

'Put us out of our misery, Lauren. Do we have life down there or not?' Frank asked her impatiently.

'Oh, we have life, Frank . . . we have life in abundance.' Lauren could not keep the huge smile off her face. 'But not as we know it, so to speak.'

'You mean new species?'

'New species, but with a twist. In fact with the ultimate twist.'

Lauren paused, enjoying the hushed expectation of her assembled team. 'The sample we pulled out of the rig last night is teeming with diatoms. Our theory about the lake was correct. But these creatures are not following the normal rules of life as we understand them. We're into exciting new territory here. We already know there's no light at all down in that lake, and now I find these samples show virtually no traces of carbon at all—less than one part in ten million. This microbial life is breaking all the rules . . . by the standards of our current science, it shouldn't be able to live down there at all.'

'So if it has no light and no carbon to sustain life, what's it's secret?' Frank asked.

'Silicon,' she said with an excited smile, 'from the volcano beneath the lake. Silicon comes from igneous rocks, and active volcanoes are a prime source. These single-celled creatures have evolved a method of harvesting it, and they've been successfully doing that in an environment that has been deprived of air, and sunlight, for at least twenty-five million years.'

'And where will this discovery lead?' Mel asked.

'That's the really interesting part. The sample we're dealing with here comes from the very top stratum of the lake, the furthest away from any volcanic energy source. The next step is to come back with a more sophisticated probe, a robot submarine, and explore the sediment layers that we know lie at the bottom. Then we might be talking a big drama, and possibly big creatures too. All we have to do is get a robot sub in there and find them.'

'How much would that cost?' Frank asked.

Lauren hazarded a guess. 'I doubt you'd get much change from fifty million. Capricorn would have to be quadrupled in size to pull off something like that, and we'd need a far bigger team.'

'Think you'd find the money?'

Lauren held up one of the test tubes. 'With these samples we can raise any amount of money we like. We've pulled off something amazing here and I think we've guaranteed the life of this research base for at least the next five years . . . and for me that is just a dream come true.'

'I'VE PREPARED the press release,' Lauren told Frank as she entered the radio room. 'It's time to tell the world what we've found.'

'Not right now you won't. The satellite unit's down.'

'What's new?' Lauren wasn't initially concerned.

'I don't mean a weather problem,' Frank told her. 'I mean the whole system is dead. I can't even get it to power up. I've had the fuse board out of the front panel, but the fuses all seem intact.'

'Have you had a go with the voltmeter?'

'Sure. I've been checking the circuitry through as far as I can, but my electronics only goes so far.'

'How's the back-up radio if we have an emergency?' she asked.

'Well, it's there if we need it. But you know how fickle it can be.'

'Let's have a look at the guts of this thing,' said Lauren.

Frank pulled back the front fascia of the satellite transmitter and they peered without much hope at the many circuit boards that were stacked within the instrument panel.

'See what I mean?' Frank said. 'We're talking chip city.'

Lauren sighed as she contemplated the workings. Like Frank, her electronics were good—but not this good. 'We'll just have to test the power output of each chip. While you're doing that, I'll get on the back-up. We should let our sponsors know we have a comms problem or they might start to worry about us if we go completely dead.'

Lauren left Frank to his task and played with the ancient back-up radio for ten minutes before she managed to raise a ground station through the waves of static. Finally, she got the message through, along with Alexander De Pierman's office number in London and the email address of the British Antarctic Survey in Cambridge.

'Tell them we're working on a problem with our satellite comms. We've only got the standard radio operational right now,' she yelled, 'so not to worry if they don't hear from us for a while. It might take us a week or more to get this sorted.'

'Roger that,' came the response. Then the connection faded.

Lauren returned to the workbench and assisted Frank with his task. They attached the voltmeter to the chips on the motherboard one by one, registering positive output for them all.

While Lauren continued with the voltmeter, Frank began to consult the circuit diagram, patiently ticking off the components against the circuit boards and trying to make some sense of the design. Finally he exclaimed: 'Look at this connector—it's empty.'

'So? There's always empty connectors in a complicated circuit system like this one.'

'I know,' Frank said patiently, 'but I've checked the circuit diagram, and there's definitely a chip missing from this one. Someone removed it. To disable the comms.'

'My God,' Lauren whispered. 'Someone in this base opened this thing up and *stole* one of the chips?'

'Seems bloody hard to believe, but, yes, that's about the sum of it.'

'Do you have a spare?'

Frank checked the spares kit, his expression of gloom deepening as he compared the contents against an inventory.

'There should be one,' he said, perplexed, 'but it's vanished.'

'Whoever did this was being pretty damn sly,' Lauren observed. 'If we hadn't had the circuit manual we would never have spotted it.'

'That's what's so frightening.'

Lauren crossed to the window and looked out into the night. 'Who asked for access today?'

'Sean had a couple of emails to send, so did Mel. Oh, and Carl was going to send a chunk of his book to a publisher. He brought me the disk last night. I was planning to do it this morning.'

Lauren picked up the floppy disk. It had 'First draft synopsis and 50,000 words' written in pen on the label.

'Did you leave this disk on the desk like this?'

Frank looked a little guilty. 'Well, Carl did ask me to keep it hidden, but I may have left it out overnight by mistake.'

'So Fitzgerald could have seen it, could have known that you were about to send it. Has he been in here?'

'As you know, this door's never locked.' Frank paused. 'You think he sabotaged the unit?'

Lauren closed the door and dropped her voice. 'Listen. I don't want anyone else on this base to know that we discovered the missing chip. As far as we're concerned, the satellite's just got a fault. If anyone asks, tell them it'll be up and running in a couple of days.'

'OK.'

'I'll sort it,' Lauren told him. 'Just give me a bit of time.'

'Well, be careful, for God's sake.'

LAUREN WAITED until Fitzgerald was well into his nocturnal weight-training session before making her move, her bare feet soundless on the carpeted floor.

Fitzgerald's room was locked, as she had expected. Lauren took the replacement key from her pocket and quietly opened the door.

Now. Where to search? Lauren thought about the options and decided to check the most obvious places first. As far as she knew, Fitzgerald would be assuming that no one had discovered his secret piece of sabotage, so there was always the chance that he had not taken too much trouble to hide the chips.

She checked the drawers one by one, and then slid each one right out so she could run her hand round the base to see if anything had been taped underneath. Nothing.

Lauren crossed to the basin and checked behind the ceramic plinth where a useful-sized cavity could easily have held something small, then she went through the items in the cabinet above the sink, removing the caps of shaving foam and shampoo to look inside.

Then to the bed, running her fingers along every inch of the metal frame, and sliding her hands underneath the sheets to see if there were any incisions in the fabric.

She then slid a chair towards the small, circular plastic fire alarm that was bolted high on the wall. Each of the rooms had these alarms, and, shining her torch on it, Lauren realised there might be enough space inside to hide something away.

She shone the torch onto the workings of the alarm, finding that there was indeed something hidden inside the alarm case, but not what she'd been expecting. She reached up and pulled the canister of 35mm film from where it had been jammed.

She put the canister in her top pocket, and had just slid the chair back into place when there was a slight noise behind her. Before she had time to turn, Lauren felt the blow to the side of her head. It was powerful, feeling more like the impact of an iron bar than a fist, then Fitzgerald was on her, slamming Lauren's face into the top edge of the cupboard and locking a muscular arm round her neck.

I'm dead, Lauren thought. *I'm dead if I don't fight*. She tried to struggle, but Fitzgerald had her arms pinned, her hands unable to strike a blow. The explorer increased the pressure, until Lauren could feel her windpipe beginning to be crushed. Her vision started to deteriorate as oxygen starvation cut in.

An age seemed to pass as Fitzgerald gradually increasing the intensity of his grip and Lauren began to black out.

Suddenly the room filled with a brilliant intensity of light and Lauren felt Fitzgerald's weight slump against her as the meaty sound of metal against flesh resonated close to her ear. Gasping horribly, Lauren forced herself upright, shrugging off the weight of the explorer from her back so that his unconscious body fell to the floor.

In front of her was Sean, trembling, dressed in a T-shirt and shorts, a fire extinguisher in his hand. He helped Lauren to the bed, where she sat hyperventilating, her face bright purple, as her winded lungs gradually got some air and allowed her to breathe.

'I thought he was going to kill me,' Lauren told him, looking down with loathing at the motionless figure at her feet.

'But what were you doing in his room?' Sean asked.

'I was looking for something. Something Frank and I thought he might have stolen.'

'Did you find it?'

Lauren pulled the canister from her pocket. 'No. But I found this.'

Sean took the film and turned it in his hands, immediately spotting the tiny scratched cross on the base of the metal roll.

'Son of a bitch. He stole my film.'

Then the realisation hit him. 'The pictures of the food and the drugs . . . I took a couple of photos inside the passenger area of the wreck. *That's* why Fitzgerald stole my film.'

'What the hell's this row?' A sleepy-looking Murdo was standing at the door in his pyjamas, staring in astonishment at the body of Fitzgerald on the floor. Mel and Frank, followed by Richard, were not far behind him.

'Fitzgerald tried to kill Lauren,' Sean told them. 'We have to immobilise him while he's still unconscious.'

The Capricorn team bent to the task, securing Fitzgerald to the bed with plastic cable ties and bound his legs together with rope.

Lauren turned to them, trying to sound rational, though her heart was still racing. 'Someone wake up Carl. I want everyone to the mess room. I want to brief you on what's happened here, and then we have to make a team decision on what we're going to do about it.'

They retreated to the mess-room table, where Murdo rustled up hot drinks.

'Take it from the beginning, Lauren,' Frank told her. 'It's time they knew everything.'

'We suspect that Fitzgerald might have deliberately sabotaged the satellite comms,' Lauren began. 'There's a vital chip missing from the transmitter, and I was in his room trying to find it.'

There was a stunned silence as this news sank in.

Suddenly, Carl was animated. 'I bet this has to do with my manuscript,' he said. 'I was due to email the first fifty thousand words of my book to a publisher yesterday. Fitzgerald must have found out and decided to wipe out the transmitter.'

'Bit of an extreme measure, wasn't it?' Mel questioned. 'What's so bad about your book that he'd go to those lengths to stop you sending it?'

'All I've done is tell the truth,' Carl said, 'but the truth and Julian Fitzgerald don't get along too well. He's threatening legal action. It all rests on the pre-expedition contract I signed before we set out. I suppose he's waiting for his lawyer to check the fine print.'

'But surely he must have known Frank would spot the radio had been nobbled?' Murdo observed.

'Not necessarily,' Frank told him. 'We had no reason to suspect sabotage. It was only because we checked through the circuit diagram that we discovered the component was gone.'

'And did you find the chip?' Mel asked Lauren.

'Not yet. But I did find a film Sean lost at the beginning of winter.'

The team turned to Sean.

'I took a roll of stills on the rescue,' Sean explained. 'I tried to process them months ago, but the roll was blank. I put it down to a camera fault. It turns out Fitzgerald switched the film for a blank one.'

'Why would he steal your film?' Richard asked.

Sean looked to Lauren and got her confirming nod to continue. 'Because I took some photos that I believe might incriminate him.'

'Incriminate him? How?'

'There were emergency boxes in the plane, packed with food and drugs. One of my pictures showed all the food wrappers and stuff.'

Richard was stunned. 'You're wrong. There wasn't any food. We didn't eat a damn thing until you and Lauren—'

'Fitzgerald ate the lot,' Sean told him bluntly, 'while you and Carl were starving to death. Every time he abseiled down to the plane he was feeding himself up.'

'I can't believe it . . . ' Richard was dumbfounded. 'No one would do that . . . would they?'

'None of you have any idea,' Carl muttered. 'The man is not to be trusted. You can't let him free again . . . he'll really hurt someone.'

'Sean. Process that film,' Lauren ordered him. 'Let's see what was bugging Fitzgerald so much he had to steal it.'

For an hour they waited while Sean went to his darkroom. He returned with the freshly dried prints and handed them to Lauren. The others crowded round as she flipped through them.

'There are the food boxes,' she said. 'Sean was right about that, you can clearly see all the wrapping and the empty cans . . . '

'And here's the drugs,' Richard said, 'the drugs that would have saved Carl and me from six days of living hell. Presumably he would have let us die out there and kept them for his own use.'

'This will ruin him when the story gets out,' said Murdo.

'Yes,' Richard added, 'and the pleasure will be all mine.'

FITZGERALD LAY SPREAD-EAGLED on the bed that was his prison and forced his mind to search for a way out.

Early experiments had revealed that his legs were tightly tied. No amount of movement could loosen the bonds that held his limbs together. For his left hand, also, there was no hope of freedom; the plastic ties were thick enough to resist even the most strenuous pull.

The right hand was different, the ties a little looser, enabling the explorer to move his arm a few inches up and down the bed strut.

Just beneath the position in which his hand was locked, a metal plate was screwed into the back of the strut—the device holding the headboard to the bed frame. One of the screws was slightly protruding and, by forcing his arm down, Fitzgerald could rub the plastic ties against the sharp lip of the screw head. Many hours of concentrated work, biting his lip against the pain, gave Fitzgerald a breakthrough: the first of the cable ties sprang open. Two more to go.

Sleep was out of the question even though he guessed it must now be 4.00am or later. If he could continue to bear the pain, he could get the hand free. Fitzgerald began again.

RICHARD GLANCED ALONG the corridor to check that no one was watching, then entered Fitzgerald's room. The things he had learned about Fitzgerald in the last hours made it impossible for him to stay away. There were too many questions burning up inside him.

Richard looked closely at the explorer, feeling his skin creep a little at the sight of the trussed-up figure, his face still bloody from the fight of the previous night.

'Are you sleeping?' Richard asked him. 'Or is that a sham like everything else?'

'What are you talking about?' Fitzgerald didn't open his eyes.

'They developed the film,' Richard told him.

Fitzgerald's eyes flicked open and locked Richard in a hostile gaze.

'And what did the pretty pictures show?' he sneered.

'I think you know.'

'I have nothing to hide.'

'That's a lie for a start. One of those photographs definitely shows empty emergency ration packs in the fuselage of the plane. You ate it all while Carl and I starved.'

'I deny it,' Fitzgerald told him. 'I never saw any food down there.'

'And the drugs?' Richard continued. 'The bandages, antibiotics and morphine? You *must* have known they were there; you *must* have known how desperately I needed them. How could you have watched me go through all that pain when you could have helped me?'

Fitzgerald let his eyes flicker for an instant to Richard's belt, where a Swiss army knife was in its holder.

'Without me pulling you out of that crevasse, you'd still be rotting there now with those two pilots.'

'I know that. I recognise you saved my life,' Richard said wearily. 'But that doesn't stop me from hating you for what you did next.'

'How do you know you wouldn't have done the same?' Fitzgerald asked him. 'Put yourself first? Don't you think when it comes to survival there's something inside all of us that is capable of that?'

Richard was white with rage. 'No, I do not. I would never let someone starve like you did!'

'I wish I *had* left you in that crevasse,' Fitzgerald said quietly.

'I can't ignore this, Julian. I have to tell this story,' Richard told him finally. 'It's my duty as a journalist.'

'You mustn't do that,' Fitzgerald pleaded. 'You'll ruin everything.'

Richard leaned forward towards the explorer. 'You were prepared to let us starve to death,' Richard said. 'I'm going to tell that story, and there's not a thing you can do about it.'

Fitzgerald's right hand snaked forward so fast that Richard didn't stand a chance. The blow was expert, straight to the temple. In an instant, Richard was unconscious.

A moment later Fitzgerald was reaching for the knife.

MURDO AND SEAN had stayed up late, taking a couple of beers at the bar as they talked through the events of the day.

'That's weird,' Murdo said as he took his beer and stood by the window, peering out into the storm. 'I thought I saw a light out near the vehicle shed.'

Sean joined him. 'Can't be,' he said. 'Everyone's gone to bed.'

'No. I'm sure of it. There! That's it again.'

This time Sean had seen it too, a momentary flickering against a window. 'Let's check it out. It might be a spark from a wiring fault.'

They dressed quickly and were crossing to the vehicle shed when they heard the sound of a snowcat engine from within. They pushed open the door and stopped in amazement at what they found. In the corner of the shed, Julian Fitzgerald was siphoning petrol from the main storage tank into a series of jerry cans. Nearby, one of the snow-cats was ticking over, the engine stuttering a little as it warmed. Hitched to it was a sledge, piled with food, equipment and an axe.

Fitzgerald froze, watching the two men warily as they entered.

'Well, well, well,' Murdo said, 'if it isn't Harry Houdini. Complete with half a ton of stolen supplies by the look of it.'

'Don't get any closer,' Fitzgerald warned them. 'I'm leaving and there's nothing you can do to stop me.'

Murdo picked up a ten-pound torque wrench from the toolbox. 'I wouldn't be so sure of that.'

'You're not going anywhere,' Sean added, 'least of all on one of my snowcats. Now, put that can of fuel down.'

Sean and Murdo each took a pace towards the cornered man, the explorer's eyes widening with fear as they approached.

'Stay back,' Fitzgerald stammered. 'I won't be stopped!'

Suddenly, he kicked out violently, knocking over one of the open jerry cans. Sean and Murdo watched in horror as five gallons of fuel glugged out, running in oily blue rivers across the wooden floor of the hut and collecting in a pool at the base of the main fuel tank.

Fitzgerald pulled a cigarette lighter from his top pocket and held it with his thumb against the flint.

'Want to put me to the test?' he asked, quietly.

'Now I know you're crazy,' Sean told him. 'Have you any idea what fire can do to us here?'

'Step back.' Fitzgerald made a movement with his hand, making as if to throw the lighter on the fuel.

Murdo and Sean retreated a few paces.

'Open the main door,' Fitzgerald ordered Sean.

Sean swung the door open, exposing the interior of the shed to whirling flakes of snow.

'Stand aside.'

The two men did as he said as Fitzgerald kicked the snowcat into gear. Seconds later he would have been gone, but the rubber of the snowcat belt had frozen slightly to the floor and the machine gave a little lurch forward and stalled.

'Now!' Murdo sprung on the explorer and smashed the wrench against his hand, the cigarette lighter clattering harmlessly away as Sean grabbed Fitzgerald's parka hood and pulled him backwards off the machine. Fitzgerald roared with fury as he pulled Sean and Murdo down, the three men collapsing into a pile.

Attempting to regain his feet, Fitzgerald grabbed at the shelving unit above him, toppling it over towards the kerosene tank, where it crashed with a resounding clatter of metal tools.

At the time, all Sean and Murdo were aware of was the shed being plunged into sudden darkness, followed a split second later by the flash of a spark and a roar as five gallons of fuel erupted into a fireball. Later they worked out that the spark had come from the inspection light that had been clipped to the side of the shelving, its bulb smashing as it hit the floor and providing the one critical spark that created the blaze that now raged out of control.

Instantly, the fight was forgotten. Sean and Murdo pulled themselves free from Fitzgerald and staggered to their feet.

'Get the extinguisher!' Sean screamed at Murdo as he beat at the flames with a tarpaulin. Behind them, he was aware of Fitzgerald starting up the snowcat and driving away.

Murdo fired the extinguisher into the conflagration, making little impact. 'It's no use,' he shouted in despair. 'The tank's going to blow.'

LAUREN STOOD at her bedroom window, the horror of the vision numbing her for some seconds. Not thirty yards from where she stood, 2,400 gallons of kerosene were burning out of control. As she watched, the wind picked up strength, directing the fireball of combusted fuel straight for the main block. Rivers of burning kerosene began to race across the ice. Lauren ran out into the corridor.

'Fire! Everybody out!' She banged her fists against each door as she ran to the entrance hall, where she threw on some clothes.

Outside, she took a step towards the fire, the ice beneath her boots slippery from the fuel. Then, from a rolling black cloud of smoke, she saw Sean and Murdo emerge.

'Fitzgerald . . .' Sean managed to quell his coughing for a moment. 'He's escaped, and he's got an axe!'

'What?' Lauren's mind struggled with this confusing piece of information even as she saw the explorer accelerating away from the base on a snowmobile, the back of the sledge heavily laden.

Then she snapped back, shouting out orders. 'Murdo. Get hold of Frank and Mel. Find Carl and Richard and get them out of the building. Fast.' She turned to Sean. 'We have to save the snowmobiles. If we lose the base, they're our only chance.'

Together they ran to the vehicle shed and pulled back the sliding door. But the interior was already an inferno, the remaining snowmobiles burning out of control.

'Leave me here,' said Sean. 'I'll save what I can. Help the others.'

Lauren ran back to the main block. As she reached the door, she saw that the accommodation block was being consumed with astonishing speed. The wind had directed the fireball like a blowtorch into the bedrooms.

There was a figure in front of her, coughing with the fumes. It was Murdo. 'Mel's out of her room. So's Frank. But I can't get down to the far end of the block because there's too much smoke.'

Lauren pushed past him, hearing a series of piercing screams.

'Help me!' came the voice. 'Help me for God's sake.'

'That's Richard!' Lauren pushed her way down the corridor, falling to her hands and knees as the smoke filled her lungs. 'He's in Fitzgerald's room!'

Lauren and Murdo dropped to the floor and crawled towards the room in which Richard was trapped. Inside was a desperate scene: the journalist tied to the bed frame, the far wall already on fire.

'Get me out of here!' he screamed.

Lauren fumbled in her pocket, finding her knife. She severed the climbing rope that bound Richard, and they dragged him out into the corridor just as the external wall collapsed into the room, showering them with sparks.

Lauren bundled Murdo and Richard up the corridor and out of the door. Then she took a gulp of clear air and ducked back inside, heading for the medical bay where Carl had last been seen.

When she got there, she realised there was no hope at all: the medical room was a wall-to-wall inferno, not even the beds visible through the hungry orange fire. Perhaps Carl was somewhere else, she prayed, out on the ice . . . anywhere but trapped in those flames.

A smoke-blackened figure emerged beside her; it was Frank.

'Help me get the back-up radio!' he called as he disappeared into the passage.

Lauren took the passage in three long strides, shouldering through the door into the radio room, where the instrument panel was already ablaze. Through the smoke she could see Frank trying to beat the flames down with his hands.

'Leave it. The radio's dead. Let's try and save the mess room.'

Choking and spluttering on the fumes, they felt their way back along the corridor into the mess room, where two figures were fighting a losing battle. Murdo had made his way back into the building and, with Mel, was trying to quell the flames with a fire extinguisher.

'Jesus!' Murdo saw the flames licking round the butane store.

'The gas!' Lauren screamed. 'That's it. I want everyone out of the base. Grab anything you can! Mel, take that sleeping-bag.'

Lauren began to push them towards the exit, shoving them in front of her as they snatched at the bundles of cold-weather clothing hanging in the lobby. Then a sudden realisation hit Lauren.

'Oh my God . . . the sample! It's still in the lab!'

Ignoring the screams around her, Lauren ran back into the burning building. The corridor was a tunnel of flame, the ceiling acting like a giant grill as Lauren counted off the doorways with her hands.

The lab. Fourth doorway on the right. Lauren crawled in on all fours, the sharp cutting edge of broken glass lacerating her hands and knees. Visibility was almost zero; she fumbled her way blindly along the edge of the workbench until she found the fridge. She opened the door, her hands closing round the smooth titanium sample tube. The specimen was still intact.

'Lauren!' It was Sean's voice punching through the smoke.

Suddenly, his hands were grabbing her by the shoulders. Lauren felt herself pulled to her feet and along the corridor. Sean dragged her, retching, out onto the ice, and manhandled her away from the inferno until they collapsed amid the others on safe ground.

An instant later the fire worked its way through to the galley, igniting the gas in an immense fireball. One gas cylinder erupted, then another, consuming the base in a hungry avalanche of combusted butane that sent dense clouds of smoke billowing into the dark sky.

'Where's Carl? Did he make it?' Lauren gasped.

No one replied.

Lauren lay coughing on the ice, her team gathered around her in shock, feeling the heat of Capricorn on her cheeks as her one and only dream burned itself to the ground.

4 THE TREK

Lauren and Mel tended to the wounds, checking what injuries each of the team had sustained. The other four sat in appalled silence, unable to tear their eyes away from the terrible carnage that was playing out before them.

Lauren had numerous painful burns to her hands and scalp where melted plastic from the ceiling had rained down on her. Murdo and Mel had similar injuries.

Sean and Murdo were fortunate in one way: both had been wearing gloves and were thus free from burns to their hands, although Murdo had a number of blisters on his face.

Frank had come off worst: his battle to save the radio had cost him third-degree burns to both hands. Even as he sat there, the blisters were filling rapidly with fluid.

Having no water to treat him, Mel packed snow round the burned tissue. 'He's the one I'm most worried about,' she confided to Lauren in a quiet moment. 'Frank needs antibiotics to prevent the tissue necrotising. We could be talking gangrene.'

'He mustn't know that,' Lauren told her. 'OK?'

As the flames began to subside, Sean noticed that Fitzgerald had reappeared, the headlight of the snowmobile clearly visible a mile or so from the base.

Suddenly, Murdo was on his feet, screaming. 'Murderer! You murderer! Come and get what's owed to you, you . . . ' He picked up a piece of metal and threw it hopelessly in Fitzgerald's direction.

'Why's he sitting there like that, gloating over the dead?'

'Calm down,' Lauren told him. 'Save your energy.'

Murdo kept up his tirade. 'I'm going to kill him,' he cried.

'Murdo, will you please keep quiet!'

The authority in her tone finally pulled the chef out of his rage.

'Everyone gather round me,' she told them, 'and try to be calm. If we panic now, we're certainly going to make things worse.'

'Worse? Make things worse?' This time it was Mel who raised her voice. 'Everything's destroyed, Lauren.'

'I know, Mel. I know. This is the most screwed up it could ever be. But I know we'll find a way out, *if* we keep our heads.'

Sean was also calm. 'She's right. As soon as they find out the radio's down, they'll send a plane out to investigate what's wrong. They'll drop us food, equipment, even if they can't land. We may have to survive a week here, but I doubt it'll be more than that.'

Lauren looked at Frank, seeing the despair in his eyes.

'That's not going to happen,' she told Sean with infinite regret. 'When the satellite went down, I radioed a message back to London to tell them we had a communications problem. I told them not to worry if they didn't hear from us . . . for a week or so . . .'

There was stunned silence as the team thought about the new implications of that decision.

'So as far as the rest of the world knows, we're just happily drilling away, minding our own business in our silent little world?' asked Mel.

'That's right.' Lauren could barely whisper the reply.

'And it might be a fortnight before they wonder why they haven't had news from us? Or it might be a month?'

Lauren nodded her head imperceptibly.

'How long can we survive here? Without food? Without shelter?' Murdo asked, gesturing to the empty world that surrounded them.

No one replied.

'That's it then.' Murdo held up his hands in despair. 'We can't raise the alarm, winter's still got weeks to run . . . we're going to die here.'

'Not one of us is going to die,' Lauren told him. 'I give you my word.' She looked over to the smouldering wreckage of Capricorn, no more now than a collection of twisted metal, melted plastic and charred wood. How she would keep that promise, she had no idea.

AS SOON AS THE WORST of the heat had subsided, Lauren ordered the team into the wreckage—their first priority to find whatever remained of Carl.

The body was not easy to locate, incinerated by the furnace heat of the fire to the point where all that remained was carbonised flesh and scorched bones. When they did find it, the team said nothing, but merely stood with their heads hung low.

They dug a shallow grave into the ice, and Carl's remains were committed with an improvised prayer from Lauren. When the burial was over, she turned once more to her team.

'Let's see what we can retrieve here.'

But the fire had left nothing. No medicine. No food.

The one commodity they could scavenge was firewood, and Lauren gave each of the team the task of gathering as much as they could. They piled the scraps of wood in a stack, and then, utterly despondent, joined together to construct some sort of shelter for the night.

Over in what remained of the vehicle shed, Sean picked his way through the debris. Finally, hidden behind the metal frame of a workbench, he found one of the sledges still virtually intact.

He pulled it out of the wreckage, calling Lauren over excitedly.

'We got a sledge,' he told her. 'We can do things with this.'

Suddenly a cry went up. 'He's back!'

Lauren and Sean followed Frank's outstretched arm, spotting the distinctive shape of the snowmobile far off on the horizon. The movement stopped. The dark shape of a human figure could be seen dismounting and standing next to the machine.

'He's watching us,' Lauren said, 'wondering what we're going to do.'

'No, he's not,' Sean said, quietly. 'He's wondering how long it's going to take us to die. When we do, he can resume his heroic expedition and then come out with some nice story about how he was the only survivor of an accidental fire.'

'You're right,' Lauren said, 'and he's got enough supplies on that snowcat to last for weeks. Maybe months if he's careful.'

'It's him or us, Lauren,' Sean told her. 'It really might be as simple as that in the end.'

THE DIM LIGHT began to fade. The wind rose steadily. The team huddled in their makeshift shelter, hastily put together out of scavenged iron. They lit a fire with scraps of charcoaled wood, holding their palms towards it for the precious warmth as thick clouds of spindrift swept in through the many cracks and holes.

They pressed in tighter against each other as the wind picked up. Towards 10.00pm, the fire began to fail, the embers dying away fast.

'Put more wood on, Lauren, don't you think?' Mel begged her.

'We've only got enough for a few hours each night,' Lauren told her. 'We have to conserve it.'

They took it in turns to use the single sleeping-bag that Mel had managed to save, taking one-hour shifts. Every few hours Mel checked Frank's hands—the blisters growing dramatically as the burned tissue reacted. Frank took the pain in silence.

By 2.00am, the shivering of those pressed against her was so intense that Lauren knew they were approaching hypothermia.

'Everybody up,' she announced. 'We h-h-have to move. We need the b-b-body heat to survive.'

There was an outbreak of grumbling protests as the team began to stagger in a rough circle.

'Flex your fingers and toes,' Lauren ordered. 'One after the other. Don't lose the feeling in them.'

The motion brought them some relief, the welcome sensation of warmth as their bodies settled into the rhythm. But they couldn't keep going for long, and after an hour Lauren called a halt.

'Back in the shelter,' she told them. 'Get close to each other.'

In no time at all the warmth they had so carefully gained was sucked out of their flesh. The cold was merciless, probing every crack in their clothing, freezing the fabric until it was as stiff as iron, numbing their limbs so that they could feel the muscles crackling as they attempted to relieve cramp.

'How long can we survive this?' Murdo's voice was already filled with despair.

Lauren looked at Mel.

'I'd say five days,' Mel said quietly. 'Maybe seven for the strongest.'

'Oh, sweet Jesus,' Murdo was crying, the tears freezing on his cheeks. 'I wasn't planning on dying just yet.'

Lauren reached out to place her hand over his. 'Just get through tonight and we'll start to work this out. We'll find an answer, Murdo. You wait and see.'

AT EIGHT, having not slept a single moment, Lauren pulled together some scraps of wood and lit a fire. She put their one saucepan on it and melted down ice until she had produced a litre of tepid water.

'Everyone has to take some water,' said Lauren. 'Dehydration will kill us way before we starve.'

They took it in turns to drink the lukewarm fluid, their lips freezing to the aluminium pan even as they sipped. The liquid tasted foul; the pot had been partly carbonised in the fire.

'I want an inventory,' Lauren announced when they had finished. 'We have to know exactly what we've got to work with.'

It didn't take her long to jot the list down on the back of an envelope, found in Sean's pocket, writing with the stub of a pencil recovered from the remains.

'Four sets of skis. Three sets of bindings. One sleeping-bag. Assorted tools. One sledge. One half-destroyed cooking pot. One compass. Two Swiss army knives. Several cigarette lighters. Various cold-weather clothes. One blanket. Scrap pieces of wood enough for a couple of weeks of night fires.'

'Anyone got any cigarettes?' Mel asked.

No one replied.

'We've got to keep searching the wreckage,' Lauren said. 'Somewhere in the debris there might be more things we can use. It'll give a focus and the movement will keep us warm.'

They began to scour the remains of the base. It was a dismal task with precious few rewards—the only useful finds were a few more pieces of firewood and some odd bits of metal, which Sean used to improve their makeshift shelter.

When they gathered together again, Lauren knew it was time for some decisions.

'So,' she began, 'bearing in mind the fact that we have no food whatsoever, how the hell are we going to survive this?'

'We'll have to hunt Fitzgerald down,' Murdo suggested. 'Follow the snowcat tracks and surprise him in the night. I'll kill him myself. That way we have food *and* the snowmobile.'

'It's too dangerous,' Lauren countered. 'If Fitzgerald sees two or three of our fitter members tracking him down, he might realise that the weaker ones have to be here on their own. The protocol,' she reminded them, 'is that we stay with the base.'

Sean was the next to speak. 'There's only one way of getting out of here alive.'

The assembled team looked at him in surprise.

'Fitzgerald's emergency transmitter. We turned it off and left it back at the crashed aircraft.'

Lauren thought about it, shaking her head emphatically. 'Sean. That plane is three hundred miles away.'

'I'm not talking about three hundred miles,' Sean told her. 'I'm talking about one hundred. That's how far it is to the barrel of supplies we dumped at the first depot, right?'

'My God, I'd forgotten about the depots,' Lauren responded.

'Here's the idea,' Sean continued. 'We set out on foot. We make a hundred-mile trek to the first barrel. That gives us food to keep us going to the second depot. We feed up again, crack the last hundred miles, then we get to the plane and activate the transmitter.'

'How can we do this?' Lauren asked Sean.

'Well, as far as I can figure, there's really only two ways. Either we split the team and the fittest make a fast dash on skis for the plane and radio for help. Or we all leave together.'

'I say we keep the team together,' Lauren told them. 'If four of us wait here, inactive, without any food, I don't believe we'd survive more than six or seven days before we died of exposure.'

There was a general nod of agreement.

'There's another factor. We don't know what Fitzgerald is going to try next. If we stick together, we've got strength in numbers.'

'Wait a minute,' Mel interjected. 'Does Fitzgerald know we put those depots down?'

There was an awkward silence as the team tried to recall.

'Damn! I told him,' Sean remembered with a moan. 'When we were on the way back.'

'Then we're screwed,' Murdo said. 'That madman will drive out there and use those supplies himself before we can get to them.'

'Hold on . . . ' Sean's expression suddenly lightened. 'I told him we laid two depots but I didn't tell him where they were.'

'What's the chances of him finding those dumps?' Mel asked.

Sean and Lauren answered simultaneously. 'Zero.'

'For that matter, what's the chances of *us* finding them?'

Lauren thought about it. 'We've got the compass. It'll be tough but we can do it. Does everyone agree we stick together?'

There was a murmuring of assent.

'Then I think we should go now,' Lauren told them.

'Why not wait until first light?'

'Because that's what Fitzgerald will figure we'll do. We have twelve hours of total darkness to put some distance between us and the base. With luck, he won't even know we've gone.'

'But when he does find we've gone, he'll put two and two together.'

Lauren considered this. 'We'll leave a decoy note, try to send him off on the wrong trail.'

'And if a real search team *does* arrive?'

'I have an idea for that. I'll arrange it before we leave.'

Thirty minutes later the team was outside and ready to go. They loaded the sledge with the firewood and the few objects and tools they had managed to retrieve, then Sean rigged up a rope harness that would allow two people to tow the sledge.

Lauren felt the rope dig harshly into the flesh of her hips as she began to ski. Then Sean took up some of the strain and the pain eased a little. Slowly and quietly, they pulled away from the base.

In her breast pocket, Lauren could feel the smooth outline of the titanium sample bottle. That was another responsibility, almost as overwhelming as the five lives that now depended on her.

FITZGERALD STEERED the snowcat in a little closer. Now he was just a few hundred yards from the wreckage of the base. It was the closest he had dared to come since the fire.

This was a trap, he knew, and he had to admit it was well done. For three days he had not seen a single sign of life from the base. They were luring him in, coaxing him closer, hoping that he would lose his caution and make the one fatal mistake that would lose him everything. If he went too close, they'd be on him like a pack of wolves.

'Do you take me for a fool?' he shouted at the ruins. ' I know some of you must be alive. Show yourselves! Maybe I can help you.'

Nothing stirred.

Maybe they were dead? The thought was enticing. Was three days and nights enough to kill them?

But Lauren was tougher than that. And Sean too. Fitzgerald knew enough about those two to be pretty confident they'd still be alive.

Suddenly he had an idea.

'I've got spare food!' he called out. 'I'm leaving some here on the ice for you now.' He tossed a tin of meat onto the ice.

Fitzgerald backed off a half a mile or so and watched for nearly an hour. No way they would resist that, he thought, no matter how much they wanted to bring him into the trap.

But no one moved. No figure emerged, stiff and frozen, from the shelter to collect the food. But it wouldn't be there tomorrow. Fitzgerald had never been more certain of anything in his life.

THERE WAS NO DOUBT in Lauren's mind that Frank was gradually losing it. Sometimes he would sing gently to himself, the same words over and again as he tripped along. Other times, he would come to an abrupt halt and stand in a daze for minutes on end, looking out across the white expanse as if amazed to find himself there.

Eventually, his conversation became stilted and confused—he couldn't hold a line of thought for more than five minutes without getting disconnected. He took to leaning on Lauren for support, resting an arm over her shoulders and sometimes tipping her off balance.

At that night's stop, Lauren pulled Mel aside. 'I think Frank's getting hypothermic,' she told her.

Mel examined Frank. 'We've got to get him into the sleeping-bag. His body core's getting dangerously low.'

Sean and Murdo prepared the camp while Lauren persuaded Frank to warm himself up. He did as he was told, and after an hour or two of violent shivering, his temperature gradually rose. He was desperate to sleep, but first Lauren insisted that Mel examine his hands.

The fingers were infected, weeping copious amounts of pus. Around the edges of the wounds, Mel could see puffy, swollen tissue. The smell was slight, but to a trained medic it was enough. On one hand, the early stages of necrosis were setting in.

'That's as far as he can walk,' Mel told Lauren later. 'If he gets any weaker, his chances of gangrene are going to shoot up. From tomorrow he's got to be on the sledge—at least until the first depot, where we can get him started on a course of antibiotics.'

This was the moment Lauren had dreaded, and it had come far sooner than she had ever imagined. After just five days, before reaching even the first of the depots, one of the team was already incapacitated. From now on they would have to find the strength to haul the sledge with Frank's dead weight on it. And what would happen if another member of the team became unable to walk?

Lauren didn't sleep that night.

FITZGERALD BLINKED with astonishment when he saw the can.

It was intact. They hadn't eaten the meat. Those starving fools had sat there with a free meal on offer and hadn't come out to get it.

How many were still alive? What condition were they in after several freezing nights? Would they have the strength to attack him? If he could just walk to that shelter and take a peek inside, all would be made clear. He could remove the bodies, drive them to the nearest deep crevasse and dump them where they'd never be found.

There was one other possibility. They might not be in the shelter at all. Fitzgerald rejected that thought as soon as it entered his mind. Impossible. They had to be in there; there was, literally, nowhere else to go without food and equipment.

Stay with the base. That was the accepted practice in such a case as this. Lauren would stick to the rules . . . or would she?

Fitzgerald found himself split. He wanted to believe they were dead . . . oh, how much he wanted that. But at the same moment he could not accept that Lauren and Sean would be defeated so soon.

No. They were waiting in there. They knew he would be itching to see if they were dead or alive. Perhaps he should just pace right up to the shelter, axe in hand, and attack them.

But why take the risk? Fitzgerald knew he held all the cards. Still, it was getting tedious, this hanging around. He wanted to get on with his journey—to drive the snowmobile back to the crashed plane, find the transmitter, and then set out for the coast . . . and the glory that was his by right.

But he had to dispose of the bodies first. And make sure that Lauren hadn't left any note behind that could compromise him. Tomorrow he'd storm the shelter, come what may.

RICHARD WAS FIGHTING a losing battle with his feet. Seventy miles of continuous cross-country skiing across the ice cap had brought the journalist to the point where each excruciating move required a major act of will-power.

When he looked back on the events that had befallen him in the past months, Richard truly wanted to cry. The plane crash, the two broken legs, the endless tedium and tension of the long winter at the base, and then the final shock of the fire. He had fought through so much, always fixing his thoughts on the world—and the warmth—he would return to. And now it was further away than ever.

It had been replaced by a new world, one in which each day began with the crackling sound of his ice-encrusted clothing as he unfurled himself from a foetal ball on the glacier. This new world was one in which the moisture on his eyeballs was glazed and frosted as the cutting wind blitzed his face, and where the few drops of dark urine he produced each day froze instantly as they landed.

The deterioration in the state of his feet had begun around the thirty-mile point. His socks—soaked daily in sweat and often frozen—began to act like sandpaper, eating away at the tissue as his heels rocked to and fro in every movement of the skis. By fifty miles the sandpaper effect had become a cluster of red-hot needles, penetrating deeper with the sliding steps, and now spreading from the heels to the soft, flat ball of the foot as well.

Richard felt his toes begin to swell, the pressure building through each agonising day as they ballooned under the bruising impact of the boots. At night—even during his spell in the sleeping-bag—he dared not take the boots off, terrified that if he did so he would never be able to squeeze the swollen flesh back into them. After eighty-odd miles, he could bear it no more. When they stopped that evening, he asked Lauren if he could borrow her penknife and head torch.

'What for?'

'I want to do some work on my feet.'

'If they need medical attention, that's down to me,' Mel told him.

'I'd rather . . . '

'Let Mel do it,' Lauren insisted. 'Take your boots off now.'

Richard lay back as Lauren and Mel removed his boots by the light of their head torches, stifling a cry as they pulled the frozen sock away from his right foot. There was a collective gasp of sympathy from the team as they saw flesh that looked more like a plate of bloody steak than a human foot. The miles had exacted a terrible toll, the top layers of skin completely eroded so that the red tissue beneath was livid and raw.

'We have to treat this,' Mel told him. 'If these blisters get infected you won't be able to walk.'

She took the Swiss army knife and flicked open the scissors attachment. Closing her mind to the pain she knew she was causing the journalist, she proceeded to cut away the dead flesh around the blisters, trimming it as deep as she could until he begged her to stop. She repeated the process on Richard's left foot, encouraging him with the thought that at least now some of the pressure would be relieved. Then, with the patient still mumbling in anguish, they replaced the socks and jammed his feet back into the boots.

Later that night, as they huddled together for warmth, Richard gently touched Lauren's arm to get her attention. 'You won't leave me?' he whispered. 'You won't leave me if I can't walk?'

'No way,' Lauren reassured him. 'If we have to pull you on the sledge with Frank, we will.' She reached out and squeezed Richard's hand. 'Think about the story you'll have to tell when we all get out of this,' she told him. 'You'll pick up a Pulitzer Prize for sure.'

FITZGERALD PARKED the snowcat a safe distance away and armed himself with the axe. It had to happen now: he hadn't slept a moment that night and he couldn't take the uncertainty any more.

He strode straight into the wreckage of the base. Don't give them any time to think, he reasoned; take them by surprise.

He smashed his shoulder into the outer wall of the shelter, sending the corrugated iron crashing down with a loud clatter into the place where the survivors would be crouching.

Nothing happened. The iron sheet had collapsed to the ground. It was obvious there was no one sheltering inside. Fitzgerald lifted it, still wary that it might be a trick.

They were gone. The space was empty. What the hell was going on? Fitzgerald stood, bewildered, his mind ticking through the options.

A note. There had to be a note, somewhere in the ruins. Whatever action they had taken, Lauren would have left a record, to tell searchers where they had gone. He began to sift through the wreckage, looking for a container, for a box or a burnt-out can that might hold the clue.

In less than five minutes he found it: a tiny piece of paper, rolled up and placed carefully in the hollow interior of a drilling bit, which had been stood on its end as a sign.

Aug 31. Capricorn destroyed by fire following incident in which Julian Fitzgerald attempted to escape from the base. Carl Norland killed. Julian Fitzgerald's whereabouts unknown but approach with extreme caution as he is mentally unstable and violent. Six survivors now set out for Chilean base in direction indicated by arrow. Lauren Burgess, base commander.

Beneath the note was a small graphic depicting compass points. An arrow pointed northeast, the direction of the nearest base.

Fitzgerald read the note again, wanting to make sure that he wasn't seeing things. Heading for the Chilean base? It didn't make any sense. How could they ever hope to make it without food . . . it was physically impossible. And yet the evidence was there in his hands.

He would follow them, wait for them to die. It would all end the same way in any case.

Just as he was about to pull away from the base, Fitzgerald paused. Something had caught his eye. Something strange about some junk that had spewed out onto the glacier. Some of the pieces looked almost like they had been placed there by hand.

It wasn't until he was standing at the tip that he had it. It was an arrow, the debris was arranged perfectly in the shape of an arrow. Anyone arriving by air—and that was the only way they *could* arrive—would see it pointing clearly away from the base.

The explorer checked his compass. The arrow pointed northwest, not leading to the Chilean base at all. So where was it pointing?

Beneath his feet he suddenly noticed a small strip of metal stuck at an odd angle into the ice. The surface around it had been disturbed.

It was lying at the tip of the arrow . . . the very place to put a second note, he quickly realised.

He scraped with his hands, finding the charred remains of a can in just a few seconds. He unfolded the note it contained and read:

Aug 31. From Capricorn commander Lauren Burgess. Ignore any other note found. It is a decoy to throw Julian Fitzgerald off our trail. Have left for the Blackmore Glacier on foot. Heading for the Antarctic Air Service plane that crashed there, to retrieve the emergency transmitter.

An indication of the bearing followed, along with the coordinates of the plane.

Fitzgerald couldn't believe his luck in finding that second note. The first note had been deliberately false. They too were heading for the plane! But how could they make 300 miles on foot?

Then a half-remembered conversation came back to him. There were depots, food and equipment left by Lauren and Sean on the outward leg of the rescue! Why hadn't he thought of that?

There wasn't a moment to lose. Fitzgerald scattered the debris so that the telltale arrow was destroyed, then raced to the snowmobile and set out in pursuit as fast as he could. As he drove, he had to make a conscious effort to calm his rage. Lauren had been clever; he had wasted days observing that ruddy shelter—so nearly been tricked by that false note.

He wouldn't underestimate her again. That much was sure.

FROM THE START of the seventh day, Lauren's nerves were in a heightened state. They were approaching the first of the equipment dumps and it was her responsibility—and hers alone—to locate it. She went through the calculations again as they plodded wearily along, checking her compass every ten minutes for the bearing and calling a halt as they made it to the 100-mile mark.

'This is it,' Lauren told them. 'By my reckoning we should be close to the equipment barrel.'

The tired team scanned in all directions but could see nothing unusual. The terrain was undulating, the surface broken by scoops and hollows; in places drifting snow had formed into hardened dunes. The light was dull, a blanket of cloud obscuring the scene and casting a watery grey sheen over the land. There seemed to be no definition in place, as if the entire scene had been sculpted from dirty bits of old cloud.

'You must be mistaken,' Murdo told her. 'I thought you said this thing had a flag on it? Surely we'd be able to see it straight away?'

'Not necessarily. This ground is more uneven than it looks. Give or take a few hundred yards, it has to be here,' Lauren insisted. 'Let's rest for a while, then get a search pattern organised.'

They rested their exhausted legs, each locked in a private world of misery as they sat on the ice. No one talked about the unthinkable—about what would happen if they couldn't find the depot.

At length, Lauren got them onto their feet and the search began.

Initially, they were enthusiastic, excited even at the prospect of the hot food and supplies that the barrel would bring. But as the day stretched on interminably, morale began to slump.

The mood when Lauren finally called them back together was one of unmitigated depression. No one, not even Lauren and Sean, had anticipated that the barrel would prove so difficult to find.

'Maybe it got blown away,' someone said, flatly.

'Or Fitzgerald got it.'

'Or we're in the wrong place. Your calculations might be wrong.'

Lauren turned to Sean, the frustration clearly written across her face. 'Come on, Sean. Think! What are we doing wrong?'

'Well, the flag obviously isn't upright any more. If it was, we'd have found it by now.'

'But what about the barrel? Why can't we see it? It's a bright blue barrel in the middle of a white wilderness, and we can't see it.'

'Maybe the answer is . . . it's not blue any more. What if it got completely coated in ice during a storm? It's the only reason I can think of that we might have missed it. It's camouflaged. Everyone's so damn tired, someone might have walked right past it!'

'So we're looking for something white. Everyone got that?' Lauren told them.

'Something white? That narrows it down nicely,' Murdo pointed out glumly, waving his arm to encompass the uniform white terrain that surrounded them.

Nevertheless, after an hour of searching, a shout went up to the south of the camp position. It was Sean, waving his hands in the air.

'Got it!' the others heard. 'Here it is!'

The barrel was on its side; one of the anchors that had held it upright had been ripped out of the ice in a gale. The flag was long gone, nowhere to be seen, and—as Sean had predicted—the blue plastic was completely obscured with a coating of ice and by a drift of snow that half covered it.

The team gathered round the barrel, elated and relieved that it had finally been found.

'You see that?' Sean pointed to a set of tracks that passed a few yards to the west of the barrel. 'I was right. Someone did walk right past it on an earlier search and never saw it!'

As they broke open the barrel and began to sort through the contents, Lauren walked over and inspected the tracks, her cheeks burning as she recognised the tread. She never told the others that those boot prints were hers.

FITZGERALD HAD DRIVEN like the wind, pushing the snowcat so hard that the exhaust had glowed red-hot in the night. He didn't dare sleep, knowing that if he could only get to that depot first . . .

He guessed he would make contact some time in the afternoon, and, sure enough, just after 3.00pm, he saw the line of black specks on the horizon. They were crossing and recrossing an area perhaps half a mile wide. They were searching; he realised that straight away.

What had Sean told him about the depots? How many were there? And *where* were they stationed along the route to the crashed plane?

Fitzgerald remembered the milometer on the snowmobile, perhaps that would hold the clue. It read ninety-seven miles. That was it! He felt a wave of satisfaction at the discovery, pleased he had thought to zero the gauge before pulling away from the base.

The depot was 100 miles from base. Simple, really.

As he watched them, he saw the team come together to a specific point. They were more animated now.

They'd found it. Fitzgerald cursed his luck. An hour or two earlier and he would have been there first. But at least he'd found them. He had to be grateful for that. The position of the next depot wasn't hard to fathom, logic told him that it would be placed an equal distance from the base, at the 200-mile point, on the other side of the Heilman Range. He could overtake them whenever he chose.

NO CHILD EVER RIPPED OPEN a Christmas stocking with more delight than the Capricorn team exploring that barrel. Seven days without eating a scrap had driven them to the point where the mere sight of so much food was enough to make them weak at the knees.

Almost as precious as the food was the medical box containing antibiotics, bandages and painkillers—including morphine. Mel took charge of the kit and began to treat Frank's infected hands.

Deeper down and packed tightly beneath the food and medical

supplies, was cooking equipment, two tents and three sleeping-bags. Lauren almost wept when she saw them.

Next the team made a careful stack of the provisions so that Lauren could make a mental list of what they had.

'By my calculations,' she told them, 'we've got enough for six to eight meals each. If we take care, we can eat at least one meal a day each until the next depot.'

They erected one of the tents, and Sean soon put the cooker to work, melting down ice and handing out a steaming plastic mug of cocoa to each of them. After seven days of tepid meltwater, the taste of chocolate was exquisite.

Then each was allowed to choose one of the precooked foil sachets of food—a process they undertook with elaborate care. Lauren chose beans and bacon, and waited her turn for the sachet to be warmed in a pan of boiling water. When she placed the first spoonful in her mouth, it created an explosion of warmth and taste that almost took her breath away.

'We'll have to get a rota system going,' Lauren told them. 'Four people will sleep while two keep watch.'

'You still think we need to mount a watch?' Mel asked her. 'We haven't seen Fitzgerald since we left the base.'

'We keep watch,' Lauren told her. 'Imagine how it would feel to come out here in the morning and find Fitzgerald had stolen all this food and the sledge during the night.'

They agreed the plan. Lauren and Sean would take the first watch. The others, desperate for the warmth, were inside the tent and into sleeping-bags within minutes of finishing the meal.

Out on the glacier, Lauren and Sean sat on the sledge, staying close to the heat of the fire.

'You think Fitzgerald's on our trail?' said Lauren.

'I hope not.' Sean peered out into the night. 'But even if he is, maybe we got lucky and he's hit a problem with the snowmobile. I don't know what kind of mechanic he is, but I sure wouldn't want to be on my own out there with a dead machine.'

Lauren looked out into the darkness. 'Maybe he's keeping just out of sight. He wants us to think he's lost us.'

'So we let down our guard?'

'Precisely.'

When their two-hour watch was over, Lauren and Sean took their turn in the tent while Mel and Murdo took over. Crawling into the protection of a sleeping-bag was a sublime moment. Lauren let the glorious warmth of the duck-down fold around her, and nestled down to sleep as the snores of her companions filled the tent.

'Sean?' she whispered.

'Yep?' His reply showed he was right on the edge of sleep.

'I wanted to tell you something about what happened between us at the base . . . '

Sean turned towards her, his face so close she could feel his breath on her cheek. 'Don't you mean what *didn't* happen between us? I think we would have been cool.'

Lauren leaned forward and kissed him softly on the lips. 'I think so too. And maybe we still will be.'

'If we get out of this alive.'

'ONE AND PULL . . . and two and pull!' Lauren called the moves as they hit the lowest flanks of the Heilman Range, the sledge graunching across the rough ice in fits and starts as the incline began to work against them. It was day eight of the trek.

There were four of them on the harness now, Lauren and Sean at the front, Mel and Murdo at the back. Richard brought up the rear, his damaged feet counting him out of the hauling duty even though he desperately wanted to help.

It was the first morning after finding the depot, and they were better fed and rested than they had been at any other point since the fire. That was why Lauren was pushing them so hard. They'd slept for a straight ten hours, and Lauren had let them eat their fill at breakfast, knowing that they would need every precious calorie for the trial of hauling Frank over the range.

She had them awake at 6.00am. By 10.00am they were navigating their way onto the first of the steep glacier ramps that had seemed so easy with the snowcats.

'Keep it coming!' Lauren urged them on as they paused to rest. 'Another twenty minutes before we stop.'

Somehow they did as she asked, leaning forward and straining in unison, the sledge grinding reluctantly up the ice for a couple more paces before they rested, gasping for breath. With every foot of height, it seemed the sledge was gaining weight.

Midday came. 'Take a break,' Lauren told them. 'Ten minutes.'

She gave them a boiled sweet each and a swig from a water bottle containing powdered orange drink.

'The harness kills me,' Murdo said, sitting heavily on the sledge.

Lauren knew what he meant. The rope had no padding and cut

ever more insistently into the flesh of their waists and hips as they fought to gain altitude. As the ascent went on these erosions became blisters, then the blisters became sores. Within a few hours, every member of the team was suffering from open, weeping wounds around their hips, one more ailment to add to the chronically blistered feet and the problems of burns from the fire.

'Can't we camp?' Mel begged after five hours of hauling. 'I'm really in pain here.'

'We keep going,' Lauren insisted. 'We can make it in one hit. Another few hours and we'll be at the col.'

An afternoon squall whipped across the mountain, slowing their progress. For an agonising hour, as visibility fell, Lauren feared they had lost their way; it would be all too easy to head up the wrong arm of the glacier and find themselves in a dead end. There was no conversation now, just deep panting as they fought against the incline.

A short while later the squall blew away, taking the dense clouds with it and revealing their position. The col was above them. They were right on target. They pulled in a zigzag pattern, exploiting the easiest angles of the slope, traversing back and forth, gaining a few feet of height on each pass.

Forty minutes later, with a last collective heave, they hauled the sledge over the remainder of the pressure ridges and made the final col; they had gained 2,000 feet of altitude in nine hours of ascent, and now the Blackmore Glacier was below them.

'Oh, God,' Murdo gasped as he saw the view, his legs giving way beneath him even as he spoke. 'Is that where we're going?'

LAUREN HAD FOCUSED her mind so sharply on what it would take to get the team up onto the high col that she hadn't even thought about the descent that waited for them on the other side.

It wasn't that the terrain was terribly steep—the height fell away in a gradient not much greater than the lower slopes of an average Scottish mountain. But it was complicated territory, riven by the dissecting fissures of crevasses and crunched-up ice.

By late afternoon they were penetrating the fractured terrain, weaving a trail beneath intimidating blocks of ice. One was shaped like a sail, another a soaring arch like a killer whale's fin. The team passed as quickly as they could beneath these obstacles, knowing that they could fall at any moment.

Little by little they made a safe descent, Sean lowering the weaker members of the team by rope where the ground was too steep to tackle on foot. By this process, they reached a gully that Sean and Lauren remembered from their rescue mission—a long avalanche chute leading in an almost straight line down to the glacier.

Sean called Lauren over. 'You think we can glissade down this?'

Lauren looked down the smooth expanse of ice. 'What if it ends up in a crevasse?'

'It doesn't,' Sean said with certainty. 'We came down it on the snowcats. The bottom runs off gently onto the glacier.'

Now Lauren recalled. 'You know, I think you're right. I think we could try it. But what about Frank?'

'He can stay on the sledge. I'll sit on the back and steer with my feet.'

Once they understood the principle, most of the team were prepared to throw themselves down the slope; anything was preferable to the pain of trying to descend on blistered feet. They followed Lauren's example, sliding on their backsides, using their feet to brake by jamming their heels into the compacted surface when they felt themselves going too fast.

After six days of walking pace the sensation of speed was breathtaking. The sledge was fastest; bearing the heaviest load, it shot past the others at breakneck speed, Sean whooping with excitement on the back, Frank white-faced and looking anything but happy at the front.

Less than five minutes of exhilarating slide put the team at the foot of the gully, where they were spat out onto the glacier.

They regrouped, smiling foolishly at each other after the excitement. The tents were erected and the stoves lit. It was Sean's turn to cook, but no sooner had he lowered the first of the food sachets into boiling water than Lauren was calling him from outside.

'Sean!' her voice hissed at him through the tent fabric.

Sean poked his head out of the front flap. 'What is it?'

'I think I saw a light.' Lauren was pointing up to the high col, faintly visible in the moonlight.

'You serious?' Sean was out of the tent in a moment.

'Yes . . . at least I thought I did . . . ' Now Lauren was uncertain.

Then they both saw it, the briefest pinprick of artificial light, glimmering in the darkness.

'You were right,' Sean whistled. 'That's Fitzgerald. He's camping up on the col. How the hell did he get on our trail?'

Lauren turned to him, her face drained of all blood. 'He didn't fall for the false note. He knows we're heading for the plane.'

'We've got to stop him,' Sean said. 'If he gets to that second depot before we do, we're as good as dead.'

'But how, Sean, when he's so much faster than us?'
'Let me sleep on it.'
'Don't tell the others,' Lauren begged him. 'They've got enough problems as it is.'

'YOU KNOW WHAT we should try?' Sean was sitting next to Lauren during one of the breaks. The team was shattered, spread around the ice, lifeless and despondent on this, the twelfth day of the trek. Progress that day had been grotesquely slow, their pulling power reduced to just a few hundred yards before they were forced to rest.

'No. Surprise me.'

'We should rig up one of the flysheets and try to sail the sledge. This wind is running about twenty knots from the south, right? And this surface is the best we've seen . . . look at it, it's like marble. We haven't crossed a crevasse or a sastruga for miles.'

Lauren scrutinised the surface, shielding her eyes to look ahead, checking for the telltale wrinkles in the glacier surface that would indicate turbulence below.

'You think the flysheet can take it? We can't afford to rip one.'

'I've been thinking about it,' Sean reassured her. 'That flysheet is guaranteed by the manufacturers to stand a wind up to force ten or beyond. It's a brand-new tent without much wear and tear. Plus we can rig it in a way that will minimise the strain.'

'What would you use for a mast?'

'We don't need one. We'd attach it at two points to the front of the sledge and use it like a spinnaker.'

'I'm warming to the idea,' Lauren told him. 'Let's take a look.'

They unpacked the tent from the sledge and brought out the flysheet. Lauren ran the fabric through her fingers, assessing its strength.

Sean handed two of the guy ropes to Lauren and took the other two himself. He opened the flysheet to the wind, seeing with satisfaction that it plumped out smoothly in the air.

The pull was surprisingly strong—strong enough, in fact, that the two of them were immediately dragged forward several yards until Sean could collapse it again.

'We'll give it a go,' Lauren told him, 'but I want someone ahead at all times to check out the terrain for crevasses and holes.'

Thirty minutes later the sledge was under way, utilising wind power for the first time. Sean and Murdo ran the operation, Sean on the front of the sledge to ensure the sail was filling out correctly, and Murdo at the back, ready to brake.

Frank lay with his head buried in his sleeping-bag, preferring not to think of what would happen if they came up too fast to a crevasse.

The sledge ran beautifully on the silky-smooth surface, the sail comfortably generating enough pull to transport the three of them at roughly twice the speed they could achieve on foot. Once they had the system going, they found they were easily outstripping the pace of the others as they tried to follow. A new sound filled their world, the satisfying swish of the runners as they ate up the distance.

Soon the foot party were miles behind and Sean called a halt so they could catch up. 'There's enough pull on this that we could take a skier on the back,' he told them.

There was no shortage of volunteers, and for the rest of the day the team took it in turns to be pulled behind the sledge.

By 5.00pm, the wind was getting too strong to handle, and Sean once or twice lost control of the flysheet completely. He pushed a little further, but within an hour one of the guy ropes had broken.

'No more sailing,' Lauren told Sean, 'but I have to admit, that was a hell of a good day's progress. Worth three days on foot at least.'

As it happened, the smooth conditions they had chanced upon that day were never experienced again. Instead, within a very few miles, they were back in the familiar chopped-up chaos of the crevasse fields, in which they would never have dared to try the sail.

THE MILES WERE TICKING off on Lauren's hand-drawn map. Fitzgerald had not been seen for forty-eight hours. By her calculations they were just three days from the second depot, but the closer they got the more nervous Lauren was becoming.

'Where the hell is he?' she asked Sean.

'Just out of sight, I imagine, keeping on our trail and waiting.'

'But waiting for what?'

Sean gave a bitter laugh. 'He has to *know* we're dead, and know where we die. That way he can bend the story any way he likes. He can't take the risk that any of us will ever be found.'

'That is so sick.'

'Also, this way he can just follow our tracks and know he's on the right trail.'

'And what about the second depot? You think he'll have figured out where it is?'

Sean sucked on his teeth. 'I'd love to say no, but if he saw us at the first depot the chances are pretty high he knows that the second one is at the two-hundred-mile point.'

'And he'll find it . . . '

Sean didn't reply.

They picked up the compass bearing again and set out for the afternoon session, four hunched figures hauling the sledge, Richard trailing far behind. The second depot, the second barrel—the target became so central to the thoughts and desires of the team that scarcely a minute went by when one of them wasn't talking about it, thinking about it or fantasising about what it might contain.

Every step was a step closer.

Their food was running low, low enough that they were down to starvation rations again.

The barrel *had* to be there. And it had to be intact.

'SON OF A BITCH!' Fitzgerald collapsed onto the snowmobile seat, his clothes sticking to him where he had begun to sweat.

What the hell was wrong with this damned machine? Forty-five pulls and the engine still refused to fire. He pulled on the starter again, despairing as no answering spark came back at him. He stared to the north, into the light fall of snow that was obscuring the glacier. What would it mean if the machine really was dead? Fitzgerald could hardly bear to contemplate the consequences.

This game of cat and mouse—a game that the explorer had begun to enjoy thanks to his mechanical advantage—would suddenly transform into something very different. They were ahead. Maybe they could stay ahead. And if they knew the snowmobile had given up, would they not come and hunt him down, six against one?

The explorer shivered, then took the starter cord in his hand and gave it one final yank. The engine gave a faltering stutter, then roared into life. Triumphant, he twisted the throttle hard, watching the revometer creep up to five, six, seven thousand revs.

Right. Which way had they gone? Just a simple matter of following their tracks. Fitzgerald drove to the north for a while until he picked up their trail. The engine continued to trip on itself, the steady throb cutting out intermittently, only to catch up again as the motion refired the cylinder.

What about tomorrow? Would it start again? The uncertainty was beginning to wear him down.

SEAN FIXED HIS EYES on the horizon, looking for the telltale dot.

'I thought of a way of . . . of solving our problem,' he told Lauren. 'How about Deep Throat?'

Lauren screwed up her face as her exhausted mind tried to make the connection required of it. 'Deep Throat?'

'It's between us and the second depot. Don't you think it would make a perfect trap?'

Lauren got it. 'Oh my God, Sean. You think we can do that?'

'It's worth a try. I'll do it alone if you have a problem with it.'

Lauren stared at him intently, doubt written in her expression. 'I don't know. It takes us into . . . dangerous territory. I've never—'

'And you think I have?' Sean protested.

'No, just that there might be questions. Later. We might have to tell our story . . . and . . . '

Now Sean got really close to her. 'It's him or us, Lauren. We already worked that one out, remember?'

'Give me some time, Sean. I need to consider this properly. This is big; it's going to change plenty of things if we do it.'

'Yeah. Like give us a fighting chance.'

For Lauren the day passed in a haze. She pulled on her harness, pushed her legs into the endless cycle of push—rest—push, but her mind was fixed on Deep Throat, on the dilemma that Sean's proposal had opened up inside her.

Lauren knew that, whatever happened, the decision would divide her permanently in some way—a tear in the fabric of her own morality, a rip, with edges that were not clean. The type of wound that gets infected easily. But she was also in the grip of the most powerful force any human being can experience—the imperative that has no equal: to survive.

Later, as they prepared one of the tents together, Lauren found the chance to speak with Sean. 'I've thought about it,' she told him quietly, 'and I think it's worth a try. But the others can't know about this. They absolutely mustn't.'

Sean showed no signs of surprise; he took her decision as a matter of fact. 'We'll do it tonight, when they're all asleep.'

AT 11.00PM, LAUREN FOLLOWED Sean's dark shadow away from the tents, keeping her footsteps in the tracks of the empty sledge he was towing. Sean waited until they were out of earshot. 'Let your eyes adjust,' he whispered to her. 'We can't risk the head torches.'

Thanks to the moon, the crevasses were not difficult to see. They bypassed the bigger ones and jumped the more slender cracks at their narrowest point.

Then Sean began to move with more caution. He stabbed a ski

pole into the snow and got down carefully onto his knees.

'OK,' he told her. 'I think this is it. I'm pushing into thin air just in front of us.' He punched a small hole in the snow bridge that lay before him, then placed the head torch inside it. Switching it on, he saw immediately that they had found Deep Throat, the feeble beam hinting at the great depth of the crevasse beneath him.

Lauren shivered. 'What about the tracks? Even if he's tired, he'll notice them disappear.'

Sean pulled a length of cord from his pocket and cast it out onto the snow bridge. Then he dragged it back. After a dozen or so casts, Lauren could already see the faint lines in the soft snow stretching out for yards in front of them.

'That's not very convincing,' said Lauren. 'What about footprints?'

Sean took a gloveful of snow and squeezed it until he had created a hard ball. This he threw out onto the snow bridge as a test. A dark hole appeared where it had sunk a little into the soft surface.

Lauren joined him, and for some minutes they were busy moulding handfuls of snow to create small craters across the snow bridge.

Sean risked a quick glimpse with the torch.

'That's better,' he said. 'It's never going to bear close scrutiny but hopefully by the time Fitzgerald works out something weird's happening it'll all be over.'

They retraced their steps, concentrating hard not to lose their trail back to the tent. Then they walked back to Deep Throat one more time, both stumbling with the utter fatigue of that long day. The end result was a confusion of footsteps and sledge tracks that certainly looked like it had been made by the whole party.

Then they returned to the tent a final time.

'That's it,' Sean whispered. 'Trap set. Now it's down to Deep Throat to do the job for us.'

AT 5.00AM THEY WOKE the others, rousing them with some difficulty from their sleeping-bags.

'We're breaking the routine today,' Lauren told them. 'We've got to get out of here right away, but we'll stop for breakfast after a couple of hours. Try to keep as quiet as you can.'

No one questioned her; there was something in the clipped urgency of Lauren's tone that did not invite further enquiry.

After a short distance, Sean left Lauren to continue with the route-finding and made his way back to the campsite. Using a ski pole, he smoothed over the trail they had just made, continuing until he had obscured some thirty or forty yards of their progress. Now the heaviest trail leading from the tent site was the false one he had marked up with Lauren the previous night.

He hurried back to the others.

Not long after daybreak the team reached a large depression, a scoop in the glacier guarded by a low pressure ridge.

'This is a good place,' Sean told Lauren. 'Let's park the crew here.'

She took off her pack. 'Let's stop for some food,' she said.

They didn't need to be told twice. Within seconds their loads were scattered around the ice, the team resting gratefully on their packs.

'I'll keep an eye out for you know who,' Sean told her quietly. 'Join me when you can.'

Once she had the first litre of water boiling, Lauren let Mel take over the food preparation and slipped away to join Sean, sure that the team were so tired they would barely notice their absence.

'Sean, I'm still not sure,' she said, as they made their way back up the glacier. 'Maybe we should be thinking about this another way. Maybe the two of us can get close to him somehow, overpower him?'

Sean stopped dead. 'Can I remind you of something? We're unarmed, he's got an axe. We've been on starvation rations for a two-hundred-mile trek, and he's been eating as much as he needs every day. We wouldn't stand a chance. The only thing about this that worries me is the fact that in eliminating Fitzgerald we're going to lose his snowmobile. That's where I am, Lauren. I'm at that point, OK?'

'Well, I'm not in the same place as you, then,' Lauren told him. 'I don't know if we have a right to do this.'

'So go back and wait with the others if you want.'

She shook her head and they continued in silence.

Not far from Deep Throat they found a prominent block of ice that was big enough to hide behind.

One hour. Two hours. Time crept slowly by. Lauren and Sean began to freeze into their positions, their muscles cramping as the cold began to bite.

Suddenly Sean stiffened as he spotted something. 'Here we go.'

The minutes ticked past as Fitzgerald weaved a steady route through the crevasse field towards them. Now they could hear the engine, shockingly loud in the still air of the glacier.

After what seemed to Lauren to be an age, the snowmobile arrived at their campsite of the previous night. Fitzgerald slowed perceptibly as he scanned the clues left in the ice, then he was accelerating once more, driving confidently down the trail that Lauren and Sean had laid towards Deep Throat.

'Oh yes!' Sean couldn't hide the excitement from his voice. 'Now a little more speed and everything's going to be over real quick.'

'This is so wrong,' Lauren hissed. 'There has to be another way!'

'Lauren, no!'

Sean lunged forward but he was too late. Lauren had left the hiding place and was already stumbling across the glacier towards Deep Throat.

'Stop! You have to stop!'

Fitzgerald could not hear her above the noise of the engine. He was fifty yards from the edge of the crevasse.

'Stop!' she screamed.

Fitzgerald glanced up and Lauren was so close to him she could actually see his jaw drop down in astonishment. Then he slammed hard on the brakes, bringing the snowmobile to a halt just half a pace away from the wafer-thin snow bridge of Deep Throat.

The explorer took in the scene: the clumsy fake tracks that petered out midway across the snow bridge, the sag in the middle that hinted at the drop below. For a while they were both silent, the only noise the brittle crack of the snowmobile engine as it ticked over.

'You can see what we wanted to do,' Lauren called out across the crevasse, 'but I think there's a better way.'

She paused, expecting a response, but Fitzgerald made none.

'Two of my team are sick, Julian, really sick. If you help us with the snowmobile, maybe we can sort things out between us. You'll have to answer for what happened at the base when we get back to civilisation. But if you help us . . . and we all get out alive, we can make things easier for you.'

Fitzgerald said nothing, just continued to stare directly at Lauren. Then he revved up the engine, turned back on his tracks and drove away, back through the crevasse field.

Then Sean was standing next to her. 'That was our chance, Lauren,' he said quietly. 'And you threw it away.'

FITZGERALD CREASED OVER and retched his breakfast onto the ice. He breathed in deeply, trying to recover from the shock.

So close. He'd been a hair's-breadth from death. And he'd been right all along. They *had* been plotting to kill him. They *did* know he was following. At secret meetings they had discussed the best way of crushing him, of sending him to hell.

And then . . . The explorer frowned. Had it really happened? He ran back through his mind. Lauren had run to warn him! In fact, she had saved his life. Why had she done that? Fitzgerald climbed off his snowmobile and stood uncertainly.

Lauren had been weak. It was her first mistake. But there was no longer any doubt about the team's intention to kill him.

Far off, he could see Lauren and her team picking their way through the crevasses of the glacier, a weaving line of dark figures heading off into the blackening void.

Things would be different from now on, Fitzgerald promised himself. So far he'd been passive, content to follow, to watch.

Now that time was over.

LAUREN SCRAPED the stubborn layer of ice off the face of the compass and checked the bearing, turning the plastic bezel until north was aligned. The red needle was sluggish and slow to swing round, the fluid inside the case close to freezing now the temperature had dropped so low.

They were seventeen days into the trek, and for the last twenty-four hours a dense low cloud had enveloped the glacier, reducing visibility to just fifty yards or less. It made progress more dangerous for the team and made navigation even more critical for Lauren; without the compass bearing they would be hopelessly lost.

Lauren's tactic in these conditions was to keep the team as closely packed as she could. 'No one loses sight of the person in front,' she told them. 'That's the rule. We can't be sure of finding you again if you get separated from the group.'

The team, terrified at the prospect of becoming lost in the whiteout conditions, did as she asked, bunching into a tight unit, the stronger ones dropping their pace to allow the weaker ones to keep up.

As night encroached, they made camp for the seventeenth time.

'We can forget about the watch rota for tonight,' Lauren told them as they settled in for the night. 'Fitzgerald couldn't find us in this stuff even if he wanted to.'

'We should get the food inside us now,' Sean said, 'while we've still got the energy.'

They melted down ice and drank lukewarm tea and a half-cup of muesli each. The muesli had to be portioned out in advance, mainly because the raisins were so sought after that they had to be counted out individually.

Next morning the fog was still with them, but at least there were fewer crevasses to worry about. They set out at dawn, making steady progress for five hours or so, bringing them to the area in which Lauren calculated the second barrel should be found.

'What can you remember about this place?' Lauren asked Sean.

'It was close to a boulder,' Sean recalled, trying to picture the terrain. 'A boulder the size of a car. If we had good visibility we'd see the damn thing from ten miles away. That's why we chose it.'

They worked by the compass, following a bearing for ten minutes, then turning as close as they could estimate to ninety degrees for a further ten-minute line. The same procedure repeated twice again brought them full circle, or rather, full square, back to the vicinity of the tent. Having drawn a blank they would pause to rest, then set out on a different bearing, five degrees to the west.

Here and there, crisscrossing the ice in seemingly random patterns, they came across the indentations of snowmobile tracks.

'Fitzgerald has been in this area,' Sean confirmed, examining the indentations, 'and recently too. These tracks would have been blown away within forty-eight hours.'

Lauren said nothing, but her heart sank a little further every time they found more tracks. Please God he hadn't found the depot, Lauren prayed; please God he hadn't done that.

After some hours of this, they abandoned the search and retreated, aching and despondent, to the tents, where they ate just a quarter of a tin of processed meat each before huddling close for the night.

The following morning, after a miserable night, Lauren joined Sean once more for a foray out into the void.

'We've got to cast the net wider,' she told him. 'I think we're further from it than we realise.'

They began the process again, going out for twenty minutes on each bearing, peering into the void in the hope of seeing something—anything—other than the spectral swirling of the fog.

At last, looming out of the frozen mist, a dark, bulbous shape emerged. The boulder was in front of them with the barrel nearby, lying on its side. The black plastic lid and metal sealing ring were scattered on the ice nearby.

Sean pulled the barrel upright. It was empty. For a while they both stood there, staring dumbly into the interior.

'Oh Christ.' Lauren's voice faltered as she realised the full significance of the development. 'He's left us with nothing. We don't even have any drugs for Frank's hands.'

They were paralysed, nailed to the spot.

'How much further can we go, Sean?' she asked him, trying to get her mind round the distance that still separated them from the plane. 'How much further can we go without food?'

He shook his head as he looked over at Lauren, his face as white as the ice that clung to it.

'And how are we going to tell the others?' Lauren asked him, the tears already welling up in her eyes. 'What can we possibly say?'

BACK IN LONDON, Alexander De Pierman was a worried man. As the days had ticked by and one week stretched into two, he had been expecting to hear from Lauren at any moment. When no call came from Capricorn, he told himself they must still be having problems with their satellite gear.

Dr Michael Collins, the director of the Scott Polar Research Institute—who were also part-sponsors of Capricorn—called on day thirteen. He too was beginning to be concerned at the duration of the blackout, and wondered if De Pierman had any news.

There was none.

But it wasn't like Lauren to leave them in the dark, they both agreed. She would know they would be itching for news of the drilling project, which should have produced some results by now.

Day nineteen. De Pierman consulted with the Scott Polar and they decided that, if there was no news by the end of the week, they would fund a flight to find out what was going on at Capricorn.

MISERY WORMED ITS WAY into their souls like a parasite setting up home in a gut. The deepest depression had struck them, a sense of exposure and helplessness as solid and intractable as the one-mile-deep ice beneath their feet.

'What's the point?' Murdo snapped at Lauren when she tried to rouse him from his sleeping-bag. 'We lost the battle and we're going to die. Better to die in a sleeping-bag than slogging our guts out there in the deep freeze, for nothing.'

'I'm taking the tents down in five minutes,' Lauren warned him. 'We'll leave you here alone if you don't get up.' She hated to play the bully, but this was the only way.

'Give me one reason . . . ' Murdo mumbled, his head turned away. 'One good reason to carry on.'

'Because if we quit now, we definitely can't win. There's still a chance, Murdo, that we can get to the plane before Fitzgerald. His snowmobile might break down . . . he might get lost in a storm . . .

fall down a crevasse.' As she spoke the words, Lauren was painfully aware of how thin they sounded.

She left Murdo to extract himself from his sleeping-bag and went to help Sean with Frank. The radio man was now incapable of using his hands at all. Every zip, every button had to be fastened for him. They helped him out of the tent and pulled him clumsily to his feet.

'Do you want Mel to take a look at your hands today?' Lauren asked him.

Frank shook his head violently. 'No, no.'

'Is it my imagination?' Lauren asked Sean when they were out of earshot, 'or are Frank's hands beginning to smell real bad?'

'They sure are,' Sean agreed. 'I've never smelt an infection like that.'

'We should watch him carefully today. I think he's sicker than he's letting on.'

The temperature was breathtakingly low, somewhere down in the minus fifties, Lauren estimated. The severity of the cold seemed to turn them to statues where they stood. The very idea of walking fifteen or twenty miles that day, with nothing to eat, seemed so ridiculous it almost made Lauren want to cry.

'How many miles to the plane?' Sean asked her quietly.

'Ninety. Plus.'

'Frank's not going to make it. He's going down fast.'

'I know. And so is Richard,' Lauren replied. 'You reckon we can pull him *and* Frank on this thing?'

Sean did not reply.

FRANK HAD A FEVER when he woke the next day and complained that his fingers were feeling worse.

'Not that I want to get a reputation as a whinger,' he told Lauren, 'but I'm beginning to feel a little rough.'

He was beginning to look a little rough, too; in fact, Lauren was alarmed by the permanent green tinge to his complexion and the sweat that she knew had begun to plague him in the night.

He finally agreed for the medic to examine his fingers. Mel winced when she peeled back the bandages; the smell was absolutely putrid, the skin black and obviously decaying.

'Well, we've certainly had a deterioration here,' she said as she examined the tissue. 'I'm going to be honest with you, Frank. You've got the first indications of gangrene in three of these fingers.'

Frank was distraught. 'Oh God. What about the antibiotics? Aren't they clearing it up?'

'No. They can keep the infection at bay but they can't beat something this strong. Also, as the days go by, your own body defences are getting weaker with the lack of food and the general conditions.'

'When does the course of antibiotics run out?' Lauren asked.

'In two days. And that's it. We only had the one course packed in the first barrel. This infection will probably progress very rapidly without the curbing effects of the antibiotics.'

'And the long-term prognosis?' Frank's voice sounded so thin and frightened it brought a lump to Lauren's throat.

Mel sucked her cheeks for a while, plucking up the courage.

'We're talking about amputation,' she said, finally.

'GET UP, RICHARD, it's time to go.'

The journalist buried his head further into the warmth of his sleeping-bag, murmuring incoherently.

'Richard! Get out of the bag!' It was a woman's voice, but he was unsure if it was Lauren or Mel.

Getting out of that bag was the last thing Richard wanted to do. This was his healing time, time to devote to thoughts of home, time to teleport his mind back to the life that had once belonged to him—if it really had been him at all. He wouldn't be the same person now, he was sure of that, if he ever got out of this alive.

A hand pulled at his shoulder, followed by the sound of the sleeping-bag zip being unfastened. Richard groaned, then reluctantly sat up, the stiff muscles in his shoulders and stomach sending dull shivers of pain though him as he moved.

He found Lauren squatting in the entrance to the tent.

'The others are ready,' she told him. 'We've got miles to kill.'

Richard heard himself laugh bitterly, a laugh that turned quickly into a racking cough. 'Miles to kill?' he spluttered weakly. 'That makes me laugh, for some reason.'

The journalist tried to get his legs to work, but they felt as lifeless as wood. He could feel the muscles contract slightly in his thighs, but they were so weak he could not lift his lower body out of the bag. Lauren did it for him, placing both her hands underneath his calves and swivelling him into a position where she could get at his feet.

She pulled at the laces in his boots, creating enough slack to open them up a little, then she slid his boots onto his bandaged feet and tightened them up as gently as she could. Richard couldn't help a whimper as some of the blistered flesh was pinched.

'I don't want to stand,' he told her.

'You have to.' Lauren stood behind him and hauled him to his feet. Richard felt the tears come to his eyes as his pulped flesh began to pulsate and flare. This moment was always one he dreaded, the rush of blood to his inflamed feet as he put his weight on them. He took a few panting breaths and waited while Lauren slid the skis into position beneath his boots. Then they set out together towards the north.

Richard did his best, he really did, but his speed was a fraction of what the others could achieve. He stared at the sledge longingly as it passed. Was there room for two on there, he wondered? And could the others pull it?

Lauren stayed by his side, supporting him as best she could and keeping up a rolling conversation. Richard was suffering so badly with the pain from his feet that he could barely pay attention to what she was saying.

Late in the morning they came to a pressure ridge blocking their path. It was a big one, Richard could see, a real epic to cross.

And that was the moment. The end of what his body could do. Now he didn't care how many miles there were to go; he had given all he had to give.

Richard felt his knees buckle as he decided to quit. That was when he discovered that the only thing that had been keeping him upright was his will-power. As for the sinews and muscles of his legs, well, they weren't going to be taking him anywhere soon . . . if ever again.

Lauren stood over him, her face resigned.

'That's it,' he told her, 'I need the sledge.'

IT DIDN'T TAKE LONG to discover that it needed all four of them to tow the two men. Previously Lauren and Sean had done most of the hauling, but now there was no escape for Murdo and Mel. The conditions were soft, the snow deep enough to make progress slow.

They tugged in unison, pushing forward on their skis and swearing bitterly as the rope sliced a little more into them with each jolting movement. They completed four miles on the day Richard threw in the towel, and now were into the second day of the extra load—one that Lauren was determined would tick off ten or more miles.

On the sledge the two men lay side by side, saying little as they were pulled along. Frank was now profoundly depressed, the gangrenous state of his fingers dominating his thoughts. He didn't complain, but Lauren could see he was hurting badly.

Richard was also sinking ever deeper into depression, his blistered feet showing no signs of healing and still grotesquely swollen. She knew there was absolutely no chance they would ever get his boots on again—not until he could get hospital treatment at least.

At midday Lauren finally called a rest stop, the team falling to the ice just where they stood, without the strength to prop themselves up against a sastruga or to sit with their backs to the sledge.

They rested for an hour, no one exchanging a single word. Then a hailstorm whipped up from nowhere, the stinging pellets of ice bouncing off their Gore-Tex clothing with a pattering sound. Still no one said a word or even moved. Anyone stumbling across the scene could easily have imagined that they were all dead.

Lauren dreaded the moment she had to motivate them to begin again—to bully them onto their feet and get them into the hated harnesses ready for more hauling.

'How many miles?' Mel asked as Lauren helped her to her feet.

'About sixty.'

Mel hung her head, shaking it gently from side to side.

'It's OK,' Lauren put her arm round Mel's shoulders, holding her close. 'We're all going to make it.'

'That's the mantra,' Murdo said bitterly, 'but does anyone still believe it?'

'It's not just a mantra,' Lauren said as they pulled away. 'It's the truth. We're all going to make it. No one's going to die.'

But for the first time her words sounded hollow, and Lauren knew why. She was no longer 100 per cent certain, not now they had so much extra weight to haul.

'Pull . . . ' she gasped, 'and pull again . . . '

Deep in her heart she was no longer sure. But something inside her was still going to try.

IT WAS TWENTY-THREE DAYS since Lauren had informed her sponsors of her radio problem, and De Pierman and the Scott Polar were now at the point where they knew they had to act. The Antarctic winter was coming to an end; the ambient temperatures might just allow a plane to land. The Antarctic Air Service promised to give it a try.

There was a weather delay, but finally the Twin Otter managed to set out for the Capricorn location. The following day, De Pierman got the news on a crackly telephone line from Tierra del Fuego. Capricorn was completely gutted by fire. The AAS pilots had been able to land and confirmed that there were no survivors.

'Did you find any bodies?' De Pierman asked them, distraught now his worst fears had been realised.

'It is doubtful there would be any. Even the metal was melted.'

De Pierman knew enough about oil-rig fires to know what they were saying. A human body is organic and will crumble to dust given enough temperature. Even the enamel of the teeth will shatter and explode if the fire is intense enough.

'How about transport?' he asked them. 'Were you able to see if any of their snowmobiles were missing?'

'We found the remains of a vehicle shed,' the pilot told him. 'There were definitely the remains of snowmobiles in there but as for how many, it was hard to tell . . . two or three at least.'

De Pierman was shattered; his one foray into scientific sponsorship had ended in total disaster, and the negative backlash would have far-reaching repercussions for both him personally and for Kerguelen Oils. More importantly, he felt a genuine sadness at the loss of so many talented people, and particularly for Lauren, whom he had come to like and admire.

De Pierman knew he would have to go public with the disaster, but his first call was to the Scott Polar to break the tragic news. The director took it badly, breaking down in tears on learning that Lauren—whom he'd worked with on several field projects—was lost.

By 5.00pm De Pierman was addressing more than a hundred reporters, giving them the news that Capricorn was destroyed, and with no realistic hope of any survivors.

Lauren Burgess was dead, he told them, and so was Fitzgerald and his team mate, the *Daily Mail* journalist and all the rest of the Capricorn crew. The response to the disaster was electric, the stunned journalists running to their mobiles to reserve the front page for this sensational new twist.

THEY OPERATED ON FRANK the following morning, after a night in which he tossed and turned in agony.

'Do it today,' he urged them. 'I really can't bear this any more.'

Lauren and Mel prepared the instruments for the operation. There was a Swiss army knife, a syringe full of morphine, a small phial of iodine and what remained of the first-aid kit that had been in the first barrel.

'Thank God we've got the morphine and the sutures,' Lauren said, looking at the meagre supplies. 'Which blade are you going to use?'

The medic flicked open the multibladed device, selecting the saw attachment. 'This one. It needs a cutting edge to be able to get through the bone, you see,' she said.

Lauren began to feel sick.

They fired up the gas cooker and began to melt down chunks of ice to create a supply of water. When it boiled, they sterilised the Swiss army knife by immersing it in the pan for ten minutes.

'We're ready,' Mel told Lauren at last. 'Bring in the patient.'

Lauren walked to the other tent, where Frank was waiting. His fever was still raging, his hair plastered to his head with sweat even though the temperature was down to twenty degrees below freezing. The others were sitting round the camp, frightened to look Frank in the eye. They knew what he was about to endure.

In the operation tent, Mel took the iodine and cleaned the wounds as best she could, trying not to gag as the rancid smell of the decomposing flesh filled the air. She noted that the gangrene had spread another quarter of an inch towards the knuckle. This operation was only just in time, she thought, or Frank would have lost the hand.

'I'm going to inject half of the morphine now to alleviate the pain of the operation,' she told Frank. 'This is going to hurt a bit. We'll save the other half for later.'

Frank screamed as she injected the painkiller directly into the infected fingers.

'All right, that's going to deaden the feeling.'

Mel waited five minutes while Lauren talked soothingly to Frank. Then she began to work with the tiny saw. He fainted, as she had warned he might. Lauren held his head up so his airway was clear, and by the time Mel completed the operation he was just coming round. Mel stitched the wounds, then cleaned them with iodine once more and dressed the hand to stem the blood loss.

The team carried Frank to his sleeping-bag, and Mel and Lauren stayed with him in the tent through that long day. He wavered in and out of consciousness as the hours went past, helped into a befuddled oblivion by the effects of the last of the morphine.

The crisis came at about 3.00am, when it seemed his fever was set to return. His temperature rocketed as his immune system fought back, his cries terrible to hear in the stillness of the night air. But by dawn he was clearly recovering. The fever had subsided and his skin colour looked relatively normal for the first time in days.

At first light they managed to get a cup of sweet tea inside the patient, and by 10.00am he was sitting up and sipping the cup of asparagus soup that they had prepared for him.

'There's no more morphine,' Mel told him.

'No matter. This pain is nothing compared to the gangrene,' Frank told them. 'And by the way, shouldn't we be getting under way?'

Lauren looked at him with astonishment, amazed at the resilience of the man. 'You think you're well enough to get back on the sledge?'

'I wouldn't want to let you down,' he said.

'I think,' Lauren told him, 'that I've never been prouder of anyone than I am of you at this moment. Not many people would bounce back after what you've been through.'

When Frank emerged and took his place on the sledge next to Richard, he got a rousing chorus of cheers from the rest of the team, and thirty minutes later they were packed up and pulling away from the camp, inching their way slowly towards their objective. Frank's incredible courage had re-energised the team when they should have been on their last legs.

As they pitched the two tents that night, Lauren felt her heart bursting with pride. 'We did nine miles today,' she told the team. 'I think we should split open one of the chocolate bars to celebrate.'

She supervised the cutting of the bar—one of only three left from the first depot—and no one mentioned that the knife used to cut the chocolate was the same one that had been used to amputate Frank's fingers just twenty-four hours before.

'YOU MIGHT THINK this is a bit crazy,' Richard told Lauren as they set out the next morning, 'but I think there's about to be a shift in the weather. My legs ache like hell when the pressure drops. Right now, they're both throbbing like crazy.'

Lauren viewed the horizon. As yet she could see no evidence of any dramatic shift in the weather, but something told her, as she breathed the bitter morning air into her lungs, that Richard was right. There *was* a detectable change in the air—a pressure shift, which could only add up to bad news.

'We could be heading for some serious weather,' she warned the team. 'Let's get some miles ticked off while we still can.'

Obediently, they put in an extra effort, covering almost two miles in the next hour. Huge snowflakes fell, dancing like thistledown from the sky, so big they seemed artificial.

'Hollywood snow,' Sean called it, holding out his hand and admiring the feather-sized flakes that landed on it. 'If you wrote it into a script, no one would believe it.'

The gentle snowfall stopped by eleven, giving way to an altogether less attractive bombardment: pea-sized granules of hail from charcoal-grey clouds that scudded past with alarming speed.

Way out to the west, perhaps as much as 100 miles off but already visible, Lauren could just detect the telltale black line of the incoming storm where it was playing on the horizon.

As they took a break, Lauren considered the terrain. 'We're on relatively high ground. See where the glacier dips down a little over there, about a mile away? Let's get there before we camp.'

The team knew it was a device, Lauren's tactic to get them to put in that extra mile—that there was little more protection where they were going than the place where they stood. Nevertheless, they did it, putting their backs into hauling the sledge, biting their tongues to prevent themselves from crying out loud as the hated harness dug its way ever more deeply into the sores on their hips.

Lauren called a halt. The wind was a force four to five, not unusual for any Antarctic day, but right on the edge of feasibility when it came to putting up a dome tent or two.

'Let's do it fast,' she ordered, hoping she hadn't left it too late.

Lauren and Sean pulled their Gore-Tex tent from its sack, the fabric immediately coming alive and threatening to rip out of their hands.

'One person on the guy rope at all times!' Lauren called over to the others. 'You let go of that tent and it'll be blown a thousand miles.'

Lauren handed the vital guy rope to Richard. He held it tight, still sitting on the sledge, his hood pulled down low around his face to give some relief from the pounding hail.

It was hit-and-miss work with the tent billowing fit to rip, but in ten minutes or so it was up. Lauren transferred Frank from the sledge into the interior, then she helped Murdo put the final touches to the other tent. The camp was made—and not a moment too soon. Just as Lauren and Sean zipped themselves into the second tent, the leading edge of the storm surged across the glacier. The previous gusts had been innocent by comparison, outriders of the real event.

Lauren knew, as she watched the dome roof of the tent begin to shudder with the impact of the wind, that they were now at the mercy of whatever the Antarctic chose to throw at them.

For twenty-four hours they lay in their sleeping-bags, hanging desperately to the fabric of the tents in the fight to keep them from blowing apart. The storm had not abated as Lauren had hoped; if anything, now into the second day, it was increasing in intensity.

At 3.00am on that second day, Lauren noticed that the central seam of the tent was beginning to split. It was a minute tear—just half an inch or so in length—but she knew if the wind got into it, the tent would be turned inside out in seconds.

'We're going to lose the tents,' Lauren yelled at Sean as she showed him the rip. 'We have to give ourselves more protection.'

'How?'

'We've got to build a wall. If this storm keeps blowing for another twenty-four hours, there's no way we can keep the tents up without a wind block.'

They fought their way out of the tent and into the teeth of the storm. Working with the head torch, Sean set to with Lauren. They used their basic tools to hack what chunks they could out of the frozen glacier. It was testing work, with the savage wind snapping in their faces, but one hour of shared labour created a pile of irregular-shaped blocks with which they managed to construct a sheltering wall about three feet high. Then it was back into the tent to wait.

The next day dragged unbearably, the wind picking up as night crept over the wasteland. Sleep was impossible; the sheer volume of the storm was enough to keep them awake despite the deep vein of exhaustion that ran through them all. Living conditions were miserable, made worse by the fine layer of powder snow that was constantly blasted through the entrances of the tents.

By 4.00am the snow was beginning to drift, the weight pressing down on the occupants of the tents until it threatened to suffocate them. Lauren and Sean went out into the whiteout every hour to shovel the stuff away with their hands, but each time they were forced back in by the cold before they could completely clear the tents.

And so the second night passed, a trial of cold, of damp, of pain for Frank with his mutilated hand.

At about eleven in the morning, the storm finally decided it would take some time out, the wind dying off to a modest force three or four, the driving snow tailing away in a succession of last-gasp flurries.

Lying in the tent, Lauren could feel the conditions begin to change. Gradually, the cracking of Gore-Tex diminished, the whipping of loose guy ropes became less frequent, until—finally—it was possible to fall into an exhausted sleep.

IT WAS TWENTY-NINE days since the team had left the base; now every step was punctuated by a long pause to rest.

The weather was still unstable, one small blizzard after another sweeping across the glacier and plunging them into whiteout conditions for hours on end. It made route-finding a nightmare, costing them time and precious energy as they were forced to detour and skirt the countless crevasses and faults.

Then they reached the biggest gulf yet: a crevasse that looked—from the fresh blue colour of the interior—as if it had only recently opened up.

'This one could be miles wide,' Sean said gloomily.

They sat on the sledge for a rest, everyone locked in their own thoughts as the wind and snow played around them. Finally, Lauren spoke. 'You take the east,' she told Sean. 'I'll recce this way.'

Lauren checked her compass and slowly walked west for some ten or fifteen minutes, keeping the crevasse edge on her right side. The driving snow was thickening with every passing moment, and visibility was poor. She decided to go on another ten minutes; in her mind was the fear that, if they pitched camp in this trap, they would never again have the physical strength to get out. She prayed that Sean was having more luck in the other direction.

Then she paused. Through the wind rush she could hear the sound of someone coughing. She rubbed the ice from her eyes and took a few steps forward, straining to see something—anything—through the snow. She checked her compass, thoroughly confused. Could she have turned a full circle? Was that noise the sound of someone where she'd left the team? Or was it Sean? She advanced a few more steps. The coughing continued. Except now she realised it wasn't coughing at all. It was more mechanical. More metallic.

Now she could see a dark shape through the swirling snow. It seemed to be red, but what could be red out here? There was someone next to it, stooping with his back to her.

Then she got it. Shit! It was Fitzgerald! Lauren froze to the spot, her heart thumping like a jackhammer in her chest as she stared in terror at the explorer's back

What if he heard her? What if he turned and saw her? She was too far from the others for them to hear a scream.

She realised his snowmobile had broken down. The coughing noise was the starter cord as he pulled it back. She could see that the fully laden sledge was still attached to the snowmobile. There was all the food . . . all the medical supplies . . .

Then she saw the axe. It was lying against the sledge, placed between her and the explorer. Now the adrenaline was pumping harder than Lauren had ever known before.

A moment in which to act . . . or to flee? Then an image of the empty second barrel flashed into her mind, and the ghastly sight of Mel sawing through Frank's fingers with a blunt penknife. She knew there was only one way to resolve this now.

Lauren moved carefully forward. She was close enough to hear Fitzgerald's curses. She picked up the axe, felt the smooth wooden handle in her hand, raised it, and aimed for the back of the explorer's head.

Her movement caught Fitzgerald's eye, a reflection in the snowmobile's mirror, perhaps, as she prepared the blow.

'Wha—?' He began to rise, turning abruptly as he did so, his cry of surprise cut off midword.

The axe struck a vicious but glancing blow into his right shoulder, deep enough that Lauren could feel it hit bone. Fitzgerald turned, the shock of the impact sending his face into contortions as it seemed his eyes would pop out of his head.

Lauren retreated a few more steps, the axe raised for a second blow, watching in appalled fascination as Fitzgerald reached up and felt the wound. He stared at his fingers, examining the blood as if he couldn't quite believe it was his.

He made a lunge for her, a roar of pain and anger coming from his mouth as he snatched at the air. Lauren turned, ducking to avoid his grasp, then she was running into the whiteout, dodging between ice pillars and scattered blocks, until she was sure she had lost him.

FITZGERALD GAVE UP the chase and returned quickly to the snowmobile, his body surging with adrenaline and the aftershock of the completely unexpected attack. He could sense that the wound in his back was serious, but there would be time for that later.

For now he had to move fast, away from this place on foot. But what could he take? And what would he have to leave? Leave them nothing. Take as much as you can tow, but leave them nothing else.

Frantically he began to dismantle the contents of the sledge, tossing packets, tins and containers of rice and pasta into the crevasse until the load was roughly half what it had been. With the drugs he was more selective, tossing out first-aid kits but keeping the morphine, antibiotics and syringes.

He gave the sledge a tug. It was heavy, but he knew he had the strength to move it. And the snowmobile? No way was he going to leave them that little toy. He couldn't get it going, but that was no guarantee that Sean couldn't. He dipped his good shoulder down and levered with all the power in his legs. The machine began to move, a few inches at a time. Within a couple of minutes he had it at the edge of the crevasse, where a mighty shove tipped it over the lip.

Hurrying back, Fitzgerald took a length of rope and tied it off round his waist. Then he looped the free end round the front of the sledge. He snapped his boots into his skis and moved away into the safety of the blizzard, navigating by his compass and changing direction with a zigzag every time he found polished ice. Leave no tracks, he told himself, or they'll be able to follow you.

As he got into his stride, he tried to pull his mind together. It was roughly forty miles to the crashed aircraft; he could do it in three days, maybe forty-eight hours at a push.

He could afford little rest now; he'd have to keep going nonstop. This was going to be a race, he realised—a race right to the end.

LAUREN LED THE WAY quickly into the blizzard, Sean and Murdo following fast on her heels. She knew it was unlikely Fitzgerald that would still be in the same place, but they had to at least try.

'This is the place,' she told them. 'He must have got the snowmobile started.'

'Shit,' Murdo cursed as he looked out into the blustering storm. 'Then we've lost him.'

Sean was crouching, examining twin grooves in the ice. He followed the tracks across to the crevasse and leaned carefully over the edge. 'Hey!' he called. 'Come and take a look at this.'

Lauren moved to join him, staring down into the darkened ice cavity. She realised immediately that Fitzgerald hadn't got the snowmobile running at all—that he'd dumped it into the nearest crevasse in an attempt to destroy it.

But the configuration of the crevasse had conspired against him. It was not sheer-sided; it was more like a series of steps going down. The snowmobile had plunged, nose-first, into a ledge of soft snow and was sitting not thirty feet beneath them. Around it were numerous small dark shapes. Lauren squinted at them as her eyes adjusted to the low light levels of the cavity.

'I can see cans!' Sean exclaimed. 'And that's one of the personal medical kits! Fitzgerald was in such a hurry to get away he didn't do a very good job of disposal.'

Lauren straightened up, thinking rapidly. 'Can we get the snowcat out of there?'

'Sure. But I might not be able to get it going.'

Lauren was already heading back into the blizzard, the compass in her hand. 'Come with me,' she told Sean and Murdo. 'We've got to make this our base while we retrieve what we can from the crevasse. Every second's going to count now. Let's go and get the others.'

FITZGERALD CHECKED the illuminated dial of his wristwatch. It was almost midnight, and time for a two-hour break. He had been moving nonstop for almost ten hours, pausing only to eat a few snacks from the mound of provisions on the sledge.

The GPS gave him the good news. He was already twelve miles into his march. This was where his superior strength and fitness would win out . . . there was no way the others could match his pace.

He managed to get the tent up, taking twice as long as usual to complete the task. He crawled inside and took off his jacket and shirt. He wished he had a mirror to see the damage.

Fitzgerald couldn't see the wound but he could feel the way the muscles near the shoulder blade had been sliced. His left arm was not so effective now. Just to clench his fist caused him searing pain. And if it got infected? He shuddered to think what the complications might be.

He lit his gas stove and watched the blue flames for a while. He took the knife with the eight-inch blade and began to twist it in the middle of the burner, watching as the stainless steel began to glow dull red. Then reaching behind his back with his right hand, he placed the blade as firmly as he could, sizzling and spitting, right into the wound. One. Two. Three. Four. Five. He moved the blade; it would be a mistake to miss some of the damaged flesh. Six. Seven. Eight. The tent was filling with the nauseating stench of burned skin and fat. Nine. Ten. He removed the knife.

Fitzgerald was not in the mood to eat or drink. He sat with his eyes wide open, staring at the tiny ring of blue flame until the gas cylinder emptied and the flame petered out.

Then he packed up the tent, hitched himself to the sledge and continued his trek into the night.

SEAN WRAPPED THE ROPE round his waist and abseiled backwards into the crevasse. A few seconds later he was kicking gently into the deep snow next to the snowmobile.

'Is it damaged?' Lauren called down.

'Seems all right.'

'Stop screwing around with that buggy,' Murdo shouted. 'Send up the food.'

Sean began to scout around the shelf, picking up the odd items of food that Fitzgerald had failed to throw far enough into the depths.

He carried on building up the stash, placing the booty in a sleeping-bag and tying it to the rope for Lauren to haul up.

There were shouts of delight from above when the team spilled the food out onto the ice.

'Hey! Been nice knowing you, Sean,' Murdo called down. 'One less mouth to feed.'

Sean smiled. It was amazing how quickly the presence of a little food had lifted the spirits of the team. That was good, he reasoned; getting that snowmobile out of the crevasse was going to take every ounce of strength they could muster.

They hauled Sean up and fell on the food, each devouring half a tin of Spam and a handful of crackers.

Lauren checked her watch. 'It's just gone midnight,' she said. 'We've got enough moonlight to work with. I suggest we get going.'

The team gathered, everyone bar Frank, who was obviously in no condition to help pull. Sean abseiled into the crevasse once more and tied a rope off at two points on the rear of the snowmobile.

'We'll bring it up backwards,' he called. 'Take up the slack.'

Sean watched with his heart in his mouth as the rope began to tighten, the fibres protesting as they stretched into the load.

FITZGERALD NOTED the coming of the dawn and decided it was time to take a break. The night had been more of a trial than he'd predicted, with numerous crevasse crossings across snow bridges that were impossible to judge properly in the dark. Still, he'd taken the risk and had come through it intact.

The GPS readout was showing encouraging news, with the crashed aircraft just fifteen miles away. The explorer broke a couple of bars of chocolate out of his provisions and ate them. The storm had blown itself out, ushering in a remarkably calm day.

The wound continued to be painful, but the imperative of reaching the target was such that the explorer was able to put it out of his mind.

All too soon, the break was over. Julian Fitzgerald popped a handful of dextrose energy tablets into his mouth and sucked them as he continued the trek.

WITH A FINAL SHOUT of 'Heave!' the team fell back as one, the snowmobile slipping up and finally breaching the lip of the crevasse. They stared at it, scarcely able to believe they'd finally achieved the objective, most of them without enough energy to pick themselves up from where they'd fallen on the glacier.

Sean pulled back the Velcro strips that held down the foam seat cover. Beneath it was a recess in which a small tool roll was sitting.

He untied it and revealed a number of screwdrivers and spanners.

'Bet Fitzgerald didn't know that was there,' he said with a smile.

In less than ten minutes, he had both carburettors stripped down, examined and repaired. He cleaned and reassembled them and replaced them on the head, taking care to position the gaskets correctly beneath. He clipped the fuel lines back on and tested they were secure. Then he ripped back the pull-start, grunting with satisfaction as the engine fired first time.

The team was jubilant.

'Pack up the sledge,' said Lauren. 'We're leaving.'

'One more thing.' Sean unscrewed the petrol filler cap and beckoned for Lauren to look inside. 'We've only got half a tank of fuel.'

'How far will that take us?'

'Hard to say. How many miles to the plane?'

'Thirty-five. Maybe a bit more.'

'It's going to be tight. It's going to be really tight.'

FITZGERALD HEARD IT before he saw it: the thin, high-pitched note of an engine carried to him on the wind.

Silence. Seconds ticked by.

He must have been mistaken, the explorer decided; there could be no engine running out here in this wilderness. Unless . . .

He scanned the glacier with his binoculars. But the machine—whatever it was—was hidden from view.

Then it emerged from a dip. Fitzgerald saw it as clear as day. Just a couple of miles behind him, a fully laden snowmobile was picking its way steadily through the glacier, a sledge running behind it.

He picked out the figures. He could see Sean in the driver's position, Lauren sitting behind him.

But *how*? The explorer had been so certain he had destroyed that machine. He felt a wave of panic wash over him as he watched them bearing down on him. They would kill him, he was sure of that.

Fitzgerald whipped the harness round him and set out for the remains of the aircraft, now less than a mile away, moving faster than he'd ever moved on ice before, the sledge bumping and tilting in his wake as he pushed his legs towards the objective.

'THERE HE IS!' Lauren had glimpsed Fitzgerald just a few hundred yard in front of them. Not far ahead of him, large shapes were dark against the ice. The remains of the aircraft, Lauren realised; they were almost there.

Then the snowmobile juddered slightly, the engine noise dying away for a few beats, then picking up again and continuing.

'The tank's just about empty!' Sean yelled.

The machine gave another lurch, the sledge bucking violently behind it as the engine coughed. Then the snowmobile coasted to a halt, the front runners sinking into the snow as the engine died. They could see Fitzgerald looking back towards them as he appraised this new development, then he continued his trek towards the aircraft wreckage, moving like a man possessed.

Instantly, Lauren dismounted, snatched her skis and sticks from the sledge and set out in pursuit, with Sean right behind her.

FITZGERALD COULD HEAR them gaining on him, the sound of their skis against the ice. *Did they have the axe?*

He knew he didn't have the time to look back.

Fifty yards. There was the aircraft wing, partly covered in snow, big pieces of engine and gearbox strewn here and there.

His legs were beginning to cramp; he could feel the muscles starting to knot as they reached their limits. The great crevasse was in front of him, the one the aircraft had fallen into. On the other side was the remains of their camp, the tents no longer standing but the fabric still visible as it poked from the winter drift. Inside one of those collapsed domes would be the emergency transmitter, but if the others reached it first . . .

The explorer thought he would have to skirt the crevasse, a detour that might mean at least an extra mile on foot. Then he saw that a snow bridge had built through the winter. It looked fragile, but now there was no choice. Fitzgerald committed himself to the thin span of ice, feeling sick as he felt it slump in the middle, the weight of the sledge threatening to drag him down into the deep void on each side.

But the snow bridge held.

Fitzgerald reached the other side, turned, and saw that Lauren and Sean were just seconds from crossing the crevasse. Next to him was a mass of metal. With a roar, he threw the metal remains out onto the snow bridge, the weight crashing with a muffled crumping noise into the midsection of the bridge and collapsing it into the depths.

Lauren and Sean came to an abrupt halt, just before the edge of the monster crevasse. In front of them, huge fragments of the snow bridge were tumbling down into the dark interior of the ice cap, and—not twenty yards in front of them—Julian Fitzgerald was standing, triumphant and untouchable.

They had failed. For the sake of a cupful of petrol, for a few yards of distance, they had failed. Lauren could feel what remaining vestige of strength was left inside her ebb and fade as she watched the explorer walk over to the remains of his old camp.

Sean, too, knew it was over; his body had given up the fight.

Lauren turned to him, her face swollen from wind blisters and radiation. 'Is there *anything* we can do, Sean? Think one last time. Once he's gone we'll never catch him again. How can we stop him?'

Sean turned to consider the engine, pulling at the twisted metal. One of the broken fuel lines was jutting from the wreckage, and as he tugged at it, a thin trickle of aviation fuel leaked from the metal line.

'There's still some fuel in these lines. If we could get enough out of this thing we could fill one of the cans with it, use it as a weapon.' Sean's voice petered out as he watched the pathetic trickle running from the slender fuel line. 'It'd never work,' he concluded wearily, and wandered off to help Mel and Murdo drag in the sledge.

Lauren leaned against the shattered engine and turned her mind one more time to the problem, knowing that if she couldn't work out a solution, all six of them would die.

FITZGERALD STOOD on one side of the crevasse, Lauren and her team on the other. He was no more than twenty yards from them, but in that moment, those unbridgeable yards were the gulf between the living and the dead.

'I found the transmitter,' Fitzgerald told them, gesturing to the yellow object strapped in the back of his sledge.

'So why don't you activate it and we can all go home?' Lauren asked him.

Fitzgerald laughed.

'Our bodies will be found,' Lauren told him bitterly. 'We'll make sure the truth will be known in the end.'

'How? By leaving a note? Who do you think will ever come to this place to find it? Besides, I'll tell the world that you all died a hundred miles from here.'

'Where are you going to call in the plane?' asked Sean. 'Just out of curiosity.'

Fitzgerald thought carefully for some moments. 'I don't suppose it would hurt to tell you my plans,' he said. 'Actually, I'm going to continue down to the coast before I put in the mayday call.'

'Eighty miles? Why go so far?' Sean asked in surprise. 'All you have to do is get out of this crevasse field and find a nice flat piece of ice. You know we haven't got the strength to follow you.'

Suddenly, Lauren gave out a bitter laugh. 'You'll get to the coast and claim you made it across the continent on foot just like you originally planned. That's about right, isn't it?'

Fitzgerald made no response to this, but merely glared at her across the gap. Then he turned away.

'One more thing,' Lauren called, her voice weak. She fished in her pocket and brought out the titanium tube she had so carefully guarded through the trek; she held it high in the air so he could see what it was. 'The sample from the lake,' she told him, the words heavy with resignation. 'Will you take it and see it gets to my sponsor, Alexander De Pierman at Kerguelen Oils?'

Fitzgerald laughed. 'And why the hell should I do that for you?'

'Because there are species in this sample that are new to science. It's my last request, if you like. We know we're going to die here now. The least you can do is let me die in the knowledge that something came of this.'

Fitzgerald's first inclination was to tell her to go to hell, but as his mind ticked over he saw another possibility.

'Species new to science? I'll do it. Throw it over.'

Lauren gave the sample tube to Sean.

'Will you . . . ?' she asked him. 'I'm not sure I have the strength.'

Sean looked at her in amazement. 'He'll take the credit for it. He'll probably end up naming one of these life forms after himself.'

'Do it, Sean,' Lauren told him. 'That sample has to be properly analysed and recorded, or it's all been for nothing.'

'Well, if you're sure . . . '

Sean reluctantly threw it across, where it plopped unharmed into the soft surface. Fitzgerald plucked it out and looked at it closely.

'How do I know you haven't put a note inside?' he demanded.

'Unscrew the top,' Lauren called out. 'The titanium tube is just an outer shell. The sample is inside in a glass tube.'

Fitzgerald did as she said. It was immediately obvious there was no note inside—the tube contained only clear fluid.

'Good enough.' Fitzgerald placed the phial in the breast pocket of his wind suit. 'Anything more,' he called back sarcastically.

Lauren and Sean said nothing.

'Then I'll be gone.'

Fitzgerald flicked down his ski goggles and hitched the harness round his waist. Then, without a backward glance, he began his trek towards the coast.

5 THE HERO RETURNS

Alexander De Pierman was sitting in heavy London traffic on his way to a meeting when the call came through.

'I've got Irene Evans on the line for you,' his secretary told him.

'Who?'

'Julian Fitzgerald's logistics manager. Says it's top urgent.'

De Pierman was perplexed. He'd had a few dealings with Fitzgerald's team during the press announcement to break the news of the loss of Capricorn and its crew, but he could not imagine what Irene Evans was calling for now, so many weeks later.

'Put her through.'

'You're not going to believe this,' Evans told him, her voice alive with excitement. 'I just got the most extraordinary news from Ushuaia. Fitzgerald's emergency transmitter was reactivated yesterday. Someone out there is still alive.'

De Pierman paused a moment while the information sank in. 'Alive? But how can they be?' he asked.

'I have absolutely no idea. But it's definitely Fitzgerald's transmitter. An Antarctic Air Service flight is on its way to investigate.'

'But after all this time?' De Pierman was struggling to comprehend what he was hearing. 'How the hell has anyone survived? And where's the signal coming from?'

'That's the bizarre thing. The signal's coming from the coast—on the edge of the continent, about four hundred miles from the Capricorn base.'

'The coast? Where exactly?' De Pierman opened his note pad and jotted down the figures as Irene gave him the coordinates. 'When will we know more?'

'In the next few hours. As soon as the flight gets there.'

By midafternoon Irene Evans was back on the line. 'I just got the call from AAS. They picked up one survivor. It's Julian Fitzgerald.'

'Did he give any news of the others?'

'They're all dead. I'm very sorry to have to tell you that.'

'Oh. Well . . . I . . . '

'I'm so sorry. I expect there was something inside you believed that Lauren and her team might have survived?'

'Call me an old fool,' De Pierman told her, sadly, 'but you're right.

All the experts said it was impossible, but you always convince yourself there might have been a factor they'd overlooked.'

'Well, there obviously was something they overlooked, or Fitzgerald wouldn't have lived to tell the tale.'

'How did he do it? And why did he end up where he did? My God, he must have a story to tell.'

'That's what the rest of the world has realised. There's going to be quite a reception waiting for him when he gets back. I'll arrange a press conference at Heathrow. I'll call you when I know the timings.'

De Pierman terminated the call and stood up, lost in thought, as he considered this startling piece of news. Whichever way he looked at it, not a single aspect of this new development made any sense. He consulted the atlas again, considering Fitzgerald's position, drawing a mental line from the place to the location of the Capricorn base.

In a flash, he had it.

The plane. The crashed plane. Fitzgerald's route would have taken him right past it. Of all the factors he had so painfully run through, De Pierman had never thought that the crashed plane might have offered salvation to any Capricorn survivors. Perhaps the transmitter had been left there? But the distance from Capricorn to the aircraft was about 300 miles. How had Fitzgerald done it?

Like the rest of the world, he would have to wait for the answers.

AS THE FRAIL, frost-ravaged figure of Fitzgerald was escorted into the press room at Heathrow, there was a collective gasp from the reporters. Could this really be the renowned explorer? He looked like he'd aged a lifetime in the last six months. Cameras flashed as he held the side of the table for support.

Alexander De Pierman was present at the conference, as was Irene Evans. They sat uneasily behind the press table and waited while Fitzgerald lowered himself painfully onto a seat.

Quickly the volume of the shouts rose. Fitzgerald tried to talk but no words could be heard. Gradually the row began to diminish. Someone handed Fitzgerald a plastic bottle of water.

'Mr Fitzgerald,' one of the more strident reporters managed to ask. 'What happened at Capricorn base?'

'The fire?' Fitzgerald said. 'It was an electrical fault, something wrong with the wiring in the base. There was a strong wind, the flames took hold faster than we could fight them . . . Then the diesel tank exploded and destroyed everything.'

'How many people survived the fire?'

Fitzgerald took another swig of water. 'One died immediately, my teammate, Carl Norland. Others were burned, and died later.'

'What happened after the fire?'

'We had no food and no transport. We realised there would be no rescue and we knew we could never make it to the nearest base. So we headed for the plane that crashed on the Blackmore Glacier. We knew there was an emergency transmitter there.'

'How did you survive?'

Fitzgerald looked into space for a long moment before replying. When he turned his attention back to the reporter, his stare was terrible, the blood-red eyes mesmerising as they fixed on the questioner.

'There were two depots with food and equipment,' the explorer said. 'Dr Burgess had put them in place when she came to rescue me at the beginning of the winter, and they were still there.'

Sitting next to the explorer, De Pierman cursed himself quietly as he heard this news. So *that* was the missing factor that he hadn't built into the equation. Lauren had put down depots that could keep the team alive. Now it was all beginning to make sense.

'How did your companions die?' the reporter asked.

'We got them all to the first depot,' Fitzgerald said, 'but there wasn't enough medical equipment to keep the injured alive. They were burned, you see, in the fire. They died of the infections . . . one after another . . . we buried them in the crevasses . . . '

The explorer's face crumpled as he wept, the reporters keeping a respectful silence as he struggled to regain some composure.

'Dr Burgess was the last,' he continued. 'My God she was strong. But even she didn't get much further than the second depot. Then it was just me and the fight to get to the crashed plane.'

'Why didn't you call in the rescue right away when you got the transmitter? What made you keep going to the coast?'

Fitzgerald took a deep breath. 'There are two types of people in this world. There are starters. And there are finishers. I made a solemn promise some time ago that I would become the first person to cross the widest point of the Antarctic continent on foot. And I kept that promise by crossing those last eighty miles to the coast.'

There was a murmur of admiration from the gathered reporters.

'One more thing.' Fitzgerald reached into his top pocket and brought out the titanium sample tube. The cameramen shuffled and bumped each other as they tried to focus on the phial.

'Most of you will know,' he said, 'that Capricorn was a scientific base. In fact, Dr Burgess's objective was to examine a subterranean lake . . . a lake she suspected would contain life that had never been encountered on earth before. The day before the fire, the team drilled into that lake and retrieved this sample. It was Dr Burgess's dying wish that this sample be delivered to her sponsor for analysis, and I honour that wish now.'

Fitzgerald handed the sample over to De Pierman with a flourish, the oil man nodding his thanks. Then the explorer broke off the interview and was escorted, with a policeman on each arm to support him, into a waiting ambulance.

The last hope had died. De Pierman had to be realistic: there was no hope for Lauren and the rest of her team now. Fitzgerald had seen them die with his own eyes, and you only had to take one look at the man to know that he too had been through hell and back.

De Pierman held up the sample tube and shook it gently. There'd better be something good in that tube, he mused, or Lauren had given her life for nothing.

ALEXANDER DE PIERMAN'S chauffeur-driven BMW pulled up outside the Royal Geographical Society just after 8.00pm.

'Wait here, please,' he instructed the driver.

De Pierman made his way through the plush corridors to the lecture hall, where he found a standing place in the crowd. Fitzgerald had become front-page news all over the world and the room was packed with hundreds of people.

The explorer stood before them as he reached the end of his address, emaciated but poker-backed, his face pockmarked with the ravages of frostbite.

'And so to conclude.' He wiped a tear away from his eyes with his bandaged hands. 'Seven days later I made it to the sea, where I finally set up the radio and called in the air rescue. But my greatest satisfaction was not from my own humble achievement—it was to be the bearer of a vital test tube from Capricorn base. I gave that test tube for analysis today and I believe the results will prove the whole enterprise worth while.'

The hall erupted into a thunderous roar of approval, hundreds of people cheering and clapping. On the stage, Julian Fitzgerald stood modestly behind the lectern, waving occasionally with his bandaged hands to acknowledge the crowd.

After some minutes, the President of the Society took the stage, raising his palms to quell the applause.

'And now, if anyone has any questions for Mr Fitzgerald?'

'I have a question for you.' De Pierman stepped forward to the front of the hall. 'But I'm not sure you'll want to hear it.'

'Alexander De Pierman was the sponsor of Dr Burgess's Capricorn base,' Fitzgerald told the crowd. 'One of those rare industrialists who put their money into the world of scientific research.'

There was a polite scattering of applause.

'Do you have some results of the test-tube analysis?' Fitzgerald asked him. 'Perhaps some that we can share with the audience?'

'I have more questions than results, Mr Fitzgerald. Are you absolutely sure that that sample was given to you by Lauren Burgess?'

Fitzgerald licked his blistered lips, giving the audience a quick, exasperated glance. 'Of course,' he snapped. 'How could I be mistaken?'

'And that sample never left your possession from the moment Lauren gave it to you until you handed it to me?'

'Absolutely not,' Fitzgerald spluttered indignantly.

De Pierman stepped onto the stage and pointed to the map of Antarctica that was projected on the screen behind Fitzgerald.

'Would you be kind enough to show me where Lauren died?'

Fitzgerald began to redden with anger. 'Sir! I no longer see that your questions are relevant. Kindly leave the stage.'

'Show me where she died.' De Pierman was insistent.

Fitzgerald glared at him and took up a pointer. He tapped it on a midway position on the Blackmore Glacier. 'As I have already said, Dr Burgess died here.'

'And the location of the crashed aeroplane?'

Fitzgerald moved the pointer, tapping impatiently again. 'Here. About one hundred miles away.'

'So, Lauren Burgess never made it to that plane?'

'She certainly did not. I was the only one.'

'Then perhaps you can help me with one perplexing thing. That test tube contained no life, Mr Fitzgerald. What it actually contained was one hundred per cent aviation spirit.'

Fitzgerald rocked visibly on his feet, clutching the side of the desk as the blood drained from his face.

'I checked the Capricorn base inventory,' De Pierman continued. 'There was no aviation fuel there at all. The only place Lauren Burgess could have got it was at the site of the crashed plane. That proves she was there and the sample container was a way of telling us that.'

Fitzgerald said nothing.

'One more question.' De Pierman spoke quietly in the deathly hush that had descended. 'If you are lying about this vital piece of information, Mr Fitzgerald, how are we to trust a word of your story?'

Suddenly, Fitzgerald was sweeping up his notes from the lecturn. 'I don't need to listen to this . . . this rubbish!' he exclaimed, and headed off the stage.

LAUREN WAS DREAMING, just as she seemed to have been doing for every moment of the weeks they had been waiting. Or were they hallucinations? In these days of wasting away, it was difficult to tell.

Frank and Sean were still by her side, but they might have been ghosts for all the conversation they offered. Days were passing without a single word being exchanged between them. Sometimes Sean held her hand, radiating heat and care into her by some magic force.

In the early stages the tent walls had become a cell, a prison, a tomb or worse. Hope was hanging on in there, but by such a slender thread it might have been spun from gossamer.

But then Lauren learned to relax. Their fate was no longer in their own hands but in the hands of Alexander De Pierman and a titanium tube filled with aviation spirit which he might or might not have received. And even if Fitzgerald had handed it to her sponsor, would the old man recognise the cry for help it contained?

Then it happened, the noise of the approaching Twin Otter as it flew towards them across the glacier. How many days had they waited? How many countless, sleepless hours had they wished for that very noise? Lauren thought her heart would burst.

She tried to speak, but her lips and throat were so blistered she could not form a single word. Instead she just squeezed Sean's hand, the answering pressure telling her that he too was still alive, and that he too had heard the sound and understood it.

The engine noise increased to a roar. Lauren tried to lift her arms out of her sleeping-bag, but found she did not have the strength. Shadows merged at the front of the tent, then astonishingly strong hands carried her out onto the ice, where the bright red aircraft sat, as unexpected and surprising in that place as an alien space ship.

Things went weird for a while, and somewhere in that black spell Lauren was dimly aware that she might have passed out. She came to in the recovery position, her head cradled on her arm, but she tried to raise herself up, wanting to know who was still alive. Had Frank died? Was Richard even now cold and lifeless in that tent?

A face loomed over her. Her vision was blurred, the edges fuzzy and lacking definition.

Lauren wondered why the face above her seemed so shocked. She could not know that her appearance was terrifying, that she looked to be little more than flesh and bone, that she had aged beyond belief. Nor could she know that her face was almost black, stained by months without washing and by the rigours of the solar radiation from which they had had no protection. Lauren's lips tried to form the 'A' of Alexander, but then a new face took over, and she felt herself lifted onto a stretcher. Then the sharp point of a needle penetrated her arm and she was lifted into the cabin of the aircraft.

A figure was carried past her on another stretcher—she recognised Frank's face. Minutes later, others were placed in the spaces on the floor. She managed to grasp a hand that was nearby, pulling weakly at it until De Pierman's concerned face came close to her.

'Are they all . . .?' she managed to croak.

'They're all alive, Lauren. You're all going to be fine.'

The engines were powered up and the aircraft bounced around as it taxied to the end of the makeshift strip. Lauren felt the engines rev strongly, then the plane accelerated fast before biting into the frigid air and gaining height.

That was when Lauren knew that this was no dream, that they really had made it. She had brought her team through it all alive.

She raised her head to look out of the window as the Twin Otter banked round in a big arc and began to head north. De Pierman cupped his hand behind her neck to support her. Beneath her she could see the creased surface of the glacier, the interior of each crevasse coloured a delicate powder blue. Far, far away, she could see the mountain range they had crossed, the dark peaks only just visible against the darkening sky.

Beyond that range was Capricorn, gone for the moment, but not from her heart. Lauren knew that one day she would be back.

EPILOGUE

It took almost six weeks in a Cambridge hospital ward for Lauren to reach the point at which she felt she could stand up and attempt to walk. On her return from Antarctica her body had been on the edge of collapse, and she had lost more than a quarter of her body mass. Her kidneys had suffered most, and she'd never be able to drink alcohol again, but she knew it was a small price to pay.

Sean had recovered faster—perhaps, Lauren had mused, because he had been the strongest from the start. Within a fortnight he was into physiotherapy, spending hours on an exercise bike to tease the wasted muscles of his legs back into life, then swimming lengths of the hospital pool to boost his arms.

When he wasn't working on his recovery, Sean would spend long hours next to Lauren's hospital bed, reading aloud newspaper accounts (often inaccurate) of their ordeal, and making her laugh. Away from the pressure of the base, and the terror of the fight for survival, Lauren and Sean finally found the ability to relax together and explore the relationship that had flared into life at Capricorn.

Once she had been discharged, Lauren had embarked on the thousand-and-one jobs that awaited her, from dealing with the seemingly unending requests for media interviews to attending the memorial service for Carl Norland.

From Fitzgerald there had been no word. In fact, following the Capricorn team's return to civilisation, the disgraced explorer had performed a vanishing act and removed himself completely from the public eye. Despite the best efforts of some of Fleet Street's finest investigators, he remained the invisible man, not even leaving an electronic trace of credit-card transactions that would enable him to be tracked. From time to time, unreliable eye-witness reports from members of the public would place him in locations as varied as Marrakesh or Benidorm, but most simply believed he had gone to ground somewhere in Britain—perhaps camping out in the wilderness of Scotland or Wales.

Lauren welcomed his absence; in fact, she dearly hoped she would never set eyes on him again. Early thoughts of revenge, or even of taking legal action against him on a charge of attempted manslaughter, were replaced over a period of weeks by the realisation that Fitzgerald's public shaming would be punishment enough.

Millions of people around the world had been shocked to learn of the scandalous treatment suffered by Lauren and her team, and the endless dissection of the story by the media would do its own job of ensuring that Fitzgerald would never find a sponsor or undertake a major expedition again. He was ruined by his own hand and Lauren was prepared to leave it at that.

When it came to the rest of the Capricorn team, Lauren had been greatly relieved at how quickly most of her colleagues had recovered. Mel and Murdo had spent less than three weeks in hospital, with their radiation and frostbite injuries responding well to treatment and little indication of long-term damage. Frank was less fortunate—the radio operator having to endure a further three operations on his gangrenous hand where the three fingers had been amputated.

'I can still turn a radio dial,' he told Lauren when she came to visit him in hospital. 'So if you were thinking of going back, I'll be first in the queue.'

Richard, like Frank, would always bear the mark of that trek across the ice: a slight limp and a retina damaged by snow-blindness would be the price he paid for his scoop. Richard's factual account of the Capricorn team's struggle for survival went straight to the top of the best-seller lists, and soon afterwards he married his fiancée, Sophie, and got the posting of his dreams.

Astonishingly, every member of the Capricorn team agreed that they would not hesitate to go back to Antarctica if an opportunity came up, with the exception of Murdo (mainly, Lauren suspected, under pressure from his girlfriend, Jan). Instead the cook returned to Scotland and, while convalescing from his injuries, planned his long-cherished backpacking journey round the world.

'I think I deserve some time out on a beach,' Murdo had explained to Lauren, a sentiment she whole-heartedly sympathised with.

But for Lauren there would be no holiday. The fire at Capricorn had destroyed every single component of her research—from the paperwork to the laboratory analysis—and ultimately, her decision to sacrifice the precious sample of lake water had removed the last piece of scientific evidence that Capricorn had ever been anything more than an expensive dream.

'We'll have to return to Antarctica,' she told Sean, 'and do it all again. We'll go back to all the funding bodies, make a new proposal, and set up Capricorn Two.'

'Anything you'd do differently this time round?' Sean asked her with a smile.

Lauren thought for a few moments. 'Maybe. You remember that self-imposed rule I had about how dangerous it is to have relationships going on at a base?'

'That was a lousy rule.'

Lauren leaned forward to kiss him. 'I know. I think I'll scrap it next time.'

MATT DICKINSON

Film-maker and author Matt Dickinson leads a life every bit as exciting as the lives of his characters. His love of adventure has taken him around the world and has involved him in expeditions to the Sahara Desert and the jungles of South America. He has also climbed Mount Everest—an experience he wrote about in his nonfiction best seller *The Death Zone*, and which also inspired his first novel *High Risk*. In order to research the background to *Black Ice* he headed off to Antarctica, a continent that has fascinated him since childhood. 'My father built an Antarctic base and carried out scientific surveys for the Royal Navy in the 1950s, so it was always a part of my life.'

The author spent time on several Antarctic bases in order to make his fictional base, Capricorn, as authentic as possible. He wanted to show exactly what it is like to live and work on a base as well as to describe the sense of isolation experienced by the research teams. 'It doesn't matter who you are, or how much money you have, when winter falls there is no way in or out, you're stuck there until spring comes around again.'

Dickinson says that he can empathise with his characters, even someone as unsympathetic as Julian Fitzgerald. 'While Fitzgerald is an exaggeration, he has certain qualities: a drive, a single-mindedness, and a very large ego, which you need in order to survive in extreme conditions. And although it may seem that the characters in my book are faced with impossible situations, there is nothing I have put them through that explorers in real life do not have to deal with on a daily basis.'

He knows what he's talking about. Having survived frostbite, dehydration and starvation during his career, Antarctica almost finished him. He and his crew found themselves caught in an avalanche while filming an ascent of Mount William. Miraculously, however, they were climbing an ice chute at the time and the cascade passed over their heads, missing them by inches. Dickinson describes it as 'the closest I have ever come to death'.

Even after near-fatal experiences like these, Matt Dickinson has not been put off his adventurous lifestyle and continues to explore, film and write about the world's wildest and most hostile landscapes.

ACKNOWLEDGEMENTS AND PICTURE CREDITS: *The Millionaires*: Pages 6–8 financial figures: The Image Bank; computer screen grab and man at desk: Gettyone Stone; man at laptop: FPG; photomontage: Curtis Cozier; Page 155: © Jackie Merri Meyer; *Only Dad*: Pages 156–158: illustration by chrisproutillustration; 269: © Frank Noon; *Gone for Good*: Pages 270–271: landscape: The Image Bank; man walking: FPG; photomontage: Rick Lecoat @ Shark Attack; *Black Ice*: Pages 416–418: footprints in snow: Gettyone Stone; Antarctica landscape: National Geographic; 539: © Colin Luke.

DUSTJACKET CREDITS: Spine from top: The Image Bank; Gettyone Stone; FPG; photomontage: Curtis Cozier; illustration by chrisproutillustration; The Image Bank; FPG; photomontage; Rick Lecoat @ Shark Attack; Gettyone Stone; National Geographic.

Printed by Maury Imprimeur SA, Malesherbes, France
Bound by Reliures Brun SA, Malesherbes, France

220AP